BATTLESTATIONS

BATTLESTATIONS

edited by
David Drake & Bill Fawcett

PRIME BOOKS

CONTENTS

Battlestation

Battlestation: Vanguard

BATTLESTATION

for Peter Heck
Welcome Aboard

for Brendan
Another Survivor

PROLOGUE

"Haven't those guys ever heard about noise pollution?" grumbled the tech, reaching up to adjust the volume on his monitors. The sound of the intruder's warp drive lowered from a deafening howl to a merely unbearable screech.

"Well, at least we know they aren't trying to sneak up on us," said the ensign, peering over his shoulder.

They still hadn't managed to pinpoint the origin of the approaching ship, but this didn't bother either of the two men on bridge watch on the Fleet Cruiser *Peter the Great*. Schlein Epsilon was technically a frontier world, but there hadn't been any combat within parsecs since the end of the Family war, decades earlier. Very few of their stellar neighbors were brave or foolish enough to challenge the two thousand worlds of the Alliance. Whoever was responsible for building the mistuned warp drive, odds were they hadn't come looking for trouble.

Three minutes later, the still-unidentified ship had dropped into normal space and was entering the system at a large fraction of the speed of light.

"They'd better brake soon," said the tech. The ship's course would take it directly into this system's star. Almost as if it had heard him, the intruder began to slow. The dials and visual displays of the control panel changed to reflect the new type of energy the intruding ship emitted as its magnetic drive attempted to reduce its velocity.

"*Merde alors!*" exclaimed the ensign, reverting to his native language. He pointed to a readout. "Does that mean what I think it does?"

"Yeah, their sublight drive just died," confirmed the tech. His fingers moved in a blur, adjusting the readings from one dial to another. Suddenly he stopped and turned toward the younger man who was his superior officer. "We have maybe three minutes to start moving for an intercept, or we don't need to bother."

The young ensign thought quickly. It would take at least two minutes to get the *Peter*'s own magnetic drive operating. More likely longer, since there was only a skeleton watch on duty in Engineering. There wasn't even time to ask the captain. If he misjudged this one, it was bye-bye to his career. Maybe he'd get lucky and find out that the unknown was some Alliance senator's private yacht.

"Get us moving," he ordered, trying to sound confident. "And sound general quarters." That would bring the captain at a run. As they moved to save the unknown ship, the ensign kept trying to match its energy profile and appearance to any known design. He kept coming up with blanks. After the successful, nearly routine interception and rescue, the reason why became obvious: the intruder was a type of ship no human had ever seen before, not even in the age of the last Great Empire.

The ship turned out to have come from virtually the center of the galaxy, from the thick "donut" of tightly packed stars surrounding the massive black hole at the galactic center. This area, known as Star Central, had hundreds of races on as many planets, many of them separated by only fractions of a light-year. Despite the closeness of civilized worlds, there was neither a united government nor any real military tradition: the few more aggressive races had either emigrated or killed one another off ages ago. Nor, with the stars so closely packed, had there been any need to develop an efficient warp drive. So when three races embarked on a desperate mission out along the spiral arm in which the Alliance was located, they had to rely upon an experimental drive that no Fleet mechanic would have allowed out of the shop. It was the highest achievement of their technology.

When scientists finally established communications with the three races of aliens aboard their unarmed ship, the reason for their nearly suicidal mission became clear. A race known as the Ichtons had recently emerged from another spiral arm and begun attacking the Central worlds. Little was known of these invaders, except that once they conquered a world they stripped it of every possible resource—including every living creature. One of fifty ships sent out from the beleaguered Gerrond home world, the ship had brought with it hundreds of hours of records and tapes of ravaged worlds to bolster their plea for assistance. Originally, they had hoped to find help closer to Star Central. But as they made their way up the spiral arm, they found the Ichtons had been there before them, pillaging and leaving whole worlds wasted in their wake. In desperation, the mixed crew had continued outward in hopes of finding anyone that might stand against the Ichtons. And thus they came to the Alliance—and the Fleet.

They were met with a mixed reaction. It had been almost fifty years since the Family war, but citizens of the Alliance worlds still paid its cost through their taxes. The defeated Family worlds had been absorbed, as well, so the war debts for both sides had to be paid. Now these strange aliens were asking the Fleet to take on an even greater enemy, one that was not yet a danger to any Alliance world. The ensuing political debate was heated and divisive.

One side argued that the Ichtons would not be a threat for centuries to come, if ever. Their opponents pointed out that each new conquest would increase the

Ichtons' strength. With the resources of the densely populated galactic core, Star Central, at their command, they would be unbeatable when the confrontation finally came. And, of course, a few politicians suspected a trap, and openly doubted whether there were any Ichtons at all.

Inevitably, the final decision was a compromise. A number of ships were sent on the months-long journey to Star Central, using charts provided by the aliens. As always, the Fleet's task began with the gathering of needed intelligence.

FACING THE ENEMY
by David Drake

1.

Oval membranes along the Ichton's lateral lines throbbed as the creature writhed against the table restraints. Two audio speakers flanked the observation screen that Sergeant Dresser watched in the room above. One speaker keened at the edge of ultrasound, while a roll of low static cracked through the other.

"What's the squeaking?" Dresser asked tensely.

"Just noise," said Tech-4 Rodriges, looking up from his monitor. "Moaning, I guess you'd say. Nothing for the translation program"—he nodded toward the hissing second speaker—"to translate."

He hoped Dresser wasn't going to nut, because the fella didn't have any business being here. That was how the brass would think, anyway. So long as the Ichton was alone, Rodriges's job was to flood it with knock-out gas if something went wrong. That didn't seem real likely; but if the creature damaged its *so*-valuable body, there'd be hell to pay.

Dresser's lips were dry, but he wiped his palms on the thighs of his fresh utilities. The uniform felt light compared to the one he'd worn during the most recent mission on *SB 781*. The scout boat's recycling system had cleaned away sweat and body oils after every watch, but there wasn't anything machines could do about the fear that the cloth absorbed just as surely. . . .

That was thinking crazy. Had to stop that *now*.

"Don't worry," he said aloud. "I'm fine."

"Sure an ugly bastard," Rodriges commented in a neutral voice.

Upright, the Ichton would be the better part of three meters tall. The creature's gray body was thin, with a waxy glow over the exoskeleton beneath. By contrast, the six limbs springing from the thorax had a fleshy, ropy texture, though they were stiffened internally by tubes of chitin. Now they twitched against invisible restraints.

"First good look I really had of him," Dresser said softly. "Of it."

He wasn't sure how he felt. He wiped his hands again.

"Huh?" said Rodriges in amazement. "But—it was you that caught him, right? I mean—you know, the real one. Wasn't . . . ?"

Light winked from the Ichton's faceted eyes as the creature turned its head mindlessly from one side to the other.

"Hey, no sweat," Dresser said. A grin quirked a corner of his mouth. The first thing that had struck him funny for—

From since they'd made landfall a month and a half ago. Rodriges thought the Ichton *looked* ugly, but he hadn't seen what the creatures did. . . .

The Ichton on the screen relaxed. One speaker squealed plaintively; the other asked in an emotionless voice, "Where . . . ? Where am I?"

"Sure, that was us," Dresser said. "*SB 781*, not just me; but my boat, my crew, you bet. Only you don't . . . I didn't really look at it, you know? Bundled it up and slung it into a stasis field before we bugged out. Scout boats don't have what you'd call great passenger accommodations."

A separate chirping punctuated the sounds the Ichton made. In a voice identical to that provided for the prisoner, the translator said, "Please relax. The restraints are simply to prevent you from injuring yourself upon waking. When you relax, we will loosen them."

"That's Admiral Horwarth, the project head," Rodriges said knowingly. "Don't know jack shit about medicine or biochem, but she sure can make a team of prima donna medicos get on with the program."

Dresser was lost in memory. He said, "When we landed, I was watching on my screen, and there was this city, a Gerson city it turned out. . . ."

Thomson was at the center console, watching the ground swing toward *SB 781* with the leisured assurance of a thrown medicine ball. Occasionally her fingers scissored over the controls without touching them.

The approach was nerve-wrackingly slow, but that was the way it had to be. Staying out of Ichton warning sensors was the only way the scout boat was going to survive. The turbulence and friction heat of a fast approach would have pointed a glowing finger straight toward them.

"Lookit that sucker!" muttered Codrus.

Dresser and Codrus didn't bother to back up Thomson, but the chance that she would have to take over from the boat's artificial intelligence was a million to one—and the chance that a human could do any good if the AI failed was a lot worse than that.

Codrus was watching the nearest Ichton colony, a vast pimple of blue light projecting kilometers into the stratosphere. Ichton strongholds began as hemispheres of magnetic force. The flux was concentrated enough to sunder the molecular bonds of projectiles and absorb the full fury of energy weapons. As each colony grew, the height of its shield decreased in relation to the diameter.

This colony was already a hundred kilometers across. It would not stop growing until its magnetic walls bulged against those of other Ichton fortresses.

Lookit that sucker.

The scout boat quivered and bobbed as the AI subtlety mimicked the patterns of clear air turbulence, but the computer-enhanced view on Dresser's screen remained rock solid. It had been a city of moderate size—perhaps fifteen thousand inhabitants if human density patterns were applicable.

The buildings tended to rounded surfaces rather than planes. The palette was of earth tones, brightened by street paving of brilliant yellow. From a distance, the soft lines and engaging ambiance of the city as it originally stood would have suggested a field of edible mushrooms.

The tallest of the surviving structures rose about ten meters. The ragged edges in which the tower now ended were the result of Ichton weapons.

A column of Ichtons had passed through the community. The invaders' weapons, derivatives of their defensive shields, had blasted a track across the center of the inhabited area and gnawed apart most of the rest of the city as well.

"Hang on," warned Thomson.

"What gets me," said Dresser, "is they didn't attack the place. It was just there, and they went through it rather than going around."

"They took out major urban centers with antimatter bombs," Codrus said. "Musta had a scale of what they blitzed and what they ignored unless it got in the way. Of course—"

"Touchdown!" Thomson said.

SB 781 fluffed her landing jets—hard twice, while there were still twenty meters of air beneath the boat's belly, then a softer, steady pulse that disturbed the soil as little as possible. No point in inserting stealthily through a hundred kilometers of atmosphere and then kick up a plume of dirt like a locating flag.

"—sooner or later, they cover the whole land surface, so I don't guess they worry about when they get around t' this piece or that."

The scout boat shuddered to a halt that flung Dresser against his gel restraints. His display continued to glow at him with images of the wrecked city, enhanced to a crispness greater than what his eyes would have showed him at the site.

Ichton weapons fired beads the size of match heads that generated expanding globes of force. Individual weapons had a range of only three hundred meters or so, but their effect was devastating—particularly near the muzzle, where the density of the magnetic flux was high. The force globes acted as atomic shears, wrenching apart the molecules of whatever they touched. Even at maximum range, when the flux formed an iridescent ball a meter in diameter, it could blast the fluff off the bodies of this planet's furry natives.

Dresser was sure of that, because some of the Ichtons' victims still lay in the ruins like scorched teddy bears.

"They're Gersons," Dresser said to his crew. "The natives here. One of the races that asked the Alliance for help."

"Too late for that," Codrus muttered. His slim, pale hands played over the controls, rotating the image of the Ichton fortress on his display. From any angle, the blue glare was as perfect and terrible as the heart of a supernova. "Best we get our asses back to the *Hawking* and report."

This was Dresser's first mission on *SB 781*; the previous team leader had wrangled a commission and a job in Operations. Thomson and Codrus came with the boat . . . and they were an item, which sometimes worked and sometimes didn't.

It didn't work on *SB 781*. Both partners were too worried about what might happen to the other to get on with the mission.

"Not till we've done our jobs," Dresser said softly. He raised the probes, hair-thin optical guides that unreeled to the height of twenty meters above *SB 781*'s camouflaged hull. His display immediately defaulted to real-time images of a wind-sculpted waste.

The immediate terrain hadn't been affected by the Ichton invasion—yet. Eventually it too would be roofed by flux generators so powerful that they bent light and excluded the blue and shorter wavelengths entirely. Within their impregnable armor, the Ichtons would extract ores—the rock had a high content of lead and zinc—and perhaps the silicon itself. The planet the invaders left would be reduced to slag and ash.

Thomson tried to stretch in the narrow confines of her seat. Her hands trembled, though that might have been reaction to the tension of waiting above the flight controls against the chance that she'd have to take over. "No job we can do here," she said. "This place is gone. *Gone*. It's not like we've got room t' take back refugees."

Dresser modified his display. The upper half remained a real-time panorama. The glow of an Ichton colony stained the eastern quadrant in a sickly blue counterfeit of the dawn that was still hours away. The lower portion of the display became a map created from data *SB 781*'s sensors gathered during insertion.

"Command didn't send us for refugees," he said. He tried to keep his voice calm, so that his mind would become calm as well. "They said to bring back a live prisoner."

"We *can't* get a prisoner!" Codrus said, maybe louder than he'd meant. "Anything that'd bust open these screens—"

He gestured toward the Ichton fortress on his display. His knuckles vanished within the holographic ambiance, then reappeared like the head of a bobbing duck.

"—'d rip the whole planet down to the core and let that out. The place is fucked, and we need to get away!"

"They're still sending out colonies," Dresser said.

His fingers raised the probes ten meters higher and shrank the image area to five degrees instead of a full panorama. The upper display shuddered. The blue glow filled most of its horizon.

Five Ichton vehicles crawled across terrain less barren than that in which the scout boat hid. Trees grew in serpentine lines along the boundaries of what must once have been cultivated fields. For the most part, the land was now overgrown with brush.

"About twenty klicks away," Dresser continued. He felt the eyes of his subordinates burning on him; but he was in charge, and *SB 781* was going to carry out its mission. "We'll take the skimmers and set up an ambush."

"Take the boat," Thomson said through dry lips. "We'll want the firepower."

Dresser shook his head without taking his eyes off his display. "The boat'd get noticed," he said. "You guys'll be in hard suits with APOT weapons. That'll be as much firepower as we need."

"Lookit that!" Codrus cried, pointing across the cockpit to Dresser's display. "Lookit that!"

A family of Gersons bolted from the row of trees just ahead of the Ichton column. There were four adults, a pair of half-grown children, and a furry infant in the arms of the female struggling along behind the other adults.

The turret of the leading vehicle rotated to follow the refugees. . . .

"You okay, Sarge?" Rodriges asked worriedly.

Dresser crossed his arms and kneaded his biceps hard.

"Yeah," he said. "Sure." His voice was husky. "Seein' the thing there—"

He nodded toward the screen. The Ichton was sitting upright. The voice from the speaker said, "Don't try to use your conscious mind to control your muscles. You wouldn't with your own body, after all."

"You can't imagine how cruel they are, the Ichtons," Dresser said.

"Naw, it's not cruel," the technician explained. "You're only cruel to something you think about. The bugs, they treat the whole universe like we'd treat, you know, an outcrop of nickel ore."

"So cruel . . ." Dresser whispered.

The Ichton's tympanic membranes shrilled through the left speaker. The translation channel boomed, "Where the hell am I? Thomson? Codrus! What's happened to my boat!"

Sergeant Dresser closed his eyes.

"Where's *781*, you bastards?" demanded the Ichton through the machine voice.

2.

"The subbrain of your clone body will control the muscles, Sergeant Dresser," said the voice from a speaker in the wall. "You can't override the hardwired controls, so just relax and let them do their job."

The words were compressed and harshly mechanical; the room's lighting spiked chaotically on several wavelengths. Were they torturing him?

Who were *they*?

"Where's my crew?" Dresser shouted. He threw his feet over the edge of the couch on which he had awakened. His legs splayed though he tried to keep them steady. He collapsed on his chest. The floor was resilient.

"Your men are all right, Sergeant," the voice said. The speaker tried to be soothing, but the delivery rasped like a saw on bone. "So is your human self. Your memory will return in a few minutes."

Memory was returning already. Memory came in disorienting sheets that didn't fit with the real world. Images that Dresser remembered were sharply defined but static. They lacked the texturing of incipient movement that wrapped everything Dresser saw through the faceted eyes of his present body.

But he remembered. . . .

The male Gerson—the tallest, though even he was less than a meter-fifty in height—turned and raised an antitank rocket launcher. The rest of the family blundered past him. The juveniles were hand in hand, and the female with the infant still brought up the rear.

"Where'd he get hardware like that?" Codrus muttered. "I'd've figured the teddy bears were down to sharp sticks, from the way things look."

The Ichton vehicles moved on air cushions; they didn't have the traction necessary to grind through obstacles the way tracked or even wheeled transport could. The leader's turret weapon spewed a stream of projectiles like a ripple of light. The hedgerow disintegrated in bright flashes.

"They sent a starship to the Alliance, after all," Dresser muttered. "The ones left behind still have some weapons, is all."

Brush and splintered wood began to burn sluggishly. The leading Ichton vehicle nosed into the gap.

"Much good it'll do them," said Thomson.

The Gerson fired. The rocket launcher's flaring yellow backblast enveloped twenty meters of brush and pulsed the hedge on the other side of the field. The hypervelocity projectile slammed into the Ichton vehicle.

Slammed, rather, into the faint blue glow of the defensive shield surrounding the Ichton vehicle. The impact roared across the electro-optical spectrum like multicolored petals unfolding from a white core.

The vehicle rocked backward on its bubble of supporting air. The projectile, flattened and a white blaze from frictional heating, dropped to the ground without having touched the body of its target.

The turret traversed. The male Gerson knew what was coming. He ran to the side in a desperate attempt to deflect the stream of return fire from his family. His head and the empty rocket launcher vanished into their constituent atoms as the powerful turret weapon caught him at point-blank range. The high-temperature residue of the sundered molecules recombined an instant later in flashes and flame.

The Ichton gunner continued to fire. Projectiles scythed across the field, ripping smoldering gaps in the vegetation.

The refugees threw themselves down when the shooting started. As the gun traversed past, a juvenile leaped uptight and waved his remaining arm. Before the gunner could react, the screaming victim collapsed again.

The turret weapon ceased firing.

The entire column entered the field. The leading and trailing vehicles were obviously escorts, mounting powerful weapons in their turrets. The second and third vehicles in the convoy were hugely larger and must have weighed a hundred tonnes apiece. They didn't appear to be armed, but their defensive shielding was so dense that the vehicles' outlines wavered within globes of blue translucence. The remaining vehicle, number four in the column, was unarmed and of moderate size, though larger than the escorts.

Diesser's mind catalogued the vehicles against the template of his training and experience: a truck to supply the new colony en route . . . and a pair of transporters, armored like battleships, to carry the eggs and larvae that would populate that colony.

The Ichton convoy proceeded on a track as straight as the line from a compass rose. For a moment, Dresser thought that the Gerson survivors—if there were any—had been overlooked. Then the supply truck and the rear escort swung out of the column and halted.

A Gerson jumped to her feet and ran. She took only three steps before her legs and the ground beneath her vanished in a red flash. Heat made the air above the turret gun's muzzle shimmer.

The supply truck's side panel slid open, and the defensive screen adjacent to the door paled. A pair of Ichtons stepped out of the vehicle. Heavy protective suits concealed the lines of their bodies.

"Big suckers," said Thomson. Her hands hovered over the console controls. Flight regime was up on the menu.

"Three of us're gonna take a whole army of *them*?" Codrus asked.

Dresser thought: It's not an army. It doesn't matter how big they are—we're not going to arm wrestle. You guys aren't any more scared than I am.

He said aloud, "You bet."

One of the Ichtons tossed the legless Gerson—the body had ceased to twitch—into the bag he, *it*, dragged along behind. The other Ichton spun abruptly and sprayed a ninety-degree arc of brush with his handweapon.

Though less powerful than the turret gun, the projectiles slashed though the vegetation. Branches and taller stems settled in a wave like the surface of a collapsing air mattress.

The Ichton with the bag patrolled the swath stolidly. He gathered up the bodies or body parts of three more victims.

"Don't . . ." Dresser whispered. Codrus and Thomson glanced sidelong, wondering what their commander meant.

The armed Ichton pointed his weapon. Before he could fire, the Gerson female with the infant in her arms stood up.

"Don't. . . ."

Instead of shooting, the Ichton stepped forward and reached out with its free hand. It seized the Gerson by the shoulder in a triaxial grip and led her back toward the vehicle. The remaining Ichton followed, slowed by the weight of the bag it was dragging.

Dresser let out the breath he had been holding longer than he realized.

"Now relax, Sergeant Dresser," said the mechanical voice. "Let the backbrain control your motions."

Dresser got to his feet, his four feet. His eyes stared at the ceiling. He wanted to close them, but they didn't close. A part of his mind was as amazed at the concept that eyes could close as it had been at the flat, adamantine images from Dresser's memory.

"You're doing very well, Sergeant," the voice cajoled. "Now, I'm going to open the door in the end of the compartment. Just follow the hallway out. Don't be in a hurry."

Dresser's right front leg bumped the table, but he didn't fall. He was terrified. His mind tried to focus on anything but what his legs were doing. The doorway lurched closer.

It was like being in free-fall. But he knew there was no landing possible from this mental vacuum.

3.

Rodriges manipulated his controls. The screen split. Its right half showed the back of the cloned Ichton shambling through the doorway, while a frontal shot of the creature approached down the hallway on the left.

"He's gonna get t' meet the brass," the technician muttered. "Horwarth and Dr. del Prato. Bet you never thought you'd be meeting an admiral and a top biochemist personal-like, did you, Sarge?"

Dresser grunted.

Rodriges touched the controls again. The right image leapfrogged to the interior of a three-bed medical ward that included a well-appointed office. The admiral, seated behind a desk of what looked like real wood, was a stocky female. She wore a skull and crossbones ring in her left ear, and her right ear was missing. To her right sat a florid-faced civilian whose mustache flowed into his sideburns.

The door to the ward had been removed and a section of bulkhead cut from the top of the doorway. Even so, the Ichton lurching down the corridor would have to duck or bang its flat head.

"Why didn't they wake him up here?" Dresser asked. He made a tight, almost dismissive gesture toward the medical ward.

Rodriges looked sidelong at the scout. "Umm . . ." he said. "They didn't know quite how you'd—he'd react when he woke up, y'know? They got me here for protection—"

The technician tapped carefully beside, not on, a separate keypad. It was a release for the weapons whose targeting was slaved to the screen controls.

"—but they don't want, you know, to lose the work. There's five more clones on ice, but still. . . ."

Dresser's face went hard. He didn't speak.

The Ichton paused in the doorway and tried to lower its head. Instead, the creature fell forward with its haunches high, like those of a horse that balked too close to the edge of a ditch.

"That's all right," said Admiral Horwarth brusquely. Her voice and the hypersonic translation of her voice echoed from the paired speakers of the observation room. "You'll soon have the hang of it."

"Part of the reason he's so clumsy," Rodriges said as he kept his invisible sight centered on the clone's chest, "is the body's straight out of the growth tank. It hasn't got any muscle tone."

His lips pursed as he and Dresser watched the ungainly creature struggle to rise again. "Of course," the technician added, "it could be the bugs're clumsy as hell anyhow."

"The ones I saw," said Dresser tightly, "moved pretty good."

The leading Ichton vehicle started to climb out of the dry wash; the nose of the last vehicle dipped to enter the end farthest from Dresser.

The scout boat's artificial intelligence planned the ambush with super-human skill. It balanced the target, the terrain, distance factors, and the available force—the lack of available force—into a seventy percent probability that some or all of the scout team would survive the contact.

The AI thought their chance of capturing a live Ichton was less than one tenth of a percent; but that wasn't the first thing in any of the scouts' minds, not even Dresser's.

The convoy's inexorable progress led it to the badlands site within two minutes of the arrival time the AI had calculated. A wind-cut swale between two tilted sheets of hard sandstone had been gouged deeper by infrequent cloudbursts. The resulting gully was half a kilometer long. It was straight enough to give Dresser a clear shot along it from where he lay aboard his skimmer, on higher ground a hundred meters from the mouth.

The Ichtons could easily have gone around the gully, but there was no reason for them to do so. From what Dresser had seen already, the race had very little tendency to go around anything.

"Team," he said to his distant crewmen, "*go!*"

Codrus and Thomson fired from the sandstone ridges to either flank. Their weapons tapped energy from the Dirac Sea underlying the real-time universe, so the range—less than three hundred meters in any case—was no hindrance.

Sightlines *could* have been a problem. Since Dresser had only two flankers, it didn't matter that they had clear shots at only the first and last vehicles of the convoy. The tops of the huge egg transporters were visible from the crewmen's positions, but the supply truck had vanished beneath the sharp lips of the gully.

The beams from the A-Potential weapons were invisible, but at their touch the magnetic shielding of the escort vehicles flared into sparkling cataclysm. Dresser's helmet visor blocked the actinics and filtered the visual uproar. He continued to have a sharp view of the vehicles themselves—undamaged at the heart of the storm.

The APOT weapons could focus practically limitless amounts of power on the magnetic shields, canceling their effect—but the beams couldn't focus *through* the shields. The escort vehicles stopped dead. Their power supplies shunted energy to the shields—to be dumped harmlessly back into the Dirac Sea—but as soon as the APOT beams were redirected, the escorts would be back in the battle.

"Mines," Dresser said to the audio controller in his helmet, "*go!*"

The gossamer, high-explosive mesh the scouts had spread across the floor of the gully went off. There was a green flash, a quick shock through the bedrock that slapped Dresser ten centimeters in the air, and—a heartbeat later—the air-transmitted blast that would have deafened the sergeant without the protection of his helmet.

The explosive's propagation rate was a substantial fraction of light speed. The blast flattened the two escorts from the underside before it lifted them. Their wreckage spun into the air.

Though the supply truck's shields were unaffected, the shock wave bounced the lighter vehicle against the side of the gully. It caromed back and landed on one side. Its shields hissed furiously, trying to repel the washed stone. The generators didn't have enough power to levitate the truck, and the ground wasn't going to move.

Mass and magnetic shielding protected the egg transporters. The huge vehicles lurched, but neither showed signs of damage. The leading transporter plowed through the wreckage of the escort. The driver of the second transporter cut his controls to the right. Bow weapons, their existence unguessed until this moment, blasted an alternate route into the sandstone wall.

The mine's unexpected ground shock lifted Dresser, then dropped him back on the hard-padded couch of his skimmer. He tried to aim his weapon.

The bow of the leading egg transporter was pointed directly at him. A panel had recessed to clear the muzzle of an axial weapon like the one carving a ramp through kilotonnes of rock. Its bore looked big enough for a man to crawl down.

Codrus caught the Ichton vehicle with his APOT weapon. The beam held the huge transporter as rigid as a moth on a pin. The screens' watery glare vanished.

Dresser raked the undefended target lengthwise with his drum-fed rocket launcher.

The launcher cycled at the rate of two rounds per second. It was easy for an experienced gunner like Dresser to control the weapon during short bursts, despite the considerable recoil: though the barrel was open at both ends, highly accelerated exhaust gas gave a sharp backward jolt to the sides of the tube.

Dresser's first rocket exploded on the muzzle of the Ichton gun. The next two green flashes shredded the bow of the transporter as recoil shoved Dresser and lifted his point of aim.

He lowered his sights and fired again, probing deeper into the Ichton vehicle through the damage caused by his initial burst. His helmet dulled the slap*bang*! of the shots and protected his retinas from the bright explosions. The rocket backblast prickled like sunburn on the backs of his bare hands.

A sulfurous fireball mushroomed from the rear of the transporter, far deeper than Dresser had been able to probe with his rockets. The shield generators failed. Codrus's weapon now cut spherical collops from the vehicle.

Dresser shifted his aim to the remaining transporter. He thought he had half the twenty-round drum remaining, but he knew he was too pumped to be certain.

A pair of Ichtons jumped from a hatch in the side of the transporter stalled in the beam of Thomson's weapon. Codrus, bulky and rounded in the hard suit that was an integral part of the APOT system, stood up on his ridge to rip the vehicle while Thomson's beam grounded its shield.

Dresser punched three rockets into the transporter's broadside. Green flashes ate meter-diameter chunks from the plating. The individual Ichtons turned together and fired their hand weapons at Codrus.

The rock beneath the crewman blurred into high-temperature gas. The Ichton projectiles were near the range at which the flux expanded beyond coherence and the miniature generators failed. If Codrus hadn't been shooting, his APOT suit might have protected him against the attenuated forces—

But an aperture to fire through meant a gap in the opposite direction also. Circuits in the APOT suit crossed, then blew in a gout of sandstone so hot it fluoresced.

"Ship!" Dresser shouted into the audio controller. He slammed a pair of contact-fused rockets through a hole blown by the previous burst. "Go!"

Ten klicks away, *SB 781* was lifting from her camouflaged hide. The AI would execute the flight plan the AI had developed. Dresser could override the machine mind, but he wouldn't have time—

And anyway, he might not be alive in five minutes when the boat appeared to make the extraction.

Bright gray smoke rolled in sheets out of the two lower holes in the transporter's plating. Flames licked from the highest wound, sullenly red, and the smoke they trailed was sooty black.

The transporter began to slip back down the ramp its gun had carved. The forward half of the vehicle was shielded, but smoke and flame continued to billow beneath the blue glow.

Thomson shrieked uncontrollably on the team frequency as she lashed the two Ichtons with her weapon. The creatures' personal shields deflected the beam—to Dresser's surprise, but if you couldn't *touch* the target, it didn't matter how much energy you poured into the wrong place.

Dresser kicked the bar behind his left boot to power up his skimmer. It induced a magnetic field in the rock with the same polarity as that in the little vehicle's own undersurface.

The skimmer lurched a centimeter upward, throwing off Dresser's aim. The last rocket in his magazine missed high. The transporter was beginning to sag in the center.

"Thomson!" Dresser shouted. "We want a prisoner!"

The rock beneath the Ichtons first went molten, then froze and shattered into dust finer than the sand that had once been compacted to make stone, and finally expanded into a white fireball that drank the Ichtons like thistledown in a gas flame. When transformed into a real-time analog, Thomson's A-Potential energy easily overwhelmed the Ichton defenses.

The skimmer wobbled downhill. Dresser steered with his feet on the tiller bar while he lay on his left side and fumbled a fresh magazine onto his rocket launcher. The Ichtons fired at movement. . . .

"Kill the fucking bastards!" Thomson screamed.

The front half of the damaged transporter began to crumple like overheated foil beneath its magnetic shielding. High-voltage arcs danced across the plates, scarring the metal like fungus on the skin of a poorly embalmed corpse.

"K—" said Thomson as her APOT beam drew a streak of cloudy red sky from another universe into the heart of the transporter. The back half of the vehicle blew up with a stunning crash even louder than that of the minefield that initiated the contact.

Because Dresser's skimmer was in motion, he was spared the ground shock. The airborne wave was a hot fist that punched fire into his lungs and threatened to spin his little vehicle like a flipped coin. The skimmer's automatic controls stabilized it as no human driver could have done, then shut down. Dresser kicked the starter again.

"Bastards!" shouted Thomson as she rode her own skimmer forward in search of fresh targets.

The explosion slammed the overturned supply truck into the gully wall again. The magnetic shielding failed; one side of the vehicle scraped off on the rock. A living Ichton, suited and armed, spilled out along with other of the truck's contents. Another of the creatures was within the gutted vehicle, transfixed despite its armor by a length of tubing from the perimeter frame.

Protein rations, bundled into transparent packets weighing a kilogram or so, littered the gully floor. The mother Gerson was only partway through processing. Her legs and the lower half of her furry torso stuck out the intake funnel in the truck body. The apparatus had stalled from battle damage.

The baby Gerson lay among the ration packets, feebly waving its chubby arms.

Thomson fired from her skimmer. She didn't have a direct sightline to the supply truck, but her suit sensors told her where the target was. The APOT beam ripped through the lip of stone like lightning in a wheat field.

Rock shattered, spewing chunks skyward. At the end of the ragged path, visible to Dresser though not Thomson, the damaged truck sucked inward and vanished like a smoke sculpture.

SB 781 drifted across Thomson, as silent as a cloud. The vessel was programmed to land at the center of the gully, since the team didn't have the transport to move an Ichton prisoner any distance from the capture site.

"Ship!" Dresser cried, overriding the plan. "Down! Now!"

The living Ichton got to its feet. Dresser, twenty meters away, grounded his skimmer in a shower of sparks and squeezed his trigger.

The rocket launcher didn't fire. He'd short-stroked the charging lever when the transporter blew up. There wasn't a round in the chamber.

The baby Gerson wailed. The Ichton spun like a dancer and vaporized the infant in a glowing dazzle.

SB 781 settled at the lip of the gully, between Thomson and the Ichton. She wouldn't shoot at their own ride home—and anyway, the vessel's A-Potential shielding should protect it if she did.

The team's *job* was to bring back a prisoner.

Dresser charged his launcher and fired. The warhead detonated on the Ichton's magnetic shield. The green flash hurled the creature against the rock wall.

It bounced back. Dresser fired again, slapping the Ichton into the stone a second time. The creature's weapon flew out of its three-fingered hands.

At Dresser's third shot, a triangular bulge on the Ichton's chest melted and the shield's blue glow vanished.

The Ichton sprawled in an ungainly tangle of limbs. Dresser got off his skimmer and ran to the creature. He dropped his rocket launcher and drew the powered cutting bar from the boot sheath where it rode.

Dresser's vision pulsed with colors as though someone were flicking pastel filters over his eyes. He didn't have time to worry whether something was wrong with his helmet optics. Thomson's shouted curses faded in and out also, so the damage was probably within Dresser's skull. Fleet hardware could survive one hell of a hammering, but personnel were still constructed to an older standard....

The Ichton twitched. Dresser ran the tip of his twenty-centimeter cutter along the back of the creature's suit. The armor was nonmetallic but tough enough to draw a shriek from the contra-rotating diamond saws in the bar's edge.

Dresser wasn't going to chance carrying the prisoner with inbuilt devices still functioning in its suit, not even in the stasis bay of *SB 781*. The tech mavens on the *Hawking* could deal with the network of shallow cuts the cutter was going to trace across the chitin and flesh. There wasn't time to be delicate, even if Dresser had wanted to be.

The air in the gully stank, but that wasn't why Dresser took breaths so shallow that his oxygen-starved lungs throbbed.

He couldn't help thinking about the baby Gerson vaporized a few meters away.

4.

There were two humans in the room with Dresser in his new body. The one behind the desk wore blue; the other wore white.

He wasn't sure what the sex of either of them was.

"As your mind reintegrates with the cloned body, Sergeant," said the mechanical voice, "you'll achieve normal mobility. Ah, normal for the new body, that is."

White's mouth parts were moving. Dresser knew—remembered—that meant the human was probably speaking, but the words came from the desk's front corner moldings. Ears alternated with the speech membranes along Dresser's lateral lines. He shifted position instinctively to triangulate on the speakers' precise location.

"I want to tell you right now, Sergeant, that the Alliance—that all intelligent life in the galaxy—is in your debt. You're a very brave man."

The voice and the location were the same—the desk speakers—but it was the other mouth that was moving. A translation system in the desk piped the actual speech out in a form Dresser could understand.

Now that he concentrated, he could hear the words themselves: a faint rumble, like that of distant artillery. It was meaningless and scarcely audible. He would have to watch to determine which of the pair was speaking—

But watching anything was easy. Dresser could see the entire room without turning his head. He noticed every movement, no matter how slight—nostrils flaring for a breath, the quiver of eyelashes at the start of a blink. His new brain combined the images of over a hundred facet eyes and sorted for the differences in the views they presented.

"It was obvious before we started that the enemy's numbers are enormous," Blue continued. "We now realize that Ichton weapons are formidable as well. In some ways—"

The desk translated Blue's throat clearing as a burst of static.

"Well, anyway, they're quite formidable."

The difficulty was that almost all Dresser now saw was movement. The background vanished beyond ten meters or so. Even closer objects were undifferentiated blurs until they shifted position. Though Dresser knew—remembered—the physical differences between human males and females, he couldn't see details so fine, and he lacked the hormonal cues that would have sexed individuals of his own kind.

Ye Gods, his own kind!

"You'll be landed back near the site where your original was captured, Sergeant Dresser," Blue went on.

The machine translator rasped Dresser's nerve endings with its compression. Its words lacked the harmonics that made true speech a thrill to hear no matter what its content.

"You shouldn't have any difficulty infiltrating the Ichton forces," interjected White. "The natural recognition patterns of your body will appear—*are* real, are totally real."

Dresser suddenly remembered the last stage of the firefight in the gully. He perceived it now through the senses of his present body. The Ichton flung from the vehicle, under attack but uncertain from where—

Sound and movement close by, a threat.

Spinning and blasting before the enemy can strike home.

Reacting before the higher brain can determine that the target was merely a part of the food supply that hadn't been processed before the attack occurred.

Dresser screamed. Both humans flinched away from the high-frequency warble.

"I'm not a bug!" he cried. "I won't! I won't kill babies!"

"Sergeant," said White, "we realize the strain you're under—"

"Though, of course, you volunteered," Blue said.

"—but when your personality has fully integrated with the body into which it's been copied," White continued, "the dichotomies—will not be quite so, ah, serious. I know—that is, I can imagine the strain you're experiencing. It will get better, I promise you."

"Sergeant . . ." said Blue, "I'll be blunt. We're hoping you can find a chink in the Ichtons' armor. If you can't, the mission of the *Stephen Hawking* is doomed to fail. And all life-forms in at least this galaxy are, quite simply, doomed."

"Except for the Ichtons themselves," White added.

The machine couldn't capture intonation; memory told Dresser that the bluster of a moment before had vanished.

Dresser's memory tumbled out a kaleidoscope of flat-focus images: a wrecked village; cancerous domes scores of kilometers in diameter, growing inexorably; an Ichton—Dresser's body in every respect—blasting a wailing infant by mistake, a waste of food. . . .

"I can't l-l-live like this!" Dresser cried.

"It's only temporary," Blue said. "Isn't that right, Doctor? I'm not denying the risk, Sergeant Dresser, but as soon as the mission's been completed, you'll be returned to your own form."

"Ah," said White. "Yes, of course, Sergeant. But the main thing is just to let your mind and body integrate. You'll feel better shortly."

"I think the best thing now is for you to start right in on the program," said Blue. "I'll bring in your briefing officers immediately. You'll see that we've taken steps to minimize the risk to you."

Blue continued to speak. All Dresser could think of was that tiny Gerson, like a living teddy bear.

5.

The screen showed six personnel entering the ward where the Ichton clone hunched. One of the newcomers was a Gerson.

In the observation room, Dresser turned his back on the screen. "How much does he remember?" he asked Rodriges harshly.

The technician shrugged. "Up to maybe thirty-six hours before the transfer," he said. "There's some loss, but not a lot. You okay yourself?"

"Fine," said Dresser. "I'm great."

On the screen, a uniformed man without rank tabs outlined the physical training program. The clone's new muscles had to be brought up to standard before the creature was reinserted.

Dresser shuddered. Rodriges thumbed down the audio level, though the translation channel remained a distant piping.

"When I volunteered . . ." Dresser said carefully. "I didn't know how much it'd bug—bother me. To see myself as an Ichton."

"Naw, that's not you, Sarge," Rodriges said. "Personalities start to diverge at the moment the mind scan gets dumped in the new cortex—and in *that* cortex, the divergence is going to be real damn fast. None of the sensory stimuli are the same, you see."

Dresser grunted and looked back over his shoulder. "Yeah," he said. "Well. Bet he thinks he's me, though."

"Sarge, you did the right thing, volunteering," Rodriges soothed. "You heard the admiral. Using somebody who's seen the bugs in action, that improves the chances. And anyway—it's done, right?"

The clone was moving its forelimbs—arms—in response to the trainer's direction. The offside supporting legs twitched unexpectedly, the tall creature fell over. A civilian expert jumped reflexively behind a female colleague in Marine Reaction Unit fatigues.

"It's going to be just as hard for him when they switch him back, won't it?" Dresser said. He turned to the technician. "Getting used to a human body again, I mean."

"Huh?" Rodriges blurted. "Oh, you mean like the admiral said. Ah, Sarge. . . . A fast-growth clone—"

He gestured toward the screen. Dresser didn't look around.

"Look, it's a total-loss project. I mean, in the tank we got five more bodies like this one—but the original, what's left of that's just hamburger."

Dresser stared but said nothing.

Rodriges blinked in embarrassment. He plowed onward, saying, "Cost aside—and I'm *not* saying it's a cost decision, but it'd be cheaper to build six destroyers than a batch of fast-growth clones. Anyway, cost aside, there's no *way* that thing's gonna be back in a body like yours unless yours. . . . You know?"

The technician shrugged.

"I guess I was pretty naive," Dresser said slowly.

Rodriges reached over and gripped the scout's hand. "Hey," the technician said. "It's not you, you know? It's a thing. Just a thing."

Dresser disengaged his hand absently. He looked toward the screen again, but he didn't see the figures, human and alien, on it. Instead, his mind filled with the image of the baby Gerson, stretching out its chubby hands toward him—

Until it vanished in tears that diffracted light into a dazzle like that of the weapon in Dresser's three-fingered hands.

INDIES

One of the political peculiarities of the Alliance was the importance of the Indie (Independent) traders to its system of interstellar trade. At the end of the Family war, thousands of no longer needed ships were sold as surplus war material. Since the larger companies had already expanded their merchant fleets massively to fulfill the lucrative contracts the war produced, they had no need for ships that were not even designed to carry cargo. As a result these disarmed scouts and cruisers were sold to Independent traders, whose ranks were swelled by Fleet personnel released as the navy shrunk to a peacetime level of staffing.

As is their nature, the megacorps and their fleets of highly cost effective merchant ships and liners monopolized the most lucrative trade routes. The Indies competed fiercely with one another for the marginal and frontier markets. They provided a vital service to thousands of worlds that otherwise would rarely merit a stop from the giant merchant carriers. When the three races arrived and made their public request for assistance, many Indie traders saw another opportunity as well. Here was a totally untapped market where there would be no competition from the megacorps. Once the star maps were released, many of the more adventurous stocked up on trade goods and began their long journey to Star Central two years before the battlestation was completed. The presence of these Indies who had preceded them provided valuable information, and numerous complications, for the Fleet station when it did arrive.

TRADING UP
by Mike Resnick
and Barbara Delaplace

"They'll ruin everything!" Salimander Smith shouted at the group gathered at the bar. "Can't anyone but me see it?" He glared at his companions. "You call yourselves traders? Hah! You couldn't sell umbrellas in a rainstorm!" He picked up his mug of Arskellian beer—provided to him gratis by the management of The Lonesome Tavern, since he was the one who'd imported it for them—and drained it.

"You're out of your mind," said one woman. "The *Stephen Hawking* is one big enormous ripe market waiting for us Indies." She paused. "I hear it's got more than ten thousand personnel aboard. That's ten thousand reasons business is going to boom."

Smith looked at her with pity. "Delilah, my dear, you're as hopelessly ill-informed as you are beautiful." She glared at him, but made no reply. "I regret to inform you that a depressingly large proportion of that ten thousand consists of Independent traders like ourselves. This ain't exactly the virgin market you think it is."

"But even if there are a lot of Indies on board the *Hawking*, so what?" protested a tall man with a luxuriant beard and long, waxed mustaches. "We have the advantage of already knowing the territory. We've already got our contacts on the different worlds."

"If they're anything like your contacts, Davies," retorted Smith contemptuously, "I'd say the new competition hasn't got a thing to worry about. Made back your losses yet on that deal for Zanther goldfish skins? I'll bet Manderxx the Nimble laughed all the way to what passes for a bank on his world." The bearded man looked uncomfortable as the others hooted with laughter.

"We can always act as middlemen and contacts ourselves to the new traders, though. There's enough business here for everyone," said another woman, who sported a massive ear broach inlaid with rare Sirel fire-rubies.

"Not with those damned insects ruining every planet they set foot on," said a third man. "They've wiped out two worlds that I had good trade deals with. I've lost markets worth millions. And don't tell me you can cut deals with Ichtons, Salimander old lizard. I tried, and just barely got out with my skin intact."

Smith surveyed the speaker with some distaste. "That's what I like about you, Harry. Your humanitarian attitude and deep concern for other living beings."

Harry eyed him truculently. "The bugs are bad for business. That's all I care about. Now that the *Hawking*'s arrived, the Fleet will wipe 'em out, and we can get back to trading for a decent profit margin."

"Not a chance," said the woman wearing the ear broach. "Those Ichtons are *tough* bastards. I think the Fleet's going to be around for a while."

"I agree," said Smith. "I've been checking with some of my contacts. It looks like we're in for a long war. Unfortunately."

"'Unfortunately'?" repeated the woman. "Smith, you've been in space too long. The Fleet'll need raw materials. They'll need R-and-R. They'll need fresh air and the great outdoors. The on-board merchants will want to trade. We'll clean up."

There was a general nodding of heads along the bar.

Smith scanned the faces. "You *still* can't see it, can you? Now that the Fleet's in the Core, things aren't going to be like they were. The Fleet means law and order. No more unrestricted trade. *That's* what's bad for business." He paused. "I've been an Independent trader—"

"—all my life," the others finished for him.

Undaunted, Smith continued. "I've seen it happen before. The Fleet moves in, the Alliance starts breathing down everyone's necks, and next thing you know, you need a permit just to lift off. I've been working the Core for—"

"—fifteen years!" they chorused.

Amid general laughter Davies said, "Oh, come off it! A few regulations won't get in our way."

"You think it'll stop at a few regulations?" demanded Smith. "You're a bigger fool than I thought! No organization stops after making just a *few* rules. And with the Fleet here, the Alliance is here. That means tariffs and duties and customs regulations. Do you really think they're going to let us keep trading rights to the worlds we've opened up when they're carrying five thousand traders of their own on that damned ship?" He stood up. "Well, I'm not going to just stand by and let it happen."

"What're you going to do—stop the *Hawking* single handed?" sneered Delilah. The other traders laughed.

"Not stop it. But I sure as hell plan to make it swerve a bit." Smith picked up his vivid cloak and shrugged into it amid a general atmosphere of disbelief. "Good night, ladies and gentlemen. I've spent enough time with fools and losers."

He went out into the darkness.

Back on his ship, Smith propped his embroidered boots onto a hassock and settled back in an antique leather armchair (obtained in a complicated four-cornered deal involving a Hong Kong merchant anxious to clear her warehouse, a Fleet services-and-supplies officer with an unlawful addiction to an illicit liquor, and an alien species known as the Nest Makers). A freshly poured beer at his elbow, he contemplated the projected fire in the holographic fireplace.

The habitues of The Lonesome Tavern were fools. Well, he'd warned them; if they couldn't see the handwriting on the wall, it was hardly *his* problem. A trader always watched out for his own interests first.

And his interests were the trading deals he'd so painstakingly worked out with six alien worlds in the Core. It had taken years for him to build up his contacts and markets—fifteen years, just as they'd jeered in the bar. Well, perhaps he *did* have a habit of repeating himself; probably came as a result of spending so much time away from people, traveling his trading circuit. After all that work, he'd be damned if he'd just stand by and let the diplomats and paper pushers and regulation makers move in and take over.

But how to stop it? The Fleet wouldn't step aside just for one man. . . . unless that man was somehow indispensable to them. *Indispensable.* To a trader, that meant supplying them something no one else could supply. Now the problem was couched in terms that he could deal with, deal-making terms. Stroking the old scar on his cheek, Salimander Smith stared into the cold flames of the hologram and pondered. . . .

Brad Omera, his face haggard, his back stiff and sore, glanced up from what was still known as "paperwork" even though paper had been out of use for centuries. I wonder if the ancient Egyptians called it papyrus-work? he thought. Whatever it was called, it seemed to follow administrators no matter what the era was.

"There's a Salimander Smith who wants to talk to you, sir," said his assistant, her face shimmering in the holotank at the corner of his desk. "He says it's vital."

"Don't they all?" muttered Omera.

"He claims to have detailed knowledge about several alien cultures we're unfamiliar with."

Omera became slightly more interested. "He does, eh? Well, I suppose he could be useful. Lord knows, we never seem to have enough alien specialists." He paused for a moment. Odds were that this was probably just another scam artist. On the other hand, they couldn't afford to overlook anyone who might enable them to establish contact with any of the races at the Core. They needed to unite against the Ichtons. "Set up an appointment," he said at last. "You never know who might turn out to be useful."

"Yes, sir. You never know."

"It's a pleasure to meet you, Mr. Omera, a real pleasure." Salimander Smith held out his hand, virtually forcing Omera to return the handshake. "I know what a busy man you are, and I appreciate the effort you made to find time to see me. I guarantee you won't regret it."

Omera surveyed Smith's gaudy clothes with distaste as he released the trader's hand and sat down again. Smith noted this—for a trader, missing the smallest detail might mean the difference between showing a profit or a loss for a year's worth of negotiating. Omera was obviously resolved not to let what he regarded as Smith's too-hearty manner and overdone clothing put him off. "My pleasure, Mr. Smith."

Bullshit. You don't like me and you didn't want to see me, but you don't want to ignore me in case I can be useful. "Let me tell you a little about myself. Can't expect a man to do business with someone he's never met before. I'm an Independent—"

"Mr. Smith, I'm a busy man, and I don't have a lot of time to spare. Let's get down to brass tacks. You're an Independent trader who's been working the Core for the past fifteen years. You've established trade relations with six alien races. Your contracts with them have been only moderately rapacious, and as a result you've made a very handsome living for yourself."

"I'm not sure I like the term 'rapacious,' Mr. Omera."

"I did qualify it, Mr. Smith. Compared to some of the Independent traders I've seen in action, you've been reasonably restrained."

Smith shrugged. "It's good for business. Alien races aren't stupid, and some of them have very unpleasant ways of dealing with traders they feel have cheated them." He paused. "I prefer a long-term, mutually beneficial trading arrangement with my alien partners. Then both sides prosper. In fact, that's why I'm here."

"To see if the two of us can come to a mutually beneficial trading agreement?" Omera's voice was cynical.

"Perhaps not a trading agreement, but some sort of understanding."

"Mr. Smith, I've dealt with a lot of Indies. Usually when they start using words like 'understanding,' they want me to bend the rules. And they generally offer a sliding scale of incentives proportional to the amount of bending they want done."

Smith's expression spoke volumes. "Amateurs, every one of them," he said contemptuously. "I have no intention of offering you a bribe."

"Well, *that's* a novel approach," said Omera. "What exactly *are* you offering?"

"Mr. Omera, as you've already noted, I've spent a long time building up trade with those alien races. I've had a good deal of experience with their customs. I know their languages and their politics. I'm prepared to offer my expertise in those areas to you."

"In return for what, as if I couldn't guess?'

"In return for recognition of what already exists," answered Smith, unperturbed. "I want exclusive trading rights on those worlds."

Omera replied flatly, "Impossible."

"You disappoint me, Mr. Omera," replied Smith easily. "When dealing with the man at the top, there's no such word as 'impossible.'"

"We're in a state of war. I'm not empowered to, nor am I interested in, working out trade deals with any Indie who comes along."

"I'm not just 'any Indie,'" said Smith, radiating self-confidence. "No other trader has my knowledge of those worlds—you yourself admitted that I was the one who established relations with them." He stared into Omera's eyes. "I'd be a valuable addition to your staff of experts."

"Somehow I don't think you'd fit in very well on the *Stephen Hawking*, Mr. Smith, valuable though you might be. And as you point out, we do have experts already, experts who are experienced in dealing with newly contacted alien races."

"Of course you do. But as you say, you're in a state of war—and time is a valuable commodity in war. How long will it take those experts of yours to become familiar with the political situation on Meloth? Politics is a passion there, and they hold elections once a month. Make an alliance with the wrong splinter faction, and you could wind up alienating eighty percent of the power brokers on the planet. You'd lose a potential ally."

"If the situation is as delicate there as you say, we'd definitely want our own experts studying it firsthand."

"If they go there without me, they might be in for a hostile reception. Melothians prefer dealing with those they know."

"A threat, Mr. Smith?"

"Not at all, Mr. Omera. Simply a statement of fact. I myself nearly got killed when I first made contact. Of course," Smith added, studying the ceiling reflectively, "Meloth's not the only planet that's hostile to newcomers."

"It's certainly beginning to *sound* like a threat. A planet that hostile should probably be placed on the interdict list. We can't have a fellow citizen"—and here Omera paused meaningfully before continuing—"landing on such a dangerous world."

Smith studied the man on the other side of the desk carefully. The administrator's face was impassive. Yes, he probably was capable of doing just that, if he felt it was necessary to further the cause of the Alliance. Omera had countered every suggestion Smith made, and had just subtly pointed out that Smith was not playing from a position of strength. I must be losing my touch, he thought ruefully. Now there was only one option left.

"Not even if that citizen knew of an even more dangerous world? A world of strategic importance?" Smith watched Omera closely.

"What sort of strategic importance?" Omera's tone suggested he'd heard this sort of thing before, but Smith's years of practice in observation suddenly paid off. The administrator had a superb poker face, but the clenching of one hand gave him away. Gotcha, you cold sonofabitch!

Smith leaned back in his chair. "Of such importance that it might help bring victory to the Alliance."

"And just what might that be?"

"I know the location of an Ichton base."

Omera's eyes were suddenly intent. "Keep talking, Mr. Smith."

"There's nothing further to say," replied Smith. "I can pinpoint the world on any map you care to show me. For a price, of course."

"How much money do you want?"

"I don't want your money."

"Let me guess—trading rights to those half-dozen worlds, correct?"

"Correct," answered Smith. "But consider what you get in return: prisoners to interrogate, captives to study, a potential bargaining chip with the Ichtons. And it won't cost you a single credit." He paused. "I'd say you're getting a bargain."

Omera studied Smith for a long moment. Smith lounged easily in his chair. At last Omera said, "I have to consult with Commander Brand."

"Consult all you like," said Smith with a casual wave of his hand. "I have nothing but time."

"Excuse me." Omera stood up abruptly and left the room.

Five minutes later Omera returned. "Agreed. Tell me the name of the planet where the Ichton base is, and I guarantee you exclusive trading rights to the six worlds you opened up."

"I have your promise on record? Exclusive rights on Meloth, Sarn, Tellikan, Arskell, Merring, and Zel?" Smith's expression had turned calculating.

"Mr. Smith, let's not become coy, shall we? You spotted my holocorder the minute you sat down. Of course it's on record."

Salimander Smith always knew when it was time to give in gracefully, particularly when he'd gotten what he wanted. "You're absolutely right, Mr. Omera, I did. Please forgive my lack of manners."

"And the location of the Ichton base?"

"Looden III. That's a system about—"

"I know where it is. All right, Mr. Smith, you have your deal. Thank you for doing your patriotic duty. And now, if you don't mind, I have other matters pressing me. . . ." Omera's face was wearier than it had been a few minutes ago.

"Of course, Mr. Omera. A pleasure doing business with you." Smith stood up, thought the better of offering to shake hands again, and left the office.

There was a man waiting for him outside, a man wearing an air of command and the uniform of a senior officer of the Fleet. "Salimander Smith?"

"Yes."

"I'm Commander Brand."

"An honor to meet you, sir."

"I understand you know the location of an Ichton colony."

"Yes, I do. As I just told Mr. Omera, it's on Looden III."

"Do you think you can pinpoint the colony's location? Lead a landing party directly to it?"

"Lead a landing party to it? Well now, you must understand that I'm not a military man," answered Smith. "Still, for the right price, and a hell of a big invasion force to protect me, I suppose we could work something out."

"The price is 173 credits a month," said Brand.

"I beg your pardon?"

"You've just been drafted as an alien contact expert. Welcome to the Fleet, Specialist Smith."

"*What?*"

"Oh, yes, indeed, Mr. Smith." Brad Omera appeared in the office doorway. "As you've admitted yourself, you'd be a valuable addition to our staff. We've decided to take you up on that suggestion."

"But you said I wouldn't fit in very well on the *Hawking*! I'd be a disruptive influence!"

"Then how fortunate it is for us that you won't be aboard the *Hawking* for more than twelve hours before you are transferred to one of our gunboats bound for Looden III."

"I thought we had a deal!" shouted Smith furiously.

"We have every intention of honoring it," said Brand. "You have the sole right to establish trade with the worlds you named, and once the war is over and you are released from active duty, we wish you good luck in your enterprise. But until then, Mr. Smith," he concluded with a nasty smile, "your ass is ours."

Omera smiled to himself as he went back into his office. Somehow he just knew Salimander Smith would find a way to turn his time in the Fleet to good use. He sat down at his desk again and wondered for a moment if ancient Egyptian administrators had ever had to worry about traveling salesmen. Probably they did. *That* hadn't changed much down through the centuries.

He sighed and got back to work.

BATTLESTATION

One of the most important lessons the Fleet learned in its war against the Syndicate of Families was the near impossibility of supporting a fleet parsecs from its normal bases. The Fleet's first solution was to stockpile materials for up to a hundred major bases and repair centers, to be transported and set up behind the advancing Fleet units. This concept was discarded after one such modular base was assembled, when the cost was calculated. The immensity of the Alliance was so great that it was becoming impossibly expensive just to guard all of its borders, much less prepare for offensive operations beyond them. Yet it was inevitable that someday such a war would have to be fought.

This next solution was to create a mobile unit capable of supporting a large fleet. Fewer of these would be needed, and they could be kept secure within the heart of the Alliance serving a useful purpose from completion. Kilometers across, the station would contain the most massive warp drives ever attempted. Only recent breakthroughs resulting from the combination of Family and Alliance science even allowed for their construction.

Unfortunately the cost of one of these mobile stations was immense. The construction of the first had been proposed over thirty years earlier, and similar proposals by the Fleet had been rejected by the Alliance Senate eleven times in the next twenty years. Eventually all the designs were filed away, but not forgotten. The necessity of sending a fleet halfway across the galaxy reopened the opportunity for the creation of the mobile base. A series of seven were proposed by the Quartermasters Corps on Port, Tau Ceti. The funding for just one was approved by a very close vote.

To the dismay of the refugees, the mobile base would take almost three years to complete. Construction of this mobile base began around Tau Ceti when someone finally realized that the base would need to defend itself. It would be operating ahead of the Fleet lines, not behind them. This would add to its cost, but give it needed "survivability." The Senate balked at this added cost. The release to the Trivid stations raised enough public support that another compromise was finally reached. The station would be armed, but almost half its space would now be set aside for private interests. In return the corporations and a consortium of Indies would contribute a portion of the cost and provide a number of construction crews. Production continued and the mobile base became the first Fleet battlestation.

GLOBIN'S CHILDREN
by Christopher Stasheff

Globin had been the human leader of a band of Khalian pirates on Barataria, leading his Weasel crews against humans of any political stripe.

Globin had become the head of a vast trading combine and the architect of Khalian integration into the human-dominated Alliance—not because he wanted to, but because it was the only route to survival for the one-time outlaws who depended on him.

Now Globin was old and tired. Well, not really old, considering that he was only eighty, and humans of his day regularly lived to the age of 130, remaining in full vigor past their centennials—but he *felt* old. And weary. And, most especially, bored.

He was satisfied that he had established a stable government on Barataria that would continue to be viable and democratic without him, and he was certain that he was no longer necessary to anyone, least of all himself.

Then the voice of Plasma, his secretary, sounded from the desktop speaker. "Globin."

Globin gave the grille a jaundiced glance, then sighed as he felt the weight of his office settle again. "Yes, Plasma?"

"A new ship has appeared at the Galactic West frontier, Globin—a ship of a type that has never been seen before. To demands that it identify itself, it responds with unintelligible gibberish."

Globin frowned. "Interesting, but scarcely vital to the welfare of Barataria."

"True, Globin. I thought it might be of interest to you personally."

Globin smiled; Plasma had been his aide for most of his adult years, and knew that inside the statesman's hide lurked the scholar that had never quite been buried under the avalanche of bureaucracy. "You thought correctly. From which direction does it come?"

"From the interior of the galaxy, Globin."

"The interior! This *could* be interesting! Is there any video feed yet?"

"None for the public." Plasma's voice hid amusement.

It was well founded; so far as they knew, the Alliance was still blissfully unaware the Baratarians had long since gained access to their sentry system's scramble code.

"Relay it to my screen." Globin swiveled about to the wall in which his view-screen was embedded, a meter high and two wide.

The screen darkened, showing night pierced with the sparks that were stars. One glowed much brighter than all the rest, and Globin reached for his controls, keying in the code for expansion. The brightest spark loomed larger and larger until it filled the screen—a collection of cylinders bound together with a coil, looking like nothing so much as a collection of ancient tin cans tied together with baling wire. And they did seem ancient—scarred and pitted by collisions with countless meteorites, splotched by mysterious burns. That spaceship had come a long, long way—and at a guess, the aliens hadn't wanted to spend much energy on force-field screens.

Either that, or they didn't know how to make them.

Voices accompanied the picture, the voices of the sentry who had spotted the ship and his senior officer.

"You're getting *what?*"

"An outrageous radiation reading, Captain. I'd guess their shielding broke down."

Or, thought Globin, they hadn't had any to begin with—like the early torch-ships, which had shielding only between the engines and the ship itself. Why shield empty space from radiation?

"Could be they're using really raw fuel," a more mature voice answered.

Globin nodded slowly. If this species hadn't bothered developing more advanced engines, they might even be using U-235. Why go after higher elements, when the lower would do?

Had they even thought of fusion?

But surely they had to, if they had come so far.

Something else bothered him. Why five separate cylinders? Perhaps one for the engines, but why the other four?

A niggling suspicion joggled his brain. Could there be more than one life-form aboard? Could they need separate environments for separate species? Or perhaps . . .

He felt the compulsion seize him, the hunger for knowledge, and knew it wouldn't go away until it was fulfilled. He would study everything he could about these aliens, at every odd moment, until he was satiated. It was the old, old hunger that had driven him into scholarship, and was akin to the lust for revenge that had driven him to find the Merchant worlds. It was the same driving appetite that had led him to learn as much as he could about the commerce of the Alliance, and had allowed him to hew out a niche for Barataria.

He hoped this hunger would work for the good of his adopted people, too.

An hour later Plasma came in with some papers needing signatures and found Globin still staring at the screen, listening to the voices, ideas whirling in his head.

❖ ❖ ❖

The conference was over; the delegation from Khalia filed out, their leader pausing to chat a little longer with Globin before they left. As soon as he was ont the door, Plasma was in. "The aliens have docked at a western sentry station, Globin! I have been recording it for two hours! They are attempting to communicate!"

Globin stared, changing frames of reference in his mind. Then he frowned. "Alien! With so many races in the Alliance, how can you speak the word 'alien'?"

"*Truly* alien, Globin! Like no creatures we have ever seen before!" The secretary turned to the wall screen, keyed it in, and selected a channel.

Globin turned back to his desk. "Let us see it as it is now, Plastna! I will view the beginning later!"

He dropped into his chair to see the collection of cylinders, scarred and pitted. It was held to the dock by magnetic grapples only—of course; there was no guarantee that an oxygen atmosphere would not hurt its occupants, so there could be no boarding tube yet.

Behind him, Plasma said, "Fighters came out to inspect, and found an alien floating at the end of a tether with his arms up and hands spread open. They took that as the sign of peace, and towed the ship back to the station. I am sure there are a triad of blast cannon focused on it even now."

And a projectile rifle aimed at each alien, Globin guessed for the top of one of the giant tin cans had opened downward, and four spacesuited figures stood on it. One was more or less anthropoid, standing on two limbs and having two others just below the sphere of the helmet—but it was broad and swollen, so much so that Globin had a fleeting notion that its suit was inflated, with nothing inside. Another stood on four legs with two more limbs extended for grasping, and a long extension behind that was probably a tail.

A tail? On a sentient being? How could its race not have evolved past the need for one?

Another alien stood on six, and one on none. All had extensions that looked like arms, though it was hard to tell in a spacesuit—but only the bearlike one had anything resembling shoulders. The one without legs was smallest, scarcely a meter long—and long it was, for its suit stretched out horizontally, floating in midair by some kind of field effect that was presumably built into the suit.

"Detail!" Globin pressed a ruby square on his desktop, and the picture enlarged. He maneuvered a joystick set next to the ruby square, and one single helmet filled the meter-wide screen. It was heavily frosted on the outside, but one square area was kept clear, presumably by heating. Reflection made the face within difficult to see, but Globin could make out a muzzle and large warm eyes. The face looked like that of a bear, but a very warmhearted bear. Globin knew it was completely illogical, but he felt himself warming to the alien.

He pushed the joystick to the right, and the bear-face slid out of the screen as the helmet of the centauroid slid in. Globin could make out sleek, streamlined jaws, and atop them eyes that were only dim glints, but enough to make Globin shiver—the creature might be sentient, but it was far from human.

He pushed the joystick once more, and shuddered again. The six-legged creature's helmet was in front of its body, not on top, and the face within bore clear convex lenses for eyes four inches across, fangs and hair shrouding everything else—at least, Globin thought it was hair; it was hard to tell through the frost.

All this time, he'd been absorbing the audio. A commentator, carefully neutral, was saying, "The ursine creature has presented a diagram of an oxygen atom; the centauroid and arachnid have presented similar diagrams of methane molecules. All have made sounds as they pointed to the diagrams, and the computer has associated those sounds with the names of the compounds. From this, we surmise that the ursine is an oxygen breather, though judging from the frost on its suit, it is accustomed to a much warmer median temperature than any Alliance species."

Globin pushed the joystick down and over—and received a shock. The horizontal alien had no helmet—only two clear bulbs, within which were antennas. They did not move; the creature might have been an inert lump. But one of the "arms" held a diagram of a molecule—no, two diagrams, Globin saw. He frowned and expanded the view, and recognized the second diagram—it was a silicon atom.

Globin stared.

"The meaning of the second diagram held by the fourth alien is unclear," the commentator said.

But it was very clear, to Globin. The creature lived in an oxygen atmosphere, but was made of silicon. He felt a prickling creep up across his back as he stared at it—a living, organic computer.

Then he remembered that that was what he himself was, that and considerably more, and the prickling went away. Still, how much he could learn from the study of such a creature!

The bearish alien touched its own chest and chuckled something that sounded, to human ears, like "Gerson. Gerson."

"The alien seems to be naming itself," murmured the commentator. "But is 'Gerson' its name, or the name of its species?"

The centauroid was touching its chest now, fluting "Silber." The six-legged alien gestured toward itself and said, in tones like metal scraping, "Itszxlksh." Then another voice, rich and resonant, thrummed, "Ekchartok."

Globin frowned, and peered more closely. The arm of the horizontal alien had begun to move toward itself—but slowly, very slowly. He wondered what means it had employed to generate the sound.

He was still watching its movement as the picture disappeared, and the commentator himself came onto the screen. "Since this scene was recorded, the aliens have been in constant contact with a growing team of Alliance scientists. They have established a very basic vocabulary . . ."

The picture dissolved back into the first.

" . . . by associating sounds with pictures of basic objects," said the commentator's voice, "then with sketches of simple action verbs. With a thousand such words entered, the translation computer has been able to enter into dialogue with the aliens, exchanging descriptions and explanations of more complex terms. With five thousand words learned by both teams, meaningful dialogue has begun to take place."

Globin nodded, so intent that he scarcely saw his secretary. The procedure was correct—in fact, it was classical. But what had they learned from their communication?

"The four aliens are representatives of four different species," the commentator explained, "and our computers have learned four different languages, plus a fifth that is apparently a lingua franca. According to the visitors' report, they are only four of a score or more of races that inhabit the stars near the galactic core."

Globin stared. Just how far had those visitors come, anyway?

Thirty thousand light-years. Of course. He knew that. Approximately. Give or take a thousand light-years.

A spacesuited human stepped into the picture, asking, "Why have you come here?" The translation computer issued a combination of growls and whistles that Globin presumed constituted the same idea in the aliens' lingua franca.

In answer, the bearish alien growled and barked. The computer translated, "We were attacked by alien beings." He pressed the top of his card, and the diagram of the oxygen atom disappeared. The card flickered and darkened into a picture of ships in space—a vast flotilla, without any apparent organization, though Globin felt instinctively that the pattern was there, if he could only take the time to seek it out. He keyed his controls to expand that picture on the "card" and found that the ships were of a design not even remotely familiar, with a strangeness about it that somehow grated, arousing apprehension and dread in equal measure.

"They came from the northwest spiral arm," the computer stated to the accompaniment of the bearish one's growls. "All efforts to communicate with them have failed; they make no response at all. We call them 'Ichtons'; in our communal language, it means 'the destroyers.'"

The picture faded away and returned—but now it showed the strange ships descending toward a tawny planet. "At first," said the computer, "they settled on several uninhabited worlds. They had tenuous oxygen atmospheres and some primitive plant life, but had never evolved sentient forms. Accordingly, we left them alone, but set probes to keep watch on them. Within a decade, we saw that their planets had become overcrowded with billions of Ichton workers. The soil had been torn away to bedrock, refuse had been piled high, and all forms of life had been exterminated.

"Then they left these used-up planets and attacked worlds inhabited by sentient races."

The picture dissolved into a scene of battle, showing a horde of insectoid creatures engulfing a band of desperate reptilian creatures who bore weapons that looked like muskets modified to fit an allosaur, but that fired blasts of light. The view narrowed, one single attacker swelling in the screen even as its image froze. Globin shuddered; the creature looked like the result of an unnatural coupling between a locust and an iguana, The trunk of the body was covered by a hard exoskeleton made up of sliding sheets. This carapace extended over the top of its head. It stood on four legs and used a third pair in front to hold a weapon that seemed to be little but a tube with a squeeze bulb on the end—but the chitinous claw rested on a button, not the bulb. There were three of those claws on each "hand." The head looked like a locust's, except for the eyes, which were much smaller than those of the terrestrial insect.

It was not so much that the creature looked fearsome, as that it was utterly, totally in contradiction of everything he had ever thought of as a sentient being—and from the silent ferocity with which it had attacked, it seemed completely soulless and mechanical.

The creature shrank back into the middle of its swarm; the tableau thawed, motion restored, and Globin watched the pocket of reptilians being engulfed by the horde. They streamed by, chitinous thoraxes and threshing legs and whipping tails, and when they had passed, there was not a trace of the reptilians.

"These are only a very few of a relatively small band of Ichtons," the Gerson explained, "but even so, they were enough to overwhelm the reptilian colony on what was once a lovely and fertile planet. The same has since happened to the home planet, and to those of three other species. On any world they conquer, the Ichtons exterminate all higher forms of life, especially sentient species, then begin exploiting the planet's resources."

The picture rose, looking out over miles and miles of barren sand.

"Where the horde has passed," the Gerson growled, "nothing remains; all life is erased."

The screen darkened; Globin moved his joystick to show him all four aliens again. The fluting voice of the Silber said, "We four races have joined together to protect our worlds. Together, we halted the Ichton advance, but only at grievous cost in lives and resources. We knew we could not hold them off for long without assistance—so we dispatched dozens of ships like this one, each with environments for representatives of each of our four species, to seek out aid for our home worlds and colonies. The Ichtons seem to have realized our goal, for they pounced on our ship as we fled our home planet. The battle was short and vicious, and our ship was damaged in the course of it, but we won free, and have come to you from the Core in only four months."

"Four months?" said Plasma. "Was their drive damaged, that they could not shift in weeks?"

"I think not," said Globin. "They seem almost to boast, as though they think four months to be excellent time. It is only conjecture, but I think their FTL drive is very primitive. After all, stars crowd densely at the Core; what need for a sophisticated FTL drive when you need never travel more than a few light-years?"

"We ask your aid," thrummed the Ekchartok, "not only for ourselves, but also for you. We believe that the Ichtons have conquered all the habitable planets of their spiral arm; if they conquer the worlds of the Core, they will begin to move out into other spiral arms. It may take a century or a millennium, but they will find your worlds, too—and then they will be virtually unbeatable; there will not be billions of them, but billions of billions. We appeal to you to fight this cancer and excise it now, while it is still far distant from you—and in the process, to aid four species who have been long blessed with peace, and have ceased to study the ways of war."

But the humans and Khalia had not succeeded in studying war no more, Globin reflected. Far from it.

He didn't bother following the debate that ensued in the Alliance Council; it had a foregone conclusion. So he was not at all surprised when Plasma burst into his office three days later, crying, "Globin! It is war!"

Globin stared, frozen for a moment. Then he snapped, "The screen! At once!"

"At once, Globin!" Plasma ducked back into the outer office, and the screen lit up with a view of the Alliance council chambers, with men in grim and very orderly debate.

"The Senate met in executive session as soon as the preliminary reports had been presented," the commentator said. "In view of the sufferings and peril of the Core races, they have decided to lend what aid they can against the Ichtons."

Globin smiled a small and cynical smile. "It is scarcely sheer altruism," he said.

"Truly," Plasma agreed. "Who does not know that the Fleet, idling in peacetime, is not always the best of neighbors? I certainly would not care to have a base on Barataria, with Fleet law virtually excluding our own government."

"Never," Globin agreed, "though we have more reason to dislike the notion than most. And there is a burden of support that accompanies a Fleet base—not to mention making your world a target for enemies, if war comes again."

"But what can they do?" Plasma wondered. "They cannot release millions of personnel into the labor force; that would cause a depression that would drain the Alliance's economy even more than the expense of maintaining the hundred thousand ships of the Fleet. They are allowing attrition to reduce the size of the burden, by refusing to replace ships that wear out, and refusing to replace personnel who retire or die—but they cannot forget that they came close, very close, to losing their war with us!"

Globin nodded. "It was almost impossible to supply so vast a force, so far from its base."

"What can they do, then?" Plasma wondered. "Create bases in the Core?"

But an admiral was standing before the Assembly, resplendent in battle ribbons and braid. "We propose to build a number of mobile bases. Each base would be capable of repairing, maintaining, and even constructing warships, on a limited basis. They would be moved by the most massive warp engines and gravitic drives ever built, and would be capable of accelerating at nearly half the speed of a destroyer. Their mass would allow them to pass through gravitic disruptions such as stars, while still in warp. Disruptions of this magnitude would tear apart a smaller field. Such battlestations would be so large as to form their own ecosystems, making them self-sufficient for food and water, and their closed environments would be capable of sustaining their inhabitants indefinitely."

"He speaks of artificial planets!" Plasma murmured in awe.

But a Senator was on his feet already, interrupting the Fleet spokesman. "That would be prohibitively expensive, Admiral! Just building such a battlestation would be a horrible drag on our already sagging economy—and maintaining it would bankrupt the Alliance!"

"The station would be self-sustaining, as I've said, Honorable," the admiral answered, "not just in material resources, but economically. Raw materials would be obtained locally by merchant corporations. To accomplish this, sections of the stations would be leased to mercantile corporations, and even to independent traders."

"Globin!" Plasma cried, and Globin stiffened, feeling the thrill pass through him.

"We would construct only one battlestation at this time," the admiral was saying. "It would be the prototype, and we would dispatch it to the Core, to aid these embattled species who ask our help. We would equip the station with a hundred ships and all their crews, plus the crew and support personnel necessary to operate the station itself. Existing, but aging, spacecraft could be cannibalized for the construction of the mobile base. Current Fleet holdings in the Alliance worlds would thereby be diminished by nearly ten thousand ships and twenty percent of total personnel."

A murmur passed through the hall, as politicians glanced at one another and calculated how much of the problems caused by the peacetime Fleet could be alleviated—and how many jobs the building of the station would supply.

"The enemy would be defeated far from home," the admiral concluded, "and an Alliance presence established among friendly species in the Core."

The Assembly chamber disappeared from the screen, replaced by the commentator. "The Privy Council continued in emergency session," he said, "and the president came forth today with an astounding conclusion."

A picture of the president of the Senate replaced that of the commentator. He was standing in front of the titanic surrealist sculpture that housed the Alliance's civilian government, its lighted windows refracted through the waterfall that covered the front of the building. It was an extremely dramatic background for announcements, as Globin suspected it had been intended to be.

"We have determined to respond to the Core's plea for help," the president said, "but in moderation—we will send only one mother ship."

Globin frowned. A token indeed.

"But that ship," said the president, "will be the size of a small moon, and will contain half of the current Fleet personnel. It will also house a substantial proportion of the Fleet's smaller vessels."

Globin's eyes fairly glowed.

"Such a vessel will of course have to be built," the president responded. "It will be named the *Stephen Hawking*. The cost will be as astronomical as its destination, but the Alliance government will pay only a fraction of it."

Globin noticed that he didn't say how large a fraction he had in mind.

"Many universities have already petitioned the Council to find room on the Fleet ships for their astronomers, physicists, and xenologists," the president went on. "They have indicated a willingness to assume the cost of their support."

Of course, most of those universities were supported at least partly by government funds, one way or another—but Globin nodded; the Alliance wouldn't have to contribute anything additional. The universities would take the money out of their research funds. They would ask the Alliance for more money, of course, but they were very unlikely to receive it.

"However, we anticipate that the major portion of the funding will come from mercantile companies," the president wound up. "The galaxy is huge, and may contain many new and valuable commodities; merchant companies will wish to explore and exploit. Several of the largest companies have already been in touch with the Alliance, asking for rights to exploit new goods the Fleet may discover. The Alliance has refused, of course, since we are committed to free trade—and therefore, no monopolies will be granted. But any merchant company that wishes to lease space on the new supership will be allowed to do so, though the rate will be very high—and from the proceeds, we anticipate being able to finance the greater portion of the cost of the expedition."

"Should we be interested, Globin?" Plasma asked. When there was no answer, he turned, demanding, "Should we show an interest?"

He saw Globin sitting frozen at his desk, eyes huge and glowing, lips slightly parted.

The Council of Barataria was in an uproar. Half of them were on their feet, gesticulating wildly. The other half were making more coherent demands, some of which Globin could actually hear from his seat at their head.

"What do you speak of, Globin? How can you resign completely from the Council?"

"How can the Council function without you, Globin?"

"How can Khalia endure without you?"

Globin sat still, trying to keep his face from showing how touched he was, reminding himself that the Council had become a prison to him. When they quieted, he began to speak, some inconsequential remarks at first, but they all quieted completely as he began to speak. Then, more loudly, he said, "It is not easy for me to leave you, my friends, but it is necessary. The glory of Khalia must be increased; the prosperity of Barataria must be continued. As you all know, our trade with Khalia has become a major element in their economy; without us, they would suffer economic disaster. But Barataria cannot merely continue as it is—it must grow or diminish, for all things change, and a people, like a single life-form, must build or decay. If other companies gain access to new resources and new markets, and Khalia does not, we will lose our share of the Alliance's commerce; our trade will eventually die."

"Surely, Globin! But does not this require that you continue to lead us?"

"Other leaders have grown up among you." Globin could see the gleam begin in the eyes of the party leaders. "The old must give place to the young—and it is for the old to lend their vision and experience to the beginning of new ventures. It is my place to lease factory and offices on the *Stephen Hawking*, and to organize and equip the exploration party that will travel aboard it, to walk new worlds and gaze into new skies—and discover new and precious substances."

The clamor began again.

When it quieted, they tried to talk him out of it, but Globin remained firm—and bit by bit, he caught them in his spell, communicated his zeal, his fascination to them. First one caught fire with the wonder and challenge of it, then another, then three more, then a dozen.

In the end, they voted unanimously to accept his resignation, call for elections, and invest in the *Stephen Hawking*.

"I don't like it, Anton!" Brad Omera, the civilian administrator of non-Fleet personnel, glowered at his military counterpart. "They can call themselves merchants if they want to, but if you scratch a Baratarian, you'll find a pirate!"

"That may be true, Brad," Commander Brand allowed, "but they pay good money, and they're hardy explorers. On a mission like this, I'd rather have a Baratarian pirate beside me than a squadron of Marines." He didn't mention that he'd far rather not have that pirate against him.

"But the Globin, Anton! The Globin himself! The arch-villain of the Alliance! The Pirate King!"

"He's a former head of state of a member planet." Brand put a little iron into his voice. "And he's a human."

"Human renegade, you mean! He's a traitor to his species, and he always will be!"

Brand didn't deny it; he only said, "He's a very skillful leader and an excellent strategist." But inside, he was fiercely determined to make sure Globin stayed in his own quarters.

It was two years between the vote in the Senate and the day the Baratarian liner matched velocities with the completed battlestation, coming to rest relative to the huge maw of the south pole port. It drifted up into that vast cavern and over near a boarding tube. It stopped itself with a short blast from the forward attitude jets. The tugs answered with brief blasts of their own, bringing the mouth of the tube to fasten to the coupling around the liner's hatch.

Inside, Globin watched the process on the ship's screens, and his lips quirked in amusement. "How fitting! The back door!"

"I see no 'back door,' Globin." Plasma frowned. "It is the southern pole of a huge sphere, nothing more."

"The huge port in the south pole, yes! The back door, for tradesmen!" Globin chuckled, aware that long ago, he would have been hurt and dismayed by the discourtesy. Now, though, it only gave him amusement, and aroused a bit of contempt for the Fleet officers who governed the ship. He knew his own worth—and had a notion of how quickly the Fleet's men would come to value their Khalian bedfellows.

The hull rang with the coupling of the huge boarding tube, and a voice from the *Stephen Hawking* advised them, in carefully neutral tones, that air was filling the lock at the end of the tube, which would soon be ready for their new passengers.

Globin rose and stretched, scarcely able to contain the excitement bubbling through him. He felt as though he were thirty again. "Tell the captains to prepare to disembark, Plasma. We've come to our new home."

With his hundreds of eager trader-warriors in their quarters, and their titanic stock of provisions, Baratarian gems, and electronic components stored, Globin was ready to face the necessary ritual of greeting the *Stephen Hawking*'s commander. Of course, many of those gems and electronic components could be fitted together to make devastatingly powerful weapons, and each Khalian had his own arsenal among his personal effects—but the *Stephen Hawking* did not need to know about that, and Globin felt no need to mention the issue in his upcoming conference with Commander Brand.

He was vastly amused at the size of the sign on the door that led to the lift tube that communicated to the world outside the decks leased to Barataria, Ltd. In Terran Standard and Khalian script, it warned AUTHORIZED PERSONNEL ONLY.

Plasma frowned at the inscription. "Do they think we cannot read their words?"

"For myself, I have no trouble," Globin assured him. "Loosely translated, it means 'Pirates Stay Out.'"

The door irised open, keyed by his thumbprint—he was the only Baratarian who was authorized—he stepped in with Plasma only one step behind him. As they rode through the light show adorning the walls of the tube, Globin found time to wonder if the humans had already christened his decks "The Pirates' Nest," or if that was yet to come.

They stepped out into a reception that was so stiff and cold, Globin wondered how long it had been dead.

"Chief Desrick." Commander Brand bowed—at least inclined—his head. "I greet you in the name of the *Stephen Hawking*."

Behind him, his first officer glowered, simmering.

Globin blinked in surprise; it had been so long since he had used his human name that it took him a moment to realize the man was talking to him. He noted the Khalian idiom "I greet you," though, and chose to take it as a compliment, though he knew it was intended as an insult—he was pointedly not being told he was welcome. Slowly, he returned the bow, actually tilting his torso forward an inch—not enough to honor the admiral as his senior, only enough to show him how it was done properly. "I greet you, Commander Brand. We of Barataria are honored by our place in the *Stephen Hawking*."

Anton Brand understood the rebuke, and reddened. He looked as though he would have liked to refute what Globin had just said, but every word had been technically correct—the Baratarians did have a physical place in the *Stephen Hawking*, though not a metaphorical one. Instead, Brand only said, "I do not think we will have occasion to meet very often, Chief Merchant, barring incidents between personnel." His tone implied that Globin had damn well better make sure there were none. "So let us agree that you will work only within the framework of the *Stephen Hawking*'s mission, and will give advice only when it is asked."

"Indeed," Globin murmured. "Such were the terms of our contract, and we will of course abide by them."

"Then we need speak no further." Commander Brand gave him a curt bow. "May you fare well on the journey, Chief Desrick."

Globin returned the bow in millimeters, stifling a smile. He turned away, trying to catch Plasma's eye, but failing—the warrior was staring at the first officer, his lip twitching as though he were fighting the urge to smile.

"Plasma," Globin murmured, and the Khalian broke his stare reluctantly and turned to follow Globin to the drop shaft, every muscle stiff with the suppressed urge to fight.

The lift shaft doors closed behind them, and Globin began to chuckle. The light show gave an eerie cast to his features as they sank down, and the chuckling swelled into full, hearty laughter.

Plasma stared, scandalized. "How can you laugh, Globin? When he has virtually insulted you!"

"No, he has not quite," Globin gasped, letting the laughter ease away. "No, he meant to, I am sure—but he succeeded only in showing what a boor he was. Let it pass, Plasma—he has little understanding, and less true honor."

Plasma stared in bewilderment as Globin, smiling, shaking his head, chuckled again. He was thinking of the upcoming, and no doubt similar, meeting with Administrator Omera.

The days passed quickly, and the weeks. They might have dragged, but Globin saw to it that his lieutenants kept their men busy with fighting practice and lessons in business and accounting. He often stopped by the practice cavern to watch the training, and took his turn in the classroom, explaining the intricacies of finance to a group of youngsters who hung on his every word. Their excitement, their enthusiasm, their restlessness, made him feel years younger. He had recruited a force of young Baratarian Khalians who did not remember the Family war, except as stories their grandsires told them—but those tales had filled them with a burning desire for glory, and their youthful lust for females stirred them with ambition for reputation and wealth, that they might each attract the female he longed for, and have the right to mate. Globin watched them hone themselves in mind and body, and beamed with pride upon them.

They asked him to teach unarmed combat as well as commerce, but he declined on the grounds of age. Still, they did notice that he practiced, too, and they strove all the harder to emulate him in both book and boot.

"But how shall we need skill in combat as well as commerce, Globin?" Plasma asked him. "Must we fight even as we bargain?"

"We must be prepared to do so," Globin answered. "We must be prepared for anything, for there is no predicting the customs of truly alien species."

Privately, though, he doubted that they would encounter any completely incomprehensible behavior. He had a notion that the principles of commerce were as inherent and universal as those of physics. He was eager to find out if he was right.

The personnel of the *Stephen Hawking* were all subdued and angry at the horrors they had just seen, as the battlestation accelerated and made the transition back into warp drive. They.had expected to find a thriving planet, geared for war, perhaps even under attack by an Ichton horde—but they had not expected to find the barren cinder of a planet that had once been the Gerson home world. The Ichtons had come and gone, and where they had passed, only rubble remained.

In the caverns devoted to their own environment, the Gerson envoy moved in a daze, seeking to help the few dozen survivors the *Hawking*'s people had discovered. Elsewhere in the ship, all the other inhabitants of the battlestation discussed what they had seen, in tones of outrage.

"How vile can they be, Globin! How insentient!" Plasma was beside himself, burning in agitation.

"It is thoroughly inhumane," Globin agreed, his face stony. "The planet completely bald! Scarcely a living being left!"

"And the Gerson emissary is a noble being," Plasma snapped, "good-hearted and valiant. How foul to exterminate so fine a race!"

"At least a few survived, and had the sense to activate their beacons when they saw our scouts." Privately, though, Globin wondered how many more survivors had not dared take the chance, and still hid on the remains of the Gerson planet, doomed to slow starvation. Certainly Brand had not taken any great amount of time to search for survivors; he had been too angry, too eager to go seek out the battle. "How are the men enduring?"

"In rage and ranting, Globin. They are young, they are warriors—and they are furious that they were not allowed to join the expedition down to the surface." He snorted with exasperation. "What did Brand think we would do—steal?" He turned to glare at Globin. "Could we not have invoked our contract, and insisted on our right to visit any planet at which the *Hawking* stops?"

"We could," Globin admitted, "but it did not seem politic, to seem to think of gain in the midst of such tragedy. That is, after all, the reason behind that contractual right—to search for marketable commodities."

"Commodities!" Plasma snapped, exasperated. "On a world milked dry, shorn clean, picked bare? What could we have found there?"

"Survivors," Globin muttered. He did not mention that he himself had been too stunned by the enormity of it, the scale of the inhumanity of the Ichtons.

But then, they *were* inhuman, were they not?

A new word was needed—"insentient." Any species capable of such unfeeling destruction could barely make claim to sentience itself. It was more like a natural force, a climactic disaster, unfeeling and uncaring for anything but its own goals. Globin began to wonder if "sentience" involved more than intellectual capacity.

Beside him, Plasma shuddered. "The tales those survivors tell! The vastness of the machines of destruction, the rolling mines and refineries, that gobbled up every trace of their civilization, all their antiquities, all their greatest works!"

"And the complete lack of feeling with which they treated the Gersons." Globin's mouth tightened. "To not even bury the dead! To do nothing but hurl them into those all-devouring machines! What do the young warriors say of this, Plasma?"

"What would you think they would say, Globin? They are unnerved, as are we; they are angered and appalled, as any feeling being might be! They speak already of revenge, Globin, though it is not their own race that has suffered!"

"Well, we can all see something of the best of us in the Gersons' emissary," Globin allowed, "and the fate of his home world has too many echoes of the defeat of Khalia; we cannot wonder if they feel the need for revenge as though it were their own."

The *Stephen Hawking* dropped out of warp drive, slowed over a period of days, and swung into orbit around the planet Sandworld (a very rough translation from the tongue of its dominant—nearly only—species, the Ekchartok). And they seemed to be not only the sole species of their world, but also the sole survivors of that species.

The alien emitted a high-pitched, keening sound as the screens of the *Hawking*'s briefing room showed them view after view of a barren, featureless plain.

"This is not as your world always was, then?" Captain Chavere, the chief of the Fleet xenologists, tried to word the question as gently as possible.

"No, never!" answered the flat, bland tones of the translator, though the sounds the Ekchartok were emitting were ragged as gravel, and its surface vibrated with contrasting wave patterns. "There were mountains at this latitude, with lakes and streams."

There was no water visible any longer, no mountains, and only vast raw gouges of valleys here and there, where titanic machines had chewed away bedrock to break out minerals. And nothing moved.

"The Ichtons have been and gone," the centauroid, amphibious Silber said. "Nothing survives in their wake; all life is eliminated, all growing things are eaten. They have scoured this world to draw from it every ounce of mineral they seek. Even their own body wastes have been processed to draw from them every molecule they can use; all that is left is the waste of their waste." It pointed, almost touching the screen where a flat, dark surface glimmered with sunlight.

"We must land and search," Chavere said, his face grim. "There may be an individual, perhaps a dozen, even a hundred, who have escaped the Ichtons' notice."

"There will be nothing, nothing!" the Ekchartok keened. "The Ichtons miss nothing; every gram, every grain, will they have sought out." Then suddenly it went rigid, totally quiescent.

The Silber stepped forward, reaching out a hand, then drew it back. "It is quiescent," said the translator. "Its suit will provide for it."

Captain Chavere hovered, almost frantic, at a loss. "What is the matter with it?"

"Shock," Globin answered. "It has gone into its equivalent of a coma, and the suit's life-support systems will sustain it."

Chavere favored him with a glare. "How would you know? This is not your field!"

"Personal experience," Globin returned. "I recognize the stimulus, and the symptoms."

Chavere reddened, but "It is logical," grated the arachnid alien, and the captain had to suppress his annoyance.

"We must search the planet! We must do that, at least!"

"Indeed," Globin murmured. "Indeed we must."

Chavere rounded on him. "You have no business in this affair, Chief Merchant! You will remain aboard ship!"

Globin had finally had enough. "I invoke the Landing Option clause in our contract, Captain. According to the terms of the agreement, when there is no condition of battle, we have the right to accompany every expedition to the surface of every planet visited by the *Hawking*'s personnel, for the purpose of investigating resources for trade."

Chavere's eyes narrowed. "Your contract? Why, what would you do on this planet?"

"Why, as our contract says," Globin murmured, "search for resources."

"But there are no resources left!"

"Nevertheless, we have the right to search," Globin reminded him.

Chavere locked gazes with him. Globin stared back, unperturbed. Finally, Chavere turned away with a snarl.

Globin permitted himself a small smile, gave a minuscule bow, and turned away to the drop shaft, Plasma behind him, showing the snarl that his chief suppressed.

As the door closed behind them, Globin said, "Select a landing party."

Chavere touched his helmet to Globin's; without a radio betraying him to eavesdroppers, he said, "There was no need for you to accompany the expedition."

"But there was," Globin returned. "I understand the need for vengeance."

Chavere scowled through his faceplate. "There is no one here on whom to revenge the Ekchartok, Chief Merchant."

"No," Globin agreed, "but there is information to be found that may show us the means of defeating the Ichtons when we find them."

Chavere's mouth flattened with disgust. "The contract only permits you to search for trade goods."

"Oh, we will," Globin assured him. "We will."

His helmet speaker demanded, "Globin? Is all well?"

Looking up, he saw Plasma with a dozen young Khalians behind him, devoid of weapons—except for the steel claw casings at the ends of the mittens of their spacesuits. Globin gave a fleeting smile to Chavere, and his smile was not pleasant. Then he turned back to his adopted children. "Nothing at all, Plasma—only myself and Captain Chavere, agreeing on disposition of personnel. Let us take our places on our sled."

"Behind us," Chavere's voice snapped through his headphones.

"Of course, the rear guard," Globin replied, amused. "Always the last."

A low growling filled Globin's helmet, coming on the private Baratarian communication channel. The young Khalians were experiencing the devastation of war for the first time, and were angered.

"But this was not war." Plasma shuddered. "This was a cold-blooded processing of life into death."

"They could not have defended themselves!" a young Khalian was saying to another. "With their cannon and ships gone, they are nothing, the slowest of the slow, small and weak!"

"But hard," his fellow demurred.

"Hard, and brittle," a third chimed in.

"But where are they all gone?" the first demanded. "To slavery? Or death?"

"If it was death," the second said, "where are the bodies?"

They were silent for a moment, considering the question. Then the first said, "Globin? Where are the bodies?"

Globin thought he knew, but he didn't want to say. "I can only conjecture."

"Then do, we beseech you!" said the second.

Reluctantly, Globin gestured toward the bare ground around them. "See how it glitters?"

There was an appalled silence. Then a young voice demanded, "Do you mean they ground them up and strewed their remains about?"

Globin was silent, not wishing to shock those he was beginning to think of as his children.

"Globin?" the first pressed. "Did they grind them to powder?"

"Worse," Globin said, as though the words were torn out of him. "They were silicate beings, after all, and pure silicon is the stuff of solid-state circuits."

This time the silence was the young's. At last one spoke, his tones filled with horror. "Do you mean they melted them down and strewed the ground with the parts of their bodies the Ichtons had no use for?"

"It is only conjecture," Globin reminded.

A low growling answered him, not of nervousness or apprehension but of mounting rage.

"What monsters can these Ichtons be, to place so little value on sentient life?" one demanded.

"Monsters indeed!" said another. "Pray we come to grips with them!"

"There is a whole planet here cries out for vengeance," a third agreed.

Globin reflected on what was not said, more sure than ever that the vision of a conquered species ground into dust awakened schoolbook memories of Khalia's defeat by the Fleet. He wasn't even sure his young warriors were even aware of this wellspring of their anger, but he was sure it was there.

An electronic tone sounded.

Amazed, Globin looked down.

"Globin!" Plasma cried. "There is a blip on the life detector!"

"I see it," Globin confirmed. "It is very faint, but it is unmistakable."

Plasma looked up and saw the other sleds speeding away. "They are going on by!" he shrilled. "Are they in so great a hurry that they cannot spare minutes to seek out a living being?"

Globin pressed down with his jaw, toggling the transmission switch inside his helmet. "Chief Merchant to Surveillance Captain. Our life detector shows a trace from the northwest."

"Too faint," Chavere answered. "We can dismiss it as background noise."

Globin glanced again at the trace. "It is a regular wave form, though it is of a much lower frequency than that belonging to any life-form we know. It should be verified."

"Look for it yourself!" the captain snapped. "We have a whole planet to cover! We can't go kiting off after every off-phase signal!"

Plasma snarled, his neck hairs lifting.

Globin glanced at him, his own face hardening. "As you bid us, Captain." He toggled his audio pickup closed and nodded to Plasma. "West-northwest."

Plasma pressed the stick, and the sled veered away from the expedition's line of travel. "Why is he so rude? By the stars, if he faced me now, I would . . ."

"Baratarians!" Captain Chavere's voice cracked like a whip. "What the hell do you think you're doing?"

Globin keyed the audio. "Just as you bade us, Captain—tracking the trace ourselves."

There was a pause, and Plasma hissed amusement.

"All right, go, and to blazes!" the captain snapped.

Globin hurried to close the pickup before it could send Plasma's snarl. "Such discourtesy should win him the death of five cuts!" the secretary snapped.

"It should," Globin agreed, "but in addition to his dislike of us, he is apprehensive—he and his crew grow nervous in the Valley of Death."

"Here is no valley, but an endless plain," Plasma growled.

"And endless death," Globin agreed.

"How shall we be revenged on them, Globin?"

"Why, by finding a survivor, of course." Globin leaned forward to peer more closely at the screen. "The trace is growing weaker, Plasma—we have passed it. Go back."

The sled swung about in a half circle.

"Holding constant." Globin frowned. "We must be at the circumference of a circle, of which it is the center."

"There is no pivot in sight but a slag heap," Plasma objected.

Globin looked up; the blue-black slag glinted in the sunlight. "It seems glassy," he said. "Perhaps it is silicon."

"Is there anything else on Sandworld?"

"It could hide a being made of silicon," Globin pointed out. "Surely it would not lack for food. Plasma, move toward that heap."

Frowning, Plasma turned the sled, then shouted with delight, for the trace was growing stronger.

It was quite strong as they settled to the ground beside the hill of glassy waste. As Globin climbed down, he glanced after the expedition's file of sleds, just in time to see the last slip over the horizon.

"How now, Globin?" Plasma asked. Behind him, the crewmen muttered.

"We take it apart, bit by bit," Globin answered. "Slowly, my children, and gently—do not dismember an ally as you seek to demolish its prison."

They whittled away at the huge hill with lasers, a slice at a time. After fifteen minutes, Globin called a halt, feeling apprehensive. "Plasma," he said, "take the sled to the crest, and tell me the reading."

Obediently, Plasma flowed back into the sled. It rose up, leveling off at the top of the hill. "The trace diminished as I rose, Globin!"

"Then it is beneath the heap," Globin interpreted. "We do not need to cut, but to tunnel. Take the portable detector, my children, and dig."

Three youngsters leaped forward faster than the rest, then hesitated. "What tools shall we use, Globin?"

"Those you were born with," Globin returned. "If you feel something hard, desist and bring the detector. Begin, now. To the center first."

The three spread out to the points of the compass as a fourth jumped around to the far side. Dirt flew; their remote ancestors had dug into burrows to follow their quarry, and the Khalian children tunneled for pleasure as human children climbed trees. A fifth followed with the portable detector that relayed its information back to the main screen in the sled.

They dug radii like the spokes of a wheel, first four tunnels, then triangulating from the circumference and two of the tunnels. The huge mass above them might have come grinding down if they had dug too many, but the detector showed them where to dig, and Plasma himself took the final tunnel directly to the spot. There, digging very delicately, he touched something hard with his claws. Carefully, ever so carefully, he dug it loose and bore it out.

It was oblong, it was flat on the bottom, it had antennas folded flat. It was unconscious, but the life detector showed it to be the source of the trace.

The Khalian warriors shouted with triumph, and Globin keyed for transmission. "Chief Merchant to Surveillance Captain."

"Of all the . . . What is it, pirate?" the captain exploded. "What mess do we have to dig you out of now?"

A score of snarls rose from the young Khalians.

Globin waved them back, smiling, but with a hard glitter to his eyes. "It is we who have been digging, beneath a mess the Ichtons left. We have found a live Ekchartok. It is dormant, but it emits brain waves."

The channel was silent for a few seconds. Then the captain snapped, "Homing on your signal. Keep the channel open."

"Give them our beacon, Plasma," Globin said. "After his rudeness, the captain deserves an unrelenting squeal."

Hisses of laughter answered him, though there was viciousness in their tone.

"How shall we repay his rudeness now, Globin?"

"Retract your claws, Plasma," Globin advised. "His embarrassment is punishment enough, but it is made worse because it is pirates of Barataria who were right, and who showed greater compassion than a human. Back aboard our sled, me hearties, with our prize."

They flowed back to their seats, Plasma asking, "What is a 'hearty,' Globin?"

"You are, Plasma—you all are. A 'hearty' is a bold and valiant fighter who delights in life, as we have this day."

Plasma sat, and turned back, frowning. "Will you not join us, Globin?"

"Yes, quite soon." Globin had taken out his pick, and was breaking loose a fist-sized sample of slag. He came back to the sled, sat down, and gazed at the glassy rock, frowning.

"Why do you bring such a piece of rubble, Globin?"

"Because," his chief answered, "I told them we would search for resources, so we must have something to bring back." But the intentness of his gaze went beyond a mere excuse.

Plasma noticed. "What troubles you, Globin?"

"Not 'troubles,' Plasma—'intrigues.' Why would an Ekchartok hide beneath a slag heap?"

"Why—did they not dump it upon him, in lack of concern, and to slay him?"

"I think not, Plasma—I really do believe they used the dead bodies as a resource, horrible as it seems. No, this one hid, and from the shape of its body, I would conjecture that it is as skilled at burrowing as yourselves, though much slower." Globin pursed his lips, thinking. "Why would a silicate life-form hide beneath a slag heap? Food, of course, since there is silicon in it—but what else? Aorta, pass me the radiation detector."

"It is here, Globin." The young warrior held out the pickup.

The detector fairly screamed.

"Transuranics," Globin explained, back aboard the *Hawking*. "Radioactive waste, to them—but potential fuel, to us. Their reactors and engines must be very primitive that they would throw away such treasure. It is well my warriors wore spacesuits, for it was only that shielding that saved them from exposure."

His chief physicist nodded, watching his men process the sample through a dozen different tests. "There are nodules of it embedded in the silicate slag."

"Will it generate power?"

"Oh, yes," the scientist said quietly. "Oh, yes—a great deal of power, Globin. If it were not for the quantity of slag holding the nodules apart, those heaps would blow up the whole planet. It is as though the Ichtons had operated a vast number of breeder reactors."

"Perhaps they did," Globin returned, "but their own technology is too primitive to make use of the product." He gave the scientist a smile. "We have learned as much about our enemy as about business."

"Business?" The scientist looked up, startled. "How is this 'business,' Globin?"

"Why," said his chief, "we are here to find marketable commodities, are we not? And what could be more marketable than Ichton slag?" He turned back to watch the tests, chuckling.

"Of course," the scientist breathed. "When will you tell Commander Brand, Globin?"

"When his fuel supplies begin to run low," Globin answered, "and he is more amenable to paying our price."

"You would not charge your own allies an extortionate rate!" the scientist protested.

"Of course I would," Globin answered. "He says we are pirates, does he not?"

"Surely you don't believe this claim that they are only looking for surviving Ekchartok, Anton!" Brad Omera was indignant.

"Surely not," Commander Brand agreed. "Why would such a search require them to set up a virtual refinery on the surface? And why would they have to ship quantities of slag back aboard in those huge canisters?"

"Oh, the Globin was very candid about that. He said that whenever they find a section that they suspect contains an Ekchartok, they bring it back up to the ship for careful handling."

"If you think you can trust what the Globin says." Brand turned to David bar Mentron, the battlestation's chief technician. "Mr. bar Mentron, what sort of equipment was it they had you build?"

"Not much more than a cold chisel with a very fine edge, sir," bar Mentron answered. "But it's in a standing frame that guarantees the chisel won't slip, and has a setting for calibrating the exact force of the blow, to the erg."

"That *is* the kind of equipment you'd need to chip away rock gradually," Omera said, frowning, "if you didn't want to take a chance on injuring a living being trapped inside it." He turned to bar Mentron. "Tell the commander about that special room they had you build."

"Special room?" Brand frowned, alert for the slightest hint of treachery.

"Just a radiation chamber, sir, you know, a laboratory for handling radioactive materials. Nothing unusual about it, for what it is—just the shielding, the lead glass, the waldoes, the locks . . ."

"*Radiation* chamber?" Brand nearly leaped out of his chair. "What would they need *that* for? What are they doing—handling transuranics?"

"They told me the slag and the Ekchartok are radioactive." Bar Mentron shrugged.

Brand stilled. "Well, that's true enough. So would I be, if I'd spent a few months under a mountain of radioactive slag."

"Yes, but that's exactly why they've taken refuge in those slag heaps." Omera frowned. "Apparently the Ekchartok can use the radiation as a sort of emergency ration, absorb it and convert it to electricity—which is all they need to keep basic life systems going inside, while they're dormant."

"Love to find out what kind of evolution that species had," Brand muttered. "How's that first one doing? Can it talk yet?'

"Only a few syllables; it's still very weak." Omera shook his head in exasperation. "You really let those pirates steal a march on you, Commander."

"Yes, I know." Brand scowled. "I read Chavere the riot act about not having followed up that trace, so he has developed a tendency to track down anything that gives his detector the slightest hiccup. He's redeemed himself by finding six more Ekchartok—in heaps of quartz rubble the Ichtons apparently had no use for, and one of them was dormant under a brackish puddle the locusts seem to have overlooked. But the fact is that in Chavere's place, I probably would have done the same thing—gone on looking for something more obvious. The trace on his life detector was so small it could have been an earthworm."

"Or a dormant Ekchartok," Omera returned.

"Yes," said bar Mentron, "but the Ekchartok emissary hadn't told us his people could go dormant."

"Understandable—the moment he saw this planet, he went into shock. But the fact remains that it was the pirates who found that live one under the slag heap, not the Fleet."

"Two more, now," Brand said, the taste of the words bitter on his tongue. "They found two others, and they're in the same condition the first was— dormant, probably in shock, but alive."

"They have?" Omera whirled about. "How come nobody told me about this?"

"Word just arrived, and the pair of them are on their way to the infirmary right now. The Globin claims they broke them out of a single slag lump in their workshop. Says they were nestled up against each other as though they were a Yin-Yang symbol."

"These slugs have sexes?" Omera asked.

"Ekchartok," Bar Mentron murmured. His voice was very soft, but Omera flushed. "Of course, Ekchartok. I'm sorry."

"Maybe the emissary will come out of shock, now that he has some company," Brand mused. "And I suppose we can't argue with what Globin's doing, if he found a couple more. But I really wonder if he needs to grind up all *that* much slag just to find Ekchartok."

"He can't be too careful, I suppose," Omera sighed, "though the pirates are certainly growing their own heap of recycled slag. And they've been bringing up an awful lot of canisters, for only two Ekchartok."

"They say the other slag lumps only had chunks of radioactive waste in them that fooled their detectors," Brand sighed.

"They say, they say!" Omera snapped. "I'd give a year's income to go in there and see for sure what they're doing."

"Then go." Bar Mentron shrugged. "The Globin's made it an open invitation."

"Of course he has," Omera snapped. "Who'd go into the Pirates' Nest if he didn't have to?"

Plasma clicked his timer and nodded. "Drill completed in sixteen seconds, Globin. If anyone who is not of Barataria should wish to come here, we will have the laboratory out of sight before he arrives."

"Not that there would be that much to see." Globin smiled. "We are doing no more than we have claimed—slicing apart suspicious lumps of slag, to see if there is a treasure therein."

"Certainly," Plasma agreed. "Of course, the treasure is far more often a lump of almost-pure transuranic than it is an Ekchartok—but who else could tell?" He turned to Globin. "Will not those who remain behind need equipment like this on the planet?"

"No—the dormant Ekchartok have survived till our coming, and they might not survive our rescue without the facilities of the hospital. They can wait in the slag until the *Hawking* returns."

Plasma nodded. "How soon will the battlestation depart for the fray?"

"In two days, Brand said. He feels that Chavere and the other rescue commanders will by then have completed scouring the planet for survivors." Globin smiled. "But for some reason, they seem to be content to leave the slag heaps to us pirates."

"They who have volunteered to stay and process the slag will be in great danger," Plasma reminded him.

"Not so great as that—they have our fastest courier, and orders to board and flee at the first sign of an enemy."

But Plasma noticed his brooding frown. "What troubles you about them then?"

"Will they obey orders?" Globin said simply. "Perhaps I should not have agreed to let them keep blast cannon and force-field generators."

"No Khalian would be parted from his weapons, Globin, you know that. And the work must continue—there may be more Ekchartoks in those slag heaps, as well as the transuranics."

"Yes, it must continue," Globin sighed, "and I will have to school myself to patience. The Ichtons have passed by, after all—they are not likely to return to a barren planet. No, certainly not."

But he did not like the word "likely."

The *Hawking* had been under way for two days when Brynn Te Mon's secretary notified him, somewhat hesitantly, of a request for an appointment.

"Send him to the science coordinator." The physicist didn't even look up from his screen, with the three-dimensional model of a very complex molecule on it. "That's what top kicks are for—to keep the bored ones away from those of us who are doing the real work."

"He asked for you by name, sir."

"Tell him I referred him to Coordinator Cray, by name."

"Sir . . . it's Chief Desrick."

"The Globin?" Te Mon looked up, startled. "What would the Pirate King want with me?"

"He wouldn't say, sir—only that it had something to do with some artifacts he had discovered while he was looking for Ekchartok."

"More likely he discovered the Ekchartok while he was looking for something he could sell." But Te Mon pushed himself away from his desk. "I'll see him, now. I've always wondered what he was like." And he did mean "always"— Te Mon was only forty, and had grown up with tales of the Human Renegade.

Globin was waiting in a small, antiseptic reception chamber. He rose as Te Mon came in. "Scientist! So good of you to spare the time. . . ."

"And I don't have much of it." Te Mon cut him off, even as he looked Globin over with a microscopic gaze. "What can I do for you, Chief Merchant?"

Globin slowly drew a small pouch out of a pocket and spilled half a dozen gems out into his palm. Te Mon caught his breath at their scintillating beauty, and at the array of colors each one refracted. "Very . . . pretty," he said. "Of course, they weren't cut when you found them?"

"No—I had one of my technicians do that. I've been experimenting with them in my own laboratory, when I found a moment. They seem to have some strange properties."

"Other than swaying the head of any nubile young lady, I can't think what."

"They make light cohere," Globin said, "and with a slight energy input, they amplify that light by a factor of five."

Te Mon stared at the gems, then snatched one up. He held it up to the light, frowning. "You know what these are, if they do as you say?"

"Of course," Globin murmured. "The key element in a band blaster that could be far more powerful than anything we have now."

"We'll run it through the tests right away." Te Mon looked back at Globin with a frown, weighing the gem in his hand. "They're for sale, of course?"

"Of course," Globin murmured.

"Success, Globin?" Plasma asked as the chief stepped out of the drop shaft.

"Success," Globin confirmed. "Contact the colony on Sandworld, Plasma. Tell them to pick up stones."

The *Hawking* dropped out of FTL mode to see the world of the Silbers floating like a blue gem in the void—a gem laced in by lines of fire and surrounded by twinkling motes.

"They're under attack!" a sentry cried.

"Battle stations!" Brand snapped, and the alarm howled through the *Hawking*. Pilots and gunners scrambled for their ships; artillerymen stood by the battlestation's huge cannon.

In the Pirates' Nest, scores of young Khalians sat in the three-place cannon ships that were more weapon than vessel, fuming and chafing at the bit.

"Globin! Will they not permit us to fight?" Plasma pressed. "I swear that if they don't, our young bloods will blow up the locks themselves and be off to the battle!"

"Bid them bide in patience." Globin never took his eyes from the screens that showed the progress of the battle. "They do not trust us, Plasma, as we all know. They will call upon us only if they are desperate."

And surely they would not be; the screens showed a horde of silver sparks swerving about the planet, lancing at satellite defense stations with ruby beams, while much larger silver dragonflies stabbed at the planet itself with columns of fire. But answering columns climbed up to meet them, and here and there, a dragonfly turned incandescent as its force-fields soaked up the energy of those gigantic planet-bound weapons, then turned into stars as the screens overloaded.

"They may be amphibians," Globin murmured, "but these Silbers can fight."

They were losing, though—there were simply too many Ichton guns against them.

"How many are there in that horde?" Plasma demanded.

"Thousands," Globin answered. "Listen!"

" . . . only a small force, our Gerson ally says," Brand's voice was saying from the screen. "A really big fleet would be more than a hundred thousand. They must have figured they didn't need more for such a small planet."

"They were right," Plasma hissed.

"But they could not know about the *Hawking.*" Globin pointed. "See! The Fleet comes!"

Yellow lines stabbed down at the Ichton ships. They reeled, swerving apart in chaos; ship after ship exploded, bright in the eternal night.

In spite of themselves, the Khalians gave shouts of triumph.

But the Ichtons rallied quickly; half of their fighters peeled off to fight this new invader. Fleet ships began to glow and explode. Then the Ichtons went after them in groups of three, singling out one ship each. Quickly, separate Fleet ships peeled off to flank and pierce the enemy, reinforcing their outnumbered colleagues.

But it left a hole in their hemisphere—and through that hole stabbed a large Ichton ship with a score of smaller ones about it. Rear guns lashed out at them, but too late—only a few died in fire.

The view shifted—the Ichton column was heading straight for the *Hawking*!

"Batteries fire as soon as the enemy is in range," Brand's voice snapped. "Home Guard away!"

Mosquitoes boiled out, filling the screen, stabbing at enemy ships in twos and threes.

"We need more, Commander," a tense voice said.

"We can't commit the reserves already!" Brand snapped.

Globin leaned forward and toggled a key. "Chief Merchant here. I've fifty ships with pilots and gunners spoiling to get into the fight."

There was a long pause; then Brand snapped, "All right, pirates! But don't wait for ransom!"

Plasma's lips skinned back from his teeth, and, truth to tell, so did Globin's—but all he said was "Ships away."

A hundred voices shrilled a cheer. The huge hatch opened, and the Khalian ships began to lance out into the night.

They turned the tide; Baratarian cruisers swarmed out about the Ichton ships that were as yet unmolested. They had to slow and turn to fight—and their cruiser was suddenly alone, without its midget guard.

Golden fire enclosed it, from the *Hawking*'s batteries. The screens glowed, but held.

A dozen Khalian moths homed on that light.

Cannon beams stabbed out from the cruiser—and daring Khalians slid in under the beams and stabbed their own fire down next to the Ichton lances, piercing through the holes the locusts had opened in their screens to let their own fire out. Three of those valiant ships danced too close to the fire and burned brightly and briefly—but three more stabbed home, then sped away, just barely fast enough, as the battleship turned into a huge fireball behind them.

Brand's voice joined the shout of triumph. Then, directly, he said, "Damn fine men you've got there, Chief Merchant!"

"They are my pride," Globin rejoined—but mixed in with the joy was sorrow for the three who had burned.

The smaller ships had burst the last of the Ichton attackers. At the planet, a very few Ichton ships sheered away to flee; the rest were cinders.

Howls of triumph echoed though the vast bulk of the *Hawking*. Brand's voice overrode them. "Kill those ships! Don't let them take word of us back to their command!"

The bright gnats swarmed after the fleeing enemy, overhauling them easily—what the Ichton did, they did by merciless efficiency and great numbers, not by speed.

Globin stayed transfixed, watching until each ruby vessel had gone dark, and the surviving destroyers shot home to the *Hawking*. His heart thrilled with victory even as it mourned the fine young pilots who would not come back.

Brand's voice sounded, closer, more intimate, and Globin knew it was a closed channel. "Your men shall have heroes' funerals, Chief Merchant. I am proud to have them aboard my ship."

Globin keyed transmission and answered, "Thank you, Commander." But he wondered how much of that pride would transmute into trust.

"But why would Brand summon you, Globin?" Plasma was beside him as they rode up the lift shaft.

Globin shrugged. "To congratulate us on our valor, perhaps, or our loyalty." But he had a notion the meeting would test that loyalty, not affirm it.

There were pleasantries and opening amenities this time, which Globin found agreeably surprising, though boring. Brand actually invited him to sit, and even served coffee. Finally the conversation turned to the recent battle, and the expenditure of energy—and Brand came to the point. "We used a great deal of fuel in that battle, Globin, and it was only a skirmish. We have enormous stockpiles left, you understand, we are in no danger of immediate depletion—but it does remind us that we will need to replenish our supplies continually."

"True," Globin agreed, "but we all knew that when we undertook the mission, did we not, Commander? In fact, the *Hawking* even has mining machinery."

"Quite so," Brand admitted, "but there is the matter of locating the raw resources. Now, gossip always moves, Chief Merchant, though I presume that, in this instance, it is based more on guesswork than knowledge . . ."

"Rumors are notoriously undependable, Commander," Globin said with a smile. "Still, what is the current rumor of interest?"

"That you and your pi . . . Baratarians have discovered a source, and are stockpiling fuel."

Globin's smile broadened. "The rumor is true."

"I am glad to hear it." Brand's eyes glowed. "And will you share those stocks with the *Hawking*?"

"Why, of course, Commander." Globin sat up a little straighter. "But you see, we are businessmen . . ."

When the drop-shaft doors had closed behind Globin and Plasma, Brand stood shaking his head, trying to recover from the price he had agreed to.

Omera was shaken, too, but he said, "Well, after all, Commander—they *are* pirates, you know."

"Chief Merchant!" The intercom in Globin's desk crackled. "Communications to Chief Merchant!"

Globin stiffened; for the communications watch to speak directly to his intercom meant they were using their emergency override. "Chief Merchant here."

"We have just received a squeezed message from the colony on Sandworld, Chief! They have detected an Ichton squadron moving toward them from the Core!"

Globin sat immobile for two seconds, long enough for Plasma to break in: "Is there any reason to think they are targeting our colony? How could they know of their existence?"

"From our communications with them," Globin answered. "We have been in contact several times a day. They had only to follow the beam. No doubt that is why our miners have sent the signal squeezed to less than a second."

"*But* why would the Ichtons pursue them? The planet is barren!"

"Revenge, perhaps," Globin answered. "It is a way to hurt us, where we are vulnerable. Perhaps to weaken the *Hawking*'s defenses. Or perhaps they have already deciphered enough of our language to know our people are refining fuel. In any event, we must aid them. All ship crews, prepare for battle!"

"But Commander Brand . . ."

" . . . knows which side of the battle line his fuel is on," Globin finished. "Leave him to me. Plasma?"

"Yes, Chief?"

"Commander Brand, if you please."

"Instantly."

It wasn't quite that fast, but it was only minutes. Brand's voice was guarded, though not overtly hostile. "Chief Merchant?"

"Yes, Commander."

"Your secretary indicates that you have a matter of importance to discuss."

"Yes, Commander. Our colony on Sandworld is under attack, or will be shortly."

"And our fuel supplies with them!" Brand saw the implications immediately. "But we can't leave the Silbers, or the Ichtons will be on them like the locusts they are!"

"Understood. Permission for all Baratarian ships to depart immediately for Sandworld."

"Permission granted," the commander said instantly. "I'll send a dreadnought to reinforce you."

"I . . . thank you," Globin said slowly.

"I'm surprised at your reluctance," Brand snapped. "Would you rather not have their support?"

"Not if we cannot agree on command, no."

There were a few seconds of silence. Then Brand said, "I'll tell the captain of the *Imperious* to follow your strategist's orders. That good enough for you?"

"More than good enough." Globin smiled, eyes glinting. "Thank you, Commander. We're off."

He snapped the key, and Plasma frowned. "What do you mean, 'we,' Globin? Surely you will stay on the *Hawking*!"

"When my warriors are all at risk?" Globin shook his tread. "I have stood my share of watches in battle, Plasma. I will go on our own battle cruiser, the *Marco Polo*—but I will go!"

Sandworld loomed in their screens—but there were no silver mites circling about it.

"Where are the Ichtons, Globin?" Plasma asked.

A cold chill seized Globin's vitals. "I shudder to think." He keyed his audio pickup. "Globin to all captains! Descend at the colony's location—and descend ready to fire! The Ichtons may all be on the ground already!"

"It is true," Plasma moaned. "Our warriors had only the one blast cannon!"

"Have faith in them," Globin said grimly. "They may be unblooded, but they have been taught the ways of battle."

Nonetheless, he was filled with apprehension.

"*F.S. Imperious* to Chief Merchant," a gravelly voice said suddenly. "We have just dropped into normal drive, and are about one AU from Sandworld. In what way can we assist?"

Globin was surprised to feel a surge of relief. "Take up station around the planet, *Imperious,* to defend against Ichton reinforcements. I believe the first wave are all aground. We are descending. Thank you."

"Jump!" he heard the gravelly voice calling, just before the connection was broken.

"A warp jump of one AU?" Plasma stared. "So close to a planet? That is horrendously dangerous!"

"It is indeed," Globin said grimly, "but he knows we need him *now* and is eager for battle. Have respect for our new allies, Plasma."

The secretary growled, but turned back to the screen. "I wish we could descend!"

"As do I," Globin assured him, "but we had need of one mother ship among our fleet, and it is only fitting that we should . . ."

"Enemy!" a joyful yelp called from the communicator.

Plasma's claw jumped to a key, and an inset appeared in the screen, showing what the fighter's sensors saw—half a dozen cigar-shaped ships with faceted sides and ruby light spears stabbing toward the great slag heap on one side and what appeared to be barren stretches of sand on the other. Yellow beams answered them, and each ship had developed a glowing nimbus as its screens drank the energy of those shafts of light.

"There are Baratarians there, selling their lives dearly!" Globin called. "Ships One, Three, Five, and Seven, all on the enemy! Ships Two and Four, hover in reserve!" He waited a second for the howl of protest to pass, then snapped, "Ship Six, land behind the slag heap to rescue the warriors there!"

On the larger screen, the ships plunged like falcons stooping on their prey, and inside Globin a crazed voice was crying, What am I doing, trying to direct a battle? I am a merchant and politician, not a general!

Fortunately, his pilots couldn't hear. Their beams of light speared down, each striking a ship, and Six fired even as it sank toward the slag heap. Five Ichton ships glowed like candle flames—and Globin saw specks scuttling across the sand between the Ichton ships and the slag heap. They had landed ground troops!

Then a sentry shrilled, "Globin! Attack from space!"

"Fire!" Globin shouted automatically, even as Plasma put another inset on the screen, showing three double-convex hexagons swelling as they sped toward

Globin's ship. The screen filled with a glare of light, then darkened as automatic sensors compensated for the glare of the force shield as it drank the energy of enemy fire; the screen flickered.

"Their beams pulse, they are not steady," Globin grated, gaze glued to the screen.

The ship shuddered, and a crewman cried out, "Screens overloaded! We are holed! Breach amidship, in cargo bay!"

They had no cargo, and one of the hexagonal ships glowed like a gem, first red, then orange, yellow, and on up through the spectrum until it suddenly flared white, and was gone.

But two more were battering Globin's ship with pulses of energy, and the deck shuddered under their feet as crewmen called out, "Holed amidships, in bay five! Holed astern in fighter deck! Holed in the bow—blast cannon three out!"

Globin felt a stab of sorrow for the gun crew that had just died, but his gaze stayed fixed on the screen, where his remaining cannon were pouring all their energy into the two remaining ships.

Suddenly, another beam lanced down from the corner of the screen, and one of the Ichton ships glowed like a ruby, then an emerald, a sapphire, a diamond—and flashed into an expanding cloud.

"Thank you, *Imperious*!" Globin shouted, his finger on the key, and his crew howled victory as the remaining ship swerved aside, turning to run—but the *Marco Polo*'s beams stayed with it, though a few made the view fuzzy as their focus shifted, trying to follow but not quite matching the enemy's changes of direction. Then the *Imperious* hove into view, its beams spearing the remaining Ichton like a specimen pinned to a board. Suddenly it flared through the entire spectrum and exploded.

"Glad to oblige," *Imperious* answered.

The crew howled with joy, and Globin with them. Then, as his crew quieted, he called out, "Remember your brothers aground, my children!"

The main screen showed what was happening on the planet's surface. One Baratarian ship was gone. Two more flew raggedly, but the beams from the six ships could not stay on them as they swerved and dipped, firing bursts at the enemy, whose screens were glowing more strongly. Ships Two and Four had dropped down to join the battle, ganging up on a single Ichton ship and avoiding the beams from the others. Six was shuttling back and forth and from side to side and up and down, playing peekaboo around the slag heap—and whenever it peeked, it spat fire. The Ichton bolts only flashed through the space where Six had just been—those that did not hit the slag heap. Many did; the slag had melted, and was flowing. The Ichton fighters were dancing away from it, still trying to shoot at something within it. Globin went cold at the thought of a gallant fighter half-buried in slag that he knew would kill him with radioactivity, firing burst after burst at the strange beings that strove to reach him.

A score of other fighters were tap dancing around the beams that seemed to come from the ground itself. Their own beams lanced the sand, but weren't hitting whatever they were aiming at.

Then three of the remaining ships glowed blue-white.

"Chief Merchant," said *Imperious*, "I can reach the ground with two beams, and still stand watch."

"Can you be sure they will not hit our men?" Globin asked, and several Baratarian voices shrilled, "Yes!" even as *Imperious* answered, "Yes, if you tell your men to avoid being directly above any of the enemy's ships, for I am squarely above them."

As though it had heard him, an Ichton ship fixed a beam straight up. Two Baratarian fighters took advantage of the opportunity to swoop in and snap solid projectiles at the Ichton—and it exploded as its overloaded screens tried to absorb the impact.

"Please, Globin!" a Baratarian voice pleaded.

"Very well. All ships avoid eight o'clock at seventy degrees."

On the screen, two of his own ships swerved aside.

"Fire!" Globin barked.

Two beams speared down from the corners of his screen to converge on an Ichton ship. It stood like a topaz for a moment, then flared and died—and, suddenly, all the Ichtons on the ground were running toward the remaining two ships. Globin reflected that if he could not hear their command channel, they could not hear his—then noticed that two Ichtons still stood near the slag heap.

"Magnify enemy at slag heap!" he snapped to Plasma, and an inset appeared with a close view of the two Ichtons. Globin looked, and thought again of the offspring of a lizard and an insect.

But these insects had sticky feet—they had become mired in the melted slag, that was apparently more akin to tar than lava.

Then, on the main screen, beams struck down from the *Imperious*, and the two remaining Ichton ships flared and were gone.

The sand was strewn with the ashes of dead Ichtons and, outside the blast circumference, a few intact but very dead specimens.

"Well done, *Imperious*!" Globin shouted. "A thousand thanks! We have corpses and two prisoners for our scientists! Oh, bravely done!"

"Our pleasure," *Imperious* said gruffly. "Your men are valiant and intrepid, Chief Merchant. Now I know why you call your ship the *Marco Polo*."

Homeward bound, the Baratarians bound up their wounds and counted their casualties. Nine Baratarians had died, three of them miners, and they had lost two of the small fighter ships. But at least fifty Ichton foot warriors had died, along with six ships and all their crews—and the *Imperious* was bringing home a rich booty of four intact Ichton corpses and two captives.

Globin had guessed correctly—the Baratarian miners had not even tried to prevent the Ichtons from landing, but had bent their energies toward preparing a mammoth booby trap instead. They had rigged their single blast cannon for remote control and had hidden it in the slag heap with its power supply—it had come dangerously close to blowing up, but had held off the ships. The heap was of their own slag, of course, not the Ichtons—no dormant Ekchartok had been destroyed in the battle. The miners themselves had gone to ground, quite literally, in dugouts walled with five feet of a kind of a cement they had improvised, at the first report of approaching ships that refused to give identity. By themselves, the colonists had killed a dozen Ichtons, and had bluffed the ships until help could arrive.

It had taken great courage, Globin reflected as he pinned medals to their bandoliers. Then he pinned new rank insignia on their commander, reflecting his excellent choice of tactics, as well as initiative, resourcefulness, and sheer ability to lead.

Now Globin was bound back to the *Hawking* in one of the small fliers with Plasma beside him. The *Marco Polo* remained in orbit around Sandworld with the rest of the fighters, a temporary guard for the invaluable transuranics, half of which reposed in the hold of the *Imperious*. Globin had taken a calculated risk on entrusting the fuel to the Fleet in advance of payment, but he did not think there was too great a chance of a bad debt.

And he was right—humans and Khalians alike thronged the staging chamber behind the *Hawking*'s landing bay, and a massed cheer went up as Globin stepped out of the airlock; the Baratarian home guard were only a thin line at the front, for behind them hundreds of humans cheered themselves hoarse.

Globin stood, blinking in amazement, then went rigid as a wave of emotion swept through him, a fierce, incredulous, exultant pride, as he realized that at last, and finally, he had become a hero to his own species.

THE STEPHEN HAWKING

Upon its completion the station was christened the *Stephen Hawking* after the First Age scientist whose theories were the basis for the development of the warp drive. The station itself was a globe over five kilometers in diameter. It left Alliance space with a mixed crew of over ten thousand Fleet and civilian personnel. Also on board were every member of the crews of the alien ship that had begun it all. Their own ship was long relegated to scrap.

The *Hawking* was so massive that before completion three construction workers became lost on its hundreds of decks and nearly died. To avoid this happening again, the walls of every deck were color-coded beginning at the top with red and descending through the spectrum to violet. Each color contained five major levels and up to three times that number of subdecks. Fleet activities were concentrated on the upper decks, red through yellow, and the civilians were concentrated on blue and indigo. Violet was almost completely taken with the warehouses packed with goods they expected to barter with the many races in Star Central. The central core of the *Hawking* was a three-hundred-meter tube running along the decks containing the massive warp drive and magnetic engines. Entrance ports were located all along the hull.

Along the hull were located 256 large aperture laser cannon. All were coordinated from a central battle bridge located in the center of red deck. Twenty-four were additionally fitted with experimental virtual reality targeting units. Backing these laser cannon up were dozens of missile tubes and literally thousands of missiles stored for station or ship use. The Fleet contingent consisted of three hundred ships, with the preponderance being scout and light attack craft. Replacement parts were sufficient to almost totally replace this fleet. Keeping track of it all was the full-time task of over a hundred quartermasters.

The journey to Star Central took over eight months. When the *Hawking* arrived, they were too late to save the Gerson home world. Most of those who remained behind had died two years earlier in the futile defense of the world. The other remaining Gersons may have been systematically exterminated by the Ichtons. No sign of any survivors could be detected from orbit. It was likely that the few dozen remaining on the battlestation were the last of the race. Feeling its way cautiously along behind the swath of destruction left by the Ichtons, the specialists began to draw conclusions from reports garnered from the intelligence ships that had preceded them to Star Central.

THE EYES OF TEXAS
by S.N. Lewitt

"I sure would like at least a chance to shower before I bring that up to the lady," Cowboy said, and grinned slowly. "Seeing as I smell like seven-year-old milk." He was covered in dust and his utilities were stained and rumpled. How it was possible to get filthy working in a clean environment on electronics he'd never figure out, but that seemed to be one of the immutable laws of nature. You open up the hull and you get dirty.

He'd been down in the bay calibrating the lasers on the *Glory*. She was a light cruiser, smaller than the *Imperious* that'd just put the bugs on the run at Sandworld. He'd heard the announcement over the loudspeaker while he was checking over the electron alignments in the controller.

Not that there was anything wrong with the *Glory*'s lasers. Far from it. But Senior Weapons Officer Logan Reyes lived by the motto that there was perfection and then there was everything else. He didn't bother with everything else. So the margin of error considered acceptable by bay crews and manufacturer's specs didn't cut it with him. Not when with a little tinkering he could eliminate at least twenty nanometers from the outer targeting range.

"I admit I have finished here for the moment, but I do need to put on a clean uniform before I go on duty. And I currently am not on duty in any case, not until sixteen hundred. Which isn't for another half hour yet," Cowboy repeated himself. "I was just doing a little tinkering on my own time."

But Vijay Deseka, the *Imperious*'s top Intel officer, was having none of it. "Those eyes will be useless in twelve hours, maybe less," he said firmly. "Dr. Blackwell needs them yesterday. And you are available now."

Cowboy wanted to argue. He was a gunny, not a messenger boy. If they wanted things hand-delivered up from the docking bay to Med Red, Mr. Analysis could just find himself some junior clerk and leave him alone. He never liked those Intel boys in the first place or the second. But the crew on the *Imperious* had just fought some fine battle and there wasn't anyone else available on the dock right at this second.

But the real reason he didn't protest anymore was that any excuse to see Doc Blackwell was fine by him. She wasn't even the kind of medic who grounded you, either, not at all. No, she was one of those xeno-types, specializing in alien anatomy. Add to that she was tall and pretty and had a smile that went kilo-watts, and hell, even Med Red wasn't so bad.

So Cowboy shook his head and took the box. It wasn't a usual gift to bring a lady. The thick-sided box smoked a mist of supercoolant condensation, and even with all the insulation his hands were slightly chilled. And the idea of alien eyes rolling around in nutrient solution made his stomach pitch and roll like nothing had done since his first training runs.

Around him the mechanic crews were all over the *Imperious*, snaking fuel feeders and electrical lines already in place and pumping. Scrubs were working on the laser ports and the larger drones were maneuvering into position. It was beautiful.

Commander Deseka gave Cowboy a withering look. At least Med Red was only a deck away. That had been done on purpose, so emergency teams would have immediate backup where casualties were most likely to be admitted. Cowboy took one of the large service lifts up one and exited into a corridor of dark crimson, a color that in merely the past six months had become indelibly associated with Medical Services and sickbay for everyone on the *Hawking*.

There was a directory opposite the lift doors and Cowboy went to check out where the Xeno labs were. He'd seen Dr. Blackwell at a briefing on the Gersons and in the gym at Bright Orange 221. But like any member of any fighter crew, he ducked Med Red like it was enemy barrage. The directory showed Xeno way in the back near the hull, and Avrama Blackwell headed the lab list.

He touched her name on the directory screen. The line remained dead for a moment, then he heard swearing in the background. A harried female voice answered. "Yes?"

"I have a little package you're looking for from the *Imperious*," Cowboy answered. "'I'd sure be glad to hand it over to you."

"Oh. Right," the woman said. "I'm sorry, we're quite busy. Could you meet me in Ophthalmology lab six? It's right next to Psychiatric Services. I think you know where it is."

Cowboy knew where it was, all right. The eye clinic was washout city, requiring gunnys and hot shots to retest every four months. To be sure the laser range and the radiation hadn't done any damage, they said. Cowboy was convinced that it was to keep themselves in a job. After all, popping in new clone eyes wasn't enough to keep them busy. Not enough accidents of that nature aboard the *Hawking*. And to get there he'd have to pass Shrink Central, the worst of the worst.

"Sure, I know it," Cowboy said steadily. "You sure you don't want me to come down to Xeno for you? It would be no trouble at all."

"Ophthalmology," the woman said.

Cowboy shook his head. Well, he'd tried. "You got it," he answered with false cheer.

Actually, the halls weren't that crowded. And when people in med uniforms saw the box he carried they gave him a curious state and then quickly glanced away.

Avrama Blackwell was waiting in the lab when he entered. She took the box from him immediately and set it in a tangle of equipment. "I'm sorry I was so brusque," she said softly. Her nose crinkled when she smiled and her large eyes glowed. "But we've got the Ekchartok survivors in Xeno now. And since they need radiation in the dormant state, the lab is lousy with it. And dealing with eyes, well . . ."

Cowboy knew what she was talking about. It was the first thing he'd learned as a weapons officer, before he knew how to play the circuits into nanometer precision. Radiation exposure was sure to damage human eyes, all the way back through the nerve. Khalian eyes, too, he remembered. And even with all the regrowns in the world they couldn't impair that level of injury. They could clone a body, but no one could replace the optic nerve. No matter how good the tech was, how minute the calibrations, nothing replaced a gunny's eyes.

"Why couldn't they clone eyes for you to work with?" Cowboy asked.

Dr. Blackwell laughed. Her laughter was musical and as warm as her eyes. "It would cost a fortune," she said. "And there are other priorities in the cloning tanks now. Priorities I can't even argue with." She shook her head.

She turned off the light and they were plunged into utter dark. Only a faint reddish glow illuminated the equipment on the lab table. Then she opened the box and took out one of the eyes with a long delicate field prong, the kind that was so low energy that it didn't glow at all, though it held the organ without touching it.

"If you want to help with the experiments that would be fine. But I've got work to do," she said.

Cowboy hesitated for a moment. To be quite honest, he was interested. But when she picked up a scalpel he decided that he wanted to know the results, not learn biotech at this late date. He'd managed to avoid it in school and saw no reason to start now.

"I'd love to be able to help you out, but I'm scheduled to go on duty at sixteen hundred," he said softly. "Would you mind telling me about what you find out? Over a beer, maybe, and a good-sized steak?"

Dr. Blackwell laughed again. "Don't leave until I give you the signal, I want to get this specimen shielded before you open the door."

He'd never been so disappointed to leave Med Red, though he had less than twenty minutes to shower and change into something respectable enough for roll call.

Combat was beautiful, Cowboy thought. Light danced around the board, red, yellow, green. It pierced the darkness and opened up the glints on the screen into explosive flowers. "Above," the green sphere of the watery Silber planet blossomed with colored blades that homed on the enemy emission traces and consumed the Ichton fighters. The small craft ignited and blew over kilometers of star-strewn space, their fragments invisible against the glare of the close-packed suns of the Core.

Cowboy sat strapped motionless at his screen, his mind as big as the battle-ground. He touched the screen gently, picking targets with the AI, directing fire. He was there, he was on top of it, he was cold as the AI plotting the fire patterns. Always been cold when the adrenaline hit, like time slowed down, and he could see into the patterns of movement, see the unexpected and preempt it.

There were others in the fleet control station on the *Glory* in the dark. The only illumination under battle conditions was the boards themselves. But Cowboy didn't care if there was anyone else there. He didn't notice them at all. It was just him and the screens and the flashes of light, the hottest, fastest game in purblind creation.

Four bugs were zeroing down to a single ungainly Silber installation, the one targeting broad sweeps through the sky and disabling at least two bugs in every pass. Maybe killing them, Cowboy couldn't tell. Over the range he could only see that they were intact.

Don't forget Miss Ellie's old Maine coon cat lying out watching the squir-rels looking deader than last week's lottery tickets all fluttering where the trash pickup had dumped them on the ground. That cat could even smell dead, for sure. Looked dead, smelled dead, lay there like carrion when the dog tried to wake it up in the sunshine. And it always got at least two good squirrels for the pot. Good eating, those squirrels were.

Now there were four coming down on the position, coming wide with shields glowing with energy burn, so that the pale wide-sweep of charged particles wouldn't touch them, swooping down like buzzards on a cold night. Hated buzzards.

And below them the Silber weapons station, hardworking, flaring desper-ately against the incoming enemy. They fired wide band again, but the bug attackers had spread and were dancing around the edges of the wave. They knew its range. And it glowed less brightly against the million stars of the Core, losing energy, draining. Still the blasts came, acid green wavering down the energy spectrum to yellow, orange, red.

Cowboy could imagine the Silbers in this post, power running low and under attack, praying for reinforcements (if Silbers prayed, Cowboy rather thought under the circumstances they would) and knowing it was hopeless. And still firing, knowing they were dead and gone but draining every last erg and drop of blood to defend their homes and families.

He hadn't known more of the Silbers than he had seen in the same transmis-sions everyone else saw. Now he could imagine the defenders below, individuals, maybe a few young kids who'd never left their mothers before, who'd never done the Silber equivalent of a night on the town and who now would never get the chance. Maybe the commander was an older guy with a baby at home who only wanted to return to his family and eat some good cooking and play with the kid.

He touched the points of light on the screen.

"High error margin," the androgynous computer voice said without inflection.

"I got override and you better listen up or you are going to be one hunk of stinking burnt junk," Cowboy muttered as he studied the display. He touched the four specs again.

They were far away and moving, the trajectories on a max evasion curve. But he could see into it, the time slowdown and his own instinct coming together at that moment to see the pattern whole and complete. He did not touch the specs again. Instead he jabbed points a little beyond them in the hard fire-control order.

The AI obeyed but felt required to lodge its protest. Cowboy didn't even bother to listen. The streaks of light he had sent searing through vacuum touched four different bug fighters and took them all out together. All four flamed in unison creating a multihued spiral in the center of the screen.

And in the microsecond it took for the wreckage to clear Cowboy searched fruitlessly for another target. In range. In *his* range, a different range than anyone else in the whole Fleet.

No joy, no joy. Frustration welled up in him and he barked an order at the board to increase range spread. The AI refused to comply. Instead there was an announcement on the speaker that pierced his concentration. "The enemy is in retreat. Go after them. Do not, repeat, do not let any of them make it back."

Cowboy licked his lips. Easy pickings, too easy maybe for his liking. But he understood what had to be done. Couldn't let the damned bugs get word of the *Hawking*, no that wouldn't do at all.

The screens changed, flowing into each other like they were melting. The navigator and the helm were taking the *Glory* around and entering the pursuit, but from his strapped and bolted position in the gun station Cowboy knew only the stream of target screens as the enemy fighters before them turned Doppler blue.

And then something caught his eye and his intuition reacted with his hand. He touched a blue spot before them and then moved his finger back and to the side. "Area," he requested brusquely.

The screen immediately showed a detailed magnification of the subregion he had indicated. It was barren. The blue spec was to one side and not turning. Still, something rang like bells in his head and he knew.

"There," he said, jabbing his finger hard against the changing screens. There was nothing in the space he indicated, and it was behind and to the side of the running bug, not in his direction of travel at all.

"We are in pursuit mode," the AI informed him.

"I don't care if we're the Dallas Cowboys Cheerleaders, we're taking them," Cowboy insisted. And he felt the quiver of the firestrike through the bones of the substructure, although he knew that was impossible. Only imagination.

But what was happening on the board was not his imagination. The blue spec he had jabbed on a screaming hunch became less blue, slowing. And as they hit high definition he saw it wasn't fighter size. Larger. And at the far edge of his viewboard a bright orange friendly appeared alone.

Whatever he had shot at was much larger than a fighter, especially compared to the friendly at the far edge. It had to be a cruiser. And as he watched it began to slow and turn, attracted by the friendly coming on hard with guns blazing full. The cruiser avoided the blasts from the friendly fighter and came around hard horizontal. Just exactly to where he knew it had to be.

And then the blaze of *Glory*'s guns hit it full power. Its shields turned it bluer than running light and for a moment he worried that it was just going to cycle harmlessly forever, an APOT feedback loop. The Ichton cruiser sat there like a burning sapphire for what seemed like eons. And then its systems went into overload and it exploded with such violence that the screen had to go to reduction eight to catch the whole show.

"So that's why they call you Cowboy," said Muller, who sat at the next board. But Cowboy wasn't listening. He was spread over a hundred klicks of vacuum as the enemy attack force was annihilated around him.

They were drinking down in civ country, in a place on Bright Green called the Emerald. Not real imaginative, though the smart money on the *Hawking* said it was named for the Emerald Isle and not the deck. This theory was borne out by the fact it was the only place on board that served Guinness Stout. Which was what Cowboy was drinking, courtesy of Sutter Washington the Third.

"Yeah, boy, you sure saved my ass," Washington said when he spotted Cowboy sitting with a couple of chief gunnies from the *Impaler* and *Kingdom Come*. "I don't know how you managed to nail that cruiser from your position, but I sure do owe you a drink and a favor. You ever in a tight spot, you know you got Sutter Washington the Third at your back, brother."

Cowboy just blinked. "I didn't know any of our people were out that far," he stammered.

Washington threw back his head and laughed. "Not many were. But I can push that baby so hard she don't know when to come. And chasing those bugs down the hole, well, they were sure pushing light. Though you know they don't have any kind of warp drive anyone'd care about. Lousy engineers, those bugs."

"Don't ever underestimate the enemy," said Chief Gunny Xia Ling. "That is the first and the second mistake. These Ichtons are not going to roll over and die because we spray Raid."

"Like I said, those bugs are lousy engineers," Washington repeated and rolled his eyes. This time Ling got the joke and they all laughed too hard.

"Well, I was in what you would call hot pursuit," Washington went on. "I was ready to fire at anything. My granddaddy was an ace in the Fast Attack Wing in the last war. You might have heard of him, Sutter Washington. So I feel like I got to live up to the name, know what I mean? So I was going hot and heavy after them. Already got two in the battle here and wasn't near ready to stop. So there we were after them as they were trying to hightail it home, and I was way ahead of the pack. Luxury pickings, what you might call a seriously target-rich environment. And I had that cruiser baby in my sights and was ready to draw on him and he turns on me!

"Can you imagine? He slows to half-light and does a one-eighty and brings guns to bear. 'Course, that means when I fire I only got a little fellow, real disappointing." Washington stopped to wet his throat a little, telling the story was thirsty work.

Cowboy interrupted. "But it doesn't matter what size the thing is to make ace, right? The little fighter or the cruiser, either works in the rating. Or have I got it wrong?"

Sutter Washington smiled slowly. "Well, in technical terms it doesn't mean nothing, but truth to tell I really wanted to do my granddaddy one better. He was career Fleet, and so was my daddy and my momma and neither of them ever got to do more than push data around a screen. So I got a lot of making up to do.

"Anyhow, I don't know how you targeted the guy. He sure had me upside down and gravy. I only say, you ever need anything, you got a friend." Sutter Washington the Third solemnly lifted the remains of his Guinness and tapped glasses with everyone at the table.

"Intuition," Cowboy said seriously. "Just pure intuition." He didn't know what he meant by that, but somehow it seemed the only explanation he could find.

"You know, some researchers think that intuition is that the brain notices and processes data we don't consciously observe."

The voice was a woman's, low and familiar. Cowboy looked up, startled. Avrama Blackwell was standing over the group drinking, her clear blue eyes steady. She was looking directly at him, "Everybody here know Doc Blackwell?" Cowboy introduced her casually.

Sutter Washington's mahogany skin went mottled gray.

Avrama Blackwell actually giggled at the young fighter pilot. "I'm in Xeno, I don't do anything with humans," she said. "You're safe."

Washington's color returned slowly. "I would rather be surrounded by bug cruisers, would rather even be with one of those grunt reaction units on the ground, than spend ten minutes in Med Red," the pilot admitted. "Anything with a stethoscope gives me the tummy wobbles." He pointed to the pocket in the pale blue medical tunic Avrama Blackwell wore over her regulation utilities. The earpiece of a stethoscope was hanging out.

She stuffed it down hastily. "Take two aspirin and call me in the morning," she said, trying to make a joke of it. The others all forced some laughter and then found excuses to leave. Immediately. Which Cowboy didn't mind one bit.

"I didn't mean to make your friends uncomfortable," she told him.

Cowboy shrugged. "Their loss," he said. "Besides, I don't think they were so much uncomfortable as just giving me some space with a pretty lady. So, pretty lady, what are you drinking?"

Avrama Blackwell knit her fingers and looked down. "Actually, I'm not. I was just on my way down to Blue U to consult a little on the civilian side, and heard some scuttlebutt that a bunch of you heroes were in here. I thought you might be interested in coming along. I don't have all the answers yet, but you might find this informative."

Cowboy drained his glass and stood. Blue U was not his idea of a good time, and surely not where he had in mind going with a woman as winning as Dr. Blackwell, but it seemed like he had no choice. He was surprised to find that she even knew the slang term for the areas set aside for civilian research and scholarship. The term usually wasn't considered complimentary.

They crossed Bright Green to the far lift, which would be closer to scientist country when they arrived on Sky. The full science complement, including offices, labs, and lecture rooms, took a full quarter of both the Light Blue and Sky decks, one on top of the other, the two joined by the large amphitheater that doubled as the ship's main entertainment hall when it was not being used to display slides of alien viruses to fifteen lab assistants.

"Are we going to talk to Brynn Te Mon?" Cowboy asked. Te Mon was the only scientist Cowboy had heard of. Normally he never ventured below Dark Green. He didn't have the money to eat at any of the expensive restaurants in Violet and didn't need any of the luxuries sold at the civilian shops in the rest of the Blues. He could get the necessities from the commissary on Yellow with the military discount, and there were flea markets there on Sundays when some of the civ merchants came up.

Avrama Blackwell shook her head. "No. Brynn Te Mon is way too busy minding the existence of the universe to be interested in something as mundane as this. No, I sent my findings and the specimens down to Vladimir Tsorko as soon as I had my data. The eyes only live twelve hours, you know. But there are some experiments that can be done when they're less alive, and there's also a biochemical analysis. That isn't my specialty."

"There isn't anyone up on Med Red who could have done it?" Cowboy asked, interested. "You had to contract out?"

"We've got two full specimens to take apart, and five fast grown clones lying in our one xeno cloning vat. And let me tell you, those cost way too much to let anyone just take them apart. Even in the interests of defense," Blackwell said matter-of-factly. "And Tsorko's specialty is radio astronomy. There were a couple of anomalies that I just didn't understand and Vladimir is, well, you'll see. A good friend. Anyway, he just came through with the results so he can explain the peculiarities I observed."

They stopped at a Sky Blue door covered with cartoons. In fact, Cowboy noticed, most of the doors down here were like that. It offended his sense of what was shipshape. Scientists were generally an unruly bunch. If they needed to put cartoons on their doors, the least they could do was use the inside.

Avrama didn't knock, she just touched the door panel. It was open. "We're expected," she explained before she went inside.

Vladimir Tsorko was a big man with a very big silvering mustache. He immediately jumped up and held Avrama by the shoulders. "Ah, my colleague, how very pleasant to greet you down here. I have looked at your specimens and run the tests as we discussed, and I have read your results. All I can do is confirm them. So I suppose I will be only a second or third author on your paper. However, I think that I have enough data to write one of my own, though it would be more in the nature of a note without further data. Of course, the more data I have the better. So if you come by any more specimens I would be so grateful. . . ."

Avrama flashed that warm, winning smile at him. "Of course, Vladimir, it would be my pleasure."

The older scientist seemed to notice Cowboy for the first time. "And who is this, your friend? Another optical specialist? If so we shall have to get the vodka and drink to all of us getting publications from this discovery! A very excellent thing, research."

Avrama Blackwell laughed again. "No, Vladimir, this is Cowboy, weapons officer on the light cruiser *Glory*. But he brought the specimens in and was interested in the tests, so I thought I'd bring him along."

"Ah, then, it is my honor to meet you," Tsorko said firmly. "And shall we get to business, then? Avrama, it is exactly as you suspected, only more so, if that is possible. I think the multiple structures you had questions about are suited to microwave reception. And the others, well, there is indeed an anomaly. However, I have a theory . . ."

"Microwaves?" Cowboy asked.

Dr. Blackwell nodded. "Oh, yes. Maybe I should go back to the beginning and explain a little."

"That would be very helpful to me as well," Vladimir Tsorko agreed quickly.

"I read your findings but you write so technically. And I have not studied any biology since I was an undergraduate, and then I threw up in the lab. I was excused from the practicums for the rest of the course. Ah, well, I had never planned on a career in surgery anyway."

Even Cowboy had to grin. There was something about the scientist that was so completely familiar. Texan, one might say, though it looked like Vladimir Tsorko had never heard of the planet called Texas or the Great Range system at all. But he had the expansiveness that made Cowboy suddenly, sharply, miss home.

Avrama Blackwell pushed the tea mug and a stack of papers to one side of the display monitor and put a stack of journal hard copies on the floor. Then she called up a series of pictures on the screen that meant nothing at all to Cowboy.

"These are photographs of the Ichton eyes," she stated, as if starting a lecture. "You will notice they are faceted, and that each individual facet is quite different. There are sections you will notice here with pupils and large sections that have no pupil structure at all. Of the facets with no pupils, there are two distinct types. One type has a strange structure that covers nearly the entire back of the retina, and the others are missing these structures. These were some of the anomalies that I consulted Dr. Tsorko about.

"However, as a first test, I placed electrodes in the cones of the retinas in all three kinds of facets, and shone light of different frequencies at them. The cones generate electrical current when they are stimulated by wavelengths they can detect." Then she paused. "How much do you know about waves?" she asked innocuously.

Cowboy shook his head. "I know that sound travels way slower than light and that some of them are no good for you. I guess I never thought about it."

"I don't know enough about waves, either," Blackwell admitted. "But sound waves and light waves are very different things. With sound you can hear ten different notes at once. If you aren't trained you might not realize what you're hearing, but a musician would. The wavelengths don't blend.

"Light is the opposite. Wavelengths blend, so you can't tell if, say, orange is the wavelength that produces true orange or a combination of wavelengths. What we see as colors are different wavelengths, and for us the visible range is from four hundred to seven hundred nanometers.

"Now, the longer the wave the lower the energy of the wave. The waves in our visible range are very small and X-rays are smaller and higher energy than that. Infrared is larger, and microwaves at the long end can be a meter from peak to peak. Radio waves cover the largest range, from ten to the minus two meters all the way up to a million meters peak to peak. Which is why I wanted to talk to Vladimir, he knows all about radio waves."

"No, my dear, I wish I could know all about radio waves," the older man said sadly. "I know only a little bit about them." And then his eyes twinkled. "But what I do not know about them, nobody else knows it either. And I shall be the first to learn. But so far you are essentially correct."

Avrama smiled at him and then the picture on the screen changed to display a chart that Cowboy thought looked like a graph of his last poker winnings. It was a lot more pleasant than the alien eyeballs, though, and he was glad of the change.

"So I tried different wavelengths of light, first in our visual range. And until I hit red there was no response at all," Blackwell continued. "So I kept going lower. It seems that the facets with pupils responded to light from visible red though infrared."

"So these bugs see heat, basically," Cowboy said, thinking about it, wondering what it meant as far as *Glory*'s fighting capabilities were concerned.

"Well, yes," Dr. Blackwell agreed, "but that's not all. I ran the same experiments on the facet without pupils. Now some of the lower energy waves can pass through wood or paper or plastic. Microwaves, for example, and radio waves of course. So I tried them, and guess what?"

"The bugs see microwaves and radio waves," Cowboy guessed. "Must make cooking dinner a real experiment in living. But what does it change? I mean, it's all very interesting and that, but what use is it?"

"Well, it might help us find their home planet," Avrama Blackwell said. "Our eyes are adapted to our sun. Obviously theirs must have some advantage to wherever they're from."

Vladimir Tsorko nodded vigorously. "Indeed. But there is still more, very interesting about this species. Avrama asked me about the eyes with no pupils. Ah, I think, this is very strange, they react to very low energy waves. But how can they focus these waves? If you cannot focus, you cannot localize. It is like sound. We cannot focus sound waves."

"But you can tell where sound is coming from," Cowboy protested.

"Indeed," Dr. Tsorko agreed. "That is because you have two ears and you can triangulate. But sound waves travel so very slowly compared to electromagnetic waves. No, to focus these you need some antenna larger than the wave. If the wave is a meter long, then you need something bigger than a meter to focus it. We use dish antennas in great arrays to focus the long radio waves and we have only the two Trilimar observatories to focus those very long waves at the bottom of the scale. But the Trilimar observatory stations have dishes the size of a small solar system and it is so very difficult to maintain them. Even with all the graduate students one could want, and really they are more interested in doing theoretical work than going EVA and patching up dish plates two weeks away."

"So they can't see those waves," Cowboy said.

Dr. Tsorko beamed. "If you are interested in perhaps a small graduate stipend when we return it could be arranged. . . ."

But Cowboy shook his head. More school was not exactly on the immediate agenda, not at all. In fact, this long lecture about waves and eyes was starting to get a little dull and he still didn't see the point of it all. So maybe they could figure out from their vision what kind of star the home world of the Ichtons circled. Maybe there would be a strategic advantage there and it was important to the effort. Right now, though, he was more concerned with cleaning out this one little pocket of space.

Those Silbers down there, now, this wasn't one bit of use to them. They needed help, and fast. Cowboy silently wished the scientists would get on with it and maybe do something like make Ichton-free Raid. After what he'd heard about Sandworld and what was happening on the Gersons' home planet, this was one enemy he had no trouble using chems against.

"You are indeed right." Dr. Tsorko didn't notice Cowboy's lapse of attention. "They can see the smallest radio waves but they cannot focus them. The way we hear sound. But, and this is very interesting, the eyes with no pupils but with a strange structure before the retina, that structure is a type of organic dish antenna for the smaller microwaves."

"Like I said, dinner is a laugh a minute," Cowboy responded. His patience was just about used up. He'd known Blue U was not exactly his idea of a rec deck. Damn, the stupid things he'd do for a good-looking woman.

"So now you can write up your paper and I can write mine, and we can let the referees decide which of us will publish first," Vladimir Tsorko said gleefully.

Avrama led Cowboy to the door. "As always, it was a pleasure to have an excuse to visit, even if it was far too short," she said brightly.

"Indeed, we have to get together for some palmyari next week, of a certitude. My treat," the older scientist said firmly, then they stepped into the Sky Blue hallway and the door closed behind them.

"What are palmyari?" Cowboy asked with some trepidation.

"Dumplings," Avrama Blackwell answered firmly. "Delicate little dumplings in sour cream sauce."

"Speaking of which, I'm starving. Would you be willing to introduce me to these dumplings tonight?" Cowboy asked, his eyes twinkling. Maybe the lecture in Blue U was going to pay off after all.

Avrama's eyes lit up as well, with mischief as well as pleasure. "I think I'm more in the mood for Chinese, and it's dim sum night at the Golden Dragon."

"I know it well," he said solemnly and stepped aside formally as the doors to the lift opened.

❖ ❖ ❖

He didn't sleep well that night and he couldn't understand why. Maybe it was the duck's feet; he usually didn't like duck's feet but Avrama chose two little plates of them. But when he left her after dinner and a stroll through the garden, without a single mention of bug eyes or any other educational topic, he couldn't get to sleep for hours.

And when he finally did manage to sack out the dreams came. Dismembered monsters were after him and he was small and afraid and in the boarding school in Sam's Town. And Jackson Byrne was there again, like all his nightmares, only now Jackson had faceted opaque eyes.

The dream followed the same structure. First Jackson erased every other line in his physics text, then the flash of the blind bomb that Jackson had thrown at him the day he moved into the Junior dorm and the headmaster's office, all reproak paneling and leather. The leather was real, butterscotch-colored even in his dream. Only the headmaster looked like Vladimir Tsorko and he was being sentenced to a life of auditing upper-level chemistry classes. Forever.

When he woke up he was soaked with perspiration and it was barely oh-dark-thirty. His two roommates were both snoring and Cowboy knew he should try to grab that last hour's sleep. What happened to the time in Weapons Command School when he could go to sleep anytime at all, when twenty minutes was enough for a good nap, and now he had trouble when the alarm went off at 0615 every morning?

Well, there was nothing he could do about it now. He knew he wasn't going to be able to drift back off, so he hauled himself out of the rack and spent the minimum in the recycle room. His utilities came out of the locker fresh enough to pass inspection. Dressed, he headed back to the bay where the *Glory* sat among all the light cruisers.

Cowboy loved the bay. He loved it when it seethed with activity, when men and women reported at a run when the enemy had been sighted, when the tech crews ran their refueling and prep after every mission. He loved it in silence when the lights were at half and the array of battle-weary light cruisers and scout boats waited in the semilights of the enormous bay. So large, so hushed, so like a church it made Cowboy want to pray.

But someone had violated the silence of the dark cycle of the ships. Crews worked round the clock, but there was no one else here now, no names on the door manifest, but a jangle of what passed for music somewhere out beyond Gremonsk still played on the wall plug. Made him think of Jackson Byrne playing that damned radio after lights out in the dorm, getting them all put on detention for a week.

Furious, Cowboy strode over and tore the offending box out of the jack. The only reason he didn't slam it against the composition bulkhead was that all hell broke loose.

A thousand watts of light came up on the registers in nanoseconds as orders boomed over the speaker. "All personnel report immediately to your assigned briefing room, bays six through nine, six through nine. All personnel report immediately to your assigned briefing room. Hot status, go, hot status."

Cowboy dropped the offending box without thought and ran top speed across the grate decking and into the hot status briefing room. The hot status team was assembled already, edgy, impatient to be gone. Cowboy recognized Sutter Washington the Third staring at the board with intense concentration and just the hint of a smile.

The briefing board glowed with bright red and tangerine displays, the data from which fed directly into the memories of every boat tasked. In enemy orange he saw a large ship surrounded by a host of fighters.

"This is what we want to get," the officer of the watch said. "It's an egg ship headed for the Gersons' world. They defend their egg ships more heavily than any other target, but these are the whole purpose of the Ichton conquest. Take out this baby and we hurt them where it matters."

There was only dead silence for a split second, and then the hot squad burst out of the briefing room and made for their craft double-time. They were out before the rotation crews arrived.

Cowboy stayed in place. His shipmates from *Glory* arrived, tousled and bleary-eyed, less than three minutes later. They didn't question him being there first. The briefing room locked cycle as the bay opened for the hot squad to launch.

This time the briefing was a little more involved. "We have sent the intercept team to attack the fighters and draw them off, if they can. We have various reports about how the Ichtons react to these tactics. It is Intel's opinion that they will not be drawn away from the egg ship, that they are instinctively pressured to protect it beyond any immediate danger to themselves."

Someone gave a raspberry cheer at the mention of Intel. Cowboy frowned. That was kiddie garbage; it had no place on the *Hawking*.

The watch officer didn't stop for a beat. "In any event, we want the light cruisers to back up the scout boats, play the heavies for them. Let the SBs take the fighters, we want the big guns on that egg ship. We have to destroy one. Not only will it be good for our effort and for our Gerson survivors, it will also demoralize the enemy. This is the crux of their mission. It doesn't matter how much territory they have taken if they can't move these babies in. Any questions?"

There were none. There was no time. The hot squad was already out there, the large schematic showed them closing fast. They were going to engage very soon now and they needed the backup of the heavier ships or they were in trouble. No questions.

They were dismissed as the bay doors went green, signaling that the bay was up to full pressure. *Glory* was ready. Cowboy ran to her with his shipmates, avoiding fueling lines and other crews without noticing them. Just one more distraction not to waste time.

The crew of the *Glory* had been together since before being assigned to the *Hawking*. They knew they were going to get the assignment, but even before they had never been the kind to let fifty years of peace make them lax. The *Glory* had won every readiness and shooting competition in her division for the past three years. And their rating aboard the *Hawking* was top ten percent. Which wasn't high enough at all for the skipper and the rest of the crew. Since they had emerged at the Core the skipper had been holding even more drills.

So that by the time the bay was ready for launch, the crew of the *Glory* was strapped in at battle stations, lights out and screens on, ready to come out shooting. They were hushed in the launch. This was not their maiden fight: They'd already been blooded once. Now there was only the task and the screens in front of them and the distance to cover before they engaged.

The screens were already reporting the hot squad closing on the enemy. Cowboy switched from schematic to actual view. The little scout boats seemed thick and not highly maneuverable compared to the sleek bug fighters. But as he looked closer he thought that perhaps the bugs didn't have the tech or weren't as concerned about it. He asked for mags on the screen and it complied. Yeah, no question, the bug fighters were old-style cockpit machines, helmeted figures sitting revealed under a transparent canopy. They fought visual, then, face-to-face because they either didn't have the instruments to keep themselves fully insulated from the field, or because they didn't trust the instruments they had.

Something about those canopies nagged at the back of Cowboy's brain as he touched the screen, commanding it back to schematic again. Easier to follow the patterns that way instead of being too involved in one particular fight. But of all the bluish blips on the screen, he wondered which one was Lieutenant Sutter Washington the Third, gunning for ace. Silently he wished the man luck, hoped that afterward they'd be able to drink another Guinness in the Emerald. That Sutter Washington's atoms would not be spread over a hundred klicks of vacuum. That his wouldn't be, either.

"Twelve minutes before reaching enemy position," the computer informed them all.

Twelve minutes. The entire universe could end in half that time.

On the screen before him, the hot squad executed a precise ninety-degree cartwheel and cut up the perpendicular vector, moving away from the egg ship pushing hard light. They executed a much more difficult fifty-degree wheel, neatly as the Fleet exhibition team, and cut back in at the egg ship from an angle that didn't give a clue as to where they had come from. Then they slowed as a single entity and regrouped formation so that instead of flying as a porcupine mass, they were strung out like an elongated arrow. And the arrow flew into place, tickling the edge of the Ichton defenses.

The shielding around the egg ship glowed like a star in the darkness. Even on the screen it quivered in the orange-colored wash that couldn't get a good enough fix to pinpoint it. Not that that mattered, Cowboy thought coldly. It was big enough that a few good hits in the general midsection should do some fairly useful damage.

But the fighters around it carried very little shielding, from the readout. Of course, they were the escort. They wouldn't be bringing this precious cargo into an embattled area.

The hot squad SBs were closing, teasing at the Ichton convoy. The lead boat of the arrow darted into the Ichton perimeter, looped and doubled back while the second SB followed in like mode.

The bugs didn't bite. They shot at the SBs when their defined perimeter was breached and Cowboy's screen erupted with red-yellow-green light. They were not anticipating the attack and were late. But they still didn't follow, weren't drawn off to pursue the enemy that must sorely tempt them.

The hot squad tried again, the SBs looking like stinging quick darts, teasing the Ichton fighters just at the edge of their formation. Ichton discipline held. They were not going to be drawn away this easily.

Cowboy watched as the blue blips of the SBs rallied and regrouped. Now they were in a double spiral. He's seen this maneuver once in a base show, one of those open-to-the-locals-let's-have-good-p.r. kind of things. It was the climax of the show, the SBs hurtling at each other, shooting down the spiral like a projectile in a barrel and crossing with only a breath between them. Then it looked like a piece of set bravado, though publicity for the show said that every maneuver and formation was part of the general battle training of all SB fighter squads.

Now Cowboy saw it in action. The spirals were good defense. The shooting lines and spirals would rotate enough that the enemy wouldn't know where the next SB would show. Using two of them should keep the Ichtons at least occupied.

Two SBs shot the spiral, laced through enemy territory, and scooped around to draw away. As they came around in position two more SBs loaded and released. These weren't so fortunate. The bugs were watching, wary, ready. They caught the first one in a green blast that bloomed and atomized. The second went evasive in the tail run, flipping and dodging and weaving. Two Ichtons pursued and looked like they were going to be drawn off, but no joy. They reached what had been defined as perimeter and turned back to their defensive position.

"Damn," Cowboy swore softly to himself. The word echoed in the silent dark of the gun station.

"Six minutes to interception range," the computer said.

"We're never going to get that egg ship if we can't get those fighters away," someone observed with frustration. Cowboy knew the voice, it was Maria Vargas, exec. And she was right.

Deep in the rush Cowboy knew perfect clarity, intuition. He could see into the patterns of combat like a crystal ball. But something hammered at the back of his mind, something fogged the sight. Everything clouded as he fought to bring it to his conscious mind. He *knew* it was there, teasing around like the SBs to the enemy. Taunting him, all the pieces jumbled like a dream. The music, Jackson's radio in the dorm, the eyes, the millions and millions of eyes. Avrama Blackwell, her crinkled nose when she laughed and her low, firm voice talking about waves and energy and eyes.

A dream, a nightmare, it swallowed him. Images overlapped, intertwined, merged with the readout on the screen.

"Two minutes to intercept," the computer said calmly.

Cowboy unbuckled his safety strap and made his way through the dark to the skipper. Captain Wurther Ali Archer stood behind the helm station, his eyes never moving from the complex-layered holo, displays there. "Yes, Cowboy," he said evenly.

"Sir, I have it," Cowboy said, trying to keep the excitement out of his voice. "We have radio communication, all the light cruisers do. And the new data about the Ichtons say they can see radio waves."

"So we should cut off those communications?" the skipper asked, honestly concerned.

"No, sir, we need to turn them on. If we put our transmitters on full, all of us, and direct them at the Ichtons down there, it would read to them like a flash of light would to us."

The skipper never looked at him but a smile crossed that grim face. "Blind them, you think?"

"Can't hurt to try," Vargas said quickly. The skipper nodded and Vargas turned to the communications center. "Li, you heard that. Post it over to the rest of the flight, coordinate settings on radio. And then give it to them."

"You really think something as low energy as a radio blast is going to do anything?" Muller groused as Cowboy strapped back into his station. "If they've got any decent hull plating this is a total waste."

"But they don't," Cowboy said. "They've got a clear canopy. Look on your realmag, why don't you?"

Cowboy saw Muller's screens flicker in the change. "Damn," Muller said. "They are some kind of idiots."

"I don't think so, Mr. Muller," the skipper said softly. "If this works it's a one-shot deal. But it's worth a try, you copy?"

But Cowboy felt no victory in Muller's soft reply. The tension was growing in a way he had never experienced before. Always Cowboy had been ice-cold. Now his palms were covered with sweat.

"Coordinate transmission ready to go now," Li said.

On the screen nothing changed. For a moment everything remained perfectly static. "Blow them to hell, you guys," Cowboy whispered. "Blow them away."

The SBs and the light cruisers began firing at the same time. The hot squad mowed through the blinded Ichtons like a McCormick combine.

The light cruisers left the immobilized fighters to the SBs and concentrated their fire on the egg ship. Its shields glowed blue, channeling the laser fire from the Fleet craft harmlessly into a power circuit. Harmlessly at first. The overloads could handle only so much power. The combined ordnance of three light cruisers stepped up the energy level exponentially.

On Cowboy's screen the shields went from orange to blue to violet to shrieking, shimmering wash. And when it finally exploded the massed shards took out nearly twenty Ichton fighters along with it, and two SBs. The screen looked like a Goanese abstract light-painting, a living flow of rich color that cycled through the spectrum, constantly revealing a new image.

Cowboy never had been much for abstract art. With the mission objective accomplished, he put his screens on passive sweep. No point in letting elation turn them into fools. There were it hell of a lot of Ichtons out there, and when they knew one of their egg ships had been blown they were going to be very angry. And it was still a good half hour back to the *Hawking*.

The Emerald was packed full that night. The whole hot squad and most of the crews of three light cruisers showed up, and the unlucky folk who hadn't been in on the kill were buying drinks for those who had. Cowboy's name was mentioned and toasted at least seven times. Maria Vargas and Li had to explain what had happened and how the radio transmissions had blinded the Ichtons in their fighters like a flash bomb until their voices gave out and someone else bought another round.

But Cowboy wasn't there to hear it. He was wearing his very best embroidered skintight and eating palmyari for the first time. They were very good, he thought. Very good indeed. But the company of one Dr. Avrama Blackwell was far better. Especially when no one was trying to get educated about science.

THE FIRST WEEKS

After eight months in warp, isolated within the *Hawking*, every member of the crew was anxious to return to normal space. During the journey there had been a number of violent incidents and even a few murders. Most of the problems were related to bad relations between the Fleet personnel, who knew it was *their* battlestation, and the representatives of the commercial interests, who were equally determined to remind everyone that *they* had virtually paid for the place. By their standards the Fleet types were there as renters, not owners. Below this surface friction were the still-healing scars of the Family war. This old antagonism was complicated by the fact that there were a number of Khalians on the *Hawking*, serving as Marines. The more fanatic of the descendants of the families had never completely forgiven the Khalia for changing sides once it had become apparent they had been merely used by the Schlein Family and its allies to harass the Alliance while the families built up their strength. Most of the murders were, as would be expected, crimes of passion.

After arrival each member of the crew, civilian and Fleet, had to face their own mortality. By the third encounter with the Ichtons it had been decided that using the *Hawking* in combat was too great a risk. This battle had been over the world of the second race that appealed for help. They succeeded in driving off an Ichton force of several hundred smaller ships and two of the giants, but the *Hawking* was twice rammed and received considerable surface damage. This only increased the feeling of vulnerability and had a negative effect on the morale of all the races on board. Fortunately some provisions had been made to deal with the problem.

STARLIGHT
by Jody Lynn Nye

He was the most famous interpretive dramatist in the galaxy, renowned and beloved on every civilized planet in the Alliance and beyond.

She was the *Stephen Hawking*'s morale and entertainment officer.

Theirs should have been a love that shook the stars in their courses.

But it wasn't.

When she enlisted in the Fleet, Jill FarSeeker had promptly been assigned to the Morale corps. She was a cheerful woman of twenty-seven, unflappable, friendly, and comfortable with herself. Though a good listener, she was also capable of speaking tactfully to the point. Spacer rank had been only a brief stop for her, and ensign rank briefer. A mere three years in the service, she had risen to first lieutenant and had been recommended for an early captaincy. Blessed with straight black hair and large, round brown eyes, Jill thought of herself in a comfortable, kid-sisterish way.

When Kay McCaul was assembling her Space and Power Use staff for the *Hawking*, she requested Jill specifically by name as her second. There seemed to be nothing that would jeopardize the assignment. Jill was single and had no family. As soon as she gave her consent, she was added to the "Orphans Brigade," and put in charge of liaising with the civilian entertainment arm. McCaul gave her the power to make decisions at every level without having to refer back to Kay herself. Although Jill was only a lieutenant, she bullied, cajoled, pushed, and prodded the other Fleet staff, even those far above her in rank, until she had the entertainment division running like a hardwired computer chip. Jill was no less formidable than Kay, but was considered to be more approachable.

Sixty channels of music and trivid available three shifts 'round were created to amuse the ten thousand passengers anytime they wanted to tune in. The rec library featured centuries of printed works, and reruns of programming from every world in the Alliance. Community access video stations were provided on each level of the battlestation, and Jill herself was the negotiating committee to whom small groups turned when they wanted to put their productions on line for general consumption. Her standards were clear—she would not stand for slander or hate shows—but within those parameters she was liberal as to what she would allow. She hated saccharine melodrama, so her roster of preference consisted mainly of meaty interviews and classics of literature and drama.

Jill's staunchest backers were the audio jocks, both civilian and military, for whom she championed nearly unlimited license. Her argument was that they were the voice of the people, into which the people could tune anytime, and that stifling them unreasonably was counterproductive. The shows became forums for arguments on philosophy and current events, and a shoulder for passengers to cry on when they could get no one else to listen to them. If there was something going wrong with the atmosphere controls, Jill was as likely to hear about it on an audio channel from one of her paladins, as she named them, as from someone who had complained to an engineer. She made Commander Brand and Administrator Omera admit that the complaints were handled much more quickly when they were aired publicly than if they remained private gripes. It didn't take a month before it was known all over the ship that Jill was the person to go to when the rest of the brass wasn't listening.

Arend McKechnie Lyseo was already in his fifties when the *Hawking* launched. He knew when they signed him to an open-ended contract that he would never return to the Alliance cluster, and considered it an adventure with which to crown his notable career. A coup for the largely unpopular battle cruiser program, the addition of the great Lyseo to its complement provided a cachet of respect, if not approval, from a larger segment of the population than it had previously enjoyed. His fan club spanned nearly the entire roster of Alliance worlds. There were other actors aboard, but none of them enjoyed the status of legend.

At first, Brand and Omera opposed letting McCaul sign Lyseo, and especially under the terms he demanded. Lyseo's contract allowed for periodic renegotiation, which they saw as a lever to extort privileges using the threat of nonappearance, but McCaul, who had had Lyseo investigated, knew there was nothing to worry about. Lyseo would never remain as a dead weight for any appreciable length of time. He was a workaholic. He might go off and sulk for a few days when he was on an ego trip, but then he would put on some marvelous heartrending or hilarious spectacle that would have everyone riveted to the trivid tanks. Throughout a forty-year career, he had a better attendance record than any aspiring performer, however motivated and half his age.

Publicly, he was magnificent. Whole audiences had been known to collapse into laughter at a single quirk of the dramatic black brows, such a contrast against his shock of prematurely white hair. A man of above average height, his frame sculpted into the long, thin lines appropriate to comedy or tragedy, he retained the suppleness of youth, both physically and mentally. Lyseo remained a current favorite when many of his contemporaries had fallen into the category of "classic" because he kept up with events, and was not shy about presenting his opinions of any of them.

"What an opportunity," he had announced at his final press conference before the *Hawking* blasted out of system, "to open up the rest of the galaxy to itself through the medium of my art."

The pronouncement pleased the top brass, who realized at last that having one of the preeminent human stars aboard and in favor of their cause meant that continuing interest in the battle cruiser would be maintained, even at the distance from the Alliance to the heart of the galaxy. That could prove vital to future funding of Fleet projects.

Every day, the slot on the entertainment network at sixteen hundred hours was set aside for Lyseo's daily performance. By written agreement it was guaranteed to last no less than a minute and no more than an hour, except by prearrangement with the Morale Office. His contract contained a clause that all of his performances would be recorded and sent back to the Alliance. No matter that it would take longer and longer for each message torpedo to reach its destination as the *Hawking* flew farther into the heart of the galaxy. It was meant, along with the factual news reports, to be a record of the journey, which would be of immense historical value. Lyseo vowed to reproduce through his art the feelings, hopes, aspirations, fears, losses, and discoveries of the warriors, merchants, and civilians aboard the *Stephen Hawking*. It was understood, though not officially condoned, that all activity stopped or slowed at 1600 so that everyone could see his newest work.

He had the best special effects holograms could produce, his own crew, and top-of-the-line production equipment, and a clothing synthesizer programmed with every garment worn by every being of any ethnicity, nationality, or planetary origin since the beginning of recorded memory. He was permitted to go where he wanted, whenever he wanted, within the ship, to gather impressions of everyday life. One further clause in his agreement that had nearly scuttled the whole arrangement was that he would be entitled to whatever quantity of power he needed, or claimed he did, to run his effects or synthesizers. His library of literature and music, when it was added to the *Hawking*'s complement, doubled the size of the memory needed to hold it.

"It is my legacy to the galaxy," Lyseo said. "Since I will not survive into the ages, my work and my philanthropy will have to speak for me to future generations."

Privately, he was nervous, easily depressed, and required constant reassurance that he was not wasting the universe's time. During these fits of insecurity, he called himself Hambone, and referred to his vast talent as a quirk.

After his first performance, Lyseo retired into his dressing room and locked the door, refusing to come out or answer communications signals.

The technicians on duty in the entertainment center sent for Jill. It was her job to handle her most famous passenger when he became difficult, a task that she did not find easy. From the time she was a teenager, she had admired Lyseo. She had watched every performance of his she could find on disk or cube. When she was informed by her boss that Lyseo was going to be coming on board, she was uncharacteristically nervous. At first, she was taken aback by the periodic snits and constant fretting exhibited by the artist whose public face she adored so much, but underneath the facade, she found a likable man. He was engaging and intelligent, and he genuinely cared for the people for whom he performed. Jill discovered that Lyseo would listen to criticism, truly listen, and apply it to himself if he found it honest. If not, it was as likely to send him into an explosive rage or an achingly pathetic depression. Lack of feedback had the potential to affect him the same way.

"It's just reaction," Kem Thoreson, Lyseo's manager, assured her as they waited at the door. "Come on, Ari, open up. You were fantastic! Everyone loved you." He kept up a steady rapping with his knuckles that Jill felt had to be as painful as it was irritating to listen to.

After a long pause, the door slid open, and Lyseo loomed over them. His eyes were mournful in the mottled mask of half-erased makeup.

"My greatest opportunity," the magnificent baritone voice intoned mournfully, "for the greatest audience a being ever had, and as you would so rightly say, I blew it."

Thoreson socked him playfully in the arm. "What are you talking about, Hammy? You were good! Wasn't he, Jill?"

Jill felt that instead of remembering, she was reliving his performance. Lyseo had enacted the chaotic arrival of the Core ship on the Alliance frontier, followed by the flurry of activity as the human and Khalian senates had decided what to do. With only changes in posture and gesture, he had gone from human to Nedge to Khalian, and back again, arguing the rightness of aiding the Core systems, while drawing the invisible sphere of the battlestation within the heart of his stage space. At the height of dramatic tension, he had held his hands framed, and a hologram of the *Hawking* appeared between them, as if he had evoked it from the depths of his self.

"It was . . . indescribable," Jill said at last, feeling overwhelmed.

Lyseo regarded her. He dabbed at a bit of makeup on his cheek with the towel slung around his neck. "That bad, eh?"

"No! It was wonderful! I . . . how did you manage to be so many people at once?"

"We are all many people," he said, waving a dramatic arm. "Sometimes I can't sleep because of the crowd. It's all tricks. Do you see, if I turn my head this way, you follow the line of my head, and the dark stripe along my cheekbone suggests a Nedge beak?"

"Why, that's incredible," Jill said, looking more closely. "And the dark smudges there and there under your eyes look like a Khalian muzzle."

Lyseo nodded. "You see how simple?"

"But it isn't simple at all," Jill argued. "It's marvelous."

Thoreson, seeing that his client's ill mood was breaking, shepherded him back into the dressing room and sat him down on a couch, talking all the while he cleaned the makeup off Lyseo's face. The great man made no protest.

"There you go," Kem said, slapping him on the back. "Good as new. You get some rest, and you'll be all ready for your next show tomorrow."

The expressive eyes met Jill's in the mirror, and the brows raised sadly. "To think of pouring out my whole soul every day, to an uncomprehending mass," the magnificent voice rumbled. "Old Hambone reduced at last to the status of the evening news."

Lyseo's self-deprecation was for Jill and Kem only. Once he stepped outside the dressing-room door, he was once again the star. Over the course of the next six months, he alternated performances based on the exigencies of ship life with items from the classics. A sly sense of humor jibed at the constant warring between the factions on board. When one cruel and much quoted parody of the most prominent Nedge merchant executives provoked a demand for an apology, Lyseo laughed it off.

"The nature of my art allows no artificial defenses to stand in the way. More to the point, my contract allows for it. Sue and be damned."

He was unassailable from everywhere but within. McCaul sent Jill to talk the merchants back into a good humor. It took some time to smooth out literally ruffled feathers. Privately Jill agreed with Lyseo's assessment of the Nedge, but since they all had to live together for a long time, it was necessary to make peace.

"You should be honored, good sirs and madam," Jill explained during their meeting. "The great Lyseo doesn't immortalize just anyone."

The Nedge looked at one another, the round eyes bright on either side of the expressionless beaks. "Perhaps there is something in what you say," Braak Rokoru mused, turning back to Jill. "But he must not do it again. My hatchlings back on Eerrik III will see, when the broadcast reaches them, and be ashamed."

"Certainly they won't see it in that light," Jill suggested. "If my parent were so featured, I would be flattered, for myself and for my nest. You could message them about it. They might want to make a permanent recording."

The Nedge inclined his head slowly, openly considering Jill's enthusiasm. "Perhaps it is only that we do not understand the human sense of humor."

Inwardly, Jill let out a sigh of relief. "Perhaps not, honored sir. I can assure you that everyone else on the ship found it funny."

Solemnly, the Nedge bowed to her. "Then we will do what you suggest. We are most grateful for your explanation."

As soon as she could possibly excuse herself, Jill fled, and had a good laugh in her office with the intercoms turned off. Lyseo's imitation of the ponderous Nedge had captured them exactly. It had been tickling at her ribs throughout her meeting, and she could wait no longer to let it out. She longed to tell Lyseo about the meeting, but suspected that once he knew, the Nedge would appear again on a 1600 show, and she didn't think she could placate them again.

Lyseo continued to fascinate her as much as he had when she was young. Whenever Jill had the time, she sat just outside of camera range in his studio and watched him work live. She regretted that it was impossible for everyone to see him this way. His personal magnetism enveloped her, drew her along in the fantasies he created, making her believe in them. A mere video of him seemed almost out of context.

Unexpectedly, the soaring audacity fell wing-clipped when the *Hawking* entered the system of the first Core world to beg for help. No planetary communication on Gerson answered any of their hails. Concerned, Commander Brand sent single-seat fighters in to do video reconnaissance. The data they sent back to base was horrific. Every population center, every domicile, every supply store, had been stripped or blasted. The carnage was evident even at a hundred fifty thousand meters. Sensors found no signs of life above animal intelligence. Word of the genocide and destruction below spread swiftly throughout the ship. The Gerson on board went crazy with grief and had to be put in restraints. After that, Jill had to put out a lot of emotional fires, and found she was counting on Lyseo's daily performance to cheer her up.

Apparently, so was everyone else. The ratings numbers showed that a record number of viewers tuned in to that day's broadcast. What they saw only deepened their feelings of hopelessness.

Lyseo, for once stripped of makeup and clever artifice, sat hunched in the middle of his stage on the floor, as the camera revolved around and around him. Arms gathering his knees protectively to his chest, Lyseo was the personification of despair. After what felt like an eternity, he lifted his head and stared hopelessly at the ceiling.

"Why did I ever leave the Alliance?" he moaned. "I was safe there. I had my friends, my family, all my comforts. I joined this fool's chase to the center of the galaxy, and for what? In aid of strangers, people who are already dead. Perhaps they are all dead, and we have come here for nothing. I will never see my birth world again. We are moving forward into the depths of the void!"

Jill, watching from a rec lounge on Orange level 2, felt her heart sink. She noted a shocked silence fall over her fellow viewers. Some of the humans sat with nervous grins on their faces, waiting for Lyseo to crack the joke. When he remained serious, they stared at him, uncomfortable and angry. After the screen faded, no one spoke for a long moment, then everyone burst out at once, most of them shouting to dispel their rage.

Jill stood up on a chair. "Now, simmer down, people," she called, signaling for attention. She tried several times to interrupt the furious chatter. No one listened. She climbed down and made her way smartly to the nearest control room. Something in the order of video sedatives was called for.

"Well, you've certainly got them talking," Jill said. Things looked bad. Lyseo was in a deep depression, and this time she couldn't use the lure of public acclaim to pull him out of it. He'd already been informed of complaints coming from the highest brass. Instead of provoking a roar of approval or a round of informed discussion, he had exposed primary fears that made most people curl up on themselves. The paladins reported no abatement in the number of frightened callers who just wanted to talk with a calm voice. She suspected that not all of them were civilian passengers.

Anticipating Kay McCaul's instructions, Jill had ordered a program of perky music, and the video terminals showed Fleet recruitment films and morale-boosting, mindless adventure sagas reaching back into a thousand years of mass entertainment. Then she went to visit the source of the trouble in his dressing room.

"I am fundamentally disappointed in the response of my audience," Lyseo said, mopping his face with his sodden tunic. "I re-create their very moods, and they turn on me. What do they want of me?"

"You frightened them," said Jill, squatting down beside his chair. "You reminded them how vulnerable they are out here."

"It was an honest assessment of the emotional sense on board this ship," Lyseo said. "I only told the truth."

"They're not prepared to deal with the truth," Jill said. "Everything that is happening is completely new to them. They are afraid of what's out there. The unknown scares them. You just reminded them of what they've been trying to suppress so they can deal with their day-to-day tasks. You're making that very difficult."

Arend Lyseo thought deeply for a moment, and sighed. "It was not my intention. I must have erred in my performance."

"Not at all," Jill assured him. "It was truly brilliant. But it wasn't what they needed to see. I'm scared, too, if you must know. I'm frightened rigid by whatever's out there!"

Lyseo stared down at her. "How miserably insensitive of me," he said. "What I do cannot make the slightest iota of difference in anyone's life if I am making it impossible for them to function. How presumptuous of me, a mere entertainer, to paralyze my viewers into immobility. I am an utter barbarian and a wretch and blind, blind, blind!" He pounded his hands on his dressing table.

Jill stood up and put her hands on her hips. "Well, at least you're not a hypochondriac," she said. "That's the one thing I just can't stand."

Lyseo gaped at her in open astonishment. Slowly, a smile crept across his lips, and he began to laugh. Jill relaxed, and grinned at him. He stood up and took her into his arms, and kissed her. Jill felt her bones melt. No matter how casually she tried to behave toward him, he was still her idol.

"You are the only thing that keeps me from despair, raven-winged maiden," he murmured into her hair. "It is your presence, your honesty, which allows me to believe that no matter what mistakes I make, it will all turn out right in the end." She raised her face to look into his eyes, needing assurance of the sincerity of his words. This man could imitate any emotion, create spun sugar out of air; it could be mere praise. She saw no artifice now, only affection and respect. He bent to kiss her again, and she responded with all her heart.

In a moment they were making love. Jill kept thinking that it was impossible, that this was one of the videos, not actual life, and certainly not hers.

"Okay, talk to me," Driscoll Strind said, picking up another comlink line. Strind, one of the most popular of Jill's paladins, had been fielding questions and frantic calls nonstop since 1615, when Lyseo's broadcast came to an end. Four hours had passed, but there were still people who needed to work out their anxiety.

"He was right!" the caller burst out shrilly, without identifying herself. "Lyseo was right. Everything he said—I felt that way. Are we going to die out here?"

"Suppose we could, citizen," Strind said calmly. "Space travel's uncertain even in this day and age."

"No! I mean could we be blown up, like those people down there? I never thought about it. I mean, when I went through the psychological tests, they asked me if I could live with never going back to my home system again. They never asked how I felt about being shredded by an alien enemy."

"You knew the job was dangerous when you took it, citizen. This is a warship. There's never been any secret about that. We're going to find the bad guys and shoot at them, and they will probably shoot back."

"But I'm a civilian! I don't want to die. Doesn't anyone care what happens to me?"

"We all do," Strind said. "It's the responsibility of the commanders to do their best to see that nothing happens to you. As for civilians getting caught in crossfire, what do you think happened to the people down there? They weren't all in the military."

"I wasn't frightened before," the caller admitted. "But I am now."

"Lyseo brought it home to you, didn't he?" Strind said, nodding into his headset as he disconnected that caller. "Well, we all want to talk about it. I asked Commander Brand to take a few minutes out to talk to us. He's here now." Strind nodded to the commander, who sat across the broadcast console from him in the semicircle of padded couch that served as Strind's studio. "You've been listening to the voice of the people, Commander. Can we have your feedback? Are we sacrificing ourselves needlessly?"

Brand cleared his throat. He hated being put on the spot, but accepted the necessity as Lt. FarSeeker explained it to him. "The way I see it, Strind, Lyseo pointed out that we could be destroyed, not that we will be. We could. You might think we were on a foolhardy errand, and wonder if we have done the right thing coming to the heart of the galaxy. And who hasn't felt that way? He told the truth. But the answer is that yes, we of the Alliance will go forth into the void to help those who come to ask for our assistance. If we did not, we would be abetting the enemy by our inaction. He made us talk about it, brought out our deepest fears. I suppose in a way we should thank him for it, but I have a difficult time feeling gratitude for a man who nearly precipitated a score of suicides. The psychotherapists report that they have been overwhelmed."

"I suppose it never occurred to anyone until now that we could die doing this hero stuff," the paladin said. "That's what I think. Now it's out in the open. We need to be kept up on the facts, Commander. The dangers. What you decide affects all of us, no matter whose department we're in."

"I acknowledge that, Mr. Strind. We'll try to keep you in the loop from now on—when it is not a breach of security to do so. That, too, is part of my responsibility in keeping the rest of you safe."

"You heard it here," Strind told his headset. "Me, I like Lyseo. He didn't get to be who he was by playing safe. He's not afraid to say what we're all thinking. Well, this situation is like any bogey in the closet: air it and we can deal with it, right? Can we have another question for the commander?"

The mood of the show improved slowly but significantly after that. The general consensus seemed to be that Lyseo had done the crew of the *Hawking* a service. The next day Jill brought a tape of the show to Lyseo and played it for him.

He paid half attention to it while putting on his makeup in the mirror and humming. The emotional storm had passed, and he was eager to go on again. He caught her eye in the glass and saluted her with the sponge.

"I don't know what I would do without you, raven-haired one." He smiled. "Will you be watching old Hambone today? I promise all will be strictly upbeat. Pure entertainment, no more. I'll save the lessons for another time. Will you?"

"Of course I will," Jill replied.

In spite of the devastation of Gerson only days behind them, and the possibility that in the days to come the battlestation could be facing destruction, loss, and pain, Jill felt she had never been so happy. Humming, Lyseo went back to his pots and sticks, and Jill left him to it.

Kem took her to one side. "You're great, Lieutenant. Sometimes it takes me days to get him out of one of his snits. Can you stick around?"

"I've got other duties," Jill reminded him. "Don't get me wrong, I'd love to. I can't. But I'll be back, I promise."

Kem clutched her arm and glanced quickly at Lyseo. "What'll I tell him?"

"Whatever you told him before I came along," Jill said. "Tell him again. I've got 9,998 other people to look after beside the two of you. If you don't like it, take it up with McCaul."

Kem gulped visibly. "No, thanks. I still have some of my hide left over from last time. The rest is still growing back."

"Good," Jill said. "Bye." She waggled her fingers at Lyseo in the mirror, and slipped out of the door.

Outside of the dressing room, Jill leaned against the bulkhead and slowly drew in a few breaths of reality. She had to stop being the starry-eyed fan and go back to her job. At the end of the corridor, Lt. FarSeeker smiled blandly at a crowd of maintenance workers waiting for a lift, her hero worship tucked away into her private thoughts.

The representatives of the Core worlds aboard were growing more agitated as the *Hawking* neared the next system feared to be under attack. The mood of the Fleet personnel was grim. Lyseo's broadcast had aided in opening communications between the two groups, but it was an inescapable fact that the station was coming closer and closer to confrontation with an unknown enemy presence.

As they approached the second system, tension was high. The paladins mediated arguments on the air as to what they would find when they arrived.

The argument was settled early when, on their approach, long-distance telemetry picked up high-level energy readings dead ahead within the system, inconsistent with the normal bursts of radiation thrown off by a star system. There was a battle going on. The *Hawking* increased velocity, and prepared to intervene.

The unknown enemy had destroyed an entire civilization on Gerson, and had left little intact to give a clue as to its origin. No one aboard could guess whether the gigantic Alliance battle cruiser would be sufficient to defeat it.

As the *Hawking* swept into a close orbit around the second planet from the star, the combatants appeared on the bridge screens. Commander Brand ordered telemetry to track the various cruisers and fighters, and tried to make sense of the battle array.

"I can't tell which side is which! Get those two Silbers up here, so they can identify the power signature of their ships," he barked.

In a few moments, the two pale-faced natives appeared, followed unobserved by Lyseo. Brand swiftly requested the information he wanted and saw it entered into the battle computer.

"Thank you, gentle beings," he said, dismissing the two aliens briskly. "You may go now. I don't want any civilians on the bridge. You can watch the action on one of the trivid tanks." He flicked a hand toward one of his aides, who bustled the protesting Silbers toward the lift hatchway. Lyseo watched them go, taking in their agitation, and the impersonal efficiency of Brand's ADC. Lyseo leaned casually against a bulkhead, taking everything in. The action on the screen excited him. His bright, deep-set eyes flicked here and there, while his body remained still, almost slack.

Brand suddenly noticed him. "What's this man doing here?" he barked. "Didn't you hear what I just said? No civilians on my bridge." The aide leaped to take Lyseo's arm and show him to the door.

"But I am Lyseo," Lyseo said, shaking off the aide's hands. "I am permitted to be here."

"We're in the middle of a battle situation, mister. Get off my bridge!"

"I invoke the clause of my contract," Lyseo said haughtily. "It will reiterate for me that I may go anywhere on this vessel at any time I so choose."

The ADC was already bent over a keyboard before his commander threw a gesture at him. "It is correct, sir. It's in the records."

"I will not be in your way," Lyseo promised him. "I will stay over here."

"I don't care what your bloody contract said. It's against bloody regulations. Anyplace you stand will be a distraction. Haul it!"

"No, sir, I will stay right here."

"Commander!" the telemetry officer shouted. "Eight small, high-powered craft have disengaged from the battle and are heading toward us. They've noticed us, sir."

"Scramble fighters," Brand barked. "And get that man off my bridge!"

The ADC and a couple of the other officers moved in on Lyseo, who crouched warily, prepared to defend himself. One of them lunged at him, causing him to jump sideways, almost into the arms of the other two men. They were big and strong, but he was nimble and wiry, with thirty years experience on any of his opponents. He squirmed loose in a trice, and was standing beside the furious Brand's chair just as the eight small ships ranged into full view. Lyseo stopped. He had never seen anything like them in his life.

"Oh," he breathed, eyes fixed on the screen. While he was distracted, the guards went for him again, and carried him, shouting imprecations, off the bridge.

"The indignity of it," Lyseo raged. He had stormed out of the lift and directly toward Kay McCaul's office. The chief of Power Use was doing her best to reason with him.

"But I understand the commander's concern, Mr. Lyseo. Why didn't you stay away from the battle bridge with a potential conflict on hand?"

"I needed to be there," Lyseo insisted. "For my art. That was where things were happening. I am drawn to conflict."

Kay McCaul shook her head. "You could have been responsible for many deaths. What if the commander became distracted while you were gathering material for your . . . er, art, and misdirected a squadron of fighters?"

"I am not blind or stupid, Administrator," Lyseo said with haughty dignity. "If he had not caused a fuss, I would have remained where I was, an immobile and noninterfering object. I am not to blame for his outburst."

Kay found his logic unassailable, but the primary purpose of the *Hawking* was military, for the defense of not only the Core planets, but also the thousands of beings aboard the cruiser. She smiled reasonably at the actor.

"Mr. Lyseo, I will ask you a great favor. I want you to stay off the battle bridge during combat. You can have any other seat in the house, but it would be better for everyone if you stay out of the commander's way. He hates an audience. Agreed?"

"Any other seat?" Lyseo asked, his black eyebrows quirking.

Kay nodded. "Anywhere."

"Where was he?" Jill asked, trying to translate her superior's furious squawk through the audio pickup in Lyseo's dressing room. The great man was in the shower, tidying up for his next performance. Jill could hear him singing loudly and cheerfully through the door, and he was drowning Kay out.

"The power center!" McCaul shouted.

"The power center?" Jill echoed. "But there's no room in there for an outsider."

"I stupidly told him he could go wherever he wanted so long as it wasn't the battle bridge. He told the technicians to check with me, and not one of them called to ask whether it was true. I would have chucked him out with my own hands if I had known. Stop him from going back there again. The techies were in a state of hysteria, having to crawl over him all the time."

Jill turned away from the pickup when she heard the singing stop and the bathroom door open and close. Clad in a toweling robe and an air of great good humor, Lyseo strolled into the room. He bent to give her an affectionate peck on the cheek. "Hello, my dear. I didn't expect to see you before today's show. What did you think of the battle our brave flyers put up? Fascinating! It has inspired me to the fullest."

"Ari, I just spoke to Kay McCaul. Were you really in the power center during the battle?"

"Why, yes," Lyseo said. "It was absolutely fascinating. In that small chamber, knowing that each new demand for power was focused to help secure a victory. Think of it!" he said, drawing an invisible panorama for her. "Discovering the sources of the demands for more energy as we rove through the battle, who needs more, and who requires less, almost as if we were seeing what was going through the lives of everyone on board for that single event, and all the time our fighters were out there in space around us, demolishing the evil Ichtons."

"There isn't a lot of room in the power center," Jill began, but her voice trailed off.

"It was a crux, a nexus," Lyseo crowed. "I could feel the tension as if I were experiencing it myself."

Jill knew that she would have to say something, but weighed her words carefully. He was so sensitive, anything that sounded too much like a criticism would make it impossible for him to function. "You . . . you won't be going back in there again, will you?"

"No, I have gathered all the impressions there that I think I will need," Lyseo said. "It's only worth one show. That kind of paraphrase can become old quickly. I don't want to bore my audience."

Jill heaved a sigh of relief. "Good. What's today's slice of life, then?"

"You'll enjoy it," Lyseo said proudly. "It'll be inspiring to all our young warriors, and the rest of us, who are young only in our hearts. It's an abstract piece, a light show, based on the grids in the power center. I intend to illumine, by starlight, if you'll forgive the joke, how it is we all contribute in our small ways to the war effort. I have dedicated it to Administrator McCaul, for her kindness in allowing me the freedom of her domain."

"I'm sure she'll appreciate that," Jill said.

Jill sat next to the light crew as Lyseo took the stage. At the left and right walls, the computer technicians who ran the lighting board and the special effects generator waited, fingers poised for Lyseo's cue. A prerecorded voice echoed through the chamber, announcing Lyseo's dedication to Administrator McCaul. The stage director counted down the seconds to sixteen hundred hours, and pointed a finger at the star. The light on the video camera directly before him went on, and Lyseo extended his arms over his head.

Throughout the chamber, tiny points of light appeared. Lyseo moved among them, gathering some of them in his hands, and balling them up to make larger ones, which he set back into the air. His skill with pantomime made it look as if the holographic projections of light were solid and malleable masses. Jill watched him with fascination, wondering what light would feel like. Lyseo accompanied his dancelike movements with a narration describing where the lights were coming from and where they were going over the course of a day. The little stars grew or shrank according to the needs Lyseo designated.

"No more to the galleys, the meals are served. Better to put more into the recreation centers. Botanics needs more, and engineering needs less."

With a trumpeting of martial music, the dance grew faster and faster. "What's this?" Lyseo demanded, staring at a little star that was pulsing with the beat of the drum. "Our ships require more. There is no more available. It will have to come from somewhere, or we will fail." He addressed the other twinkling lights. "Will you all give something of yourselves?"

The other lights sparkled eagerly, and he gathered part of each one's substance to add to the failing light. Under his hands, it became larger and stronger until it dwarfed all the rest. Lyseo sprang aside to avoid a dark red ball of flame that swept out of the darkness toward the small lights. The white globe swept between the red comet and its intended victims. The adversaries met in a crash of glaring light. Images of the Ichton fleet engulfed the red globe as it circled the white, now clad in a shell like that of the *Hawking*. Lyseo continued his declamation while the fight continued. It was thrilling and inspiring, guaranteed, Jill felt, to make everyone on the *Hawking* feel as if they were part of the battle, part of the great movement to liberate the Core planets. Lyseo whirled around the red globe, showing that it was weakening. The performance was working up to a grand and exciting climax when suddenly the lights dimmed, and the giant globes of light blinked out of existence. The special effects generator whined down to a dull hum, and shut off. The technicians sprang forward to see if they could restore power.

The interruption hit Lyseo like a blow to the solar plexus.

"No!" he shouted into the darkness, beating at the air with his fists. "Bring it back! I am not finished!"

"I'm sorry, Ari," the lighting director called, running an agitated hand through her short blond hair. "I was just on the horn to the power center, and they've cut us off. They need our juice for the weaponry. We're under attack!"

"I demand that they restore power," Lyseo shouted, drawing his fists down against his belly. It was a tight, fierce gesture that did nothing to salve the ache inside. "They can't simply interrupt me like that!"

"No can do, Ari," the young woman said, shaking her head. "We'll have to wait until it's all over."

"I have a contract that entitles me to whatever power my performance demands, and I demand that it be restored to me. Kem!"

"Right here, Hammy," the manager said, stepping into the low beam of the security lights.

Lyseo rounded on him. "Go down to the power center, since they ignore our summonses, and tell them to turn on the juice to my generator. I don't care what's going on topside." He flung a dramatic finger ceilingward, and stalked from center stage toward his dressing-room door.

Shocked, Jill rose from her chair and advanced on Lyseo, cutting off his dramatic exit.

"Hold it just one millisecond," she demanded, planting one hand on his chest. She glanced over her shoulder. "Kem, you stay right here. Ari, what do you think you're doing? Were you just blowing smoke, or do you really believe we should each work for the war effort?"

Lyseo stopped and regarded her with a bemused expression. "Of course I do, my dear. I mean it sincerely. I like to think I do my part."

"Then would you please stop invoking your precious contract and let the troops get on with their jobs up there? You sound like a spoiled brat, carrying on that way. If the power center cut you off, they knew damned well what they were doing. It wasn't to annoy you, it was to save lives. Possibly even your life."

"But to interrupt me in the middle of the flow—it was as if someone physically assaulted me," Lyseo pleaded, trying to make her understand. Jill opened her mouth to reply.

Suddenly the lights went out entirely, and Jill felt the floor drop a few inches under her feet. She staggered against Lyseo in the dark, and the two of them crouched onto the floor.

"We've been hit," someone whispered. "The station's been hit."

All around the black chamber there was a rising murmur of voices. Within moments the safety lights returned. Jill clambered to her feet, and headed for the door.

"Where are you going?" Lyseo called, hurrying after her.

"There are going to be ten thousand scared people out there, and I'm their morale officer. I have to find out what's happened and let them know."

Lyseo sounded almost desperate. "*I'm* scared, too. Please, please stay here with me, Jill. You have a shipwide frequency here. You can communicate with anyone you like without leaving. Stay with me."

"Ari, I can't. I've got a job to do."

The panicked look she knew had replaced the expression of arrogance on Lyseo's thin face. She remembered, with a pang, the sensitive, insecure side of him. Jill felt herself melting, and steeled her resolve. She was concerned for him, but couldn't afford to waste time in beginning damage control. The *Hawking* couldn't afford morale problems, not now.

Lyseo reached out for her hand. "I need you. Please stay."

Jill forced herself to draw back. "There are ten thousand people aboard this cruiser who also need me. What about them?"

"The needs of the many outweighing the needs of the few?" Lyseo threw at her bitterly. "And old Hambone is one of the few?"

He was going to have another temper tantrum, and Jill refused to coddle him through it. "If you like. If you didn't insist on being one of the few, I might be able to help you, too. I love you, but you are the most spoiled sentient being I have ever met in my life!" Jill looked around and saw that everyone was staring at them. She gasped. She had told off the great Lyseo, and right in front of a roomful of people! Jill felt color mount in her face, and turned to flee the room.

Lyseo grabbed her wrists before she could pull away. "Say that again."

"No," Jill cried, refusing to meet his eyes. "I can't believe I said it the first time. I'm so sorry. I shouldn't call you names."

"Please?" he coaxed her. "Before the line about the spoiled brat. I know I deserve that, but won't you?"

"I love you," Jill said, after a long moment staring at his feet. "I don't think I've ever said that to anyone but my parents."

"Then I am doubly honored." He turned her hands over one at a time and kissed her palms, a gesture that sent a tingle coursing through her. "My dear, with that to hold to my heart, you can go and help the multitudes, and I'll know that I'll have a part of you here that they can never touch. That small phrase alone gives me security I find nowhere else and with no one else. As soon as the lights come back up, I'll do my little part here to help out."

"I'll be back later," Jill promised.

"And I'll be waiting," Lyseo said. "Now then, people," he shouted, clapping his hands as Jill drew away, "let us try a technical rehearsal, shall we? I want to be absolutely perfect for our lads and lasses. From the top, if you please."

After the Ichtons were driven back, Commander Brand called back his forces to repair their vessels and heal their wounds. During the late shifts, Jill's paladins began to receive calls from viewers who had watched the most recent performance by Lyseo.

"It was terrific," a woman told Driscoll Strind. "I put it on disk so I can watch it over and over again. To think that when we put lights down during an attack, it actually helps the military to do their job."

"That's a simplistic explanation of it, citizen," Strind said, punching the cutoff button and switching to another call. "I think it has as much to do with moral support as electricity. Keep it up, folks. With your help, we're going to win this one."

Jill and Lyseo lay curled together on the couch in his dressing room listening to the audio channel.

"You made my job much easier today," Jill said, smiling lazily up at him. "I've never known morale so high. If pure optimism could stop the Ichtons, they'd be history."

"Ah, but without you, it would have been impossible for me to continue with my work," Lyseo said. "Audiences are fickle, but no matter what lies ahead, I will conquer the galaxy all by myself if I may count on one who will always care for me."

"I always will," Jill said, and shyly admitted, "I always have."

Theirs was a love that might have shaken the stars in their courses, but it wasn't. It was merely a comfortable, quiet center for both of them in an increasingly chaotic environment.

THE ICHTONS

A Preliminary Briefing for *Hawking* **Personnel**
Unrestricted Release

The Ichtons appear to have evolved in a different spiral arm than the races of the Alliance. It is difficult to determine how long they have been ravaging their way across space, but the number of gutted planets discovered to date implies a very substantial period, perhaps even several millennia. We can assume they are experienced and adept at this practice.

Physically the Ichtons resemble both a terrestrial insect and mammal. The trunk of an Ichton's body is contained in an exoskeleton of considerable strength. Their multiple appendages are furred, contain an internal bone structure, and resemble the arms and legs of an earth gorilla or Altarian sermet. Their three-fingered hands are quite strong and capable of delicate work. They are believed to be egg laying, but nothing is known about their young.

As has been the case with all sentient races discovered to date, the Ichtons are individually aware. While it is convenient to attribute insect traits to the Ichtons, this is a fallacy based upon the similarity of their appearance to Terran insects. There appears to be no group awareness or similar connection between Ichton individuals, though they do tend to organize into groups and may be assumed to be highly social. Instinct may play a large role in the decision-making process of the Ichtons. Those few captured seemed almost unable to cope at first with the radically different environment. This may be the main source of Ichton motivation on all levels. Intelligence of a level equal to the average human is merely another tool to fulfill their instinctive needs. A high level of instinctive motivation might explain why those Ichtons we have been able to communicate with are unable to understand the resentment of other races at being overrun and their planets pillaged. When asked why their race acts in this manner, all the prisoners taken to date simply could not comprehend what was being asked. Again, all those likely to directly engage any Ichton force should remember that this type of motivation does not make them any less dangerous as an opponent.

COMRADES
by S.M. Stirling

"Out of my way, furcoat!"

Captain Alao ber Togren checked half a step as she came out of the adjutant's tiny office.

Shit, she thought, quickening her stride. *Somebody—someone non-Fleet and human and* civilian—*was throwing species epithets around.*

A high chittering sound echoed from the narrow corridors.

Someone was throwing insults at a Khalian *who was also a* Fleet Marine. *The consequences were not likely to be pleasant, unless she got there soon.*

The Marine officer walked with her right shoulder brushing the wall; the *Stephen Hawking* was the largest self-propelled object humans had ever built, with more than enough room to carry ten thousand crew from Alliance space to the Core of the galaxy—but it had been built by the Fleet, and Fleet Marine quarters shaved space as if this were an assault boat, not a battlestation.

Stensini, she thought disgustedly as she turned the corner and saw who the human was. *I might have known.*

"Stensini, *back off,*" she barked. "You, too, Senior Sergeant Yertiik. Carry on."

Like half her troops, Yertiik was Khalian—she made a long-accustomed mental effort and refused to even *think* "Weasel"—and quick-tempered even for that race. He let his fur drop flat under his coverall and moved his hands away from the hilts of the nonregulation knives at his belt, but the air stayed full of the wet-dog smell of his anger and a low chirring sound. His eyes stayed fixed on Stensini as he stalked away, as stiff as the short legs and undulant spine allowed: staring was aggressive bad manners to his race.

"Ah, glad to see you, Captain," the human civilian said, then froze.

Anhelo Stensini was a big man, muscular and blond; the Marine officer was a stocky 160 centimeters, with bristle-cut black hair, a beak nose, and a complexion the color of teak.

"Wish it was mutual," Ber Togren said neutrally, after a moment.

She could smell her own sweat, under the neutral ozone and pine smell of recirculated air. *I could brig him,* she thought wistfully. The *Stephen Hawking* was technically on battle alert. The Gersons had been among the Core races who came looking for allies and found the Alliance, and the battlestation had found their system under Ichton—enemy—control when it broke out of FTL drive. There had been a skirmish, nothing but an occasional shudder through the massive fabric of the battlestation to her Marines or anyone else not in the Fleet's defensive units. But technically, they were under martial law and she could . . .

"Unfortunately, we're going to be seeing a lot of each other," she said with a slight sigh.

The blond eyebrows rose. "I was just coming by for the artifact boxes," he said.

"Tums out they want to take a look at Abanjul," Ber Togren said. According to their Core informants, that was one of the first planets the Ichtons had taken when they appeared in this neighborhood. Deserted by now, although many of the forces attacking Gerson had come from there. "Sending us on a corvette. Think there may be some bugs left. Deserters, stay behinds, whatever."

"Ichtons are not insects, Captain," Stensini corrected absently. Then the meaning of what she had said sank through, and he paled. His specialty would be needed.

"Whatever."

Krishna. The civilian was a sentiologist, a student of intelligent life; and, oddly enough, a xenophobe. Although only toward Khalia. Fifty years before, there had been a war; at first the Alliance Fleet had thought their enemies were the Khalia, muskeloid aliens, cannibalistic pirates. Then they had found the *real* backers behind the Khalia, the families, and the Weasel war had gotten serious. Toward the end the Khalia themselves had changed sides, with an eagerness that was only partly due to the Alliance dreadnoughts orbiting their home world. They just loved to kill, was all.

Stensini's father had been one of those human oligarchs of the Family Cluster; he hated the Khalia for what they represented, a lost heritage, betrayal.

Ber Togren hated them for a much simpler reason; Khalian raiders had hit the Fleet research outpost where her parents worked. What was left of her mother had been found in the raider's food locker after the pursuit caught it. Her father had spent the rest of the war in the 121st Marine Reaction Company, the Head-hunters, collecting weasel tails; then he'd retired, paid for an orthowomb to hatch the frozen ova he and his wife had deposited, and raised her on war stories.

Naturally, she hated the Khalia. Almost as much as she loathed the Family rich kids who thought they'd lost the war, because they came out just obscenely wealthy instead of omnipotent. If Ber Togren had been in charge, they'd have really lost.

Have died. All of them.

"Get your kit together," she went on. "And don't even bother complaining to anyone, because this is Brand's idea." Anton Brand was Fleet commander on the *Hawking*. Not exactly God, or even the close approximation a Fleet ship captain was, but near enough. "You're the sentiologist they assigned me."

Shit.

Abanjul was dead. It *smelled* dead, a stink of acid and chemicals and raw earth and a little rotting organic matter. The area around the stealthed landing boat was chaotic, a wilderness of tumbled hills of some fine powdery material colored in sand red and scarlet and livid yellow. Cold wind blew it into the faceplates of the Marines and scientists, and several tonnes of it had made convenient cover for the prefab shelter, the new hill already looked as ancient as the others. The talclike substance was Sahara-dry, too fine-textured to hold water, but there were pools of blue-tinted liquid running on the hard clay substrate beneath it. The sun was setting; Abanjul's star was a G4 like Sol, but from here it was a swollen red ball covering a quarter of the horizon, haloed by banners of color like nothing she had ever seen. The landing boat was gone, and the corvette would land only on receipt of the correct codes. That had been sensible, at least.

Ber Togren flicked up her mask. Dust settled on her lips, tasting of metal and rust.

She spat. "What *is* this stuff?" one of the troopers muttered.

"Mining by-products," a technician answered automatically. "Pure silica, traces of alumina and heavy-metal salts. Oxides of a number of things. Oxygen content in the atmosphere's dropping noticeably already. Couple of millennia and it'll be negligible, unless what's left of the oceans recover, which—"

A high, thin keening cut through the quiet whistle of the wind. Half a dozen Marines went into crouches, until they saw it was a friendly. One of the Gersons. The ursinoidlike aliens were wearing light environment suits and she could see the short-muzzled face quite clearly. The black button nose was dry and grainy-looking, a sign of ill health, and wet something ran from the eyes and nose and mouth. One of the technicians made a move toward the Gerson, stopped when the alien's own superior went over to it.

Thud. The senior Gerson had kicked the other one in the ribs—the teddy-bearlike aliens had skeletons quite close to the mammalian norm—and shouted something at it. Normally the Gersons' language sounded rather pleasant, like a combination of bees humming and choral song. *Thud.* More harsh shouting, and the prone Gerson picked itself up, still mewling, and staggered back to the ship.

"Uncharacteristic," Stensini murmured on their private channel. He was in charge of the civilian team. "Very uncharacteristic of Gersons. They're under considerable stress, of course."

Ber Togren ignored him. "All right, you people," she said on the unit push. "Let's get dug in and camouflaged. And remember, maximum priority is prisoners. Second priority is reasonably intact corpses." Command priorities, she left unspoken; grunts tended to put a higher value on their own ass than the brass did. They were Marines, though; mission first.

Stress, she thought, looking around. Ber Togren had been born—decanted—stationside, and had spent most of her life in space or hostile-environment habitats; what she saw around her was not too bad, in itself. The Core holos of this part of Abangul had been taken before the Ichtons arrived, an anthropology mission to study the primitive natives, and showed rolling hills covered with silvery-green trees.

"Yeah, fairly considerable stress," she muttered.

Gerson was occupied by the Ichtons now, and in a generation or two it would look just like this.

"It is good to see you back," Chief Worker hummed.

He had an individual name, compounded of his smell and markings on his exoskeleton and some of the tones the tympani along his thorax made when they vibrated, but there was no need to use them here.

Fighter sounded a *recognition* and pushed past into the warren, his patrol with him. The worker waved his unit out to unload the trucks; those were big vehicles slung low between five-meter balloon wheels, but shabby, patched. Like everything else in the improvised warren.

"Fuel," Fighter hummed. "Seventy-seven kilos liquid hydrocarbon; three tonnes of protocarbon foodstuffs, supplemented; assorted machine parts, some electronics."

"Excellent!" Chief Worker replied. "Our reserve was running low and the hydroponics facility is behind schedule."

He turned and limped away; the right limb of his forward pair of legs was missing halfway down. Ichtons had little curative medicine and no artificial limbs. There had never been any need for such; replacements for injured individuals were in plentiful supply and much more efficient than feeding the wounded.

Fighter turned to one of the technicians. "Any more activity?" he hummed.

"None since the last indication, Fighter," the technician hummed. "Definitely a fusion-impulse engine of some sort. Apart from that—" The operator's forelimbs moved in a fluid gesture of resignation, the three-fingered hands clenching. The equipment was cobbled together, here in an off corridor of the abandoned mine. Everything had been second-rate to begin with, and nothing useful had been left in the evacuation.

Including us, Fighter thought bitterly. Including us. "Do you wish to make contact?"

"Negative!" The ultrasonic whine of the Ichton's tympani keened upward until the technician winced and turned his faceted eyes away.

"Then how shall we arrange for evacuation?" The technician must be desperate to question a military order.

"We are not even certain it is an Ichton vessel," Fighter hummed. "Carry on. Passive sensors only."

"We are to avoid contact?" said one of his patrol, newly promoted to warrior status and fingering his converted mining laser uneasily.

"On the contrary," Fighter replied. "We will mobilize all trained"—half-trained, his mind filled in mordantly—"personnel and investigate at the end of this diurnal period."

The others of the patrol split off, each speeding up a little as they headed toward their dens and their mates; none of them had been allowed breeding privileges before the evacuation. They would have been evacuated, if they had.

Fighter stepped wearily through into the main brood chamber. Half a dozen incubators lay grouped around the infrared lanterns, each holding two eggs. None of the clutch of females had laid more than two, not on the minimal rations available, but they would all be hatching in a month. The creche mother was aestivating in the far corner; her exoskeleton was mottled with age, and her mind wandered—this world had been polluted enough to reduce the life span well under thirty years, Fighter himself was twenty-eight—but she was the best they had. At the vibrations of his entry she stirred and unfolded her limbs.

"You!" she hummed in the female tongue. It had less vocabulary than the male, but its intonations carried power. Deep within himself Fighter felt needs stirring, to protect and guard, a flash of guilt. "You! Facilities *inadequate*. Conditions *bad*. Hatchlings endangered!"

"They will improve," he soothed. They stood and groomed each other's cara-paces, until the old female sulked back to her corner.

Fighter's mandibles ground together as he wearily sought his niche and ate, longing for the digestive torpor that would let him forget his worries.

We are breeding, he thought. Of course; they were Ichtons. This world is no longer fit to support us. Equally obvious; the people would not have aban-doned it, if it was. Abandoned Fighter, in a recuperative coma from a training accident . . . Few had been left behind, but the absolute numbers had been quite large. Fifty billion of the people had inhabited Abanjul in its prime, a few generations after the native sapients had been exterminated. Most of those judged not worthy of evacuation—in coma sleep, packed into the transports like cargo—had suicided when they found themselves left, or starved. Ichtons had had a technological civilization for a *very* long time, and they were not good at surviving on their own with no reason to live.

Fighter had not. Fighter had found others, built this little base, scrounged and improvised. Now they were breeding, and that had solved most of the morale problems. Any male of the people knew there was work worth doing when eggs and hatchlings were about. The others were content, but the data tormented him. In only twenty generations the atmosphere would be incapable of supporting life. Their descendants would be thousands by then, and they would have to establish a self-sufficient sealed environment. Could they? And their numbers would be growing exponentially, doubling every decade, on a planet stripped bare. Impossible to construct ships and escape . . .

He let his nictitating membranes dim his vision, the warm incubators blurring into a heat-source glimmer. Several of the eggs had been sired by him.

If the ship is not Ichton, we will take it, he decided. We will not follow the people. The thought was heretical enough to make him stir in the sleeping niche, the hard chitinous surfaces of his body scraping at the padding. Why? They have already judged us unfit. We will take the non-Ichton ship—some of the crew, if necessary—and we will find a habitable planet.

A wild dream. Stumbling across an ecology that would not kill them would be difficult, the more so as they would not dare seek one pretamed by a sapient race. They would have to take an uninhabited planet, or one with pretechnological sapients that could be exterminated piecemeal. Ichtons did not need energy weapons to fight, and they bred very fast.

Fighter glanced back at the eggs. Anything necessary, he would do.

"Nothing. Absofuckolutelydamly *nada*," the sensor operator said.

Ber Togren rocked back on her heels and looked around. They were on the roof of a complex of buildings; Stensini and the others said they had been electronics-heavy administrative headquarters of some sort. Now they tumbled in ruin almost to the horizon, except where they ran along the edge of a green-acid sea. The . . . buildings, she supposed . . . had been made of concrete. Concrete with single-crystal silica fibers and silica fumes added, which gave it roughly the consistency and tensile strength of medium carbon steel. The Alliance hadn't used either for a very long time, but she supposed it was cheap and effective and the Ichtons didn't waste resources on fancywork. Evidently they hadn't wasted time getting the machinery out of it, either; from the looks, they'd just used a plasma gun wherever the walls were inconvenient.

Despite herself, Ber Togren was starting to *like* the Ichtons a little.

"There were heavy-duty superconductors in the structure," the tech went on. "Cermet stuff. And dick-all I can get below, but it all goes down *deep*."

"No more of the—" Ber Togren stopped herself; if there had been any more of the modulated discharges, the technician would have told her. He was a Marine, she didn't have to draw a picture for him.

Sodding hell, she thought, going to as close to the beveled edge of the rooftop as she could and flipping up her visor so that she could pop a hard candy into her mouth. They had spent two months looking at traces that turned out to be bits of equipment giving up the ghost, and seen a *lot* of ruins.

This was a waste of time and personnel. The corvette was off looking at the rest of the system; the Ichtons had used the other planets and asteroid belt rather intensively. But for Abanjul, just the landing party. There were a lot of people on the *Stephen Hawking* but not all that many Marines. Not nearly enough to look for a couple of dozen bugs who didn't want to be found, on an entire *world*.

"Either Anton Brand is a complete fuckup, in which case we're all doomed, or—"

The technician swore mildly. "Now, that was a surge," he said. Then he frowned. "Captain, I can't tell you right off, but either it faded in and out, or it got closer and then farther."

"I—"

Anhelo Stensini looked at the odd angular script on the tunnel wall and swept the reader's pickup over it; the light of the jury-rigged lantern was dim and red but more than enough for light-enhancement equipment. The acid smell of the Abanjul-now atmosphere was a little less down here, but the readouts said there was a worrying concentration of heavy metals, particularly mercury. They would all need a course of chelating drugs before lift-off.

Fascinating, he thought. There had been plenty of bodies, and from the tissue samples, the Ichtons had had time to adapt to large-scale industrial pollution, plus radiation levels that would fry a rat's genes. Not engineered, it was too messy for that. Just good old-fashioned Darwin.

The reader beeped. *All broodcare technicians will assemble evacuees at the third landing below,* it said.

Behind him the two Weasel hired killers were chittering to each other. The Alliance gunsel with them was fiddling with her communicator. He ignored the noise, continuing a slow, careful scan of the corridor. It was twenty meters in diameter, a pure cylinder with walls of fused rock, slanting down almost imperceptibly to the west, under the dead sea. Armored doors spotted the walls at patterned intervals, flush with the surface.

"Hey, Yerti, we're out of touch," the human Marine called.

The chittering stopped. Stensini felt a tug at his elbow, and turned to see a Weasel face peering up at him from shoulder height. It was encased in the long-snouted helmet, with the muzzle-protection wings folded back, and the teeth showed wet and pink as the thin carnivore lips curled back. Academically he knew it was the equivalent of a nervous frown, but he jerked his arm back. He might have pushed, if the Weasel had not been carrying a long curved knife in one paw and a short bulky-looking slug thrower in the other. His stomach lurched and spat acid into the back of his throat; it had been *behind* him with that, all the time. Usually he could make himself forget, but it had had to remind him, the treacherous little vermin were always looking for an opportunity to—

"Gum dis wey, nu, nu, nu," it chittered and barked at him. "Toksiik, Anna, gover me me me." Then it thrust past him, glancing down at a display woven into the soft armor. "Zummmthing is—"

A door swung open down the corridor with noiseless speed. Stensini only saw the beginning of it, because something struck him very hard in the stomach and he fell down, just in time for something else to hit him on the back.

The first blow had been Yertiik's, kicking back and using him as a jump-off point in his leap. The second had been the other Weasel bouncing off his shoulder blades because they were under his feet. A *thing* was in the doorway, whipping at Yertiik with a long bar held in its forward pair of limbs. The Weasel twisted in midair and landed where the upright part of the—the *Ichton's*—body met the horizontal portion, and his hand was stabbing with the knife so rapidly that the arm blurred and there were the crisp *pockpockpock* sounds of density-enhanced steel crunching through exoskeleton. That was lost in the long *crakkks* as Yertiik fired his machine pistol in bursts through the open door and the rounds exploded off whatever lay behind. Toksiik somersaulted past the fight, flinging in a stick of bouncer grenades as he did. More doors were opening, flooding low-level light into the corridor, and a dry rustling sound.

Anna Steenkap's hand fastened on his collar and dragged him ruthlessly backward. She was firing bursts from her assault rifle one-handed over his head, the muzzle blasts slapping at his head, and shouting into her pickups. Anhelo Stensini was looking over her shoulder when the door *behind* them began to open. Steenkap could not possibly have been able to hear it, but she still managed to drop the civilian and turn herself and the muzzle of her rifle three quarters of the distance before the Ichton in the doorway fired his weapon. Most of her upper torso disappeared into a blood mist with a quiet chuffing sound. Something thin and very cold sliced into his legs.

Captain Ber Togren threw herself down and to the side without breaking stride, landing on her shoulder blades and firing. Half a dozen assault rifles tore into the Ichton before it was halfway through the ceiling hatch; bits of body and gobbets of body fluid dropped down on the Marines.

"Report, Beta Platoon," she said, backflipping herself onto her feet.

"Found Toksiik," the voice said. "And what's left of Anna. No sight of Yertiik or the civvie. *Shiva, watch it*—" A blast of static, most likely from the aura of a plasma discharge. "Shiva and *Vishnu*, Captain, we can't hold this. It's like a fuckin' cheese."

She nodded bleakly. The Ichtons didn't seem to have much weaponry; half of them didn't have real weapons at all, just tools like welding lasers and the equivalent of staple guns. Most of them weren't very quick on the uptake, either. On the other hand, they were completely willing to die, and they knew this heap of tunnel-spaghetti like it was home. Which it was. There seemed to be a fair number of them, too.

"Pull back," she said. Pushing farther was just going to lose more of her people. Too bad about Steenkap, and Toksiik had been efficient for a . . . Khalian. Losing Stensini was going to put her in very bad odor with the brass, but she would worry about that when the time came.

"Captain." The home-base push. "We gotta anomaly here."

She froze, motioning her escort to guard positions.

"Exactly what?"

"Sonic reading. Sort of like frying bacon—"

She blinked. "That's . . . *Get out! Get out* now, *get out of there!*"

"Captain, we—"

Silence.

"Ma'am?" One of the platoon leaders. "What *happened*?"

"I think we all died," Ber Togren said. Then her voice snapped out: "All right, consolidate on the roof. Move it!"

Anhelo Stensini cringed against the cold stone at the whistling shriek from the nearby . . . cell? Compartment?

"Die, die, please die and stop doing that," he mumbled. The Weasel had lasted . . . there was no way to tell how long. It was completely dark here, and there was usually little noise. He was very hungry and thirsty when the dry rustling of the Ichtons came for the feeding. Water that tasted like poison and was, rations from the Fleet stocks. Very occasionally one came with a light, dim and ruddy, and chalk. Then it sketched and he gave it words, and it never forgot and never made a mistake twice. When it went away the darkness closed in again. How long? Days, many days; weeks, maybe months . . . sensory deprivation destroyed your sense of duration first of all.

Another long whistling scream. "Die!" Stensini screamed. "Die and shut up. Die!"

A long bubbling moan. The worst of it was he thought the Weasel probably would die, if only he could.

"I am uncertain as to my interpretation," the bioanalyst hummed uncertainly.

Of course you are, Fighter thought. You were not worthy of evacuation with the people. He felt his forelimbs quivering with long-held tension, his membranes were slow and sticky as they wetted his eyes. The muscles at the base of his forelimbs ached sharply where they spread over the thickened area of exoskeleton. Several of the trainee fighters with him had folded into limb-wrapped lumps of exhaustion in the corners, aestivating.

Aloud he hummed confidently: "Your logic train seems sound. The small, more heavily furred species is utilized by the taller?"

"Yes." They both flexed fingers and nictitated in puzzlement. The Ichtons sometimes utilized sapients prior to their extermination; as sources for biocircuits, for research, sometimes for casual labor in their own disposal. Utilizing such a species for high-risk functions such as warfare seemed inefficient. . . . A scritching sound brought Fighter and several of his aides around, manipulators darting for their bladecasters, but it was only a pair of hatchlings playing tag up the walls and over the ceiling. Fighter scooped them down and handed them to the brood mother, who carried them away with a sharp chirr of reproach.

"Perhaps the smaller are biological constructs?" Fighter hummed, returning to the business at band. There had been theoretical studies on developing such from wild sapients, but in the end it had always seemed non-cost-effective to waste habitat on constructs that could rarely perform more efficiently than Ichtons. Bioanalyst ground his mandibles. "They seem entirely wild—unless a methodology unfamiliar to our concepts was used in their construction."

"Yet they show equal geneloyalty!" Fighter hummed, with a *tock-tock-tock click* of his mandibles to indicate extreme puzzlement. All Ichtons were of the same genotype, and had been since the time of legends. Ichton loyalty was faultless; that of other races dubious, accordingly. Here there were bonds without any sharing of genes at all, which was madness and chaos.

Think, think, Fighter told himself. This was not his training. He was an instructor of surface troops, no more. You will do this because you must.

"First, we must determine the balance of power," he said. "There are time constraints. We do not know when the alien vessel will return."

"Here the poor bastards come again," the technician said.

Ber Togren nodded soundlessly. They were all wearing improvised sound-boots cut out of the insulation and scanty padding of the two transports left. Not much fuel left for either; not much food or ammunition, much of anything. They had enough water but a declining supply of filters. . . .

The area they were on looked fairly good, solid red sandstone cut into gullies hundreds of meters deep. There were cirrus clouds high above, and a cold wind flicked grit into their faces. Here and there a patch of lichen—something like lichen—struggled to grow. They had a good triangulation on the spot now, although whatever the Ichtons used to cut rock was incredibly quiet.

You have to avoid the cities, she thought. It had cost them, to learn that. Not easy, most of this continent had been built over. But in the cities there was too much cover, and the tunnels were too numerous and close to the surface, the Ickies could come up under you with virtually no warning. It looked like the Ickies spent a lot of their time underground anyway; they'd found bits and pieces of hydroponic tunnel farms that must have been thousands of kilometers long when Abanjul was a going concern. Yeah, the cities are bad. Out in the open country all you had to worry about were the deep transport tunnels that laced the whole planet. They'd been sealed and vacuum evacuated originally, but the Ickie holdouts could still use them and still burrow up. You could hear them, though.

Unless there was a maintenance shaft near. That was pretty bad, too.

"*Ready,*" a radio voice whispered in her ear. Lying pressed to the gritty pink surface of the rock slab she felt a vibration, then for an instant she could actually hear the Ickies boring up.

"Wait for it," she said softly. "Nobody jump the gun."

Nobody did. The circle of rock in the center of the mesa began to tremble; it was a feeling like fear through the soft armor between her stomach and the stone, shaking gut against bone.

"Now," she whispered.

Pdamp. The explosion wasn't very loud. The string of cord around the Ickies' drillhead was thinner than thread, but the explosive propagated at near light speed. You were safe enough a few meters away in open air. Closer, rock shattered into powder and burned white because it didn't have time to move away fast enough. A flash of white light ran around a circle, and within it sandstone collapsed downward in chunks and blocks. Rock hit her again, an angry blow this time, then trembled beneath her like a lover. Something huge and metallic swayed through the air in the maelstrom of churning blocks. Then a plasma lance cut across it like a bar of orange-red light, and it blew up. *That* was loud. Her face shield and earphones cut it to protect her senses, as the center of the drill zone collapsed downward.

Figures dashed forward, and the satchel charges dropped into the hole. More explosions, and the technician relayed the sound of things falling far down in the rock. Everyone else stayed ready, and when the lone Ickie crawled out someone put a neat four-round burst of prefrags through its central exoskeleton. They had learned. You didn't waste ammunition when no more was coming, and apart from a risky head shot the central body mass was the best place to get them. There was an internal skeleton—sort of an extension of the exoskeleton and an internal frame for the limbs—but the Ickies were still squishy inside and *real* vulnerable to hydrostatic shock. The problem was that the Ickies showed plenty of ability to learn as well; faster than humans or Khalia in some ways, slower in others.

Pordiik came up beside her, pushing back the wings of his muzzle guard. "Gat was haff haff herd," he barked; her ear translated automatically. His pelt was looking a little mangy; patches of her own hair were loose. Too many trace elements in the air and water, no drugs. They were all tired most of the time, too, and nothing healed quite right.

"Yeah, pretty half-hard," she replied.

"Why tey bodder wittt us us us?"

That was a difficult question. The Ickies held more than half the expedition, captured when the base camp was overrun—*assuming they haven't just eaten them or whatever*—and more than half its equipment. Including the main transponders, which meant that nobody here could communicate with the corvette until it went into low orbit, if then. Properly handled the main transponder could be used to jam the weaker signals from the transports and helmet coms; nobody had thought to bring along a tightbeam light sender.

"I think I've figured that out," Ber Togren said. "Look, these Ickies are the rejects, right? The ones the others couldn't be bothered taking off."

Pordiik laughed, snapping several times, his tusked jaws clumping. "Not good good to be here before tey leff leff."

For a moment Ber Togren blanched at the thought of trying to fight a ground action on this planet when there were fifty billion Ickies and a functioning civilization.

"Yeah, so, they're not fools. They know Abanjul's going down the shithole—couple of generations, you won't be able to breathe."

Pordiik made the Wea—she corrected herself again—Khalian equivalent of a shrug. "Couppple of gen-gen-genrations, ev'rone dead."

"Ickies don't think that way. One of the few good things that bastard Stensini figured out from the records. So . . . what have we got that the Ickies here want really, *really* bad?"

"Urrk." Pordiik raised his nose skyward, in symbolic surrender. "Bud tey tey haff te transponder."

"And Stensini knew the codes. He's probably dead." She sighed. "You know, for a while I thought Anton Brand was an idiot for sending us to find a few thousand Ickies on a whole planet. How could we find them if they hid? Now I know *I'm* the idiot. He knew the Ickies would come looking for us—he just didn't figure I'd fuck it up so bad." She grimaced. "Live and learn."

"Learn otter ting ting," Pordiik said, pushing himself up with the extended stock of his machine pistol. It was time to police up and move out. "Learn not to look at my tail tail with knife and trophee in mind," he concluded.

Ber Togren stood thinking for a moment. True enough, she conceded. Brotherhood of the about-to-die, that's us.

Stensini's face looked hollow and gaunt and mad-eyed on the screen. Better than mine, Ber Togren thought bleakly. Much better than Yertiik's, which was naked and eyeless. Not much was left of the rest of him, although he wasn't quite dying, since the wounds had been inflicted carefully under antiseptic conditions. Saliva worked around the thin sagging carnivore lips, and a trickle of sound.

"—so *tell* them, you stupid bitch, *tell them I'm telling them the truth!*"

Stensini was screaming, and she cut the gain down on him. It was under-standable, of course. From what he said they didn't bother with lights, much. The Marine officer swallowed slightly: complete darkness, and the Ickies moving in it. . . .

"Why don't you believe Stensini's code?" she said to the Ickie that had called itself Fighter Izader; his image held center screen. The interior of the transport was dark otherwise, the air blessedly clear. She needed to be able to think, and they had to spare the fuel to filter and compress.

"Because the subordinate species has also given us a code, and several crucial symbols are different," it said. There was a high whistling background; it was using a modulator to bring the vibrations of its tympani down to the level humans could hear. "This code was supplied only after extreme coercion," Fighter was saying.

They learn fast. This one speaks better Standard'n I do. But then, it had learned from Stensini and his techs. Ber Togren was a promoted ranker from a long line of grunts. Dad had had better things to teach her than upper-class diction. For a moment Yertiik's face reminded her of the picture of Mom. Mom's gnawed bones, at least. *Quite possibly chewed on by Yertiik's grandparent . . .*

" . . . since the specimen put up such resistance, there are grounds to believe that it is speaking correct information. It is also evident that the human Stensini is a status rival of Ber Togren. We know status rivalry. Perhaps this status-conferring information is not shared within the genotype, but only with a noncompetitor subordinate species?"

"The Weasel is just trying to save itself," Stensini barked.

"This is possible," Fighter agreed.

"Why should I confirm or deny?" Ber Togten said softly.

"You and your genesharers will die soon, without reproduction," the Ichton said seriously. "We have that which you need for survival. If you can survive for some time, your Fleet will send rescuers. If we have your ship, we will depart. The people have no use for us, but we will go elsewhere to expand the realm of the people; we have proven our fitness. Thus all benefit from a temporary truce." The Ichton was leaning forward; Ber Togren had an eerie feeling it was desperately trying to convey sincerity.

She sighed, looking at Yertiik. *Beyond help.* "Yes, there's only one sensible answer," she said.

Fighter looked up. The humans and their subordinates were grouped nearby, and the thundercrack across the sky bespoke a hypersonic transit. He signaled to the technician, and mentally inventoried the huge piles of supplies; they must take all that was practicable, for a primitive world. The hatchlings whistled through the lattice of their traveling cages, already becoming torpid with traveling-aestivation.

"You shall awake to a boundless feast," he murmured, and watched the tech's manipulators touch the keyboard.

"Kali damn you, Yertiik," Ber Togren said, looking down at the limbless body, still barely breathing. Khalia were *tough*. She was glad he was unconscious, though; they felt pain, too. "You didn't leave me any fucking choice at all."

Across the shallow valley from her, the Ichton was ordering the code transmitted. Yertiik's, and quite genuine.

Fighter looked up. It had been worth the effort, worth resisting the temptation to curl up and dream away the effort and grief and pain. He had won, for his people—his own people.

For a moment there was sunlight.

GUNG HO
by Judith R. Conly

Grandmother's children cut their teeth on Fleet medals,
on glory tales of conquest and heroic sacrifice,
of battle companionship grown to life bond
and heart's partner exploding in tragic loss
along the mine-studded course to stable alliance.

Father's comrades gleamed with the reflected glow of legend,
and smugly accepted inherited tranquility
with eyes averted from parents' unsightly scars.
Their patrols wore tracks in the space between the stars,
and their shift-end dinners appeared on schedule.

We, the restless heirs of memory and routine,
trained to revere past generations' rites of valor,
retrace history-blessed patterns of combat
with no adversaries but our ancestors' shades
and the boredom-born hazards of careless assumptions.

With erstwhile enemies who have echoed our yawns,
now we congregate in decades-suppressed anticipation.
Through the battered lens of new neighbors' desolation
we gain grief-focused perception beyond united borders
and rediscover our uniforms' peace-deferred promise.

Together we gather, admiral-shriven of guilt in our joy,
excitement-fueled, to transport our sphere of protection
in defense of disparate strangers' kindred cause.
To repel the ravenous avalanche of devastation,
we launch our laser-bright ranks toward victory.

CIVILIANS

One of the greatest assets of the *Hawking* was also the source of the greatest complications to its performance. This was the large number of civilian specialists and merchants that comprised nearly half of the battlestation's inhabitants. While technically under martial law when in a war zone such as Star Central, these were still civilians who were unused and unwilling to become very military.

Among the most difficult types of civilians for the Fleet to deal with were the dozens of top scientists who had joined the mission for a wide range of reasons. Often eccentric and aware that they were terribly vital, some of these civilian experts often had to act as the sole resource for their specialty for the entire station. With the round-trip from Star Central to the nearest Alliance world taking nearly a full year, the analysis of vital information often had to depend on the insights of a single individual.

BLIND SPOT
by Steve Perry

Gil was inserting a smokestack on the model of the *Toya Maru* when the woman walked into his shop. The model was of a Japanese ferry that had sunk in the Tsugaru Strait on Earth in 1954, killing over eleven hundred people. He held the tiny stack in place long enough for the bond to set before he put the miniature vessel down on his bench and ordered the work light to dim. The voxlume obediently dialed itself down by half and the pix he was using for reference faded from the tabletop.

The woman was tall, wearing green skintights that showcased a sthenic and most attractive figure, and he guessed she was about his age, thirty. Her jet hair was chopped short, worn very curly, and her features were not quite balanced enough to be called classically beautiful. Her nose was a tad too long, her lips a bit too full, her green eyes large and on the edge of *sanpaku*, the tiniest bit of white showing under the irises. No, not classically beautiful, but the combination of features was synergistic and quite striking. Amazing that the *Hawking* was large enough so that he had never seen her before. And surely he would remember if he had.

"Yes?"

"I'm looking for M. Gil Sivart."

"You've found him."

The woman glanced around, and if she was impressed with what she saw, it didn't show. Gil's model shop was deep in the Dark Blue small-biz section, halfway to the hull. The place was not much bigger than the main room of a personal residence cube, jammed between the much larger cloned spidersilk shop and the kung fu school, but it suited Gil's needs. It didn't require a lot of room to build ZZZ-scale models—a couple of magnifying cams, a few microsurgery tools, and a moldmaker table would just about do it. Of course, there were some exhibits set up, but a two-centimeter-long version of the *Titanic* or the *Hsin Yu* under a magnifier hardly needed a landing bay for display.

"Were you looking for a model?" he prompted.

She sighed. The words tumbled out, all in a rush: "No. I need your help. Somebody murdered my lover and I want you to find out who."

❖ ❖ ❖

Gil opaqued the front window, the plastic going indigo to match the level color, and had his security computer lock the door. "Have a seat," he said.

The woman sat.

"You are . . . ?"

"Linju Vemeer. I work in sensor construction on Bright Green, that's J1."

"Well, M. Vemeer, I watch newsproj. I don't recall hearing anything about a murder."

"It was a week ago," she said. "A robot on Orange 5 pinned Hask to a hatch and . . . crushed him." Her emotions welled, but did not spill into tears. Gil could feel her pain almost as a tangible thing in the air.

"I do remember something about that," he said quietly. "A terrible accident. Near the hull."

"It wasn't an accident, M. Sivart. Hask was too careful a man to let a drone just roll up and kill him!"

"Have you said so to ISU?"

"Yes, loud and repeatedly. Internal Security thinks I'm a grieving mate whose brains have been short-circuited by my loss, though they didn't put it quite like that."

"Why should I think otherwise?"

She looked at him. "You're a pretty large man and you work out, right?"

"I have an arrangement with the kung fu school next door, yes."

"You would go maybe a hundred eighty-five centimeters tall and, about ninety, ninety-one kilos?"

"Pretty close to that."

"Could you stop a C-class drone, a sweeper, say, from pushing you off a walkway?"

"I expect so."

"Well, Hask is—was—ten centimeters taller and fifteen kilograms heavier than you, M. Sivart. He was a weight lifter, he could benchpress almost three hundred and twenty kilos. He could have torn that drone apart if he had seen it coming, certainly he could have pushed it away or flipped it over."

"If he had seen it coming," Gil said.

"His *back* was pinned against the hatch," she said. "He was looking right at the thing that killed him. He couldn't have missed it."

Gil thought about that for a second. Yes, that seemed on the face of it odd. Still, this was out of his area of expertise. "I'm afraid I couldn't be of much help to you. I sometimes do favors for people, to facilitate the, ah, return of certain things that have . . . gone missing, when nobody wants ISU to get involved, but I don't have any official standing. Station authorities might take a dim view of somebody meddling in an ISU investigation."

"There is no investigation," she said. Her voice was bitter. "How could you interfere with something that isn't happening?"

"I'm sorry—"

"I can pay you whatever you ask," she said. "Hask left me his insurance. DOJ—death on the job—pays a quarter of a million stads. I'm rich—but he's *gone*."

"It's not the money—" he began.

"Look, I don't have anybody else! Please!"

Gil looked at her. She was in pain. She was going to start crying in a second and this was obviously something she needed to do to get past this tragedy. A vital man, her lover, had been cut down unexpectedly. She had to deal with that and make some sense of it, only she couldn't accept the explanation. So here she was, asking him for his help. That was usually his problem, he couldn't turn away from somebody who really needed him. Especially women who were not-quite-classically-beautiful. A character flaw, no doubt, but one he had learned to live with, being that he didn't have any choice. So what would it hurt if he asked a few questions? He could talk to the cools and the medics, likely confirm what they thought, and make Linju Vemeer feel as if she had done all she could to put her dead lover to rest. It was little enough. Besides, he was a puzzle addict, and there was a little piece here that didn't seem to fit. He would worry about that until he found out where it went.

He looked at her and nodded. "All right. I'll check into it."

Now she did start to cry. "Thank you," she said. "Oh, thank you."

Accident reports were generally unclassified, and Gil had no trouble downloading the file and storing it in his personal flatscreen. He scanned the text, scrolling through it rapidly. It seemed straightforward enough. Burton Haskell, aged thirty-one T.S., had been found by a coworker in the induction space between the third and fourth hulls on Red 2 one week past. He was apparently dead upon discovery—here was the medical report, cause of death a crushing chest injury that ruptured the heart. M. Haskell had been an inspector/supervisor for two years, a sensor installer for a military hitch for four years before that, and had worked in other aspects of electronic construction since graduation from secondary ed, having been with the *Hawking* since construction began. No brothers or sisters, parents both deceased in a shuttle accident ten years back. Not officially married, but an SO of record, Linju Vemeer, listed as beneficiary on his insurance policy.

Gil smiled, his mind working. The classic triangle of any crime was constructed of three sides: means, motive, and opportunity. A quarter of a million HS standards was certainly motive. But Gil didn't think Linju had killed her lover, not if the cools had signed off on it as an accident. She would have to be incredibly stupid to stir up an investigation if she were the killer and already cleared of any crime. She didn't seem that stupid.

He went through the rest of the information. ISU had sent a man as a matter of form, there was the name of the officer. Here was the medic's name and that of the worker who had found the body. He would start there. Assembling a puzzle was not all that difficult if you had a knack for it. Like constructing a tiny model, it was simply a matter of basic logic. First, you gathered pieces, then you put them together. If they didn't fit, you went out and found some others that would.

Gil glanced at his chronometer. A couple of hours before midshift change. He could take a lift up to Dark Green and enjoy a nice stroll to the medical center. Or he could go all the way up to Orange, to the ISU substation and locate the investigating cool and see what he had to say. Or walk to the hull and catch the slant tube to Bright Green and the coworker. In truth, he could visit all these people via the com; he could link and find out what he wanted without ever leaving his shop. But there was no substitute for personal contact, he had found. Pheromones didn't traverse the com, neither did subtle body language, and sometimes these things told you more than words.

All right. He would go and gather a few pieces of this puzzle and see what they looked like.

The air in the induction hull felt stale, it smelled faintly metallic, something like the injection mold Gil used to form model parts did when it was cooking perma-plast. The supervisor had cleared him to talk to the man who'd found Hask.

"M. Rawlins?"

The man's head was depilated and he had a mandala tattoo in shades of true red and blue inscribed on his bare scalp, making it hard to focus upon. He was thin, medium height, and wore installer's recycled gray-paper coveralls and biogel slippers. According to his public information file, Rawlins had been working here for six months; before that, he had been employed by Kuralti Brothers, one of the larger commercial merchants in the galaxy, at various of their six branch outlets on the station, transferred in from one of their planetoid-class stores in the Tado System. He was a sensor installer, one of the dozen who had worked under the late Haskins.

Without making it obvious, Gil tapped at his right breast pocket, activating the tiny ball recorder he carried there. True, it was a violation of civil privacy, but he was gathering information, not legal evidence; he'd never present the little steel marble recording to any official scrutiny, it was only for his personal use.

"Yeah?"

"I'm Gil Sivart. I wonder if I might ask you a couple of questions about M. Haskins? I cleared it with your supe."

"You a cool?"

"A friend of M. Vemeer's."

Rawlins shook his head. "I feel sorry for her, you know, but Linju's got a bug up her twat about this. Talking about somebody killing Hask."

"I understand you found him?"

"Yeah, I was the first one to see him dead. I was scheduled EVA, to the outer hull to do security scanners, you know, Dopplers. The drone had squashed him against the V-wall lock."

"How would that drone have done that?"

"Well, it's a garbage ram, it shoves stuff into the recycle chute to the hoppers on five. Normally there's a canister there, when it gets to a certain weight, the drone dumps it into the lock."

"Why would M. Haskins have been there?"

"It looked like he was trying to fix the lock. It was jammed, something out of the last canister that got dumped, that happens. He was big enough to make the drone think it had another load waiting, so it went to dump him."

"Isn't there a safety of some kind?"

"It was turned off. It's usual to run a bypass when you work on a lock, the door won't open with the safety off."

"And the drone doesn't have a human recognition circuit?"

"Most of 'em do, but this was an old one, a Brooks bug brain, it hadn't been upgraded yet."

"Strange set of coincidences, isn't it?"

Rawlins shrugged. "Accidents happen. Last year a hatch tech got spat into vac without her suit and there's five different safeguards that missed her. Karma."

"Haskins was a pretty big and strong man," Gil said. "He was looking right at the drone when he died. Any ideas as to why he didn't just shove it away?"

Rawlins shook his head, irritated. "Look, f'l'owman, I'm supposed to be an installer, I didn't design the station, okay? It was bad juju and I'm sorry he's got to be dead, but don't ask me."

"His SO is in pain and she's looking for reasons."

"Tell Linju I said I'm sorry. You can tell her I said I think she's off the track here, too."

"Thanks for your time, M. Rawlins. I expect you're right."

The cool shook his head. "Officially, it's an accident," he said.

Gil had offered to buy the man lunch in exchange for his time, and the pair of them sat at the little cafe a lot of the military noncoms liked, F3, where orange shaded into yellow. The cool drank splash, a mild form of beer, and Gil sipped at coffee. The cool's name was Millet. Once again, Gil's recorder was running.

"Unofficially?"

"Well, my opinion is suicide."

Gil blinked. "What makes you say that?"

"Hell, he was looking at the drone when it got him. He had to have let it happen. Guy like that could have picked the damn thing up and thrown it one-handed, he wanted, he was a big sucker, muscular as a gorilla. I think he wanted to get around the suicide clause in his insurance, so he made it look like an accident. Only thing that makes any sense."

"He didn't have any enemies who might want to see him dead?"

Millet shrugged. "Maybe, but not any we could find. He spent a lot of time in the gym, he was well liked, nobody with any grudges. Nice guy, minded his own biz, didn't step on anybody's toes. We did a shallow scan on everybody who could have been in there with him. That's not a high security area or anything until you get outside, but the doors are wired to record anybody who comes or goes. There were a couple dozen workers in and out of there that day and we checked 'em all. Nobody made the scanner squeal. So it had to be an accident or suicide."

Gil nodded. "Thanks for the help."

"No problem."

At the medical center, the shrugging continued.

"What is your interest in this, M. Sivart?"

"Haskin's significant other has some questions about the death."

The medic, a portly woman of fifty, shook her head. "No question about it. He got squashed like a fly."

"Any drugs in his system?"

"No, he was clean."

"I see. Any history of depression?"

"Not in my records, no."

"Could something have happened to him before he was crushed? Some illness or trauma hidden by the injury?"

"Yes, of course. We would have found an infarct so it wasn't an MI, but a nodal malfunction is possible, though I don't think this was the case. Not a CVA—a stroke, we'd have seen that. The man was very well developed, he had an excellent cardiovascular system."

"Thank you, Doctor."

After he finished with the medic, Gil walked to the tube that would take him back to his shop. So far, it had played out about as he had expected. The one anomaly was the dead man's physical position when he died. It nagged at Gil, but by itself wasn't enough to indicate homicide. Murder was rare on the station; there had been a couple during the out voyage, but both of those had been easily solved, crimes of passion. A man had been stabbed by his lover when she caught him in bed with her mother; the other was a fight in a bar that had escalated, the killer waiting outside for the victim and bashing him over the head with—of all things—a bicycle. No mystery either time.

On the way to the tube, a beeper signaled the start of a military drill. Gil stopped walking. The tubes would be closed for the duration of the drill, could be two minutes, could be ten, depending on the computer scenario. Already all decks above Yellow would be buttoned up, and Military Command Center would be issuing orders to affected personnel. Sometimes the civilian population was included in the drills, having to rig for combat, but those were fairly rare. If it was military only, then the commercial comchans would still be working. Since he wasn't going anywhere, he put in a com to Linju Vemeer.

"Yes?"

"Gil Sivart, M. Vemeer. I'm checking some things. Was M. Haskins depressed about anything?"

"Depressed?"

"Unhappy. Distressed in any way."

"No. Why do you ask?"

"The possibility of suicide has been raised."

"Suicide? That's crazy! Hask would never do that!"

"You sound very certain."

"Listen, the night before he died, he and I were together. We had a wonderful time. We were talking about getting a formal cohab contract. He wanted to have children. So did I."

"And you say the evening was pleasant?"

"We drank wine, had a meal that he cooked, and then made love five times. That pleasant enough?"

Gil stared at the com unit. Well. A man who had made love five times in a single evening certainly didn't seem to be a candidate for suicide, unless fucking himself to death was the way he wanted to go. And considering fathering children argued against it, too.

"Thank you," Gil said. "I'll get back to you."

Hmm. Just for the sake of the puzzle, assume that it was murder. The means was evident. What would the motive be? Who had the opportunity? If you knew one, you could get the other, but which would be easier to determine?

The all-clear chime sounded. The drill was over.

Gil headed toward the tubes.

The kung fu class lasted an hour and a half, after which Gil usually did a short meditation alone in his cube. Because he was sitting quietly on a floor cushion trying to clear stray thoughts from his mind, he heard the sound he probably would have missed had he been watching the trivid or listening to music. A tiny *click* in the hallway outside his cube.

He thought about the sound. His cube was the last one in a feeder hall cul-de-sac two hundred meters or so away from his shop. He had chosen the unit because it was at the end of the hall and thus apt to be quieter than most. There wouldn't be any foot or cart traffic going past, just the residents of the two cubes slightly uphall from him, neither of whom had much company. The old man to Gil's left was retired from his former job as a food service tech and was generally asleep by 2100. The cube to Gil's right belonged to a woman having a liaison with two other women a level down, and she spent most of her time in the larger cubicle belonging to one of them. So—who's there?

Came another *click*. It was right outside his door.

He sat there for another two minutes, but his meditation was shot, he might as well satisfy his curiosity. He unwound his legs, stood, and moved toward the door.

The door slid open and Gil stepped out into the hall. Nope. Nobody home. The question was, what would have made that clicking sound? It was familiar, though he couldn't place it at the moment. Still, the hall was empty and there was nothing to indicate anybody had been there. He turned to go back into his cube. Another mysterious noise in the night, probably some kind of plastic or metal stress—

Wait a second. The circuit breaker.

The plastic cover to his cube's circuit breaker had a latch on it, so when you opened or shut the little plate, the latch made a small noise. And the breaker was immediately next to the door, where they were for nearly all the cubes on the station. They could be locked, to keep bored children from playing their little switch-off-all-the-lights games, but hardly anybody ever actually used the locks, certainly Gil didn't. The lights hadn't gone off, there hadn't been any interruption of power in his cube, so why would anybody have opened and closed the panel?

Gil reached for the circuit breaker's cover and opened it. There was the *click*, sure enough.

Whoops. Hello?

A black plastic nodule about the size of his thumb was stuck to the board, just over the cube's shower circuit.

A cold finger jammed itself into his bowels. Gil recognized the device. There was a similar, smaller unit augmenting the battery of his molding table. Damn! A power pusher!

Since all water had to be recycled on the station, there were shunt circuits built into showers, fountains, sinks, toilets, and whatnot for proper recovery of gray and stink water. And since water and electricity were a dangerous combination, special care was taken to be certain that amperages and even voltages were kept very low in those systems that came into contact with people.

The device stuck to his circuit breaker was a specialized piece of hardware, used to amplify and focus electrical current. A kind of superconducting capacitor with microcomputers and a Henley's Loop, a pusher could take regular power, store and step it up on the order of fifty to a hundred thousand times, then discharge it as needed, over a programmed period—or all at once. Thus it could allow a small battery to operate even a very heavy machine for a time, inducing the needed current by focused broadcast.

Gil stared at the pusher. He felt cold. If this thing were operative, and if it were set as he suspected, then the next time he stepped into his shower, he would have been in real trouble. The five or six volts of operating current in the thin wires of his shower, the head and floor and wall recovery systems, would suddenly have become maybe six hundred thousand volts, with a big rise in amperage, too. The wiring would surely have overloaded and spewed much of the excess juice into the water showering down upon him and puddled at his feet. And a wet body grounded in more water has little electrical resistance.

He would have fried like soypro in boiling oil.

And if he hadn't heard that small sound in the hall, it was likely they would have succeeded. He could have died in the shower and not have been missed for a few days, giving the murderer plenty of time to come and remove the pusher. An unfortunate accident, it would seem, some freak induction thing with the shower, and wasn't that too bad?

If somebody wanted him dead, then they had to have a reason. Unless they were unhappy with a model he'd sold them, then that reason must be connected to his other activities. He got along with the kung fu class and he didn't have any major enemies he knew about due to his personal history, not on the station, anyway. The thieves he had brokered with various organizations were usually grateful to him that they weren't going to do locktime or brainscramble. That left the investigation he was pursuing. And if somebody was willing to kill him to keep him from continuing it, then Haskin's death surely hadn't been an accident or suicide, because who would care?

Despite his brush against death, Gil smiled. Seems as if he had gathered more parts to this puzzle than he had figured. Things were getting interesting.

In the morning Gil called Linju Vemeer. They arranged to meet for breakfast. "This won't cause you a problem with work?" he asked.

"I don't need to work any longer, M. Sivart. Hask saw to that."

"Call me Gil."

"All right. Gil. Might as well call me Linju."

The restaurant on Green 3 was an "outdoor" cafe, with tables outside of the place where it opened into the deck park. The small trees and open space had been carefully created to give the illusion of a much a larger area, and it was pleasant to sit sipping coffee with a handsome woman, watching children play under the artificial sun on the live grass in the park.

"You were right," Gil said. "Hask was murdered."

Her face tightened, then relaxed a little. "How do you know?"

He told her about the incident at his cube. She was disturbed by it and said so.

"Have you called the cools?"

"No. Not yet. I would rather have something more to give them when I do."

"It could be dangerous for you to continue. I would understand if you stopped."

He smiled. "I'll be careful. I put a lock on my breaker."

"This doesn't make any sense, you know. Why anybody would want to kill Hask?"

Gil said, "Well, if we believe that he was killed and we know how, all we need to do now is figure out who or why. Either of those will eventually give us the other."

"What will you do?"

"I'll have another talk with ISU. Maybe I can narrow things some. Oh, and one other thing. If the killer tried for me, he or she might also feel disposed to try for you."

She looked startled. "Me?"

"If you were gone, they might assume the investigation would stop. It wouldn't, but they might not know that."

She looked at him. "What would you advise?"

"Simple caution. Don't walk down any deserted corridors alone. Keep your doors locked. Take care when you shower. Call me immediately if you see or hear anything suspicious."

"I will."

After she left, Gil walked toward the tube station and entered a lift to take him to see Millet. He didn't really think Linju was in danger, but it didn't hurt to be careful. As the tube, only half filled with passengers, lifted, the newsproj lit and began to rattle on about what was happening on the station and in the galaxy beyond. A group of visiting Gersons, those teddy-bear-like aliens, were enjoying their tour of the *Hawking*. The amphibian race of Silbers were engaged in battle with the Ichtons, the latter's fleet having laid siege to, and nearly having sacked, the Silbers' planet. In the financial news, a number of major businesses had recently suffered reversals, including among them the Luna Industrial Complex, the Milview Starfreight Lines, and the Kuralti Brothers chain of stores.

Gil listened idly to the news. Sometimes he forgot that the *Hawking* was an instrument of war, sailing the vacuum of deep space to fight against the Ickies who would, if not stopped, wipe out every other race they met. A single murder didn't seem like much compared to planetcide; still, he couldn't do much to affect a war but he might be able to help here. Life, after all, was lived in the details.

Indeed, it was the small details that added up to make the whole. For instance, he knew that whoever had meant to kill him was technically adept. It required a certain amount of knowledge to know how to use an electrical pusher, and to come by one without it being missed or accounted for. Gil had done a search of pubinfo files and had discovered that there had not been any sales of this particular model and brand of pusher to private citizens recorded in the last month. Likely it had been stolen. If he could find out where the pusher had come from, it would help the search for whoever had taken it. He had an idea about who that might be, but he needed more.

Gil met Millet. They stood in the back of the big rec room on Dark Yellow watching the skaters slide in their smooth boots across the low-fric surface.

"I checked you out," the cool said. "You have some friends in high places."

Gil shrugged. "I've done some favors for people."

"Yeah. I heard."

"Do you suppose I could get a copy of the names of those people who came and went to Haskins's location on the day he died?"

Millet shook his head. "That wouldn't be likely, no. The privacy rules wouldn't allow us to reveal that outside official channels. Why do you want it?"

"Because I'm sure he was murdered."

Millet sharpened, his eagerness apparent. "You have proof?"

"Not yet. The list of names might help me get it. As would the results of the scans."

Millet shook his head. "I can't reveal them. It would be my ass if anybody found out. Talking invasion of privacy, civil torts, like that."

A skater fell in front of them and laughed as she slid spinning across the floor. Other skaters leaped over her or veered to the sides to keep from tripping.

"You're a patrol officer," Gil said. "Senior grade?"

"That's right."

"So you could get to be a subcommander if a slot came open?"

"Yeah, me and ten other seniors. Lot of competition for the nonmilitary openings."

"A nice rise in status and pay, though, right?"

"Yeah. What are you shooting at here, Sivart?"

"Well, let's suppose here that you uncovered a murder and another attempted murder and caught the perpetrator. Would that give you an edge for promotion?"

"An edge? Yeah. Sharp enough to cut anybody else out of the way."

"Suppose that I could give you that? I figure out who it is *and* give you the reason and enough evidence to justify a deep scan. You get all the credit."

Millet watched the skaters circle past. He was silent for maybe thirty seconds. Then, "What do you get out of it?"

"I get to solve the puzzle. And you owe me a favor."

Millet looked at him. "That's it?"

"That, and the gratitude of a not-quite-beautiful woman."

"Ah."

"Well?"

"Let's go someplace private," Millet said.

Gil had in his flatscreen a no-print-no-transfer copy of the lists he wanted, courtesy of the ambitious Millet. The names were simple enough, there were thirty-four of them. And although he wasn't a tech, the results of the truth-scans were easy enough to follow. They were only shallow scans, verifications of questions asked, as opposed to deep scans that could dig into the memory and unconscious mind of a subject, were he willing to speak or not. Still, shallow scans worked better than basic lie detectors. When asked about the death of M. Haskins, none of the thirty-four people questioned registered any direct knowledge of the cause.

Gil sat in his shop, waiting for the molds of several hair-fine extrusions to finish producing the tiny model parts. Something was definitely wrong with this picture.

If, as he had good reason to believe, Haskins was murdered, then either the door scanners had missed somebody or the truth scanners had erred. Occam's razor said that it was the latter: the door cams were difficult to rascal, they were hardwired and fed into a central recorder, whereas the truth scanners required human operators. Assume the killer was one of the thirty-four. Then he or she had lied about it and the shallow scan had missed it—or been altered.

Gil plugged into the library and downloaded several files on the history of electroencephaloprojic readers. It took nearly two hours for him to finish reading, and it wasn't until the final section that he found what he was looking for. He smiled.

Gil put in a com to Millet.

"Did you know that a shallow scan can be beaten?"

Millet said, "I've heard that it is possible. Some hypnotic drugs supposedly'll fuzz the test. But we do drug scans on everybody to check for that."

"There's another way," Gil said. "By telling the exact truth."

"Huh?"

"Suppose you ask me if my name is M. Gil Sivart. Is there any way I can truthfully answer that no?"

Millet rolled that one around. "I don't see how, that's your name, isn't it?"

"Not precisely. I have a middle name, too, it's Meyer. Technically speaking my name is Gil Meyer Sivart, so I could say no to your question and be telling the truth."

Millet considered this. "Yeah, I can see that. But you'd have to be real clever to get through a whole session without slipping up," he said. "And it wouldn't fool a deep scan."

Gil went on. "But if you had an idea of what they were going to ask you and you had time to set up your replies, the machine would never blip because you would be telling the literal truth, right?"

"You're reaching."

"Oh? Assume you're the killer. The tech asks, 'Do you know how M. Haskins died?' And you take his question to the limits of knowledge—you don't know the precise cause of death, yes, he was crushed by a robot, but what *exactly* killed him? Unless you had access to the autopsy report, you couldn't say for certain, could you?"

"Come on. What if I asked you point-blank, did you kill Haskins?"

"Nobody asked that question. I have the list right here. And even if they had, the killer could have safely answered no and have been telling the truth. *He* didn't kill Haskins. The *robot* killed him. Yes, he *caused* the robot to do it, but he could have touched a control and turned away, say, not looking the actual event, and would have been able to deny that he had seen Haskins die."

"This is real iffy stuff here, Sivart."

"I know. But it opens up an otherwise dead end."

"You won't get a legal order for deep scans on thirty-four people, not unless we are talking about espionage, station security. You'd have to bring the military in on it. Even so, they'll hear screams way out in the spiral."

"I think we might be talking about just that," Gil said. "But maybe I can narrow it down. I'll get back to you."

Gil went to see Linju at her cube. Partially this was to ask her some questions, partially it was to see where she lived. She was on Basic Green, a quarter of the way from the hub, in a neighborhood that was much like Gil's own. With her new credit line she could easily move to one of the luxury places, on Dark Yellow, or even down in the Violet, where a lot of the commercial rich folk lived. Double- or even triple-sized places with all the perks that money brought. A lot of his sculptures occupied display tables down in Violet, given that he didn't give them away. Truth was, Gil could probably afford one of those places if he wanted, the going price of one of his models being as high as it was. He didn't need the room, though, and his ego wasn't so fat it needed an expensive address to drop into polite conversation. That was too easy, to get snared in the mine-cost-more-than-yours trap.

Linju met him at the door. She wore a long robe of pale green silk that was belted at the waist. The robe covered her, save for a flash of leg when she sat, but it was thin enough to cling in interesting curves and hollows. After appreciating those interesting places, he remembered to look around. The cube was clean, furnished in basic extruded furniture, a lot of cushions on the floor. A couple of paintings were hung, acrylics, one of two nude people embracing, the other of a group of children playing in a water fountain. There was a small statue of a dancer in a ballet pose on a table near the door, bronze or resin cast to look like bronze. There was a rack with infoballs slotted, books, and holovids. Here was a place where you could feel comfortable, and he did.

"Chair or a cushion on the floor," she said.

He chose the floor. So did she.

"What have you found out?"

"Not as much as I need for legal reasoning," he said. "I want to know more about Hask's work. What exactly did he do?"

She thought about it for a few seconds. "You know that the military subcontracts out a lot of things. Hask worked for Sensor Systems. They do a lot of different projects, but their biggest contract was to install and maintain the external hull pickups. Doppler, radar, light-spectrum visuals, magnetics, like that. It's an ongoing process. FTL screws some of them up, microdust and stray hydrogen atoms knock them out of tune or even off-line."

"Go on."

"Hask checked on the installations, making sure they were working and encoded properly. He had about a dozen people on the team; he was responsible for making sure what they did came up to milstan specs."

"I would have thought the military did that themselves."

"They're supposed to, technically, but they're stretched thin. The officer in charge might suit up and go EVA for form's sake, but basically he signs off on the subcontractor's inspection—if he knows him. Hask spent most of the trip out doing this, plus he was ex-military himself, so the military guys knew his work was clean. Once a year there's a major systems check and if everything passes they figure they can trust you. Hask's sections always passed. He had the fewest glitches on the station last test. He was proud of that. Hask would laugh and screw around with the best of them, but when it came to his work, he was tight, he didn't goof off."

Gil considered that.

"Any help?"

"Yes. We know he was murdered and we know how. I think maybe I've got part of a reason why, and that gives me some possibilities as to who.

"One more question. Do you know when the last major system check was?"

"Couple months ago. No problems."

"So there wouldn't be another such test for maybe ten months?"

"That's right."

"In which time the station would be likely to see more action against the Ichtons."

She shrugged. "Military hasn't said for sure and of course they wouldn't, but that's the scat."

He nodded. "I'll call you soon. I think we're getting close."

At the door, she touched his shoulder. "Gil?"

"Yes?"

"It means a lot to me to put this to rest."

"I know."

"I appreciate all you've done, even if you don't figure it out."

The weight of her fingers through his tunic was small but much of his attention was gathered on the spot; suddenly it had grown warm almost to the point of heat. There were a lot of things he could have said, but he only managed a somewhat flustered thanks.

As he walked away from her cube, Gil grinned wryly at himself. Careful there, Sivart, your professional judgment is about to fall off a high-gee mountain. And it would be all too easy to take advantage of her grief. Not something a decent man should do.

Hell of a thing, ethics. Tended to get in your way all the time. Damn.

Back in his own cube, Gil listened to the recordings he had made with his sub-rosa device. Rawlins, the man who'd found the body; Millet the cool; the medic; Linju. There was a piece missing, one crucial part. He felt it tapping at the perimeter of his mind, a small thought he could not quite catch. It was a key, if he could only slip a net over it and grab it, it would somehow open the hidden door.

He went through the flatscreen's material for the fifth time. Nope, it wasn't there, whatever it was he wanted.

He accessed the library computer and began searching and researching material he had read before. Along the edge of the computer's image, the on-line charges blinked and grew. This was going to cost him a nice piece of change, all this blind skipping hither and yon. He almost had it, he was sure of it, he had a reason, though it was iffy, it didn't quite make enough sense to nail down and call it that, but it was *almost* right, he knew it. Damn!

He was watching the on-line charges get bigger when it suddenly came to him. Of course! There it was, right in front of him, crap, how could he have missed it?

Gil grinned. Had it been a micrometeor it would have taken his head off because he'd been too stupid to duck.

He ran through his recordings and nodded to himself. With a specific idea in mind, the library obediently gave him the correlations he needed. There it was, plain as white bread.

Time to go and talk to the murderer.

❖ ❖ ❖

Rawlins's skull tattoo was beaded with sweat as he stacked honeycombed plastic crates of sensor components on a lift. He was alone in the storage room when Gil arrived.

Rawlins looked up. "Sivart? What do you want?"

"A confession would be nice," Gil said.

"Confession? What are you talking about?"

"Killing Haskins. Trying to kill me. Espionage. Anything else you'd like to unburden yourself of."

"What, are you crazy?"

"I don't think so. It took me a while to put it together, but anybody who looks carefully can see it."

Rawlins stepped away from the stack of crates and stood facing Gil from five meters away. His hands were empty. "See what?"

"Why you did it. It went past me at first, the motive, because I was too close in, I couldn't see the larger picture."

"What is this larger picture?"

"Oh, you know that. I'd guess you are in for a full wipe at the very least. Me, I'd shove you out a lock if capital punishment were still legal."

"You are crazy," Rawlins said. He put one hand behind his back.

"Nope. And I have enough to get a judge to go for a deep scan to prove it."

Sweat ran down Rawlins's face. He blinked it away, appeared to consider things, then pulled something from under his back coverall flap and pointed it at Gil.

"Well, well," Gil said, "what have we here?"

"It's a heartstopper," Rawlins said. "Induces cardiac fibrillation out to about twenty meters, in the hands of an expert. I'm an expert."

"So that's how you managed to get Haskins set up in front of the drone. I expected it was something like that."

"No, you didn't, or you wouldn't be here. Who have you told?"

"Nobody, yet. I wanted to get your confession recorded first." He pointed at his breast pocket.

Rawlins laughed, a nasty sound. "You don't think I'll get to play with that recorder after you, if I want? You *are* crazy."

"You'd be surprised," Gil said. "I scored very well on my last psych test."

"All right. Let's cut the scat. How much?"

"How much are you offering?"

"Don't play cute, pal. If you aren't greedy, you can retire in comfort. Half a mil."

"What I'd really like is to see you swing from a yardarm," Gil said. "That's an old nautical term. They'd tie a rope around your neck and hang you by it. Death by choking, or, if you were lucky, a broken neck."

"You're not in any position to be threatening anybody." Rawlins waved the weapon.

"Another accident will be hard to explain."

"There won't be an accident. You'll just disappear."

"I might have told somebody where I was going and why," Gil said.

Another laugh. "No, I don't think so. I think you're one of those guys who thinks he can handle anything. All that kung fu stuff you play with, the kind of work you do for the corporations to keep the cools out of it. Yeah, I checked up on you, pal. You're gonna make the carp in the recycle ponds real happy when they find you chopped up in their food. This is a discom, sucker."

Rawlins aimed the heartstopper and pressed the firing stud. There was a high-pitched burble from the device.

Rawlins's grin faded as Gil's grew.

"Can't trust technology, can you?" Gil said. He pulled the crow strip on his tunic open and revealed a thin and glittery gold mesh vest concealed under the clothing.

Rawlins threw the heartstopper and tried to rush past, but Gil ducked, then slid over and snapped a fast counter sidekick up. The fleeing man more or less impaled himself on Gil's heel, whacked himself smack on the solar plexus, and stopped cold, unable to breathe.

Gil stepped in and swung a backhanded hammerfist to Rawlins's temple. It was a solid strike, he felt it all the way into the middle of his back, and it stretched Rawlins out full length, unconscious before he hit the floor. It was unnecessary, the hammerfist, but it made Gil feel a lot better. His hand would be sore, but it was worth it. He touched his personal com.

"Officer Millet? I have a present for you."

Once again in Linju's cube, Gil sat sipping at tea.

"Very good," he said, nodding at the cup.

"Yes, sure, it's wonderful. Come on, Gil."

He smiled. "Okay. Once we were pretty sure that Hask was murdered, the first question that has to come up is why? Since nobody seemed to have any personal grievances against him worth homicide, then that left his work. The killing was carefully planned and executed, so that argued against a crime of passion."

Linju nodded.

"What he did was inspect sensors, equipment essential to the battle worthiness of the station. So I figured that it was either something he had discovered or was about to discover that somebody didn't want found out. That narrowed it down to the people who worked for him."

"But they all had passed a scan," she said.

"Right. So I dug around and found a way that you can rascal a shallow scan. That opened it back up again. Hask had a dozen people working for him, but some of them worked pairs, some of them were off-duty, and some of them were EVA when he was killed. That left me with two possibles, one of whom was Rawlins.

"I went over the scans; and I went over the tape I made of my first conversation with Rawlins. When I listened to it enough times, I realized he had evaded some of my questions, but very skillfully. When I asked if he knew how Hask had come to be where he'd been found, he sidestepped it. I didn't realize it at the time. Very sharp."

"So you suspected Rawlins all along?"

"He got better as a prospect after I found the pusher on my circuit breaker. He was a tech, he knew how to work such stuff."

"Then why didn't you turn him in?"

"Before I could point the cools at him, I needed a reason. Why would Rawlins in particular want Hask dead? What did he want to hide that bad?

"Rawlins was an installer. He put sensors onto the outer hull itself, the first line of defense against any incoming threat." He paused, waiting to let that sink in.

It only took a second. "He was sabotaging the sensors," she said.

It pleased him that it didn't get past her. "Yes. And according to what Millet found out from the military, they wouldn't have found out about it until the next full-scale test of the system. Until then, they would work well enough, unless triggered by an esoteric combination of radio and radar pulse. Once activated, there was a computer rigged to reroute the feed from fully functional gear so they would still *seem* to be working, but in fact would leave a rather large blind spot in the system.

"The military is reluctant to say just how big this gap would have been, or if it would have constituted a real danger, but I suspect that the hole created would be enough for an attacker to slip an antimatter spike or maybe a ceepee beam through it. It's classified information, where the hole was, but depending on where it was, it could cause major damage. Maybe even destroy the station entirely."

"Christo," she said.

"Exactly."

"So Rawlins was a spy? An agent of the Ichtons?"

"Well, yes and no. That was my problem. There's no record of Rawlins leaving the station since he arrived, no indication of how he would have been contacted by them. There are ways, of course, but it's not as easy as the trivid dreadfuls make it out to be.

"My problem was that I was looking at the motive wrong. Little versus big. On the near end, we had Hask discovering the tampering, and that was a problem for Rawlins that had to be corrected. Probably he called Rawlins on it and Rawlins stalled him long enough to set up the murder. We'll find out for sure when they do the deep scan. But there didn't seem to be anything in Rawlins's background to show him as a traitor in the employ of enemy aliens. It was when I was watching how much my library charges were going to cost me when I remembered one of the oldest rules in investigation, something I should have been looking at all along."

"Which is . . . ?"

" 'Follow the money.' "

"You see, the Ichtons don't try to communicate with men, at least they haven't so far. They squat on a planet, kill everything that moves, and take over. While they might have a lot to gain by taking out the *Hawking*, they probably wouldn't have any idea whatsoever of how to go about hiring a human agent."

"So, who . . . ?"

"I was in the tube, on my way to see Millet when I heard the news," he said. "There was an item about galactic companies that weren't doing too well. One of them was the Kuralti Brothers."

"The big stores?"

"Yep. And I found out from Rawlins's records that he had worked for them for several years. They have half a dozen outlets here on the station."

He waited to see if she would put it together. After a moment she did. "My God. Rawlins was going to help destroy the station and kill ten thousand people and friendly aliens for the *insurance*?"

He nodded. "War insurance is very, very expensive. And it pays off very, very big—but only if the loss is in actual combat. If this station went *boom!* under the guns of an enemy alien, there would be sufficient documented records of it transmitted to require that the insurance company pay off policy holders. I would bet that the Kuralti Bothers have unusually large policies for the six stores on *Hawking*. And that they found some way to let the Ickies know just where to shoot."

She shook her head. "My God."

"I expect Rawlins bribed somebody to allow him access to some kind of escape ship. When the shooting started, he would have slipped away. Risky, but he was being well paid."

"Hask died so somebody could make a profit," she said.

"Yes. People have been killed for a few coins in their pocket. We are talking about billions. Big money blinds some people to everything else."

"You took a big risk facing Rawlins alone."

"Not really. He worked with electronics. I figured he must have used some kind of cardiac stunner on Hask; a neural tangler would have shown up on the autopsy, but the fibrillation damage was covered by the drone. That's why Hask was facing the thing, so his heart would be crushed. He was probably almost dead when it hit him. I wore a faraday vest I borrowed from Millet, so I wasn't in any real danger."

"He could have used a needler or a zester," she said.

"Nah. Too risky. No chance of calling that an accident."

He stood. "I need to be be getting along. Officer Millet wants to buy me lunch. To celebrate his recent promotion to subcommander."

She walked him to the door. "Listen," she said, "I'm still grieving over Hask. I expect I will be for a long time."

He looked at her and nodded, not speaking.

"Maybe," she said, "maybe you might feel like calling me in a month or six weeks?"

"I would very much like to do that," he said.

She raised herself up on her toes and kissed him lightly on the lips, the softest of touches, then pulled back. "Thank you for all you did," she said. "And what you probably could have done—but didn't. Call me."

When the door closed quietly behind him, Gil let out a long sigh. Well. Maybe ethics were useful things after all. Lunch with Millet would be good, but a month from now, things could be a whole lot better, couldn't they?

Oh, yes, indeed.

THE EDGE

Outnumbered by a factor of thousands to one, the crew of the *Hawking* had a few advantages that they had to make full use of. One of these was their more efficient warp drive. The warp drives used by the Ichtons, and most of the races inhabiting Star Central, were incredibly inefficient by Alliance standards. It took any Ichton ship almost a week to cover the same distance as could be traveled by the slowest Indie tradeship in a day. The most modern Fleet scouts were as much as ten times faster when under warp than their equivalent Ichton vessel.

The Ichtons did not use scoutships as such. Perhaps their communal instincts mitigated against the smaller vessels and isolated duties. More likely their greater numbers simply allowed them the luxury of making every reconnaissance one made in force. As the swarm of hundreds of mother ships and their escorts moved from system to system, the Ichtons would invariably send ahead smaller fleets comprised of several cruisers.

Counterbalancing the Alliance edge in technology to the dismay of the Fleet representatives, was the almost complete unwillingness of most races to even acknowledge the Ichton threat. Even when a race did recognize the danger, which might not directly affect them for generations, they often chose to fortify their own worlds and send only token forces to support the *Hawking*. The *Hawking* was, after all, crewed by outsiders. Their explicit intention to organize all the planets of Star Central under their coordination often appeared a greater threat to the local leaders than the distant Ichtons.

THE STAND ON LUMINOS
by Robert Sheckley

Frank Livermore was on his way to the blue briefing room, where the assignments for his section were being given out. Frank was more than ready, too. He was tired of waiting around while the high brass sat in their plush conference rooms on the *Hawking*'s upper levels and decided the fate of middle-level officers like Frank. He might be assigned to outpost duty on some lonely, deserted little world where he'd be expected to watch for the arrival of the Ichton fleet, and then try to get out at the last minute. Or he could be assigned to one of the task forces that civilization had set up in various locales as part of their great effort to contain the Ichtons before they reached the home worlds.

"Hey, Frank, wait up!"

Frank turned, recognizing the voice of Owen Staging, the trader, who had made his acquaintance early in the trip. Staging was a big, barrel-chested man with a boxer's pug nose and the forward-thrust shoulders of a belligerent bull. He was a tough man, cynical and profane, who managed to stay popular with everyone aboard the *Hawking*. Frank liked him, too, though he neither entirely trusted Owen nor subscribed to his ethics.

"Where you off to in such a hurry?" Owen asked.

"They've called a briefing session," Frank said.

"About time," Owen said.

"These things take time," Frank said.

Owen shrugged. "Where do you think they'll send you?" the trader asked.

"You know as much about it as I do," Livermore said.

"I just might know *more* about it than you do," Staging said.

"I don't get you," said Frank.

Owen smiled and laid a forefinger alongside his nose. "I got a kind of idea about where they'll send you."

"Where?"

"Hell, no sense talking about it yet, it's only a hunch," Owen said lazily. "Tell you what, though. Come have a drink with me after you get your assignment, Frank. In the Rotifer Room, okay? I've something to tell you I think you'll like to hear."

Frank looked at Owen with mild exasperation. He knew how the trader loved to pretend to have inside information. And perhaps the man *did* have such knowledge. Some people always seemed to know what was going on behind the closed doors in the upper-level boardrooms where senior officers conducted the day-to-day business of fighting the war against the Ichtons.

"All right, I'll see you there," Frank said, then hurried off onto the express walkway that led to Blue Briefing B.

The small auditorium had seating for about five hundred people. Frank noted that it was about half full. It was a circular functional room with no pretense to grace. There was mellow indirect lighting, as in many places on the *Stephen Hawking*. The place looked somber, shadowy, and official. Frank found a seat in one of the front rows between a bearded gunnery officer and a uniformed woman from Ship's Stores. Frank couldn't remember seeing either of them before. It was strange, how long you could live on the *Hawking* without meeting any appreciable number of its ten thousand mixed personnel. At the end of a five-year tour of duty you rarely knew anyone beyond the core group of ten or twenty people with whom you had immediate business. Although most of the *Hawking*'s great expanse of space and its array of stores, shops, buildings, and structures of all sorts were pretty much open to everyone, people tended to live pretty much in their own section and to limit their friendships to people with similar job descriptions.

The gunnery officer sitting beside him unexpectedly said, "You're Frank Rushmore, aren't you?"

Frank looked at the man. The gunnery officer was in his late sixties, like Frank. He had that tired, somewhat cynical look that some officers got when they stuck too closely to their specialty for too long. Officers are not encouraged to sound off about matters outside their own competence, of course. Phlegmatic and incurious, that was the desideratum; but some measure of the simian quality was needed if a man was to stay mentally alive.

"Hello," the gunnery officer said. "I'm Sweyn Dorrin." He was broad-faced and clean-cut except for the tufts of hair on the points of his jaw that proclaimed him a follower of Daghout, a mystery cult that had made some inroads into the loyalties of Fleet personnel in recent years. Dorrin did not look the religious type, however. He had a dull and incurious look about him, as if hardly anything was worth his while to consider, or even to wonder at.

Yet he was wondering something now, perhaps just for the sake of the conversation, for he asked Frank, "Do you know where they're posting you?"

"My superior hasn't discussed it with me," Frank said, not particularly wanting to talk with the man but unsure how to extricate himself without seeming rude. "Do you know?"

"Of course," the gunnery officer said. "My CO said to me, Dorrin, you're the best man we've got on Class C Projectile Spotting Systems. No combat zone assignment for you. We need you to train new troops. They'll be moving you back to the secondary services depot at Star Green Charley."

"Good for you," Frank said.

"Thanks," the gunnery officer said, ignoring Frank's irony. "What about you, Frank?"

"How do you know my name?" Frank asked.

"I used to see you at the Academy outpost at Deneb XI. They said you were a square shooter."

Frank knew he had been a good officer, conscientious, thorough, but never flashy, never seriously considered for higher ranks. They'd never put his name forward for promotions above and beyond what fell to him through seniority. He was twenty-nine years in the service, and what had it gotten him? A lot of traveling, a lot of staring at the insides of spaceships, a lot of leave in strange places, a lot of women he didn't remember the next day, and who didn't remember him the next minute. That was about all the years in the Fleet had brought him, and he wondered now why it had all gone by so fast. Retirement time was coming up and he wasn't sure what he was going to do, retire with thirty years or take another hitch. There was a war on, of course, and some would say that now was not a time to be leaving the Fleet. But there was always a war on somewhere and a man had to think of himself sometime didn't he? It seemed to him that a man owed something to himself, though Frank wasn't sure what that something was.

The gunnery officer wanted to talk about old times, but the assignments officer had entered the auditorium and obviously wanted to get on with it. This officer's name was James Gilroy and he had been doing this for a long time, leading out the assignments as they came down to him from the Fleet Planning Offices.

Frank's speculations were stopped when he heard the assignments officer call his name.

James Gilroy's dry voice said, "Mr. Rushmore? You have been given a special assignment in sector forty-three. Lieutenant Membrino will meet you in Room IK and give you the requisite information and documentation."

Frank groaned inwardly. He had just come back from a three-month mission in his single-man scoutship. He could have used some time off, a chance to have a little fun in the honky-tonk bars on the Green-Green level of the *Hawking*. But he made no protest, saluted, and left the conference hall.

Lieutenant Membrino was quite young, no more than his early twenties. He had a small mustache and a serious case of acne.

"You are Mr. Rushmore? I have all the data right here for you." He handed Frank a small black plastic satchel and motioned for him to open it. Within were star charts, a stack of printouts, and an assignment list. In a separate envelope were his orders.

Frank read that he was to go to the planet Luminos, and there present his credentials as a messenger from the *Stephen Hawking*. Once he had established his bona fides, he was to inform the inhabitants of the planet of their situation apropos of the Ichtons. A position paper on Luminos followed. The gist of it was that Luminos was in the path of the oncoming Ichton space fleet.

"I don't understand," Frank said. "Why does someone have to go there and tell them? Why not just send a voice torpedo?"

"They might not pay attention," Membrino said. "Luminos is a new world, and the Saurians are not very sophisticated in the ways of interstellar politics. Their electrical technology is scarcely a generation old. They're still pre-atomic. They have only recently encountered the idea that other intelligent races exist in the galaxy other than themselves. If we sent a message, it would simply confuse them. They have had so little experience of other races that a lot of them still believe some of their own people might be trying to pull off a hoax. Whereas if you appear in a scoutship that employs a technology a thousand years beyond anything they've got, and deliver your message . . ."

"I get the idea," Frank said. "In how much danger are they?"

"That's the sad part. According to our best calculations, Luminos is directly in the Ichton invasion path."

"How much time do I have before they show up?"

"It looks like three weeks, maybe a month. Enough time. But you'll have to move lively, Mr. Rushmore, to get in and out of there without getting into trouble."

The Rotifer Room was an expensive eating spot and nightside hangout much frequented by the better-heeled members of the *Hawking*'s personnel. This tended to limit it to upper ratings and wealthy or at least affluent traders. Frank had often passed by its discreet entrance on Green-Green with the plastic palm tree copied from the logo of the ancient Stork Club of Earth. He had never gone in, not because he couldn't afford it—anybody could buy a drink at the Rotifer—but because his tastes tended toward the egalitarian and he was more than a little uncomfortable in close proximity to wealth and position of a sort he had never attained.

Owen Staging was waiting for him inside, seated at a table near the small, highly polished dance floor. This was not an hour when people were dancing, however. Not even the orchestra was present. The place was empty except for Staging and Frank and one or two couples in dark corners, and a discreet waiter in black tuxedo who moved around noiselessly, making sure everyone had drinks.

"Take a seat, Frank," Owen Staging said. His voice was vibrant, with strong chest tones. The big trader was wearing a shirt of some iridescent material decorated with many bits of cloth and metal sewn on to it. The fashion was a little too young for him to carry off successfully. His wristwatch was a genuine Abbott; aside from keeping time it also regulated his body's autonomic systems, checking and smoothing out any disparities when they deviated from Owen's previously established norm. The Abbott also had an automatic yearly adjustment for aging, and in most ways took the place of a personal physician, with advantage, some would say. The big trader looked the picture of health. He was in his late fifties, the prime of life, a big man, on the corpulent side, with large fleshy features and lank blond hair cut in a short brushcut. The smile on his face came easily and seemed genuine. This is a pleasant man, you would have said to yourself. Then, a moment or two later, you would have thought, But there is something about him . . . You'd mean something unpleasant, but you wouldn't know just what it was. Perhaps it was the flat, appraising way Staging looked at you, sizing you up and deciding what use you could be to him. That might have been it. At the present moment, however, the trader was all affability as he pushed a chair out for Frank and clicked his fingers for the waiter.

When the waiter came with the wine list, Owen pushed it aside. "Try some of the Vivot Clique '94, Frank. The sommelier didn't even know he had it until he was looking for something else in his Violet deck storage bay and found this. Pricey, but worth every credit of it."

"Just a beer," Frank said to the waiter.

He was uncomfortable around the trader, but had come to think of him as his friend. They had done a lot of drinking and talking together on the long trip out to Star Central. The trader had been affable and had shown interest in Frank.

"So what assignment did you get?"

"I'm dispatched to a planet called Luminos," Frank said.

"Luminos?" The trader's yellow eyes closed as he thought for a moment. Then they snapped open. "Luminos! Right on the edge of the war zone, isn't it?"

"I'm not supposed to talk about my assignment," Frank said.

"Come on, Frank! What am I, an Ichton spy?"

"Of course not," Frank said. "It's just that some things are best kept private."

"I already know," Staging said. "So they're sending you to Luminos? It's a useless assignment."

"Well, someone's got to warn them," Frank said.

"But why you? It's a rotten assignment, Frank. You just got back from a long one-man run. You'll be weeks getting to Luminos in a scouter, and once you get there there'll be nothing for you to do. The Saurians of Luminos won't want to talk to you; not after the news you bring them. And there'll be no traders there to talk to because the whole thing's in a war zone. And while you're being bored to death on this provincial little planet, there's a good chance you'll be rather messily killed if the Ichtons come through earlier than expected."

"Somebody has to do this sort of work," Frank said. "That's what the Fleet's out here for. We have to warn all intelligent races who are in the path of the Ichtons."

"I know that, Frank, but it's more than a little futile, isn't it? What good will a warning do them?"

"At least it gives them a chance."

"But what can they *do*? They can't move their planet out of the Ichtons' way."

"I know," Frank said, feeling defeated but stubborn. "But we have to give them the chance anyway."

Owen Staging leaned back and sipped his tall, dew-beaded drink. Ice cubes tinkled as he raised his glass in a humorous gesture. "What I don't understand, Frank, is what's in all this for you?"

"Why should there be anything in it for me?"

"Don't give me the humble crap, Frank. I guess humanity owes something to the men and women who are fighting to keep them alive and free. Twenty-nine years in the service putting out your all for humanity and what do you have to show for it? Just another crappy assignment that won't make any difference anyhow."

"Now look," Frank said, "that's enough. You can make a case against anything. Service in the Fleet is honorable work and the Fleet has been good to me."

"I'm not saying otherwise," Owen said, "but it *is* a little ironic, isn't it, that this assignment that is going to be a dangerous bore to you could be a source of considerable wealth to me?"

"What are you talking about?" Frank asked.

"If I could go in to Luminos," Owen said, "I could follow up on a very fine business opportunity that has just come my way."

"I'm not going to take you into area forty-three with me," Frank said. "I go into Luminos alone. Anyhow, you know the rules; no traders are allowed in war zones."

"I had no intention of going," Staging said. "Luminos is very soon going to be a dangerous place to be in. I don't get my jollies off by taking risks. War is your business, profit is mine. I'd like to make a profit with you, Frank. A profit for us both."

Frank looked steadily at the trader's tough face for a moment. He'd been expecting something like this. Ever since the trader had begun to curry favor with him back at the beginning of the trip, Frank had had the feeling that the man wanted something. And, in a way, Frank didn't mind. He liked the trader, liked his rough jokes and easy manner. And if the trader *did* want to win his favor, what was so bad about that? No one else cared that much for Frank's opinion on anything. It was flattering that the trader, a bold and successful businessman, did, whatever the reason.

Frank's face was expressionless when he said, "Profit? I don't know what you're talking about, Owen."

The trader dug two stubby fingers into the breast pocket of his twill jacket and fished out a brown chamois bag. The neck was held shut by a cunning knot. Tugging at the knot, Owen collapsed it and opened the neck of the pouch. He turned it upside down and teased it gently. Out of the sack rolled what looked like a pebble. But no pebble had ever possessed that fiery pulsating rose color. Looking at the gem Frank felt a brief touch of vertigo, and a feeling that he was entering a strange blue twilight zone where he was suddenly very far away from himself and very close to something he couldn't put a name to.

"What is that thing?" Frank asked Owen.

Owen put the stone down on the table between them. He gently poked it with a forefinger. "That's a Gray's fire stone," Owen said. "It's one of the rarest things in the universe—a psychomimetic mineral that can amplify and alter the mood of whoever holds it. Notice how it changes colors as my hand gets close to it. It responds to each holder with a unique array of colors. The scientists still don't know what that means."

Frank said, "I've never seen or heard of anything like this."

"That's because you don't read the fashion news," Owen said. "Gray's fire rings have made a great splash on the fashion scene in recent years. In fact, they've become the most important accessory of the year according to *Universal Humanoid Stylings* magazine."

Frank lifted the gem and felt it pulse in his hand. "Are these very rare?"

"Only a few hundred of them appear on the market every year. You can imagine what price the top designers pay for them."

"Where do they come from?" Frank asked.

"That has been a mystery for a very long time. It was definitely confirmed only last year, Frank. These stones are from Luminos."

"The place I'm going to?" Frank asked.

"The very same," Owen said. "You see, Frank, if I were going there, I could trade for these stones. I have a dozen outlets back in civilization that are ready to bid against each other once I have them."

"Well, you'd better forget about it," Frank said. "You know very well that no traders are allowed in a war zone."

"No," Owen said, "but there *is* something you can do for me, Frank."

Frank thought for a long moment. "Why would I want to do something for you, Owen?"

Owen grinned and said, "In order to do an old friend a favor. And to earn a considerable sum of money for your retirement fund, partner."

"Partner?"

"I want to go into business with you, Frank."

"You want me to get Gray's fire stones for you?"

"That's it, Frank. And we'd split the proceeds fifty-fifty."

"But what would I trade for the stones?" Frank asked.

"I've got something the Saurians are going to want," Owen said.

"Are you talking about whiskey?" Frank asked.

"No," Owen said, "though they could probably use that, too, with the situation they're in. But I'm talking about something they really need, given the present circumstances."

"Well, what is it?"

"I'm talking spaceship engines, my friend. That's what the Saurians are going to need, since all hell is going to break loose in their neck of the woods pretty soon now."

"Where did you get the spaceship engines?" Frank asked.

"I've got a cousin who works in General Offices Surplus and he has a friend in job-lot disposals. They're just starting to dispose of the L5 components."

Frank knew that the L5 had been the heart of the drive shield mechanism in recent years, and of the cold fusion warp generator that made FTL travel possible. It was a unit of considerable antiquity as such things go, nearly ten years in steady production. Frank was not surprised to find that the old model was superceded by a new one. What did surprise him was that Owen had gotten his hands on some of them so quickly. He must have acquired them hours after they were decommissioned, before the big planetary dealers got a chance to bid. Or had the situation been rigged to give him sole bid?

"What are you going to do with the L5s?" he asked Owen.

"I already told you," Owen said. "I am going to give them to you on consignment. Then I am going to stay here on the *Hawking* and wait. You are going to put those engine components in your hold. There's plenty of room; there's only thirty-one of them and they weigh only a couple hundred pounds apiece. You will take them to Luminos where they'll be hot items once you tell the Saurians what's in store for them. Once that's established, you trade engines for gems at the best rate you can get, bring back the stones, and we both make a nice profit."

"It's a pretty smart deal," Frank said a little sadly.

"What's more important, it's an open and aboveboard deal between you and me."

"You forget that I'm an active officer in the Fleet and you're a civilian."

"There's no law that prevents an officer from trading on his own account."

"As a matter of fact, there is such a law."

"Oh, *that,*" Owen said. "No one pays any attention to that old statute anymore."

"I do," Frank said.

"That's what I like about you, Frank," Owen said. "You're honest and that means I can trust you. That's why I'm going to put thirty-one L5 engine components into the hold of your scoutship and not even ask you to sign a piece of paper. I know you, Frank, and I know you'll be honest with me on this matter."

"I'm not taking your engines," Frank said, "and that's that."

"Are you so afraid of doing a humanitarian deed?"

"Since when is selling engines for you a humanitarian deed?"

"It's selling engines for *us* and it's humanitarian because those poor Saurians need all the help they can get."

"Why not just give them the engines, then?"

"Because I had to pay for them," Owen said. "I won't be able to keep up my good deeds unless I get paid for them."

Frank saw nothing strange in this proposition. The self-serving nature of it disturbed him, however. "I don't like the idea of making a profit on people's misery," Frank said.

"Then give your percentage to charity," Owen said. "Just make sure I get mine. Seriously, Frank, you'll be helping the Saurians in the only really tangible way you can. You'll be giving them a chance to defend themselves and a way to strike back at the Ichtons."

Frank didn't much like it, but he found the logic inescapable. Thinking it over, it seemed to him that by selling the engine parts to the Saurians he would be doing something for them. And it was perfectly in line with his orders to warn the Saurians of their imminent danger of attack. So he could follow Owen's scheme, do his duty, and also provide for himself in his old age. What was wrong with making a profit? Everybody else did it! Why should he hold out? And as for becoming a partner with Owen Staging, well, what was wrong with that? He could do a lot worse He had done a lot worse most of his adult life, serving in the Fleet.

"All right," Frank said. "I'll do it."

Owen Staging stuck out a meaty red hand. "Put her there, pardner."

Luminos was a small planet in the region of the galactic center. Although close to its neighbors, it was far enough from the next planet bearing intelligent life to require a full-fledged space era technology for trading and cultural exchange. This technology the Saurians of Luminos had not yet achieved, though they were right on the verge of it when the Alliance contacted them.

On Luminos, even electrical generators were still fairly recent developments. The Saurians were only one or two generations away from gas lighting.

After a long boring trip in space, the planet became visible on Frank's viewscreen as a blue and green globe, laced with stringy veils of white cloud. Frank began radioing while still well out to space. He got no response. He turned toward the planet's surface, moving in a shallow deceleration curve. Soon he could pick out cities and roadways, the usual indicators of civilization.

The Saurians still weren't making any attempt to communicate with him, nor had they responded to his own broadcasts.

As Frank piloted his scoutship down low through the atmosphere, his radio finally crackled into life. A voice demanded in the Southhoe dialect used by many races of the Star Central region, "Who is that?"

Frank identified himself as an officer of the Fleet, detached from the *Hawking* and sent to the planet Luminos as a special messenger bearing important news.

There was a stunned silence at the other end. A Saurian said, "Just a minute . . ." There was a delay of several minutes. Frank continued to decelerate. It was a bit of a bore, having to go through all this confusion, but that was how it often was with races that had little experience with others not of their kind. Every race that came to spacefaring went through the shock of discovering other forms of intelligent life where before they had thought they were alone. This was bad enough. What was worse was discovering that these other forms of intelligent life often brought with them problems nobody was ready for. This seemed to be the case with the Saurians.

The Saurian came back on the air. "Just a minute, I'm getting my orders . . ." There was another delay, then the Saurian said, "We're putting aside a special landing area for you. We are calling officials from all over the planet to be present for your arrival."

"No need for all that," Frank said. "I come with news of an urgent situation that I need to bring to the attention of any responsible official."

"Don't tell *me* about it," the voice said. "I'm just an aircraft landing officer."

Down on the ground, huge crowds had gathered. They were overflowing all the runways except the one assigned to Frank, where a cordon of uniformed police kept a semblance of order. After landing and closing down his engines, Frank allowed small tracked vehicles to approach his craft. They maneuvered the scoutship to a section of the field where a reviewing stand had been placed and grandstands hastily erected. The crowd was already in place when Frank finally emerged. A covering of royal velvet led from his spaceship to the most elaborately decorated spot on the reviewing stand. Frank walked down this and was greeted by a small, splendidly dressed group of Saurians.

At first Frank and the Saurians just looked at each other, because they were physically quite unalike. Frank looked like a typical man. The Saurians looked like typical dogs of the Airedale variety, with a bit of hyena thrown in for good measure, and with opposable thumbs on a fingered hand rather than the claws more common among the canine species. Frank was not prejudiced toward creatures of shapes other than his. Multiplicity had long been the rule in the great assembly of star-roving peoples. The Saurians, however, were new to the situation, and they gawked at Frank and passed comments among themselves in lowered voices, which, nonetheless, Frank heard and understood.

"Looks like he's descended from a monkey, don't you think?"

"Yes, or possibly a baboon."

"I wonder what color his ass is?"

"Jethro, not so loud, he'll hear you!"

These Saurians and their boorish comments were about what you'd expect from an unsophisticated new race first encountering one of the high galactic civilizations.

Meanwhile, the opening ceremony looked like it was becoming a flop. The Saurians stood around in their splendid uniforms and looked uncomfortable and unsure what to do next. Frank had been trained for these situations. He took two steps forward, raised his right hand with the fingers opened in a universal gesture of peace, and said in a clear voice, "Hello, I am a friendly messenger from a place beyond your sky. You do know about other races in the galaxy, don't you?"

"We've heard," the eldest of the Saurians said. "But we still do not entirely believe."

"Better believe it," Frank said. "There are many worlds out there, and many different kinds of people, and not all of them are friendly. In fact—"

He stopped. The eldest Saurian had raised a hand in a universal gesture that asked for a pause or break or change of venue.

"Yes," Frank said. "What's the matter?"

"It sounds," the Saurian said "as if you have a serious matter to discuss."

"Yes, if you consider an approaching race of venomous insects a serious matter."

"I must ask you," the Saurian said, "not to say anything about that at this time."

"Why ever not?" Frank asked.

"What we have here is a stranger-welcoming ceremony. That must be completed. Then we can turn to the information-disseminating phase of our relationship. Also, you can't tell the information because there is no one present to tell it to."

"There's you," Frank pointed out.

"I am what we call in our own language a hectator second class. That means I take trash in and out of buildings. You simply do not give official messages to someone like me."

"Suppose I tell one of these fellows," Frank said, indicating the other two Saurians.

"No," the hectator said. "They are my assistants, which is to say, even less than nothing."

"Surely I can tell someone! What about all these people here?" Frank indicated the big crowd of alert hyena-headed Airedales in the reviewing stand, watching the proceedings with the greatest sign of interest.

"Audiences always turn up when something happens," the hectator said. "They come for the show. But they aren't going to listen to you. It's not their job."

"Look," Frank said, "I've got to give my information to someone and get out of here."

"It's a problem," the hectator said. He thought for a minute. "You could always write it out, and I'll see that it gets to someone who knows what to do with it."

Frank was tempted. This assignment didn't seem to be getting anywhere. But it was his duty to make sure that the Saurians really understood about the Ichton danger. Besides, there were the spaceship engines he'd taken aboard for Owen. Now that he had overcome his qualms about selling them, he was suddenly interested in doing so. He could really use some money for his retirement. Selling the L5s presented a fairly honorable way of earning it. He just needed to be patient.

"I'm going back to my ship now," Frank said. "I want to tell my information to someone quick. Otherwise I'll broadcast it to your capital city through my loudspeakers."

Hectator said, "That would never do. No one would listen. The officials always interpret and explain matters of any importance for the people."

"But this is urgent!"

"Oh. In that case, wait right here. I'll go find out what they want to do."

The hectator went away and whispered with a small group of Saurians at one side of the reception platform. After a while the hectator came back.

"They said they'd send someone to talk to you tomorrow."

"But didn't you tell them this is urgent?"

"They said that they're not prepared to accept your unsupported word on that this early in the game."

The next morning an official came to call on him. Before Frank could speak, the official raised one pink-fingered paw.

"You must understand," the official said, "we officials don't really run anything. Luminos is an anarchy with no one really in charge. But people like to have rulers they can follow when that seems the best way to go, and blame when the officials turn out to be wrong. So we appoint people. It makes things easier."

"Your local arrangements are no concern of mine. I've brought news of the utmost urgency."

"So I gather. But I'm not the one to tell it to."

"That's what the hectator said."

"And very correctly, too. What would we do with mere hectators running the government?"

"Why can't I tell it to you?"

"Because I'm not supposed to be told anything important."

"Who is?"

"I think you'd better speak with Rahula."

Over the next few days Frank learned that the Saurians had many ceremonies of an extremely boring nature and he was supposed to be the centerpiece of all of them. They mainly involved a lot of bowing and posturing, all of it performed with fixed smiles on everyone's faces. The Saurians were extremely cautious, though perhaps "suspicious" would be a better word. It was obvious that they were not a sophisticated people. They kept sneaking looks at Frank, like they couldn't quite believe he was there. Their newspapers had front-page stories about him, getting all the details wrong and pointing out in tedious detail how Frank was a sample of man from the future and going into endless specious detail on how the Saurians stacked up against him. All in all, it looked like the Saurians were having a bad case of culture shock.

From the first minute of his arrival Frank was trying to get the Saurians to discuss the Ichton situation with him. But they didn't want to talk official business or to get down to anything important. "Look," they told him, "don't get us wrong, it's a very great pleasure to have you here with us. We're really honored, if you know what we mean, but before we can discuss interstellar matters we need to finish the new interstellar conference hall. Then we'll have a place worthy of receiving an ambassador like yourself. Believe me, we want to consider your important tidings just as soon as we are set up for it."

"Look," Frank told them, "this matter of the Ichtons, it won't wait . . . ."

But they wouldn't listen. They would just smile and back away from his presence, leaving him finally talking to himself. Othnar Rahula was the only one who would even pretend to listen to him.

Othnar Rahula was a member of the Saurian aristocracy and was in every way a being to be reckoned with. He was handsome as Saurians go. His ears were always cocked attentively, a sign of good breeding in man and beast alike.

Rahula was affable but there was a mystery about him. Frank couldn't figure out what sort of job he held or what his position was in the Saurian scheme of things. He seemed to be important, and other Saurians were in awe of him, but he never seemed to do anything. It was not polite to ask directly, so Frank decided to put some questions to the Saurian servant who brought his dinner.

"What government post does Rahula hold?" he asked Dramhood, the servant.

"Government post?" Dramhood was puzzled.

"All the government officials seem to defer to Rahula's opinion. Yet he doesn't seem to have an official function."

"I understand what you mean," Dramhood said. "Rahula has a function, but it's a natural one, not an official one."

"What is it?"

"Rahula is this year's official Exemplifier for the Saurian race."

Upon further questioning, Frank learned that the Saurians worked on a role-model system. Every year the high priests of the culture, duly elected by newspaper vote, went to an ancient monastery high in the mountains, there to confer and decide who would become this year's role model for the inhabitants of Luminos. Rahula was that year's standard-bearer of cultural self-identity, the one the other Saurians wanted to model themselves on.

This custom, Frank learned, had some interesting consequences. What the role model did was what everyone wanted to do. What he believed quickly became what everyone believed. What he thought was what was on everyone's mind, and what he considered unimportant hardly counted at all.

After a week on Luminos, Frank had been unable to get any response to his threats and warnings about the Ichtons. His mention of the spaceship engines he wanted to sell had met with polite disinterest. This led Frank to conjecture that the Saurians had by no means reached their full intellectual potential yet. In fact, as Othnar Rahula remarked one afternoon, sitting in the cabin of Frank's scoutship, where Frank had asked him for tea, "We've just entered into the idea of even having a potential. We've just discovered intellect and all of its pleasures. It's like we've just woken up onto the stage of galactic history and here you come telling us we're in danger."

Frank said, "I'm sorry if your intellect is taking a beating by discovering you're not the only kids on the block."

"I understand your metaphor," Rahula said. "I think it does not apply in our case. Or, perhaps, it does. I don't know. I just know that it's pretty shoddy when you come here from a superior civilization and tell us that we are about to be wiped out by a race of large carnivorous insects."

"So you *were* paying attention to what I've been talking about all week!" Frank said.

"Yes, of course. But frankly, Frank, your news is too important to take seriously. Besides, I mean, if it's so important to do something, why don't you sentient beings with battle fleets do something about it?"

"Maybe I haven't somehow made myself clear," Frank said. "We, the allied forces, are doing everything about it that we can. The war has been going on for years. Either we destroy the Ichtons or they wipe us out."

"Well, it may be as you say," Rahula said in a tone that left no doubt as to his uncertainties.

"You simply are not acting in a realistic manner," Frank said.

"Is that what you asked me here for?"

Frank shook his head. "The real reason I've invited you to my ship is to try to convince you of the emergency one last time."

"It's easier for us to believe you're mistaken in your facts about the Ichtons," Rahula said, "or that you are drunken or drugged or a crazy person. It is very difficult for us to think that our entire race may be going down the tubes in a couple of weeks due to an alien invasion we can't do anything about. If the Ichtons come, we will bargain with them. We are a clever people. We will come out all right."

"Your strategy of bargaining," Frank said, "is based upon a delusion. I have something to show you." Frank touched a button on the scoutship's switchboard. Well-oiled motors sprang into instant hum. Rahula sat up, startled. The great tuft of silky blond hair that depended from a knob in the center of his forehead rustled with the sound almost that of a snake shedding a skin.

"You have started the ship's engines!" he said.

"I'm taking you for a little ride," Frank told him.

The spacecraft doors clanged shut. Machinery hummed into life. Red and green lights flashed, then steadied.

"I don't want to go for a ride!"

The generators kicked in, and a low throbbing replaced the sudden, high-pitched whine of servos. Lights flashed on the banks of dials above the instrument panel. There was a soft chittering sound as circuits opened and closed.

Rahula said, "You must let me out of this ship at once. I have a luncheon appointment in fifteen minutes."

"You're going to see what I want to show you," Frank said. "Think you can bargain with these guys? I'm going to give you an idea of what it means for a planet to come up against the Ichton horde."

"But I really don't want to see this," Rabula was saying pettishly as the scoutship moved through Luminos's upper atmosphere and then into the darkness of space.

It took Frank only one FTL jump to get to the location he wanted. It was a system of one planet and three moons circling around a red dwarf.

As they came within visual range, Rahula could see that the place had an oxygen atmosphere and possessed the deep green-blue colors of living matter. But as they came closer though, he saw that most life had almost been expunged from the surface of this place. Sweeping low over the planet, Rahula saw that no birds flew in the sky. They passed over dry ocean bottoms; the very water had been sucked away and put into tanks for Ichton use in other places. The land had become mainly desert, and there were miles-deep scrapes where the surface had been strip-mined, ruthless machinery tearing apart the fundamental rocks to get at the valuable minerals and rare earths. A vast cloud of smoke lay over the land, hugging the mountain contours in great, greasy coils. Here and there were shallow ponds that had not been entirely sucked up by the Ichton salvaging and reclamation operations. Higher magnification revealed that these ponds were pustulant with noisome lower life-forms.

They swept over the land at what would have been treetop level, had there been any trees left standing. Beneath them, miles and miles of rocky devastation sped hypnotically past their eyes. And this scene, monotonous and horrifying, repeated itself endlessly as they traversed the planet, until Rahula finally cried, "Enough, Frank, you have made your point. What is this place?"

"This planet is called Gervaise. It is a sister planet to the Gerson world that received similar treatment at the hands of the Ichtons."

Rahula was silent during most of the flight back to Luminos. His soft, shiny brown eyes seemed turned inward. His blink rate was up; he seemed to be thinking very rapidly indeed. When they came down on the landing field at Delphinium, capital city of Luminos, Rahula turned to Frank and said, "How many of those ship's engines do you have to sell?"

"Thirty-one," Frank said.

"And what do you want for them?"

Frank took a deep breath. "My partner and I want to get ten fire gems per engine."

"So many? But it would take us years to find a quantity like that."

"Well, make it five per engine, then. If you all worked together, your people could probably get that together in a matter of weeks."

"Perhaps we could," Rahula said. "But meantime, we can't kid ourselves any longer, the Ichtons are coming toward us and there's no time to waste."

"Nor any need to waste it. I will let you have the engines now, if you give me your promise to pay the agreed-upon price of five stones per engine."

"Yes," Rahula said, "I agree to that. Now bring us back to Delphinium. I must arrange transport for the engines."

"Are you sure you can speak for your people?" Frank asked. "Will they agree with you about the engines?"

"I believe what I'm doing is correct," Rahula said. "Therefore the others will also think it correct. They will do what I do. It is our system."

Frank had to admit that having all the people believe what you believed was a political advantage few races ever possessed. Overnight, and as though by magic, all of the Saurians were aware of the menace that confronted them from space, and, rather than being blasé and evasive about it as before, were, like Rahula, suddenly and deeply concerned. Within minutes after Frank's talk with Rahula, through a sort of racial telepathy, which was immediately reinforced by unprecedented coverage in the newspapers and television, the Saurians all knew they were about to be attacked by the Ichtons, a six-limbed insect species of unparalleled ferocity. Everyone also knew and approved of trading fire gems for spaceship engines.

The Saurians sent several heavy trucks to carry off the thirty-one L5 engine components. The trucks brought them to an industrial complex in a park not far from the capital city. On radio and TV, Frank heard about the organizing of the search for fire gems. Expeditions were quickly organized and sent out to the little-visited regions of the planet near the polar caps, where fire stones had been discovered in the past. Great numbers of Saurians were enlisted into this search, which was supported by all the considerable resources of the planet. Soon the first fire gems began to arrive. Rahula made himself personally responsible for ensuring that Frank got what had been promised him. That meant that all the Saurians considered themselves responsible. It was one of the best-secured debts in the history of loaning.

For a few days Frank could take some time off from the concerns of war. He visited the best-known wonders of the Saurian world. These included the upside-down waterfall at Forest Closet, the Twisted Volcano at Point Hugo, and the Glass Dance Floor at Angelthighs. These were not the spectacular sights for which some of the worlds in the region were known. But they were very special, and carried a load of sentiment. Frank especially liked Forest Closet with its ranks of whispering willows. It was disagreeable to realize that the Ichtons were about to cancel all possibilities, good or bad.

It took the Saurians eight days to collect all of the promised fire stones. There were 155 stones in all, and the presence of so much concentrated mood essence in crystalline form was more than a little overwhelming. There was a special ceremony in which Frank accepted the fire stones on behalf of himself and Owen Staging.

Next day, Rahula took Frank out in one of the surface cars and brought him to the main factory where the engine components were being built into fighter bodies. Frank was a little surprised to find that the Saurians were planning an active defense of their planet. He had somehow assumed that a government group would try to save their own lives, escaping to another world in the ships they could build before the onslaught of the Ichtons. He had seen this happen before. It was typical behavior.

But not for the Saurians. With rapidity and efficiency, they were putting their planet into the best state of defense possible. Under the goad of this emergency, they produced great quantities of jet fighters and equipped them with improved models of the basic jet fighter engine. These were for defense in the atmosphere. To fight between the worlds they had constructed separate bodies to house the thirty-one spaceship engine components purchased from Frank. Their ship designs had been purchased from reliable off-planet sources. Looking these plans over when he was taken for a tour of the factory, Frank could spot some mistakes. Luckily, they were matters he could correct on the spot.

A voice tube torpedo arrived for him. Captain Charles Mardake, head of his section, wanted to know when Frank would be back. Frank sent back a reply in which he explained that the situation on Luminos was still fluid, and that although the Saurians were now working actively in their own defense, they still had a ways to go and therefore Frank could still be useful here. The Ichton attack was still not imminent and so he was exercising his discretion and staying on a while longer.

That morning another message rocket was recovered and brought to Frank in his ship. It was from the office of the Fleet observation corps. They reported that the Ichton fleet had diverted slightly because the big insects had to take care of a larger planet that lay close to their invasion path. It was a planet where high gravity beam installations had been causing problems to some of the outlying Ichton ships. "So the main horde is going to miss you," the report went on, "and that's the good news."

However, the message went on, the bad news was, some Ichton squadrons were being sent to check the flanks for overlooked worlds that could be usefully stripped. One such squadron was coming directly toward Luminos. It consisted of between five and ten cruisers and would be there in about a month or three weeks. They appeared to be Stone-class cruisers and were judged very dangerous.

The message was a blow to Frank's hopes. He had begun to believe that the world of Luminos might be overlooked, but this news dashed that possibility. A group of even five Ichton battle cruisers was potentially as devastating to Luminos as the arrival of the entire battle fleet. The Ichton ships were of a technology far superior to anything the Saurians had been able to put together. Not only that, there was also the matter of battle savvy. The Saurians had never fought a modern space war. Their own wars against each other would have to be considered the equivalent of the bow and arrow struggles of primitives.

But the Saurians were prepared to fight, and the raw youngsters piloting the thirty-one ships built around Owen's L5 units had a lot of esprit de corps. They had memorized some of the fighting tactics as taught by the standard training manuals. But they were a long way from being prepared to face up to the reality of a murderous opponent. They needed more training.

Frank decided abruptly that he would take the situation in hand himself. He announced through Othnar Rahula that starting that very day he was giving classes in spaceship tactics as they pertained to planetary defense. There was no lack of enlistees for his crash course. The Saurians picked up the main concepts with great rapidity. Soon Frank was able to lead the thirty-one new ships in simulated battles in Luminos's troposphere. By rapid shuffling of personnel, and keeping the ships occupied all of the time, Frank was able to train a good number of Saurians in spaceship tactics. The civilian population, meanwhile, made its own preparations, working day and night to get guns of appropriate mass and shocking power online in an attempt to defend the cities against the onslaught that now might be no more than days away.

Another voice torpedo arrived. It was a message from the trader Owen Staging. "Frank," it said, "I don't know what you're staying around there for, but please get out. Now! You've done all you can. Maybe a lot more than you should have. It's time you got out of there. Remember, you owe me something, too, like half the stones. That's a joke. But seriously. C'mon back, partner. We've got a great future ahead of us!"

Frank was resting in his bunk aboard his own spaceship when the trader's message came. Soon thereafter there was a warning signal from a long-distance satellite warning station: first elements of an Ichton battle group had been detected at the fringe of radar receptivity.

Frank stood up, and with a heavy heart activated the switches that closed the main airlock. Yes, like it or not, it really was time to get out. He had almost cut it too fine. He'd gone right down to the wire with these Saurians. He would have liked to take station with them and have it out against the Ichtons here and now, but he knew that he couldn't do that. His loyalty was to the Fleet and it was to the Fleet that he had to return.

Losing no time getting aloft, Frank directed his ship to an asteroid belt that formed a maze of rocky moonlets in space near Luminos. He knew he should be kicking back up again into FTL drive, but he couldn't resist waiting long enough to see how his protégés did against the Ichton battle group.

Long-distance radar reported the progress of Ichton spacecraft into the Luminos system. Five cruisers were identified. They were some new class, smaller than Stone class, less well shielded, a sign, perhaps, that some of the Ichton manu-facturing units were having to cut back to simpler models. Although they were not Stones, they were still formidable.

For Frank, it was getting very late indeed. But still he delayed in the asteroid belt, waiting for news of the engagement.

Five Ichton ships in line-ahead formation suddenly clashed with the thirty-one Saurian ships in three half-moon formations. Beams flared, shields ran up through the spectrum as they staggered under the energy of multiple strikes. In the first five seconds of combat, seventeen Saurian ships were disabled or vapor-ized entirely. But two of the Ichton ships were out of the fight, and a third looked like it wouldn't last much longer. The matter seemed to have been decided in that first instant of colliding energies. The Saurians were still hanging in there.

The surviving Saurian commanders learned fast. There were some things about space combat that had to be learned on the spot. No amount of theo-retical reading, and not even well-designed simulation equipment, would do. Learning was greatly stimulated by surviving that first engagement.

Now the third Ichton ship was down, dissolving into the raging maw of its own wild-running main engine. Two to go! A group of Saurian ships led by Othnar Rahula surrounded the fourth Ichton cruiser. The smaller ships buzzed around the cruiser like maddened flies. Electrical potentials danced off the edges of ships' shields in wild coruscations of curling force as more energy weapons came to bear. In that confined area space itself heated significantly for a moment. The beleaguered Ichton ship blew out its rearmost shield, tried to rig a temporary one, and was caught without adequate defense when Othnar Rahula swung his ship around and slammed a volley of torpedoes into the stricken cruiser. Brilliant explosions shuddered out into the blackness of space. The Ichton cruiser was still trying to reply with her guns when her FTL equipment vaporized and she was gone as though she'd never been.

Meanwhile, Frank had been dawdling in the asteroid belt, not wanting to turn on his FTL just yet because he wanted to know what was happening.

Then the remaining Ichton ship suddenly began to lose power. The blast from its drive jets faltered, the color of its propulsive flame lances changed from golden yellow to cherry-red. It wobbled, yet somehow remained in precarious control, and began to descend into the atmosphere of Luminos. The landmasses of the planet rushed up to meet it, and so did a full squadron of Saurian jet fighters. Colored a metallic liquid black, except for the white markings on their wingtips and tails, these fragile machines clawed up into the stratosphere, higher and higher, until their engines began to flicker and die out through lack of oxygen. They fell back to denser atmospheric levels. The Ichton spaceship now had descended to meet them, still fighting for control, less agile than before, but still moving at a speed no jet ship could match. The fighters replotted their trajectories and flung themselves in for the kill. The high, thin air of Luminos was alive with explosive projectiles from the jets' wing guns, hammering at the Ichton cruiser's screens. The projectiles bounced harmlessly off, as did the rocket torpedoes and small guided missiles. The Ichton ship seemed to be recovering its poise and getting more maneuverable by the second. And it seemed that its commander was realizing that the Saurian aircraft could do little or nothing against his screened spaceship.

The Ichton commander ignored the fighter attack and turned his attention to the planet below him. Explosive rays lanced out from the cruiser's underbelly. Big chunks were torn from the heart of the large city beneath him. A pall of oily black smoke rose into the air. The Ichton spaceship slowed to a deliberate pace. It seemed determined to do a really good job, destroy anything that crawled or swam or flew, strip out the minerals and other valuable things and take them off to the Ichton fleet.

The fighters seemed useless against the well-shielded Ichton cruiser. Seeing this, Frank realized he was going to have to do something. He activated the controls, and somewhere inside of himself it occurred to him that he didn't have to do this, not really, he'd just been sent here to warn these guys, he wasn't supposed to be getting into the fight, he wasn't supposed to be dying for them. But that thought had no time to take hold, because Frank was filled with the simple need to take action and preserve a situation that was threatening to go very badly for the side he had decided to fight for. It didn't occur to him that he had returned somehow to one of his original intentions, formed back when he first joined the Fleet, concerning what to do with his life, how to spend it, what it was for. He knew it was not for making a profit like Owen the trader, but for some other reason, something that bad to do with serving humanity in the broadest sense, against its enemies like the Ichtons.

Frank found the Ichton ship in range and fired. As he had feared, his rockets bounced harmlessly off the ship's shields. The Ichton ship fired back. Frank managed to elude the missiles, not trusting his shields to take too heavy a load. When matters quieted down for a moment he saw the Ichton ship coming after him again. He countered. It was stalemate.

There was nothing Frank could do. He and the Ichton canceled each other out. He was going to have to try something different if he was to have a hope of putting the Ichton ship out of action before it destroyed the planet Luminos.

There was one thing still left to try. It was a very old tactic, and it dated back to the days when ships were made of wood and sailed on water. He could ram. It was an almost unheard-of maneuver in the modern world of space combat, but circumstances made it possible now.

Frank put the controls on manual and aimed his scoutship directly at the Ichton cruiser. He watched, fascinated, as the image of the enemy ship grew in his viewplate from a tiny dot to a vast metal war machine of incredible and still growing proportions. Frank felt himself tense as the moment of impact grew closer and closer. And then . . .

Before his eyes, he saw what looked like a meteor arc in from the side and impact with the cruiser. To Frank it looked like an act of God. It took his tired brain a moment to figure out that it must have been one of the Saurians in a fighter craft, ramming the Ichton from the side. The Ichton cruiser exploded in a silent blossom of light and energy, a light that bounded up and down the visible spectrum and seemed to light all of space before it died.

"Nice job, Frank," Owen Staging said. It was a week later. Frank had returned to the *Hawking*, filed his report, and was awaiting further orders. He had also taken it on himself to issue urgent requests to Star Central.

He had told the examining board, "Gentlemen, the Saurians need to be supported in their efforts against the Ichtons. I respectfully request that we send them considerable more military assistance than we have done before."

"They're not a very big power," one of the admirals on the examining board said.

"No, sir, they're not," Frank said. "But they won't quit on us. And that's worth quite a lot in this day and age."

A temporary aid package was approved on the spot. Frank found himself quite a hero back at the *Hawking*. He'd taken a chance, exposing himself for so long in Ichton-dominated space. He'd helped a friendly planet pull off a victory. It was a small one, but it was nice to have any sort of success among the many defeats that had been inflicted by the Ichtons.

Frank didn't particularly want to discuss these matters with Owen Staging when he met him, this time at the Wahoo, a common sort of tavern on Green 2 that was a favorite with Frank.

"Here's what your engines sold for," he said to Owen, taking out of his backpack the hefty chamois bag that contained the gems.

"You did well, partner," Owen said, bouncing them up and down in his hand. "Although you did leave your departure until very late."

Frank shrugged. "I want an advance on my share in folding money."

"Of course, partner, of course! I've got it right here for you." He took a cashier's check out of his pocket. "It's unusual to use paper anymore for transactions, but I thought you'd like it. I know you're an old-fashioned man at heart. There'll be more after the sales."

Frank glanced at the check, folded it, put it in his pocket. "This will do for a beginning. But I'm afraid it's going to cost you more than that, Owen."

"What are you talking about? Half was our agreement, and it was very generous on my part if I do say so myself."

"It's going to cost you three-quarters."

"I'll see you in hell first!" Owen snapped. The trader got to his feet. The expression on his face was not pleasant. His fingers slipped around a hardened glass tumbler as he turned to face Frank.

"You won't need that, either," Frank said. "You're not crazy enough to attack an officer of the Fleet."

"Your commission expired yesterday," the trader snarled.

"Correct. And on the day before that, I reenlisted."

"But our agreement! You were going to resign from the service and be my partner!"

"Sometimes people lie," Frank said. "You told me that yourself, Owen. And you told me it was all right, that was the way human beings were."

"What are you trying to prove, Frank? What do you want with so much money?"

"Guns and ships cost plenty. While the Fleet brass tries to decide how much to help the Saurians, I'm going to send them what they need."

"You're using my money to buy those people weapons?"

"Yes, yours and mine, too."

"Frank, I don't think I understand you."

"I understand you, though," Frank said. "There are a lot around like you, Owen."

"A lot of what?"

"Civilians. You people just don't know what the score is, really."

"Maybe not," Owen said. "I don't understand you at all. But maybe we can do another deal one of these days." He held out his hand. "No hard feelings?"

Frank shook his hand. "None at all, Owen."

He watched the man walk away. He'd never understand men like the trader. But he didn't have long to ponder about him. He had to start the flow of weapons flowing. Weapons to the Saurians.

ORIGIN OF THE SPECIES

The preliminary analysis of the data obtained by deep exploration of the Ichtons' arm of the galaxy was hardly reassuring to those commanding the *Hawking*. It appeared likely that the Ichtons had been methodically pillaging their way down their arm of the galaxy for tens of thousands of years, not just one or two millennia. Some civilian specialists even brought up the possibility that the Ichtons weren't moving toward resources, but like the barbarians that caused Rome to fall were actually running away from something even nastier. *Hawking*'s officers decided to refit one of the Fleet's few brainships for an extended probe up that arm in the hope of finding the edge of the Ichton infestation. This would give them some idea of the scope of the resources controlled by their adversaries. It would also serve a number of additional purposes that even those making the mission were not aware of.

KILLER CURE
by Diane Duane

She disliked him from the first moment she saw him . . . which was not a good state of affairs, since he was her new brawn.

Maura was MX-24993 now. She had just begun growing used to it. It wasn't that she hadn't liked her last brawn. She was an intelligent enough woman, and kind; but she brooded, and Maura had never been the brooding type. All her young life working with Fleet she had leaped into missions without a shade of concern for herself. She knew life was short, but hesitation and caution were not going to prolong it. Cecile, her brawn, had been an expert on the Ichtons, as much as anyone was; and she brooded. Maura had never understood why she wasted her time. Now Cecile was gone, and Maura had been called into *Hawking* to have the new engines installed. Also the new brawn.

He was very young, by her standards, at least; surely no more than twenty-six or twenty-seven years old. His records were still being uplinked to her computers, and she would have exact data later. But at the moment, she looked, and saw the young, handsome (almost too handsome), slender form, in Fleet fatigues, come striding into her control room as if he already owned it. Well, perhaps he was part owner, but it was not an auspicious beginning.

His name was Ran Nordstrom, and he was out, apparently, from Helsinki—the city, not the planet. He was very fair, very blond, even to the eyebrows and eyelashes. The eyes were a surprise: they were very green where you expected blue, and they were frighteningly enthusiastic. That worried her. Maura had seen enthusiasm. It tended to create dead brawns. But also, at the ripe old age of two hundred she had long since put excitement and enthusiasm behind her.

"It's just a training run," he was saying. Maura looked at him out of her introspection. "Oh, really," she said. "What makes you think that?"

"Well, I mean, look at the brief." He cocked his head. "Twelve pages of dithering that boils down to 'Go find somewhere where the Ichtons haven't been.' That'll take us about a day, especially with the new engines. . . ." He grinned at her. Or in her general direction, the way a blind person looks more or less toward the source of a sound.

Maura put aside her annoyance. They could teach you to look at a brain's column while at school, but some brawns never quite got it, preferring to treat the brain as a whole ship, rather than someone located.

"The question is," Ran said, "where will they send us after that?"

Maura chuckled at that. "Son, in this business, and these days especially, you learn not to look too far ahead. Just when did you graduate?"

"Four months ago, on the *Hawking*."

Maura sighed, but kept the sound to herself. A virgin brawn. What had she done to deserve this? But she was going to have to make the best of it. And if as he said, this mission was going to take less than no time, all the better. For longer-term problems . . . well, there was always divorce if things didn't work out. Or the Ichtons, who sometimes provided much more permanent separations.

She would not let them anesthetize her when they put the engines in. Maura had heard all the stories about the trauma of seeing yourself operated on, but she was not convinced. She took a nerve block, yes; she shut down the neural and bioneural transmissions to the parts of her that were involved, and then watched them open up the panels and slide the black boxes in.

They weren't really black boxes. They were shiny silver—shells, like hers, modules; everything installed in the drive compartments and sealed away, under ultra-clean conditions.

"There's someone here to see you, Maura," one of the engineers said during the installation.

She was reading just then, and didn't actually hear him. "Who is he? What does he want?" And how did she know it was a he?

"Says it's your brawn. Says he wants to see the engines go in."

Maura could think of several reactions to this, but suppressed most of them. "Tell him his security clearance isn't high enough," she said.

The technicians guffawed. "A bit sensitive about showing him our private parts, are we?"

Maura didn't reply. Maybe she was. Or maybe—? She didn't know what she thought, really. This was one of the newest technologies of Fleet, these jumper engines. Only the fastest scouts had them, and she was going to be one of the fastest, now. She was being seriously overengined for her size. They plainly meant for her to go a long, long way. How far? she wondered. And where? There was an awful lot to the galaxy. The thought of having Ran with her for who knew how many years—It was ironic to be the fastest thing on jets, and not be able to run away from your problems, because you were carrying them around inside you. . . .

They finished with her, and she watched them finish sealing her up—making the neoneural connections. Very gingerly she felt the new engines. They felt hard and shiny and cold yet. Very slowly the fingers of her probing slipped inside them, like a stiff glove. She worked the logic probes around, touching the engines' intricacies. The new cesium arsenide/cold helium circuitry was in now, that allowed the fast shunt of the Olympus engines to work the way they did. Where the usual neural current paths in the average engine felt like water running, this felt much different. Most peculiar. It had weight; it slipped in globules, like mercury, but moved faster than it should—squirted, almost—like something under pressure, at the molecular or subatomic level rather than any higher one. It was all very strange. A new feeling. . . . One was in serious danger of becoming enthusiastic about it. She set herself to doing system checks, and waited for Ran.

He started moving his things in the next morning. It was a very small collection, for weight's sake, as it always was—but very eclectic. He had hard books and solids and vids, and a couple of paintings, rather well done in the Neoimpressionist style; though small, as they needed to be for approval for on-ship transit.

"I can't wait to leave," he said. She knew, and it made her head hurt.

"Listen, Ran," she said. "Have you ever seen an Ichton?"

"The reconstruction? Yeah." He shook his head. "Nasty buggers, but we'll beat them."

"Yes, well," she said. "I just want you to be clear about something. If we run into any, we're not going to hang around."

This time he looked right at her column, with an expression of such shock that Maura almost laughed out loud. But she managed to restrain herself.

"What do you mean?" he said. "I saw the weapons they were installing in you!"

"They're mostly defensive," she said. "Haven't you read the briefings? Don't you know the kind of armaments the Ichton ships carry? We've got just enough to singe their tails with, and then we run away. So don't get any cute ideas."

"Wouldn't help me much if I did," Ran said. "You've got control of all the weaponry anyway."

At least he knew that much. "Your business is to stay alive," she said. "So is mine. We have more important things to do than fight. If we run, we run. That's life."

He didn't actively look sulky, but them was still an air of vague disappointment about him. He opened his month, then closed it again as if thinking better of something he had been about to say. "There anything I can bring you from stores?" he said. "Not that we'll be out there that long anyway. Just something to while the time away."

Maura had to chuckle. He had no idea how short this mission was going to be if he kept on in this vein. "I'm fine," she said, "but thank you for asking."

He went out and fetched another small carton with his spare uniforms in it, and a few other pieces of bric-a-brac. They genuinely were bric-a-brac; one of them was a small Staffordshire china dog, its paint well worn off it. "Where'd you find that?" she said, interested in spite of herself.

Ran laughed. "It was my mother's. She had it from her father . . . it's been passed down, oh, four or five generations now, I guess. The member of the family who's going farthest away always gets it. It's well traveled, this critter."

It looked it. Its paint was faded, and it had a faintly cross-eyed expression, like someone who's taken too many jumps too fast. "Amazing it hasn't been broken," Maura said.

"Most of us tend to keep it under our beds," said Ran.

"What? You don't put it out on a shelf and let it take its chances?"

Ran raised his eyebrows. "Crockery shouldn't take chances," he said. "People, though . . . that's another story." And he glanced at the column and walked away.

Maura swore softly to herself. Brawns! What was she going to have to do to this one to calm him down?

They left the next morning. Maura had been cautioned to put a lot of distance between herself and the *Hawking* before she jumped the first time. For my good, she had thought, or for theirs? It was well known what happened if a jump engine happened to malfunction . . . and the first time a brain used one, there had been accidents and miscalculations. . . . It was easy enough to understand. What happened when you suddenly had a new part of your brain installed that worked forty percent better and faster than the rest of it? There were sometimes mishmashes, problems with coordination. For a human being to move an arm or leg fifty percent faster might not make any difference, but when the motor control involved was running a matter-antimatter conversion engine, and the mix suddenly went south . . . well.

Ran was sitting in the chair in the control room, drumming his fingers on the arms of the chair, trying to control his excitement and nervousness, and doing very badly. "Have you had time to look over the navigation plan?" Maura said.

"I saw it three days ago. It's fairly straightforward. A hop-skip-and-jump setup: hop to the system, skip any planets not populated or showing signs of interference. Survey what's there, then move on to the next star."

"It's a fairly extensive list, wouldn't you say?" she said. "Forty star systems, with an option for forty more?"

"Piece of cake," he said. Somehow Maura had known he was going to say that.

"There's some in the galley," she murmured. "First jump. Five minutes, counting from—now. Do you have trouble with fast jumps?" she said.

He blinked. "I've only done it once. Didn't bother me much. It felt—" He shrugged. "Like going up in an elevator, actually. That pit-of-the-stomach feeling."

Maura had never been in an elevator, but she knew that pit-of-the-stomach feeling. The sudden, bizarre pressure all over the hull, where there couldn't be any pressure; the sense of not discontinuity, but of wrongness. That was the strangest thing about it. It was more a pang of conscience than anything else; there was a sense that it was morally wrong to be jumping. As if the laws of the universe were for the first time speaking and telling you directly that they were being violated, and they didn't like it. Maybe that was just a side effect of being in a shell—the tendency to perceive physics directly, instead of through the film of less-sensitive senses. "Well," she said, "then you won't mind this one. It's only forty light-years or so."

He gulped. Maura found it briefly satisfying . . . and then was ashamed of herself. There was no point in deriving enjoyment from the discomfort of her brawn, even if he was a total prat.

The engines built power. There was no sound of it. They were quite silent; no moving parts, not even any moving plasmas, remained in the engines. The antimatter mix was coming up to the correct richness. That was the secret of making these engines move smoothly, Maura had been told; not just dumping the masses together, but keeping the mix slow and low at first, then enriching it as you went along. George, of GB-33871, had told her that it was very similar to making a cream sauce. Add the active ingredient slowly, taste as you go along, heat gradually, not too fast so that it doesn't curdle. Slow and easy. . . . It'll be worth waiting for when it's done. George was a little strange, being about four hundred years old now; he would make jokes about being near the end of his service life. But he had survived a lot, and strange or not, his advice was worth listening to . . . even if he couldn't eat his own cooking.

Maura didn't say anything further, but sat there and watched Ran sweat, and counted the minutes down. *If only he knew that I hate this as much as he does. . . .*

They jumped, and found the first star, a little K0 with no name but a string of numbers and letters out of the catalog. There were three planets: two gas giants, and a third of Earth type.

Maura said nothing for a while, letting Ran get himself up and stalk around the cabin with the air of a man just released from prison. Trainees were only taken on the shorter jumps. Maura wondered if this one had finally gotten further into him than the pit of his stomach, after all. He looked haunted. "What news?" she said. She could easily have found out by using her own sensors, but you had to let a brawn do something.

He was leaning over the computer, looking at the readouts. "Infested," he said.

"How much?" They had been using percentages to talk about how much of the planet was domed-under. The Ichtons did not waste much. The strip-mining of old Earth was positively environmentally kind compared to the way the Ichtons used the planets that became theirs. Anything that could be termed a natural resource, however rare or common, was used. Everything was taken; mined, drilled, dug up, scalped off, and the proceeds shipped off to those domes to make . . . heaven knew what. The materials for more domes, Maura thought. This planet would have showed, to the human naked eye, a handsome blue-green ball; nothing strange about it. Unless you looked down to its southern hemisphere, and saw the blot that was not the color of earth or sea; the blot that under higher magnification could be shown to glitter balefully, like a many-faceted eye. A thousand domes, ten thousand, a million, packed together and expanding. The eye glittered at them.

Maura breathed out. "What percent?" she said again.

Ran was still looking at the readout screen. "About ten," he said. "There's a lot more undermining going on than shows at the moment. They're under all the seas contiguous to that continent, and spreading. Maybe they're trying not to attract too much attention here."

"Too late for that, then," Maura said. "Anything noticeable in or near the other planets? Orbital facilities?"

"Nothing."

"All right. Then we move on."

Ran went back to the couch and strapped himself down again, with an unhappy look. "That last jump—" Maura said.

"It was all right," said Ran, and finished his strapping. "Let's go."

"As you say," Maura said, and took the next jump without even bothering to count it down—fifty light-years, this time.

And she did it again, and four more times after that, and barely let him have long enough to stretch his legs in between. Each time they found the same infestation; sometimes lesser, sometimes greater. Ran was beginning to frown, and to look frazzled. After the twelfth, she said, "Are you sure you want to keep going?"

"Oh, yeah," he said. "Let's get this done."

For her own part, she was finding it very hard to be cool. She could see, as if it were with her own eyes, what he couldn't; the detail on those domes. There was always a sort of no-man's-land around the domed zones, protected by force-field from intrusion; a wide barrier, just dirt or rock. Very often, on the far side, there would be large or small groups of the indigenous species—just looking. Sometimes they were trying to attack—futilely, of course; sometimes doing nothing, just gazing in horror at the sudden inoperable cancer growing on their world. She wondered whether the numbers, the figures and statistics, called up anything in Ran's mind—any image of something real. She was familiar enough with his train of thought, anyway. Even if relatively young as brainships went, Maura knew what to expect. "Honeymoon syndrome," as it was somewhat derisively called in the corps, the actual opposite of a honeymoon—when two people who didn't know each other were thrown together to do highly dangerous and professional work, in a relationship that one way or another wound up being more intimate than many marriages.

She kept offering him chances to stop, but he wouldn't. Rolling up to the twentieth planet, she said to him, "Look. That's enough for one week."

"I want to keep at it," he said.

"I'm sure you do. But I for one want some rest, and I am not going any farther. You can get out and walk if you like."

"I just want to get this job done," he said.

Maura looked at him. Sensors picked up the elevated heartbeat. The sound of his EEG rattled against another sensor like pebbles shaken in a can. Agitated. Mustn't let him get into this state again. "Look," she said, "I'm sure you want to keep going. But we have more work to do."

He turned away from her, the color rising in his face. "It can't all be done in a week," she said, trying to be gentle.

"It can!" he said, wheeling on her. "It's only the tools that are ineffective. Not the mission. Not the goal." And he strode off toward his cabin.

She looked after him from another camera. I could lock his door, until we settle this. I could lock him out, as well as in. . . . But she let him go in and shut the door unhindered, and lie on his bed.

Maura didn't bother waiting for him to come out. She had her own business to take care of on this mission. She idly pulled a copy of his records, and ran her optical scanners over it.

The picture was much the same as the man she saw now. A picture of the parents: one dark-haired, one fair. The fair hair came down through his mother's side. One brother, also in the Fleet; lost, some time ago, at Balaclava. Several postmortem commendations—he apparently had been leader of a fighter squadron that had managed to take out several Ichton ships, before being destroyed. That was the pity of it; no speed or cunning mattered, when you were dealing with odds of fifty or a hundred to one. The Fleet might be more maneuverable than the Ichton ships, but there were always more of them, no matter how many of you went down fighting valiantly.

The lost brother . . . who knew what effect that would have on Ran? She thought of Loni. It had been a while since she had thought of her. They weren't sisters, really, but they had come into the brain facility at the same time; they had worked together and trained together, and played the games shell kids play together—chasing each other around the center at high speed and putting the lives of many at slight risk. They had had a good time together. Then they had both been commissioned as brainships. Loni had gone on in Fleet service after her payoff, and was last seen near the Rift. Her last communications were untroubled. But there had been reports of Ichton fleets out that way. No news ever came back, no wreckage. Nothing but silence where Loni had been.

Maura considered this bit of her history in conjunction with Ran's, and snorted to herself. Was some amateur shrink out there trying to do a good deed? The Med Psych people out at *Hawking* had been known to pull such stunts every now and then. Well, Maura was having none of it. There was nothing wrong with her.

Nothing that seeing Loni again wouldn't cure. . . .

There was of course no chance of that. Maura laughed hollowly at herself, not caring whether Ran heard her or not, and went back to her hobby.

She had been dabbling in code holography for a long time. It was very enjoyable to encode holograms of places that didn't really exist, or ones that did. That was a challenge, too—to engrave pictures of places she had seen pictures of, and compare them to the originals. Image processing without the image, that was all it was. A very basic sort of pastime for a brainship, but it pleased her.

She was doing an unabashed pastoral that had so far cost her several weeks labor; a not-very-subtle takeoff on some paintings she had seen dating back to Earth's seventeenth century. Rolling hillsides, green fields, hedgerows, various stock animals wandering about; nattily dressed young men and young women in long dresses and carrying frilly parasols, standing under trees and admiring the view. But the view was clearly not on Earth—it was the upcurving interior surface of a Dyson sphere, with the "afternoon" sun hanging up in the midst of it all.

She was working on the clouds in that sky, some hours later, when Ran woke up with a start. For amusement's sake, she put a copy of what she was working on up on the screen in the control room, so that he could see it. He didn't come into the control room for a long time. He made his breakfast first, and took a long while over it, before finally wandering in. There he stood, and looked at the picture. "Nice," he said.

Maura chuckled at him. "Thank you. How did you sleep?"

"Badly," he said. "Can we get started?"

"In a little while. I'm still running some system checks." This was not strictly true. There was one check she had left running all night—engine status—but she let it stop now.

"And how are the engines doing?"

He might be an annoyance, but he was an observant one. "Greenline optimum."

"But you weren't expecting them to be doing that."

"Young man," she said, "you will have the courtesy to ask me what I think, not tell me." When he merely raised his eyebrows at her, Maura said, "No, I didn't expect that. I expected—some slight hiccup, some change in the wave form. It's not as if these are standard components . . . or, rather, not as if you're hooking these components into a standardized system. There is one very idiosyncratic component." He nodded. "These engines tend to react one way with one brainship, another way with another."

"And you were expecting them to malfunction?"

"No, but to produce some idiosyncratic—" She sighed. "I don't know what. Are you about ready?"

"I have been for a while," he said.

They started out again. This time it was a longer series even than the last. They were almost halfway through the list by the time they were done, and nothing was working out the way Maura had planned. He was supposed to be weary and frazzled at this point; she was supposed to be cool and collected, and in control. But he got cooler as the days went by, and the planets—the ravaged shells—the percentages got higher and higher. She was getting frazzled. The sight of the species of many worlds, standing, staring across the no-man's-land; the sight of ocean creatures scrambling out of water and dying in the air, unable to deal with the alien presence that was changing their seas, polluting the water or drinking it dry. Fourteen planets, all complexed—all infected, from ten to thirty percent, sometimes more. Icecaps being mined off for their water, atmospheres being pumped away, pressurized, shipped out in cans; planetary crusts being mined straight down through the discontinuity layers for the liquid metal inside them.

They paused long over one planet. So much of its core had been mined out that there was now no sign of the robust magnetic fields that should have been there. Its rotation had slowed. Half of it was baking, half freezing, and a slow nutation was dragging the frozen side around for its turn, ice giving way to fire.

"We're all going to die," Maura heard herself say.

Ran's head snapped around. "What?"

"They're all going to die."

He looked at the viewscreen. This world was a watery one, better to look at than most; the damage wasn't visible. But the sensors clearly showed, under those oceans, the terrible changes in the temperature of the ocean floor, where Ichton drilling through the crust was exposing magma to the sea bottom, and the seas were slowly coming to a boil. Only the changing color at two or three points of the world, from a dark blue to a lighter one, betrayed that anything was happening at all. It was a very gradual change—you almost might not notice it, unless you were far enough out in space and could see the spots. Ominous, like the spots on Jupiter.

"Die?" Ran said. "Yes. Eventually, so we will."

Maura gulped and tried to turn her attention elsewhere, for the little time while Ran was completing his readings. There was really nowhere else to look. The dead black of space, or this dying blue. She peered around the ship here and there, glanced into his cabin . . . saw that the crockery dog was sitting on a shelf, on a pile of books. "Came out from under the bed, did he?" she said, trying desperately for levity.

"What?"

"The dog."

"I suppose we all have to come out sometime," Ran said.

They went on, through the weary day, and through another. On the morning of the fourth day in this series Maura could barely stand the sight of Ran; but he got up more energetic than ever, somberly eager to get about their work. They were almost through their list of star systems, anyway—there was that small consolation. No more than ten left to get through. . . . But Maura found herself dreading the next jump, even as Ran strapped himself in and waited for her to report herself ready.

I could plead engine trouble, she thought. *Except that I have this feeling he'd know there wasn't any. And I wouldn't give him the satisfaction of knowing I was having trouble carrying out this mission. . . . Besides, wasn't she a good member of the Fleet, always doing her duty without stint or shirk? What kind of chance would humanity and its allied species have against the Ichtons if everyone just quit working whenever they wanted to?*

"All set," she said.

They jumped. The jumps had been bothering Maura more and more over the past couple of days, while Ran sat there as unmoved as if he were watching an entertainment. It was not so much the physical sensation of the jump anymore, but the sure knowledge of what they would find on the other end of it. Maura prayed for uninhabited planets, for mistakes in the list—there had been a couple of these, and they had come out to find no planets around a star at all—but these were unmercifully few . . .

"Here we are," Ran said. She looked around, got a glimpse of the star, a ravening-hot blue B2, and scanned for its planets. Found three of them, gas giants, and the fourth, a barren rock swinging in close orbit: and the fifth—

Baleful, a single huge, gibbous eye, faceted, it glittered at her. There was no land to it, no sea, no icecap, no air. Nothing but the hard outline of glass and plex against naked space: a million million domes, overlaid on the corpse of a world, dry, empty, dead. . . .

She began to weep.

Ran was staring at her.

Maura didn't care. She moaned, and sobbed, and cried, and the inside of her hull rang with it. System alarms went off as her blood chemistry and EEG went askew; she ignored them. Ran sat and watched her column, and Maura spared only a second to wonder why he looked so horrified, yet still so calm—then lost herself in her grief again. *Death, nothing but death, that's all we'll find from here to the Core. We've watched this problem get worse and worse as we've come farther and farther up this arm of the galaxy. The Ichtons have left nothing but corpses from here to the heart of things. If we had hopes of settling anyone out this way, they're dead now. And what will happen when they finally come upon the Alliance worlds, and Earth?*

That was when more alarms started going off, and there was abruptly something to look at besides the poor husk of a planet that hung below them. Maura wished there weren't. She had to fight with her grief now, try to force it down. She thought she had had enough practice at that, but it was harder work than she thought. "What is it?" Ran was saying, up out of his seat now and looking really upset for the first time. "Maura, listen to me! What's happening?"

"Trouble," she said, and gulped, still looking for control. "Far perimeter."

"What is it?" Ran headed back for the control seat.

"Ichton fleet. What else, out here where there's nothing but us?" She paused, gulped again, straining her "eyes" out into the darkness. The traces were faint as yet.

"How many?" Ran said.

"Hard to tell. They're out at the far fringe. Could be a hundred—could be two." She reached a finger of probe back into the engines, feeling for their readiness. They were ready enough—She poked them again. There was a slight sluggishness about them—"Not now," she muttered. "Oh, not now, when you didn't show anything all the rest of the time!"

Ran watched her, then looked over at the small screen by the command chair. "Do they usually move that fast?" he said.

She glanced back at the Ichton fleet. "No, they don't!" she said. They were coming up much faster than usual, faster than she had ever seen in many engagements. "This is no time to act this way," she said to her engines, poking them again, more sharply, trying to jar that abnormal wave form out of existence. "Wake up!"

They came on-line, but not at the level of response she would have liked. "Shall I take gunnery?" Ran said.

Maura burst out laughing. "Against them? Here," she said, patching the controls for gunnery through to his console. "Do what you like. I'm leaving!"

And she ran. There was nothing decorous about it; she just ran. The problem was, the Ichton ships were running right up behind her. Second by second they slipped away from the fringes of her sensor perimeter, into prime-detail sensing range. There were a hundred fifty-four of them. They had been massed, originally, in their usual free-flight "pack" formation. They were spreading now, the first of three steps toward an englobement. Then after they englobed, they turned their weapons onto any unfortunate ship in the middle, and blew it away. Was this how Loni went? Maura thought. Likely enough. Caught all by herself, out in the rear end of nowhere—

Maura had no desire to stay around for such a party. But it began increasingly to look as if she was not going to be offered a choice. She went on standard evasive for a few minutes, changing course four, five times. Distantly, from Ran's cabin, came a muffled crash; she looked for a fraction of a second and saw the crockery dog lying on the floor in pieces. Too bad. . . . She had other worries. She was trying hard to give the Ichtons the impression of a ship running panicked and with no plan in force. The second wasn't difficult, since, distraught as she was, she had no plan. This situation had been in many a mission simulation, but the results had always been so hopeless that Maura had long since decided the best solution to an englobement was to be several parsecs to one side of it, and accelerating outward. She was in no position to do that; the Ichton left flank of the englobement group was reaching out toward her. Now she ran, just ran, channeling power to the engines, pushing them as hard as she could. And triggered the jump—

—and nothing happened—

She was so shocked, she couldn't even swear. Maura looked at Ran, but there was no help there: he was busy at the gunnery console, programming her few bombs for what looked like an optimum spread, a pitifully ineffective stroke against the force that was chasing them. The beam weapons wouldn't be much help, either. She flipped desperately into diagnostic mode, and her world filled up with numbers and figures. That suspicious wave form was missing now, missing completely—but at the same time, she couldn't jump. Don't tell me the thing was necessary to the engines' functions, there was nothing about that in the docs—! Maura began stepping down power to the jump engines, taking pressure off the systems she had been poking before, while at the same time pushing herself along at conventional boost, as fast as she could. Even without the new equipment I should be faster than any Ichton—

No one seemed to have told them that, however. They were gaining, and the righthand side of the englobement was catching up to her now. Another lobe coming in at twelve o'clock— Dimly she could sense Ran firing several of the beam weapons in chord: there was a strike on one of the Ichton ships "above" and behind them. Then another, and two ships of the hundred fifty-four puffed into vapor and vanished.

As if it's going to be much help—the globe was tightening around them. The beams lanced out again, and another ship vanished: one of the "coordinator" ships,

Maura suspected, for the lobe of Ichton ships "above" them began to fall back slightly from the others, and lost some of its coherence. "There!" Ran shouted.

It was the only chance she would get. Maura turned all her attention inward, ignored Ran and space and the Ichtons and their billions of dead; looked for that wave form, and when she couldn't find it, picked another and coaxed it, willed it, pulled it into the right shape. Down in the engines, something felt as if it turned over and started to wake up—

"Now! Maura, for God's sake, now!" She ignored him. Not ready yet—not ready—almost out of reset—

"*MAURA!*"

Her engines opened their eyes and looked back at her.

Reset—

As the righthand and lefthand arms of the restored englobement locked around her, Maura jumped, hard and high. The wrong feeling twisted her gut, harder than she had ever felt it.

They came out in clean space, empty of stars, or planets, or Ichtons.

For a few minutes Maura just drifted, and made no sound. Ran was looking at her in concern; she let him. Her navigational systems spent the time finding several Cepheid variables they recognized, and determining position from them. They were a long way from the Core.

"Maura?" Ran said at last.

She was almost too tired to answer him. And too frightened, and too sad, and too upset.

"What, Ran?" she said finally. It came out sounding more like a moan than anything else. And then, to her utter surprise, a joke occurred to her. "You're going to tell me we should get back to work on the rest of the list, huh?"

"No," Ran said. "We can go home now." He got up from the control chair, went over to the main console, and tapped at the console keyboard, just a few characters. "The mission's over."

The knowledge came on in the back of Maura's head, like a light. She gazed at it in horror and growing anger.

"You are from Psych," she whispered.

Ran nodded. "Personal Intervention," he said.

"A fardling shrink! So the whole new-kid act was just that. The tantrums, the nerves . . . and the engine malfunctions were your fault, then. . . ."

"Judiciously applied stress," Ran said, "is one of the best ways to produce a result. Striking at the heart of someone's strength. In your case, the engines . . . and your perceived ability to get out of any problem that came after you, or just generally 'rise above it.' Impair that, and all kinds of interesting issues come up to be handled. Like your detachment from your work, which has been increasing noticeably over the past few years."

"'You could have gotten us both killed!" she yelled.

"Of course," Ran said. "I was willing to take that chance, for both of us. Me, I'm expendable. But a dysfunctional brainship is worse than a dead one, in Fleet's opinion."

He got up from the console and walked back to his cabin. She stared at him as he went, shocked speechless for a moment. But only a moment. "Well, isn't that just fine!" she shouted after him, making her voice follow him down the hall by the speakers set there. "And what goddamned sonofabitch sent you here to do me over? What gives you the right—"

"No one sent me," Ran said. "You can't be 'sent' on a kill-or-cure. You volunteer."

She stared at him. Ran stood in his room and gave her camera pickup a crooked sort of smile. "You wouldn't make it easy for me, either," he said. "I could have done all this in virtual experience, if you'd let them knock you out to put the engines in. But no, you had to play it stoic. Typical of you, actually."

She fumed, but helplessly. That was the worst part of it. He was right. "Too much detachment," Ran said, "is a bad thing for brain or brawn. You get callous, you get uncaring, your reaction speed goes down, you get one or both of you killed. Why do you think Cecile left you? She saw what was coming, and didn't feel like getting killed. Fleet Psych noticed the problem. Decided to do something about it. The only question was what."

"So they sent you to freud me over," Maura said.

"Don't talk dirty. Who has time to freud people anymore? We need cures, not progress. For too much detachment, the cure is reattachment to the realities of the world, by the most violent means possible. The Ichtons seemed like a fair bet. Not combat with the enemy, by preference—that's only made you more detached, in the past. But rather, contact with their victims. Intensive contact, the worst that could be found. And when *Hawking* Defense let it be known that they had this mission waiting, well, you were the obvious choice."

"Two birds with one stone," Maura said sourly.

"Two birds," Ran said, "yes." He bent down to pick up one of the shards of the china dog, and turned it over in his hands. "As I said, we would have preferred to do this in virtual reality, controlling the circumstances more carefully."

"'Virtual,'" Maura scoffed. "Not much danger in that."

"Cures work there," Ran said. "But so does death. If you had died, so would I have. Just as if it were real."

He kept smiling that annoying smile at her. She wished she could say something that would wipe it off his face, that would let him know how upset she was, how she hurt. But then again. . . . how long had it been since she hurt, since anything hurt? There had to be something wrong with that. . . . "I suppose I should thank you," she said, "for risking your life for me."

"Don't bother practicing manners on me, Maura," Ran said. "You're much too angry to care about being polite at the moment. I would say rather that you're more concerned about seeming sane to other people, when you're none too sure yourself that you are. As for me, I was doing my job. So were you, both while we were out there, and all the times before I met you . . . while what you experienced was crippling you slowly. The Fleet takes care of its own, dead and alive. Even if sometimes the caretaking does annoy the shit out of them. So jump for *Hawking*, now, and get this information back where it will do someone some good. And then, after you've dropped me off, you go back out again and do what you have to do—taking care of yourself, now, as well as of your brawns. That'll be thanks enough for me. And now, with your permission, I'll start clearing my things out."

He had never asked her for permission for anything before. It was a little strange. Maura watched him start putting things away. I'll be glad to see the back of him, she thought.

All the same . . . I wonder what the next brawn will be like?

NO WIN

The meeting was short and the conclusion clear. They had fought over twenty Fleet actions, won almost every one of them, and saved over a dozen worlds, temporarily. They were also losing the war. There was no way that the *Hawking* and any number of Star Central allies would be able to stop the Ichtons using only military intervention. There certainly had been limited successes, thousands of Ichton ships destroyed at the cost of only a few dozen Fleet vessels lost. That wasn't enough. There were tens of thousands more and the Ichtons had infested so many worlds it was likely they were building warships faster than the Fleet and all their allies were destroying them.

Another solution had to be found. To do this a lot more had to be learned about the Ichtons. And they had to find these things out quickly, while there were still worlds in Star Central left unmolested, no matter what the cost or sacrifice necessary.

A TRANSMIGRATION OF SOUL
by Janet Morris

One minute, Sergeant Dresser missed his human body. The next, he didn't. Loss. Relief. Pain. Pleasure. Awkwardness. Dexterity. Confusion. Command.

Command. He must take command of his body. Of his mission. Of his emotions. Of his life.

But he couldn't. He was lost, twice lost, and deep in an alien jungle that fouled his feet and arms and dragged nearly invisible tendrils across his face, trying to scratch him and catch him.

Dresser was lost and alone. So alone. Barefoot and nearly naked. Exposed.

His breathing was too loud. His heartbeat was out of sync. His stride was uneven.

Where was everybody?

He thrashed before him with his arms, trying to beat back the jungle. He mustn't get caught here. Caught in a web of sticky stuff that would hold him forever. . . . Caught, and prey to the hairy carnivores of this stinking, rotting world.

If he could have managed it without falling, he would have run. But he couldn't run without falling, not in this weak light of an alien sun; not in this jungle so hungry to eat him. If he fell, something in the murk might jump out and wind him up in its arms or its leg or cocoon him in some viscous mass and he would be trapped.

Trapped until eaten. Trapped and struggling.

He was whistling in fear. He could hear the pathetic sound of it. The keening of his heart came up through his body and made an awful sound that was not the sound of a soldier.

Take command. Take control. The hairs on his head itched. He rubbed them against each other. . . .

He stopped short and stood there, as still as he could manage, wavering on his feet. Sergeant Dresser stood there, counting his arms. Two too many. His head itched.

Remember who you are. What you are.

Take command. Take control.

Dresser was a volunteer for a mission too terrible to be contemplated, not that there was any way out but to go on with it.

Remember what you aren't: a human being. Not anymore.

Breathing hard and listening to his own pulse that pounded so wrongly, he wanted to retch. But his head itched too much. And the sound of fearful whistling wouldn't stop.

Then he remembered that the hairs that itched weren't on his head: they were on his antennas. It was the itch of terror and it was nearly overwhelming. And the terrible squeak of fear, so paralyzing, a sound that might give him away, came from rubbing those antennas together.

He had to stop it. The sound of so much fear made him ashamed. The sound of it could give him away.

He was still a soldier, even if he was a bug soldier. He reached up with his combat knife and began hacking at his own antenna, sawing away at the base of his skull. The pain took a long time to run down into his brain, and . . .

. . . He had to stop the sound, before it brought all his enemies down on him . . .

The pain finally stopped him. Blood rushed into his eyes and made everything twice as dim and ominous.

His gut churned. He was bleeding. He could hardly see. He could barely smell. He couldn't hear the keening sound anymore, though.

That was something.

He dropped to his knees and hung there, on fours, staring at the knife in his hand. There was flesh on the knife. His flesh.

He had to get hold of himself. He needed his antenna; he needed every sensory clue he could get to help him maneuver this alien body through a twice-alien landscape not its own. He needed every edge he could get.

The knife edge glittered in his gray hand. Ugly hand. Alien hand. Bug hand. But a knife was a knife, all over the galaxy—maybe all over the universe. He needed the knife and he was willing to see it through faceted eyes as long as he could take comfort from having it in his hand.

And he needed the strong gray hand holding the knife. He needed to remember that he was a soldier. And he needed to smell his way home, if he still could.

Feel his way home. Stumble. Crawl if he had to. Wriggle through the loamy dirt with all its hidden threats and sweet/salty delicious smells. Find the group. Find himself.

Take control. Take command. He was a soldier. He was still that.

He had to remember who he was. What he was. He was Dresser, but he couldn't say that. Couldn't form the words. Couldn't really hear that way anymore. Couldn't make that sound. Not that sound.

So then, what did you do, when you were a bug and you had to find your way home?

Get up, that was what you did.

He was still a soldier. Take command. Take control.

He had to get up, before something dashed from the shadowy jungle and caught him in its jaws. He had to find the others. He had to get on with his mission.

He had a mission. One hell of a mission. The most important one of his life. Maybe the most important one of anybody's life.

It had cost enough in lives, to put him here.

He remembered a bit of combat, an exploding globe of force; a blue glow that both attracted and repelled him: home; the enemy. Home sign. Enemy spoor. Both and neither.

Jesus God, what had he let himself in for?

He was in the body of the enemy, shoehorned in here like a wrecked pilot punching out of a derelict vehicle in an escape pod.

But worse. There was no place to go home to, when you were a man in a bug suit.

Or a bug with a man in your head.

He shook his, and the antenna he'd hacked at twinged warningly.

He raised his head to the sky that must be up there somewhere and screamed his name as loud as he could.

Dresser! he wanted to shout. *Now you've done it, Sergeant Asshole. See where your macho bullshit got you this time?*

But nothing came out.

He tried again, as hard as he could, to bellow at the sky. Somewhere up there, his guys were waiting for his report. He had to take control. Take command.

Or was it the other way around?

He heard his own voice, screeching: *Greel.*

He screamed it three times and then had to drop his head to shake the blood from his eyes. Green blood. Green. Greel. Greel. Greel.

What the hell did it mean when you wanted to say your name and it came out sounding like that.

Greel.

Not even close. If his head didn't hurt so much, and if the blood wasn't still streaming over his face, he'd have banged his forehead on the ground.

Stupid fool. Why'd you volunteer? Huh, Dresser? Why?

Dresser couldn't remember why. He didn't care why. He wanted to check in with his controller. Hear his name. Have somebody validate him.

Maybe he was a bug with delusions of humanity.

But he knew better.

He was Sergeant Dresser. If he played his cards right, he'd come out of this war a hero. Somebody had said to him, a world away when he awoke in this body, "Your men are all right, Sergeant. So is your human self. Your memory will return in a few minutes."

Maybe he was still waiting for those minutes to pass. Maybe he was still in the experimental station.

No way. No such luck.

His mind wanted to hear him say that he was Sergeant Dresser, but he couldn't say that. He didn't have the lips for it.

What was in a name if you couldn't say it?

He was Greel, anyhow. He knew it. His body knew it. The name felt good along his entire length. It made his thorax warm and he felt, for the first time in this nightmare shadowscape, safe. Greel. Greel. Greel.

Mama come and get me. Brothers, gather 'round. Greel is here.

Alive. Safe. With stories to tell and a dark spot inside full of wisdom. Knowledge such as none have ever had. Feast with me, feast of my knowledge, and learn all of my stories if you can.

Dresser pushed himself to his feet and didn't realize he was licking his own blood from the knife until he began to chew a severed chunk of his antenna. Chew your own flesh.

Dresser's heart shriveled.

But the antenna was in his mouth.

It tasted good. It tasted of home and hearth and salts so precious that they'd heal any hurt.

He sucked at the knife until the blade was shiny because every drop of precious blood was in his happy mouth again. He examined the knife with his eyes and with his antenna, making sure it was spotless, perfectly clean.

Then he put the knife in its sheath on his belt and trudged on, feeling stronger. He held his head up, so that the blood didn't run into his eyes.

He knew he was leaving a trail for the carnivores that had overrun this place and destroyed the balance of nature here.

But he couldn't stop to worry about it. He had to find his unit. Take control. Take command.

He was a soldier. Lost or not, alone or not, he was still that. Both of his souls knew it. Both of his hearts were sick at the way he'd broadcast fear all around him.

He was disoriented, but that was no excuse for hacking himself up like that. You didn't try to kill yourself. You didn't maim yourself. You didn't weaken yourself or make yourself a target. Especially now, when the enemy was everywhere, lurking in a jungle of alien spirit on a planet only a fool would die to save.

All around. In the jungle, full of shadowy, creeping, choking growth and hiding vermin. In the huts of the carnivores that ate all the other food here. In their skies. And beyond. Even beyond the sky, enemies were hiding—stinking things with obscene desires and infectious ways.

Coming to get him.

He bolted. He ran unseeingly through the thick growth until his heart nearly burst.

When he stopped, bent nearly double in pain, he had no idea where he was in relation to the original bearing he'd taken.

He was doubly lost. Doubly afraid. And mortally alone.

Dresser didn't know how to stop the fear in his heart, but at least this time his new body wasn't broadcasting that fear by rubbing its antennas together.

One antenna was swollen, stiff and short and caked with blood.

So he'd stopped his new body from broadcasting that telltale fear. He'd win this war yet. Take control. Of his flesh, at least. Take command of his exoskeletal, six-limbed, horror-story self.

Do his mission. Get home. Get out of this despicable body and eat out on the war stories for years to come.

Sure he would. Tell Codrus how he'd been so freaked when they'd dropped him in the jungle that he'd hacked off one of his cloned antennas before he realized what he was doing.

And ate it. Funny how that made you feel better, when you were an Ichton on an alien world.

He was getting the hang of it. Sure he was. This place gave both of his minds the willies and was wrong to both sets of his senses, the remembered ones and the actual ones.

He'd give anything to see this world through human eyes. See the trees he knew were there. See the grass, so green, underfoot. See the local teddy-bear inhabitants for what they were, not as enemies. See the sky, blue with fleecy clouds, not gray and grainy and muzzy and dark.

So he missed being human. So what? If this had been an easy job, anybody could have done it. He had to find the nest, or whatever it was.

Find his target. Do the infiltration.

Find the group. Report to group leader. Section Leader Greel, reporting. . . .

Oh, man. This was harder than he'd thought it was going to be. He turned in place and his good antenna waved violently. The wounded one only twitched.

But he caught a directional telltale, a sound, a waft of homelike scent, of female musk and warm metal.

This was so damn bizarre, being down here this way. Harder than anybody'd thought it was going to be. Harder than anybody'd warned him it would be.

Being human was a piece of cake, next to being a three-meter tall soldier bug who'd lost his unit.

He reached up to brush the sweat out of his eyes and saw the ugly bug hand just as it swiped bug blood from his bug eyes.

This was one creepy-crawly mission, that was for sure.

But somehow he felt better, having sensed a new direction.

Finally, his limbs seemed to know how to behave. His head still hurt, so he carried it to one side, favoring the hacked-up antenna. Well, he had a war wound. Close contact with the enemy, he'd tell them when they asked. Lost his helmet that way, too. And his battle suit, along with most of his weapons, in life-and-death combat with one of the sluglike monster soldiers of the enemy. Escaping with his life had been a near thing.

Ha. That was the truth, in a way. Only he had to make sure they didn't realize that he'd brought the enemy back with him—that the enemy was within him, inside him, a part of him?

No, that wasn't quite right. Take command. Take control.

Whose bright idea was it to make an infiltration agent wear a cloned bug body, anyhow?

He couldn't imagine how he'd had so much trouble moving through the growth before. Now he was on the right track. His path was clearly marked.

Olfactory clues nearly sparkled before him. His four legs churned with a professional efficiency. He knew where he was going. He found a clear place without even thinking about it.

His antenna hurt. Some enemy had jumped him, after the battle. He'd been out picking up chunks of dead carnivore—as bad as the hairy things tasted, food could not be wasted.

He remembered. One of those slugs had come out of nowhere, shooting.

He touched his chest, remembering the pain, the blast overpressure his suit couldn't absorb or deflect.

One of those slugs had overpowered him. They were so slow-moving, they were hard to see when at rest. But this one hadn't been at rest. Greel had struggled, but it had nearly hacked him apart.

He remembered the terror. When it got him out of his suit it was going to eat him alive. It was peeling him as if he were a Meal, Ready to Eat.

He wanted to wipe the alien memories away. But they wouldn't go away.

And at the end of all the alien memories waited Dresser—the unpronounceable name, the alien identity—and the key to resolving all this confusion.

Dresser understood everything important. Take command, take control. Do the mission. Report back.

Almost everything important. He couldn't fathom how to find his way home, through the growth, to his cloned body's unit. . . .

Dresser felt as if he were coming up for air, breaking the surface of a dark deep pool.

For a moment intent sparkled like sunlight, mission overcame misery, and Dresser was fully in control of everything—except his limbs, his senses, and his body. Even the pain receded. It belonged to somebody else.

Then he sank back, inexorably, as if an undertow were pulling him down.

But he had no choice. He was drowning in unresolvable stimuli, in knowledge that wasn't his and impulses he couldn't sort.

This body had once belonged to someone named Greel who'd known how to use it—who *still* knew how to use it. Greel knew everything necessary for Dresser to survive. How come they hadn't warned Dresser about this, when he'd been briefed?

You couldn't be yourself *and* somebody else—especially when that somebody was as alien as this bug, whose body had its memories of personality genetically imprinted in its every fiber. You couldn't try to be a human in a bug suit and succeed well enough to survive.

But Dresser had to do it. Somehow. Or he'd die here.

And he didn't know what to do next. But Greel did.

Dresser couldn't see right. Greel saw just fine.

Why the hell hadn't somebody warned him that this was a suicide mission?

Darkness full of memories that Dresser couldn't sort lapped at him, threatening to close over his head like oily water. Dresser panicked.

Panic shut down every reasoned impulse, even doubt. It nearly shut down thought.

Take command. Take control.

Take . . . a step.

Move! Blindly, he rushed forward at hellish speed. He crashed onward, away from confusion, toward certainty.

Away from the alien presence in his head. Away from the ghost of madness.

Toward home. Toward help. Toward his own kind.

He kept his wounded head to one side, to ease the pain that was driving him home.

Greel knew the road back. He'd helped build it. The road was broad and clear of the mold that grew over this world so thickly.

He could nearly make out the encampment's identifying signature.

It was going to be good to be home—or, at least, among soldiers, among the force, among his own in their home away from home—among the people.

How did you lose your weapons, brother?

Say again the story of escaping from the slugs.

Tell the tale of capture, of being stripped of your suit, and of your triumph and escape.

Now, all together: Sing of valor; sing escape; sing return, brothers and sisters.

Mama, our valiant Greel is back with us!

Sister ReScree, your beloved section leader is full of wisdom, back again.

Under a canopy of blue, the people sat to feast the dead and sing. Around them were ranged the fierce-armed cars of their battle and the deep-dug engines of their home and hearth. And these space-going sons and daughters of a race of voyagers sang sweet songs: all who'd found a home here, on a distant shore, sang of where they'd been, and what they'd left behind. And brave songs, too, they sang: songs of a new home here to fight for and to win. All together, they raised their voices to praise their hundred heroes newly fallen, and one more.

In the place of honor, Greel sat, saying long songs of strife and woe, his mutilated antenna waving stiffly, his voice soft as a soldier's song always is when loss and death make victory partial and life so sweet.

He was witness to the battle, sole survivor. He had braved the clutches of an awful enemy and survived.

Sweet was the feast they gave him, of dead brothers and lost songs, sitting all around the sacrificial ground where a festival for heroes was laid.

Drink was there, and meat of long acquaintance. Everyone tasted the souls of dead friends and lost comrades, of lovers who could only be redeemed through ceremony.

Immortality was close, for the dead. It hung over the festival site and it sweetened the meat of the departed. It made every mouthful of lost heroes' flesh a sacrament to be savored before swallowing.

And in all the remembering of all the dead and gone, Greel took part with his lies and his split soul crying out for redemption. But Greel could not redeem his sins before the family, before the ancestors, before eternity.

The enemy was within him, looking out through his eyes. The enemy didn't understand how beautiful were the songs of dead heroes.

The enemy was repelled at the most sacred ritual. But the enemy dared not move or speak or do any obscene thing at all.

This was Greel's place, Greel's world, Greel's seat at the heroes' table.

All spread before them, on a long cloth of gold, were the hearts and eyes and heads and hands of a hundred departed heroes. On plates and dishes of copper lay the brains and tongues of the dead.

And as the extended family of the Four Hundredth Unit of Mother Sree feted its dead and ate their wise flesh, Dresser was only an obscene dream that had overcome Greel in his terrible ordeal.

There was no enemy within him. There was only the new life ahead, and the new struggles to come. There was only this moment to revere the dead and take them into every living soul.

The bodies of their heroes, whatever had been salvaged, were ready to eat. Lying in state.

Greel had come home just in time. Woe if he had not, and missed a chance to eat the flesh of his beloved group leader, of whose eye and of whose brain he was privileged to taste.

The stories of his beloved group leader took a long time to tell. Each who ate must stand and say his part. And when those tales had all been heard, then the heroes who'd died while Greel had lived must be eaten, too, and learned by all.

Learned by heart. Learned by hearth. Never forgotten, but becoming one with every other soul.

And Greel was honored, strengthened, and filled with wisdom he hadn't had before.

Singing and dancing and night-long prayers left every soul among them better. Even Greel's uncertain tale and the lies he told went into every heart with reverence.

But though he was ashamed, Greel could do no different. He had eaten of his group leader's eye, and now all eyes were on him.

His sister ReScree, who led the unit for Mama Sree, was watching him with soft and inviting looks.

He had survived a test of soul. He was group leader now.

Before him was the greater portion of his former group leader's brain, to prove it.

Such a gift was more than he deserved, and he tried to tell the true story of unworthiness, but Dresser stopped his story, froze him with fear.

Take command. Take control.

The threat was clear. The struggle inside him made him shiver with its onslaught. And he understood the warning for what it was. Let loose this evil phantom from inside him and he would die. Should he be found out, the thing within would die as well. Then what?

All the smells and sights, all these memories and gifts from brothers and sisters will be lost if you say wrong things. No one will eat of you. You will be desolate and forgotten, a rotting carcass left behind to become nothing forever.

No one could imagine the horror inside Greel. The worst horror anyone could comprehend was being Missing In Action, lost to the group, lost to the people, lost to history, to time itself.

And Greel would suffer all those punishments, if Dresser were a real presence in him, not just a figment of stress and sadness.

But Dresser was a figment. Must be. Would be. Around Greel were all his comrades. In his heart was a battle song. And in his veins ran the blood of heroes stretching back a million years.

Grief in Greel came pouring out in a long song. He ate all of the group leader that was left, and as he became one with his predecessor, he faced death.

Memory so clear that life was circumscribed by it. Fighting on, against terrible weapons. Facing heartless enemies and giving back no ground. Standing firm as melting armor and screaming troops assigned an agonizing doom.

And soft sweet breath of peace.

Death ran through him, as it must, and made him stronger. He faced it and faced it down, and sang a new song of rebirth on its far side while all his family sang harmony.

Too many fools had been less than they could, group leader used to say. So Greel said it now, and delight came among the gathered throng, laced with melancholy.

Everyone who missed their dead embraced, and the honored Sister ReScree eyed him, then got up on her four feet and keened.

He did, too.

Such an invitation was not to be denied. Such an honor was granted few soldiers. He would breed tonight, in the honor of the dead—of all the dead, but especially in honor of his beloved group leader, whose soul was now inside him.

He would be honored by the womb of ReScree, and all their eggs would be heroes of the blood.

He couldn't cry enough for joy, or sing enough for vengeance upon the slugs. The day would come when all his offspring would go forth from this sad ball of bloodied home, into the black universe, hunting the terrible, soulless slugs who'd put a memory in Greel's heart worse than a glittering blade.

The memory of Dresser would be among those memories that the children carried. Greel's get would have his every memory of violation more terrible than death.

If he had eaten an enemy honestly, and then found so awful a taint remaining in him, he might have found some way to refuse ReScree, despite the honor.

But this thing in his head had not come to him through hungry victory, or by way of the jaws of strife. And refusing would dishonor his dear departed group leader, and make an end to Group Leader Greel, whom he'd just become.

He wanted life too much. He wanted ReScree too much. So only the children would know what had truly happened to him, what was real and what was not.

And if the mighty Sister chose, then ReScree would eat his head when the breeding deed was done.

If she ate him, then the guilt inside him would be hers to bear.

If he pleased her, and she let him live as the previous group leader had lived, then he would be twice honored among the people. At least until the children hatched. And then?

Only time would tell.

History was only truth, and truth would come with time. When the children hatched, they would seek out slugs with all the hatred that Greel had in his heart for the phantom in his soul. They would make a crusade against this most hideous enemy that lodged within a hero's heart and hung there like a ghost.

If ghost this were, this Dresser in his mind, haunting him, then that ghost would beget ghost upon ghost in the minds of all the children of the people, for millennia.

He knew this truth to be unshakable, when ReScree's four legs brushed his own. He knew ecstasy such as only one in a thousand soldiers ever knows.

And he knew risk beyond reason, the helpless risk of passion, when only his mighty sister's forbearance would say if he would live to fight another day.

In such an embrace, even life was less than the chance to give the gift of life.

As his body grew great and strong, and then exploded in upon his nerves, and then spent itself within her, he understood all of life's mysteries.

It was a gift beyond all other gifts, an honor beyond comprehension, that Greel had come to this moment, where an open womb invited him to true immortality.

He closed one last time on his destiny, and waited, unable to move even an antenna, barely breathing.

If she chose to destroy him, now, to take his flesh and use his sustenance to nurture her brood with him, nature had decreed that he could not resist, even if he wished to try.

But Greel didn't wish to try. He was a soldier, but now he was a father of a generation. And he knew that there was no honor as great as this, which had come to him partly because of all he'd suffered.

So maybe the ghost of Dresser, the slug, would go into the children's souls and wreak havoc, and maybe not.

ReScree got up heavily, all his juice dripping out of her, and turned to face him. Her eyes were as bright as suns. Greel could see himself, his chin propped upon the ground, reflected back from the facets of those eyes: tiny Greels, as many as her womb would spawn, spent, helpless, a thousand husks of a thousand heroes waiting to live or die.

ReScree raised herself up on her hind legs. She pawed the air above him.

And she began to sing.

While ReScree was telling him all her stories, life was fuller than a great, round abdomen of promise, and he had no shame that he begged for his life and took it when she offered the favor.

After all, he had bred her, but now there were within him all the former group leaders who thought that they, too, could do as much. Each wanted their turn. Each promised life for memory of life, as long as Greel's strength held out.

Later, when the dawn was nearly come, the mighty Sister left him. Exhausted, shriveled, and nearly dead of ecstasy, Greel lay by himself out under the blue canopy of the encampment and stared at the sky beyond.

Had he done a dreadful thing? Was he dishonored? Was his taint a disease that would spread and make heroes into cowards?

Was he himself a coward?

Had he accepted honors under false pretenses? Had he begged for his life because life was full in him, yet, or because the alien thing in him had not the grace or the wisdom to know how to die?

Not even ReScree's passion had killed him. Was this a great moment in history, or the worst? Had he sown seeds of rebirth, or of his own people's destruction?

He'd soon find out. He was group leader, now. He'd found the strength of his predecessor and the strength of a hundred predecessors in the sacrificial meal. He'd survived through all, despite all. Despite even the ghost within him.

ReScree had looked upon his virile heroism and found him good. She had taken him to her, and granted him another season. So he was in some way worthy of the favors granted.

History is only what it is, never what it isn't. And Greel was now a father of history.

A father.

So few ever became one.

He wanted to sing, but he was spent and sad and full of doubts and fears once again. There was this creature in his head again. In his heart again. In his soul again.

Sergeant Dresser of the slugs.

And the creature wanted to destroy all his children.

This Dresser, this slug whose blood he could not remember sucking, whose flesh he could not remember eating, was all inside him like a fever.

This Dresser, this thing inside him, was more powerful even than his just-departed group leader, insistent and demanding, wanting him to get up and go out into the night, beyond the blue perimeter, where it could begin its evil work.

Unthinkably evil was that work. The thing called Dresser wanted to keep Group Leader Greel's children from being born. Even more horridly, it wanted to keep this planet from being cleaned, from being food, from being home.

It wanted everything that Greel did not want. It wanted slugs everywhere, triumphant slugs with the blood of the people on their shoes. It wanted a universe where only slugs lived.

Dresser wanted to exterminate the people altogether. Dresser was appalled and repelled by the most tender rituals of antiquity. Dresser didn't believe in immortality. Dresser only believed in death.

And the thing called Dresser that was lodged within Greel's heart and soul was strong. It wanted to use him for its perverse desires. It had been lying in wait for him, all this time.

Now it was clawing at him. Now he was weak. And it knew his every thought. It knew he was weak. It was chanting to itself, deep inside him.

Take command. Take control.

No.

Take command. Take control.

Greel had done that. He was group leader now. He had become a father.

Take command. Take control. Report, quick. Get out of here. Get up. Reconnoiter. Get into the transport. Into the power station. Into the ships. Check out the hardware. Find the weak spots. Warn the guys.

No.

Sleep.

No.

You're dead, you damned bug.

No. I am reborn.

You're dead. We grew you in a tank.

No. No. No.

Greel almost screeched in fear, then. But suddenly he couldn't move. He was imprisoned within himself.

His body was not his own.

Fear came up from his belly and tried to swallow him whole. He nearly lost his battle with Dresser, with the evil within him.

And he called for help, silently, within his heart and within his soul.

Help.

He couldn't give up. He couldn't find the strength to resist. He couldn't bring death home with him, he who had so recently brought life to his mighty sister.

He wanted, suddenly, to die. He wanted Dresser to die with him, then and there. He held his breath. He tried to stop his heart.

He would die before he destroyed his own children. He wished that ReScree would come back and find him. He could convince her to kill him, if he could not find the strength to stop his heart.

He slowed it. He counted its beats. Heart, stop. Body, die.

Die and take the evil with you.

Die, die . . . die . . . die . . .

Once more, he called for help.

And his group leader heard him, as group leader had always done. The group leader whose brain he had so recently eaten had been through many trials, including death. He did not want to die again, so soon. And before his time, another had fought on distant shores and eaten many alien minds and hearts, and died and died again. He, too, wanted to live, to fight this enemy and destroy this threat.

So all the ancients within Greel's stomach now rallied and, making their desires known, began to fight against this devil spirit.

The survival of all their children was at stake.

Life as the people knew it hung in the balance.

A society can do no greater good than provide for its children. Food for the children was here. Life for the children was here. This planet was a womb in the making.

They could not let it go. They could not pick up and leave. They could not do anything but fight for all their children and their children's children who would be born here and go from here among the stars.

Take command. Take control.

Help.

All the spirits of his ancestors spoke in Greel's heart. They harangued his weakened soul. Greel must fight the invader.

Take command. Take control.

Help.

He had special wisdom. He had the black wisdom of the enemy within him. ReScree had spared him to lead the fight.

And fight he would. Take command. Take control. Death was an earned reward, to be achieved in glory and heroic deeds.

Death was no refuge from the truth.

If Greel had not been possessed by the ghost of his enemy, he would have remembered that.

So Greel could not die now, in shame, fear, and anguish.

He must fight through to the end of the battle against this most horrid of enemies.

And when the fighting was done, and the worlds made safe for the children of the people, when every threat was countered and all the food was eaten— then the children would all remember the nature of the slug enemy that, by luck and fate, had become a story known to Greel.

Group Leader Greel had wisdom enough inside him, now, from feasting upon his kind, to understand that the spirit of Dresser was a gift, not a curse.

And though only his own heart and his own souls knew what special truth he had discovered, that truth would make the people strong enough to destroy this enemy forever. The children were at risk.

Therefore, Greel had no choice.

Despite his labors of the night, despite his captivity, despite his honors and his feasting, he pushed himself to his feet. Time to go inside. Get new armor. Appoint a new section leader in his place. Choose new weapons.

Time to plan a sortie against this enemy. As soon as the mourning time was done, they must strike.

Before the slugs struck them.

On his four feet, Greel wavered. A strange hesitation overtook him.

He managed three steps, then four, toward the open door of the unit home. Then he collapsed, exhausted.

His antenna ached beyond measure. His heart was sore. He had given his all in ReScree's embrace.

No matter how urgent, he could not begin his offensive now.

He had to sleep. He had to wait. He had to digest. To recover, if he could.

Sleep. Sleep.

But sleep was a shiny place of peace, and between him and it was all his guilt.

He wanted to go back to the ceremonial ground, but he couldn't move. He wanted to sort out the confusion in his head, but he couldn't sing. He wanted to find ReScree and warn her that perhaps the children might not be . . . as other children.

But he couldn't even do that.

He was too tired. He was too weak. He was too guilty that he had coupled with a sister when he knew he was infected with . . .

With what?

He wasn't sure. He was too tired to be sure of anything. Not even all the wisdom of the former group leaders within him could help him, now. His trials were beyond even their experience, and their souls were already merging with his.

Greel was too tired to do any more.

He was safe, back with his people. He needed to sleep, pass away the memories and let wisdom absorb itself into him. Sleep. This was the way of it after feasting the dead, and breeding the living. He couldn't put off his body's needs much longer.

He should have realized that he was too tired to do anything more.

When he was rested, this phantom would be nothing but a false memory.

There would be no doubt, when he was rested, that he was a group leader and greater than any group leader before him.

Had he not triumphed over the slug enemy? Escaped the hideous doom of a death without ceremony, without rebirth in the bodies of his peers?

Was he not, now, Group Leader Greel, consort of ReScree, and forgiven for risking himself to a nameless enemy grave?

He lay there, helpless and torn within himself, on the ground, until ReScree sent orderlies to help him inside.

He pretended to the sleep of heroes. It was due him. He'd forgotten, somehow, that eating the family brought a great lassitude.

The ceremony always made the great ones weak. That was why children were born from the frenzy, why breeding was ritualized at the time of death.

Otherwise, how would there be more people?

Otherwise, how would the best survive?

And if there was truly an evil within him, then that evil would be absorbed by the wisdom of time itself, as evil was always absorbed.

He didn't need to be afraid for his children.

Only for himself.

Dresser was so goddam happy to be out of the bug encampment that if he'd had lips, he'd have been whistling. The whole mission was a real screwup. A gut-twister. Enough to make you forget you'd volunteered.

He was angry at everything. He flailed at the thick jungle with his armor-plated arms and blasted helpless trees with his bug weapons as he drove his one-bug recon vehicle through the jungle at breakneck speed.

Whenever he depressed the firing stud on his bug-style armored jeep's control panel, little globes of force spat out of the muzzles of the two forward guns. The globes coming out of the barrels looked like bubble stuff fired from a giant air gun—until they began to do their lethal tricks.

He was carving a few new paths to nowhere, but the bugs wouldn't ask any questions he couldn't answer. And he had to get a handle on the capabilities of these bug weapons, if not an understanding of the science behind them. He couldn't make a damn thing out of bug science.

It wasn't easy to get at technical intel here. There were bug science types who were born with hardware affinities, and all sorts of inherited infor-mation from bug techs who'd come before them. But Greel wasn't one of them.

His body was a shooter's body. It thought like a soldier, not like a scientist or like an engineer. When something didn't work, it got a replacement unit from supply. At best, it could cannibalize pieces of fried equipment. . . .

Wrong word.

The bug orgy, complete with other bug friends as the main course of the dinner, still made him queasy when he thought about it.

Anyway, when he thought about stuff like that, this bug body got all excited and the bug personality started to give him trouble.

Greel, stay asleep. You need the rest. You fucked your little bug heart out, and now you've got to do a bit of on-site perimeter recon. After all, you're the specialist in slug—in human behavior.

You bet he was.

Greel's close encounter with the slugs—with the humans— had helped him get one mother of a promotion.

Dresser geared the jeep up into its fastest mode, and then had to back off before he crashed himself into a tree. These jeeps were wheelless, and they had two sets of clutches; four pedals in all.

He tried not to think about the details. When he didn't think about that extra pair of feet, they seemed to know what to do just fine. Muscle memory, he'd been told by the techs, would help him out at times like these.

And it did. His guys had done lots of homework. He wasn't blaming them. He was doing pretty good.

He steered the jeep toward the bug "road," and onto it.

He hoped to hell he knew where he was going. He was almost sure he did.

You had to give credit to the DR&E guys who thought up this mission. Directorate of Research and Engineering had really topped out on this one. All you had to do, to handle the normally delicate stuff of infiltration bug style, was sort of curl up in the back of your head and let the bug body do its thing.

This bug body came complete with an autopilot that did bug stuff whenever bug stuff was appropriate.

But how the hell was he going to report to his human handler about the bug fucking and what it mean to humanity, if those eggs hatched knowing as much about slugs—about humans—as Greel now knew?

Shit, what a mess.

Well, never mind. You can't explain what you can't explain. Nobody up on the ships was going to want to think about what would happen if the next generation of bugs hatched. The mission was to make certain that the next generation didn't hatch.

And never mind the bit about bug dinner parties with bug officers as the main course.

Well, promotions were always hard-won, in any man's army.

You had to do the best you could.

When Dresser got back to his human body he was going to parlay this mission into a couple pay-grades worth of special expertise.

Especially since the next generation of bug babies all had him as a father. Sort of.

No matter how hard he tried, he couldn't imagine how the hell he was going to get any of what had happened to him into a cogent report.

Luckily, his new status as Top Bug for this installation made him the last word in security for the area.

So he could probably make sure personally that none of those bug babies of his ever grew up to eat any of the teddy-bear natives of this planet. It was a nice planet once, before the bug infestation.

It could be a nice planet again. Would be a nice planet again.

Thanks to his bug girlfriend's decision not to eat him alive.

Jesus, how had he gotten into this?

And, more to the point, what kind of report could he give that would get him extracted, soonest?

Maybe he could say that ReScree might change her mind and eat him. If he got eaten, whoever chowed down on him would know everything he knew.

Talk about ways to blow a mission.

But nobody would believe him when he told them they'd better get him out of here because his very death could give—and every secret human capability and plan as well. They'd think he was making it up, grasping at straws, manufacturing excuses.

They'd think Dresser had lost his nerve.

Death was real different for slugs—for humans.

Maybe he was taking the wrong approach.

Maybe the new equipment he had with him would help. Command would want to examine all this stuff: the jeep, the weapons, the command and control hardware.

You couldn't really make much of it without his bug sensibilities.

Maybe he'd give a technical report, along with a request that he and this gear be extracted together so he could show them how it worked, back home.

On that ship. Not home. "Home" was bug-think. The bugs couldn't go home, once they'd left a place. They made one interspatial journey, one landfall, and that was it. They had to make a home wherever they ended up. Must be a lot of bug colonization ships that never found a landfall as good as this one. When that happened, they just ate each other and fucked their brains out until they all died of lack of life support.

So was the history of the people. So was the fortune of the Hundredth Mother and her Unit, to have found such a fertile, food-bearing home.

Here they'd stay until a new generation could be launched to the stars from this home. . . .

Dresser shook his head so hard in his helmet that his wounded antenna twinged.

Shit, this bug-think had to be controlled. He had to find a way to control it. Otherwise, Greel would come awake and then there'd be trouble.

Let the bugger sleep.

Ha.

But it wasn't funny. He couldn't do this mission without the bug expertise that came with this body. Had they known, back on the *Stephen Hawking*, that the body would come with an inboard intelligence as well as with operating instructions? Known and not bothered to tell him?

Or was Dresser just the luckiest sonofabitch this side of *Scout Boat 781*, his old command?

Whatever the truth, Dresser wanted to be extracted, and fast. He could give them more relevant data than they'd ever dreamed he'd find out.

Troop strength. Site reports. Logistics. Battle plans. Long-term strategy. Doctrine. Order of battle.

You name it, Greel knew it.

And there was no use wasting all this critical intel dithering around on a standard infiltration mission. . . .

Jesus, they hadn't known squat, shipboard.

The realization broke over Dresser so suddenly he almost veered off the road and hit a tree. If they'd known what he knew, up there, they'd never have sent him down here in the first place.

They'd have kept this Greel body up there and interrogated it until it died of stress or its own will.

But they didn't know anything about the people. They hadn't known anything about Greel.

They couldn't have known. Dresser started the jeep again: rest right rear foot on pedal. Push down on button with right front foot. Stomp bar's left side with left front foot. Pump with left rear foot until angle relative to ground is achieved. . . . Piece of cake.

They couldn't have known, up on the ship, what kind of bug body they had. They didn't know a section leader from an orderly. They still didn't know what it meant to have your infiltrator become an agent of influence.

Shit, if they knew, maybe they wouldn't let him come in, after all.

Maybe they'd keep him down here, hardware or no hardware. He could read the compass directions of the bug world, now, and translate them into his own with hardly a second thought. He'd better figure this out, fast. He was almost at the coordinates where the communicator was secreted, and he didn't want to draw attention to the site by spending too long there.

If the real advantage in this war is understanding the enemy power source and technology, so that we can counter the enemy's weapons, then they'll let me come in.

If they decide the advantage is in understanding enemy psychology and having an ear in the planning meetings, then I'm stuck here for the duration.

Dresser really wanted to be able to make a case for the former. It was human-think to expect to learn about bug tactics and throw a monkey wrench into enemy strategy by infiltrating the bugs' planning sessions.

The enemy's senior war planners were mostly dead and living in the back-brains of their descendants, anyhow.

You couldn't really skew the family's thinking. The people had no choice but to stay here, to live here and die here. They couldn't retreat. They had no way off the planet once they'd made landfall. They'd cannibalized their interstellar vehicles to make the systems they used to chew up these planets.

They'd stay here until there were enough young bugs to do the work, and then they'd start rebuilding a spacefaring capability, using up the planetary resources to fuel the expansion.

When they were done, the new generation would be starborne, thousands upon thousands of them. But the cycle was nowhere near that stage.

They were digging in, still in colonization stage. And so you had to eradicate them. . . .

Dresser started to feel sick. The dreaded psychic undertow began tugging at him. He could barely see. Barely control his limbs.

Don't be scared, Greel. Go back to sleep. Everything's fine.

He let memories wash over him of vast clouds of colony ships leaving a used-up world. He stopped the jeep as the memories overwhelmed real-time stimuli. He put his head on his arm and concentrated on maintaining control.

Take command. Take control.

When the memories subsided, he resumed driving toward his contact coordinates.

Ol' Greel had the clout to come out here, alone, with all the newest bug hardware. It was a lot easier to control the bug body when it wasn't afraid. Originally, it had been naked, afraid that some snake or anteater or teddy bear would come out of the jungle and eat it.

The bugs were real picky about how they died.

Now that he had to frame his report, he needed to be very careful not to make Greel afraid that he'd eradicate Greel's offspring—their offspring. Dresser began trying to feel parental about the eggs.

It wasn't easy. He wasn't the guy for this part of the mission. They should have used a psychologist. Or a xenobiologist. He was just a soldier. A shooter.

But maybe that was what he and the bug had in common. This bug, no matter how high he'd come in his hierarchy, was still a soldier.

And the trouble with cohabiting a body with another soldier was that soldiers were tough, disciplined, and resourceful.

They knew that some things were worth the ultimate sacrifice.

Dresser had one advantage over the bug body and its innate intelligence: he didn't give a damn how he died. He didn't care about the disposition of this carcass, or any carcass he might end up inhabiting, including his own.

Dead was dead, to Dresser.

So when he got to the contact point, he didn't flap because he couldn't find the APOT transceiver right away. He wanted to give his report, you bet.

But if he couldn't, he was willing to wait and try again. Or kill himself and his bug body if he thought that was the only way to protect what he'd already gained on this mission.

And he'd gained plenty, he thought, rummaging around in the undergrowth for the transceiver. But maybe not enough to die for. He just needed to keep the bug body under control by letting it know that he'd kill it where nobody would ever find it, if it gave him any shit while he was trying to make his report. Kill it where nobody'd ever find it to eat it. Kill it where everything it knew would die with it. Forever.

It didn't want to die alone.

He sympathized with it, but not enough to be afraid to crawl around on the ground. The bug body was having its equivalent of the heebie-jeebies, down on all sixes in the bush: it had a hereditary fear of spiders, snakes, and most furred mammals.

Even in its suit, it was beginning to drool a brown fluid from its anus: when it was this tired, it couldn't control its bowels if it was afraid.

You had to ignore the stuff you couldn't control.

You just kept your mission in your mind. You just kept doing the job.

Eventually, you were supposed to win that way.

Only sometimes, you didn't.

Where was the damned communicator, anyhow?

When he found it, he was nearly weak with relief.

It had an inboard autotranslator, thank God.

He sat there in the grass and burst out the first identifying transmission.

It seemed to take forever to get a response from the *Hawking*.

When he got it, it made him want to cry.

Nobody was buying his story.

"But I'm telling you, you ought to extract me and this bug buggy I got here. I got weapons. I got intel. I got everything you need."

"No way," came the response. "Not if what you say about your infiltration is true."

What had he said? He didn't remember saying anything.

"What do you mean?" he chattered in bug speak, and the machine translated.

Had he blanked out? What the hell had he said?

"Confirm," said the voice from his ship, "that you're group leader of the Hundredth Unit, that you're in the planning sessions, that you're able to call strikes and plan incursions and determine force mix."

"Confirmed," he admitted. He hadn't meant to tell them so much. He remembered now what he'd said. But he'd been light-headed when he'd said it, giddy with contact, trying to make them see reason. . . . He'd just been trying to explain why they ought to bring him in. Bring him back aboard ship.

Bring him. . . .

"You just get next to that big female and stay there," the voice told him. "We don't want to rock the boat. Keep up the good work. *Hawking*, out."

All he could hear was static.

He wanted to cry, but these eyes couldn't. He wanted to laugh, but he had no lips.

The alien body was already up off the ground, heading back toward the safety of its jeep.

He was hopping up into it before he realized that he was singing a soft, happy song of parenthood, of home, and hearth, and children.

BATTLESTATION: VANGUARD

Dedicated with thanks to
Jim Baen
who used to work with the Fleet
and our newest crewperson, Katherine.

PROLOGUE

Fleet battlestation *Stephen Hawking* had been in action close to three years, fighting a lonely battle against the predatory Ichtons. It had lost nearly half the warships assigned to it—destroyed or too badly damaged to carry on the fight. Morale had taken a severe blow right at the start, when the battlestation had arrived only a few weeks too late to prevent the annihilation of one of the races they were supporting. Then, the allies' defeat in the Battle of Gerson, and the subsequent loss of the Gerson home world, had shown them just how overwhelming the task ahead of *Hawking* was.

Fleeing from Gerson and gathering her resources, the *Hawking* prowled between the stars, avoiding contact with the major Ichton fleets. The damage inflicted in the Battle of Gerson had made it clear to everyone on board just how vulnerable their position was at the far end of a supply line two hundred thousand light-years long. While the Fleet personnel had volunteered for the mission of saving the three worlds of the races whose representatives had traveled so far to ask for help, not everyone shared their sense of dedication to the mission. Even the surviving races in the Core preferred to spend their limited resources defending their own planets, rather than rallying around the battlestation.

Likewise, many of the merchants whose companies had subsidized the building of the *Hawking* were preparing reports recommending that they cut their losses. In practice, this meant abandoning the battlestation and fleeing for safety, even though the journey to the nearest Alliance world, three months away at top speed, was nearly as risky as staying to face the Ichtons. Already a few of the more timid Indie merchant ships had been gone suspiciously long without returning for fuel or repairs. It was a toss-up whether they had fallen prey to the enemy, or were burning up the parsecs in a headlong flight back to the Alliance.

The survivors manning the *Hawking* had good reason to feel vulnerable. Skirmishing with the Ichtons went on constantly. The buglike enemy had come close to destroying the *Hawking* once already. None of the promised reinforcements had appeared; they could be months away, if indeed the notoriously stingy Alliance Senate hadn't already decided to withdraw support from an apparently failing campaign so far from home.

With morale so low, it was no surprise that a few of those who had been attracted to the mission by the promise of quick riches turned elsewhere in hopes of guaranteeing their own survival.

DEADFALL
by Scott MacMillan

"Payday," Harvey grumbled to himself. "You line up for almost a half hour, then you stick your pay card in a slot in the wall, and guess what?" He pressed a button marked "Adjust" to the right of the small screen. "After this thing gets through deducting what you've spent, you're lucky if you've got enough credits left for a six-pack."

The small screen went blank for a moment, then flashed Harvey's ID on the screen.

KIMMELMAN, HARVEY JOHN.

Harvey pressed the button marked "Yes."

ENTER PERSONAL IDENTIFICATION NUMBER.

Harvey tapped in his six-digit number, waited a few seconds, and pressed the button marked "Enter."

ONE MOMENT PLEASE.

Although the liquid circuitry of the machine rendered it totally silent, Harvey liked to imagine that from somewhere behind the polished stainless-steel walls he could hear the whir and click of small gears meshing in engagement as the central banking and finance computer debited his Earned Credits Account.

KIMMELMAN, HARVEY JOHN. The screen seemed to darken slightly as if it were scowling at some sort of economic male-factor.

ECA AUDIT SHOWS SIGNIFICANT DEFICIT.

"Great," Harvey snorted. "Just great."

PAY CARD RESTRICTED TO ESSENTIAL PURCHASES ONLY FOR NEXT 24 PAY PERIODS.

Twenty-four pay periods . . . "Jeez," Harvey groaned, "that can't be right."

"Got a problem, amigo?" The man in the dark blue boiler suit standing behind Harvey sounded mildly concerned.

"I'll say I've got a problem," Harvey answered. "This machine is all screwed up. It says I'm two years over my credit limit."

"Well, are you?" the man asked.

"Hell, no. I couldn't be more than maybe two or three days over at the most." Harvey scowled at the small screen.

PLEASE REMOVE YOUR CARD.

"You haven't loaned anybody your card, have you?" the man asked.

"No," Harvey lied. "I haven't." *Except for that bimbo up on Dark Green Ten,* he thought. *If she . . .*

"Well then, it's probably this pay station," the man in the boiler suit said, derailing Harvey's train of thought. "All kinds of crap contaminating the circuitry down here in Violet One and Two." He put his own card in the machine and tapped in his code as he spoke. "Look," he said, pointing to the screen. "The damn thing shows me having way more pay credits than I should."

"That's great for you," Harvey said. "But I'm still busted until I can get up to Twelve deck next month and sort this out with someone in Finance."

The man in the boiler suit gave Harvey a wicked grin. "How much you need to hold you over till then?"

"Huh?" Harvey asked, a little slow on the uptake.

"Look. I've got more than enough 'extra' pay credits here to cover anything I'll need for the next month. So why don't I just transfer some of them into your Additional Credit Account? You can then transfer them to some of the clubs on Dark Green Ten and enjoy yourself next time you're heading up north." He gestured toward the overhead deck with his index finger. "Come on"—he gave Harvey a conspiratorial grin—"my treat."

Harvey thought it over for about two tenths of a second. Since it was a simple transfer from one account to another, there was no way he could get into any trouble with Finance or the Internal Security Unit.

"Thanks," Harvey said, slipping his pay card into the slot marked "Transfers" on the wall next to the screen.

"Okay . . . now we press a couple of magic buttons"—the man's fingers tapped out a coded response on the keypad—"and your card gets credited with an extra two pay periods." The Pay Link machine began digesting both cards.

"So, what do you do down here in the T decks?" the man asked as the machine transferred the funds.

"I'm a ballastician," Harvey said with a serious look.

"Ballistician?" the man asked, not sure that he'd heard correctly.

"Yeah." Harvey grinned. "I move ballast around to keep the station trimmed. It's important to keep everything evenly dispersed down here in the south pole, otherwise the *Hawking* would wobble on its axis. That'd screw up the gravity, mess up the gunners' aim, and spill that high-priced booze up in the Green Zone."

The man in the boiler suit laughed at Harvey's joke as he withdrew both cards from the slots in the wall.

"Careful where you point this, amigo. It's loaded," he said, handing back Harvey's card. "See you around."

With a brief wave he turned away from the machine and headed down the gangway to a freight belt. Grabbing one of the handles he stepped onto the freight platform and rode the belt up to an intermediate freight deck and vanished between the rows of neatly stacked containers.

Harvey turned back to the Pay Link and inserted his card in the slot.

"Jesus!" he half gasped. "This is a small fortune." The two pay periods that had been logged into the credit memory of his card represented more than eight of his own pay periods. Whatever the guy in the blue boiler suit did, it sure paid a hell of a lot better than running a forklift down at the south pole.

Harvey took his pay card out of the machine and stood there for a few minutes, absentmindedly tapping it on his thumbnail. In less than five minutes he'd gone from busted to flush, courtesy of . . .

Harvey realized that he didn't know his benefactor's name. He put the plastic card back in his wallet and headed over to his forklift, wondering if maybe he shouldn't have followed his mother's advice: "Never take money from strangers." Shrugging then, he stuffed his wallet into his back pocket and climbed aboard his forklift.

Pressing the starter button, he made a series of mechanical growling noises as the unit rose silently from the polished floor on its pale violet tractor beam. Then he made a sound that he imagined resembled the crunch of shifting gears as he headed back to the freight bays on Violet Four deck.

The *Stephen Hawking* carried several thousand megatons of cargo in her holds on Nineteen and Twenty decks. Foodstuffs, toilet paper, and a host of other nondurable items were stacked and racked beside trade goods from other planets, surplus military hardware, and contraband items confiscated from the occasional tramp freighter that had been unsuccessful in running the Alliance trade monopoly blockade. As the nondurables were consumed by the ten thousand-strong crew, Harvey Kimmelman and his forklift raced around the hold, constantly shifting containers from one side of the ship in the other in order to keep the giant man-made planet rotating smoothly around its central axis. The work was not particularly demanding, but Harvey enjoyed it.

Harvey spent the next three or four days in silent apprehension as he waited for the Central Finance Records Division to discover their error and track down all of the extra pay credits that had been downloaded onto his pay card. But as the days slid into weeks and no one from Internal Security came to question Harvey, he began to realize (or at any rate believe, which in his case was just as good) that somehow the computer that did the continuous credit audit somewhere up on one of the L decks hadn't discovered the error. When a month had passed and still no security men came to drag him away in the dead of night, Harvey was convinced that he'd avoided detection.

To Harvey, that meant only one thing. In ten days, when his periodic recreational leave came up, he was going to Green One and have a real blowout. And if at all possible, he was going to find Frosty Hooters and ask her to explain how the six-pack of joy juice she used his card to buy ended up costing him two years' pay. Once he'd settled things with Frosty, he might even treat himself to a few days in one of the orgasmatrons. . . .

The digital readout on the control panel of Harvey's forklift interrupted his idle speculation concerning autoerotic stimulation on Green Seven: *15MK: T7.021.690.*

"Okay," he said through clenched teeth. "Fifteen thousand kilos to shift. All in a day's work for"—his voice produced an instant echo effect—"Harvey Kimmelman-man-man-man, Space Ranger!" He provided a few more sound effects as his forklift silently glided between the neatly stacked rows of color-coded freight containers.

As he reached sector 021.690 on T7 deck, Harvey lowered his infrared scan shield, focusing its laser beam on the bar coded manifest that occupied the lower right-hand corner of the nearest container.

> OWNER: Griewe Galactic Novelties
> CONTENTS: Entertainment Chips
> PRODUCT COUNT: 192K Gross
> BALLAST WEIGHT: .0175M ton

Turning the control on the dash of the forklift, Harvey adjusted his scanner to read only ballast weights as he cruised along looking for a heavier container.

"Come on," he said as he moved along the aisles. "Gimme a nice heavy combat vehicle or maybe a bunch of heat-shield tiles. Something *real* heavy." His voice dropped two octaves on the word "heavy." "Anything," he said, "as long as we find it before the cargo computer tells me what to start moving."

The cargo computer was faster, and inside of ten minutes had not only located the precise items to be moved but had told Harvey where to put them. Sixteen hours later Harvey made his way back to the work sector to get the last of the containers. As he positioned the forklift to make maximum use of his tractor beam, he heard giggling coming from behind him.

Swiveling around in his seat, Harvey saw the silhouette of a woman standing on one of the containers, her figure a seductive dark shape in front of the high-intensity work lights. Her hands rested on her hips, and her shapely legs were spread wide, the intense backlighting filtering through her gossamer dress.

Harvey tried to shield his eyes, to get a better look at the girl. She giggled again.

"Harvey Kimmelman!" The voice was warm and inviting. "Imagine seeing you here!"

Squinting into the light Harvey couldn't make out her face, but he did recognize the voice.

"Frosty?" he asked in a tentative tone. "Is that you up there?"

"You remembered!" she cooed, jumping down onto the deck. "How sweet."

Standing next to his forklift, Harvey could see the delicate features of her face, the gentle curve of her throat, and the firm roundness of . . .

"Sure I remembered," he said, forcing himself to look into her eyes. "A man's not apt to forget a beautiful girl like you. Especially after the time we had up on Green Ten," and he thought, *Especially after you took my pay card and ran up two years' worth of credits buying a six-pack.* Harvey suppressed an overwhelming urge to climb off the forklift and throttle her.

"So, did you come to visit?" Frosty asked, puckering her cherubic lips into a delicious smile.

"No," another voice said. "He's working. Isn't that right, Harvey?"

Harvey turned and saw a man in a blue boiler suit step from the shadows of the stacked freight containers.

"Long time, no see, huh?" he said as he walked over to where Frosty Hooters stood, still smiling vacantly up at Harvey.

"Yeah, I guess so," Harvey said, slowly recognizing the man in the boiler suit as his benefactor at the Pay Link machine.

The man slid his arm around Frosty's waist and gave her a little kiss on the cheek. "Frosty, could you leave us alone for a few minutes? I've got something I want to discuss with Harvey," he said.

"Sure, Forsythe," she said, kissing him on the lips. "Bye, Harvey." She waved. "Hope to see you again sometime." Turning, she vanished into one of the aisles between the stacked freight containers.

Despite his anger toward her, Harvey felt a twinge of jealousy tug at him somewhere behind his belt buckle. Forsythe watched Frosty vanish between the containers and, when he was sure she was out of earshot, turned back to Harvey.

"Well, amigo, I suppose you're more than just a little curious about what's going on." He gave Harvey the same grin he had used back at the Pay Link more than a month ago.

"Yeah, you could say I'm curious," Harvey replied. "I don't get too many visitors down here in the cargo hold."

"Harvey," Forsythe said through a public-relations smile, "I know I can trust you, so I'm going to let you in on a little secret." He walked over to the side of the forklift. "Can you switch that thing off for, say, half an hour?"

Something told Harvey he shouldn't do it, but he said, "Sure," and almost involuntarily switched off his machine.

"Good. Now, hop down and come with me," Forsythe said with a conspiratorial grin.

Harvey did as he was told and followed Forsythe between two rows of neatly stacked containers.

"If you don't mind, do you suppose you could fill me in on what you and Frosty are doing down here?" Harvey said before they had gone more than a few meters into the labyrinth of stacked freight.

"Not at all," Forsythe said. "We work down here."

"Bullshit! You don't work cargo." Harvey stopped in his tracks and grabbed Forsythe by the arm. "So what are you doing here?"

"Easy, amigo." Forsythe brushed Harvey's hand off his arm. "I didn't say I worked in cargo."

"Oh, yeah? Then what do you do?" Harvey asked in a voice like old leather.

"I guess you could call me a packager. I take ideas, people, concepts, and put them together in such a way everybody walks away smiling." He grinned at Harvey. "Even you, amigo. I'll have a smile on your face in five minutes flat."

"How so?" Harvey asked, not sure whether to follow along with Forsythe or head back to the forklift.

"Simple. Just walk down to the end of this row of containers and turn left. You'll like it. I promise." Forsythe gestured down the corridor formed by the dully gleaming containers.

Harvey shrugged, and walked the hundred or so meters to the end of the stack of containers. When he reached the end he stopped and looked back at Forsythe, who waved.

"Go on," he shouted. "Go on."

Harvey turned left and froze in his tracks. There, not more than ten feet in front of him, was Frosty Hooters, in all of her pagan, transgalactic, naked glory.

"Hi, Harvey," she said. Then crooking her finger, she beckoned him to follow her as she turned and scampered down the narrow aisle between the containers.

"I told you I'd make you smile."

Forsythe's voice made Harvey jump.

"Holy crocodiles!" Harvey exclaimed. "What's going on here?"

"Come on." Forsythe sounded like he was speaking to a confused child. "I'll show you." Taking Harvey by the arm he led him down the aisle to a dark green container. As the two men approached the end of the container it swung inward, revealing a hidden entrance.

"In here," Forsythe said.

"Why?"

"Trust me. I put a smile on your face, didn't I?" Forsythe gently tugged Harvey toward the opening, and Harvey reluctantly followed him in.

The door of the container hissed shut with a metallic click, and for a few moments the men were wrapped in total darkness. Then a soft blue light slowly filled the interior, changing in hue from a pale azure to a rich warm violet. Harvey could feel his skin prickle as the light increased in intensity.

"What the hell?" Harvey said as his skin began to tingle.

"Relax," Forsythe said. "Just a little decontamination, that's all." He nudged Harvey in the ribs with his elbow. "Gotta be clean for the ladies."

The door at the other end of the container opened and Forsythe led Harvey into the chrome-plated lobby of a deep-space sin bin.

For a moment Harvey was stunned by the gleaming black walls, the white tables, and the red patent-leather divans. Jaw slack and eyes wide with amazement, he tried to take it all in: the hot, glowing colors of the neon lights, the soft-as-moss carpet beneath his feet, and the almost-sensual musky smell of the air.

Forsythe threw himself down on one of the divans and signaled to one of the girls at the bar.

"Drink?"

Forsythe's voice brought Harvey back to semi-consciousness.

"Huh? Yeah, yeah, sure. A beer."

Harvey gawked as a well-muscled Telluran at the bar smoothed her delicate pink fur while the bartender poured out their drinks. Picking up a small tray with the beer and Forsythe's lemon vodka on it, she walked over to where the two men sat.

"Here you are, boys," she said with a voice that sounded like the purr of a satin cat. Her fur stood out provocatively as she handed Harvey his drink. "Just let me know if you want anything else."

Harvey thought he was going to faint.

"Calm down, amigo," Forsythe said over the rim of his glass. "She only serves drinks. You know the law."

"Yeah. They can only, uh, mate with their own kind."

"Species," Forsythe corrected him. "Otherwise it's fatal for their partner. Complete sensory overload."

Harvey grinned. "I hope that wasn't what you had in mind when you said you'd put a smile on my face."

Forsythe laughed. "No, but that's good, amigo. Real good."

Harvey set down his beer, pleased that Forsythe had laughed at his joke—although he had been only half joking when he said it. "Forsythe, I don't want to sound naive but just what kind of place is this?"

"I guess you could call it a very special nightclub," Forsythe said, tossing back the last of his lemon vodka. He watched Harvey's reaction out of the corner of his eye. "It's very discreet, caters to some very special clients, and is more or less legal."

"What do you mean, 'more or less' legal?" Harvey asked.

"Well, I have an entertainment license for a small bar up on Green One.

Packed, it can serve maybe twenty people. All very intimate." He signaled for another round of drinks.

"One day about three years ago"—the Telluran brought the drinks and Harvey felt his blood pressure begin to rise—"we were remodeling after a couple of Indies did a fair amount of damage to the place during a private party. That's when I discovered that there was an old service elevator that ran right through my club to the cargo decks." He sipped his lemon vodka before continuing. "So, I decided to expand. Down here.

"I had a company Earth-side design a modular nightclub and finessed a permit that gives me permission to operate anywhere in the Alliance, provided I stay at least one thousand meters from any of their clubs." He gave Harvey a quick grin. "That's what I mean by semilegal. I'm only 980 meters from their nearest beer bar."

"So, who comes here?" Harvey asked. "I've been pushing cargo for two years, and I've never seen anyone down here before today."

"That's because we're careful. Our customers are very important people," Forsythe said, finishing his drink. "They can't go slumming in the Green Light district or be seen crawling out of some sleazy orgasmatron at four in the morning. That's why they come here, amigo. They have a good time, they go home, and nobody knows."

"Well, that's all very interesting," Harvey said, setting down his half-empty glass. "Maybe someday I'll be rich enough, or important enough, to be one of your customers. But for now I've got some cargo to shift." He stood up to leave. "How do I get outta here?"

"Same way you came in, amigo. Only before you go, I'd like to offer you a job." Forsythe gave Harvey a long, sincere look. "I think you're just the man I need down here."

Harvey's new job was simplicity in itself. Forsythe had a specially constructed container that served as the shuttle between the access elevator and his private club. Harvey would move the container to the door of the elevator at the end of his shift and then, after dinner and a beer, he'd wander back to the freight deck and, climbing on board his trusty forklift, return the container to the front of the club.

Harvey had been shuttling the container back and forth for nearly six weeks when a strange thought hit him. Every night he took a container full of people to the club. Who, he wondered, was taking them back to the elevator? Two days later, at the Pay Link machine, Harvey raised the question with Forsythe.

"I've got another driver on the payroll who works the graveyard shift," Forsythe said as he downloaded a stack of credits onto Harvey's pay card. "Not that it's any of your concern."

"Sorry I asked," Harvey said as Forsythe withdrew his pay card from the Pay Link machine.

"No problem, amigo," Forsythe said. "Look, I'm going to be closed for the next few days, so why don't you go topside and enjoy yourself. Take Frosty with you. God knows, with what I'm paying you, the two of you can have quite a blowout." He regarded Harvey for several long seconds. "I'll set it up. You two can stay in one of the hotels on Green Two. Well? What do you say?"

Harvey could only think of one thing to say.

"Great. When do we leave?"

"You can leave tonight, after the customers arrive." Forsythe handed back Harvey's pay card. "Frosty will join you tomorrow at the hotel."

"I can't go tonight," Harvey lied. "I have to cover for a pal on the morning shift."

"Okay, amigo. Then blast off tomorrow." Forsythe smiled. "You're rich, do what you like."

That evening Harvey collected his passengers as usual and transported them to Forsythe's club. Before he lowered the container to the floor, he hopped out of the forklift and stuck a wad of gum that he had been chewing to the underside of the container. Climbing back into his forklift, he lowered the container into place, and then went back to his quarters.

The next morning Harvey gunned his forklift to life while producing a cacophony of mechanical sounds, including the squeal of rubber on concrete at he pulled away from the loading dock. Soon he was easing the forklift between the rows of containers to approach Forsythe's club. He glanced around casually as he stopped it and hopped off, bending down to examine the edge of the container he had placed on the floor the night before. Oozing out from under the edge of the dark green container was a wad of pink bubble gum.

Quietly, and without any sound effects, Harvey drove back to the loading docks. He didn't know what was going on in the club, but one thing was certain. The container he had dropped off the night before hadn't been moved. On the way back to his quarters he tried to decide what he should do.

In the shower he toyed with the idea of going to Internal Security, but decided against it. If Forsythe's operation was legitimate, his visit to Internal Security would cost him his job—a job, he reflected as he toweled himself dry, that had paid him nearly a year's salary in less than two months.

Harvey finished dressing and tossed a few things in an overnight bag. No, he decided, he wouldn't go to Security. Not until he'd had a chance to talk to Frosty about what really went on in Forsythe's club. Switching off the lights, he left his quarters and took the express elevator to Green Two.

The lobby of the Hilton Hotel exuded an aura of expensive elegance that made Harvey feel slightly ill at ease as he waited for the desk clerk to confirm his reservation.

"Ah, here it is," the balding man said as Harvey's name came up on the screen. "Suite 1121 . . . Mr. Kimmelman and Ms. Hooters." He looked up from the CRT and gave Harvey a smile that looked as if it had been pickled in alum. "Just follow the guide to your room, sir."

A small robot glided to a stop next to the desk. Harvey set his bag on it and then followed it across the lobby and down a series of well-carpeted corridors until at last they came to suite 1121. The robot opened the door, allowing Harvey to enter first before it followed along with his bag.

By the standards of accommodation on the *Stephen Hawking*, the hotel suite was big. Harvey figured it to be at least four or five times the size of his quarters down in the south pole. There was a small video room with several comfortable-looking chairs opposite the three-dimensional video wall, and next to that was a bedroom with a huge bed. Beyond the bedroom was a bathroom, and through the open door Harvey could see Frosty reclining in a deep bath filled with the most wonderful-looking suds.

"Hi, Harvey," she called the moment she saw him. "Come on in, the water's fine!"

Harvey didn't bother to undress, but simply stepped into the tub and slid down next to Frosty.

The next thirty-six hours blurred into a nonstop orgy of indulgence. For the first time in his life Harvey was rich, and he was enjoying it. He and Frosty went shopping, took in a concert, ate in the best restaurants, and made love. It was after a particularly satisfying bout of lovemaking in zero-gravity mode that he had almost decided to forgive Frosty for having scammed two years' worth of pay credits, and was seriously thinking about marrying her, when she managed to break the spell.

"Gee," Frosty said, "it's a shame about the Club, isn't it?"

"What do you mean?" Harvey replied, trying not to think about her long fingernails as they slowly dragged their way across his belly.

"Well, just that Forsythe may have to close it down," Frosty said.

"Close it down? Why?" In his mind's eye Harvey could see little pay credits with wings flying out the windows of his dreams.

"Well," Frosty said coyly, "it's because business hasn't been all that good."

"Well, I sure seem to bring a lot of people there every night." Harvey reached down and took Frosty's hand in his own. "What do you mean that business hasn't been good?"

"Just that we don't get very many customers. Sometimes only one or two show up, and most of those leave early." Frosty's other hand was teasing the inside of Harvey's thigh.

"What do you mean they leave early?" Harvey moved closer to Frosty, forcing himself to concentrate. "How could they?"

"Well, I don't know how they leave, but they do. I've even asked Forsythe about it, and he just shrugs and says, 'They've gone.' " Frosty laid her head on Harvey's chest. "I thought maybe you took them back."

"How many came last night?" Harvey asked.

"Silly," Frosty replied. "It was just you and me. . . ."

"Not last night then," Harvey said with some exasperation, "but the last night you worked at the Club. Before we came up here?"

"Oh, that's easy," Frosty cooed. "Four. Two regulars and two new guys. But the new guys didn't stay long; they left after about an hour."

"How did they leave?" Harvey asked, afraid of what the answer might be.

"Well, Forsythe said you took them back." Frosty lifted the covers on the bed and looked down toward their feet. "You're not paying attention," she said.

But all Harvey could think of was the wad of bubble gum oozing out from under the container. It hadn't moved all night, and if the two new customers had left, then someone else had taken them.

"Frosty," Harvey asked, "is there a back entrance to the Club?"

"I don't think so, Harvey," she said. "There's the bar and the casino, then the playrooms, a kitchen, and the dorms." Frosty pulled her face into a cherubic pout. "I've been everywhere in the Club, but I've never seen any other entrance except the one you came through when Forsythe hired you." Her face brightened suddenly. "Unless there's another entrance in the hen house!"

"The 'hen house'?" Harvey asked.

"I think that's what it's called. At least that's what one of the regulars called it. I remember that Forsythe actually got upset and told the man he'd have to leave." She smiled at Harvey. "Can we . . ."

"What do they do in the hen house?" Harvey asked, interrupting Frosty's playful request.

"I don't know," she said. "But I'll show you what we do in the playrooms." She pressed against Harvey as she reached across to turn off the lights. "Oooo," she cooed in the darkness. "Now you're really paying attention!"

The next morning Harvey went down to the desk to check out of the hotel.

"How much do I owe you?" he asked when he finally managed to attract the desk clerk's attention.

"Name, please?" The overhead lighting gleamed on his bald head.

"Kimmelman. Harvey Kimmelman." Harvey tossed his pay card on the polished desk, secretly hoping he still had enough credits to pay the bill.

The bald head bent over the CRT and tapped away furiously at the keys. "Ah, here you are," he said without bothering to look up. "Three nights with Ms. Hooters . . ."

The desk clerk stopped in midsentence. "Yes, Mr. Kimmelman, everything is in order." His tone of voice had become very deferential, and Harvey wondered if the man was about to transform into a toad right before his eyes.

"So, what do I owe?" Harvey asked, a slight edge to his voice.

"Why, nothing, Mr. Kimmelman. Your stay has been with the compliments of Hilton Hotels." Slight beads of perspiration glistened on the desk clerk's sandy-colored forehead. "I hope that everything was to your satisfaction?"

"Sure. Just fine," Harvey said, picking up his pay card. "See you again in a couple of weeks."

Picking up his overnight bag, he headed out the doors of the hotel and across the bustling mall on Green Two. As he stood waiting for the express elevator to take him back to the south pole, he mulled over what he knew of the Club and what he had learned from Frosty. By the time he was strapped in to a deceleration seat, he had reached a simple conclusion: Things didn't add up.

It didn't take a tech level one propulsion engineer to know that the Club wasn't raking in enough to pay him the sort of cash Forsythe was splashing around. That meant that the money had to come from some other source.

Forsythe's Club on Green One? Maybe, but Harvey doubted it. Blackmail? Frosty had said something about regulars, but it was doubtful that they would be able to come up with enough credits to cover his salary week after week, let alone take care of Forsythe's operating expenses.

The express elevator hit four g's on stopping at the south pole, and despite the gaseous suspension of the seat, Harvey still felt like he'd left his stomach up around Seventeen deck. Untangling himself from the harness, he left the elevator and went straight to his quarters.

After the opulence of the Hilton, Harvey's quarters seemed almost claustrophobic. With his bed folded into the wall the room measured not quite three meters by four. It contained the regulation folding chairs, a small video screen, a bookshelf, a closet, and a mini-galley where Harvey could reheat a meal purchased from the vending machine in the corridor if he didn't feel like dining in the chow hall.

The soft plastic walls were teal blue with stainless-steel trim, and the self-cleaning carpet a ubiquitous gray. A door next to the bookshelves led to a small bathroom that contained the one luxury that made the small apartment worth every credit it cost: a genuine liquid shower complete with hot and cold taps.

Harvey surveyed his domain, wondering if it would still be his when he finished poking around the Club. The thought surprised him. Without realizing it, he had devised a plan and now he was putting it into action. He tossed his bag onto one of the chairs and headed out to the cargo decks.

On board his forklift, Harvey snapped down the safety visor on his helmet.

"Rig for silent running." His voice had the harsh metallic crackle of an old P.A. system.

Easing the machine out of the loading docks. Harvey made a series of sonar pings until he was sailing down the wide aisles of Violet Two. Navigating his way through the islands of stacked containers, Harvey finally sighted his first port of call.

He eased his forklift into the docking bay accompanied by the sound of tugboat engines thrashing the briny sea into foam. The central cargo computer had less memory than all the inhabitants of the *Stephen Hawking* combined, but it did serve one very useful purpose: it kept track of every piece of freight, every bit of cargo, and every single container on Violet One and Two.

Leaning over, Harvey took one of the mainframe cables and plugged it into the bayonet socket on the side of his machine. Keying in the coordinates of Forsythe's Club, he asked for a profile of freight distribution on the deck. Within a matter of seconds, his on-board display lit with a schematic of the containers, a virtual floor plan of the Club. Harvey entered the information into the memory of the forklift's computer and then disconnected from the central cargo terminal. Without a sound he glided down the freight corridor, headed for Forsythe's Club.

Taking a printout of the area as a map, Harvey parked his forklift twenty meters from the Club and proceeded on foot to Forsythe's container complex. Easing himself between the tightly packed rows of containers, he slowly made his way toward the front. Finally, at the end of one of the narrow corridors, he dropped down onto his stomach and carefully peered around the corner.

The dark green container that Harvey had placed in front of the Club four days earlier was still anchored to the floor by a wad of pink bubble gum. Harvey pulled back and stood up, hesitating for only a moment before he began back-tracking to a point where he could circle around to the back of the Club.

The rear approach was going to be more difficult. Here the containers were stacked three deep, and it was obvious to Harvey that he wasn't going to be able to climb on top of them without some sort of assistance. Trotting back to the forklift, he hopped on board and, accompanied by the sound of squealing tires, drove the machine around to the back of the Club.

Harvey pointed his scanner at the bar code on the top container.

ALLIANCE MORTUARY STORAGE
HUMAN REMAINS

The next two containers were the same.

So that's how he avoided having his containers moved, Harvey thought. *He's running his Club in the middle of a graveyard.*

A shudder ran up his spine. Alliance regulations were crystal clear about the remains of the dead. Once placed in storage they were not to be moved or tampered with. Some species had unusual notions about proper respect for their dead. Harvey couldn't remember what the penalty was for "mortuary disturbance," as the regulations called it, but he was sure of one thing: It ranked with murder, arson, and treason in Category A crimes.

Taking a deep breath, Harvey locked his tractor beam onto the topmost container and lowered it gently to the ground, followed by the next one. Then, locking on the bottommost container, he moved it slightly to the left, opening a gap of about forty-five centimeters. He replaced the top two containers, then drove back around to the front of the Club.

Climbing down from his forklift, Harvey made his way past the dead of the *Stephen Hawking* and squeezed his way into the complex of containers that housed the Club. Inside the walls of cargo that surrounded the Club, Harvey was surprised to discover that Forsythe's containers were packed in a tight cluster that left a clear three-meter path around most of its perimeter. At one corner of the cluster one of the containers was moved forward to where it butted up against the wall. This, Harvey surmised, was the entrance to the Club.

Working back from the entrance, Harvey mentally ticked off each of the containers. The bar and casino in one; the playrooms in another; the dorms for the girls and the kitchen. And behind the kitchen, the hen house.

Harvey leaned against one of the containers, trying to get his bearings. Behind him, coming from inside the container, he thought he could hear a high-pitched whine. Pressing his ear against the smooth green container, he strained to catch the sound again. Faintly, over the pounding of his own pulse, he finally heard it.

Instinctively he tried to mimic it, the way he reproduced the sounds of everything from a crash-diving submarine to an FTL engine with warp failure. The whining sound grew louder, as if whatever was making the noise were drawn nearer the wall of the container by Harvey's mimicking sound. Stepping back from the container, Harvey was convinced that he'd located the hen house. Whatever Forsythe was up to, the answer was in that container.

Two sides of the container were flush against the others, while the third side left a gap of slightly more than half a meter between it and its neighbor. Harvey slid into the gap and pressed his back against the container, wedging himself in place. Slowly, hand over hand, he crawled up the side of the container like a mountaineer moving up the crevasse of a stone face. When he reached the top, he spread his arms across the opening and pushed himself onto the top of the container.

From this vantage point he could see the layout of the containers and the small courtyard that separated the hen house from the rest. Crouching low, Harvey trotted along the top of the container until he reached a point above the courtyard. Lying flat on the roof, he lowered himself over the edge until he was hanging down the side with his arms fully extended. Pushing away from the container with his feet, he let go and dropped the last three meters to the deck.

The courtyard wasn't more than five meters on a side and, to Harvey's immeasurable relief, there were two doors that opened onto it. One led into the hen house and the other, if Frosty's description was to be relied on, led into the kitchen.

Harvey pulled back the kitchen door just wide enough to look inside. The stainless-steel galley seemed deserted, and he quietly closed the door.

Harvey pushed the hen house door open and slowly eased his way into the container. He found himself in a small, empty room lit only by a pale green work light. Closing the outside door behind him, he stepped across the room to another door. Before he could reach the door latch, the light began to change color and Harvey felt a prickling sensation all over his body as the by-now ultraviolet light completed its process of decontamination.

As the light level slowly faded back to a pale lime-green Harvey opened the inner container door. A thick, musty smell rolled out and filled the small room, reminding, him of the odor he had noticed when Forsythe had brought him into the Club nearly two months before. Stepping through the door he found himself in a room racked with shelves from floor to ceiling, each shelf holding something about the size of a man contained in a black plastic bag closed with a heavy zipper.

At first Harvey thought that he was in one of the mortuary containers, and for a moment a wave of pure panic crashed over him, threatening to drag him under in a sea of terror. He took several deep breaths with his eyes screwed shut against what he had seen. Then, as he felt himself calming down, he opened his eyes once again.

The body bags were still there, but even in the dim light of the container Harvey could tell from their shapes that they didn't contain bodies. Carefully he unzipped one of them. Inside he found a set of Fleet battle armor, complete with helmet and plasma gun. He opened two more bags and found more armor and weapons. In the semidarkness of the container he managed a quick count. Enough equipment to outfit a hundred men.

It didn't make sense. What would Forsythe want with all this gear? A hundred men in battle armor could take over a ship. . . .

The realization of what he was looking at hit Harvey between the eyes with the force of a hard ball coming off a Major League bat. Forsythe was planning a mutiny.

For just a moment Harvey's knees seemed about to buckle under him, and the room seemed to sway around him. He reached out to steady himself against the shelves when he heard the noise. It was a high-pitched whine that warbled up and down, much clearer than when he had first heard it outside on the cargo deck. With a deep breath, Harvey walked past the body bags filled with weapons and stopped in front of the steel door at the far end of the container.

Unzipping one of the bags, Harvey eased out a plasma gun and checked its charge level. The small needle in the dial set into the stock swung up to the top of the green band. Even on maximum power, he had a hundred shots before he'd have to replace the magazine. He set the firing selector to three-round burst, switched off the safety, and opened the door.

The smell was overpowering, a rotten, fetid, decaying stench that caused

Harvey to double over in a retching spasm that sprayed his lunch across the floor of the container. Struggling to stand up, he dragged his sleeve across his tear-filled eyes, blinking hard to see what was in the room.

The room was filled with long, narrow tables about chest height, covered with plastic trays filled with rotting compost. Floating in the semi-liquid slime were hundreds of rusty ivory-colored oblongs, bobbing gently up and down in the decaying filth.

Skulls, Harvey thought. *Probably all that's left of the bodies of the Fleet Marines who owned the gear in the other room.*

Just then one of the skulls floated to the surface of the liquid compost and slowly rotated toward Harvey, a trail of black slime wrapping itself around its forehead. Harvey watched in morbid fascination, at any moment expecting the empty eye sockets to fix him with their hollow stare. The skull slowly turned and then sank back into the ooze. It took Harvey a full minute to realize that the skull didn't have a face. It couldn't. It was an egg.

For some reason, the realization that he was looking at an egg didn't surprise Harvey in the least. He had come to the hen house to find—

The high-pitched whining started again, interrupting his thoughts. Rising and falling, it seemed to be calling something, as if it expected an answer.

Harvey moved forward in the semidarkness, edging his way toward the keening sound. As he moved between the tables he saw the eggs rising and falling to the tempo of the whining sound, almost as if they were children responding to a lullaby. The whining increased, and from the tables Harvey could hear a clicking sound as the eggs tapped against one another.

And lower, beneath the sound of the whining and the tapping, there was a scratching sound. The sound a cat makes when it is scratching at the door to be let out.

Crack.

Harvey spun around at the sound, ready to blast anyone behind him.

Crack.

This time it was next to Harvey, and as he continued to back down the aisle he watched the eggs on the table next to him rise and fall, rise and fall, in time to the whining sound that seemed to be filling the room.

Crack.

A dark fissure appeared on one of the eggs, a musty red fluid seeping out.

Crack. Another fissure appeared, and a tiny hand with three opposed digits poked its way through the crack, picking at the shell, trying to get out.

The crooning stopped, and for a moment the only sound was the tapping and cracking of the eggs. Then a shrill scream exploded behind Harvey. Instantly he spun around and found himself less than three meters from a female Ichton.

Instinctively Harvey pulled the trigger, and three rounds slammed into the Ichton's chest, sending it staggering back against the wall. Harvey turned to run and knocked over one of the tables, sending the eggs crashing to the floor in a welter of liquid compost. The female reared on her hind legs, screaming furiously at Harvey, and launched herself at him.

Diving under a table, Harvey slipped in a gooey mass of compost and Ichton hatchlings and slid into another table. Giving a might heave against the leg of the table he sent it tumbling down, its precious eggs smashing as they hit the floor of the container. The hatchlings squirmed on the floor, squeaking in agony as they tried to burrow into the compost for warmth.

The female Ichton bent down and moved forward, trying to scoop up as many hatchlings as she could and place them in the compost trays between the still intact eggs. Harvey watched her through the targeting system of his plasma weapon. He could see three closely spaced wounds on her upper thorax, one of which seemed to be suppurating, the result of having partially penetrated the Ichton's exoskeleton.

Harvey lay perfectly still, waiting for a clear shot at one of the Ichton's powerful legs. On the targeting system the room seemed as bright as the cargo decks outside, and Harvey was just squeezing off his shot when he felt something jab into his leg.

His shot went wide, with only one round even grazing the Ichton's leg. Looking down as he scuttled closer to the door, Harvey saw a hatchling hanging on to his pants leg, trying to stab him with a shard of eggshell. He scraped it off with his boot, its still-soft exoskeleton popping as he crushed it against the wall.

The female continued to busy herself rescuing hatchlings, and seemed to be ignoring Harvey, despite the injury to her leg. Propping himself up into a crouch, Harvey brought his weapon up to his shoulder. Scanning over the female Ichton, he tried to decide where he was the most apt to kill her with his next shot when he heard a faint whining sound behind him.

Jerking around, Harvey fired in the direction of the sound, just a heart-beat before the second Ichton let loose a blast from its weapon. The three slugs struck the Ichton under the chin, throwing her own aim wildly off. The spray of micro-slugs from her weapon ricocheted off the wall of the container and flew around the inside of the hen house like a swarm of angry hornets. As she fell forward, her lifeless hulk crashed into two more of the tables, smashing more of the eggs onto the floor.

Leaping to his feet, Harvey dashed to the door, firing over his shoulder in blind panic as he went. Behind him the remaining Ichton screamed as it bounded on in pursuit, apparently oblivious to its wounds. Harvey slipped and fell as he ran past the body bags filled with weapons, sprawling full-length on the floor of the container. The Ichton became tangled in its own legs trying to squeeze through the narrow doorway, giving Harvey barely enough time to scramble to his feet and stumble into the courtyard.

For a brief moment Harvey considered shooting the Ichton as it came out of the container, but a voice at the kitchen door changed his mind.

"Harvey!" Frosty shouted. "This way!"

Bounding to the door, Harvey grabbed Frosty by the arm and dragged her across the kitchen.

"We've gotta get out of here! Which way to the door?" he demanded.

"Ooo, Harvey," Frosty cooed. "You're so forceful!"

"The door!" Harvey barked. "Where the hell is it?"

"There." Frosty pointed to a thick-necked Telluran who stood blocking the door to the Club. "Behind him."

"Move it, pygmy!" Harvey yelled, covering the seven-foot-tall tower of muscle that blocked his way.

"You're bug meat, pal," the Telluran said, drawing a slug gun from under his cook's apron. "You and—"

Harvey fired twice, the six slugs from his weapon blasting a hole in the Telluran big enough to step through.

"Come on," he shouted, dragging Frosty over the smoldering remains of the Telluran. "We've—"

Harvey's voice was drowned out by Frosty's scream as the Ichton pushed its way into the kitchen.

"Go, go, go!" he shouted, pushing Frosty through the door and into the Club. "I'll cover you!"

He swung the muzzle of his weapon up and fired three quick bursts from the hip.

The Ichton slowed slightly in its advance and looked around the kitchen, blinking its honeycombed eyes. Unable to distinguish the exact shapes of Harvey and Frosty, the Ichton sprayed the room with a burst of automatic fire, unleashing a torrent of micro-slugs that ripped through the kitchen like a buzz saw. Harvey dived clear, and rolling behind the bar for cover got off another burst at the Ichton.

Two of the plasma slugs grazed past the Ichton, but the third slammed into its left front leg, shattering the insectoid's knee. The Ichton reared up in pain, its finger still on the trigger sending a full-auto burst into the ceiling of the kitchen. Bellowing in agony, the Ichton came forward on three legs, scuttling sideways like a wounded crab.

Harvey dashed across the Club and made a dive for the door, rolling onto his shoulder as he hit the floor, coming up with his weapon blazing as the Ichton leaped toward him.

"This way!" Frosty shouted, holding open the door that led from the container to the cargo deck.

Firing a burst over his shoulder, Harvey raced out of the con tainer and onto the deck. There, not twenty meters away, was his forklift.

Harvey sprinted past Frosty as he raced to the forklift. "Go get Security!" he shouted as he climbed into the cabin of his machine.

Hitting the starter, he swung the forklift around to face the container that had been used as a shuttle for the Club. Running forward, he hit the tractor beam and locked in on the container. He was just about to hoist it aloft when a slug crashed into the frame next to his head.

Diving for cover, Harvey threw himself off the forklift and onto the cargo deck. Bone cracked as he hit the ground, and a blinding pain seared up his arm. Struggling to get up, his broken arm dangling at his side, Harvey heard Forsythe's voice coming from near the entrance of the Club.

"Harvey, you blew it!" Forsythe was angry, and his voice edged on the hysterical. "You were one of the chosen, amigo, but you blew it. You could have been a survivor, one of the kings. The Ichtons would have let you live, it was part of the deal. But not now, amigo. Not now."

A shot rang out and another slug slammed into the forklift. Harvey raised his head above the edge of the cab just enough to see Forsythe moving toward the forklift, a small pistol in his hand.

Harvey weighed up his chances of surviving where he was and decided that Forsythe would kill him before Frosty returned with Security. He raised his head slightly to see if he could reach his gun where it had fallen on the floor of the forklift's cab.

Another shot rang out, and Harvey ducked back down and then half stood up, darting into the forklift to grab his gun.

Forsythe fired twice, but missed. Crouched next to his machine, Harvey fumbled his weapon to his shoulder and, with his good hand, switched it from "Burst" to "Full Auto." Moving around the back of the forklift, he took a deep breath, then dashed toward the nearest stack of containers, blindly spraying a burst at Forsythe as he ran.

It worked. Forsythe flattened himself on the deck as Harvey's shots passed harmlessly overhead. Recovering, he rolled into a kneeling position and let loose a string of shots in Harvey's direction.

The Ichton cautiously stepped out of the shuttle container and onto the cargo deck. She held her shattered foreleg folded up tight against her abdomen, and a thick mustard-yellow fluid continued to ooze from the wound on her thorax. Using the container for cover she cautiously peered around its edge, her multifaceted eyes picking up the patterns on the cargo deck as a mosaic of shapes, colored only by their infrared heat values.

She could detect some movement in front of her, and the fine fibers in the joints of her elbows tingled to the bark of Forsythe's pistol. Cocking her head, she tried to decide if the moving heat pattern crouched on the deck in front of her was friendly or not. Unable to decide, she brought up her weapon. The eggs, the hatchlings, had to be protected. The thing in front of her wasn't an Ichton, wasn't important to the swarm. She pulled the trigger.

A thousand plasteel fléchettes spun out of the barrel of the Ichton's gun, separating from one another until they reached the outer limits of their static charge adhesion and formed a pattern precisely ninety millimeters in diameter. Each fléchette had three stabilizing fins that wound themselves in a spiral the length of the shaft, imparting a 1500 rpm spin to the projectile that turned it into a lethal drill no thicker than a hypodermic needle.

The first blast caught Forsythe in the back and drove him to the ground. Within three tenths of a second, another two thousand fléchettes bored into the pulped flesh and bounced crazily off the deck, rattling into the stacked containers around the Club. Forsythe's legs jerked spasmodically against the deck for a few moments and then went still.

Harvey was frozen in place by the awesome destructive power of the Ichton weapon. Staring at what was left of Forsythe's body, unable to make his legs obey the command to run, to get the hell as far away as possible from the Ichton, the only thought he had was that he was next—that in a matter of seconds, he'd be reduced to a pile of quivering pulp like Forsythe.

Fear saved Harvey's life.

The Ichton leaned out farther from the container, looking for the enemy that had destroyed the eggs and killed so many hatchlings. Her eyes picked up a mosaic of shapes and colors, but nothing that she could identify at the distance. There was no movement, and the dull orange heat shape ten meters away was identifiable as a machine. Satisfied that there was no living threat in front of it, the Ichton stepped back behind the container to continue looking elsewhere.

Harvey's legs came back to life. Running to the forklift, he climbed into the cab and grabbed the tractor beam joystick. Pushing it forward, he began raising the container.

The wounded Ichton sensed movement behind her and turned and fired wildly into the side of the container, sending a shower of fléchettes ricocheting in all directions. Limping back from the container, she brought her weapon up, ready to fire at the first sign of movement.

Hunched down in the cab of the forklift, Harvey slowly brought the microphone of his bullhorn to his mouth.

The Ichton thought she detected movement of some sort on the dull orange heat shape. Slowly she rotated her head, hoping to detect some movement on the facets of her eyes. In the upper periphery of her vision she saw the container overhead as if it were some sort of dark rectangular cloud. Around her she saw the smooth green walls of the containers, the dull gray flooring of the cargo deck, and the slowly cooling remains of Forsythe.

The Ichton concentrated on the dull orange heat shape of the forklift. Inside the container she had left were eggs and hatchlings that needed her, while outside was danger to her brood. Better safe than sorry. She raised her weapon to her shoulder.

There was a metallic chirruping. The Ichton cocked her head to one side and moved her elbows outward to trap more of the sound. The chirrup came again, this time followed by a low whining sound, much like the lullaby she had crooned to the hatchlings as they struggled to be free of their eggs.

She made a high-pitched warbling whine, cocking her head and elbows to catch any sound of an answer.

The chirrup struggled to duplicate the sound, but couldn't.

It had to be a hatchling, one that had somehow been dragged or carried out of the nest. If they were to continue to avoid detection, she had to rescue it.

It chirruped again, and she took a hesitant step forward.

Harvey watched as the Ichton stepped into the shadow of the container held in the tractor beam of his forklift. He chirruped into the microphone—and then turned off the tractor beam.

From nearly eight meters up, the sixteen-ton container dropped onto the deck with a deafening bang, crushing the Ichton to a yellow smear.

Harvey smiled to himself and clipped the microphone back onto the dash of the forklift. Switching on his computer, he accessed the mainframe on Twelve deck and typed in a brief coded message. Then, swinging down from the cab of the forklift, he headed toward the Club. As he passed the spreading pool of mustard-yellow slime that oozed from under the container, he made a popping sound, like someone stepping on a bug. Bending down, he picked up the Ichton's gun in his good hand and headed back into the Club.

When Internal Security arrived with Frosty, they found Harvey in the hen house, ankle deep in broken eggshells and rotting compost and dead hatchlings. Security set up a command post in the bar, and while the security officers helped themselves to free drinks and a medic worked on Harvey's arm, their commander interrogated him.

"So let me get this straight," the security commander said. "You were moving an empty container when this guy, er . . ." He turned to one of the security men. "You got a make on the meat pie outside?"

The security man shook his head.

"No? Okay." He turned back to Harvey. "So you saw this guy come running out of here with the Ichton hot on his tail. The Ichton shoots the guy, and you drop the container on the bug. Right?"

"Yup, amigo. That's exactly how it went down." Harvey smiled at his interrogator. "Any more questions?"

"No, not right now." The security commander stood up. "You can go. We'll call you if anything else comes up."

"Sorry," Harvey said, "but I'm not leaving."

"What do you mean, *you're* not leaving? This is a security matter, and I'm sealing off all of these containers." He signaled for the two security men at the bar. "You're going. Understand?"

"What I understand is that under the Alliance Salvage Laws, these containers were unrecorded enemy possessions. It doesn't say anywhere that they have to be outside the ship, just not in the memory banks already. Only that mess in the back has any intelligence value. As the sole surviving combatant they are now mine. Even the permits for the bar up on Green will take weeks to revoke." Harvey held up a printout from the computer in his forklift, mimicking a trumpet as he presented it. "If you'd care to read this, you'll see that I filed for salvage eleven minutes and twenty-one seconds before you arrived."

The security commander snatched the printout from Harvey's hand. His scowl turned to a frown as he examined the document. It would take months, maybe years to sort this one out and there was a rumor of imminent combat. Legal technicalities weren't his problem and the Ichtons were dead. And there was no way to guess how the upper command would react to the incident. No use rankling a potential hero, and he might want to come back here when he was off duty. He waved the two approaching security officers off with a shrug.

"Now, unless you want to start paying for your drinks, I'm going to have to ask you all to leave." Harvey's smile was hard enough to cut diamonds. "Okay, amigo?"

The security man glared at Harvey, tried to smile, then handed back his deed to the containers.

"Okay, Kimmelman." He turned to the two security men who were now standing next to Harvey. "Come on, men, we're outta here."

The two men followed their chief to the door, where he turned and gave Harvey a last glowering look.

"I'll be back for the bug box, Kimmelman," he said, then turned and left the Club.

Frosty came over from behind the bar and sat down next to Harvey. "Are you going to be all right?" she asked, stroking the back of his neck.

Harvey stretched his injured arm. The medic had done a good job repairing the broken bone, and aside from the tickle of the current and a twinge of pain as he pulled Frosty closer to him, Harvey could tell that he'd be fine in a few hours.

"Better than ever," he said, giving Frosty a smile and a little squeeze. "Now, why don't you show your partner-to-be the playroom?"

Frosty cooed with delight.

OLD GRUDGES

Elsewhere on the *Stephen Hawking* there were the sectors owned by those corporations rich enough to have purchased their own floor or wing. Along with the megamerchants were a number of companies financed by the governments of their respective worlds. Among them perhaps the most unusual, and certainly the most flamboyant, was that of the Baratarians.

Barataria was actually a group of asteroids that had originally harbored fugitive Khalians who had refused to accept their defeat by the Fleet. Eventually, like most Khalians, they realized that the Families, and the Schlein family in particular, had used them, and used them badly. This led to a grudge that was passed on undiminished to the next generation of Baratarians. Like the pirates of Earth, many of the Khalian pirates found legitimate or somewhat legitimate ways to invest the wealth taken from both Fleet and Family ships. This wealth gave them considerable leverage in the chaotic period after the war when the Khalian and Family economies were in shambles. As a result the Baratarians became prosperous merchants and dubious, but valued, members of the Alliance.

Their leader had been a misshapen human known to them only as Globin. His warped exterior hid one of the best minds in all humanity. Globin's decision to retire after almost seventy years came as a relief to the Fleet sector commander. There is nothing like having an only mildly socialized genius and ex-pirate under your command to keep things lively. Globin's decision to spend his "retirement" as the head of the Baratarian mission on the *Hawking* presented the battlestation's commander, Anton Brand, with some perplexing problems.

HEARING
by Christopher Stasheff

Selena Schlein dreamed. She lay in cold sleep, very cold and very deep, so cold that her mind had the illusion of warmth, so cold that the stream of life had ebbed to a trickle—and as she slept, she dreamed a nightmare.

For she dreamed of the Fleet, whose ships chased those of her family over the sky—which couldn't be; they didn't know of the Schlein family. At least, so far as anyone knew, they didn't know of the Families—but there was no telling what their spies had ferreted out, and in her dream, the Fleet had found them, and had chased Selena's exploration ship to the center of the galaxy, even though they couldn't have, even though part of her shouted silently, No! It wasn't that horrible Fleet, it was those implacable insects!

But in the nightmare, the pursuing ship loomed larger and larger in their viewscreen, and her husband Hans was shouting, "Get the women into the lifeboats!" but she was protesting that, no, she would rather remain there by him, to die with him if it was necessary, but the whole ship shuddered as the Fleet vessel grappled it, one of the bulkheads fractured and split open like an egg, and an alien form slipped through, but it wasn't the dreaded Fleet uniform, nor one of those horrible bugs, it was even more horrible, it was one of those vicious, savage Weasels, the Khalians, whom the Families' agents had so successfully suborned into attacking the Alliance, but now it was a Khalian, but Dobie and Harl who were carrying her away to stuff her into the life-pod, strapping the tubes with the needles to her wrists, and she was screaming, "No! I can fight, too!" but the drugs were taking effect, the world was growing dim, then vague and fuzzy, then totally dark, and she relaxed with a flood of relief, safe in the darkness even as her heart ached for Hans, frantic with worry for him, but her fear and worry were distanced somehow by the darkness. . . .

But the blackness was lightening, her eyelids trembling, trying to open. She fought to keep them closed, keep the safe warm darkness wrapped about her, but it wasn't warm anymore, it was chilly, and she shivered, it was cold, so cold, and her eyelids opened all by themselves, to look for warmth . . .

And the nightmare slammed back, her two worst fears coupled together, for there, not two feet from her face, hung the monstrous Khalian face under the Fleet uniform cap, its furry snout split in an evil, gloating grin, and Selena screamed, thrashing about, trying to escape, but horrible soft arms held her imprisoned, and she screamed and screamed and screamed, until the warm fuzzy darkness came back to shield her, and free her from the responsibility of wakefulness.

Globin looked up at his secretary. "But how would it be if the Gersons had been a sentient race that had nothing in common with us, Plasma? If they had been, let us say, thinking plants—or living stones?"

"Speak only of what is possible, Globin," Plasma said with a rare show of real anger. "This we know: Giant bugs seek to destroy beings like us, with warm blood, and that is all we need to know."

"So it comes down to like and unlike," Globin sighed. "Is there no more to Right and Wrong than that?"

"Of course not, Globin! The Ichtons seek to slay the folk of other races and take their planets, as they slew the Gersons and laid waste their home!"

"That is true," Globin said, nodding, "and surely it is wrong to steal and murder—but right to defend, and kill in defense of others' lives."

He was quite well aware that the Ichtons must surely believe—if they were truly thinking beings, rather than mere biological calculators evolved to solve technological problems of slaughter—believe that their own conquests and genocides were right, and that men of his own species had once believed the same. It did not make the Ichtons any more morally sound, but it did make Globin wonder.

He wondered even more that he should wonder. Who was he to ponder questions of right and wrong—he, Globin, traitor to his own kind, pirate king, space-thief, and murderer, responsible for the deaths of many who had been killed when their ships had been taken by his men—more accidentally than intentionally, true. His orders had always been to take without killing if possible, but to kill if it was necessary, but responsible nonetheless. So he was a murderer, yes, and could not deny it. His only justification was loyalty to the Khalian pirates who had adopted him when men of his own kind sought to slay him, and that had always sufficed—till now.

Why did it suddenly bother him? he wondered. Now, when he had lived one hundred years out of a probable hundred thirty—now, when he had turned his pirates into legal merchants and made their peace with the Alliance; now, when he had resigned his place among the Baratarian Khalians and taken a horde of young and eager volunteers to help defend the weaker races at the Core of the galaxy, against a marauder who annihilated all in its path, without reason or cause save its own greed. Surely there could not be a cause more right, nor a moral issue less ambiguous!

But Globin was keenly aware that the Ichtons, more alien than any species he had yet encountered, could hardly be said to think as human beings did, nor even as mammals did—and he was also aware that learning how they thought was the only real path to stopping them. Defeating them completely was improbable—there were simply too many of them, too many ships, too many conquered planets, and more disappearing into their collective maw all the time. It would be as much a feat of diplomacy as of war to make them stop, as it had always been—as MacArthur had helped the Japanese to realize that commerce was a more certain path to dominion than military conquest, and Gorbachev had played peacemaker between the United States and China.

But when he began to try to learn how the Ichtons thought, he began to wonder about their own ideas of morality—and thus, so late in life, had begun to ponder the issues that had for so long been clear. Oh, they still were—clear for him, clear in terms of what he must immediately do; but on the cosmic scale?

The viewscreen on the wall lit, and an excited Khalian looked out at him, tense with the enthusiasm of youth. "Globin! Plasma, tell Globin at once! There is a life-pod! Our scoutship has caught it!"

Globin was on his feet. He would have to move fast; any such detritus brought in was common property of the whole ship, and the humans of the Fleet would have overheard Platelet's message. "What is in the life-pod, Platelet?"

"Terrans! Females! Globin, come and see!"

Globin stood stunned. "Terrans? Here? So far from home, from any Terran home? How could they have come? None are being sought by the *Hawking*."

"Ask it of them yourself!" Plasma was already halfway to the door. "Globin, come quickly!"

The life-pod was clamped to the underside of the Khalian scoutship, seamed and cratered with the impacts of space junk. But its cargo had already been transferred to the Khalian ship, and were now being carried through the airlock—

On stretchers.

"They screamed when they saw us, Globin." Platelet looked up, his eyes huge, for a Khalian. "Screamed, and called us monsters, and begged for mercy. They would not be quiet no matter how much we reassured them, so we sedated them. It is best if they see you first, when they waken."

But one last Terran woman came walking, behind the stretchers of her mates. Globin caught his breath; she was beautiful, even under the dirt and caked sweat of a long sojourn in the life-pod, even with the strain ravaging her face, and her golden hair dulled by dirt. But her eyes were huge, and frightened.

Plasma nudged him, and Globin came out of his reverie. He stepped over to her. She looked up, terrified, like a doe about to run at sight of the hunter—then saw a human face, and relaxed.

Almost collapsed.

She sagged against Globin's chest. It was unexpected, and he fell back a step, then braced himself and took her in his arms, making soothing sounds. "There now, the ordeal is over, you have come to safe harbor, you will be all right. . . ."

She seemed to melt against him, but made no reply.

Emboldened, he held her away just a little, and said gravely, "But you must tell me, child. How did you come to be here, so far from human space?"

The girl watched his face intently, with a little frown. There was something odd about that gaze, something troubling, but Globin set it aside for later analysis and said again, "How did you come to be here?"

"Speak more slowly," the girl said in an odd flat voice. Globin would have interpreted that as sarcasm, but the intentness of her gaze made him realize that it wasn't.

"How . . . did . . . you . . . come . . . to . . . be . . . here?" he asked. "What . . . happened . . . to . . . your . . . ship?"

Then he realized, with a shock, what was odd about her gaze. She wasn't making eye contact. Her gaze was lower, watching his lips. A strange feeling went through Globin, a shivering thrill at the strangeness of it.

"We came to study the Core," she said. "Men and women, many married."

"The *Dunholme* Expedition," Globin breathed. He remembered the story, discovered in the Schlein family archives after the surrender, and released to the media. Even in the Alliance's triumph, the expedition had been heralded as an example of devotion to science. A dozen couples had embarked on a virtual suicide mission, for the Core was so far away, at the speeds attainable a century and a half before, that there was very little chance the people would come back alive. The ship would, but they would not. It was a monumental case of self-sacrifice, choosing to spend virtually their whole lives cooped up in a single ship—never mind that the ship was so large as to be a tiny world in itself—and forswearing having children, for they had no right to commit unborn people to such an existence.

Of course, some of the critics had noted, these were people to whom science was so important, so thrilling, that what they were giving up was balanced by the opportunities they were gaining. Others had noted the psychological profiles of the people aboard: they were mostly misanthropes, who had felt rejected by others, and rejected society in turn (How well Globin had understood that!), though they got along well enough with one another, enjoying the society of fellow rejects; and none of them really wanted to have children. The two qualities seemed to go together, somehow.

But they had never come back. Oh, they hadn't been expected to, not for a hundred years—but they had set out a hundred fifty years before, sent by the wealthy and ambitious Schlein family, striving for more wealth and greater power among the Merchant Families, sent to find some secret of Nature that would give them a huge edge over their rivals. But the long-delayed war had come to the Schleins, and cut them away, and Globin had grown old waiting for the *Dunholme* to come back, grown to the age of eighty yearning for the knowledge they would bring, had set off with the *Hawking* for the very core to which they had gone, fuming at them for not having sent back their data.

But when they had confronted the Ichtons, he knew what had happened to them—or guessed. Now he had merely to confirm it.

"The *Dunholme* Expedition?" he asked the girl again, then remembered to say it a third time, slowly. He was beginning to realize what was wrong with her.

She nodded. "We were attacked by the insects, but we escaped—and the FTL drive was damaged. We fled for months, fleeing at light speed, but their pursuit ship finally caught us and disabled our engines completely. The men put all the women in a cryogenic chamber, this life-pod in which you found us, while they worked to make the ship come alive again, knowing they would probably die trying. The last one alive was to release the pod, so that we at least would have some hope of rescue—and praise Heaven it has come!"

"But they were all mature men and women on that expedition," Globin protested, "in their thirties or forties, and you are scarcely twenty, if that."

The girl nodded, her eyes huge and luminous—and Globin felt his heart twist. He berated it silently, and himself for an old fool, and made a conscious effort to focus on her words, not her face alone.

"They had agreed not to reproduce," the girl said, "but had not forsworn love-making, and most of them were married. What went wrong with the contraceptives, I do not know—but there was an accident, and I was born."

Globin frowned. "That was dangerous. With so little space, if others had followed your mother's example . . ."

"But they did not," the young woman said firmly. "Everyone deplored the bad luck, my mother most of all—but with every breath of condemnation, she smiled with secret delight. At least, that is what my father said, as well as all my aunts, with a touch of envy. You see, they had all reared families already, but they tell me that nothing raises the desire for one last child so much as seeing someone else pregnant."

"So you grew up aboard ship," Globin said, frowning, "and never knew what it was to live on a planet."

"Never," she said, "until now."

Globin resisted the smile of amusement that pushed at his lips. "This is no planet, child, but only a ship, albeit a very large one."

"And I am no child," she said firmly, "albeit I am much younger than you."

Globin gazed at her a moment, then inclined his head. "Your pardon, fair lady."

"Of course." She smiled, and her face was a sun.

Globin held his gaze on her while he waited for his blood to stop effervescing. Then he said, "So you never knew of the Khalian War."

"They have told me of it," she said evenly, "and have showed me the holocines shot during the worst of the battles. The Khalians looked terrible, then. They do not look so monstrous now."

"You are not seeing them in combat," Globin pointed out. "Did your parents not tell you of the horrible things they had done?"

"Yes, but I could understand only the broad outline." The girl tapped her ear with a forefinger. "I am deaf, you see."

She said it matter-of-factly, as though it were the most natural thing in the world. Globin sat immobile as his hardened old heart softened amazingly with pity; she had adjusted admirably, or developed iron-hard emotional defenses.

Unless . . .

Unless it *were* the most natural thing in the world.

"Deaf from birth?" he asked.

The young woman nodded. "Cosmic radiation, we think—the ship was not entirely proof against it. Though Heaven knows, there were enough other sources available. It took them a year to understand why I did not respond to sounds, but only moved my lips. Then, slowly and painfully, they taught me to speak—but by the time I could understand a large enough vocabulary to comprehend the accounts of Khalian atrocities, I was old enough to be skeptical, too, and to think that no living being is inherently evil."

So that was why she had been afraid, but not terrified. What the other women knew as contemporary terror, she had known only as history—and could not have been raised with species hatred, for she had not comprehended the gory details.

"I would have said so, too, at one time," Globin said grimly. He was thinking of some of the more unpleasant examples of his own species.

The young woman misunderstood. She frowned. "Do you speak of the insects?"

Globin had to consider that before he answered. "I do not think they are evil in their own minds," he said, "assuming they have minds, as we know them. But as a species, they are as evil as a cancer."

"But no more than a cancer," she pointed out. "After all, a cancer has no mind, no will; it does not intend to cause pain."

Admiration for her mind kindled in Globin now, and he warned himself to beware. "Exactly. It *does* evil, but it may not *be* evil. As with the Ichtons—that is what we call these marauding insectoids. For now, though, we must fight them."

"Of course," she said with perfect composure.

"And that is all you knew of your parents' universe?" Globin asked. "Only the broad outlines of the war?"

"Oh, I learned the details when I was in my teens," she said. "It all seems like a story in a book, though, for that is what it was."

Globin held her gaze while something shriveled inside him, at the thought that he was history to her. "What of the Khalians after their war with the Fleet?"

"I was told that the war was ended," she said, studying his face, "ended many years ago, and that most of the Khalians had joined with the Alliance. Some, though, would not be appeased, would not stop fighting, but became pirates, so that they could continue to prey upon the ships of the Alliance. They told me also that a human renegade had clawed his way to command of all the pirates—a misshapen creature called the Globin." She shrugged. "Surely he could not have endured long—a lone human among his blood enemies."

Globin took a deep breath, turning away, then remembered that he had to face her while he talked, or she would not be able to understand him. "One human did—a Captain Goodheart. His ship was blown up by a Family squadron."

She frowned. "They told me of Captain Goodheart—scary tales for darkness. Was not this 'Globin' his assistant?"

Globin nodded. "Globin led the search for Goodheart's killers. He found them, though it took years—and all the Families with them."

She stood rod-still, galvanized, eyes wide. "What happened then?"

"War," Globin told her, "between the Alliance and the Families. The Khalians, learning that they had been used as the Families' tool, screamed betrayal and allied with the Fleet, seeking revenge."

Her face was ashen; she had to moisten her lips with her tongue. "And the end of that war?"

"The Fleet and its Khalian allies defeated the Families. Their worlds were occupied; they paid reparations."

"They were conquered," she whispered. "All because this Globin found them?"

He could see from her face that she knew the fate of those who were conquered, but he found he could not lie. He nodded, and felt his heart plummet.

But it revived at her next words. "I cannot believe that he was so thorough a villain—that he must have had reasons for what he did, other than money."

Globin nodded, with relief. "You are right." But he was annoyed with himself, too; her opinion of him should not matter so much. "What is your name?"

"Lusanne," she said. "What is yours?"

"People call me 'Globin,' " he answered.

She would not scare. No matter what he told her, no matter how much of the gritty truth, she would not scare. She was only interested—perhaps "fascinated" would be a better word—for she was confronting a living legend, a character from the pages of history.

And she was very curious. Globin decided she must be a natural historian.

But while he discussed history with her, he had to manage the present, with an eye to the future. Both were summed up in one name: Brand.

❖ ❖ ❖

Commander Brand had raised the roof, or at least the ceiling; his voice almost shook the speaker off the wall. "Globin, what the hell do you think you're doing holding human prisoners?"

"None more human than I, Commander," Globin told the image on the screen, "though you may find that hard to believe."

"Any prisoners taken are under the authority of the Fleet, Chairman! Any shipwreck survivors rescued are under my jurisdiction!"

"With the commander's pardon," Globin said, his old tone of authority reasserting itself, "the survivors were rescued by a Baratarian corporate vessel, taken to the Baratarian sector, and are currently the guests of the Baratarian Corporation."

"Damn it, Globin, they're Schleins!"

"And very sick ones, too," Globin said, authority turning into iron. He reflected that Brand's intelligence network was, as always, excellent. "It would be very dangerous for them to be moved just now, Commander. With all due respect, in consideration of the survivors' welfare, I must respectfully decline to allow them to leave the Baratarian sickbay until they are restored to full health."

"They're human *women*, Globin! And you've got 'em being nursemaided by a bunch of Wea . . . Khalians!"

"Khalian doctors," Globin snapped, the iron transmuting into steel, "under the direction of my personal physician, Dr. Arterial—who is a graduate of Camford University on Terra, I might remind you, as well as of the College of Physicians of Khalia."

"But he's not human, Globin!" Brand took a long breath, then said, "My quarters. Chairman. Right away—if you please." The last was very grudging, but Brand knew the contract—and the laws to which he would answer if the *Hawking* returned to Terra—and, moreover, knew that Globin knew them, too.

"It is always a pleasure to accept your kind invitations, Commander," Globin returned evenly, then rose with a satisfied smile. "Plasma, if you would join me?"

The *Hawking* was a huge ship, so by the time Globin and Plasma arrived at the commander's office, Brand had had enough time to both calm down and think things through—so, as Globin came through the door, he was all sweetness and light. "Now see here, Globin. I think we can both agree that the ladies' welfare is foremost."

Globin breathed a secret sigh of relief. He was more than halfway home free. "Yes, Commander, I can agree with that."

"Well, these women are Schlein family. How do you think they're going to feel if the first thing they see when they wake up is a Khalian muzzle?"

Globin remembered how the one woman had reacted already, and said slowly, "Your point is well taken, Commander." Of course, Brand knew just exactly how well taken it was; Globin didn't doubt for a second that the commander knew about the one woman who had half waked, screamed, and lapsed back into unconsciousness.

"Well, that's all I'm asking—just to have Terran doctors treat them." Brand held up a hand. "No, I'm not asking for your Dr. Arterial to be excluded from his own sickbay, or for any of his assistants to be kicked out—I'm just asking that human doctors be allowed in there, too."

"And that they be the first one the revivees see." Globin nodded slowly. "I'm afraid I cannot disagree with you in any degree, Commander—as long as we are only speaking of five or six doctors, and they are coming to our sickbay, not the other way around."

"Done!" Brand grinned like a shark. "I'll have them down there in five minutes, Chairman!"

Globin decided that Brand would pay for that grin.

But it would take time to decide how to exact that penalty. Oh, Globin knew what it would be—he would keep the women in the Baratarian Quarter. But how to achieve it would take long days of thought, and nights of letting the elements of the problem link themselves up while he slept.

While the problem stirred itself around in the back of his mind, and the physicians labored over the other survivors, Globin allowed himself the luxury of the company of the youngest Schlein.

And a pleasure it was, for she showed not the slightest distaste at his presence. He took her for a tour of his domain, the Baratarian Quarter of the ship. They visited the workshops, the mess hall, the lounge, and ended by strolling through the park. Lusanne looked about her with bright and eager interest in all the strange sights. "So vast," she whispered.

It was only five hundred meters in diameter, and fifty high, but the walls and ceiling were painted to give the illusion of a limitless expanse of plain rolling away to an imaginary horizon, to fulfill the need of shipbound creatures for open spaces. Globin realized with a shock that the poor child had never seen open fields or sky, any sky but the star-strewn night of the Core. She might have been afraid, but instead she was eager, and his admiration for her, already high due to the courage he perceived in her, rose still more.

She would far more likely have been afraid of the Khalians who rose from the long grass now and then, bounding away in frenetic joy at escaping the close confinement of their quarters for a few hours, or strolling slowly by, chatting. Always Khalians, always fur and leather, never human skin and clothing. Raised to fear Khalians as other children feared bogeymen, Lusanne might have shrunk gibbering in terror—but she greeted every encounter with the fresh enthusiasm of a child let loose to discover its world—or a scientist given free rein to examine whatever she wished.

"So I am a pirates' prisoner?" she asked in her oddly uninflected diction.

"Scarcely!" Globin stifled a chuckle. "You are a guest, Lusanne, and we are no longer pirates. I guided the Khalians of Barataria into legitimate commerce forty years ago. They are a legal merchant corporation now and obey all laws."

"Forty?" She looked up, startled. "But our ship departed on its expedition only thirty years ago!"

Globin stared at her, amazed, realizing just how long she and her shipmates must have been drifting in that capsule. He said gently, "It has been one hundred fifty years since your parents began their quest, Lusanne."

She stared. "Can we have been in that life-pod for so long?"

"Perhaps not," Globin said slowly. "You said that the Ichtons—excuse me; that is what we call the insectoid race that attacked the *Dunholme*—you said that your ship fled for several weeks, at nearly the speed of light?" She nodded, and Globin said, his suspicion strengthened, "There is a time-squeeze effect; for each week that passes near the speed of light, years pass on the surface of a planet. So you may not have been in the capsule longer than a decade or so—but between your long sleep and your long escape, twelve decades have passed."

Tears formed at the corners of her eyes. "Alas! For my father and the brave men who died with him! For even if they escaped the Ichtons, they must be dead by now!"

Globin remembered that she had said the last man alive had released the pod, and knew that the men for whom she mourned had almost certainly died. "They died that you might live, Lusanne," he said softly. "Surely there can be no greater mark of a man's love than that. Let the tears flow, Lusanne, for they must fall sometime. Let them fall."

Her face reddened, her fists clenched, but the tears began to flow in earnest.

Globin felt his heart twist, and held out his arms. Lusanne came into them like a child to be comforted. He folded his arms around her and patted her back gently as the sobs racked her body and she clung to him as though to a life ring in a turbulent sea. Globin rested his cheek against her head, savoring the warmth and the sensation of her body pressed against his, concentrating on every touch, every pressure, to be sure he would remember every detail, for he had never held a woman in his arms before and knew he probably never would again.

Finally, the tears slackened, and Lusanne pulled away from him, eyes downcast. Globin's handkerchief was instantly in her hand; she dabbed at her eyes, then blinked up at him with a tremulous smile, and he felt his vitals turn to water. "Thank you," she said. "I had not known . . ." Her voice trailed off.

"Emotional shock," Globin explained, and wondered if it was true of himself, too. "You've had a traumatic experience"—he managed a sardonic smile—"culminating in rescue by a pirate."

"But you said you are no longer a pirate." Her eyes were wide and very blue.

"I am not," he told her. "The Khalians elected me their leader, and over a decade, I managed to move them more and more into legitimate trade. Finally, our commercial ties were so strong that the Alliance virtually had to offer us membership, or lose too much gold to us in trade. As part of the treaty, and to save their collective face, we agreed to cease piracy, which we had almost eliminated anyway."

She stared, horrified. "You are of the Alliance now?"

"We are," he said gently, "and the war with the Families is over."

She began to tremble. "Yes—the war with the Families. Will not your Khalians hate we Schleins?"

Globin bit his lip. He said gently, "The Khalians realized they had been used by the Syndicate, betrayed, so they joined with the Alliance. The result was foregone, but tedious."

Her face was pale. "What is left of our homeland?"

"Your homeland is intact." Globin was terse. "But its armaments, and the factories that built them, are gone."

"They are defenseless, then," she whispered.

"The reparations are paid," Globin told her, "and they have nothing more to fear from the Fleet. Oh, there were atrocities, yes, but as few as the command could manage. Your countrymen are humbled, and many died in the war, but they are by and large intact. They could have fared much worse—and the Fleet that fought them now protects them."

Lusanne watched out of the corners of her eyes, uncertain. "Will the Fleet not seek to revenge itself on us women, if they find us?"

"They have," Globin said gently, and waited for it to sink in.

It did, and she pulled back with a gasp. "Not you!"

"Not really," Globin said. "There are few Fleet personnel in Barataria's decks—but those decks are leased from a Fleet battlestation, and the overall command of the ship is Fleet."

"Then we are lost," she whispered.

"No," Globin said, "you are saved. The men of the Fleet might still harbor hatred for the Schlein family, but even they will certainly be courteous to civilians—which you are, especially since the war is long gone."

"Only courtesy," she whispered.

"Only that," he agreed. "But you are in the midst of Khalians here, and young Khalians at that, to whom your government's treachery is only a tale from a history book, and whose fathers' desire for revenge has been slaked, and forgotten—for that is how the Khalians are. You are safe among these, my adopted children."

She darted a curious glance at him, but all she said was, "I must tell all my aunts about this."

Globin nodded. "Come—let us see how well they have recovered."

Behind the glass wall, the women were sitting, still dazed and groggy. The Fleet doctors moved among them, their faces masks of impervious politeness—though now and again, one slipped, and the contempt showed through.

Lusanne shuddered. "Must we be left to the cold care of such strangers as these?"

"Only until your aunts are restored to full consciousness and mobility," Globin assured her. "That has been the subject of some spirited discussion between the commander of this battlestation and myself."

That was a huge understatement, he reflected as he thought of Brand's fury over the intercom, and the hatred that still seemed to echo in his voice when he said the name "Schlein." So now, as Globin stood with Lusanne gazing at the groggy women sitting upright in their flimsy hospital gowns, supported by their raised mattresses, watching their human and Khalian physicians with fearful eyes, Globin deliberated about the next phase in his campaign against Brand.

He was certain that he was right to want to keep the Schlein women in his own bailiwick. These were not women who had undergone the defeat of their home planet, and been chastened by it and come to be grateful for Alliance clemency, but women who were still mentally at the height of deceptive war, regarding the Fleet doctors as their captors and hated enemies, and the Khalians as their despised but lethal pawns. In Brand's territory, the best they could expect would be ostracism; at worst, they would be targets for the long-buried vengefulness that they themselves would reawaken.

Globin's recruits, on the other hand, were all young Khalians, who would not really think about the Schleins having been traitors to either race, for to them, the war was only a tale told by their elders, albeit a very vivid one. Like Lusanne, they would be more curious than vengeful, and willing to be patient, coaxing their prisoners ahead into the modern day, and waiting patiently for friendship.

There was no question—the women had to stay in Barataria.

But how?

"Let us go in," Lusanne said. "I can see what they are saying to one another, when the doctors' backs are turned."

See what they say? Globin frowned down at her, then remembered that she was reading lips. "Yes, of course. Let us go in."

They came into the recovery room, and every woman instantly locked her gaze on to Globin, apprehension deepening at the sight of one more strange male. Then Lusanne's presence beside him registered, and they relaxed—a little.

"Thank heavens, child!" Selena croaked. "We were afraid you were dead!"

"Very much alive, Aunt Selena," Lusanne assured her. "Our rescuers have been very courteous and gentle with me. I would like to introduce you to our host, the chief executive of the Baratarian Corporation."

"Thank Heaven!" breathed the tallest, a woman in her fifties with tousled, auburn hair, still beautiful even though she was drawn and wan with the strain of her long coma. "A man who isn't a Fleet officer!"

"Be quiet, you fool!" snapped an aging matron. "That's not a man, it's the Globin!"

The auburn woman stared, horror coming into her eyes.

The women all shrank back against their mattresses in alarm. "The Globin!"

"Am I so notorious as that?" Globin blinked around at them in mild amusement. "I had not thought that my reputation would reach all the way to your home world!"

"We have heard," Selena said, her mouth dry. "We have also heard that you treat your captives well, because you expect their governments to ransom them."

Globin nodded gravely. "But I am no longer a pirate, madam, nor are my Khalians—and Barataria is no longer a pirates' nest, but the home world of a commercial conglomerate."

There was a stir among the women, and Selena glanced at Lusanne for confirmation. Lusanne nodded ever so slightly, and hope lighted Selena's face. "You have become legitimate, then!"

"We have," Globin acknowledged. "But we will still extend every courtesy to our guests. Indeed, the Distressed Spacefarer's Law allows no less."

"It does not require 'every courtesy,'" Selena said with irony, "but we are grateful for all that you have given us thus far." She had rallied; pirates might be dangerous, but businessmen would strike a deal, and Selena, scientist or not, had been raised to business. "We are, then, aboard one of your Baratarian ships?"

"I fear not, madam. You are aboard the *Stephen Hawking*, an Alliance battlestation operated by the Fleet."

Instant consternation spread throughout the recovery room—consternation verging on panic. "So that is why those doctors were so cold, so hostile!" the auburn woman cried, and Selena snapped, "You cannot surrender us to them, sir! You must not!"

"Peace, peace, Aunt," Lusanne said. "The war has been over for years!"

The women stilled, staring at her, huge-eyed.

"What war?" Selena whispered. "The Khalians were defeated three years before we left!"

"The war between the Fleet and our Families." To Lusanne, a whisper was as good as a shout. "The war is history, and the wounds have healed."

"But how can so much have happened in so short a time! You were not even born when we left! Only twenty-six years ago! Could our home world have fallen so quickly?"

"Madam," said the Globin, "how old am I?"

Selena turned and stared, suddenly registering the lines, the wrinkles. "I had thought it was only space tan," she whispered.

"I fear it is more," the Globin said. "In fact, I have been told that I am uncommonly well preserved for my years, especially in view of the strains of my life in administration."

Selena's lips parted, but her voice was a bare whisper. "How . . . how long?"

"You have been in cold sleep for several decades," Globin said gently.

"Several?" Selena licked dry lips, swallowed, and asked, "How long?"

"Many years," Globin answered, and Lusanne said, "We have been on our journey for a hundred fifty years, Aunt."

Selena reeled, squeezing her eyes shut. Lusanne was at her side in a second.

"No, no, child, I am not going to faint," Selena muttered. She recovered her poise, pushed Lusanne away, and said, "So the battle is lost, and the rancor has cooled—but not completely, as we have seen from our doctors." She glanced nervously at the medical team who hovered behind Globin. "All in all, I think we might be safer here."

"You are my guests for as long as you wish to remain." Globin inclined his head graciously. "Or at least for as long as I can stall off Commander Brand."

"And how long will that be?"

"At the least, until you are completely restored to fitness and peak physical condition. How did you say you felt, madam?"

The Klaxon sounded.

Throughout the Baratarian Quarter, Khalians scrambled for battle stations. The Klaxon's braying modulated into words: "Enemy approaching! Enemy penetrating screens! Enemy attack on south pole!"

The quarter rocked at a sudden blast that rang through the hull into every cubicle. The Khalian crewmen stumbled, throwing themselves against walls for support; a few fell to the floor. Then they were up again and running as the Klaxon yammered, "Hull penetrated at cargo hold South 24!"

South 24! Globin had a momentary vision of trade goods spilling out into space by the gross, trade goods fired by energy weapons within the hull, trade goods trampled under . . . Then he shook it off—if they didn't manage to repel the Ichtons, all the trade goods in the galaxy wouldn't do them a bit of good. He yanked open the cabinet on the wall and pulled out his rifle, then hauled the door open and went into the corridor. At his age, he knew better than to run, and his crew knew better than to let him near danger—but Plasma had dashed off after the attackers, gray muzzle or no, and no one would see the Globin coming out to the fight. . . .

He was amazed at himself; his self-image was still fixed at twenty, when he would have shied away from any combat in sheer terror. But a lifetime with Khalian pirates, and Goodheart's careful instruction in unarmed combat, had given him back the courage the boyhood bullies had stolen, and he went toward the sound of battle, not away from it.

Then the deck lifted against his feet, and the walls shuddered. He lurched against a bulkhead, but kept his feet while a chorus of screams broke out ahead. Globin stared, then ran. It was only a few steps to the sickbay. . . .

"Hull holed in Khalian sickbay!" the Klaxon blatted. "Infantry to sickbay!"

Globin swerved into the doorway, remembering to leap aside so other defenders could come in—and they did, in a stream; but a fireball blossomed in the doorway. Khalian screams shrilled; Globin shrank back, turning his face to the wall while the light faded. Then he turned and saw dead Khalians on the floor. His heart wrenched at the sight, but more of his young Weasels were leaping in and dodging to the sides, and there was no time for grief. Globin turned ahead and saw the huge insectoid shapes grabbing at the Family women. They shrank back shrieking, looking about them wildly, clawing at the walls. The oldest one had found a plasma holder and was beating at a carapace; the Ichton tore it out of her hands and turned its rifle toward her, but younger women jammed chairs between them, and their screaming was beginning to be as much in anger as in fear. Lusanne had a bit more presence of mind than he would have expected—she had found a pole lamp and was stabbing the glowing tube at the Ichton's eyes.

It was valiant, but would do no good. Globin steadied himself, resting his barrel on a bedstead. He aimed for the insect's eyes and waited for a split second when there would be no human head in the way. Auburn hair swung aside; Globin pressed the trigger. The energy bolt flashed. Women screamed as they leaped aside, giving Globin a clear field of fire. He shot again and again.

The Ichton's shrilling was at the upper edge of his hearing, tearing through his head, and the monster swung its firearm about, blasting blindly. The women hit the deck. Globin realized, with satisfaction, that he had burned its eyes out. He lowered his aim to the thorax and fired. His bolt smashed in; three more of the Khalian crew joined in, focusing on the thorax. The monster bucked, then fell dead.

Globin looked up and saw that his crew had seen what he had done, and were imitating. Bolts flared at Ichton eyes; bug rifles spewed in every direction, but hit only the walls. Khalian fire focused on thoraxes and burned through.

Then Plasma leaped in front of him, chittering in rage. "Globin! If you die, we are all lost! Get back, get away!"

A dozen young Khalians leaped in, a living wall between them and the Ichtons—but the living bugs were retreating, firing as they went back out through the hole they had blasted in.

"That is a long tunnel," Globin said to Plasma. "We are nowhere near the hull."

"But there is vacuum somewhere at the other end," Plasma snapped. "They are fainting from loss of air!"

And indeed, the women who had thrown themselves down were not rising. Here and there, a few Khalians were falling, clawing at their throats. The air being sucked in from the rest of the quarter had sustained them thus far, but it was almost exhausted.

"Lusanne!" Globin cried. "Quickly, Plasma! The oxygen!"

Plasma moved more quickly than his chief, and a few of the youngsters saw what he was up to as he cracked the valve on the oxygen cylinder in the clinic. Some leaped to help him, finding other green cylinders; others caught up blankets and sheets and slapped up a quick barrier over the hole.

Moving more slowly, Globin brought an oxygen mask to Lusanne—but she was already working her way to her feet, and pushed the mask away. "Selena— my other aunts—they need it more than I."

Globin sighed and turned to help the Schleins who knew from personal memory what had caused the animosity between them.

"All told, we got off very lightly," Brand told the hastily assembled conference. "It was just a raid by a couple of destroyers, backed up by a battlewagon. The big ship sat back and helped pour fire into one point on our shield until it overloaded, causing a sector to collapse. Then they sat back and provided covering fire while the destroyers broke in and started shooting their way toward the sickbay. When they found out they were dying faster than we were, they pulled out. All told, we lost four of the Schlein women and six of our own crew, plus thirty wounded. All things considered, it could have been much worse."

"Let's hope they don't think to try it with a larger force," someone said grimly.

"We know they will, now," Brand said, his face heavy. "We'll just have to start shooting if they come anywhere near. That's pretty obvious, though. The real question is, why?"

Everyone was silent, avoiding one another's eyes. It was the question they'd been hoping not to have to think about.

Brand turned to Globin, pointing at the cross-sectional map of the ship. "They attacked your quarter, Chairman. That might have been accident, but coming into the hold and blowing their way through wall after wall until they came to the sickbay—that was deliberate, very deliberate. Why?"

He turned back to the assembled officers. They all frowned, looking back; then one voiced the thought that all were thinking: "The women."

Brand sighed. "Good. Then I'm not the only one who sees it. But . . . why?"

The officers exchanged puzzled glances. Then one said, with an apologetic half laugh, "Because they're beautiful, of course."

The reaction was out of all proportion to the joke—if it was a joke. Everyone took it as such, though, laughing till the tears came. Brand took it well, grinning as he looked about them, stifling a chuckle of his own. After all, it *was* hilarious— giant insectoids thinking human women attractive. It was almost as funny as the notion of one of the bug queens exciting desire in a human male—and every one of them must have thought of that, too, for when the laughter had begun to slacken, it suddenly redoubled in a new wave. When the noise had subsided, though, Brand frowned, serious again. "Okay. What possible interest could they be to the bugs? And how could the swarm have found out about them, anyway?"

There was only muttering for a while; then Globin had a sudden inspiration. "Commander! They could never have seen the women before, or the Schleins would not have lived for us to find them!"

The conversation stilled; everyone turned, amazed. "Why, that's very true, Chairman," Brand said slowly. "They could only have seen the Schlein vessel."

"But they destroyed the ship," someone else pointed out, "and all the male Schleins aboard."

"Yes, Commander, that tallies with what the women have told us," Globin corroborated. "The men ejected them in a life capsule and stayed to fight."

Someone else said slowly, "Why did the men stay?"

It was a good question, and the apparent answer was so obvious that no one had ever thought of it. They looked at one another in surprise.

"Yes," Brand said slowly. "Once the women were safe, why didn't the men escape in the same fashion? Obviously, because they couldn't."

"Of course!" cried a captain. "If they all ejected in a life-pod, the bugs would have blasted them out of this space-time! The men had to keep the fight going long enough for the women to get lost in the depths!"

The room was very quiet for a few minutes, as each man contemplated the courage of those Schlein men, fighting to certain death, knowing they stood no chance of winning, but also knowing that each second they bought would give their loved ones a little longer to recede into the dark and cold of interstellar space. Even here near the Core, there was enough room between stars so that one tiny, hundred-foot-long life-pod would be indistinguishable by radar from a thousand other asteroids—if it were beyond the reach of telescopes.

"So the bugs knew someone had escaped," Brand summarized, "but they couldn't find them. Why would they be so fanatical about killing them, though, once they'd been found?"

"The Ichtons are fanatical about everything," someone said.

"Sheer cussedness," someone else suggested. "They hate not finishing something they've started."

"No." Brand shook his head. "They've always been very logical—we've seen the records, we know they've gone past hard targets to find easy ones, and not come back until they had so much strength massed that the hard targets had become pushovers. It's not like them to take a risk of any kind, let alone what amounts to a commando action against overwhelming odds. They had something to gain from this, more than just a sixty-year-old grudge."

"More to the point," someone else said, "they must have had something to lose."

"Of course!" Globin was on his feet, eyes wide with sudden understanding. "That's been bothering me for a while—why would they have taken the trouble to eliminate a single ship, one that didn't even bear enough armament to be a military vessel? Why bother swatting a fly?"

"Unless," Brand said slowly, "the fly has come too close to your lunch."

"Or your heart," Globin said grimly.

Brand's eyes glowed. "Yes! They saw something, Chairman. They saw something on their viewscreens that they shouldn't have seen—and the bugs have to make sure they don't tell anybody. When your men found the life-pod, the bugs must have picked up the radio transmissions—we know they have some kind of intelligence service. They wouldn't have had to understand very much to know that your people had found something. A little thought, and a bit of record-checking, could have told them what."

"Seems kind of farfetched," an officer said slowly, "for them to find out that much just from some half-understood radio transmissions."

"I don't like to think of the alternative," Brand said grimly.

Neither did anyone else—that there was a traitor aboard or some kind of listening device. The atmosphere grew strained; they knew that Brand couldn't discount the possibility, now that he'd thought of it, and that Internal Intelligence would be very alert for any signs of treachery from now on.

"Still, it seems possible," Globin said slowly. "A lone picket who picks up a sudden flurry of language-noise, then gets close enough for his long-range sensors to see something heavy being towed in. . . . Of course, he wouldn't attack himself, not if there was a chance he'd be shot down instead of bringing back important information. No, I don't think it requires a spy."

"Maybe not," Brand conceded, "but it does require the Schlein women being a lot more important than we thought they were. Chairman, I really must insist they be moved into the Fleet sickbay, where they can be guarded more securely."

Globin bridled, but kept his tone soft. "I beg to differ, Commander. This incident has set back their convalescence by several weeks; it is very important that they not be moved."

"But your sickbay's shot to pieces, Globin! You can't take care of them anymore!"

"Repairs on the sickbay are almost complete," Globin demurred. "The survivors are comfortable in the recreation room in the meantime — and your counselors are helping them to cope with the shock of the invasion."

"We must have them submit to hypnosis and memory scan, Chairman! It's absolutely vital!"

"Agreed," Globin said easily, "but they cannot be subjected to any such exertion until they are fully recovered. You know that, Commander. Ask your own physicians. What good is a dead source? How much water can you draw from a dry well?"

Brand was still a moment; his eyes narrowed. "There is one among them who is fully recovered, Chairman. I have seen her walking in your company."

"What, Lusanne?" Globin shrugged impatiently. "She is scarcely more than a child, Commander. What could she know? What could she have understood from what she had seen?"

"Her information is vital, Chairman!"

"But it cannot be gained without her consent," Globin said, his voice iron. "Hypnosis will not work on an unwilling subject. There is no point in the scan unless it is voluntary."

"Then ask her, Chairman!"

Globin sighed. "Very well, Commander. I shall ask."

Lusanne drew in upon herself, her eyes wide. "Must I, Globin?" Then she answered herself. "Yes, of course I must. If it might save lives . . ."

"But you are afraid," Globin interpreted. "It will do no good if you are afraid, Lusanne. You would be too tense to achieve the trance. Even if you did, it could not be deep enough."

"What could I have seen that the Ichtons would care about?"

"Nothing, probably," Globin said, "unless everyone on your ship saw it, too. But in all probability, they did not—only those who were on duty on the bridge at the time would have had the chance."

Lusanne nodded slowly, frowning. "That would make sense. . . ."

"Who was on the bridge?" Globin asked softly.

"Of my aunts? Only Selena, and Maude and Mirabile—they were the only ones of command rank. The rest of us couldn't have cared less. There were only a few of the men, too—no one wanted to take time away from their experiments, to do it. Someone said it was like having to be chairman of a mathematics department."

"Perfect irony," Globin said, and reported it that way to Brand. "They may be trying to kill people who do not have the information they fear, Commander. The ones who did know, they have done in already."

"It's possible," Brand admitted, "but we must be sure. Can't you persuade her, Chairman?"

"I probably could," Globin said slowly, "but she is afraid of the Fleet, Commander. Your doctors have not hidden their hostility very well."

"And the scan would be unsuccessful, if she's so fearful," Brand sighed, sitting back. "Very well, Globin. We'll work at creating an atmosphere of trust. Let's just hope that the Ichtons don't manage to rob us of all atmosphere of any kind, first."

But Brand couldn't be stalled forever. A good long time, true—his own doctors admitted that the women were thoroughly depleted by their long sleep; muscle tone was gone, digestion was delicate, and nervous systems were recovering rather slowly from thirty years of dormancy. Still, even Globin couldn't delay physical therapy with any good conscience—the women's lives depended as much on their physical fitness, as on their dwelling place. So the day came when Brand invited Globin to a conference again, and demanded, "They are restored to health. We want them."

And Globin, with the utmost courtesy, replied, "Your pardon, Commander, but they wish to remain my guests."

"The war may be over, Globin, but those women were not residing on any of the planets that surrendered and are not yet included under the terms of that treaty. They may have information about the Core that we need, and may not wish to accept the armistice."

Globin stood rigid, hoping he was mistaken about what the commander had not said. "Just how strong an interrogation do you intend?"

"What?" Brand stared, taken aback as much by the iron tone as by the words themselves. Then he realized Globin's meaning and leaned back with a long whistle. "Oh, no, Globin, what do you take me for? Of course we don't intend torture! But the women are human, and must reside among their own kind!"

Globin relaxed, but only a little. "I would send them in an instant if they wished to go, Commander, but they are . . . apprehensive."

"Apprehensive? About what?"

"About their reception among Fleet personnel, Commander. Even their doctors treated them with a contempt that was only slightly veiled."

"We are only human, Globin. You can't be surprised if the presence of Schlein family members straight from the middle of the war brings back old . . . antagonisms."

"Not surprised at all," Globin said dryly. "Under those circumstances, *you* should not be surprised if they find the company of my young warriors more congenial."

"We must have them, Globin!"

"They are my guests, Commander. I shall not ask them to leave."

Brand slammed a fist down on his desk like a gavel. "You are bound by the regulations of the *Hawking*!"

"As you are bound by the terms of our contract," Globin returned.

Brand's face turned stony. "I will convene a formal hearing. The arbitrators shall decide the issue, and their judgment shall be binding upon both parties as is stipulated in your contract!"

"To arbitration I shall submit." Globin's tone made it quite clear that he would not submit to Brand.

The hearing chamber, somewhat ominously, was also the room intended for court-martials and any other legal proceedings that might have arisen during the voyage. However, its architecture didn't suggest the majesty of the law—more the boardroom of a corporation. There were three tables, joined to form an "I"; the stem, the longest table, was taken up by a double row of officers, corporation executives, and a few high-ranking civilians, such as scientists and doctors. Two of the faces there were Khalian; only one was Baratarian.

At the head of the "I" were Brand and his counselors; it was the head because that was where Brand was sitting. However, an enlargement of the Alliance seal took up most of the wall behind him, whereas the wall at the foot was blank, with a paleness that suggested the holotank it truly was valuable for the conferences for which this room doubled. Even in so large a ship as the *Hawking*, every space had to be used for at least two functions.

Globin sat at the foot of the table, with Selena Schlein, Lusanne, and Plasma, who was surrounded by a leader and its recordspheres.

Brand brought down a gavel. "This hearing may begin. Let the record show that on this date, the Fleet invoked its authority to take into its care any distressed space travelers taken aboard the *Stephen Hawking*, and that the Baratarian Corporation has refused to surrender its prisoners."

"We are not prisoners," Selena Schlein snapped.

"Objection," said the military attorney next to Brand, and the commander said, "Sustained." Then, to Selena, "Please do not speak unless you are recognized. For the record, please tell us your name and—"

The alarm blared.

Everyone sat bolt upright.

"Battle stations!" a voice snapped over the sound of the Klaxon.

"Ichton ship has penetrated inner defenses! Commander Brand to the bridge, please! All personnel to battle stations! Enemy is within range, but his shields are holding, and his fire is concentrated on a single zone of ours! All personnel to battle stations! Conflict is imminent!"

"Adjourned!" Brand struck the gavel down one more time, even as he rose and turned from his seat.

"Back to our quarters," Globin snapped, and they rose, he and Plasma to either side of the ladies. Dr. Arterial stepped up from the witnesses' seats to stand in front of them, and the single Baratarian officer fell in behind. In formation, they went out the door and toward the drop tube.

"They cannot really manage to board so huge a ship as this!" Selena protested.

"The *Hawking* is big, but that only gives it a greater area to defend," Globin returned, "and the Ichton ships are big, hard, and mean. They have probably spent a dozen ships and all the lives on them, to bring a single cruiser so close— but there are as likely to be three as one, and—"

The floor lurched out from under them.

Howls of anger split the air, and smoke filled the hallway. A huge insectoid form came looming out of that smoke, fire spearing from it.

Their little formation wheeled about; the young Khalian who had been the rear guard was suddenly the point. He drew his weapon in a single clean motion. . . .

A piercing, high-pitched tone stabbed their ears, so loud that it sent a singing pain right through their brains. The young Khalian dropped his weapon, clutching his ears and rolling on the floor in agony. So did Globin, Selena, Dr. Arterial; Globin fought to pull his hands away from his ears, but found he couldn't bear the shriek emanating from the Ichton.

Lusanne scooped up the young Khalian's fallen weapon, aimed, and fired. A small box on the Ichton's front blew into bits.

The shrieking tone stopped.

Lusanne's fire tore at the Ichton. Terran shouts and Khalian shrilling echoed down the hall, triumphant; a fallen weapon came skidding toward them. Selena pounced on it and opened fire on the Ichton, but it kept coming, looming closer and closer. The fire from its weapon was a mad spray now, tearing at the walls and the floor, battering all about them, but not hitting.

Globin finally managed to draw and fire.

The addition of his weapon was enough; the Ichton dropped. Its body jerked as fire tore it apart. Finally, the pieces lay still.

Another loomed through the smoke behind it.

Their fire tore it to shreds.

That wasn't all there was to the fight, of course. It raged on for hours, and for the first time in decades, Globin was in the thick of it, trying desperately to protect the women, who were trying desperately to protect him. The other Schlein women caught up discarded weapons and remembered childhood training; they became a battle unit. Decades of daily exercise paid off; Globin's old heart labored; but it did not fail him. Lusanne, Selena, and the other Schleins fought on by his side with their scavenged weapons, snatching up charge packs from dead soldiers as they came upon them.

The new noise boxes were in constant use; it was an experiment, but more than a dozen Ichtons had them. Globin would hear the shrill screech and urge his little squadron toward it—after all, any direction was as likely to bring the ladies to safety as any other. As they came closer, they were disabled by the piercing tone, but Lusanne, with unerring accuracy, exploded box after box. Globin began to wonder about her hobbies.

Finally they linked up with a squadron of Marines, who formed a circle around them, and Globin and Plasma gratefully let the younger generation take the brunt of the fighting. His young Khalian fell, and until another squadron of soldiers joined them, Lusanne filled his place in the circle, side by side with a young blond giant who fought like a very demon and cheered her on to victory. "After them, woman! Oh, what a lass! Kill every last one of the stinking bugs! Don't even *think* about mercy—'cause *they* won't! By the stars, I've never seen such a woman as you!"

He couldn't know that the object of his admiration couldn't hear his praises; she fought shoulder to shoulder, and could not see his lips. She could only sneak quick glances at him as he fought—but that she did often, her glances became longer and longer, almost gazes of awe.

When the battle was over, and the amplified voice of Brand told them that surviving enemies had retreated, that all other hostiles were dead, and that the hull was sealed—then, finally, Lusanne could look up in admiration at the big soldier who towered over her and was amazed to see him gazing raptly down at her and breathing, "You are the most remarkable woman who ever lived!"

"But—I am deaf," she protested.

That rocked him for a second, but only a second. Then he said, "Thank Heaven you are, or we'd all be dead this minute!" And he seized her and kissed her.

They froze, lip to lip, for what seemed an unconscionably long time, and something seemed to unknot and flow inside Globin's chest as he watched—but he smiled sadly, and nodded, for yes, this was how it should be, youth to youth, without some dried-up old misshapen man in between.

Love inspires trust—and Lusanne was willing to undergo the memory scan, if her Sergeant Barkis was there to hold her hand. Of course, the psychiatrist and the interrogation specialist were much warmer toward her now, and made no secret of their admiration for her courage under fire; that did no harm, either.

Her three aunts who had been on the bridge were interrogated, too, about the few days preceding the attack sixty years before. All their testimony agreed they had discovered a new planet; everyone on the ship had been very excited about it, so the bridge had relayed the pictures from the visual sensors to the big screen in the lounge. They had gone considerably closer to try to determine if the planet could support life. It could; they had come too close, and Ichton ships had boiled out into space to attack them.

That was all the three aunts remembered. But Lusanne's memory held an extremely clear picture of the viewscreen when the planet was first identified— and the astronomers were able to identify the stars at the outer edge of the screen. From that, they could make an excellent guess at the location of the planet.

"A home world," Brand said with immense satisfaction. "Maybe not *the* Ichton home world, but certainly an Ichton home world. Young lady, you have done us an invaluable service."

"But how?" Lusanne protested, eyes wide in bewilderment. "How can I, when all of us saw it on the big viewscreen in the lounge? Why could I, when my aunts couldn't?"

"Because they use all their senses, Lusanne," her sergeant said. He pressed her hand, and she turned to watch his lips. "They don't emphasize what they see as much as you do," he explained, "so your visual memories are much sharper, much more detailed."

Lusanne stared at him, startled. "I held the clue because I'm deaf?"

"Sergeant Barkis may have found the answer," the psychiatrist agreed.

Globin could see the fear in her eyes, so he hastened to reassure her. "Yes, I know—that makes you an even more vital target for them, you, and you alone. But not if they or their spies discover that your secret is out, and that we all know of the home world now."

"How can we tell them that, though?" she asked in conster-nation.

"By the most direct message possible," Brand said, and keyed his intercom. "Bridge! Astronomy is sending up a set of coordinates they got from Psych. Set a course for the Ichton home world!"

"Aye, Commander," the bridge responded.

Brand sat back, gaze glittering. "Now the Ichtons really will attack!"

They did.

WEAPON OF WAR

With only limited space available there were no ships larger than a cruiser brought to the center of the *Hawking*. The fact that all the warships and dozens of merchants had to be carried within the *Hawking*'s hull on the six-month journey to the galactic center had mitigated toward the *Hawking* carrying a larger number of smaller ships. Many of these were the almost-unarmed scouts, specially equipped to find and warn the races threatened by the Ichtons.

The smallest of the combat aircraft were the Fleet SBs. Designed to serve as patrol ships among the shipping lanes inside the Alliance, the SBs were the smallest ships capable of warp drive. Too small to carry engines capable of powering laser turrets that were effective at anything but near point-blank range, the SBs' sting came from the two dozen missiles jammed into launchers that occupied nearly half the ship's length. Individually the SB was little threat to any larger combat ship as both sides protected them by antimissile laser banks. A squad of six to ten SBs could launch enough missiles simultaneously to overwhelm even a small cruiser's defenses. The cost was often two or three of their number destroyed in the attack. Needless to add, the SBs attracted only the most reckless, and often creative, pilots.

In the six months after the fall of Gerson, the *Hawking* fought a series of delaying actions against three large Ichton fleets that were moving on parallel courses around the galactic center. The Fleet warships were slowly losing this battle of attrition when two of the Ichton fleets simply disappeared. After a week, Anton Brand ordered all the remaining ships to concentrate on the remaining large fleet. In a number of sharp actions, the Fleet forces joined with those of nearby allied races to shatter this third Ichton force. This victory gave a needed boost to everyone's morale. Everyone except Anton Brand and those of his staff, who realized that there had been virtually none of the dozen of mother ships normally found at the center of any Ichton formation. The Ichton fleet they had destroyed had obviously been meant as a distraction, one that had succeeded and further bled the remaining Fleet forces as well.

While the larger Fleet ships had engaged the Ichtons, the smaller SBs continued to patrol at the edges of the area of conflict. It was one of these forces that discovered not the new combined Ichton fleet but one of the many supply convoys needed to maintain it.

CHARITY
by S.N. Lewitt

Charity is incumbent on each person every day. Charity is assisting anyone, lifting provisions, saying a good word . . . Removal from the way of that which is harmful is charity.

—Hadith of the Prophet Muhammad

"Dawn Leader, we have bogers four o'clock, axis Z. Repeat, four o'clock, axis Z."

Dawn Leader didn't say anything at all. He spun the heavily armed SB as hard around as he could up the axis Z, bringing guns to bear on the enemy. The computer blinked into targeting and then fired the volley on autoselect. Slow, so screamingly slow, he thought. The best they could rig in the limited space and energy requirements of the SBs, but the smart controls weren't near the reflexes in any true ship of the line.

And it was too late. The SB *Dawn Walker* exploded in a million colors across ten klicks of raw space. And the shards of that explosion tore up the smart missile he had launched only nanoseconds ago.

Shards that should have torn through the enemy fighter, but instead were directed harmlessly around it. An energy shield, up and in place. Made no sense for the Imps of Shaitan. What did they care for an individual to live or die? They had no concept of Paradise. No, it was all to insult their human prey, to throw a challenge across the battle lines instead of fighting like honest men.

Group leader Hassan Ibn Abdullah was furious, and he knew that was exactly where the enemy wanted him. Angry and ready to make mistakes. He could hear their laughter in his head, if the Ickies laughed at all. And he knew better than to imagine it. The thought only led to mistakes.

"Dawn team, report," he ordered briskly.

Element one was in good shape; element two was a little too far from the group. Hassan ordered them back. And three, three was gone. *Dawn Walker* and *Dawn Singer* both.

The four SBs, even armed as they were, were not the ideal craft in which to fight the Ichtons. SBs had never been designed as primary fighters. They were only scoutships for transport and exploration, and rigging them with the heaviest guns they could carry was not going to make them a match for the Ichtons' protecting horde.

And Dawn Group hadn't been on a combat mission. At least they hadn't thought it was a combat mission when the assistant head of Planetary Astronomy had briefed them. In fact, Hassan had been upset at that briefing. He had wanted to be in the attack group, not given some Cub Scout assignment.

"We've got some readings that indicate there may be a habitable planet in this system," Rhys Davies had said softly. Dr. Davies always talked as if he were lecturing undergraduates in the intro class he didn't really want to teach. "And my department has been asked to find a place to settle the Gerson survivors." This was said with distinct distaste.

Not that anyone, even Davies, could possibly want not to help the few remaining Gersons. He merely resented being forced to be application-oriented when there was obviously so much more important theoretical work to do. Hassan had come to expect this attitude whenever he had to deal with the Science staff. Which meant that he dealt with them as little as possible.

"In any event, it is well out of the heavily trafficked areas and the military advisors have said it is not in the general thrust direction of the swarm. There is no reason to believe that the Ichtons have ever found this sector, and hopefully they will be eliminated before they do."

For the first time Hassan found himself agreeing wholeheartedly with Davies. If not with the assignment. He wanted to be out there doing some damage, not playing human probe.

That was an uncharitable thought, he knew. The Gersons had already lost so much, their home world, their people. The few survivors were not particularly happy aboard the *Hawking*, no matter how comfortable the civilians tried to make them. So Hassan tried not to protest, to hold it in his mind that this was a great service.

Maybe it wasn't killing bugs, but there were lots of bugs out there. More than enough to go around. Plenty left for him and the rest of Dawn Group to kill. They could spare a few hours for an act of charity.

Still, Loe Sebeng had their SBs fully armed and loaded and in top shape. "Never know what you might find out there," Sebeng had muttered, shaking her head. "Never know. Too damned much garbage around this place anyway. Want to dump some garbage while you're out?"

"We might be on routine," he protested. "But we're not the garbage scow."

Sebeng had given him one of her rare smiles. "Well, you're armed as far as I can make you. The only ammunition you're not carrying is what won't fit."

Hassan had been pleased by that much, but resigned to one more routine patrol. If they found a place for the Gersons, well and good. If not, well, there were plenty of bogers to go around.

Which was why the convoy out here was such a surprise. No one had anticipated it. And Astronomy should have been able to pick up on all that leaky
radiation from primitive drives. They should have spotted this from the other
side of the big black donut it was so bright. And he and Dawn Group had just
blundered into it.

A single scout group shouldn't be alone with a four-freighter enemy convoy.
No, a destroyer should be out in this mess, sweeping up handfuls of those little
Ichton fighters that protected the big ships, sweeping them up and cracking
them open. Even the Ickies couldn't live in hard vacuum.

Why wasn't there any cover? Why hadn't Astronomy picked up that bright
red-hot trail when they did the survey routine? The questions flew through
Hassan's mind and he dismissed them. No time to think about that now. Just
time to do what was necessary. Get the four survivors back to the *Hawking*.
Better to let the brass know about the little convoy over in this sector, ready to
pull out and invade disputed space. Which by Ichton standards wasn't disputed
at all. They didn't believe in disputed space, weren't genetically capable of recognizing any claims other than their own.

"Break hard around the rock, kids," Hassan said. The casual ease of his voice
masked his tension. The tiny moon ahead of them was really no more than
a glorified asteroid caught in orbit around an inhospitable planet. Puny for a
moon, but big enough to give the Dawn Group a little shelter. They split, two
elements going in opposite directions and jinking hard against their expected
trajectories. That would confuse anything but a real smart-read missile, and
would be hard to follow even if it could be read.

The moon seemed enormous this close. Hassan skimmed his SB down so
close he could feel the drag of the flying lunar dust, barely a meter above the
surface. Let them follow that, he thought in fury. His signature IR should be lost
in the background reflection of the surface itself. Even a smart missile couldn't
take him there.

As he rounded the lunar curve, his stomach clenched again. There was a
moment of terror, thinking that the rest of the group had not made it. And then
he saw them, each one planing the horizon and appearing in the shadow of the
only shelter they had.

"No one followed us, boss," said *Dawn Breaker*. That would be Solange des
Salles. There was a question at the edge of her voice that came through even on
the private line.

"There seems to be a pattern here," Hassan said. "Did any of you note when
pursuit dropped off?"

"At about two klicks from their destroyer, looked like to me," Martin Hong
answered. "But that's an approximate, boss. I was too busy taking care of business to get their exact address, if you know what I mean."

Hassan thanked him and sighed. Marty always did manage to embellish even a simple report. But Hong's observation coincided with his own, and with Bradley in *Dawn Tiger* and des Salles again. So. That should mean they were safe enough behind this rock for the time being, until they could slip away after the convoy had passed.

Hassan was not about to bet that there wasn't going to be any pursuit at all. Good Muslims didn't gamble, and a serious stint in Tactical School had shown him why. So far, it was the one taboo he hadn't broken. Yet. Besides which, he didn't like the idea of sitting still like a convenient target while there were enemy nearby. It made his skin crawl.

Part of Hassan Ibn Abdullah wanted to stay, to keep on blasting ammunition until the entire load Sebeng had stocked was gone. He knew better. They needed some bigger guns out here. More important, Intelligence had to know about these movements. There was something brewing in the Ickie strategy that they had not anticipated, and it was worth all their lives, let alone their kill ratios, to get the news back.

"So it's time for all good Dawn Riders to get back to Mama," he muttered. Then his voice became louder and more distinct. "Let's take it in slow formation, ride this shadow down, and use the radiation background cover of the planet to slip atound. Then we can head straight home. Those Ickies are going in the other direction, and they'll be there when we get back with some reinforcements."

"Ah, boss, c'mon," Marty Hong half teased and half pleaded. "You wanna share all the glory? I could win my Silver Cluster out there."

"You think the taxpayers got nothing better to do than buy you new boats?" Hassan clipped him short. "Let's get back to base and tell the tech toys all about this convoy."

One by one, in a stepped formation, the Dawn Group departed. Their single SBs drifted down toward the dead planet below and disappeared against the background radiation. Which was very high. This place had more radioactive elements than the *Hawking*'s drive. It would be a major find for whoever could exploit it, but deadly to live on. Even the Ichtons, it seemed, had decided to pass it by.

Hassan, in *Dawn Leader*, came around last. On the far side of the planet the team regrouped for their jump back to the *Hawking*. Far enough from any gravity well to slip free, they disappeared into speed where the enemy could not follow.

But Hassan Ibn Abdullah did not feel any relief even when he saw the battlestation before them, larger than the moon he had used as a shield. Which made no sense. Here he was safe. The enemy possessed nothing, nothing at all that could damage the battlestation. It was like trying to blow a minor star. The great docking bays around the north pole were cavernous black, beckoning. He herded in his little group, smaller by two than when they had gone out. But the sense of well-being, the break in tension that had always signaled homecoming before, did not touch Hassan. Not even when the airlock had cycled through and he was standing on solid deck in his "indoor" blues.

"We weren't expecting a convoy out in this direction," Hassan said, debriefing to the tack officer of the watch. "We were just on an exploratory patrol since this wasn't a sector we'd done more than survey. We were under orders from the Science section, to be honest. But after we took a look at the rock, which would be real interesting to a merchant and absolutely no good to resettle our Gerson survivors, we came around to take a quick peek at the rest of the system. And we ran into what had to be a major column movement. I didn't see anything I could identify as an egg ship, so I don't think they were moving to take possession of a new place. At least not right now. But there may well be another population under attack out there that we don't know about."

The tack officer's face remained completely unreadable. "Thank you, Group Leader," the tack officer said. "You can go now."

Hassan knew better than to try to make his case more strongly. Instead he rose and left the debriefing room with all its glow maps and screen charts. The misery that pressed down on him didn't leave, even though he was off duty now for twelve hours.

Solange des Salles had waited for him outside the briefing room. She settled into a long stride that matched his as they moved away from the offices. "Tanya and Lee are on duty now," she said casually, naming her roommates. "My place?"

Hassan grinned. "How about a little later?" he asked. "It was a stretch. I want to unwind a little first."

Solange nodded, shrugged, and left. Much as he and des Salles had a useful arrangement, he already had other plans. He had a serious date with the rack.

But even as exhausted as he was, Hassan couldn't sleep. Instead he lay awake in the dark haunted by his last year at home, the year he had made the decision to join the Fleet. To become a warrior, a protector, one of God's Chosen.

A warrior earned Paradise, if he fought in defense of Muslim people and for God. There was no reason to worry about death, though Hassan had worried often before formulating his application on his father's ornate writing desk. His worries had been normal boy fears. What if he died in a fire, or crossing a street, or got kicked in the head in a soccer game like Sa'ad Ibn Ibrahim? Then he would surely go to Hell, since God saw into his heart and knew all the times he had missed prayers and had broken fast during Ramadan. All the times he had the opportunity to give charity but passed them by, or, worse, did not even recognize them. No matter how many times Mr. Ali in Religion class tried to quiet their fears and remind them of how God had promised Muhammad to count each believer's good deeds as ten and each of his sins as one, Hassan was quite sure that his total was in danger.

There had been only the normal boy things until Rashid's older brother Farid had been killed in the vacuum accident. Farid had been a fixture in Hassan's life, the counterpoint to Mr. Ali. Farid had taught them all to be bad.

Farid had been out working on the communications software, doing the overhaul that Sho-Co promised would bring in all the new Omni transmissions on full-time broadcast. Al-Shabir was on its way to becoming one of the main-line worlds, not a secondary franchise consumer. So when the stress points on the ancient Maktab orbiter went critical during a crew visit, there was very little left to bury. Sho-Co took the blame and paid indemnities to all the families. It controlled the Omni in seventy-three systems

Hassan had gone out with Rashid and his brother Farid the week before Farid had died. He was the first young person Hassan had known who had died, excepting Sa'ad in the soccer game. But Sa'ad had been seven years old and the imam had assured everyone in school that he was in Paradise now and didn't have to study quadratics or memorize the Koran anymore. Farid was different. Hassan was older and be knew that Farid had been very far from Paradise.

Farid Ibn Salah had enjoyed what he could in his short life, and what he enjoyed most was horrifying his elders. He had done a good job of it, intro-ducing Rashid and Hassan to home-brewed whiskey and "hard" tobacco in the bubble pipe. He never said his prayers, even proclaimed himself an atheist. Though once he did say to Rashid that he wasn't, really. Just that he was young and he thought the mullahs didn't understand that and hated all the techs who didn't adhere to the old ways. That was all. And after all, Farid was young. He could make up for all the mistakes later, when he was older. Once he had made his point.

He hadn't gotten the chance. Hassan had heard about the accident and gone to Rashid's home, miserable and afraid. That Farid could die and go to Hell, Farid who was always so full of life, so ready with a joke, that frightened him. It had frightened Rashid, too, and the two friends had finished off the last of Farid's imported stash of Johnnie Walker. The next morning, hung over, he couldn't go to school. He could barely move. At least his parents believed it was only grief over Farid's tragedy and let him stay home from school while they went to work. He had turned on the Omni and there had been the ad screens.

They had said that the Fleet was once again looking for young fighters to seek out the evildoers who would annihilate sentient species. The Fleet was the defender of all humanity, and so by extension was the defender of the Holy Places and the Peoples of the Book. There had been marching music in the background and holos of great warrior heroes from the earliest days of Islam,

Abu Bakr and Ali, Akbar the Great and Salah-El-Din. There were glittering machines and uniforms glittering even more from decorations.

Despite the splitting headache of his hangover, Hassan Ibn Abdullah had immediately gone to the interactive and requested the application and filled it out then and there. His father would be proud of him he was sure. And his mother would not be too disappointed about his not graduating from Caliph Umar University and sitting in the Majlis. She would understand that he would have a better chance to get elected if he was a war hero, and she would be sad but not object.

The acceptance had come by the next morning. And Hassan Ibn Abdullah was duly inducted into the defense of Mankind, and incidentally his own hope of salvation.

He had never questioned the rightness of that decision. Indeed, as he had progressed through training, winning more opportunities to advance, to become a fighter and then a group leader, he had only had his first impression confirmed. This was where he belonged. God had placed him in this Fleet for a true purpose.

And it had been easy for him, too. There was something poetic and whole about the way groups moved in combat, patterns of victory and defeat that came as clear before his eyes as the fanciful flowers and birds on the carpets in his parents' home. He had enjoyed the physical training, more demanding than soccer practice. And most of all he had loved learning to fly.

Piloting an SB was like becoming a bird, one of the great hunting hawks his grandfather had showed him when he was small. He felt like them, strong and fast and utterly unafraid, swooping and skimming over the surface of a planet, free and utterly alive in space.

Talent, his instructors had called it. He had been promoted and given more opportunities to take classes and advance. Things that were never taught at home became his daily work. And people who were not like those at home became his closest friends.

It was not that he left the faith of his people. It was merely that he wanted to be liked by these people, his new peers. He wanted to spend time with them, to fit in. He had been very young and felt very alone. There wasn't anyone else from Al-Shabir in his training group. He wasn't sure if there was anyone else from Al-Shabir in the entire Fleet.

And certain of the restrictions wore down slowly. After refusing too many times he couldn't stand being alone anymore and had joined the rest of his group in the bar. And he really hadn't intended to drink alcohol, truly he hadn't. The image of Farid in Hell haunted him. But when the group ordered pitchers and Solange des Salles had poured him out a glass and put it down in front of him with a wink, he hadn't wanted to refuse. Al-Shabir seemed very far away, and these people were his group. It wasn't like he had never drunk alcohol before. It wasn't like anyone else he knew was worried about going to Hell. After a few times it seemed very silly, very old-fashioned, to stand off from his friends. He couldn't deny it.

Not the beer, not the wink either. He hadn't been wrong. And while Solange was too strong, too insolent, too independent to be the kind of girl he had dreamed about, she had thick blond hair and a wide engaging smile and freckles on her nose. She was exotic, tempting, drunk.

Being a bad Muslim didn't mean that he didn't believe. It only meant that he knew he had guaranteed his own safe conduct after death. He didn't have to worry anymore and he wanted to enjoy all the advantages. He never doubted that war was the one path he had to salvation.

As he had never doubted victory. There was no other possibility. A believer was always victorious. He had been raised on the history of the Battle of Badr and the conquest of North Africa. The only time they failed was when they fought those who were also People of the Book whose faith was stronger, who were more committed in their duty and their prayers.

Hassan Ibn Abdullah had always thought that obvious. And working with the men and women of the Fleet, with his group and even the Marines on board, he had never had a moment of doubt. That the Ichtons were completely godless was a proven fact. And if many of his colleagues and associates were not of the best moral character, there were plenty of others who made up for them. Among the Muslims aboard the *Hawking*, the small chapel was always filled to capacity and many worshipers were stuck in the hallway during the Friday noon service.

There were better Muslims than Hassan on the *Hawking*. But Hassan Ibn Abdullah of Al-Shabir had never minded. They weren't warriors. They weren't guaranteed. Some of them weren't with the Fleet at all. One of the civilian technicians, Ahmed Al-Dookhi, had seen him going into the Emerald Isle with Solange des Salles and Marty Hong and the rest of his group, and had tried to talk him out of it. Reminded him of his obligations and what was forbidden.

It didn't matter that things were forbidden. They were the Elect, there was no question in his mind. So he spent more time with Solange, sampling other pleasures that were normally outside the realm permitted on Al-Shabir. After beer came the whiskey and the rum, which he never really liked.

Solange introduced him to the sausages she enjoyed from her own home, not telling him at first they were made from pig. He had been horrified when he discovered it and Solange had laughed. She had been sitting naked on his bed, glasses of wine balanced on the floor, a plate of cheese and crackers and sausages between them.

"Really, this is so much worse than all the rest?" she had asked in honest confusion.

And Hassan, after careful consideration, had to agree that it was not. And that he didn't belong to Al-Shabir properly anymore. He was all Fleet now. Just like the others, his friends, his lover. He told himself that again and again over the next days until he didn't have to say it anymore. The words appeared in his head along with the beer and the sausage and Solange.

But in the dark, trying to sleep, Hassan Ibn Abdullah found the source of his unease. The idea of that convoy, so far from the fronts, disturbed him on more than a professional level. He could see them, imagine all the space between the millions of stars, all fdled with the Ichton swarm. Nothing stopped them, nothing could turn them from their purpose. And their purpose was an evil one.

The legion of Shaitan advanced through the darkness a planet at a time. There were billions of them who had no part in the fighting, who didn't even know or care it was going on. The devil had won. And Hassan's faith was shaken down to the core.

He could be a bad Muslim. He could violate every stricture in the Koran. But he could not accept that God would give those, those bugs a victory over men. That was beyond comprehension. That was a bad dream.

He gave up on sleep, got up and washed and put on the civilian dress of his home. The plain white robe and headdress were exotic on the *Hawking*, but it still was more comfortable to Hassan than the dark trousers and shirts that felt like just one more uniform. The long white *dishdasha* made him feel connected to the person he used to be, not the amalgamation of characters he found himself playing now.

He left the military levels and wandered down onto Green Three where some of the more affordable shops were clustered. He wanted to look at the people more than the goods, at the relaxed cheer that pretended normalcy. As if anything here was normal. As if it was normal to be shopping quite securely in the middle of a war zone where people were running out and dying.

"Hey, Hassan, I owe you a drink, boss." Marty Hong came over, clapped Hassan on the shoulder, and tried to steer him in the direction of the Emerald Isle, Marty's favorite watering hole, the only Irish pub on the battlestation.

But something had snapped inside Hassan. He felt isolated, outside Marty's camaraderie. Suddenly it seemed like everything here was as alien as what he found on the planets of the Core. The corridor of Green looked dirty, full of the refuse and detritus of another culture. Alien, not for him. He shook his head. Marty shrugged and went off, confusion on his face at Hassan's refusal. For the smallest fragment of time Hassan wanted to run after Marty, say it was just a joke, and join whoever was off duty down at the watering hole.

Something held him back. From the very depths of his mind came a word he had not heard in a very long time. A word he had not heard since he had joined the Fleet. Haram. Forbidden.

It made him think of the clean places back home, the expanses of shoreline rippling pristine in the sun. Or not so clean. There had been bright filth all over Al-Shabir, hard glints from the litter, the beverage cans and food tins strewn over the sand reflecting in the moonlight. That night he had gotten drunk with Farid and Rashid they had sat out on the rocks and watched the warm ocean tide, emptied the bottle of imported whiskey that Farid had brought back. Haram. Emptied it and thrown it out into the sea where it had floated and glittered in the dark water. It had been ugly and small and unclean, just like everything in his life.

He turned sharply and went directly back to the hull elevators, muttered "Orange Four" at them, and waited. The doors opened silently and he was back on the barracks level again. He was only glad that being a group leader, he had private quarters even though his rank didn't rate the luxury.

It was thought that group leaders might need some privacy to talk to members of their groups, and they surely didn't rate private offices. The one overcrowded space they shared to do the required records work and sign in for their briefings was never quiet enough for a serious discussion, let alone secluded enough for one that would go better without others present.

Now he was glad only that he had a place to go to be alone. Completely alone. He walked the nearly half klick of corridor around to his door and sealed it shut behind him. The panel would have the privacy indicator lit so no one would interrupt.

It had been a long time since Hassan Ibn Abdullah had said the required prayers, had found that need in himself. He had spent too many years trying too hard to be the proper Fleet group leader. On Fridays he went for public services at noon, but otherwise was more concerned with fighting than with other obligations. After all, he was a warrior. He was guaranteed Paradise.

Now, however, he felt overwhelmed. He had not come to terms with the enemy before, with their enormity and the strength of their drive. They could not be the Chosen of God, the ones assured of victory. And yet, and yet . . .

He could not clear the vision from his mind. Hundreds, thousands of the tiny fighters. Each one armed better than the SBs. All of them swarming together around a nucleus of destroyers and frigates marching out under orders. Marching across the sky, marching in the dark masked by the myriad planets and stars of the galactic core.

He tried to drive the image from his mind and concentrate only on the words that flowed from him. Verses of the Koran came unbidden, the language rippling like flowers in a breeze. Like the enemy convoy stealing around in secret.

And it all came together, a single inspiration. He rose from his prayer rug with a more grateful heart than he had ever experienced. The vision was complete, perfect, and it encompassed him. Hassan knew the keen pleasure of it even though the image was hideous, frightful. He could see the beauty because he could see past it and into what it meant.

God had spoken to him, directly. He had no doubt. Now he only had to get the tracking from Astronomy.

Not even bothering to change out of the white *dishdasha* and headdress, he ran out of his private quarters and to the lift as if he were on first assault and they were under attack.

He got down to Astronomy in the Civ sections and started banging on the indigo door with Rhys Davies's name lit on the plate. He slammed his fist against the steel until his hand ached.

Davies opened the door. "Why can't you use the bell like a normal person?" the scientist groused. "Did you find anything useful?"

Hassan shook his head. "What happened?" he asked Davies as if the other understood everything that had gone on in the past sixteen hours. "Why didn't you find the convoy in your data?"

"What convoy?" Davies asked, then turned his back on the pilot without inviting him into the office.

Hassan didn't bother waiting for the invitation, but pushed his way through the closing door and after the planetary specialist. "There's an Ichton column moving through that system," he informed Davies hotly. "Bleeding radiation all over the place. You should have been able to spot them in your observations. You do make observations, right?"

Davies turned suddenly and cocked his head. "A column movement that we didn't see?" he asked, ignoring Hassan's anger. "Let me pull the records."

He touched a keypad on his desk and the wall display lit with a bright orange backdrop, then dissolved into star fields Hassan didn't recognize. In fact, they changed and became something else entirely, graphic plots of color that didn't make particular sense to the pilot.

"These are the spectrographic prints," Davies said. "Now, let's try again. You said that the convoy was coming around LLR-1182?" The display shimmered and changed again. Now hot yellow filled the screen with streaks of blue and green and pink smudges across the face of it.

Davies ignored him. "Hmmmm. Yes. Yes." The astronomer's face glowed with excitement.

"Yes, what?" Hassan demanded. He couldn't make any sense of the display.

"I'll have to do some more looking," Davies said.

Hassan was so curious and frustrated that he wanted to shake the heavyset older man. "What? What is it? What do you see?"

Rhys Davies licked his lips. "I never thought it would be a practical application. Of course, I'm not in stellar architecture. We'll really have to do a full
departmental study to get the complete picture. I'm not sure really . . ."

"Please, please tell me," Hassan begged. This man was going to make him
crazy.

"We may have a signature for the Ichton drive," Davies said simply. "It's dirty,
you're right. But against LLR-1182 the element signature is hidden under the
star's own element band. Every star has a spectrographic signature. Elements
exist in different proportions everywhere, and each one has its own color. But
against that signature the drive emissions are masked. Wait."

The screen became more yellow and the green, blue, and pink moved around.
The colors started to flash. Hassan felt a little dizzy. The scientist said nothing
but "Hmmmm." And then Davies smiled.

"I can see it," he said finally. "They're using the stellar radiation to mask their
movements. You wouldn't think they'd be able to. And they don't do it all the time. I
wonder . . . Only certain stars would be suitable. It wouldn't be hard to check."

Hassan thanked Davies emphatically and then hurried out. He understood.
There was more and no doubt the astronomers and the intelligence analysts
aboard would create a detailed picture. Maybe it would even indicate something far different from what Hassan saw in his own moment of inspiration.
But he didn't think so.

The Ichtons had a camouflaged route. Possibly it could even be traced back
to their home planet. Even if it wasn't quite that direct, they had worked out this
area to keep their movements hidden. Secret.

Hassan could barely keep from dancing in the corridor. The idea overwhelmed him. There were indeed more than enough bugs to go around. It
would be a charity to them to remove them from the universe. From harming
decent species' lives and homes. Surely this was the greatest charity of all.

In the sudden extreme clarity that surrounded his thoughts, Hassan Ibn
Adbullah realized perfectly why the warrior merited Paradise. It was not fearless-
ness or commitment or any of the things that he had thought. It was charity. In
the truly just, war was the highest expression of charity to others. And everyone
in Mr. Ali's class knew that God loved charity above all other virtues.

Hassan managed to get back to his own quarters and change into his
working blues. He didn't think he would impress the tactical staff in his native
dress. And this had to be done right. He was anxious and excited, but to hurry
wouldn't help.

So he made a proper appointment through the proper channels, filed the
paperwork with more routings than strictly necessary, and changed. The duty
roster on his screen rippled as the new appointment came through. He had a
meeting in twenty minutes with the division's tactical superior and staff. But

Hassan Ibn Abdullah was perfectly calm as he took the lift from Orange down to a Briefing Red on the operational front.

"This could be part of an overall assault plan," the tack said softly. There was no denying the interest in his face; Hassan felt more than vindicated.

"I would expect it is, sir," he agreed. "It seems that they are trying to bring in more ships and fighters behind cover and converge on us without us expecting them. I think we've got them a little frightened."

The tack smiled without humor. "Very possibly. That would be the way we would do it. Only the Ichtons aren't us. And I'm not sure we have any idea of what they would do or why. Although that's my best guess. Astronomy promised they'd have the readings up to us as soon as they'd isolated the pattern. But that could take days."

Hassan nodded. "I realize that, sir. Dr. Davies briefed us. But maybe in the meantime we could make life a little less comfortable for the bugs."

"Ichtons, Mr. Ibn Abdullah. Our enemies are sentients, not bugs, and the minute we forget that we're in trouble," the tack repeated by rote.

Hassan ignored the routine warning and went on. Only the high tacks ever bothered with those fine distinctions. He knew perfectly well what he meant and he wasn't about to underestimate the enemy even if he used the wrong terminology. "Well, sir, they were sticking pretty tight in formation. They wouldn't even follow us out to the moon we hid behind. They're avoiding the rocks and keeping to empty space. And staying between the orbits and the sun, for camouflage I'd guess. But they aren't expecting to be hit out there. They're just sitting begging for an ambush there."

The senior tack shook his head. "That convoy will be nearly through by now," he said. "And since you already engaged with them they know that we know . . . And, honestly, we can't afford the forces to sit and wait until another convoy tries to come through using the same trick. We don't have enough manpower as it is, and we're short on armed SBs. Which you should know. Hell, we could hardly spare the garbage scow."

Hassan had known and ignored the fact. Sebeng always managed to make sure the Dawn Riders were equipped to the teeth. He had been so certain, so clear about what needed to be done.

In his mind he could hear the voice of Mr. Ali chanting over and over again, *It is charity to remove something harmful from the way.* The garbage scow. The empty Johnnie Walker bottle floating in the tide, reflecting light like a beacon to the thing that was unclean. And Hassan Ibn Abdullah began to laugh.

"Sir, could I take the garbage scow out for a run?" he asked when he got his breath back.

The tack officer's eyebrows went up abruptly. "Why, Group Leader?"

But Hassan Ibn Abdullah was laughing so hard that it took several moments to catch his breath to explain.

There was a convoy. Maybe not the same one. Hassan Ibn Abdullah couldn't be sure. But there were Ichtons out there, using the masking radiation of this star to keep their movements out of sight.

Only now Astronomy knew what to look for. Astronomy even found a fun problem in the tracking, something that could interest theorists like Rhys Davies.

Not that Hassan cared. He only cared about what he was doing, about this moment. The garbage scow was large and unwieldy. It had not been made for a human driver in general, but the calculations were too intuitive to be left to a machine. Hassan didn't even know how to explain it properly.

The dark folded around him. He took the tug out slowly, dragging it around the column from the orbital side. And he opened the hatches. Refuse from the *Hawking* spewed into space. Beer cans and bottles from the bars, bits of meal covers and shiny wrapping paper from the rich inhabitants of the south pole. He guided the barge gently forward, running it out as fast as he could, trying to outdistance the column.

There were fighters after him. He tried to jink but the scow balked and bucked under him. Damn. He pushed on ahead, continuing to spray the entire sector with debris, waiting for the hit.

Only it didn't come. He saw them in the scan between the slivers of bright garbage, saw them coming straight in on him and then fluttering around, lost. A few feeble attempts to fire and a single smart missile dropped into the dump and was unable to fix on a target. Was unable to find a target.

He pushed forward, hoping there would be enough. That Sebeng had packed the hauler as full as she did the SBs' holds. Already his plan was working, was beautiful. So beautiful that he could barely contain his pleasure.

He came around full and cut off the front of the convoy. Here they had better shots at him as he upped the pressure in the refuse chamber. Pieces shredded finer with the higher energy surge and the whole segment of his own position between the planet and the star had blotted into garbled haze.

The garbage was all reflective. And it was shining all that energy back at the enemy. The radiation from the star and the nearby planet, the power leaking from the Ichton drives, the communications bands and all the scanners, everything was being broken and bounced among a billion billion crashed fragments of landfill. Like grains of sand, each one a mirror on the shore, the chaff drifted into eddies and rifts, spread and spun insanely through the Ichton convoy.

The enemy tried to fight back. They fired energy weapons that were immediately dissipated by the chaff. They tried smart missiles whose targeting devices were completely stymied. Even their navigation and orientation were affected and what had once been a neatly purposeful convoy through camouflaged space started to resemble the kiddies' bumper car ride at the Eid Al-Fitr fair.

Hassan could appreciate the view only through the windows in front of him. This was no fighter, it wasn't even a patrol SB and so his own screens were as confused as the enemy's. And so he never saw the large Ichton destroyer that was on his tail and that ripped the garbage scow neatly in two down the keel, adding even more to the confusing backwash.

"Dawn Riders, open fire," Dawn Leader commanded. They came from behind a chunk of moon, something irregular that had most likely been an asteroid captured by the planet's gravity. They had ridden this way before.

Solange des Salles, acting group leader, read out the coordinates. That was unnecessary. The attackers could see targets strewn across the environment like loose cut gems on a jeweler's velvet. Targets that lay drifting helplessly, surrounded by chaff, unable to navigate or fire. Blind.

"It's almost a pity to just pick them off," Marty Hong said.

Three SBs, even loaded with all the ammunition Sebeng could pack into their holds, could only account for three quarters of the disabled Ichton column. The Dawn Riders didn't protest when the frigate *Viceroy* arrived on the scene and began mopping up the remains.

That night the Dawn Riders bought all the drinks in the Emerald Isle in the name of Hassan Ibn Abdullah. They drank and threw the glasses against the wall to commemorate his victory. And his death. Credit for the full column, by popular demand, was given to him alone.

"And he can't enjoy it," Marty said, trying to keep sentimental and drunken tears from his eyes. "He's dead."

"I don't think so," said a stranger in a white robe. "But he wouldn't enjoy the beer. He died properly, and in Paradise no one is ever drunk."

Des Salles listened, and then ordered another round. "Here's to you, Hassan," she said as the rest of the Dawn Riders raided their final round. "Looks like we're gonna have to do all your drinking for you now. Looks like you got to be a good Muslim in the end anyway."

RX

A massive Ichton force had gotten between the *Hawking* and their strongest ally, the Emry. Anton Brand reacted by attempting to call all the Fleet and the allied race's ships back to the station, a difficult task considering how thinly they were spread. As the *Hawking* gathered its strength, it began to edge slowly toward Emry. Isolated and outmaneuvered, the crew of the Battlestation *Stephen Hawking* fought two battles. The first was against hundreds of small and large Ichton units. The other battle was against themselves.

The level of stress, already considered unbearable, increased geometrically as the *Hawking* crept toward Emry and a confrontation with far superior Ichton forces. Occasionally a small Ichton force would discover the *Hawking*, forcing yet another change of course to avoid ambush. Those fighting on the ships or inside the station had nowhere to run and only the prospect of greater danger to look forward to. Under this burden any psychological problem became severe. It was the responsibility of a few members of the medical staff to assist those who need their help the most. Repairing their minds as well as their bodies. But who watches the watchers?

MEDIC
by Mercedes Lackey
and Mark Shepherd

Dr. Althea Morgan paused in the hatchway to her office, leaned against the cold metal, and sighed. This job was not something she was looking forward to, but it was better than the alternative.

Thinking.

Although being cramped in that tiny cell of an office was almost as bad as thinking.

It's a good thing they don't allow claustrophobes in space.

Her so-called "office" was about the size of a supply closet, and had just enough room for her desk, chair, and terminal—and, if the visitor happened to be the size of your average ballet dancer, room for one other person as well. At least she had a chair. Visitors got to perch on a narrow metal flap that folded down from the desk.

Why did I ever agree to be staff administrator, anyway?

She squeezed past the end of the desk and settled into her chair, steeled herself, and reached for the computer terminal to turn the Cyclopean monster on.

It immediately chided her for not touching it since the *Elizabeth Blackwell II* hit norm-space by beeping at her. *Angrily,* she thought. Then it presented her with a flood of memos about how crowded her message-queues were, followed by a directive from the Admiralty about saving queue-memory.

I know, I know. She hadn't turned the damned thing on because she hadn't *seen* the damn office since they hit norm. She hadn't seen anything except the surgery, the prep room, *her* room (damn little of that), and the corridor between her room and surgery.

Nominally, she was the director of the medical personnel aboard the *Elizabeth Blackwell II*. In actuality, she did as much hands-on work as any of her staff, right down to holding bedpans if it came to it. And during the last few weeks, there'd been a lot of hands-on. She'd taken all of the Neuros, most of the Neuro-musculars, all of the Spinals, and even a couple Thoracics.

Or, in the jargon of the no-nonsense first-in surgeons of the Fleet—the Heads, the Hunks, the Backs, and the Chests.

For a moment, she buried her head in her hands, overwhelmed not so much with memories but with a flood of *impressions.* Things had happened too quickly for memories. The *Blackwell* served the same function as the old MASH units had for ground-based troops; she was only one of many, but sometimes it seemed as if *Blackwell* was the only one of her kind out here. All alone, except for the Big Ship, the *Stephen Hawking*. That was what *she* called it, the Big Ship; she had not set foot on it for weeks, and to her it was a great deal like returning to Heaven. She had never been there, and probably wouldn't go there until she died—she sent a lot of people there, though, and none of them ever came back.

Or if they did, she didn't recognize them.

Blood; that was the primary memory. Blood, lots of it, in all the variations of red. And internal organs. Many kinds, often not human. Sometimes fluids she didn't even recognize as blood, forms she had never seen before, organs with functions she couldn't even guess. The medicomp knew, though, good old many-eyed Argus; and the replicator could reproduce the fluids, the organs, from a cubic mil of clean tissue. Nothing fancy; that was for the Hawkins. She just saved them, patched them, and got those all-important clean samples; the Big Ship made them whole again, grew them new lungs and spleens and *feshetti*, carved them faces that looked like faces and not nightmare-horrors. Whoever had said that combat in the modern world was clean had never been on the *Blackwell*.

More memories. Operating with one eye on the comp screen and one on the patient. Comp over the table, Eye of God, beloved Argus, that told her and every other surgeon everything she needed to know about her patient, including where her hands were in the welter of blood and God knew what. The comp that guided her hands.

Not the same comp that was bitching at her now, beeping at her, chiding her for her inattention. *That* was Admin. Cyclops. The Eye she hated.

Well, there was one advantage to not logging on for weeks, even months. There was a lot of crap she wasn't going to have to deal with. Computer-sent messages have a short life span. Administrative crap had an even shorter half-life.

She typed slowly, cursing the ancient, outmoded keyboard. Anyone over the rank of CPO in the military side had a Voice-Response-System. Anyone with any kind of rank had a VRS. If she had had a secretary, the *secretary* would have been issued a VRS. But, in the usual FUBAR of the military, because she was an administrative head and *should* have had a secretary to deal with all this garbage, she didn't need a VRS.

Never mind irreparable nerve damage that made her hands shake so much that she could stand in for the drink mixer in the ship's lounge. Never mind that her secretary had been co-opted to man guns somewhere on the Big Ship. Never mind that *somewhere*, without a shadow of a doubt, there was a friggin' closet full of VRSs doing nothing on the Big Ship. There might even be one hidden somewhere on the *Blackwell*. No VRS for Admin personnel. End of story.

Thank the Deity-of-Your-Choice for mass queue-purges.

First mass purge: all social notes. Not that there were a lot, but there was no point. Somewhere there was a reg that said that on so called noncombat ships there must be regularly scheduled social events for the purpose of crew morale. So Cyclops scheduled them and reminded everyone to attend; probably even programmed the ship's mess for refreshments that no one came to eat, then sent bitchy notices about food wastage.

Second purge: all ship-to-ship general notices older than yesterday.

That freed up a lot of queue-space, and mollified the damn Cyclops enough so that it stopped *beep*ing at her. Now all it was doing was issuing reminders every five minutes or so.

Now selective purges. Anything personal older than a week ago. Most of the personal notes were stupid; residue of interstaff quarrels and infighting, reminders of things that she would never have forgotten anyway, and if she didn't remember them, they hadn't been worth remembering. Requisition orders older than a month; if someone hadn't chased her down for her thumbprint in person, they'd found a creative way of solving the shortage.

In general, that was how things got taken care of on the *Elizabeth Blackwell*, you either chased Morgan down for the print, found something else that would do, or did without. There were some ingenious jury-rigs on the *Blackwell*.

That took care of the nonsense. Now came the work.

The only part that she cared for were the personnel files of new staff. Not that she hadn't met them all by now, but buried in the files were the little things that made a face into a person. That Trauma Spec Jharwat Singh Rai was a near concert-level violinist. Or Sanders, the head ward nurse, was the champion Swords and Spellcast player in the Fleet. Or that Orthopedic Surgeon Ledith Alsserth from the Indies collected old Earth jazz recordings, even though his people had never so much as seen a saxophone. She wasn't even certain one of his race could *play* a saxophone.

So she left those until last, as a reward for good behavior. It was amazing how much paperwork accumulated whenever they docked with the Big Ship; the transfer orders were enough to fill twenty megabytes alone, and that was in compressed mode. *Why* do the stuff in triplicate, when "paperwork" didn't exist in hard copy anymore?

Never mind. She could fill them out. It didn't matter. As long as she kept busy, she wouldn't have to think. Think about how the ultimate weapon the Fleet had built, the *Stephen Hawking*, the *battlestation* that was never supposed to see close combat, had just been through the trash-masher. How there was an even bigger enemy armada than the one that had trashed them coming down the Throat right now. Straight for them.

How the cavalry was not coming over the hill. Not out here, back of beyond of anywhere. Not when they already *had* all of their eggs in one basket.

No. Better not to think. She would take care of her job; let the ones in charge try to think of a solution. She had plenty to do. If work on the *Blackwell* ran out, she could volunteer for reconstructive surgery on the Big Ship. There was plenty of that. There was always plenty of that.

More crap to wade through; complaints. The *Blackwell* had taken some scrapes and minor hits, and systems were cranky. Very cranky, Minor malfunctions all over the ship—including, predictably, the mess hall, reducing the already minimal palatability of the food down to the flavor of flour paste. Not that *she* could do anything about that, but she got the complaints from her staff anyway.

Just hope nothing major breaks loose before the overhaul crew can get to us.

By the time she had waded through the last of the muck, her trembling hands and wrists ached, and she was only too glad to be able to simply page through the files without having to type anything.

It would be nice if she could have a pair of StediGloves in here—but those required the medicomp to operate.

And of course, since there were no requirements to extend Argus's all-seeing Eye into the office, there was no way to get the Eye in here. Administrators had no need for the Eye—what, was she going to do surgery on the desk?—and neither did secretaries.

So, Eye, no gloves, no steadying influence on her hands. Have a nice day.

"Hell, even *chaplains* have VRSs," she muttered, and called up the first of the files.

Working from bottom rank up; nursing staff first. As always, she heard the voice of her mentor in her mind's ear. Good old Doc Glock. "Nurses. Get to know them *well,* girl—they're your lifeline, your extra hands, your other eyes. Got three things going wrong at once; put your ops nurses on two of 'em. Chances are they'll do as well as you. Need a third eye, put your nurse on the comp and have her read the damn thing back at you. *Let* 'em close when you're done if there's another on the table waiting for you, let 'em do what they can. Let 'em do any damn thing if they're capable, and to hell with regs. This won't be Saint Simeon's; there won't be anyone looking to book them for practicing medicine without a license, or to sue you for malpractice. *Let 'em work right up to the limits of their capabilities, and thank 'em afterward.* You won't be any less a doctor. Those boys and girls and whatevers are gonna be damn glad they're still alive when you're done with 'em, and they won't care who or what did the work. . . ."

As she called up pictures, file (usually from graduation) and current, she didn't get many surprises. Other than the usual—how the trim and ultra-proper loosened up; the young and shiny and eager got some of the shine rubbed off.

How the ones so sure they were God Almighty you could see it in their eyes learned they were mortal after all.

Nothing like getting the shit scared out of you a dozen or so times to get rid of those anal-retentive tendencies. The *Blackwell* had gotten a fair share of close calls, and even a few minor hits. That's why the *Blackwell* was armed—and had the best legs in the Service.

Now Althea was well into the smaller corps of surgical doctors and trauma specialists. New chest-man; that was good. Even better that his specialty was Xeno. That was probably why she'd only seen him over coffee in the lounge. She was human Neuro; for Xenos, even with neurological damage, a chest-man with Xeno specialty was a better choice than a human with no Xeno experience. She tagged him mentally for call-up when the time came; two sets of experiences sometimes saved a "kid" of whatever race that one alone couldn't. Not if, *when*. For the time would come that she would need him, as night followed day.

There were no surprises until she came to the last file, highest rank. The new Chief of Surgery. File image; bright, cheerful, new-and-shiny. Laughing eyes. Nice girl.

Whom she did not recognize.

What the hell?

She called up a recent image; it was like seeing images of two different people, and *this* one she knew. Except that she'd had no idea this was her CoS. For a moment she toyed with the idea of a ringer—though *why* anyone would try and place a ringer on the *Blackwell* she couldn't imagine—but the tissue typing done just last week matched the one in the file that went with the graduation image.

Two different people. And the second one was a nonentity. No expression. Hair cut to a short little fuzz. Nothing in the eyes.

That was why she hadn't thought the woman was even a full doctor. There was *nothing* about Celia Stratford that was remarkable. The file was a blank. No hobbies. No interests. No friends. . . .

Fifteen transfers in fourteen years.

What?

Her first thought was that the woman was a major troublemaker—or attracter. But there were no discipline hash marks against her in the records; nothing, in fact, but glowing commendation after commendation. All the transfers were voluntary. *Requested.*

The longest she'd stayed in any one place was two years; the shortest, six months. She'd been on the Big Ship until the hookup before this one; she'd requested transfer again, and she'd gotten it. Then the fluke—because she had an outstanding record, and because Althea's old CoS had gotten conscripted elsewhere, the computer threw her into the CoS slot with an automatic upgrade.

Fifteen transfers in fourteen years. A nonentity. A mystery. A puzzle to solve, to stave off thinking.

Just what the doctor ordered.

She ordered a copy of the file—and any others that Celia was mentioned in—transferred to her Pers area. Later, she could warm up the terminal in her cabin and look it over lying flat on her bunk.

She gazed once more into the eyes of the nonentity on the screen, before dismissing the image. There was a person in there, with a reason for all those transfers. And Althea Morgan was going to find her.

Ready or not, Celia, here I come.

Still groggy from the jump, Celia wove her way through the breakfast crowd in the mess hall. She shrugged and stood in line, wishing she could be invisible. Over the years, through trial and error, she perfected her body language to effectively broadcast, to a wide area, *stay away*. All except the most imperceptive individuals could read her posture, the folded arms, the hostile look, the stance that turned slightly inward. She was more comfortable being by herself, and made no secret of it to the world.

It's better this way, she thought, waiting in the incredibly slow line. *It's better to have no friends than lose the ones you have to those damned intelligent grasshoppers. If I never see another insect again, it will be too soon.*

The cafeteria, if one could call it that, was small and cramped, like everything else on the ship. There were perhaps thirty people in here, mostly medical staff in their traditional whites, with a few ship's support in green coveralls thrown in to keep the eye from going snow-blind. The ship's captain, whom she had met briefly when transferring from the *Stephen Hawking*, along with the higher ranking doctors, would probably be taking meals in the officer's mess. She couldn't help but laugh, remembering the XO orderly's expression when he told her she had that option, and she had declined it. Apparently nobody ever did that.

I'll be more invisible with the larger numbers, she told herself. *If I mix with a group of senior staff I'll be expected to make small talk. Here, I can be quiet without raising eyebrows or questions.*

As she had expected, breakfast was the usual dull military fare. All reconstructed soy made to resemble, if you had a vivid imagination, eggs, bacon, and ham. Or for those of other persuasions, oatmeal, bagels, and cream cheese. The coffee more than made up for the pseudomeal; somewhere in the brew's distant ancestry, there must have been at least one or two real honest-to-God coffee beans. That, or the replicating equipment on this ship was more advanced than the mess on the *Stephen Hawking*. Not likely, given the rest of the meal.

It doesn't matter, she thought, selecting a table (thank God) that was sitting off by itself. *As long as I don't know a soul, I'll be happy with bread and water.*

Checking her watch, she saw that she had two hours before her shift officially began. *Of course, they'll expect me there an hour early. Good thing I came when I did. If this is slow for this place, I'd hate to see what it looks like during a rush.*

Everyone around her seemed to be in the advanced stages of waking up and not particularly looking for company.

For all intents and purposes, just like her.

Another trick she learned a while back; early breakfasts usually insured privacy.

How long has it been, anyway? she thought, playing with her make-believe bacon. *Ten, eleven years?* She added the years, surprising herself with how long it had *really* been. *Great Good God,* Celia thought, dropping her fork. Fourteen years. *My, how time flies when you're having* fun.

She remembered the way it had been, in the early days, shortly after graduation. *I was so young, so fresh, so . . . stupid.* Janet Walter had been her roommate all through med school and her best friend since their freshman year, so it was natural that they should ship out together, to the same ship's hospital. Janet could make a good joke out of just about any bad situation, and acted as the perfect counter to Celia's own unpredictable mood swings, made worse by the nasty little border war they were cleaning up after.

Being a doctor seemed so very heroic then. Working near a war was even more so. Or so all the holos, the books, the newsvids said. Her teachers told them that they were going out to bring life amid death. That they were special. Important.

And it certainly felt important. She had been prepared for the horrors of battlefield surgery; she had spent her internship in a charity-hospital trauma unit. She had been prepared for the chaos, the constant stress.

What she hadn't been prepared for was that the medical personnel might be a target.

She didn't even remember who they were fighting. Or where. It could have been any battle in any conflict. It might not even have been the enemy; it might have even been an accident, so-called "friendly fire." The details were not important; what was important was that up until that moment she had no idea what it was like to lose someone important, someone close.

She closed her eyes and bent her head over her pseudo-eggs as the memory overwhelmed her.

She'd been asleep, off-shift. The ship rocked; that woke her up. She grabbed for the light switch; her overhead died, and emergency services went on-line, the red lights, the wheeze of the ventilators. She didn't even remember dressing or running down the corridor to the surgery. Just being there, as body after body came under her hands. Waiting for Janet to come pounding in from her room.

The last person she expected to see come in on a stretcher was Janet.

And she was the last person Celia expected to see *die*.

Curdled, blackened burns covered her body, and Janet's screams still haunted her sleep. Her best friend was so racked with pain that she didn't even recognize Celia.

Celia had not lost control of her emotions, at least not during the procedure. She had calmly and coolly applied the plastic flesh that would hold Janet together until a burn specialist could see her, until someone from Rad could see how much of a dose she had gotten.

Triage; minor, major, grave. Janet got the red band—grave—but there were lots of red bands. Too many; the ship had taken a major hit to the crew quarters. She had learned later that Janet had been with that young ensign she'd met in the mess. The young ensign's body had shielded hers from the worst of the blast.

Too many red bands, and not enough doctors to see to them. Celia had lacerated spines to put back together; heads with the brain laid bare. Everyone was busy, there were too many bodies, too many seriously injured.

The red band wasn't enough. She had wanted to shout, to drag the burn man over to Janet, to point out that this was another *doctor*, one of the fraternity. But her professional etiquette prevented her.

Janet's screams had stopped suddenly.

Even in the tumult of the overfilled trauma ward, the other moans of agony, the shouts of doctors and nurses, the wheeze of machines, Celia heard that horrible silence.

She had whirled, staring across the room, patient forgotten. Janet gazed upward, eyes open, mouth frozen forever in a silent scream.

Dead. In a room full of doctors and nurses, of lifesaving machinery, she was dead. Even after the training, the years of schooling, Celia still hadn't a clear idea back then of how fragile life really was.

We had breakfast together. She was laughing, talking about her new boyfriend, about how wonderful working in a war zone was. Why were we hit? We were a hospital ship, damn it! Where were the people who were supposed to be protecting us?

To this day, a million questions hammered at her. They had then, and none of them had ever been answered. The answers, she knew deep down inside, wouldn't bring Janet back.

Nothing would; not technology, equipment, or training. Janet would not come back.

The rest was a blur. She had a dim recollection of turning back to the table, of turning back to her work, with tears streaming down her face; more burn victims, some worse than Janet was, some not as bad. Not for her; hers were the shrapnel recipients, the fractured skulls and broken bones. Somewhere in there was the first time she had seen the results of decompression, though why anyone had thought the ER could actually do anything with the mess on the gurney escaped her.

She went to bed; when she woke, there was nothing inside.

When Janet died, Celia decided later, her emotions died with her friend. A hidden gear, a thrown switch, put her in a detached, unfeeling, mechanical mode.

She remembered the next few weeks, the vague sense of moving with a purpose, with no real sense of joy or pain. No sense, really, of anything. *Nothing.* She got through each day, just barely. When she went to her room to cry, nothing happened. The tears wouldn't come.

And they never did, Celia thought. *Will they ever?* She shook her head. *Probably not. After fourteen years, what would be left?*

She had requested an immediate transfer then. She wasn't sure why, not at the time. All she knew was that like a wounded creature crawling away to lick its injuries in private, she needed off that ship, since leaving her profession altogether was out of the question.

But when she made the request, they had denied it!

Only then did some kind of emotion wake; rage. She barely restrained her anger when she had her conference with the Chief of Surgery, a large, aggressive bitch of an old woman who refused to listen to her.

Her supervisor informed her in no uncertain terms that she was needed on that particular ship in that particular slot. She had no experience in combat medicine, and she was lucky to have a chance to gain some of it where she was.

The CoS made working in that nightmare that had killed Janet sound like a *privilege.*

And one more thing; regs. She didn't really have a choice. She wouldn't be allowed a transfer for another year. Only senior staff were allowed transfers.

Celia could have strangled her then.

She returned to her cabin in a state of barely controlled rage. But somehow, in the interval between the end of the interview and the beginning of her shift, she came to the startling realization that she was only a working part of a larger machine, the workings of which were decided by other, more important people.

What, Celia had asked, *would I have to do to get transferred?*

Become the best damned medic we have, the supervisor informed her with a self-serving sneer. *That is your only ticket out of here.*

Then I had better get back to work, Celia replied, and proceeded to *become* the best damned doctor, the best damned surgeon, the Fleet had ever seen.

Then she went a step further; she went back to the books for further surgery specialization. She surprised everybody by picking up the old manual skills, the kind used in the most primitive of field conditions; old-fashioned surgery with scalpel and sutures. Except for a few who kept their hands in because they were assigned to ground-based MASH units, most surgeons didn't even bother picking up a metal scalpel once during their whole careers.

With every patient that came past her, she remembered Janet, and put as much energy into saving that person as she would her best friend.

It became a challenge, to be the best so that she could have the most freedom.

In the end, she had the freedom of the Fleet. Not only did she have a ticket off that particular ship, she discovered that she could write her ticket to wherever she wanted.

And she discovered something else. There would never be another Janet. There had been too much pain in losing the first one. So she started running away, whenever people began coming too close.

For a while each change of location helped keep her isolated, but inevitably she began forming acquaintances. Acquaintances had the potential to become friends.

There must never be friends.

She was never sure what criteria she went by, or if there was anything specific that went on in her head. But at some point in every assignment, she realized that her time was up.

Time for a transfer. Before I get too close to these people.

She sensed something distantly wrong with her attitude, as well as her lack of feelings, and like a good little professional, she sought confidential help from a psychiatrist. She was a little hesitant about seeing a man, but she didn't have a lot to pick from. Dr. Reynolds was the only shrink on the ship. It was him or the chaplain, and she had long ago lost any faith in a higher power of any kind.

Dr. Reynolds soon became "Walter," then "Walt." With each session, some grueling, she relived Janet's death, and bit by bit Walt peeled away the layers of her psyche, like the skin of an onion. She didn't like what she found there, but Walt didn't give her a choice. He forced her to face herself, and learn to deal with what was there.

Slowly, the feelings began to return. But not the kind of feelings she expected, or even *wanted.*

Textbook case, Celia. Like so many fools before her, she was falling in love with her shrink. And he was happily married.

She never told him why she stopped seeing him, but she somehow never had time to schedule another session, and after a while, the comp stopped reminding her. Celia avoided him fairly easily; her schedule and his didn't exactly mesh. She went back to repressing her feelings, which she did with relative ease. She was pretty good at it by now.

Then the mine struck the ship. Weeks later, the technicians couldn't quite figure out what race had made the bomb, but whoever made it knew what they were doing.

It might even have been from a race centuries extinct, made for a conflict that someone had won or lost when man was still fumbling about in his own solar system with sublight spacecraft. It might have been something from their current enemy. Wherever it came from, the device had drifted through several layers of security, deftly evading them all before it impacted on the hull.

Celia was on duty when it happened this time. A quarter of the ship had decompressed, killing large numbers of crew before automatic doors sealed off the damaged sector. Those who weren't killed probably wished they had been, in the few minutes that were left to them.

Decompression is such a nasty business, Celia remembered thinking. Of the thirty patients brought in, they lost twenty. Before she went off duty, they brought in one last survivor.

Walt Reynolds. He was gasping for air with ruined lungs when the stretcher floated past. Celia stood there, frozen, for several moments, before she realized she was the only surgeon who wasn't busy with someone right then.

He looked at her with frightened, bloodshot eyes as she put the oxygen mask over his face, checking his skin for the instant frostbite that often accompanied decompression and vacuum exposure. She looked in those ruined eyes, laced with scarlet ruptures, remembering how reassuring they had once been, after gently exposing her mental wounds.

Triage. Minor, major, grave.

She knew before she got started that Walt was going to die, but her training stepped in, seized control of her body.

I'm the best damned doctor on this ship, she thought, wondering why that was important then.

But even the best damned doctor in the universe couldn't save someone with no lung tissue left to breathe with. Not when all the mech-lungs they had were plugged into other people.

When Walt died, she felt nothing, nothing at all.

After that, her career became a series of transfers, initiated whenever she thought she was getting too close to someone. There were many ships in the Fleet, but not all of them had—or were—medic units.

Then there was only one option left open to her. The *Stephen Hawking*. Heading out near the Core, facing yet another brand-new enemy, where the fighting was the heaviest.

The *Stephen Hawking* was a huge ship—but not big enough. Only too soon, she had to run again.

They were losing more ships than ever now, and even medical craft like the *Blackwell* weren't immune to fire, friendly or otherwise.

As she knew.

The Ichtons didn't care what they destroyed. To transfer would mean suicide, sooner or later.

Celia transferred.

And now—now none of it mattered, really. When the huge Ichton fleet had been detected days before, she remembered thinking not so much that she was going to die, but that the running, finally, was over. Instead of the understated fear that those around her were showing, she felt calm, almost serene. In a way she was grateful for the approaching fleet; her heart welcomed them.

The running is finally over.

She would have gone on, wallowing in these cheery thoughts a little longer. But a sudden lull in conversation made her look up, and she noticed the staff administrator had just entered the mess ball. An older gal, she had that seasoned look of someone who had been in medicine a long, long time. *What was her name? Dr. Morgan. Althea Morgan. Neurosurgery and Personnel.*

She had a searching look, a little frown on her face as she scanned the mess. *Who is she looking for?* Celia wondered.

Althea's eyes passed over everyone in the mess hall, then settled on Celia. A smile swept over the mature features, leaving no doubt that she had found who she was looking for.

Celia panicked. *Oh,* shit. *She's looking for* me.

A hunch told Althea that Celia would be hiding out in the mess hall, and as usual her hunch proved to be correct.

There she was, huddled over her plastic tray, sitting alone, eating by herself.

No big surprise here, after reading her file.

When their eyes met, Althea could almost feel the panic she saw there.

Celia's file said she was forty-two, but she looked much, much older. *Well, she has seen a lot of action—but that much action?*

Even from where she stood she could see stress lines in Celia's face, and she wasn't close. On the other hand—the woman wasn't taking any pains to look attractive, either. Not even close.

Forty-two and a veteran. Did I look like that when I was her age? she wondered. Well, it really didn't matter, did it? What was important was what was going on inside that head, not outside it.

She put on her friendliest smile and approached her table, hoping the woman wouldn't flee before she got there.

"Well, he*llo*," Althea said, flashing that all-important smile. "I'm Althea Morgan. You must be our new Chief of Surgery, Celia Stratford."

Celia stood still for a moment, then offered a weak smile. Slowly, like a caged animal reaching uncertainly for food, she extended her hand. "Very pleased to meet you," Celia said, but Althea was far from convinced that she was. "What, ah, can I do for you this morning?"

Althea looked down, at where Celia had put her hands after the tentative handshake. They were gripping the table sides, and the knuckles were turning white. Had she met Celia before seeing what she could do in a surgery, this tense display would have been alarming. But apparently she left the strain and discomfort behind when she went to work; her work, so far, had been exemplary.

Good thing, Althea thought. *Or this girl would never have made it past the first day!*

"Please don't think of this as business, per se," Althea said soothingly. Oh, it was business, all right, but not the kind Celia would think of. *If there's a neurotic working for us, it's my business to find out.* "I was just going over the new personnel files and saw yours, and realized we hadn't actually met."

"I see," Celia said.

That fits. Monosyllables. Not unfriendly, but there's nothing there to make anyone want to continue a conversation, Althea thought, and consciously turned off the frown that started to form on her own face. *Well, let's see if I can't get past the first barrier and see what your next line of defense is.*

Althea chuckled, hoping it didn't sound as artificial as it felt. "You know, in the good ole days of medicine, or anywhere else for that matter, the medical director would be the first person the new transfer would meet. But now, with all our computers . . . well, you know how it is. There's not enough human contact, in my not-so-humble opinion. Especially in our profession. Machines do enough as it is; we shouldn't let them take over our whole lives."

"My mentor made the same observation," Celia said icily. "But at the same time he pointed out that the technical advances in our field have made it possible for the surgeon to concentrate entirely on his specialty and not on extraneous nonsense."

"What, like doctor-patient relations, and bedside manner?" Althea grinned. She'd gotten a response, a negative one, but a response. *Let's jab the needle in a little deeper.* "Frankly, my dear, you can call me old-fashioned, but I think that kind of attitude sucks."

She had deliberately chosen the single most offensive way to phrase her reply, short of marine-class obscenity. She hoped fervently for anger.

Something to show that the personality was only buried, not amputated. She had a shrewd idea, now that she'd had a look through Celia's files, of where the problem was, and at least part of the cause. She'd left old Cyclops on a search-and-categorize mission that ought to keep him from pestering her with any foolishness for a while. He was looking for something specific; people with whom Celia had either extended professional or social contacts who had died violently—on the same ship where she was stationed. Good chance that she would have been in the trauma center when they came in.

Meanwhile, she was going to stick some pins in the girl and wake her up. She got her response. "Battlefield conditions are no place for bedside manner, Doctor," Celia said with a spark of anger in her eyes.

"Oh, I beg to differ." Althea raised one eyebrow. "A little personal attention just before the anesthetic hits can make all the difference between someone fighting for his life and giving up. I've seen it happen too many times to discount. And it doesn't take any time at all—I mean, you have to read Ar—I mean, the medicomp screen anyway. You just pay attention to what it says about that kid on the table, lean down while your nurse is spraying your hands, and say, 'Hey, soldier, we're gonna get you back to that pretty little bundle of fur in no time, with a fancy scar to prove you're a hero.' Or maybe, 'Don't sweat your boyfriend, honey. The *Hawking* crew is warming up a brand-new face for you right now. Want to pick out cheekbones when you wake up?' Or even, 'Show these humans what you're made of, soldier. You're worth a dozen puny bareskins!' "

Celia's hands were shaking as badly as Althea's. "You're making them into people—not patients—"

She shook her head. "Not at all. They already *are* people, and their lives are mechanical enough. I just remind them that other folks know they're people, too. Let them know that somebody cares that they were there, that they live through their injuries. I even talk to them while they're under."

"You *what?*" Celia was properly horrified. Actually, Althea had disturbed quite a few medics with her little eccentricity before they saw the results. "That's insane! How could—"

"That's good medicine," Althea corrected. "Or haven't you read your studies of the effects of anesthetics on the conscious mind? Most species listen to and understand *and are affected* by what they hear when they're under. In fact, you've got a pipeline straight to the raw psyche right then, bypassing all the usual protections we put on what we hear. Tell a patient something while he's on the table and he'll take it as from the mouth of the Deity-of-His-Choice. So I tell them they're doing fine, make jokes about the mess they got themselves in, tell them that the staff on the *Hawking* is going to put in some improvements that'll wow the extremities off their mates. Lots of times I get kids pulling through that had no right to."

The rest of the staff had recognized that she was having *one of those conferences* with a new doctor; the mess had mysteriously cleared of personnel. *Good. Because I'm getting to her, and she won't perform with an audience.*

"I—didn't know—" Celia whispered, her eyes dark with *some* kind of emotion. "But—what if they don't—pull through? You've made them into people for you, and what if—"

"What if they aren't faceless simulacra anymore?" Althea gentled her voice; there was an edge of hysteria in Celia's words that she didn't want to push just yet. "What if they die?"

There was no doubt what the emotion was in Celia's eyes now. It was pain. She didn't say anything, she didn't even nod. She just sat there in frozen silence. But her eyes begged for an answer.

"Celia, that is the price that we pay for being mortal. People die—of *stupid* things. I lost my mother when a house fell on her." She shook her head, her mouth twisting in remembered pain, but still able to see the absurdity. "Some idiot was moving a living-unit with an inadequate lifter; he dropped it. It went through the pedwalk and crushed my mother in a shoe store two levels below. Imagine how I felt the first time some poor innocent reacted to a bad mood I was in by asking sarcastically, 'What's the matter, did a house fall on your sister?' Shit happens. You work through it, and live."

Celia shook her head, and to Althea's joy, there were signs of tears in her eyes.

"We pay doubly, because we are physicians as well as mortals," she continued. "We have the skills to save lives—"

"But sometimes we can't—" Celia choked, and then shut her mouth tightly.

"Sometimes we can't," Althea agreed. "That doesn't mean we should cut ourselves off from feeling. Not even pain. Pain lets us know we're alive; so does love. Maybe that's why we've come running out here to get ourselves killed, trying to keep them from turning the rest of the universe into their private lunch counter. I don't know. I *do* know that no matter how much *feeling* costs, I'm not going to stop—because when you stop feeling, you're dead."

Okay, wrap it up, quick. Get out of here so she can recover from what you just shot at her. Althea glanced at her watch and swore. "Damn! I'm in surgery in an hour. I'd better grab a bagel and get out of here." She reached over and patted Celia's icy hand. "It was good meeting with you, Celia. I expect we'll be seeing a lot more of each other, now that I know who you are."

She made a quick exit, snatching a bagel for form's sake, and headed for her cabin, restraining her feeling of triumph.

Good work, there. Got some real emotion out of her. She palmed the lock on her door with anticipation. *Now to see what Cyclops has for me, and see how close to the bone I came.*

She hit the Enter key on her terminal before she even sat down on her bunk, and to her immense satisfaction, Cyclops had found not one, but two possibilities.

The first . . .

Omigod. Med school roomie; best friend. Requested assignment to same ship. And, yes, Celia had been in the trauma room when her roommate came in. The hospital ship itself had taken a hit, and every skilled hand on board had been summoned to duty.

Probably watched the poor thing die. Althea looked over the old records with a professional eye. *God. Gamma rays just sheeted through that compartment. Those weren't blast burns, not entirely . . . The girl was dead before they took her to the trauma room, just nobody knew it. Not even Jesus Christ himself could have done anything. But I'll bet Celia never knew that.*

Then two years later—

Her shrink. Shit, doesn't it figure. And he would be a classical Freudian, too, which means he encouraged her to fall in love with him as part of the therapy and I'd be willing to pin my job on the fact that she didn't know he was Freudian. She'd have been better off going to the chaplain, at least he had Gestalt training.

She lay back on her bed and laced her hands under her head. *Celia, Celia, what am I going to do with you? Are you bright enough to actually* listen *to what I'm telling you? I hope so. Because I can't have you on my staff otherwise. You'll wind up killing people and never know you were doing it. But you're ready to rejoin the world. I can sense it.*

Or else you'll crack, when we need you most.

And if it comes to a choice between helping you out of your morass slowly, or getting you out of the way, I'll commit you on a Psych charge, girl.

Because while I have compassion for you, I have no pity. I have no time for pity. None of us does.

Stunned, Celia watched Althea get her bagel and leave the cafeteria. They had spoken maybe four minutes, five tops, but it felt like she had just gone through one of those grueling hour-long sessions with Walt: like a glass of ice water had just been thrown in her face.

Like she'd just been peeled bare, right down to the bone, then casually put back together.

What is she? she wondered. *How did a paper pusher in administration, a surgeon, get to be so good at getting inside people?* During their brief discussion Althea neatly dissected her as if she were some kind of frog, or if she were psychic, or both. *She's in Personnel. She must know everything about me. Janet, my transfers. Walt, the transfers.* Celia had never felt more exposed in her life, and it was *not* a feeling she was comfortable with.

Her cold breakfast sat untouched in front of her as she wavered between anger and revelation. The ice Althea had just chipped away revealed wounds, not flesh, and she wasn't certain what she should feel just then.

Some of the things Althea said were just plain crazy—

Or were they? She *had* heard some of them before, like the part about talking to the patients who were under. All the times when she might have done such a thing in surgery, she remembered being so busy with the technicalities of the operation to even consider it.

Still, it sounded a little wacky, even with evidence to support it.

Or did it sound wacky because *she* didn't want to believe it? Didn't want to think that some muttered remark, some unthought curse, might have pushed one of her own patients over the edge of survival?

She sure knew the right buttons to push. Celia shuddered. *Who does she think she is, anyway?* She reached for the anger, and found that it wasn't there. *Damn it, where did it go?* she thought. *I have to be angry about this . . . don't I? If I'm not angry, then what does that mean?*

That I believe what she's trying to tell me. The exchange rolled over and over in her mind, and Celia tried to analyze it further, looking for the hidden meaning that must have been there. But wasn't.

"When you stop feeling, you're dead," she whispered. *That's what she said. And damned if that's not how I've been feeling all along.*

Her soul seemed to decompress. A feeling of release filled the void that she had willed all these years; sense that a burden had gone, a feeling of light and weightlessness.

I can be a doctor and be human, too, she thought. *They're people, not patients. Let them know it.*

Then, another thought; the recollection of Althea's face, the graying hair. The lines of care and pain that not all the laugh and smile creases could erase.

She's lost people, too, and not just her mother. And she lived. She can laugh. She has friends, I know she does—

Then, greatly daring, trying the thought to see if it hurt; *I'd like to be her friend.*

She looked up, feeling silly that she was the only one left in the mess hall. She got up and consigned her breakfast to the disposal; she felt strange, as if she'd been hit with some kind of psychotropic drug, and had no idea what it was going to do to her. But even that was better than the emptiness that had been her constant companion all these years.

Leaving the cafeteria, she entered a triangular hallway of bare steel girders; pretty Spartan for a medical ship, but she knew that the paneling had been stripped earlier for more important sections of the *Blackwell*. Only a few crew and medical staff wandered the halls. The day for most had begun. Celia glanced at her watch, and, seeing she was late for her shift, walked a little faster.

From somewhere beneath her came a loud *whump*.

It rocked the floor and walls so hard she stumbled and went to her knees. Simultaneously a red alert alarm began wailing in the hall, followed by the flashing red light near every intercom.

What the hell? she thought madly. But her battlefield training took over and she kept her head low in case something else might explode or fly through the air, working her way over to the wall to clutch at an exposed girder.

Is this finally it? she wondered, calculating the proximity of the Ichton fleet, which should still be quite far away. *Must be something else, but what?* The red alert sounded only if a life-threatening situation occurred *on* the ship, or if the ship itself was in danger.

Considering the intensity of the explosion, and the fact that they were still docked with the *Hawking*, it was probably the former. She found a rude laugh somewhere inside her. *Ironic, if I die now. At least,* she thought whimsically, *I'll have some peace of mind if I do.*

A sharp pain in her right leg hindered her as she tried to get up. Blood had soaked the leg of her uniform, vivid against the white fabric. She swore softly and rolled the leg of her pants up; she found it was a long and shallow gash, bleeding messily, but not immediately threatening. A special patch in the ER would stop the bleeding. Fine and dandy. That's where she was going anyway. She'd probably cut it when she fell; there was certainly enough crud lying around in the halls because of the repairs going on.

"Shit happens," she said to the ship as she hobbled toward the ER. Now, behind her, she heard shouts, and some other ominous, unidentifiable sound. One of the shouts became a scream; she quickened her pace.

Here we go again, she thought, going into surgeon mode. *This isn't just a job. It's a fucking adventure!*

When she got to the lifts, she discovered that whatever exploded had apparently taken them out as well. *Great,* she thought. *It's only two flights. Not bad, even with the artificial gravity. Here's hoping* that *stays up.*

It took several more minutes than usual to get to ER. When she finally got there, all hell had broken loose.

Most alarming was the group of doctors huddled around the medicomp CPU, as if it were a patient, not the marvelous tool the staff had come to depend on. The main screen was blank; one of the doctors slapped the monitor on its side, as if to urge it to life. Nothing happened.

There were no patients there yet, but she had a sickening feeling there soon would be. "She's here," someone said. The room became silent, and one by one all heads turned to her.

One of the doctors, an older surgeon just months away from retirement, hung up a phone. Dr. Powers's expression was grave. He saw her, and slowly padded his way through the others. The crowd parted, letting him pass.

"Dr. Stratford," he said, glancing briefly at the leg wound. "We should get a patch on that."

"In a moment. What *happened,* Doctor?"

"It appears," he began, addressing all present, "that a water boiler in the crew section has exploded, due to residual damage from the last battle. It's a nasty situation down there, and it's taken out the airlock along with a few other goodies. We won't be able to transfer patients to the *Hawking* until the dock crews get a temporary lock set up, and cut through the old one. Until then, we're on our own. Ladies and gentlemen, get ready for a long night."

Celia knew them was more; Dr. Powers didn't disappoint her.

"The explosion created a power surge—and repairs had taken the breakers and power cleaners off-line. The surge took the medicomp and a lot of our electronics out as well." Powers took a deep breath. "Here's what we're faced with. We have some telltales, the ones built into the tables. EKG, EEG, body temperature. We have stand-alone equipment, like the oxygen, blood replacement, and suction devices. No laser scalpels; they were slaved to the medicomp, and until we get a tech up here to get them unhooked, they're useless. No StediGloves."

"How're we going to know where our hands are?" someone wailed.

Powers gave him a look. "Eyeball. This is going to be metal scalpel and suture time, kids. Nurse Ki'ilee?"

An odd-looking anthropoid with arms far too long for its uniform stepped to the front of the group. "Thir," it lisped.

"Find the autoclave and all the manual gear. I think it's in one of the holds with the spare IV equipment. Requisition whoever you need to trot it up here and get it set up. On the double."

"Thir!" The nurse saluted sharply and ran off. Powers turned to Celia.

"According to your records, you spec'd in field surgery." He looked at her as if he expected her to deny it.

"I did," she replied.

A tiny bit of relief crept into his expression. "Then you're the best CoS we could have right now. What do we do?"

She froze for a moment—then her mind went into high gear.

"We'll be getting patients in here in a moment—" She examined the room. "Triage in the hall; there won't be room in here. God forbid it happens, but if there are any medical personnel hurt, they get priority. You, you, and you—" She pointed to three nurses. "You're triage and hall prep. If you spot any paramedics out there, put them on triage and get back in here."

She turned her attention back to the huddle of doctors, as a secondary—explosion? Or the crew of the *Hawking* trying to get in to them?—shook the floor. "Each one of you pick three nurses to help you; you'll need them. One holds clean instruments, one assists, and one operates the breathing equipment. Put a bucket or a pan under the table for dirty instruments." She thought quickly as the nurses and doctors together started setting up what they could; even as she thought, the anthropoid nurse arrived with a bulky container on wheels and a line of ships' personnel with boxes.

"You sailors!" she snapped—and the men and women came as close to snapping to attention as they could. "You stay here. Nurse, these people are yours for the duration. You set up the autoclave and start sterilizing instruments You sailors, you take clean instruments to the doctors and take the used ones away, back to the nurse. *Spray your hands every time you touch something that isn't clean.* Nurse, tell them what you want."

The nurse stood up taller with the new increase in status, and began issuing orders in its soft lisp. Celia surveyed the room, and noted the dismay and despair on some faces.

"Stop thinking about this as an impossibility," she said gently. "I've done this hands-on. Scalpels are the same, they just don't cauterize, so there'll be more blood. Nurses, if you're assisting, keep the suction going and blot delicate areas with sponges. Doctors—how many of you have done real suturing?"

Only two. "Nurses?" A couple more. "All right, has anyone ever done needle-and-thread sewing? Handwork or embroidery?" Three, including a paramedic who had just wandered in. "Fine. You six are the closure specialists. Doctors, you do internals, nurses, muscle tissue and major vessels, hand workers, final closure. We'll run this like an assembly line."

She got them set up; patients would come in the door to the nearest empty table. Anyone *not* working on someone would prep them, then keep them going until the first available surgery-team could take them. Then surgery, then closure, then out the door and the anthropoid nurse's team would clean the table for the next.

"Get them patched together and keep them alive," she ordered, and did a quick mental reckoning. "I don't think it'll take the *Hawking* more than a few hours to get to us. Give them that much time, and we're home free. It doesn't have to be pretty or neat; it *does* have to be good."

"Doctor?" One of the nurses waved her hand in the air. "What are we doing about anesthetic and blood?"

No blood analysis at all; that was the medicomp's job. "Can we get by on locals and injectables?" It was a lot easier monitoring the dosages on those.

Powers turned to the anthropoid, who nodded. "We haf jutht rethupplied," it said.

"Okay. Save the inhalants for major thoracic wounds; use your own judgment. Blood—shit."

She shook her head; the replicators were probably gone, too, or the nurse wouldn't have asked the question. "Stored where we have it, hyperoxygenated universal, where we don't, and species-specific plasma or Ringers if you don't know what the reaction to universal will be. A few hours, people. That's what we need to buy them. Okay? Don't forget those clean samples; the *Hawking* will need them. Okay, on station—go—"

That was when the first wave hit.

Celia tried to be everywhere, looking over shoulders, advising, cajoling, coaxing. The first wave wasn't so bad; not nearly as bad as she had thought. No decompression; lots of burns, some pretty horrible, but nothing that needed really major surgery. Her fledglings gained confidence as they sutured their first gashes, as they cut bits of shrapnel from arms and legs. Nurse Ki'ilee was everywhere, turning her little corps of recruits into a real team. She lost a few in the first couple of minutes, as weak stomachs couldn't handle the gore of the OR—she gained more by sending the unsteady out to wake up the rest of the med personnel and haul them in.

It was just as well that they had that first wave to practice on, because when the second wave came in—the victims who'd been pried out of their wrecked rooms—needed every bit of confidence that they'd gained.

Here were the major injuries that Celia had feared; yellow bands weren't coming in the door at all, just red. Severed limbs (put it on ice, stop the bleeding, kill the pain, stem the shock, let the *Hawking* handle it), torsos ripped open, spurting arterial wounds, punctured and collapsed lungs. . . .

Celia shoved doctors aside when they hesitated, taking over and scolding and swearing at her patients like some kind of cross between a first sergeant and a mother hen. "What in hell were you doing in bed, anyway? You're gonna have to get yourself back up off that bunk in double time, mister, you hear me? Making all this shit for me to do—" Encouraging? It was the closest she could come. At least she was filling those unconscious ears with the sure message that they were going to live.

They were people. They were her responsibility. And suddenly she found herself caring, caring passionately, that they would live.

"Celia!"

The urgency in that voice made her head snap up. Someone across the crowded OR waved frantically at her.

Dr. Powers. He wouldn't call her unless he needed her.

She wriggled her way between the tables, across a floor slippery with cleaning solution and much-diluted blood—Nurse Ki'ilee was making certain that the OR stayed as clean as it could be. But when she reached Powers's side and he made room for her, his white face did not prepare her for what she found on the table.

Dr. Althea Morgan.

Her mind froze; her body wanted to run and her soul screamed.

Not again—not—again—

Powers gestured at the massive chest wound. It looked as if she must have been reading something off her terminal when the explosion occurred; shards of razor-edged plastic and glass had ripped into her body, somehow sparing her face.

I can't—I can't—

"I can't do this," Powers said numbly. "I haven't got that kind of skill."

"Nobody does—alone," she heard herself saying. "Pull Urrrlerri off whatever he's doing, and get me Nurse Merfanwy. And then take over for Urrrlerri."

She found her hands reaching for instruments; found herself going to work on the worst of the slashes, a puncture that threatened the lung.

Found tears streaming down her face and soaking her mask. "*Damn* you, Althea Morgan," she snarled as the two assistants arrived, and she put Merfanwy (incredible visual acuity and sight in the low UV) on picking out the near-invisible shards of glass, and Urrrlerri (tentaclelike fingers with incredible flexibility) to work on the abdomen while she did the lungs. "*Damn* you, you old bitch! How dare you talk to me like that and then do this to me? You psychotic bitch from *hell*! What did you think you were doing? You're going to come out of this, you monster, I'm going to drag you out of this by your damn *hair*! If you even *think* of dying, I'm going to pump you so full of stim you'll *dance* over to the damned *Hawking*! You hear me? You hear me?"

Oblivious to the sideways glances from the rest of her operating team, she continued to rage at Morgan under her breath, alternately cursing her and telling her that she'd better not abandon her *friend*, leaving her to face the coming Ichtons alone.

Ignoring the tears that threatened to blind her until her nurse sponged them away, her hands worked with maniacal speed; patching, suturing, making whole.

Then it was over—someone wheeled Althea out—

And there was no more time to agonize, for a sucking lung puncture was on the table in front of her, and another patient to curse back into life. Then another, and another—they had Walt's face, or Janet's or Althea's—

And she gave them all her curses, her tears, her skill—told them all they were needed, that they *would* live or she would, by all the gods anyone ever swore by, come *after* them!

Suddenly, silence.

The OR was empty. Not even a green bracelet in sight. She blinked once, looked around at the equally weary bodies around her, and slowly pulled off her facemask.

There was someone at her elbow; someone she didn't know, but in medical white, *clean*, with a look of concern and a little name tag that said "Dr. R. S. Rai."

"I'm from the *Hawking*," he said, slowly, carefully. "We've got all your patients, Doctor. You did incredibly well, you didn't lose anyone who made it this far."

"We didn't?" she replied ingenuously.

He smiled. "Not one. Six hours on your own and not a single one."

"Oh," she said vaguely. "That's fucking wonderful." And she let him lead her off to a bed.

"So," Althea said the moment they let Celia into her room, "I'm a nasty old bitch, am I? And you were going to pump me full of so much stim I was going to dance over to the *Hawking*?"

She grinned at Celia's look of shock. "Told you that people heard what you said to them." She lowered her voice, conspiraorially. "Did you know that there's now a story going around about a foul-mouthed angel who wrestles victims right out of the hands of Death and then kicks their butts back to their bodies?"

She laughed out loud at the look on Celia's face, even though it hurt.

"I—uh—"

"I bet you didn't even know you knew those words." She reached out and took Celia's hand. "Look—I snooped into your records, so I know about your friends. I'm sorry, Celia—"

"But enough is enough," the woman said, herself. "You were right. All I was doing was—anesthetizing. As soon as it wore off, something was bound to break."

It was Althea's turn to be surprised, and Celia smiled—the first time she'd actually seen that expression on the woman's face. "I've had some time to think—and to get a little help. I found a good female shrink on the *Hawking*, and an even better chaplain. Oh, I'm still a mess, but we all are, right?"

"Right," Althea said softly, with a silent salute to her own legion of dead. "That's part of the price we pay, we survivors. Beats the hell out of the alternative."

Celia nodded, and the life in her eyes brought back a hint of that laughing girl of the graduation picture. "Speaking of beating the hell out of someone—" she said, a hint of humor starting to show—"I figured I'd snoop in *your* records while I was temporary admin head. And I found out that you fancy yourself as a *go* player." From behind her, she whisked out a board and bag of stones, and placed them on Althea's tray table. "So I thought I'd show you just where you really stand in the *go* hierarchy around here."

Althea raised an eyebrow. "Is that a threat?"

"No." Celia's smile turned wicked. "That's a promise."

"Care to make a little wager on that?"

"Sure." Celia licked her lips. "I take on the paperwork—against *you* taking on me." Her look was challenging. "You're degreed in head-shrinking. And I don't intend to lose."

Althea felt a warm rush of irrational happiness. "The game or the friend?"

"Either." A shrug. "Maybe we don't have much time. So I want to learn how to enjoy what time we have left. I figure you can do that *and* help me get my head straight."

"You're on." She selected black. "You know—I *am* the kind of person your parents warned you about. You're about to learn things they never taught you in med school."

Celia just laughed. "Why do you think I made that bet?"

REINFORCEMENTS

It was confirmed that, as Anton Brand had feared, the two missing Ichton fleets had united and were moving toward Emry. In their effort the invaders were bypassing a number of usable, inhabited planets. This was a change of procedure that worried all of the strategists of the races united to fight them. Beyond the Fleet's more effective warp drive, only the Ichtons' predictability had so far enabled them to be met and defeated, even locally.

One of the worlds bypassed was that inhabited by the Squarm—a young race, by local standards, that physically resembled Earth's walruses. Initially reluctant to abandon the defense of their world, when the Squarm leaders realized how easily the Ichtons that had already passed would have overwhelmed their defenses, they agreed to contribute half of their space navy to the Fleet-led effort. The other half was retained to defend the planet against the numerous smaller bands of Ichtons appearing more frequently in the Core systems. Other nearby races followed this example, almost doubling in number, if not quality, the forces based on the *Hawking*. The appearance of allies gave a boost to the nearly negligible morale of the *Hawking*'s crew. It also placed a strain on the station as it strived to support almost twice the number of ships it had been designed for.

The decision was made to intercept and divert the Ichton fleet. This would buy time for the Emry to complete the construction of new factories designed to build new orbital defenses based upon the most effective Fleet weaponry. The planet Emry was also supplying many of the resources needed to maintain and repair the *Hawking* and had to be defended if they were to continue the defense. So the battle began, but Brand had underestimated the determination of the Ichtons to punish and destroy any opposition. Rather than turn to face the new threat posed by the Fleet, the Ichtons' combined fleet continued on toward Emry at full speed. Dropping out only to navigate, re-form, or snap at their pursuers. Unable to use its superior speed without leaving all their ally's ships behind, the *Hawking* found itself in a stern chase. They followed the Ichton fleet, with individual units pushing ahead to engage their rear guard. The decisive battle Brand sought had, instead, degenerated into a running fight covering hundreds of light-years and several weeks. One in which the constantly reinforced Ichtons more than held their own.

The arrival of over a hundred destroyers of the hundred forty dispatched from Tau Ceti months earlier was a second tremendous morale boost for the crew of the *Hawking*. Their crews were exhausted from the seven-month journey to the Core, but Brand had no choice but to throw them instantly into the battle.

Along with mail, spare parts, and the latest trivid programs, the reinforcement fleet also brought a few unwanted visitors. Dealing with them proved a new challenge for even the combat veterans on the *Stephen Hawking*.

TAKEN TO THE CLEANERS
by Peter Morwood

The lieutenant ran one finger around his tunic's high collar, as though the garment were strangling him, then set all to rights again with a quick downward tug at the hem. Despite hours of pondering over real and imagined errors, he still wasn't sure how he had pulled this particular duty; but he was fairly certain that he wasn't going to like it much. There were too many cold eyes and rattrap mouths among the budgetary fact-finding commission for that.

"If you'll all just step this way. Yes, that's right. Stand well clear of the doors, please. Mind the gap. All present and correct? Good. Now then. Welcome aboard the Battlestation *Stephen Hawking*, ladies and gentlemen, welcome aboard. I'm glad to—"

As the commission formed up in an untidy gaggle and its shortest members pushed to the front, his voice faltered. At least the blink of disbelief that had accompanied the stumble in his words had gone unnoticed. He hoped. The shrouded mike of the wall-mounted com unit beckoned. "Er, excuse me just one second." His thumb hit the Transmit button just one second after that.

"Channel five, engage privacy mute. Joe. Hey, Joe, you there?"

Course I'm here. Where else would I be?

"Hah! Where else would I be? sez you. Do you believe this guy? Don't gimme that crap. I dunno where you'd be. Just run me a translator check. Right now."

Why d'you need a trans—

"Uh, Joe, in case you haven't noticed, the why is because you didn't tell me there were Weasels in this bunch. Are the little fleabags getting a proper salutation?"

Yeah, sure they are.

"Gender and all?"

Gender, rank specifics, even line-family enhancements.

"Jeez, makes a change."

Gimme a break. We just finished a war with the furry little creeps. You think I want to start another—

"Look, just give me some warning next time, willya? Okay? Yeah, yeah, you, too. And your mother . . ."

The lieutenant let his face relax from the fixed grin it had adopted as com control came on line, Expression #27, We're Fine, We're All Fine, How Are You? and though his facial muscles wanted to go straight into #42, Sod This for a Game of Soldiers, he managed to resist the temptation. Rule One where the Civil Service was involved, never let the Buggers in the Suits know what you're thinking.

"Sorry about the interruption, ladies and gentlemen. Fleet business, security clearances, all that sh—stuff, you know how it is."

I don't think.

"My name is Neilson, Lieutenant Robert Neilson, and Commander Brand has assigned"—*ordered*—"me to look after you folks during this short guided tour of the *Hawking*. I'd like to take a few minutes before we start to advise you all of a few points—" *which shouldn't need repeating but then we're dealing with Suits and not real people, aren't we?*

"First, this station is on full active status, so military personnel will expect to have priority for use of the on-board transport net. Second, given the size of the *Hawking*, Internal Security recommends that it's in your own interests not to go wandering off by yourselves. Yes, ma'am?"

Ohshit.

The woman who spoke was of that sort who, in an earlier historical period, would have worn a tweed two-piece suit and terrifying spiky-framed spectacles. Even though she, like the rest of the commission, was wearing the name-tagged coverall issued to all visitors who might be entering a variety of shipboard environments, she still managed to suggest that indefinable air of tweediness. Neilson concentrated for just long enough to get the gist of her question, then tuned out the rest.

"Yes, ma'am," he said at last, "I understand that an economic analysis commission doesn't expect to be treated like tourists." *It's far too good for you.*

"Then, Lieutenant, since you understand, evidently your superiors also understand." Even her voice sounded tweedy, like the nightmare of a librarian. "As the representatives of the Defense Committee who financed this battlestation, why do we need a chaperone in the first place?"

"Because, ma'am, none of you know your way around." *And little fingers pushing little buttons could smoke half of this sector.*

"Are we considered incapable of asking for directions?"

"No, ma'am. Of course you could ask for directions, but as I said"—*and why weren't you listening?*—"this vessel is at active status, and—"

"Lieutenant, do you mean, ah"—the man, a classic career civil servant whose coverall should have been in pinstripe, was fumbling for the military terminology through the filing cabinets of a brain taught to work in signed triplicates—"that we are at, ah, general quarters?"

"No, sir, not general quarters. If we were at general quarters I wouldn't be here." *And neither would you.*

"But even allowing that active status is more peaceful than general quarters, surely a civilian would have less call on his or her time than a military . . . ?"

"I doubt a civilian guide would be as useful to the members of this commis sion as—"

"Or is the military trying to keep this commission all to itself? What is the civilian administrator's view?"

"Sir, the administrator was consulted on the matter. Both Administrator Omera and Commander Brand thought it would be simpler if a Fleet officer acted as guide. It's a matter of security." *Mine.*

The tweedy woman said something to her neighbor that Neilson couldn't quite catch, but her tone was clear enough that he could guess the content of the words. He had heard something of the sort before. "No, ma'am. Not so that the commission's access can be restricted. Quite the reverse. As Fleet personnel, I'm cleared to take you anywhere on the *Hawking.* A civilian guide would be restricted to civilian sectors only."

"And why is that, pray? The various civilian interests represented on board have put quite as much money toward the development of this station as the military."

"That's as may be, sir. It remains equally true that a civilian has no busi ness to be in the military sectors. Yourselves excepted, of course, but then the bureaucratic arm is a sort of honorary military." Neilson allowed himself to sink a small pin. "I believe that has to do with funding. Now, if you'll all just follow me." He cleared his throat and shifted into lecturing mode.

"The nine deck levels immediately above this location are military in func tion. Further, there are eleven decks below that are entirely scientific and civilian. What isn't widely understood is that, despite popular and romantic representa tions, the Fleet does more than just seek out new life-forms and new civiliza tions, and then blows them up. Unlike the Ichtons and the Khalians—excuse me, sir, it's true and a matter of historical fact, you can't deny twenty years of war—we are not aggressors. No sir, the *Jrgen Stroop* was a orbital bombardment platform purposely built for a single operation, Case White—yes, sir, economi cally built, from scrap parts—and never actually used. But given the existence of such aggressive species as I've already mentioned, it's hardly surprising that a vessel like the *Hawking* needs to be well-armed. . . ."

The little group had not gone very far along the corridor before a piercing scream shattered the silence and scattered the little gaggle of bored bureau crats. Even though he knew he was safely on board an Alliance battlestation, even though he *knew* that there was nothing more dangerous behind him than a bunch of civil servants and a couple of tooth-drawn Weasels, Lieutenant Neilson was still flattened against the nearest bulkhead with his side arm drawn before he took time out to look back toward the source of the noise.

He relaxed at once and returned his gun to its holster, watching as a small shape fled meeping past him and back into the safe shadows beyond the pools of maintenance-level light.

"Shoot it! Why don't you shoot it?"

The only thing that Neilson shot was a puzzled glance back toward the party he was escorting, and most particularly at the tweedy lady, who was now giving the impression that she wanted to be standing on a chair with her skirt pulled tight around her legs. Since the regulation coveralls were—for good or, in her bony, long-shanked case, ill—fairly form-fitting, and most certainly didn't come equipped with any sort of skirt, this took some doing, but she managed all the same.

"Shoot it, ma'am? Why would I want to do that?"

"It's some sort of nasty alien!" Quite apart from the wording of the Alliance charter, simply being alien had long ceased to be any good reason to shoot something. There was a very satisfying embarrassed pause as the woman straightened herself up, brushed herself down, and generally tried to pretend that nothing untoward had ever happened. It didn't really work, but Neilson suppressed his grin and gave her the benefit of the doubt.

"No, ma'am. That's a Rover-SAC."

"A what?"

"A Rover. A Semi-Autonomous Cleaner."

"Dear God, I thought it was alive."

Lieutenant Neilson breathed out gently through his nose, so that the breath could not be used for all the comments that came simmering up inside him. Finally, he allowed himself just one. "Ma'am, Fleet sentiologists have identified more than three hundred life-forms since the *Hawking* moved coreward. They've had wings, legs, fins, tentacles, gastropodal traction, and even gaseous substructures. But so far, no wheels."

"What does it do, Lieutenant?" Neilson shifted his gaze and shrouded everything behind it with a slow blink. That sort of question could only come from a career civil servant who hadn't been listening to anything that anyone had said.

"Sir, it cleans, sir."

"Are you telling us that this facility has spent fiscal revenue on self-propelled cleaning devices?"

I just did. "Yes, sir."

"Lieutenant, have you any idea of how much such things cost?"

I'm flight crew. Why should I? "No, sir. But probably much less than the expenditure of putting FODed equipment to rights. Foreign-object damage is something you just don't want to know about, sir. Also I would guess that the Rovers cost less than maintaining a janitorial staff big enough to deal with a station of this size. Sir."

"Thank you, Lieutenant. Carry on."

Neilson knew the tone of that thank you, just as he knew the tone of the muttering that followed him down the corridor, and he was heartily glad that he was nothing more than a guide. Before this bunch left the battlestation, somebody somewhere on *Hawking* was going to be justifying the bars on their cuffs and the salary that went with it.

"Why 'semi-autonomous'?" said a dubious voice behind him.

Because autonomous units won't let their union members wash the windows, thought Neilson with a grin. "Sir, I think I could show you better than try to describe the difference. This way, please."

The control room wasn't too far from their intended route, and it was as busy with humming readouts and glowing monitors as any other on the battlestation. Even though he knew what it was all about, Neilson found the place appropriately impressive, and from the noises at his back, so did the members of the commission.

"What is this, Lieutenant? Internal security?"

"No, sir."

"That man at the control board, with the joystick, is he some sort of pilot?"

"No, ma'am. He's a janitor."

"A *what*?"

"A janitor, ma'am. He monitors the Rovers—on an intermittent basis—and makes sure that they're only doing what they've been programmed for. Hence semi-autonomous."

"All of this"—the disbelief was palpable—"just to keep an eye on a lot of self-propelled vacuum cleaners? I'm very glad you brought us here, Lieutenant Neilson. This is exactly the sort of gross overspending that our commission was—"

"Overspending, sir? Hardly. If anything, this facility's undermanned. And the Rover-SAC isn't a vacuum cleaner. At least, not just a vacuum cleaner."

"I think you'd better explain yourself, Lieutenant." The voice had one of those deceptively gentle tones, like a razor blade concealed in soap. "This, this blatant display has done very little to favorably influence the commission so far as allocations of funds from the next fiscal year are concerned."

Meaning, give us good reason to pay, or we won't.

"Ma'am, the commission was supplied with all necessary documentation—" Neilson began.

"Documentation is one thing, Lieutenant. Personal observation is another matter altogether. I know which I prefer."

Neilson took the insult—to himself, to the Fleet, to the veracity of the Service—without turning a hair. As one of the two Khalian commissioners wandered past, nosing and poking at things in a way that he would never have dreamed possible on an Alliance ship, hair was, however, much on his mind. If the commission wanted personal observation, they could have it. "Then, ma'am," he said, "it might be worth your while to question Mr. Leary."

"Mister who?"

Just the man sitting at the console. The one with Leary on his name tag. "The janitor, ma'am."

"Then bring him here."

"It would be better if the commission went to him, ma'am. He's quite busy just at the—"

"I said here, Lieutenant. And now."

"Ma'am, I really don't think—"

"Lieutenant Neilson, all this pretense of industry isn't fooling anybody. Janitor Leary, come here please. . . ."

Neilson backed hurriedly out of the cross fire as Leary, never impressed by Suits at the best of times, made it plain that he wasn't going anywhere for anybody right in the middle of his shift. For just a second Neilson thought the old man was going to say why, but he needn't have worried. In the tradition of janitors from long before man took his first faltering steps into space and left little trails of moondust that somebody had to sweep up, Leary subsided back over his controls, muttering as if they were somehow to blame.

A Rover-SAC whirred by, paused ever so briefly, then meeped to itself as Leary hit the override and trundled on. Neilson winked at it, and grinned.

"Janitor Leary," said the tweedy woman, her thin veneer of patience wearing out after several fruitless attempts at being polite, "if you value your position on this battlestation, you'll do as this commission requires, and do it now."

"Do it," said Neilson, leaning over the console and tapping it with one finger. "Just make sure you've logged a record that you left your post subject to unnecessary duress, and McCaul can't say a thing. No matter what happens." Another Rover-SAC purred into the room, and, like the first one, hesitated as if trying to make sense of conflicting signals. Halfway out of his seat, the janitor reached out to his control board, but Neilson slapped it away. "Leave be," he said briskly. "The Suits are waiting."

They weren't the only ones. The Rover-SAC ambled along a bulkhead and scooped up a few minuscule scraps of garbage, but the little machine's heart—or processor, anyway—didn't seem to be in its work. Neilson watched it thoughtfully, wondering how something that was little more than a knee-high six-wheeled box of tubes and brushes could convey such an impression of nonchalant whistling. Every few seconds it stopped while its small sensor suite ran a check on its surroundings, almost as if it was expecting something to happen.

Like, for instance, the duty janitor to explain what was and what was not genuine trash—except that the duty janitor was also trying to explain his existence to a group of unsympathetic civil servants. That meant the Rover-SAC had to make up its own tin brain, and in common with all such dim-witted machines, it reverted to default programming. Part of that default required the collection of loose fibers and particulate matter . . .

. . . And it was unfortunate that one of the Weasels was halfway through a molt.

As the Rover-SAC lunged at the Khalian's left leg and started giving the limb a vacuum-and-rotary-brush grooming the like of which the Weasel had never experienced before in all its life, the Khalian jumped half its own height off the deck and shrilled something that its translator flatly refused to handle. It didn't help matters that the Rover's suction system was strong enough to keep it firmly attached and brushing away even when the Khalian left the ground, and within only a few seconds the leg had no further problems about shedding fur.

At least, not until some grew back.

As the rest of the commission stood dumbfounded and as Neilson and Leary came close to bursting in their attempts not to laugh, three more Rovers appeared in the doorway. The attentions of the first—still attached, still brushing, but working on the fleeing Weasel's tail by now—had left enough particulate matter of one form or another that none of the cleaning machines hesitated even for an instant. With the merest hint of tire squeal, they made straight for the Khalian commissioners, chased both of them three times around the console, followed them through the door in a whirl of rotating brushes, then down the corridor and out of sight.

"Of course," said Neilson unsteadily, "we could do away with the janitor and refit the Rovers with artificial intelligence. You know, the stuff the military use. But Leary's cheaper in the long run. . . ." He broke down in helpless sniggering for a few minutes, then hauled himself back to something like composure. "Either way, you'd better make your minds up soon. There's three hundred Emry due on *Hawking* day after tomorrow, and the Rovers'll want to brush down every one of them. . . ."

IMPERATIVES
by Judith R. Conly

The twin siren calls of duty and desire
have launched our legions of need-driven soldiers
to conquer another hatchling-fragile foe.
Their concern-rooted hold on bountiful homeland
as precarious as their biped balance
cannot muster sufficient strength to withstand
our avalanche of dominating drive to victory.

Performing devout service to instinct's compulsion
to protect and provide for potential mates
and nourish the unborn heirs to our future,
we cleanse our new nest of its erstwhile occupants
and assemble the skeleton of our civilization
to shield the female flesh that will fill it.
Then, content with a world secured,
we follow our obsession onward through the dark.

Yet, even as we strive to pour further lengths
of rainbow-blood road across the spectrum of stars,
I cannot always succeed in suppressing
vain idle speculation about the imperatives
of those children of such alien swarms.

COUNTERINTELLIGENCE

When they conquered the Syndicate of Families at the end of the Khalian War (see *The Fleet*, Volumes One through Six) they had absorbed the Family-controlled worlds there into the Alliance. Now, two generations later, most former family members considered themselves patriotic Alliance citizens. Perhaps only the Schlein family had retained their antipathy for the Alliance and the Fleet. As the youngest of the major families, the Schlein had run the intelligence branch of their space navy. When the Alliance prevailed, Fleet Intelligence determined that they no longer needed the services of any part of the Schlein organization. But the Schlein refused to disband.

After so many decades the Schlein family no longer engaged in active sabotage or outright attack on Alliance officials, but even seventy years later they still maintained a shadow organization based upon their old intelligence stations. It is hardly surprising that several Schlein descendants were ordered to join the civilian ranks on board the largest fighting station the Fleet had ever constructed. There to continue their tradition of passive resistance and dislike for the "Khalian traitors and oppressive Fleet."

Except for a distinctive success in planting a few agents among the Ichtons themselves, the Fleet intelligence branch had little success for the first two years of the defense. Driven by instinct to preserve and expand their race, captured Ichtons proved stubborn even in the face of death or mutilation. It fell to a renegade Schlein agent and embittered Gerson survivors to realize that the best way to counter instinct was with instinct.

YOU CAN'T MAKE AN OMELET
by Esther M. Friesner

"Sundry alarums," the drunken man muttered, "and diversions." Peter Schlein tried to get off his bed and only succeeded in rolling himself onto the floor. Outside, the chaos that was officially, emphatically not anything for anyone on Green Eleven to concern themselves about thundered on.

"Which is why they've got every last set of blunderfoot Fleetledeets in this whole godforsaken metal marble ram—ram—ram*pag*ing, that's what, through the halls so an honest man can't even have him a drink in peace without getting sort of killed. Four—four—*four*, I think, or was it five? Ah, fuck it, *four* cycles they been at it now, and still no one knows what all the whizmadoo's about. A man's got a right to know!"

He staggered to his feet and leaned against the dear, familiar wall of his cabin. "Don't you agree, O my muzzy brother?" he asked, apparently of the bulkhead. Had he been alone, he would have kissed it, glad to be safely home again, and to hell with looking like a candidate for the psychs.

But he was not alone, nor was he actually having a nice chat with the wall.

"It is not my place to say, sir," came the rumbly reply. Big, solemn, brown eyes regarded Peter Schlein with such completely nonjudgmental acceptance for the man as he was—warts and all, constructive criticism be damned—that for an instant Peter wished at least three out of his seven ex-wives had been Gersons.

That was the *djroo* speaking, of course. Only a drink as insinuating and deadly sly as *djroo* could convince Peter Schlein that he should have married a giant teddy bear. *Djroo* had an awfully strong voice. By cycle's end it would be screaming inside his skull. Schlein already owed his life to the towering, fur-covered ursinoid presently staring at him. It was this same Gerson—Iorn by name—who had, on numerous occasions previous to this, figuratively saved Peter Schlein's skin, soul, and sanity from the horde of miniature Mongols who wreaked hangover havoc every time the man crawled back under the *djroo* samovar and turned the tap open all the way.

"Urrrh . . . Iorn, when you've got a spare seccie, would you mind mixing me up a little of that *dee*-lightful little spring tonic of yours?" Schlein sounded pitiful when he wheedled, but he had found it the tone of voice most likely to obtain promptest reactions from the Gerson. Orders, however politely couched,

smacked of shouting, and shouting bespoke scenes. When Iorn was—*assigned?*
bonded? given into Schlein's service? Schlein couldn't say which—he was briefed
that it would be the politic thing to respect the Gersons' cultural preference
for not making scenes, even in private. Good advice, this, given the size of the
average Gerson.

The once-bright leading light of the Schlein family might have lost much,
but political savvy was bred so deeply into his DNA that it would only abandon
him five minutes after he was declared clinically dead.

Which, he reflected, had almost happened.

The Gerson turned from his contemplation of *homo inebriensis* and busied
himself briefly in the very compact, very efficient, very frivolous, and most
certainly *very* discreet kitchen-*cum*-bar at the far end of Schlein's living quarters.
A private kitchen—complete with the requisite accompanying pantry-supply
channels of dubious legality—was the stuff of legend aboard the *Hawking*. It was
an indulgence whose clandestine construction had required sizable "understand-
ings" with the slickest of the Indie traders, but every time Schlein tasted Iorn's
latest culinary or potable concoction, a small, *djroo*less voice inside told him it
had all been worth it.

Even when the drink was going to taste as close to Khalia tailfur as this one.

The work of moments produced a thick *uberglas* beaker filled with a frothy,
somewhat viscous solution the color of old cheese that was presented to Schlein
on a silver tray. "Your tonic, sir."

"Uh . . . thank you, Iorn," Schlein said. He downed the concoction in three
gulps and shuddered as each swallow walloped the relative circadian daylights
out of his stomach. He set the beaker down with much the same sense of relief
at Duty Done as Socrates must have showed the hemlock.

Freed now from the threat of alcoholic retribution, Schlein managed to add,
"I mean . . . thanks for it all. Everything you did. Not just the tonic." The words
sounded inadequate, even to a man who was accustomed to giving short weight
in all his personal dealings. "If you hadn't come into the lounge just then, I think
that nest-fouling Khalian would've done for me." He addressed the bearlike
Gerson in its own tongue—linguistic ability was what had landed Peter Schlein
aboard the *Hawking* instead of in a richly deserved prison cell somewhere halfway
back across the galaxy—but he dealt out the insult to his absent whilom opponent
in its native language. Profanity for the Gerson, Schlein had learned, went paw in
paw under the selfsame shunned aegis of making a scene.

Iorn attempted to shrug his sloping, shaggy shoulders. It was not a gesture
suited to Gerson anatomy, but the alien's excruciatingly precise code of behavior
encouraged him to make any effort necessary to treat with others in ways
familiar to them. "It was my *ghruhn*, sir Schlein," he replied. "My . . . pleasure."
He retired to the kitchen.

The translation was even more inadequate than Schlein's watery thanks, and the family man knew it. *Ghruhn* was more duty than pleasure, backed by the Gerson convention of doing what you had to do amiably, like it or not; but if you were Gerson you had damn well better *make* yourself like it. *Ghruhn* was how obligations—however unpleasant, distasteful, or downright revolting—were forcibly given both the mask and the substance of something the bounden party had wanted to do all along. As Schlein watched Iorn potter around with some mysterious new cookery project he reflected that next to the *ghruhn*-burdened Gerson, Old Earth samurai came off looking like a pack of whiny, self-indulgent shirkers.

Which was why Schlein's—*servant? batman? bearman? aide-de-drunk?*—Iorn had waded into a battle that was none of his instigation or concern and rescued him. Schlein had an abstruse sense of what was funny to say to a half-seas-over Khalian, the Khalian had a knife—surprising that was all it had—and Iorn had an unasked-for field day wiping up the floor of The Emerald with the weasely creature.

"It doesn't go with the job description, you know," Schlein called at Iorn's back as the Gerson popped a pan into the oven. An exotic, somewhat disturbing smell permeated the air until the recyclers kicked on and sucked it out. "Saving my neck. How's the—uh—arm?"

"It's nothing." Again Iorn attempted a shrug. He returned from the kitchen area and extended his hairy paw, the better to show off the expert job the medics had done. The shaved patch was almost unnoticeable, the stitches hidden by the same thick pelt that had thwarted or deflected much of the Khalian's wild, drunken slashings.

An uneasy silence fell between master and "man."

Then: "Will there be anything else you require of me, sir Schlein?" It was Iorn's way of quitting for the day, as if this day had been no different from any other.

"Hm? What?" Peter Schlein shook his head a little clearer. Iorn's tonic prevented hangovers but didn't do a damned thing toward diluting the immediate effects of strong waters. "You're going?"

"If there is nothing further required of me. Tomorrow is my day parted from you." The Gerson phrased it so that his day off sounded like the saddest cycle of his life. Which was impossible, if you knew what the Ichtons had done to his home world. "May I be forgiven tomorrow's service?"

"But wait. Not so fast. How 'bout a re—re—re*ward*, yes?"

"It was my *ghruhn*," Iorn repeated, and shambled for the door.

In vino veritas, but Truth sometimes boots Common Sense clean out of the picture. Peter Schlein flung himself after the hulking Gerson and latched on to the creature's left paw. "Hold on a seccie, friend. I mean—family honor, you know. My life—much or little as they care for it back home—it's still—I'm *Schlein*, dammit! I've got to give you *something*!"

"Kitchen privileges," said the Gerson levelly, "such as I presently enjoy are quite sufficient, sir Schlein." Iorn gave his nominal master a hard stare, a gaze with enough ice water in it to shock the family man into near sobriety. Schlein released his grip on the huge teddy bear's paw, both of them behaving as if the recent outburst had been purely accidental, the participants innocent bystanders.

"Yes, but—but you've already *got* those. At least let me have some of my Household escort you home," Schlein muttered. "All that to-do out there"— he nodded toward the door that gave on the Green deck corridor—"I think I remember what a rough time you had getting me back from The Emerald, checkpoints and all, never would've happened if I'd had the foresight to take Household along. Ex-Fleetledeets to a man, they are. To a woman. Thing. That's their whole job, after all, dealing with other military hoseheads. Why there's all this botheration going on in the halls and no hard info . . . hmph! Some silliness about searching for—I don't rightly know what." He shook his head. Gently.

"Ichtons, sir," said the Gerson with as much emotion as a human butler might say *socks*. "They're loose, you know."

"WHAT!" Too late, too late the netherbrained reminder that shrieking your head off in front of a Gerson is sure to be construed as Making a Scene. Peter Schlein's face went chalky enough to blend with the no-color of his platinum-blond hair. Had he owned a chin, it would have been trembling madly. "D'you mean to say the Ich—the Ich—the bloodthirsty fiends have *escaped*?" He cast his infantile blue eyes upward toward either Heaven or the Fleet installations on the *Hawking*'s upper decks.

"Only two of them, sir," Iorn replied. "If rumor is correct. There have been no official statements issued."

Schlein pressed a hand to his brow. It came away clammy. "And they—the Fleetledeets—they're searching this level for them?"

"All levels. Thoroughly. It will take much time." From the oven, a bell went *tling*! "Ah, good, it's done. I almost forgot." The Gerson showed his fangs in an Earth-approximate smile and headed for the kitchen as if Ichtons escaped strictest Fleet custody every day.

"Oh, don't bother, don't, I'll take care of my own dinner tonight," Schlein said hastily. His skinny form was far more agile than the Gerson's fearsome bulk and he nimbly darted past Iorn to reach the oven first. "It's the least I can do for you." He opened the hatch and reached in.

Later he couldn't recall whether his shriek of pain had been louder than Iorn's bulkhead-rattling roar. He remembered thinking that he did not recognize the cooking vessel he pulled from the oven, that ordinary pans were not supposed to retain heat that way, and that a sensible man would certainly let the offending dish drop, even if it did mean that it shattered and splattered all over the floor. There were people to clean up the mess after. When you were Schlein there was always someone else to clean up after you.

He really didn't think Iorn was justified in batting him so hard across an already weakened skull that every light in the Peter Schlein private universe flickered out.

He woke up with Iorn's face looming over him, the Gerson's breath smelling like a bizarre combination of old meat and violets. Another memory came tippytoeing into his battered brain, one of an All Decks Alert stench wafting up from the cook pan he had so unceremoniously dropped.

He tried to sit up and found it remarkably easy. His head was clear, all vestiges of the *djroo* purged from his system by Iorn's magical blend. That was to the good: he would have hated to confront his present situation drunk, because it was hardly bearable cold sober.

"Where the—?" He turned his head this way and that, but it was too dark to make out any object farther than arm's length from his eyes. He could feel that the bed he rested on wasn't your standard *Hawking*-issue bideawee. It rustled too much, was loosely covered with a coarsely woven throw, and again, the *smell*—!

"Sir Schlein honors us," said Iorn to the dark.

"Us?" the family man could only repeat, at a loss.

"Honor is done," came the response, and the sound of large bodies with the tip-off Gerson gait of shamble-rock approaching. Two more of the huge ursinoids emerged from the blackness to stand beside Iorn, though one was considerably smaller than the other.

For the first time in a short life ill spent, Peter Schlein felt like the goldy-haired girlie in the nursery tale his *madonnamech* had played for him at bedtime in the fargones. The bears in the story had wound up tearing the juvie trespasser limb from limb, in the righteous vindication of the private property laws, but that was only a cautionary *fabula*.

Wasn't it?

"Welcome to my home, sir," said Iorn in a voice so neutral Peter was hardpressed to divine whether his once-harmless servant had mayhem in mind. "Our thanks for your presence." He spoke his native tongue here.

"Think nothing of it," Schlein replied in kind, with only the slightest hesitation. In truth he was very good at what he did, linguistically, when he was functional enough to do it. If he sounded a bit dubious, it was more from wondering what Iorn had in store for him now.

We're all the way in down-below Violet, where these eetees have their home-from-homes, he thought. *Which explains this away-in-a-manger excuse for a bed. Violet Nineteen deck, maybe even Twenty, for all I know. Half the world away from home for me, and all the way to hell and gone from those top-crawling Fleetledeets for sure. Never did think I'd want to see one, but* autres temps, autres *temptations. Too easy to ask how he got me here. The sight of Peter Schlein being hauled uncon- scious around the* Hawking's *so damn common the kiddies set their chronos by it. Anyway, once we hit Indigo levels, the quartermasters don't look twice at anything they can't check in or ship out, and here in Violet where there's just eetees and cold, cold storage, who's going to interfere with a full-grown Gerson on business bent? Mutation! Whatever the fuck I did to twist Iorn's tailypo, he's got me at his mercy for it now, in spite of all this finicky show of ceremonial hospitality. If things could get any worse than this for me, I'd bleeding like to know how!*

And somewhere the God that family Schlein had written off so long ago as a poor business partner laughed and complied.

"Sir Schlein will forgive us if the lighting of our humble home is less bright than what he is used to," Iorn went on. "It is an unfortunate necessity. Among the Gerson, guest-right is divine, and first-come guests must be accommodated in all things, even at the expense of later-come guests' preferences."

"Then . . . I'm not the only one you've—" *Careful, Peter, careful! A Gerson can rip your arm off single-pawed and absentminded.* "—invited?"

"Didn't I tell you he was wise, Mate?" In the dark, Iorn sounded cheery enough. "Perceptive. I always said how deeply I was indebted to the psychs for having granted me my employment as— What did they call it?"

"Therapy," came a second growly voice, a whit less throaty than Iorn's. "So that you would refrain from future outbursts of slaughter."

Iorn chuckled, Peter cringed. "All wisdom to the psychs," the Gerson said. The words unadorned were a simple, ritual statement of high regard for the brainpokers, but Peter Schlein picked up on the linguistic music of intonation that translated Iorn's remark to mean, *I took those fools to market and back and came home wearing their asses for a hat!*

Peter's eyes made adjustments. The Gerson whom Iorn called "Mate" plopped herself down beside him so that he could see her a little better. Her muzzle was somewhat blunter than Iorn's, though her fangs looked just as sharp. The smallest Gerson pressed itself close to her back. There was more glittering around its head than Schlein could put a reason to. In the warmth of Iorn's quarters he felt cold.

And then Iorn gave him cause to feel colder. "Sir Schlein is kind, as always, Mate. You will learn this as I have, the longer he honors us with his company. Certainly one who speaks our tongue so well—taking into account the Ten Degrees of Courtesy almost as well as a homeborn—will offer us his help in entertaining our first-come guests as they deserve."

Something chittered and whined in the dark. Something large rustled in a corner of the room that Schlein still couldn't see.

"Ah!" Iorn sounded pleased. "They are hungrier. They are almost always hungry." He lumbered off and the shadows swallowed him.

"They're here," Schlein said, half to himself. "Ichtons." There was no denying it, once he got past the mental obstacle of a flatly pronounced *It's impossible!* Peter Schlein had once been dragged along up-level to view some of the *Hawking*'s prized captives, in the empty Fleetledeet hopes that the Family man might be persuaded to enlist his considerable linguistic skills in the cause of in-depth decoding of Ichton communications. No one had to tell Schlein *or* the Fleetledeets that there's more to translate in a language than merely what is said.

He would never forget the skin-crawling sight of the captive Ichtons, and he would never forget their *smell*! Which was why he didn't need his eyes to confirm what his nose had just told him. Impossible or not, they were here. Looking back, Schlein believed it was the horrific thought of spending so much time near that god-awful Ickie stink that made him refuse to cooperate with the Fleet. He had declined the honor by pricing his services in a way to make the family back home proud, and gave the despised popgunners to know that if they coerced him, he'd be only too happy to translate . . . wrong. There were other, lesser linguists aboard the *Hawking*, some even Fleet personnel. None as good as Schlein, but good enough to make do. They let him off.

Who would do the same for him now? The chirring in the darkness grew louder, accompanied by a bone-shattering clashing sound. "How in the name of downtrade he managed to bring two full-grown Ickies—oh, God, they're really fucking *here*!"

"Yes, they really fucking are. And what we are to fucking do about it I do not fucking know," said Mate. Schlein hadn't expected a response at all, not from her, less so in his own tongue, least of all using that sort of language. What he could make out of her expression was proud and self-satisfied. "Iorn has been teaching me," she explained, pleased with herself. "To learn to address all guests in their own speech is my *ghruhn*. Oh! Apologies. It is my *fucking ghruhn*."

Peter Schlein made a mental note to stand vigil over his own vocabulary around Iorn in future. If "future" was a word he could still use as more than a bad joke.

"Do you—do you suppose your *ghruhn* might include explaining why your hubby has turned your happy home into an illegal Ichton shelter?" he asked. "Or why he decided to invite me to join this little exercise in getting us all deep-spaced when the Fleetledeets finally get their search parties all the way downball to this level?" Sotto voce he added: "If there's any shred of my nerves left after finding out I'm in the same room with the fuzzybuggies."

"You have no ease, honored sir? You fear our first-come?" Her voice was richer and deeper than Iorn's. Courtesy served, she had returned to speaking Gerson. The little one at her back—little only beside herself and Iom—slipped around to insinuate itself into her lap. It was pretty big for such babyish snuggling, but Schlein reflected that he really didn't know enough about how fast Gersons matured to be a critic.

"Well, my dear hostess, to tell you the truth—"

It was then he saw it. Total dark would have been a blessing, even if it left

Schlein blind, but there was light enough to let his eyes suck more and more sight from the blackness—the pattern if not the color of Mate's tunic, the shimmer of moisture at the tip of her snout, the gentle curve of the paws cradling the smaller Gerson to her chest. Now through the pounding waves of sickness in his gut he could not keep himself from staring even while he prayed not to see.

Half the child's head was torn away, replaced by a silvery shell that glittered with a compact array of multicolored lenses and telltales. The bearish snout was gone, and the lower jaw; a simple, flexible tube ran from the convex metal muzzle cup-shaped like a surgeon's mask down into the throat incision. Idle clasps and fasteners dangled from the gap where the small Gerson should in a rational universe still have a right upper limb.

"He will not wear it," Mate said softly. Eyes fully used to the dark, she had seen where Schlein's gaze ultimately came to rest. "The medics have been very kind to us—our debt endures—but he refuses to wear the 'tronic arm that they have made him. It is too hard, he says. It reminds him too much of—"

How can he say anything? Schlein wondered, staring at the nearly faceless creature in Mate's arms. Aloud he said, "They did this to him? The Ichton?"

Mate's heavy head nodded. "Iorn fought with the rest of our city; no good. We were able to escape to the caverns, awaiting help, but it was so deep, so dark in there, so close and crowded—" Her paw tenderly stroked the metal face cup as if it were responsive flesh. "Nn'ror was always impetuous, like his father; a leader. He would not mind his elders. He stirred up the others of his year, brought them out of the caverns by a secret way—spying on the enemy, he said, to learn their weakness so that someday he and his followers could attack them, defeat them, drive them away."

"They caught him?" It really was a stupid question.

"All of them, his year-friends, Nn'ror, all. It was yet in the time before they made our world ash. They reaved the surface, then. As nearly as we could have any news, we heard they meant to use all they could find for the maintenance of their hatchlings." Her gaze fixed itself on the child's mangled face. "Ours was always a good world for raising children."

Hesitantly, as if acting on its own, Schlein's hand stretched out to touch the small Gerson's ravaged face. Mate saw, and nodded ever so slightly, allowing it. The child flinched away when Schlein's fingers came within brushing distance of its shell—sensors in place and functioning, top-of-the-line synthetic nerve replacement, nothing too good for these martyrs to the Ichton scourge. Every sentient on the *Hawking* knew what the Gersons had suffered; everyone was more than willing to make excuses and allowances for anything a Gerson survivor might do.

Which explained, perhaps, why Iorn had managed to spirit off the captive Ichtons unhindered, undetected. Folks tended to look the other way when a Gerson passed, going about his business. *If we give them what they need or want, maybe they'll go away,* Schlein thought. *And if they go away, we won't have to look at them, and remember what they went through, and live with the dead scary thought that such things can happen in this galaxy and maybe not so big a maybe—maybe next time we'll be the ones it happens to.*

"Almost all the others were fully . . . taken by the hatcheries when Iorn and the others were able to learn where they were and stage a raid. It was easier than they hoped. They did not yet know that word had come to the invaders to move out, that the resistance elsewhere had made our home not worth the effort to subdue, that it would be burnt in retribution and example. There were so many other worlds to be had, so easily. Nn'ror and perhaps two others of his year-friends still lived, left behind with those few eggs that had not hatched. Those two—" Mate shuddered. "Those two Iorn himself had to kill."

Speechless, Schlein tried to force an unwilling mind to form a picture of towering, shaggy, benevolent-looking Iorn killing children of his own kind. What could bring any sane, feeling being to that point? Part of him didn't want to know, part would go mad if he stayed ignorant.

"Why—why did he kill—?"

"For kindness. They could not live long with what parts of them remained uneaten," said Mate, and Peter Schlein vomited noisily into the bedding.

Peter Schlein never dreamed he would turn out to be such an apt short-order cook.

"At least the recipe's simple," he said, taking the dish from the oven. "You're a good teacher, Iorn."

"It is my *ghruhn* to instruct you as you desired, sir Schlein," the Gerson rumbled. This time he sounded as if he had gotten some actual pleasure out of fulfilling *ghruhn*. "I ask your pardon for my unfortunate temper before, when you dropped the dish. It goes against our way to keep a guest hungry."

"To say nothing of wasting good food," Schlein replied. The smell wafting up from the cook pan was still rank enough to make him turn his head away. "Whew! How do you stand the stink of this?"

"With the philosophy, sir Schlein, that at least they do not smell quite so bad cooked as raw."

"So you feed Ickie A to Ickie B, in installments, and contrariwise?" Schlein set the steaming dish on the counter, picked up a spatula, and poked the bubbling contents. He could have sworn that something poked back. "And, uh, how long do you think it'll be before the two of them are all . . . done?"

"Not soon enough." Iorn's expression was stern. "Word comes that Fleet has redoubled search efforts. There may not be time enough left until they are discovered. Their deaths are not my cause."

"Aren't they, then? Because at the rate you're going—I mean, they do have mighty healthy appetites, these fuzzybuggies. Do they know who—what they're eating?"

"From the start. They are untroubled by it." It was no hard guess to make that Iorn wanted the Ichton to be *very* troubled before they died. "I do not understand their samespeech, as you do, but I would give my heart's self to know why this is so, why they can live unsorrowed by what is an abomination among my kind, yours, nearly all sentients I have known."

"Look, Iorn, I don't pretend to speak fluent Ickie, but I'm willing to hazard a could-be for you," Schlein volunteered.

"I would be obliged."

"As you were for kitchen privileges; I know." Schlein kept a lid on his esophagus, trying very hard *not* to think of what it was Iorn had been cooking in the same oven as the family man's food. "You see, though it's not a custom we Terrans are any too proud of, we have been known, in times past, to nibble the odd fellow man. Strictly ceremonial reasons. In the far-gone oldens, when you defeated an especially valiant enemy, you did him the honor of eating his heart, thereby gaining his valor for your own. Or if he'd been cunning, you munched his brain. D'you get the idea?"

"I do." Iorn nodded sagely. "And if he was admired for being the father of many young, then you—"

"Oh, no, no, no, no need to get carried away, is there? Ahahahaha." It almost sounded like laughter. "However, we don't do that anymore."

"No?" The ursinoid's brow furrowed. "We do not abandon our own customs so lightly. Meaning no offense, sir Schlein."

"Don't suppose it was *custom* that made you coldcock me so's you could drag me downball just to meet your—ah—first-come guests?"

"I admit it was the inspiration of the moment. I was rather put out by the loss of my so carefully prepared dish, through your mishap. It did mean I would have to procure more of the raw material, thus lessening the time I would have to entertain my honored Ichton guests according to their merits."

"Just so," said Schlein, turning greener by degrees as Iorn spoke of "raw" material, knowing what he did of Iorn's "entertainment" of the Ichtons. "Spur-of-the-moment forsooth. I mean, it was hardly the sort of invitation one reads about in all the best etiquette books."

Iorn showed teeth. "Would you have come had I invited you any other way?"

"Not this century."

"And it *is* our custom to take mortal offense when our offers of hospitality are declined. So you see . . ."

Indeed he did, especially the way in which Iorn pronounced "mortal" so that it almost rhymed with "fatal."

"Well, all that aside, I'm glad you *asked* me to drop in." Schlein regarded the still-seething surface of the Ichton casserole grimly. "I only wish you'd done it earlier on. I'd've had a chunk of Ichton *au poivre* myself, just to get the ball rolling."

"You would devour them, sir Schlein?" Iorn looked puzzled. "But I believe you said that Terrans no longer—"

"We don't eat people. These are Ickies. And since you did say your goal wasn't to destroy their bodies so much as their minds—though there's a lot to be said for shredding the fuzzybuggies straightaway, Fleetledeet strategy be damned—maybe the sight of a mere human chowing down on their formerly private property might shake 'em up like they deserve to be shook."

The Gerson parsed all this slowly, then brightened. "An excellent idea!" he roared, and wasted no time in catching Peter Schlein upside the head with another most effective backhanded blow that removed all possibility of objection.

"Look," Peter Schlein said, trying to keep the shrill note of desperation out of his voice. "I was hungry."

Captain Conway stared at the skinny little family man before him and tried to link the pathetic picture he saw to the concept of "monster." No use. Though the evidence garnered by the search party was irrefutable—they'd burst in and caught him in flagrante, trying to floss a piece of carapace out from between his front teeth, for pity's sake!—some concepts still refused to merge in the human mind.

Fleet or not, Captain Conway was human, even if the *Hawking* was his first "real" assignment. He took a deep breath and got a stronger mental toehold on reality before saying, "Schlein, in the Fleet we don't eat our prisoners."

"Well, that's all right, then," Schlein replied, all sweet reason. "I'm not Fleet."

"But you are here on Fleet sufferance."

"So if I fuck up what happens? You send me home?"

Captain Conway passed a hand over his brow. This was just the way the interview had been going ever since the leader of Team Crater had returned to announce that the prisoners were found and in what condition they had been found and then threw up all over Conway's desk.

"Schlein, what do you think would happen if I let it slip out to our allied eetees that you'd been—reducing the chances of us learning more about how Ickie minds work?"

"I'd get a medal? A parade? All due respect, Captain, but Iorn's hunger for privacy to the contrary, I'm wagering word's already out about how your precious fuzzybuggies used their own captives. Children, sir! Fed piecemeal to their young. If we preserve them alive, we might someday learn all the wonderful, apparently rational-to-them reasons why they can take other beings' babies and use 'em as meat for their own. Apart from the great and marvelous contribution to sweet, holy Science, who gives a shit?"

Captain Conway pulled back involuntarily. Passion had transformed the wispy family man into something with backbone, something almost worthy of Fleet respect. What Schlein said about the Ickies was true, if you believed the Gerson survivors' reports. Iorn was not the only one to tell that tale, though he had been hardest hit by it. Records were clear the futile rage within the huge ursinoid had triggered more than a few violent episodes aboard the *Hawking*— barroom brawls that ended just this side of needing a body count—until the psychs suggested placing Iorn in a position of service where Gerson *ghruhn* might siphon off the creature's wild anguish into productive channels.

Productive! There was a laugh. Unless you called adding a few truly arcane chapters to *Child's Guide to Intergalactic Cookery* productive.

"Don't start looking for a place to hang that medal quite yet, Schlein," Conway said. "Even if every eetee aboard agrees with what you did in practice, they're compelled to object to it on principle. If we show ourselves to be no better than the Ichtons, can their victims ever trust us?"

"Ah, the moral edge." Schlein sounded weary. "Once upon a time, I liked to believe it'd cut warm butter, but I learned better. I did what I did. Hand me over to the eetees and let's be done with it."

"But *why* did you do it, Schlein? And tell me 'I was hungry' one more time and you're going to have an unfortunate 'accident' on your way to confinement."

Conway's fist was truly impressive, particularly when held so close to Schlein's gently bred nose. Schlein swallowed the first upsurge of instinctive panic, then said, "Call it . . . a favor to a friend."

"No good." The list lowered. "Your friend Iorn's in custody, too; him and his family."

"What?" Schlein sat up straighter. "Mate? Nn'ror? They've done nothing."

"The psychs thought it best to separate them. Unhealthy—family atmosphere cited."

"Separate . . . So Iorn's in solitary—"

"All three of them are. The psychs reported—"

"One psych can kill more poor suffering bastards with his triple-damned *reports* than all you Fleetledeets and your bumblasters combined. Mate and Nn'ror did nothing, I tell you! Look, not even Iorn's guilty here. It was—it was all *my* idea! I can prove it, too. Iorn was my servant, his *ghruhn* wouldn't allow him to disobey anything I asked of him. He couldn't have done any of it without me, my kitchen, my fucking start-to-finish *complicity*, for the love of Chomsky!"

Schlein rose from his seat, his face contorted. "You march right out of here and tell your buddies to let Iorn's family go, or at least lock 'em up together. That kid of theirs needs his kin. He's teetering on the edge, and he'll take his parents with him if he goes over. Or haven't enough of the Gersons died to suit you? Try breaking *that* news to your supermoral do-the-civvie-thing eetees! See how happy they are with you Fleetledeets then!"

Conway had no trouble getting Schlein to sit down again. One firm shove to the breastbone did the trick, even if the little man took a wild swing at the Fleet captain before subsiding. Gasping for breath, Schlein managed to add a last verbal jab to his tirade: "Especially when they find out that all your precious Fleet intelligence you got from studying those captive Ickies wouldn't fill a thimble next to all I learned about 'em over one friendly little . . . *lunch*!"

It was Conway's turn to sit down. "Say what?"

Schlein grinned. "You'd be amazed to learn all the new Ickie words—nay, cultural-linguistic concepts, may they flourish—that I was able to pick up while chewing the fat with our *honored guests*." He used the Gerson term there and savored Conway's bewilderment until he offered the translation. "It looks like we—*I* guessed right. One Ickie getting the nibblies on another is socially acceptable. They're even got a whole catalog of courtesy terms to describe the gallant donor, beginning with the noble fuzzybug who sacrifices his substance for a battle comrade and rising in honor until you reach the noblest Ichton of 'em all, one willing to lay down his spare parts for the nourishment of the egglayers and the hatchlings. Not that he wants to; it's the least pretty of deaths. Those newborns are terrifying and *mean*."

"You actually learned those terms?"

"And many more." Schlein made a self-effacing bow, no easy task in a chair. "I was called the inverse of every one of them as soon as I told my dinner companions just what it was I was eating with such relish. There is something terribly, terribly irking to an Ickie when he realizes his sacred flesh is being devoured by a lesser being, one who cares Khalia-squat about the all-precious hatchery. Food means a lot to the fuzzybuggies. The only appetite they haven't been able to govern is appetite per se. Ol' metabolism's got 'em , and got 'em bad. Give 'em enough time and they come up with a slew of airtight rationalizations for why it's okay to eat Grandma. My sister was like that about chocolate. I perceive a *waste not, want not* subtext. Perhaps I'll do a monograph on it someday."

"You'll do it now and forward it to us immediately, if you know what's good for you. The more we know about the enemy—"

"Trade you," said Schlein.

"Trade?" Conway's fingers curled around the armrests of his chair.

" 'Course. Until someone tells me different, I'm Schlein. Trading's our life. Family ghosts would show up en masse to beat the ectoplasmic shit out of me if I didn't try to get something out of you in swap for what I know."

"There isn't much trading you can do in deep space without a suit," Conway said meaningfully.

"There isn't much Ickie interpretation you Fleetledeets can get out of my corpse," Schlein countered. "Come on, O captain mine, you know you want me on your side. You did before, if you'll check your own records, and you want me even more now, with what I've got to share."

"Our own methods will uncover everything you've learned."

"So they will, given time. How much of it can we waste? Be a sport, friend. All I'm asking is the release and reunion of Iorn and his family—no sense you holding on to innocent parties, anyhow—and in exchange I'll give you my full cooperation, professional services, and first dibs on the soon-to-be patented Schlein Method of Ickie Interrogation guaranteed to yield results undreamed of, swiftly and accurately."

Captain Conway steepled his fingers in thought. All that Schlein said was true. He was the best linguist the *Hawking* had to offer, and if his results did derive from less-than-conventional methods, at least they were *results*. Fleet could use results.

"Point One: We will release the Gerson family," Conway said at last. Schlein beamed. "In exchange for which consideration, you will serve Fleet interests—"

"Of course. I said I would."

"—*by becoming Fleet*. Point Two: Your enlistment buys their freedom. Got it, Cadet Schlein?"

Peter Schlein's face fell. "This is going to kill Father." Then he perked up. "This is going to *kill* Father!"

"Point Three: You will have to develop an equally successful alternative to your so-called Schlein Method at once. We will not eat Ickies. It isn't—it just isn't *Fleet*."

Schlein smiled. "We won't have to."

The captive Ichton looked up at the scrawny Fleet cadet who came boldly into its cell, whistling. It was accompanied by a Gerson carrying a tray. The Ichton's interest flared unexpectedly when the uniformed Meat addressed him in an almost-fluent version of the losser Dialect, saying, "Breakfast!" The Gerson set down the tray and shoved it through the small, temporarily disrupted zone in the Ichton's confining forcewall.

"I know it's not much," said the Meat, brushing aside a lock of its pale blond headfur. "But we Fleeties do insist that all our guests belong to the Clean Plate Club. Oh, doesn't translate, does it? Simple: no more for you until *that's* all gone. Or until you choose to have a little chat with me about, oh, all sorts of things! Nearly anything you've got to tell me about you and yours will be fascinating, I know. And you'll like the food much better. You *are* hungry, aren't you? Born hungry, I hear. Well, don't waste time picking at your food. Before too long, it may be picking at you."

The prisoner stated at his plate; at the holy, the horrific shape of the Ichton egg that was just beginning to hatch.

Iorn tugged at Peter Schlein's arm. "Let us leave them alone, sir Schlein," he suggested. "Family reunions should be private affairs."

"For a while," Cadet Schlein agreed. "Though I'll bet not for long. Exit," he directed, "pursued by a bear."

NET PROFIT

The distant sound of cannon has always been hazardous to morality. As it began to look doubtful whether the Ichtons could be stopped before reaching Emry, or even afterward, many of the less reputable merchants and Indies turned to bottom-line philosophy first attributed to Earth's long discredited Harvard School of Business. If the *Hawking* was soon to be destroyed, then any action needed to ensure their own personal gain was justified. After all, at their current rate of expansion the Ichtons would take another two hundred years to reach the Alliance itself. Best they return a success or spend their remaining years in opulence, even if later generations had to fight a bit harder.

Too often this attitude meant profiteering at the expense of the war effort. As the running battle continued, a new concern came to dominate those of Omera and internal security. How to prevent their own people from thwarting the war effort in their rush for gain? Or more often simply how to keep the level of chaos acceptable on the civilian decks?

Even the news of the destruction of an Ichton mother ship in a six-destroyer ambush personally led by the son of Fleet Admiral of the Red, Auro Lebario, failed to slow the frenzied rush for a quick gain. New sources of profit were sought. Some of these were found among the growing population of allied races occupying the lowest levels of the *Hawking*. Since the *Hawking* carried enough weaponry to dominate any one of their worlds, most of these allies found it understandably difficult to fully trust the selflessness of the Alliance battlestation, even while recognizing the necessity of cooperating with it.

JOINT VENTURES
by Don-John Dugas

It was already hot when I stepped into the lift for Violet Eight. Not too bad. Like a slow oven. But when the door opened onto the corridor, it got really hot: thirty-two centigrade if it was ten. The air was misty, the humidity was so high that the ceilings dripped. Every time I came here it was like this: overpowering, like boiling alcohol, boiler rooms, and reptile cages. The violet walls looked nearly black after the brightness of the green decks where I spent most of my shifts working for Omera. I wondered how they justified the damage the unplanned humidity did to the station's life-support system. Maybe they figured the two hundred ships the aliens living here seconded to Fleet command balanced out the trouble.

I turned down another corridor. The violet walls reflecting off the grilled metal decking in the bad light made everything look dirty. I passed an exhaust blowing steam. It crawled lazily down the passageway. I followed it until I came to her door.

"You see your boyfriend today?" I said after I'd kissed her. As usual her cooling system was doing about half the job and I peeled off my shirt as I entered.

Viv, wearing only a clinging T-shirt, walked farther into the apartment. The invitation wasn't very subtle. But then I wasn't there for subtle. The Institute had gotten her a great place—two rooms all to herself. Not bad for a university sentiologist on a grant. Shame it was down here among the gators.

"You bet."

"Handsome as ever?" I asked.

"Beautiful," she said, clearing aside a scribe unit and some more junk so I could sit down. "He was in the caf for almost three hours today. Just sat there again, tapping his fingers."

Viv was an antiquarian who had turned out to have a talent for dealing with other races. She had silky blond hair, a most generous figure, just where it should be, and the biggest and deepest brown eyes I had ever gazed into. Said I was an antique of sorts, but never explained. With her legs, I never questioned what she saw in a low-paid, civilian security investigator. Every day Viv worked near the caf, talking with the gators, getting to know the way they thought. The Institute was paying her good money for the culture profile and she was earning it. I'd seen the pile of disks cluttering up her apartment. The gators were the most important of all the races that were supporting the Fleet against the Ichtons. Physically very different, but surprisingly like humans in their attitudes.

Last week Viv told me she had spotted him. She'd described her mystery man as between twenty and thirty, with the body of an unarmed-combat instructor and white-blond hair. His only flaw seemed to be that he wore glasses, but Viv said it made him look sensitive and intellectual. And he just sat there for hours, motionless, staring at some spot on the bulkhead. She'd guessed that he was another scientist working with any of the dozen alien races that had settled into the lower levels of the *Hawking* and asked me to look out for him, let me know more about what he did and where he went. I went to the caf, a dingy place at the upper end of the color that dealt with several races, but he had gone. Then we had that mess involving the Ichton attempt to bribe their way aboard the *Hawking* on an Indie so they could breed larvae and I'd had no time.

The next day, in bed, she'd informed me that at precisely the same time, he was there again. And the next.

"The guy's in a rut," I said. I had been on Violet Eight for less than a minute and was already sweating freely. She opened up the small galley freezer, pulled out an icy one, slid it through her auburn bob and down her neck for the cool, and threw it to me.

"I'm telling you, he isn't normal," she said. "There's something funny about the way he's been acting."

"I'm sure it's nothing," I said, opening it. "Probably got the hots for one of the caf workers. Or maybe he likes the smell of gators."

"Squams!" she said angrily.

"Sorry." The Squams were an allied race. They looked like a large, multicolored walrus that had been shoved into an alligator coat and weren't very comfortable with the result. They walked on all fours, thick hands at the bottom of each foot. For fine work they used a beard comprised of a dozen long, silky fingers just under a wide, smooth-toothed mouth. On the upper decks most people had never seen a real Earth gator, so the nickname had stuck.

Viv looked at me like I'd just given my kid sister a haircut with a steak knife, then flopped down on the bed beside me. "Today I watched him while I pretended to type. He sat there for nearly four hours without moving anything but his fingertips."

"Like this?"

She knocked my hand away. "I'm serious!"

"All right," I said. "Forget the caf workers. I think he's got the hots for you."

"Yeah. Right," she said.

"Why not? You said you always went for lean men."

She traced the old scar that ran across my left pectoral with her fingertips. "Almost always."

We fooled around for a while after that. Afterward, she said, "That woman was there again today, too. I've seen her at the Handi-Mart."

"Pretty?" I arched an eyebrow.

"Very. Distinguished-looking."

"Hmm. Sounds like my type." I watched her reaction and took another pull of beer from the bottle, now warm.

She shot me an amused look.

"Well, that's it," I said. "Mr. Handsome sits across from Ms. Beautiful."

"Or vice versa," she said. "Who cares? Someone's leering at somebody."

"That's all you ever think about." But she smiled.

"I'm a cop in a small town with some big-town tastes," I said, trying to forget the big-city trouble that had forced me to volunteer for the *Hawking*. "Besides, since I haven't seen your mystery man yet, I don't have anything but your say-so to go on."

"Can I help it if he shows up while you're working?"

"Go on, laugh if you want," she said. "Just the same, there's something about him. He scares me now." She looked at me and I believed her. "He doesn't even move his eyes behind those glasses."

"You sit close enough to see whether his eyes move?"

Viv knew I'd caught her out. "All right. I went over to have a closer look. I wanted to see if you were right about . . . perspectives. I thought the woman was alone at first, but one of the Squams I talked with told me she was there to watch two hatchlings!"

It was kind of unusual for a human to nanny aliens, but the *Hawking* was a human station. The richer aliens had figured out that a human could do a better job of keeping their offspring out of trouble on it. Most also figured an armed battlestation was a lot safer place to raise them than their own worlds with the Ichtons busily invading one about every two months.

"She stays all afternoon?"

"No," Viv said. "She arrives around 1200, an hour or so before he shows up. They leave almost at the same time, though—around 1730. She spends all her time talking to the Squamlings—teaches them English, I suppose—while she knits."

"Knits?"

"Scarves, I think."

I let that pass. "The parents of those kids must be pretty rich if they can afford a nanny," I said. "Have any of your gat . . . Squam friends told you who they are?"

"I haven't asked."

She was quiet for a minute. "I wonder if he's there to spy on someone."

"Why do you say that?"

"He's never in the caf at any other time. I asked one of the waitresses to keep an eye out for him. He always paces back and forth just outside the door before he goes in, like he's waiting for a signal."

"That's new."

"No. Jannie—that's the waitress—says he's done that since he first started coming in."

"What's the beautiful nanny doing while he's walking around?"

"I don't know. She lives near the caf on Violet Seven. When I've seen her at the Handi-Mart she's always buying a lot of stuff and usually she has the Squam kids with her."

I looked at her. "Maybe I should bring down an application form."

"For what?"

"Security. You could replace Kenvich—or Omera."

"Ha-ha. You'll see."

Around 2000 I made dinner. Afterward, we decided to leave the dishes and walk over to the caf for a drink. Viv rooted around in the junk for her sweatpants. She'd gotten about as much as she was going to get out of these gators and had already found a new place on another deck. Half her things were already packed. The other half were strewn all over the floor.

As for me, I had no choice but to put my shirt back on despite the heat. Walking around with your blaster showing is considered unprofessional in undercover cop circles.

The walk to the caf was quiet. Most of the residents in Violet kept to their own special environments. After eight hours walking through the rec areas, keeping the Indies from getting too rough, it was nice to be able to relax with your girlfriend. Even if you had to do it in a sauna.

We walked toward the lifts, then turned right. We came into a large open area, a kind of city square the amphibious aliens had put together themselves. Some of the condos connected up to Violet Seven, giving the place a split-level effect.

The most expensive places faced onto the long, shallow tanks in the center of the square. Squams, old and young, lay on their backs in the pools. They were happiest when they had plenty of humidity to keep everything going smoothly. The steam vents they had rigged up from the heat-dissipation system were okay, but there was nothing a Squam liked better than a nice soak in that green, reclaimed water.

Viv made some noises at a few of the Squams sitting on the curbing around the pools. I just smiled. We were always getting lectures by the Fleet sentiologists on how to deal effectively with all the Alliance races represented on the *Hawking*. The warm-fuzzies (as we usually referred to all the vaguely mammalian races) you could pretty much treat like everyone else. It was the hard-skinned, cold-blooded ones that I couldn't get used to. They were just so completely *different*.

As we made for the caf, a Squam male (Viv had taught me how to tell them apart) stopped her. They hissed at each other while I looked around. He was impressive. They all were. He measured a good two and a half meters from claws to crest. His horny skin was a dull gray-brown and there wasn't an ounce of fat on him. He looked like a giant swimming machine—all muscle and shoulder—wrapped in a boxy alligator bag.

But the thing that stayed with you was the eyes. Nothing lived in those faces except for them. Black. Deep-set. Shining. Unknowable. Never moving, never dilating. Once in a while, the greeny-white membranes would sort of roll up in something like a blink, but that was all you ever saw.

I took a last drag and threw the soggy cigarette into a can and looked into the crowded caf.

"Hey," I said.

Viv hissed something else to the Squam and turned around. "What?"

"Is that him?"

Her gaze followed mine through the big plastic-walled front with the frosted edges and the glitzy chromium fittings. Beyond the chairs and a couple dozen heads, I had seen a white-blond human.

"That's him!" she said.

It felt like I was meeting an in-law for the first time.

"What's he doing here so late?" I asked.

"I don't know!" She said it like it was indecent for him to be there.

"Let's go." She took my arm and we went into the caf.

It was dark inside and there was a steady flow of clientele. There were a couple of admin types getting stupid on the funny Squam beer. Some girls from the rec decks were helping them. The staff were mostly human, with one or two Khalians thrown in. Except for Romeo, the rest were pure gator.

There was an empty table next to his and we took it. While I sat with my back to him, Viv scoped him out from over my shoulder.

"Hey, Viv," a woman in a tight synthetic T-shirt asked. "The usual?"

"Hi, Jannie," Viv said. "Yeah."

"Soda water it is." The waitress looked at me.

"Whiskey," I said. It wasn't the real stuff, but it worked.

"Single malt or blended?"

"In a glass'll be fine."

She didn't smile.

"He been here long?" Viv whispered, nodding at the man.

"Since you left," Jannie said before walking away.

"Well?" I said quietly. "You going to ask him to the prom?"

"I don't know," she said. "He looks like he's asleep."

His eyes looked white in the reflection of the halogen light strips in his glasses.

"You said he doesn't move much."

She looked at him. "His fingers aren't even moving."

Jan reappeared with the drinks a few minutes later and Viv paid. We talked for a while about the profile she was working up and what she was planning to do after she got back from the Core.

"You want to teach?" I asked her. That's what most sentiologists I'd met wanted to do.

"I doubt it. I've got other interests."

"Yeah?"

She leaned forward. "You don't think I took this job just for the fun of talking with other races, do you?"

"I was under the impression that this was the kind of fieldwork some sentiologists wait a lifetime for," I said.

"I'm more interested in, shall we say, planetary resources."

I smiled. "You want to be an Indie instead of a sentiologist."

She laughed. "Indie? They're poor. I want it big time—merchant or nothing! How many people do you think have the cultural and linguistic background to trade with the Squams? Ten? Twenty? Three of us."

"Anybody can talk to them with a translator," I said. I had never seen her so animated.

"Anybody with a tie-in to a Fleet battlestation mainframe, you mean. Otherwise not enough to really do a deal."

I saw her point. "So you're going to get a job with the merchants cutting deals with the Squams." The Squams were one of the few expansive races we had found in the galactic center, they occupied almost seven worlds and were looking for more when the Ichtons arrived.

"That's it."

"What about the Institute?"

"They'll get their culture profile."

"And so will some merchant."

"Why not?" she asked. "They've already paid for it."

Double pay. No wonder she could afford a bigger place.

"He still there?" I asked a few minutes later.

She looked over my shoulder. "You . . ." Her face went pale and she stood up. Her eyes were fixed on the man behind me.

"What is it?" I said, turning as I followed her eyes. Under his chair a small pool of blackening blood congealed with some kind of transparent fluid. He was very dead. Viv screamed.

Almost an hour later the forensics team had finished with the scene. After that, it took only a minute for the med team to bag him up and haul the body out of the caf. I was just finishing with Jannie when Kenvich walked in. His Fleet uniform was perfect, right down to the freshly polished Military Intelligence pips on the collar.

"What's the situation here, Detective?" he said.

"What the hell are you doing here?" I asked.

He folded his arms together. "You know the drill, Bailan. Security is supposed to be informed on all felony calls. Informed immediately."

It had been like that ever since they'd declared martial law on all levels after Gerson and it stank like moisture-reclamation tanks under a whorehouse.

"Handsome over there got in the way of a needler," I said, pointing to the black body bag the medicos were carrying away.

"Boys said you were first on the scene. Notice anything?"

"I was less than a meter from him when the lady there"—I hooked my thumb at Viv—"spotted the blood. Prelim assessment puts the time of death around 1700, but we'll know for sure soon."

Kenvich looked hard at Viv, then back to me.

"How long were you here?"

"About a half an hour before she spotted the blood."

"You sat next to a stiff for half an hour and you didn't notice a damn thing?"

Kenvich was a weenie. I'd known officers like him in the Marines and I hadn't been impressed.

"Right, Kenvich."

"*Captain* Kenvich."

"Asshole," I said.

"What was that?"

"I said 'Yes, sir,' *mon capitan.*"

He glared at me and looked at the plastic caf front. The frosted edging as well as the clear windows were unmarked. "Shot from outside while the door was open?"

"That'd be my guess," I said, "which means whoever offed him is one hell of a shot or had really good sights and a stable platform. Could've been someone passing by or from the condos across the square."

Kenvich grunted. "About the victim," he said. "Confine your investigation to the external elements of the case as much as possible."

"What?"

"You heard me."

"Trying to steal a little thunder, Kenvich?"

He moved in close. "Listen, mister. You do what I say, when I say it. In case you'd forgotten, you're under martial law. It's only out of courtesy to Chief Omera that we're letting you civilians handle this at all. And as for your wiseass remarks, this comes straight from Internal Security HQ: leave the victim out of it as much as you can."

"Great. How about the murderer?"

He gave me one last look and went over to talk with a couple of the uniforms who were questioning people.

I walked over to Viv. "When you're ready, I'll take your deposition."

"Me?"

"Absolutely. You're the only person who can give us something useful to go on."

"What about his ID? His room?"

I moved her into the corner. "He didn't have any ID on him. Nothing in his pockets except for a card key to a storage container, location unknown, and a *lot* of credits. No distinguishing features. So far we have nothing on the guy."

Viv looked at me.

"Don't say it," I said. "Either Fleet Intelligence is already in on this or they will be in about two hours. And I mean in. Security's already dicking around. It's only a matter of time before the big boys want to play, too. Let's hope we can get this thing rolling before they put a lid on it. You ready?"

"Sure."

I got a recorder from one of the uniforms and came back. "All right. Did you notice this man today?"

She smiled. "Yes. When I arrived here this afternoon he was in his usual place."

"And the blond nanny?"

"Yes. She was over there, as usual."

"And in the last eleven days you never once saw them speaking. Is that correct?"

"Yes. From where they sat, they couldn't have without shouting. They were about eight meters apart."

"And they'd sit there, motionless, all afternoon?"

"Except for her knitting and talking to the young Squams."

"Always knitting? For nearly two weeks?"

"Yes."

"You didn't notice what type of knitting it was, did you?"

"No."

"When did this woman leave this afternoon?"

"Around 1700."

"1700. Just about the time the forensics boys think he bought it. Did the woman leave before or after 1700?"

"I don't know. I left around 1615 and she was still there. Why? Do you think she . . ."

"I don't know. We won't know anything beyond what you've told me until the lab finishes. You don't know where she lives, do you?"

"Yes. Liz at the Handi-Mart said she lives on Violet Seven, just above the caf."

"And how about the Squams she works for?"

"Across the square in that condo."

"That's all you've learned?" I said.

"Is it enough?"

I laughed. "If you hadn't taken an interest in your boyfriend, I'd be in a real jam now. You've given me something to go on."

"The blonde?"

"The blonde. That reminds me . . ."

I walked over to a com and called HQ. "This is Bailan. Cal, pull the file on Violet 7.135.280."

"You got it, Detective," the kid said on the other end. As com operators went he was a good one, no silly questions and backed up about ten of us and occasionally came to our rescue with a squad of uniforms if things got rough. I heard the sound of a keyboard.

"Rugh Hass, Squam Indie. Nonresident landlord."

That meant he paid the bills but didn't live there. "Any other listings for Hass?"

More keys being punched. "Yeah. Violet 8.135.310. Big place on Violet Eight."

I figured that put him in the condoplex across the square. "Put a plainclothes on the first address. If a blonde comes out, stay on her and call me right away."

"You got it."

I hung up. "I've got to get going," I said to Viv. "Why don't you turn in?"

"No way. This is too interesting. Where are you going?"

"I've got to go up to Med Green. The body boys should be finished pretty soon and I want to get the report in person."

"Why?"

"Transmissions and files can be intercepted. I know we're under martial law, but I'll be damned if I'm going to let Internal Security or Military Intelligence screw this up."

"Okay. Will you be back down later?"

"I don't know. I'll try."

"If you are, I could use some consolation."

Twenty minutes later I was warming my heels outside Dr. Obor's lab on Green Five. She saw me through the window and came out in her operation greens. Behind her I could see him on the slab. His white hair made the victim look like a statue waiting to be posed and placed. Not human anymore, no one that loved or hurt.

"Hey, Bailan."

"Doc."

"Do I get to wash up first or are you going to grill me right here?"

"We'll compromise," I said. "How about you tell me in the scrub room?"

We walked in. She took off her gloves and started to clean up. "Death was almost instantaneous. The victim was shot from between twenty meters and eighty meters away. The projectile was a six-centimeter ceramic dart with a triangular cross-section. Standard round."

"Where was he hit?"

"In the skull," she said. "One point seven centimeters above and behind the right ear—that's why there was so little external bleeding."

"Any idea how fast the dart was moving?" I asked.

"I'd say that based on the penetration about 270m/second."

"Pretty low velocity," I said. Whoever did it could have used a silencer. "Okay. What about the victim?"

"Human. Mainstream. White male. Caucasian. Twenty-eight years old. Evidence of extensive physical training, probably tank swimming and unarmed combat. And get this. Implants."

"Where?"

"In the fingertips. Very simple mobile keyboard linkup with squirt-transmission capability."

"I better check how many of those we have aboard."

"Eighteen," she said, smiling as she pulled off her booties. She was a pro. "None of them match up. This guy isn't on any *Hawking* files."

Or maybe he wasn't on the kind of files normal people had access to. "Anything else?"

"Excellent health. Remarkable physique . . ."

"Yeah, I heard that from Viv."

She raised an eyebrow but didn't say anything. "Scar on left shoulder indicates reconstructive surgery," she continued, "probably from a blaster deflection or laser wound, about three years ago."

"How about the clothes?"

"No labels. Very used and shabby, except for the underwear and socks."

"How so?"

"They're practically new. The pants are pure silk."

I didn't know what to make of that so I kept my mouth shut.

"The shirt and pants were permeated with very fine hybrid flour—not pure, but mixed with traces of rice. His glasses are hard-tempered acrylic with a slight amber tint."

"Shooting glasses?" I asked.

"Shooting glasses," she confirmed.

"Fingerprint matching came up with a big zero," she said. "Like I said, no one on the database has heard of this guy."

She looked at me. I didn't say anything.

"That's it," she said finally.

"All right, Doc," I said, going for the doors. "You've been a lot of help. Really."

She smiled. "Tell me about it sometime."

Back on the lift, I tried to imagine him. Not as the corpse on the table, but as a living man, twenty-eight years old. Handsome, fit, putting on the cheap old clothes over the expensive underwear before heading off to a little caf on Violet Eight.

Where did he go? What did he do until 1300? Did he always dress like a bum or did he change somewhere? How was it possible for him to sit there for hours every afternoon, staring at a point in space, while quietly typing? And where was the computer he had been typing into?

How long had it been going on?

Where did he go at night? Did he have a private life? Who did he see? Why the flour and traces of rice in his clothes?

All these questions kicked around inside my head as the lift dropped me back to Violet Eight. I retraced my steps back to the square and walked into the condo. A human guard—more of a doorman really—stood inside the lobby.

He wasn't terribly impressed by my badge. He kept his knees from knocking together long enough to say, "What the hell do you want?"

"Which of your tenants employs a nanny?" I asked him. "Beautiful. Blond."

"Agnes Wunderlei?"

"Could be. Every afternoon she takes two Squam kids across the square to the caf."

"That's Agnes," he said. "She works for Mr. and Mrs. Hass, resident aliens. Squams."

"Which is theirs?"

He pointed down the hall. "Second door on the left, pal."

"What do they do?"

"Mr. Hass is listed as being in speculation and arbitrage. The missus is a tech aboard one of those fancy destroyers the Squams brought into the Fleet."

"Either of them here now?"

"Mr. Hass just went out, but she's still here I think."

"And Agnes?"

"She doesn't live here."

"Thanks," I said, making for the hall. I clipped on my translator and rang the bell. I could hear it ringing inside, but nobody answered. I rang again. At last the door opened.

She was well over two meters tall and she knew it. Her scales were smooth, tapering to frosty edges of near-transparent tissue. The skin on her neck lightened evenly into a pale powder-green and her eyes were true jet, not the charcoal color that a lot of the females had. From what Viv had told me about their aesthetic, she would be considered a real knockout. She was wearing a silk floral-print dressing gown.

"Yes?" she said. The translator turned her hiss to a flat monotone.

"My name is Bailan," I said. "I'd like to speak with Mr. or Mrs. Hass. I'm from the police."

"May I see your badge?"

I showed it to her.

"Very well."

She opened the door reluctantly, holding the gown closed tight in front of her. I walked in.

It was a magnificent apartment. The walls were tiled all the way up to the intricate moldings of the high ceiling. The furnishings were tasteful, the ornaments expensive.

"I'm sorry if I seem rude," she said, "but I'm alone with the children. How did you get here so quickly? It can't be fifteen minutes since my husband left."

"You were expecting me?" I said, hoping the translator would disguise the surprise in my voice.

"You or somebody. I didn't know the police were so quick. I suppose my husband is on his way back?"

"I don't know."

"You didn't see him?"

"No."

"But then how . . . ?"

I wasn't going to help her.

"Do you mind waiting for just a minute?" she stammered. "The children are in the kitchen and I'm always concerned little Rugh will try to put his sister in the oven and dry her out."

She walked away, her claws remarkably quiet on the tiled floors.

I heard her saying something in the next room. When she came back there was a faint smile on her snout. She showed me her teeth.

"Please excuse my manners," she said, "I never asked you to sit down. I do wish my husband were here. He's the only one who really knows the value of the jewels. After all, he bought them."

Jewels? And why was she so impatient for hubby to get home? She seemed almost afraid to speak.

I kept my face as neutral as I could.

"We've heard of so few robberies here," she said, still stalling. "I guess it must come from living in such an enclosed community."

"When did you get home tonight?" I asked.

She gave a start. "How did you know I went out?"

"I know you work and where."

"You work fast."

"I was already in the neighborhood."

She was wondering what I had meant by that. I let her wonder.

"Have you checked her room? I'm the only other one who ever goes up there. Besides, it's a real mess . . ." She hardly suppressed a sigh of relief as footsteps pounded outside the door and paused. A card key slid through the lock. "My husband. Dear? In here!"

This one was getting his vitamins. He was closer to three meters than two, filling the room like a fist fills a boxing glove. His head barely cleared the ceiling and the disk case he carried looked like a cigarette lighter in his horny fist. He looked at me.

"Darling," she said. "The detective got here ahead of you," she said. "I was telling him you'd be right back."

He looked down at me with polite interest, but I could sense an air of defiance in him. "I beg your pardon," he said in English. Perfect accent—even too perfect—with just the slightest trace of hiss. "I'm afraid I do not understand, Mr. . . ."

"Bailan," I said. "Detective Bailan."

"Detective Bailan," he corrected himself. "But how odd. And you wanted to speak with me?"

"In your capacity as employer of the nanny, Agnes Wunderlei."

"Oh. But you cannot mean that you have already recovered the jewels? I know this all must seem peculiar, but the coincidence is so curious that I am still trying to understand it myself. You must realize that I have only returned from Security headquarters where I lodged a complaint against her. I come home and I find you here, and you tell me . . ."

It was hard to tell with something that couldn't sweat, but he seemed nervous. It was clear the wife had no intention of leaving the two of us alone.

"What was the nature of the complaint?" I asked him. His wife went stiff.

"The jewel robbery, of course," he said. "Agnes did not come for the children this morning, nor did she call. When I went to her room, she was gone. While she was at work, my wife realized it might be good to check our valuables. She called me. When I looked, it was clear why Agnes had gone."

"You went to her room?" I said. "The doorman said she didn't live here."

"She lives on a higher deck, directly above," he said. "Our building connects through a service passage."

"I see," I told him. "You went up and the box was empty."

"Exactly."

"What time did you check the box?"

"Around 1800."

"So you stayed with your children?"

"Yes," he said.

I turned to her. "And you returned . . ."

"About 1830," she said evenly.

"Why did you wait until nearly 2200 to lodge the complaint?" I asked him.

"I had left dinner cooking all day," she said, a little too fast. "We didn't think . . ."

"I should like to know what you were doing down here," Hass asked me. "Is it usual for Security to assign people in our residential area?"

It was apt to get racial pretty fast unless I could get out of it. "I'm not from Security. Like I said, I'm just the police. And I was off duty."

"But you were questioning my wife in your official capacity, were you not?"

"Yes."

"Regarding what?" he demanded. "I'm sure Alliance Relations would be very interested to hear that the police are invading people's homes. . . ."

"And listening to what people tell them?" I said. His righteous act was starting to bug me. "You can't say it's my fault. Since I got here, you've done nothing but talk about some jewel robbery that doesn't interest me in the least. If you want to get tough, we can do that, too. Right now I'm here investigating a much more serious crime."

"More serious?" she said. There was a lump in her throat.

I kept my eyes on the husband. "You didn't hear about the crime that was committed this evening in the caf across the square?"

"No," she said with some relief.

"I fail to see," he said, "what concern . . ."

"This could be of yours?" I said. "As far as I can tell, none. I'm just interviewing people who might have seen something."

"Murder?" the wife gasped.

"I don't recall I mentioned the nature of the crime," I said, "but as it happens, you're right."

The husband shot her a cold look through eyes that were half-lidded in warning.

"We have reason to believe your nanny was acquainted with the deceased. What time did she disappear?"

"Sometime between 1830 last night and 0800 this morning," Hass said without any hesitation.

"That would be logical," she chimed in.

"Okay. Can you show me her room?"

They looked at each other. "Very well," he said. "Let me get my key. I'll show you up."

He took me upstairs and through a converted utility shaft. He had a tight squeeze getting through. When we got to the other side, we were on Violet Seven. Through the grilled deck I could see the square below us.

We came to a door. The key was already in the lock. Hass pulled it through. The door opened.

I looked at him. "Your wife just said she was the only one who came up here."

"Of course. But sometimes I . . ."

The lights came on automatically. The room was bare and cluttered at the same time. Only one corner seemed clean. I walked over to the small dresser and opened it.

"She left without her clothes?" I wondered aloud.

"She's not very bright," he said. "After all, how far can you run on a battlestation? Of course, if she's sold the jewels she could easily buy a new face, new ID. As I told the man at headquarters, they're worth in excess of two hundred thousand credits."

"Free enterprise," I said. I walked over to the bare patch on the deck and went down on my knees. Two levels of the deck had been cut out with an oxyacetylene torch. About sixty-five meters down and across, I had a clear line of sight through the plastic front of the caf.

"How long has she been with you?" I said.

"We hired her when we arrived on the *Hawking*—about a hundred days ago."

"You found her through an ad?"

"Her references were impeccable," he said. "And she spoke perfect Squam within weeks."

I stood up and filed that one away.

"Mr. Hass," I said. This was going to be a tough one. "By any chance—and this is just a routine question, you understand—by any chance was your relationship with Agnes anything more than employer and staff?"

It was just a shot in the dark, but oddly enough, he paused. He looked more concerned than he had been. "Will my answer be a matter of record?"

"It'll never come up."

If he knew what the hole in the floor meant, he'd know I was lying. "Yes."

"Here or in your apartment?"

"Here, of course. She was of great help in my trading business, unofficially. She often entertained potential clients, or . . ." he hesitated. "Sometimes I would find it expedient to entertain certain clients of my own and she would absent herself. With so many of our men serving on ships many of my race are here alone, without the benefit of husband or family. It is almost my duty . . ."

"I can take it from there." Or could I? Jesus. "I asked because I noticed that a button of your tunic has fallen off. I just found one like it under the bed."

I held out the button. He took it with surprising speed.

"When was the last time?" I said.

"Two days ago."

"Did you see Agnes last?"

"When I was entertaining my last guest here. She waited until I arrived and then left. She often waits in a nearby caf for . . . me to leave."

"She didn't act unusual?"

"Not at all."

"Did you know if she had any visitors?"

"Visitors?"

"Any . . . males?"

His snout seemed to disappear into his long neck. The teeth came out. It wasn't comforting. "The question never came up," he said flatly. "However, had Agnes had a lover, I would in no way have known. That would have been her own business."

He almost seemed jealous. Hell, he weighed a ton and was a different species. Still, I had to ask. Maybe white hair was her lover and this hulk decided to play the jealous type.

"Can you tell me where you were today between 1700 and 1900 hours?"

"Of course"—I think the Squam actually smiled—"I was with my children, we spent the entire time by the pool. There were dozens of neighbors there that I spoke to. Such outings with their father are vital to the younger ones' development. I am totally dedicated to my mate and our hatchlings."

"I see. Well, thank you for your cooperation. It's late and I think that pretty much covers it."

"Fine. Shall we go back down?"

I wondered if a minute had gone by when he wasn't lying.

After Hass had taken me down and shown me out, I stopped back at the concierge's desk. He was reading one of those sleaze mags, the kind that came with the disposable vibrator gloves for three credits ninety-five.

"You get everything?" he asked.

"Were you here around 1800 last night?"

"Sure."

"Did you see Agnes bring in the Squam kids?"

"Like I see you here now, pal."

"Did she usually come out here or did she go up to her room after she finished?"

"She always came through here."

"Did she yesterday?"

"Yeah. Mrs. Hass got home late. It was nearly 1900 when Agnes left. She ran outta here in a big hurry."

"Thanks."

I lit a cigarette and walked over to the caf. It was almost 0100 now and the place was empty. I called in to HQ and got Cal at the desk to punch up a list of the employees at the Violet Eight Handi-Mart. Only one was named Elizabeth. With any luck she hadn't gone out.

The com rang five or six times before someone picked up on audio.

"Yes?" a bleary voice said.

"Ms. Taeder? I'm sorry to bother you so late, but it's police business."

That seemed to get some respect. She turned the visual on. A small woman with big collarbones stared back at me. Her kinky brown hair was dragged back all the way. It made her look like a greyhound. Behind her was a hole of a room, just a foldaway bed, a small video, a commode, a dry-shower, and a dresser. She looked like any checkout girl, only a little more so.

"What is it?"

"My name is Bailan. I'm investigating the disappearance of a woman named Agnes Wunderlei. I understand she did all her shopping at your Handi-Mart."

She looked surprised and worried. "I hope she's all right."

"She's just gone missing," I said. "We'll find her." That was me. Bailan of the Space Scouts. We find anything. "Can you tell me anything about her?"

"Umm . . ."

"Anything at all."

She worried her lower lip for a couple of seconds. Then something clicked. "She wasn't a domestic."

"What do you mean?"

She blushed. "Off the record?"

"It depends. Try me."

"Well, you know, we give sort of a rebate to servants so they'll do their shopping with us. One credit back for every ten of their employers' money they spend with us. It's good for business."

She looked at me like she expected me to call the fraud squad right there.

"Yeah?" I said.

"Well, the first time we gave her the money, she just stood there stupid."

"And after that?"

"Oh, she took it, but more to fit in than for the money."

"I see. So what do you make of that?"

"She acted like she was rich. Rich and well educated."

"How so?"

"We get all kinds down here. Herfets and Emry off Five. But especially Squams. Lots of different languages. Hell, I wear my translator all day."

"Sure."

"Well," she said, narrowing her eyes, "every time Agnes would come in, it seemed as if she was listening to them. Like she understood."

"How can you be sure?"

"She never wore a translator, but every time somebody would make a joke, she'd smile like she understood."

"Anything else?"

She shrugged. Her shoulders were bony and overworked. "Noth . . . Well . . . No. Forget it."

"What?"

"You'll think it's stupid."

"Tell me."

"She knitted."

"What about it?"

"Well, I saw what she was working on a couple of times when she was waiting at the register. It was junk."

"People have different tastes," I said.

"That's not what I mean. My mom used to knit. What Agnes was working on wasn't anything, just knots. Just one long web of knots."

It was nearly 0200 when I got back to my room. I grabbed a cup of rehydrated coffee from one of the machines down the hall and gulped it back. I stripped down and went for a shower. As the caffeine and the cold water started to splash together, I considered the options.

If Hass had caused Agnes's disappearance, the theft of the jewels was a good way of diverting suspicion. It was attractive, but it proved nothing. It was also, I had a hunch, not true. Then again, this Agnes might very well have boosted the jewels.

There was another possibility, and I would have to start giving it some thought.

I toweled off and walked back to my room. I grabbed the com and dialed headquarters.

"Police Headquarters, Carroll here . . . Jesus! Bailan, where you been?"

"I've been on Violet Eight since I called you. What's up?"

"All hell's broken loose up here. You got a priority/Umbra message—I think it's from Security—burning up the hard disk. Omera's got a copy, too," he added. We went way back.

"Great." It was just like Kenvich to go tattling. "I'm at my place now. Can you mail it, Cal?"

I saw him reach for the terminal off-screen. "Sure."

"Anything else?"

My terminal powered up automatically as the message came through. "You bet your ass," Cal said. "Some Squam Indie named Hass called Alliance Relations about you. Said you'd been rousting his family."

"They always do."

"Yeah, but they usually don't turn up dead a couple of hours later."

"What?!"

"The call came in a few minutes ago. Some maintenance guy found Hass clogging up the drain in one of the pools they got set up down there. Security stepped in right away—we're out of it."

"How did he get it?"

"Somebody emptied a needler into him close-up. Very messy."

I pulled on my pants and checked to see my blaster was charged. "Hey, did the blonde ever come back to Violet 7.135.2807?"

"No."

"Thanks, Cal. I'll take it from here."

He shook his head. "Don't be stupid, Bailan. Kenvich is already gunning for your ass. Says you've been exceeding your authority—been screaming about security risks. Don't make it any worse. Hit the sack and let the chief sort it out tomorrow."

I looked over at my rack. It was calling to me.

"Talk to you later, pal." I hung up and pulled open the memo with the mouse.

It wasn't from Security. It was from Fleet Intelligence. After quoting the regs at me for two pages, they finally cut to the chase. Hass and his wife were Squam agents. In fact, *the* Squam agents aboard the *Hawking*. Hubby collected data from various moles and sleaze-bags while wifey transmitted from the Squam ship she was a techie on. Very neat.

The thing was, Counterintelligence fed them almost everything they were getting. In a weird way, this kept everybody happy. The Squam government trusted us more because Fleet would confirm what they already knew to be the "truth." In turn, they trusted us more and so were more cooperative—essential if we were all going to eliminate the Ichtons.

I didn't read the cease and desist part of the letter—I headed for the lifts instead. As the elevator dropped I tried to figure out other ways for the pieces to fit together, but they kept coming up the same way.

I was sweating again when the door finally slid open on Violet Eight. I stepped into the passageway. A Squam with a needler in his fist walked toward me. I was going for my gun when somebody killed the lights.

The blaster coughed twice in my fist. His head and upper body broke apart with a flash as the plasma took him. I saw him twitch before it went black again. The deck shook as the big lizard hit hard. A hatchway hissed open close to where I stood and I heard more claws on the decking.

I dropped onto the wet deck and rolled. A heartbeat, then the whine of a needler spray ripped the air.

What sounded like hundreds of ceramic toothpicks zinged and ricocheted down the passage. The hair on the back of my neck stood up as the air whistled and tore over my head. I wanted to slip down between the slick grating, but all I could do was hold on.

One of them went into my calf. Maybe more than one. That was the way with needlers: it started to hurt only a few minutes after you'd been hit, unless they hit you somewhere important. Then it didn't hurt at all.

More scratching. Closer this time. I was in trouble. My blaster would light the passage—and meep like a torch. Needlers had no flash. I heard their labored, reptilian breathing as they came down the hall. There were two, maybe three of them in all. I held my breath. They came on slowly, listening and sniffing.

I reached up, groping for a door or anything. We were all out of luck. They were only a meter away when I opened up.

I fired as fast as I could, shooting and shooting. They screamed and twisted and I kept firing, lighting the place up like a Dore illustration. A few droplets of the plasma spattered back onto me. I scrambled back on the steamy floor, wiping myself as best I could.

Every alarm in the place went off. I checked my blaster and looked back. There had been only two of them after all. Molten heaps bubbled where they had been. I looked away, staggered against one of the sickly violet walls, and lurched off toward Viv's.

I found a vidcom and called in. Carroll said they'd meet me there.

Her door was open. Back in her T-shirt again, she had almost finished packing. Three big plastic crates stood where the bed had been. The rest was bare.

Her hand was wrapped around the butt of a needler, a strip of cloth in between so she wouldn't leave prints. She knew who it was, but she didn't look at me right away. When she did it didn't mean anything much. She just lifted the mean little pistol a little and slid along the deck toward me, her lips tight-set.

But I had my blaster out myself. We looked at each other across our guns. Maybe she knew me, I hadn't any idea from her expression.

I said, "You killed them, huh?"

She shook her head a little. "Just Hass. He did Paolo."

"So that was his name."

"Yes. He worked for Counterintelligence. He was Hass's case agent."

Kenvich was going to go strategic.

"Put the gun down," I told her. "You're through with it."

She lowered it a little. She hadn't seemed to notice the blaster I was pushing through the air in her general direction. I lowered that, too.

"Why did you cap Hass?"

She looked up at me. "He got panicked after you went to his place. He came down here, convinced you were going to uncover the whole thing. He was going to blow it."

"He was renting you the information before passing it on to the wife."

"Right."

"And you sold it to the highest bidder via Paolo."

She nodded a little. "Most of the time our buyers would get the Fleet movements before the orders were even posted."

Profiteering. It was an old scam with a new twist. The merchants would come in and spread rumors that the Fleet was on the way and as the panic began to spread, they could buy up everything that wasn't nailed down at rock-bottom prices before moving on. Needless to say, it also compromised mission security with the enemy.

"You fed the info to Paolo . . ."

"But we couldn't be sure if Intelligence was onto him," she said.

The penny dropped. "The knitting."

"Just old-fashioned Morse code," she said. "I knew it would take a long time, but I couldn't risk being seen with him."

"The grain they found in his clothes. What was that about?"

"He had a transmitter set up in a container of long-storage grain on Twenty deck."

She didn't seem to mind telling me. It was almost all there.

"Why the elaborate setup?" I said. "What went wrong?"

"Two weeks ago, Paolo sends me a message. Says he wants more money."

"So pay him."

"I did. Three days later he says it's not enough. Says he's going to turn me in to Intelligence and take a big fat promotion unless he gets a lot more."

"So you told Hass Paolo was Intelligence. Hass sends over the hard-boys and it's *Adios, Paolo.*"

She didn't say anything after that. She just stood there, looking small.

"Who was it set me up?" I said finally. "You or Hass?"

She looked at my blood-soaked pants. She lowered the needler and took a step toward me.

I brought my blaster up.

"You're a bad horse, Viv. I'm not betting on you anymore."

I made a broad, disappointed gesture and moved a little closer. She backed up. I should have taken the chance when she gave it to me.

"So what's the plan now? Change apartments and find a new supplier?"

"Sure."

She said it like I'd asked her to go on a Ferris wheel. "Tell me," I said, "was it worth it?"

"What do you mean?"

"The money."

She looked at me like I was stupid. Maybe I was.

"Are you kidding?" She laughed. "Since Hass rolled over, I've cleared over 1.3 million credits. Tax-free and in the clear."

I didn't like what her definition of "in the clear" was. "The merchants pay pretty well."

"I would say the most valuable commodity going is knowledge, wouldn't you say?"

"'Grace is given of God," I said, "but knowledge is bought in the market.'"

"Dickens?"

I shook my head.

"Whatever. The point is, there's plenty of cash to go around. It's evident from tonight's fiasco that I need someone who can handle it when things go bad. Why don't you join me?"

I looked at her for the last time, really. There were a lot of things she might have said, that I maybe would have fallen for, but that wasn't one of them.

She saw it in my eyes.

Viv jerked up the needler and squeezed the trigger at me. She did it without moving a muscle of her face.

Nothing happened. It puzzled her in a vague, month-before-last way. She turned the gun around, still careful about the cloth wrapper around the grip, and peered into the muzzle. She shook it and then remembered I was there. I hadn't moved. I didn't have to, now.

"It's on full auto, but that yellow telltale means the clip is empty," I explained. "You left them all back in Hass."

She moved to go and I raised the blaster. The motion shifted my balance and the wounded leg almost gave way. A pain rose and my vision closed to only a narrow hole. I fought back and found myself nauseous, but leaning against the wall. Viv had moved a few steps, whether to help me or grab the blaster was a good question. She looked toward the door and took a few steps. The question in her expression was clear. I wasn't sure myself. Part of me knew I could simply let myself fall and no one could say I hadn't tried and passed out. The pool of blood at my foot was all the excuse I needed.

Two images fought each other in my mind. One was the memory of her soft body so desirous in my arms. The other was the cold, motionless slab of flesh in the morgue up on Green that had been her partner. For a long time neither of us moved.

When I heard the sound of the security overrides on the door and Cal telling the rookies to stay alert as he opened it, I knew what I decided no longer mattered. He'd read the report I'd filed after the fight in the hallway and figured out where, even wounded, I had to be going. Good police work. Though sometimes too efficient backup can be a pain.

I let go and let myself slide slowly down the wall as Cal came through. Viv gave me a look that hinted she somehow felt betrayed. It really didn't matter, but I was just too hot and too tired to care. Letting Viv go now would simply have delayed things. Hass had been right about one thing. There was nowhere to run on a battlestation.

STERN CHASE

A Royal Navy adage is that a "stern chase is the longest one." There is also an old army saying, "Hurry up and wait." Perhaps the most draining part of any modern battle is that generally everyone is bored most of the time. Hours of mind-dulling tedium are interspersed with minutes, even seconds, of furious combat. Spacemen would arm, prepare, and then warp for hours to drop back and engage the Ichtons in a few minutes of carefully planned combat. Those lucky enough to survive then fled back to the relative safety of the main fleet or, farther back, to the *Hawking* itself.

In that sense the *Hawking* had proved a success in its appointed mission. The battlestation had more than proved itself capable of supporting large forces at an unimaginable distance from their home base. Further, it now had provided both a base and safe port serving a large fleet under combat conditions for almost three years.

To those Fleet personnel serving on the Battlestation *Stephen Hawking*, this record was a matter of pride. Unfortunately there was little time for satisfaction as a constant stream of broken men and ships returned and had to be made ready to return to the battle. This continuing grind of unbroken crises had to begin taking its toll. Fatigue alone became a major factor in Anton Brand's calculations. Also of concern to the *Hawking*'s commander was the tenuous morale of the allied races.

Brand attempted to break off the pursuit after nearly twenty days of constant small battles. As the Fleet ships pulled back, the Ichton warships followed. There could be no respite. Too many ships had warped back toward the *Hawking* and any lapse in the pressure would release major Ichton formations from guarding the mother ships. Freeing them to attack the *Stephen Hawking* itself or nearby allied worlds.

So they continued as best they could. Fighting without respite. The not so lucky returned their torn and shattered men and ships for repair. Everyone assisted in maintaining the faith of the allies. Sometimes this last was hard to accomplish. This was even more difficult when it appeared the ally's world might be the next Ichton target.

THE HANDMAIDEN
by Diane Duane

"Don't just stand there," Kashiwabara said. "Hold the retractor."

I'm not just standing here, Sal thought. But all the same she took hold of the J-shaped thing and pulled. "Not that way," Kash said irritably. "Welder, Junie. Thanks. More toward you, Sal. That's the way."

Kashiwabara was up to her elbows in the man, her eyes screwed half closed. To Sal she looked like a child at school, engaged in some particularly engrossing piece of work with modeling clay. It was not clay she was working with, though, but flesh, some poor man's intestine. At least Sal thought it might be intestine. She had a general impression of wet glistening rounded shapes, of squelchy wet noises: and she wanted nothing more definite than that. This was hardly her proper business, and she didn't intend for it to be so in the future, if she could help it.

O God—she started, and lost the thread again, her eyes widening in dismay as the air abruptly fizzed red around them all. "Didn't think it would spurt like *that,*" Kashiwabara said, her voice bemused, her hands suddenly moving very fast, perhaps three times as fast as before. "That one, right there, Junie. The one next to it. Thanks. Should be right under there— *There* it is. Jeez, look at the state of it—how is the boy still with us? Guts."

"A good anesthesiologist," said a mild voice from the head of the table, down past the glow of the sterifields.

"You shut up, Belle. Don't take the man's credit. You barely know where to put the tubes. Junie, where's the dish?"

"Here. Kash, is that going to be enough left?"

"You kidding? More than plenty. Twenty cells is enough to clone from in situ. In a week he'll have a nice new spleen. Get the one down to Path, Junie, the ghouls'll want it. Where's the dittosplen?"

O God, Who holds all lives from their beginnings to their ends, Sal thought, *keep this man in mind—* Man, though: it was hard to see him as a man, at the moment. More a collection of tubes and oozing liquid, with the fields shimmering over everything and making it look unreal, like something out of a vid. Sal shook her head, abruptly angry with herself. There was a hell of a way for a chaplain to see one of her charges, as a thing rather than a—

"Getting to you, Sal?" Kashiwabara was looking across the body—the *man*—at her, with an expression that had just a little malice about it. No more than usual, she consoled herself.

"No," Sal said. That was only partly true. When she had first seen the man brought in, only survivor of the Ichton attack on her little fleet, he had looked like someone much more in need of prayer than of the surgeons—burned, explosively decompressed when his suit gave: the debridement alone, before the surgery, had left Sal sure she was working with a corpse. People did not just lie and take the dreadful peeling off of burnt material and flesh fused to it that the man had undergone—not if they were alive. They woke up, and screamed. Sal's nightmares rang with those screams. But the man had simply lain there, in shock so profound that he had noticed nothing; and then he had gone into the OR. Kashiwabara had taken all of ten minutes over him now—a surprising amount of time for her.

"He'll live," Kashiwabara said, in the matter-of-fact tone of voice of someone announcing the score of a football game some light-years away. "Whether he'll like it—" She shrugged. "Fuser now, Junie. Thanks. Let go of that, Sal. Just take it out and throw it in the bucket. Junie, count the retractor out." Kash took the fuser and wielded it, closing the operative site with negligent skill. "It's not my table," Kash said, to Sal this time. "I just patch them up. After that, they're your business." Her eyes were direct, cool, almost merry. Sal's eyes burned. She looked away.

"Who's next?" said Kash.

"Khalian," said the circulating nurse, glancing at the wall screen. "Head trauma, enucleated eye, possible brain trouble. Contrecoup, they think."

"Poor Weasel," Kash said in that same cool voice. "Pull out a head tray and get him in here, and prepped. Him? Her?"

"Him."

"Your table?" Kash said to Sal.

It was her table, of course. But she said, "I'll pass on this one. Back in a while."

Kashiwabara nodded. "I need a new skin," she was saying as Sal shouldered out of the OR. "Try getting me one a size larger—"

She leaned against the wall of one of the many corridors up in the Blue and fought to slow her heartbeat down. People passed her, glanced at her, glanced away with expressions of pity or concern. With the battle going on over their heads, everyone was busy: but her uniform singled her out for their pity. It was standard Fleet uniform except for the dog collar, and the tabs with the Uniform Religious Insignia on it, the circle with the dot in the middle. "The Holy Ovum," Ricky Woods had called it while they were in the Fleet orientation course together, how many years ago now? . . . And there had been quite a few other names, most of them rife with innuendo. Where was Ricky now? Sal wondered. Was she even alive? . . . Or in the body, rather. Sometimes, of late, in the rush and fury of a war that could mean the end of whole civilizations, it was hard to remember that there were more important things, more meaningful things, than mere physical life.

So she had always believed, anyway.

And do I believe it now?

Sal pushed the thought away, straightened herself up, tried to look a little less doleful. There was nothing more depressing, to the onlooker, than a depressed minister. Her job, here and now at least, was to help people find their way to their strength; and if she chanced to be able to be useful in some other way as well—like holding a retractor—she did that. Though it was hardly her primary function.

Not that some people seemed to realize it. *Make yourself useful,* Kashiwabara had said, very casually. *Or is it just my own uncertainty showing? We all have these periods of not being sure what we're for—but this one has lasted longer than usual. What real good have I done anyone here? Sometimes I think I should just go out on combat duty and get killed like the rest of them—*

Her pager beeped. She sighed and pulled it out to look at its little screen. It said, MY OFFICE, PLEASE, IMMEDIATELY. F.

Sal took herself off along the corridor in a hurry. Frank Arnasson was no one to keep waiting, especially in the middle of a war: nor at any other time. He was coordinator for Inhabitant Resources aboard *Hawking,* and Sal's immediate superior. He did not take his own position seriously, since it involved coordinating things as disparate and low profile as Food Services and Janitorial; and Frank always growled about how his title and a few credits might get him a cup of soup on some benighted world where no one knew any better. But there were few people who could quicker get you in deep trouble than Frank if he suspected that you weren't doing your job.

She took the lift down two to Blue Three and trotted along the corridor to 270, where Frank's office was. Sal paused only long enough to get her breath back and yank her tunic into place, then buzzed.

The door snapped open for her. She stepped in and saw Frank hunched behind his desk as usual, eating something, a food bar of some kind. Nothing unusual there: Frank was the worst person she had ever seen for snacking at his desk—he never stopped. Standing across from him, though, watching him with an expression that at first glance seemed like mild interest, was an Emry.

Sal paused there as the door hissed closed behind her, and the Emry turned to look at her. It was in Fleet uniform, very dark and simple, but oddly decorated with something unusual—a silver chain, very massy, like the ceremonial chains that Sal had seen in pictures of mayors from some parts of Europe, back on Earth. The chain shifted as the Emry tilted its head to look at her, revealing a glint of gold on the low-cut collar of its uniform. It was the Holy Ovum.

Frank put aside his food bar and folded his hands, looking at Sal, too. His honest, ugly face, big and blunt, with its potato nose and little eyes, smiled slightly as if she were the solution to a particularly thorny problem.

"Fleet Chaplain Salvatora Arkas," Frank said, "Fleet Chaplain Ewa n'Vhuurih."

The Emry bowed, a graceful gesture, but his head did not bow, and his eyes never left Sal's. For a moment she was lost in those golden eyes, then she blinked, taking in the beauty of the dark pelt with its faint pattern of darker spots, and the long nose with the abrupt patch of pink at the end. This, fortunately, was one aspect of her chaplaincy that was easy for her. She had never had trouble seeing the Creator in species that were alien to her own. The problem, perhaps, was that she had sometimes been too good at it, and this could be impolitic, when all the energies of one's highest superiors were being vested in hating one of those species or, worse, manipulating it.

"Chaplain," Sal said, wondering how she looked to those golden eyes. And the question rose immediately to mind: What sort of religion do they have? No one had even mentioned the word in connection with them before.

"The chaplain," Frank said, "is the Emry's first member of your service. I want you to make him welcome, show him around, see that he's properly oriented . . ."

The Emry made a gesture that looked like someone casting something to the ground in front of himself: plainly ceremonial, though what it might mean, there was no telling. A touch of excitement began somewhere down inside Sal. *How do they see You?* she said to the One Who listened. *What might we find out from them? Thank You for this opportunity—*

"I thank you for your help," the Emry said. "This means a great deal to us."

Sal shivered slightly. The translator might convey words, but the voice was more clearly that of an animal than any alien voice she had heard before: it was almost furry around the edges.

"You're very welcome," Sal said. "Have you been quartered?"

"Go on, go on," Frank growled, and picked up his food bar in one hand and a stylus in another. "Take care of the amenities elsewhere. You two have work to do, so do I—"

Sal glanced at the Emry and found what looked like the same expression of slight amusement there. They headed for the door together, and as it closed behind them, the Emry said, "A sudden sort of creature."

Sal laughed. "He is."

"I am up in Yellow," the Emry said. "A comfortable enough little den. It is diplomatic quarters, if I understand these things correctly. Perhaps better than I would normally be given, if those here understood my function. Or if I did." His jaw dropped in that amused look again.

Sal nodded. "We all spend a while trying to find out exactly what we're supposed to be doing here," she said. "For humans in our service, at least, there are certain basic duties. Rotation through the various kinds of religious service—there's never time to do them all in one day, so we take turns—"

"We," said the Emry. "There are more than one of you, then?"

"Normally there would be." It was surprising that Sal's eyes could still start stinging again over *this* issue: she had thought it was settled. "There were three of us on board—enough to cover, it was thought. We managed, just barely. But some of the ancillary craft needed coverage, those staff went off to take care of business there—" Sal shrugged. "One of them was killed during an Ichton attack while he was performing a wedding. The other—we have no idea what happened to the ship: it just never came back. Probably Ichton again."

So uncaring, said the raspy voice in Sal's memory, *what else should it be in this part of space?* That had been Larry's constant refrain, always a little sad, always with a slight edge to it, as if he held God personally responsible for the mismanagement of the whole galactic situation, and was daily expecting Him to do something about it. Larry had gone about all his work with that same slight impatience and irritation, but always unfailingly good-natured: he was one of the most simply loving people Sal had ever known. And now he was gone, with the captain and the first officer of the little ship to which he had traveled. Doubtless, though, he had gotten the job done. Sal was sure they had been married for at least several seconds before they were dead.

"And now you are alone here," the Emry said.

Sal raised her eyebrows. "Inasmuch as any of us are ever really alone," she said, "yes."

The Emry looked puzzled at this, and his tail thumped. It was a short one, making the gesture look peremptory, almost annoyed. *But there's no telling,* Sal reminded herself. *I must be careful not to anthropomorphize the gestures of a species we don't know very well as yet—*

"I should like to see what you do in a given day," said the Emry, "if there is no prohibition against it."

"I think that was the general idea," Sal said. "No, there's no prohibition. Come on, I'll show you the chapels."

They went up three levels and made their way about halfway around the curve of *Hawking*. "Here we are," Sal said, and touched the door panel. It slid open: they went in.

The Emry looked around, blinking solemnly. "But there is nothing here. Just a table."

Sal laughed. "The dangers of a nondenominational chapel. We can dress it as necessary. Shinto, Jewish, various flavors of Christian, Buddhist, you name it."

"Flavors," the Emry said thoughtfully as Sal went over to the holography panel. "This is a matter of taste, then."

Sal chuckled at the joke . . . then wondered if it was one, as she saw that puzzled-looking expression on the Emry's face again. She touched the panel and said, "Here's one of the standard Christian configurations."

The light on the bare walls shifted, and a radiance grew near the ceiling, as of stained glass somewhere above; the cross, very plain, appeared over the table, which was now made plain as an altar. "Solid artifacts we keep stored in the next room," Sal said. "Candles, canopies, and whatnot. The usual equipment." She looked curiously over at the Emry and said, "Do you use such things?"

He shook his head, looking up into the radiance. "No," he said.

Sal looked at him. "I'm sorry . . . I don't know what to call you."

"H'ewa," the Emry said.

"H'ewa . . . I'm very curious, but I don't want to break any prohibitions either, and I have no idea what sort of rules you might have about your worship—"

"Very few," H'ewa said, and blinked. "You mentioned—'Shinto'?"

Sal nodded and touched the panel again. The light shifted once more, falling into squarish patterns of brightness and dark, evoking a feeling of screens pulled across a source of light outside. The sound system cut in and from somewhere off in the middle distance came the sound of bass voices intoning one of those scalp-raising triple-voiced chants to the Jewel in the Lotus. "I know a few of the chants myself," Sal said, "but they're hard on the throat. Not any of the serious ones, though, the healing chants: almost all the masters who knew them died a long time ago, and the recorded ones just don't seem to work the same. . . ."

H'ewa nodded—that gesture, at least, they seemed to have in common. "You would use this room fairly frequently for your—'worship,' then."

"Yes. You do it otherwise?"

"It is not a personal matter? One must have a special place to perform it?"

Sal shook her head. "Not necessarily. Some religions feel that worship works best in groups, that's all. Other say not: that each person makes his own choices, and needs no mediator between himself and the First Cause."

"What do you say?" H'ewa said, looking again at Sal. It was a direct expression, a little challenging.

"Well—" Sal leaned against the wall. "I was trained first as Church of Mars, of course, and your first training tends to color your thinking somewhat. So I tend to believe, in common with other people of my sort, that God made the world, but the world became marred: so to redeem it, He descended into it Himself, first as man, and in other times, in other shapes, to draw the natures of those kinds of beings into His own."

H'ewa nodded, but his face was getting that perplexed look again. " 'Believe,' " he said. "You don't *know*?"

"Well, historical proof is an oxymoron half the time," Sal said. "Hard enough to tell what really happened ten minutes ago, or ten hours, as opposed to what a 'historian' would say. But—" Then she stopped, seeing the look of perplexity on H'ewa's face intensifying. "No," she said. "No, of course I don't *know*—that's the whole point of faith. No one can ever *know* for sure, or have Deity proven to them past all doubt. The mere physical nature of the universe won't permit it. Belief is all we've got."

"But other 'flavors' say differently?" H'ewa said. There was a sound of urgency creeping into his voice.

"Well, some say that knowing is possible, but unnecessary for the assured soul." Sal was beginning to sweat, not least because she had no idea where all this was going. "Some say that neither God, nor the universe symptomatic of Him, care whether you believe in them: that belief itself is unnecessary. Just as believing in the table is unnecessary, because it's there whether you believe in it or not. Even if you can't perceive it."

H'ewa turned away, looking troubled. "H'ewa," Sal said, "I want to help, truly I do. Tell me what the trouble is."

The Emry turned back to her. "Who knows?" he said. "Who knows what the truth is?"

What is truth? someone had said a long time ago, and washed his hands. Sal wished she could do the same. "None of us know," she said. "All we can do is go on as we've done in the past, and look for new answers. We thought—I hoped you might have some new answers for us."

H'ewa bared his teeth suddenly. It was an alarming expression, and Sal stepped back involuntarily, then stopped, seeing the desperation still in his eyes.

"I was sent to find out what I can," H'ewa said. "I must try to do so, even if you don't know. But we thought you did—about this First Cause: this God. It is a great disappointment."

He sighed. "Show me the rest," he said.

Sal opened the door and showed him out, her mind in an uproar too great even for prayer.

Several hours later Sal had shown him the hospital wards, and what a chaplain did there, visiting the sick. She had also done two or three counseling sessions that she really didn't need to do, but scheduled gladly enough, to give her some kind of routine to fall into while that golden-eyed regard was with her. With the counselees' permission, H'ewa had sat through the sessions, his handsome ears swiveling to follow the conversations, eyes blinking gently. Sal wondered if it was her imagination that her counselees were being a little more forthcoming about their own troubles than usual. Maybe it was the fascination of the stranger: or maybe that H'ewa was an uncommonly good listener, in the way of someone very uncertain of what they're hearing, who therefore concentrates on every passing word.

They broke for a meal after a while, H'ewa going off to his quarters—apparently the Emry preferred to eat in private. Sal, for her part, went straight off to Frank's office. He was eating, again, or still. He looked up at her as if she were excessively unwelcome, but that was par for the course with him.

"I don't think the Emry *have* a religion," Sal said before he could get started. "Who put that creature in a chaplain's uniform? Was it some kind of joke?"

"If it was a joke," Frank said, putting down one of the eternal food bars, "it was a big one. Right from the top, that lad came. Some relative of one of the people who run the planet, sent here at their orders. And the orders specified chaplain—it was a six-sigma translation, so don't blame it on an error in syntax."

"But they don't have any religion," Sal said again, feeling helpless. "They don't know what God is, or gods, *any* gods, as far as I can tell! They don't know what religious services are, or priests or ministers of any kind!"

"Maybe they want to find out," Frank said heavily. "Possibly they think they're missing something, seeing that so many of the other species in the Alliance have such things. Who knows how they think of it. A weapon. An advantage."

Sal's eyebrows went up. That struck her as a very inappropriate way to consider religion.

"And don't you go getting judgmental," Frank said. "I know that look. Sal, all I'm sure of is that this situation is politically provocative. Apparently our lad has orders to go back to their high council, or whatever it is, and report to them after his visit—and I hear rumblings that what he says will make some kind of difference to their alliance with us and with the other Indies. This is too important a matter to screw up, so whatever you do, you'd better do a good job of it, Sal, or by whichever God's turn it is in the rotation today, I'll have your butt in a sling. Now get out of here and let me finish my dinner."

Sal smiled thinly, thinking (and tempted to say) that no one had ever seen Frank finish a meal before, and it was unlikely to start happening now. But she thought better of it—the remark was uncharitable, anyway: how he handled stress was his own business. She went away to see about the evening service.

There was no one there for it, which was a common enough variation when *Hawking* was in battle. The other main variation was that a given service was filled to overflowing, whether the people attending were of that denomination or not. The need for reassurance, for consolation, sometimes seemed to flow through the station like a wave. Other times, like now, people were just too busy. At such times, Sal particularly remembered the old prayer attributed to Cromwell before battle—though she herself doubted that that cold young man had ever said any such thing: "O God, Thou knowest how busy I must be today:

if I forget Thee, yet do not Thou forget me." She made it her business on such days to remember God on behalf of all the people who didn't have time.

The rotation said that today should have been the Zoroastrian service, but plainly no one would care, and Sal was feeling shaken: so she went back to the old familiar, the C of M service, which would console her, if no one else. The holography installation had filled the chapel with the pale, cool, rose-tinged light of one of the old Martian underground sun temples, one shaft of light coming down from the pierced ceiling to fall on the altar, which now looked like a plain slab of sandstone. The cup and plate were of stone as well, not orna-mented, not polished. Only the bread and wine had not changed. She was just in the act of lifting the cup up into the light and pronouncing the words cele-brating the Change when the door opened.

Sal had long learned to ignore such things. She kept herself where she belonged, in the moment of miracle, until it was finished, paying no attention to the silhouette in the doorway. It vanished, the door closing. Only a short shadow, standing back there in the reddish darkness, watched her she caught the gleam of golden eyes.

Sal finished the service as she had done for some time now, with the old optional prayer for use "in times of War and Tumults"—*not that most times aren't that, one way or another,* she thought. "King of Kings and Governor of all, whose power no creature can resist, to whom it belongs to justly punish wrong-doers, and to show mercy to the repentant: Save and deliver us, we beg You, from our enemies: abate their pride, assuage their malice, and confound their devices: that we, being armed with Your defense, may be preserved evermore from all perils, to glorify You, the only Giver of victory—"

"Does anyone truly have such power?" came the quiet voice from the shadows, the beast's voice. Sal shivered a little for the pain in it.

She finished what she was doing, took off her stole, and made her way back into the shadows herself. "So I believe," she said, folding the stole up, "but that won't be good enough, will it?"

There was a moment's silence. "We have need of certainties," H'ewa said. "Now more than ever."

"A lot of us have been looking for them, too," Sal said, "for a long time. Without much success."

Frank's words were much with her at the moment. She had been trying to figure out for the past little while exactly what she could do to be of help to H'ewa, to the allied species, to the Independents . . . and had found no answers. *Frank is on his own this time,* she thought.

"But some success," said H'ewa.

"It depends on who's judging it."

H'ewa sighed. "Our world," he said, "needs saving. All the ships, even this one—with all its power—seem able to do little. The Ichton fleets are all over this part of space, and all your might is only able to barely hold them away from us. What kind of civilization is it that can only survive with the help of aliens and strangers?"

Sal sighed, too. "Ours has been that, on occasion," she said. "If one thing that's been lost in the past years in our sense of ourselves as being competent to deal with the world . . . maybe that's not a terrible loss. Certainly those of us who believe that there is a Master of the universe also believe that our sense of ourselves as surrogate masters sometimes gets in the way of any real interaction with It. . . ."

"But you have not interacted with it," H'ewa said, "at least, not to any effect."

"We think we have," Sal said. "But our idea of effect, and Its idea of effect . . . are two very different things."

H'ewa shook his head again. "These are not the answers I came looking for," he said "I need to know; where can help be found, if not in all these ships and armaments? We had hints, from other people like you, that help might be found in other ways. Spiritual ways."

"It depends on what you mean by help," Sal said. "Victory? Triumph over one's enemies? I have no guarantees of help from the First Cause, the Powers, whatever you prefer to call them—on that account."

"Nothing like that. Just peace," H'ewa said, and that terrible pain was in its voice again, like the voice of a beast caught in a trap. "Just to be left alone."

Sal shook her head. "As for the second, whether it's available in the universe anymore, if it ever was," she said, "is a good question. You can ask an all-powerful God for things, but even the omnipotent is helpless against simple nonsense. Like saying, 'Oh, God, please turn blue into yellow.' Were we ever, any of us, really alone—in a universe in which every part affects every other—to be left that way again? By each other, let alone by other species—however mindless or well intentioned?" Sal breathed out. "As for peace—we keep asking. We're told, in most religions, that someday we'll get it. Or it will get us. But rarely while we're breathing. Life seems to be mostly about problem-solving, the way most species see it—and the more problems you solve, the bigger and more complex they get."

They were quiet for a moment as the shaft of sunlight slid away from the altar. "You spoke just now, up there, of a coming again," H'ewa said. "One of these—Powers—saying it would come back. That evil would die."

"But not when," Sal said, shaking her head. "Never that: no data on the future. As for the rest of it . . . all the stories of the Powers coming into the world, actually into it, to intervene . . . are in the past, a long time ago. Very old. Increasingly, we seem to be the ones who do the intervening. The Powers may speak . . . but they don't *do* much. We seem to be the ones who do the doing."

"We are not doing it very well, it would seem," said H'ewa.

Sal laughed, not as bitterly as she might have. "We never have," she said, "but we do what we can with what we've got. You're quite right, about the weapons not being enough. It's hard to stop using them, though. Right now, we don't seem to have much choice. If we stop shooting at the Ichtons, they'll roll over us and dome us over in a matter of minutes."

H'ewa bared his teeth again. This time Sal felt no need to step back. "I think we will not let them do that," he said. "And in the meantime . . . we will not wait for the Powers, either."

"It's not recommended," Sal said. "'The gods help those who help themselves'; that's a popular refrain in a lot of places. They may not help with hardware, or logistical support . . . but there are other ways."

H'ewa looked at her a moment, eyes glinting gold. Then he moved toward the door and went out.

Sal went to her prayers, distressed, and not knowing what else to do about it.

The next morning, when she went by the address H'ewa had given her for his quarters, she found the door standing open, and a cleaning robot working busily inside. "Where is the occupant, please?" she said to it.

"Vacated," the robot said, and kept dusting under a chair.

Sal put her eyebrows up and went off to Frank's office. He was eating at his desk and barely looked up at her. "What did you say to him?" he growled. "He was up all night in the library, ransacking the computers. Then left on the shuttle about half an hour ago, back to Emry."

"Nothing offensive, if that's what you're worried about," Sal said. "I gave him the truth—as much of it as I could find in such a short time, anyway. It seemed to be what he wanted."

"You'd better hope so," Frank said, looking, at least on the surface, relieved. "Well, go on, do you think I have all day to sit here jawing?"

Sal smiled at him and went off to the wards to visit some of the people she had missed yesterday—some of them missed on purpose, because they were a touch xenophobic and wouldn't have cared for the presence of an alien while Sal was ministering to them. She couldn't get rid of the memory of those golden eyes, blinking at her conversations, listening to the people she had been talking to; the comical swivel of the ears, but also the intensity. . . .

"Sal, they've got incoming in OR, a lot of it," said one of the nurses from the doorway as Sal got up from the last bedside. "You free? Some of them may need you."

"On my way." She pulled her stole out of her pocket and headed for the lift—OR was one level down. It was a madhouse when she got down there, but that was nothing new. The scorched-bacon smell was nothing new, either—she knew it of old, and hated it. More burn cases. *At least they'll be alive. But will they like it—*

As usual for large emergencies, Sal took herself into the prep room, where triage was taking place. There was already a sad row of plastic-sheeted shapes over on the side of the room; dead, or soon to be: too hurt to waste time with, in any case. The second group, those awaiting surgery but not critically enough wounded to need it right away, was fairly large. Sal deafened herself for the moment to their cries and stopped long enough to pronounce the general absolution over those already dead, then turned back to see to the cat-two people—trying to make out who was conscious, who needed a hand to hold, who was dealing with their pain sufficiently to notice someone with them.

She was almost past him before she saw the sheen of the dark pelt, the darker spots, and the flesh under it, startlingly pale, except where the burns blistered it. His jaw worked, but no sound came out.

Stricken, Sal dropped to her knees beside him. For some time he didn't notice she was there, just worked his jaw. A slight, slight moaning came from him: not the sound of the beast, now, not at all, but that of a child in pain too great to otherwise express. After a while, this stopped, and one eye opened. The other was burned closed, or burned away entirely—there was no telling, nothing but a mass of blistered, furless flesh all down that side of his face.

It took a while for the eye to see her, for the sight to register. She was already speaking the words softly, whether he would understand them or not; in the middle of the prayer he said, rough-voiced, halting: "Who are you talking to?"

"You and God," she said. "Now shut up!" She was horrified at her own tears as she went on with it. " 'Lord, visit and relieve Your servant here, for whom we pray. Restore him, if it be Your pleasure, to his former health—' "

"One of us at least is here," H'ewa said, his jaw dropping briefly. "Not for long, perhaps. They caught us—halfway—"

He coughed bloody froth, could not go on for a moment. "No matter," he said. "I had made my report: last night."

Sal stopped praying and stared at him. "On what? The existence of God?" She was tempted to laugh through the tears.

H'ewa hissed—maybe it was laughter, too, or pain. "Just so."

"And what conclusions did you come to?"

"Noncombatant," H'ewa said. "But possibly available for discussions."

She shook her head, in amusement and bitter rue. "What will this mean for your people?"

"In the war? Nothing. But after we have all survived it—we will have one more thing to talk about, perhaps. For a long time. We have been looking— We thought we were the only ones—"

There was more blood, this time, and less froth. Sal knew this sign. It meant lungs that had had more vacuum than was good for them: many vessels ruptured, maybe a big one. "I need a reassessment here!" she cried, but all the staff were busy, running around like mad people: and those golden eyes met hers, stilled her.

"Now that I have done some of the doing—" said the voice of the beast, calm, as if speaking to a child. "Talk to these Powers for me, so that I can—see how it is done. It is practice. You will have to—do the same again, for others will come looking, in a while. You will have—quite a few visitors."

Sal swallowed, and on the impulse of the moment changed prayers. " 'God, giver of all good gifts, who has made varying Orders in Your scheme of things, give Your grace to those called today to Your service, replenish them with the truth, so that they can faithfully serve You—' "

Much too much blood, this time. "Junie!" she shouted, trying to get the attention of the only nurse she knew well, but no one came. H'ewa turned his head, and exhaled blood, and nothing else. His eyes did not close, but their gold began to tarnish.

Sal wiped her eyes and went on with it, even to the last line, for though breathing might stop, the nurses had always told her that hearing was the last thing to go. " 'You are a priest forever,' " she said, " 'even after the order of Melchisidech.' "

She stood up then, as one of the other nurses came along, knelt down by the body, touched the control on the stretcher, and steered it into the OR. Sal watched them take H'ewa's corpse away, and knew it was hopeless; but at the same time, could not lose an odd feeling of anticipation. *Apostle to the Emry? Not apostle, that's too high. Missionary?*

" 'I am the handmaiden of the Lord,' " it said in the documentation. Sal smiled a sad smile. " 'Let it be done to me as you say,' " she whispered.

Meantime—

She went off to kneel by a man whose arm had been blown off, checked the tourniquet, and began to pray.

IN DANGER'S WAY

As the two opposing fleets converged on Emry, the intensity of the battle grew. Enough Fleet ships had been eliminated to force lulls in their attack that allowed the Ichtons to regroup. The Ichtons had themselves suffered heavily enough that they were finding it difficult to protect the mother ships and the tens of thousands of soldiers and millions of eggs they carried. But no one could fight harder than an Ichton protecting those eggs.

The *Hawking* arrived at Emry to find the planet already under attack. Anton Brand held the battlestation in the system's Oort cloud, where it could hide among the cometary debris. Even so the constant parade of ships to and from the station would soon divulge its location. Nonetheless, Brand made every effort to disrupt the Ichton attack. Fierce battles erupted as the Fleet and their allies tried to tear their way through the more numerous Ichton attackers and destroy the mother ships. On the second attempt a sortie from the surface of Emry actually succeeded in tearing apart one of the massive Ichton vessels. This made the remaining Ichtons meet the next incursion in an almost suicidal frenzy. Two days later the siege of Emry continued unabated.

Reluctantly Anton Brand stripped the *Hawking*'s escort until every functioning warship had entered the battle. Soon even hastily commandeered armed merchant ships joined the battle. Anton Brand had at this point committed every ship that carried a weapon except the *Hawking* itself. The station was simply too valuable as a base to risk in combat. But this meant that before the final stages of the conflict had been joined, Brand had committed all but his last reserve.

Under sublight drive the sheer bulk of the *Hawking* made the battlestation slow and hard to maneuver. This meant that the three hundred laser cannon and two hundred missile tubes that served as the station's final line of defense had to be manned constantly. All were needed to drive off the occasional Ichton sortie against the station itself. Already stretched to the limit, the Fleet personnel turned to the civilian levels for reinforcements. Considering the low level of morale, this was not an easy task.

SHOOTING STAR
by Jody Lynn Nye

"Never!" Lyseo announced with a look of horror. He glanced up in outrage from the image of his face in the makeup mirror to those of his two visitors.

"C'mon, Hammy, we need you to bang the drum. It's just a few little training films. So what?"

The scene: Lyseo's dressing room. The characters: Arend McKechnie Lyseo himself, Fleet Lieutenant Jill FarSeeker, and Kem Thoreson, Lyseo's personal manager. The time: perhaps badly chosen.

"So *what*?" demanded Lyseo. "I did training films before I took up performance art, me bucko. I even did a recruitment film for the Fleet." He drew himself up from his chair into a perfect attention stance, and forty years dropped from his mobile face as it formed into a look of terrified obedience. "Lyseo does not repeat himself."

Morale Officer FarSeeker sighed. She was a small, businesslike woman of twenty-nine, with a thick knot of straight black hair tied up at the back of her head. "What constitutes repetition, Lyseo?" she asked patiently. "You've done Old Earth classics a thousand times."

"But never the same way twice," the actor explained, his long hands describing the cone of a spotlight before him, obviously peopling it in his mind with actors. "Ah, the differences you can bring out, the nuances of emotion!" He regarded her sternly. "How many nuances can there be for 'slide bolt home, making certain the power supply is disengaged before disassembling'?"

Jill FarSeeker laughed, losing her composure. "All right, they are boring, but they're necessary. Be reasonable."

For her, Lyseo allowed a tiny smile to touch his eyes. He gathered up her hands in his and kissed them. "Lyseo is never reasonable either. Why me?"

"McCaul's idea, really. We're running out of trained gunners, and frankly, our only remaining pool of beings from which to draw is the civilian population of the *Hawking*. It's a frightening concept to most of them, so our demonstrator needs to be a civilian. The Fleet won this engagement, but casualties were higher than we expected. We've only got a few days to enlist some volunteers, while the *Hawking* cleans up in this system and we move on to the Emry's. Our scouts report we're going to face a massive force there, and we need backup techs.

The Emry are already skirmishing with the enemy, so time is short. I could use someone from the theater company, but Kay wants the most visible, most impressive, most charismatic personality on board the ship to be the center of these videos. Your presence alone will make more people watch them."

With every erg of praise, Lyseo was visibly softening. "These monstrosities won't be beamed back to the Alliance, will they?" His daily performances interpreting his impressions of life on board the *Hawking* were broadcast toward the Alliance star cluster to be collected on museum-grade video cube as his legacy to Art. The Fleet concurred in the practice, seeing Lyseo's visible support of the *Hawking* and its allies as a way to help secure funding for domestic projects as well as keep interest alive in the battlestation project itself. The same charisma was vital to engender enthusiasm in the instruction program.

"Not if you don't want them to be," Jill promised him. "They're strictly for internal use. We need to be able to put trained personnel onto the warships, and we need them soonest. You can help greatly by cooperating."

"I am already helping. The first encounter is fixed for 11:35 exactly, the second eight hours and ten minutes after that. I think you'll be well satisfied."

"That's all for morale," Jill pointed out. "Once you've raised their spirits, we need to channel them for maximum effectiveness."

"Do not spout your military jargon at me," Lyseo said, holding his head between his hands. He smoothed back his mane of white hair and straightened up, every move as graceful as if it had been preplanned. "All right, I will do it—but under one condition: I get complete creative control."

"That's reasonable, Jill," Kem put in, seeing that his client was ready to give in. He put an arm around Lyseo's shoulders. "Ari's got a reputation to protect. He can't be seen doing bit-bite dialogue."

"Okay," Jill replied, allowing herself to seem beaten. "Can we start today after your performance?"

"That would be acceptable," Lyseo said grandly. He put a hand each on their shoulders and ushered them toward the door. "And now, if you'll excuse me, I have my regular job to think about. Heavens around us, a regular job! Poor old Hambone."

The dressing-room door slid shut behind them. Jill heard the lock engage.

"So much for the early lunch he invited me to," she complained, looking at her chronometer. "Well, that's all right. I have other things I can take care of."

"He's thinking about your videos," Kem assured her. "You know how he gets when he's got a new project to chew on."

"I suppose I do," Jill sighed. "At least we got him to agree. I thought it would be harder than that."

"You applied the soap just right. Lieutenant McCaul owes you a raise, getting Hammy to agree without a week-long fuss."

Jill shrugged. "He's the best performer for the job. Otherwise, I wouldn't be bothering him. With his support behind the training program, which otherwise could look like enforced conscription, my job will be a lot easier. It's going to be tough enough to sell the idea to grocers and hairdressers that they need to learn how to run laser cannon. I refuse to give them 'Your Starship Needs You' pablum. These are all adults, and they deserve to know the truth about their situation, but I have to prepare them first."

Thoreson sucked in his breath over his lower lip. "You're right, sweetie. Sorry I made it sound like a video contract coup. There'd be riots if you don't handle this right."

"There may be riots anyhow, Kem," Jill sighed. "I simply hope I've set enough backfires to keep from having to fight an internal battle while we're engaging the Ichtons on the outside." She squeezed Kem on the forearm and headed toward the lift.

"Lieutenant!" Jill's office door slid open on a breathless woman she recognized as the day hostess of The Emerald, the fancy restaurant on Green deck. "Trouble!"

Jill was on her feet before she thought to ask. "What kind of trouble?"

The woman, about fifty standard years of age, wiped her round, pink face with her sateenoid sleeve. "Master Lyseo and a man are having a loud argument in the lounge. I tried to separate them, but they got around me. *He* told me not to interfere." Jill didn't have to ask which one "he" was. "They're *throwing* things. Can you do something before one of them gets hurt?"

Jill grabbed the hostess's arm and hustled her toward the lift. "What are they arguing about?"

"The other man—I don't know him—made some kind of disparaging remark about the last battle, you know, that we're losing by inches, and we'll be eaten alive by the Ichtons. Master Lyseo was just about down his throat in a millisecond."

Jill groaned. She pounded on the lift panel, as if hitting the buttons would make the transport come sooner. It wasn't like Lyseo to enter into an argument in public. If someone tried to drag him into a fight, he was more likely to zing his opponent and walk away.

The transit from Blue Fifteen to The Emerald took just a year and a half longer than forever. Jill was nearly bouncing up and down in impatience to get there and see what mischief Lyseo had managed to raise in the half hour since she had seen him.

To her relief, no one else had become involved in the altercation. Lyseo and a human male in an Indie's flight suit faced off across ten meters of cleared space in the restaurant lounge. There were broken dishes on the floor against the wall behind Lyseo, and an upside-down plant half out of its pot not far from the trader's feet.

The trader sneered at Lyseo, but did not close the distance between them. The impresario was looking uncommonly dangerous, and the Indie probably didn't dare to see what the older man was capable of. Jill eyed the man. He looked slightly familiar, reminding her of someone with whom she'd had recent contact. She wondered if he was one of the paladins, one whom she didn't know well; or one of her "problem children," a discontented civilian who had passed the psych tests showing that he was fit to join the *Hawking* but who couldn't resist stirring up trouble in a group. There was no time to check out her database; tension was escalating right in front of her.

"It's a crock!" the man barked, his voice cracking with passionate fury. "The Fleet brass are feeding us a line of sewage that we can ever beat the Ichtons! We've lost too many ships, too many pilots. We might as well give up and go back—admit it!"

"Admit it?" Lyseo boomed, filling the room with his magnificent voice. "Never! The Fleet will not fail in its mission. Perhaps you're too young to remember it, sonny, but the odds were just as great in the Family war, which they won rather handily."

"Handily," the man mocked, striking himself under the chin with the edge of his hand. It was a gesture of insult. Lyseo glared. "After fifty years of war, pops, in case you've forgotten. We're finished. You people make me sick. I'm tired of being cooped up with people like you in this centimeter-square can prison. We're too vulnerable. We have to draw back."

"Retreat? In the name of all traditions, boy, how did you pass the psychological screening? Don't think of the *Hawking* as a soap bubble that could pop on the suntides. Think of it more as a leukocyte in the bloodstream of the galaxy, here to wipe out an intruding organism." The man snorted, and Lyseo raised his voice further. Jill stepped forward to intervene, but an upswept hand stayed her. "If you don't think we have a chance, then throw your strength into our effort, boy," Lyseo said. There was a ragged cheer of encouragement from the restaurant patrons at these words. He thrust out a hand toward them. "See? Your fellow *prisoners* agree. Stop telling us what can't be done, and help with what *can*."

His oration earned him a scattering of applause. Reddening, the young man realized that he was surrounded by an audience. Jill decided now was the perfect time to intervene and diffuse the situation, but she wasn't quick enough to stop the Indie from reacting. He cast about for something else to use as a weapon. His eye fell upon a huge flowered vase sitting on a shelf on the wall. The hostess beside Jill moaned and clutched her hands together as the man seized it. He threw it at Lyseo, and she shrieked. Jill gasped.

With magnificent reflexes, Lyseo snagged the vase out of the air by its rim and tossed it to her. With her jaw agape, Jill caught the ceramic um and wrapped both arms around it for safety. To her amazement, she noted that it was a lot lighter than expected, and much sturdier. Surreptitiously, she tapped one side with a knuckle. It gave off a dull *tank-tank* sound. It was a fake, made of extruded plastic. Then she noticed the time. On the fancy chrono on the wall, it was just past 11:45. So this was the morale-raising exhibition. The confrontation was a setup, engineered by Lyseo.

She was so involved with her discovery that she missed most of the parting shot the artist fired at the retreating trader, in which he declared that the Fleet was stronger, more enduring, more intelligently run, more adaptable than its opponent, however great its numbers, "And we shall be victorious!"

There was a round of frenzied applause. Lyseo affected then to notice that he, too, had an audience, and bowed, a little sheepishly, to his public. The restaurant patrons and a crowd who had gathered from surrounding levels at the rumor of a fight in The Emerald gave him a standing ovation. He waved jauntily to them and strode to greet Jill with a kiss. Gallantly, he took the vase from her hands and restored it to its pedestal.

"Next performance at 1900 hours," he whispered in her ear as the hostess hurried over to see that the expensive *objet d'art* was unharmed. "No autographs, please."

"Why, you fraud," Jill said admiringly. "Who was he?"

"One of your underrated and overworked theatrical company, my dear, only slightly disguised. He'll be master of his own repertory guild one day. Does a splendid burn and dudgeon. Shall we sit down, my dear? Did I not promise you lunch in this overpriced beanery?"

"Yes, but do I dare eat it with you?" Jill asked, shaking her head doubtfully. "You have shocking manners in public."

He threw back his head and laughed. "I promise you that all the crockery will remain on the table, and knives will be used for no other purpose than severing bites of food."

"It was a great performance," Jill admitted after they had ordered. "I was completely convinced. How do you do that so well? Your speech was perfect, it was so . . . so stirring."

"I believe in what I said," Lyseo replied simply, hands extended palms upward. "Otherwise I would not have risked my life, which I hold precious, in such a venture as this space station. You ought to know by now which things are the greasepaint and which things hold true throughout. Among those things that are true is that I love you, and you bring bright starlight to me in the midst of the void. There's little enough I can do to return this sublime, matchless favor."

He raised his glass to her, and Jill returned his toast. Even after nearly two years of daily contact, his words, his voice, had a way of making her quiver all over. While their love affair was hardly eternal bliss, Jill was happier than she had ever been. All her life, she had admired Lyseo's work. In the Alliance, it was hard to find many higher up in the entertainment pantheon than he. She was amazed to find herself hopelessly crazy about the man behind the public image, the sensitive, flamboyant, easily moved personality that relied on her, trusted her for her honesty. He didn't need fans; he had billions of them who loved everything he did, good or bad. Jill just loved the man himself.

Lyseo was in a good mood. The day's performance was a humorous pantomime that involved the master entertainer transforming his lean frame into semblances of each of the allied races, one after another. Soon, a catlike Emry was chasing a fluttering, birdlike Nedge all over the stage. The Nedge fled, in spite of the Emry's insistence that he was trying to be friendly, and that any suggestion of aggression was all a misunderstanding. Jill, sitting in the control room at Lyseo's insistence, howled along with the technicians. She dashed tears out of her eyes at the little Emry pouncing after the terrified Nedge, trying to make friends.

"Damn, he's good," the Khalian director said. "My cheek muscles hurt from grinning. You'd think we had a stageful of actors. How can he do it, day after day?

"He never repeats himself," Jill said, watching the Emry herd the birdman into a corner, where he rubbed up against him, kitten style. "I love it, but I wonder how much it will do for interspecies relations."

"Are you joking, esteemed ma'am?" the director asked, hissing with laughter. "The Emry delegation already called asking for holocopies to use in their diplomatic training packets—for use in those very intersystem relations after we've saved their system." Jill noticed that the Khalian meant when, not if, and approved his optimism. "When Master Lyseo showed up and asked to observe them, they thought they'd soon be featuring in a show. They think Lyseo has a point."

Jill admitted that he did. With the appearance of new allies, members of the Alliance were having to adjust to the values and characteristics of each. Lyseo had found the one sure key to helping such diverse races understand one another: humor. Of all their new contacts, the Emry were the friendliest and least likely to need further exhortations to their emissaries to use tact. She wished the same could be said of others. In Jill's opinion, the Saurians, whose ravaged home planet definitely justified their grief, also demanded significant concessions based on their status as galactic orphans, making it impossible to feel much sympathy for them.

Besides, those aboard the *Hawking* were beginning to wonder if they themselves would survive much longer. The classified message from Commander Brand ordering training of any qualified civilian in station defense continued to distract her from enjoying her favorite entertainment. How long could they continue to supply manpower to run the ships and guns? In worst case, what if the battlestation itself had to participate in an attack? There would be nowhere safe for damaged ships to run to, no hospital facility free of enemy fire. Help-less isolation, in the midst of the galactic center, terrified Jill as much as it did any of the nervous civvies or Indies on board. In the meantime, the *Hawking* made its way toward the Emry system with all speed. Brand must have liquid refrigerant in his veins.

The thought of a last stand with all resources committed had already occurred to someone who phoned in to Jill's paladins, the audio jocks who kept the action going over the sixty broadcast channels circulating through the battle cruiser. It had been an uncomfortable rumor for the better part of the last month, undoubt-edly since it became evident how difficult it was to wipe out an Ichton fleet. Inde-pendent traders plying the newly opened space lanes collected gossip and spread it among the civilian population of the *Hawking*. Jill had had to perform minor works of wonder to keep morale from plummeting each time more was discov-ered about the Ichton culture, or when the Ichtons staged surprise attacks on the Fleet. The fact that there hadn't been suicides was a miracle.

She couldn't take credit for the best of the spirit-raising. The morale laureate belonged jointly to Lyseo and Driscoll Strind, Jill's self-confessed knight in denim armor and the most popular audio jock in the ship. Strind, with his cool head and calming, deep baritone voice, maintained order and restored perspective on his daily show, and wasn't afraid to go all the way to the top brass to get answers his listeners needed to have. Strind had credibility ship-wide. He was Jill's fervent supporter and unmentioned second choice for the instruction videos.

It might have been easier if she had simply approached the paladin first. Getting Lyseo to buckle down and recite the words in the simple script was a lot harder than she had even feared it might be.

"There are three hundred laser ports on the surface of this vessel," Lyseo complained, eyeing the minute gunnery chamber in the rear of the "south pole's" food service center. "Or so this uninspired missal tells me. Why choose this dreary outlet for me to do my piece?"

"Because it's well out of the way of daily operations, and ninety percent of the extant installations match the configuration or have elements in common with this one, including those aboard commissioned attack vessels," replied Gunnery Captain Thano Carrin, Jill's official consultant on the project. He was what she classified as "regular army," a specimen of the by-God, by-the-book military mind. "We want the information conveyed in this exercise to have the widest utility."

Lyseo winced, and Jill stepped in to translate. "You mean most of them look like this one," she said. Carrin nodded.

"Right. All the low-power gunports are identical. All that's needed when the alert sounds is for the person or persons closest to the port to strap in and connect the communicator to his, her, or its aural appendages, and fire away at the bugs—on command from the battle bridge, of course. They're really very simple to use. Anyone could do it."

"If anyone can," Lyseo said dangerously, "then *get* anyone. Anyone else."

Carrin turned red with impatience. Kem Thoreson leaped in to the rescue. "Yeah, but no one can show them how to do it better than you can, Ari. Go on."

Jill recognized Lyseo in a difficult mood, and stepped in. "Let's get the take done quickly, and get it over with, shall we?" she suggested.

With a calibration visor strapped around her head and resting firmly on her beak, the Nedge camerawoman set up holopoints around the inside of the gun turret, then placed a small, circular red light near the end of the sights and one to the side of the chamber next to the controls. "If you face the one that lights up, Master Lyseo, we'll be able to synch captioned credits in the edit."

Lyseo took his place in the gun emplacement and adjusted the seat to fit his frame. With a wink at Jill, he slipped on the communications gear and settled back. Captain Carrin pulled a headset from a wall niche and put it on.

"I'm taking the place of the battle bridge, citizen," he said. A tinny echo of his voice was audible from Lyseo's earphones. "I'll tell you what to do and give you target sightings to fire at. This is what you'd hear if this were an actual attack."

Lyseo nodded and tapped the earpiece with a long forefinger, the little gesture dynamic with focused energy. The actor's whole stance depicted fear, determination, and excitement all at once. Jill began to feel a sense of urgency, as if there were a real battle going on, and he was part of it. That was Lyseo's gift. He could make even a make-believe situation seem real and exciting.

Carrin ran him through the mechanics of operating the gun and how to read the screens. The actor was a quick study, picking up the mechanics accurately after one or two essays. "You are number 231. The Ichton ships fly slowly, but you have to take into account the fact that you're on a ship moving many times that of your opponent. Your own speed can ruin your aim, so unless you're an ace, let the targeting computer follow your mark. Once you've acquired your target and the computer locks on and verifies you have an enemy ship, not an ally, fire using the hand control."

Lyseo nodded, his eyes sweeping the skies and the tiny screen at eye level for imaginary enemy craft.

Carrin burst out suddenly, "Number 231, enemy at 245 degrees, 1500 klicks off center! Target and destroy!"

The gunner's head went up, eager eyes sweeping the darkness to the left of center. His laser's muzzle followed as he moved the hand controls, tracking the enemy craft. There was a muffled beeping as the computer locked on to a piece of space debris. Carrin glanced at the heads-up display to make certain that Lyseo's target wasn't live, then shouted, "Fire!"

The red tracer beam lanced out of the gun, striking the fragment of rock and ice, which exploded in a glorious display of white and hot yellow. "Well done, 231," Carrin congratulated him. Lyseo's shoulders relaxed.

The cinematographer signaled him to begin his lines. "To insure the continued defense of this space station and our newfound allies, the civilian and military administrations of the *Hawking* want you to know how to operate the defensive emplacements aboard the station and its attendant vessels when our commissioned comrades are wounded or disabled."

He swung around toward the second camera spot, raising a hand for a sweeping gesture. "Our numbers are few, but our spirit is great. *You* are a vital—OW!" The hand had whisked up past his chest and smacked solidly into the edge of the bulkhead. Lyseo curled up over his hand, hissing.

"Cut," the Nedge squawked into her throat mike. "Are you all right, citizen?"

"Confound it!" he shouted, his voice echoing in the metal-walled corridor. Jill winced. "Why are we using such a miserably small cubbyhole as this?"

"It's a typical laser station," Carrin replied, a little bewildered.

"I can't work in here," the star declared. "There isn't room for me. Look at my hand!" There was a dark purple bruise like a whip mark coming up across the back of Lyseo's palm. His knuckles were white.

"It should be all right, citizen," the Nedge said imperturbably, "if you keep your gestures small. Do you want to start again?"

"Why in blazes should I? This isn't Shakespeare or Eerk Kraakknek."

"Perhaps another location, with more elbow room, would be the answer?" Jill offered. She smiled hopefully at Lyseo. Her hope of getting the filming over in just a few takes was fast becoming a forlorn one. The crew gathered up the equipment and followed Captain Carrin to the next laser port. A Khalian gunner recognized the great Lyseo first and the captain's bars on the officer consultant second, and scrambled out of his seat with whiskers a-twitch.

Lyseo climbed into the seat and looked around him. "No." He crossed his arms, refusing even to put on the headset. "The lighting in here is dismal. I want another one."

"What?" Captain Carrin demanded. "This one is fine. It's big enough to jump rope in."

"I have full creative control," Lyseo reminded him. "Take me to a suitable setting, or let me go back to my dressing room. I have other engagements."

The little Khalian looked disappointed until the actor patted him on the back. "It's not your fault, little friend. Fortunes of war, fortunes of war, that is all."

The Khalian brightened, but he was the only happy being in the corridor. Resigned, the camera crew loaded up and trudged down the beltway, stopping at each laser port. Lyseo found something to complain of in each one, and rejected them in turn.

"I swear that if you're marching us around the perimeter just to get a rise out of us, I'll make the camera tech save all the takes and beam them straight back to the Alliance," Jill said warningly.

"I am quite serious about finding just the right place to make your dull little video," Lyseo replied. "It could only be your charms, raven-winged maiden, that led me to agree to such a tedious proposal. It will waste all the rest of my day and most of my night."

"Only if you don't cooperate," Jill observed. "We're only days out of Emry space. We don't have a lot of time to waste on theatrics, not especially yours."

"You wound me," Lyseo said plaintively. "I serve Art. Wouldn't you prefer that these videos be of the highest caliber that may be achieved? I promise the next setting we choose will be the last."

"All right." Jill allowed herself to be mollified.

"Yellow alert," the loudspeaker said as they emerged from the lift on the next level. "Yellow alert. Ion trails from Ichton-type ships have been detected in this area. Please stand by for any further instructions. That is all."

Well, that wasn't terribly surprising. The system had to be full of Ichton spoor, from the ships that had retreated from the battle with the Fleet. The indicators ran on automatic, sending the alarm directly to the computer without relaying it first through a living operator. The announcement repeated in several languages and on screens at the lift stations. Jill mentally crossed her fingers that the shrinks and the paladins were ready for another panic attack. The passengers waiting for the lift immediately looked nervous. One of them abandoned the queue and hurried down the aisle toward a cross-corridor. The others muttered among themselves as they boarded.

"Everyone's nervous," Jill commented. "There shouldn't be another Ichton for light-years around us."

"Every moment, it becomes more vital to strengthen our defense," observed Lyseo, carefully watching the faces of the people who passed him. The crew stopped a robot transport vehicle going toward the nearest laser ports and loaded the equipment aboard. Lyseo shook his head at the first few, all occupied by gunnery staff on alert, then, to Jill's surprise, nodded thoughtfully at the fourth. She signaled the robot brain to stop and let them off.

"What do you think, citizen?" asked the Nedge. "Will it do?"

"Plenty of room to swing about in," the actor said, surveying the alcove more closely, "even for my overblown posturing. Well lit, clean, almost ideal."

"I'll settle for almost," Jill said, and turned to the crew. "Set up, please. I'll clear things with the gunners."

Like the Khalian on the upper level, the two human female officers were delighted to make way for the great Lyseo.

"Will anyone be able to tell it was our port he sat in?" one asked. "Maybe if you let me leave the picture of my mother in it? She runs the arcade on Blue Fourteen. She'd be so proud."

"Certainly," the actor replied, glancing at the small holo of a middle-aged woman in a smock. "Her image will act as a reminder of those for whom we are fighting, and why we must succeed."

Both sergeants giggled and sighed while he clambered into the cockpit and strapped in. The emplacement was twice as wide as most of the others to make room for a second laser and operator.

Carrin hooked himself up to the corridor-side headset and ran Lyseo through the operations once again. Lyseo checked the mechanism of the new weapon, getting used to the differences between its action and the one with which he had worked before. When the actor nodded that he was ready, Carrin started him off with mock targets. The Nedge muttered quiet directions to her crew. She made quiet clicking sounds of approval to herself as Lyseo provided them with good action shots full of expression that also showed clearly how the hands were placed, and what use should be made of the monitors and computer.

"Gunner 198," Carrin barked, "target coming around to you at 90—that's three o'clock, mister—maximum range."

"I hear you, sir," Lyseo responded, swiveling the laser to meet it.

"Red alert," the computerized voice announced over the tannoy. "Red alert. All crew to battle stations. All civilians to secured areas. Ichton fighters approaching. Red alert."

Jill slammed her palm against a wall-mounted communicator. "Battle bridge, this is Lieutenant FarSeeker. What's going on out there?"

The reply crackled through the speaker. "A bunch of orphan fighters without a mother ship, Lieutenant. Looks like they're on a suicide mission to do what damage they can because they can't get away. Secure to quarters or battlestation. Out."

"Out," she replied.

Jill's eyes widened. A sneak attack! The Ichtons must have set up an ambush inside the Oort cloud surrounding the system. People and vehicles hurried in all directions through the wide hall, rushing toward their stations. An alarm went off, and there was shouting and the squeal of straining machinery.

"Target destroyed, sir," Lyseo told the headset microphone crisply, and Carrin nodded in response, as lost in playacting as the dramatist himself.

On the small amber screen under Lyseo's nose, the unmistakable formation of Ichton fighters moved into target range The first sign of them that was visible to the naked eye was the gleam of the small lights at the extremes of each small ship.

"Multiple targets approaching at 135 degrees, 10,000 klicks from center," Carrin recited automatically, and stopped, surprised, as he realized that this enemy was real. One of the gunners sprang into her seat and strapped in. "Get him out of there," she barked, gesturing at the actor.

"Sir, may I take over for you now?" the other gunner asked, holding out her hand to the actor.

"I have it!" Lyseo announced, tracking it with his laser and paying no attention to the young woman. The chair swiveled around and downward.

Startled, the officer glanced at Carrin for orders. Carrin looked at Jill. Jill shrugged. There were 256 laser emplacements arrayed about the *Hawking*. Sixty or more were covering this quadrant of the space station's defenses. If one was manned by a neophyte, it shouldn't hurt anything. Carrin nodded once, sharply, giving approval. The camera crew, who had started to take down their equipment, hastily reconnected everything.

"Steady . . . steady," Lyseo admonished his targeting computer. "Hold it right there, you! Yes! Permission to fire?"

"Given," Carrin said, hearing the word echoed a second later on the helmet from the battle bridge. Lyseo squeezed the trigger, causing the red beam to lance out into the darkness. Other red needles joined it, converging on a target a long way off. There was a tiny explosion of white that bloomed and winked out.

"He got one," the Nedge said excitedly. "Well done, citizen!" The crew cheered.

Lyseo wasn't listening. With the single-mindedness for which he was famous, he had immersed himself in what he was doing, and doing it incredibly well for having had only one lesson, Jill thought.

The *Hawking*'s fighters scrambled within seconds, and green dots joined the white ones on the small amber screen. Lyseo's chair swung first one way and another as he lined up on targets. He shot at several more, but the computer confirmed no other kills besides the first one. Dozens of red tracer lights lanced out alongside his, searching for the touch of Ichton craft. The Fleet fighters were also getting kills several seconds before the gunners' eyes registered that their targets weren't out there anymore. White fire bloomed occasionally from above or below them as a plasma torpedo launched from the larger cannon at the *Hawking*'s poles.

There were fewer than sixty Ichton fighters. In minutes, the battle was at an end. The loudspeaker announced that the enemy had been destroyed, and the siren emitted two blasts for all clear. The corridor was filled with cheers and hoots of relief. Jill was relieved, too. The *Hawking* could defend herself, in an emergency. She hoped she never had to live through it again.

Lyseo fell back in the chair with a gasp, as if he had been swimming underwater. He glanced up at the camera at his shoulder, which was still recording.

"There," he said, drawing himself up with dignity. "Now, if *I* can do it, *anyone* can do it."

"Wonderful," crowed the Nedge.

"That was really well done, sir," one of the gunners said. He turned to look at her. "You've got a natural eye for it."

Surprised eyebrows arched into his hairline, Lyseo glanced over at Jill, who raised her hands and began to applaud. She was joined by Carrin, the film crew, and the two gunners.

"Encore!" Jill called, her eyes filled with mischief. "Encore!"

"My dear young lady," he said, grinning at her affectionately, "Lyseo *never* repeats himself." Unbuckling the straps, he eased himself out of the seat and stretched. "That was a fascinating experience, citizens, but I have no wish to repeat it. Besides, I have an appointment." He took Jill's arm and steered her away toward the nearest lift.

"Where are we going?" Jill asked, looking over her shoulder at the crew. The Nedge cocked her head, asking for permission. Helplessly, Jill nodded back. The crew began to put away the equipment. There was plenty of good footage, and it would make a dynamic training video. There was the ring of truth in every single frame. The first chance she got, she'd call up Driscoll Strind and leak news of the video to him. People would be clamoring to see it before they thought about the fact it was meant to drag them out to do active duty. There might be a number of volunteer gunners, all Lyseo fans who wanted to emulate their idol.

As for Lyseo himself? "Come, my dear," he urged, escorting her into the lift. "If we hurry, you can catch my next surprise performance. I'm planning to have a duel in the video library. Data cubes at thirty paces. My opponent takes a dive on the fourth toss." He grinned, the lazy, magnificent smile that Jill loved. "I always prefer to fight battles that I know I'm going to win."

THE LAST RESERVE

Napoleon is often quoted as saying that the army with the last reserve wins the battle. After three days orbiting the Emry system, it was apparent to Anton Brand that without his introducing some new factor they would be unable to drive the Ichtons away from the already-battered Emry home world.

In an attempt to give the Emry some relief Brand ordered a complete withdrawal. He had hoped the Ichtons would follow his ships outward, as they had during the earlier parts of the month-long battle. Instead they used the pause to redouble their attack on Emry. It was apparent that the Ichtons were continuing their new policy of destroying all opposition at any cost. He would have to recommit quickly or lose the planet.

Six hours after the withdrawal a squadron of the largest of the Fleet ships made a near light-speed run through the Emry system. Streaking past the Ichton screen they managed to destroy two more of the ten remaining mother ships. But the Ichtons responded quickly by throwing up a barrage ahead of the fast-moving ships. Moving too rapidly to avoid the missiles and mines, the Fleet force lost three of their eight heavy cruisers. This was too high a price and Commander Brand forbade any repeat of the maneuver.

Two days after the loss of the cruisers the battle had degenerated into a series of strikes on the Ichtons who had formed a widespread globe around their mother ships. This globe then settled into a distant orbit around Emry and when they were not directly engaged by the Fleet ships the Ichtons returned to the merciless bombardment of the planet. Anton Brand had not left the battle bridge since ordering the withdrawal four days earlier. He had slept only in short naps, unable to pull himself away from the battle. Finally Dr. Althea Morgan appeared and threatened to declare him medically incompetent unless he slept.

As it turned out, Commander Brand only got three hours rest before the dramatic conclusion of the battle.

BATTLE OFFERING
by Katherine Kurtz

The catastrophic fate of the Gerson world left scant reason to suppose that the enemy was anything other than pitiless and brutal. More than an hour of visual recording brought along by the last of the Gersons to escape told of planetary devastation almost beyond imagining, and on a scale hitherto unknown in Alliance memory except as a result of natural disaster.

For the gentle, bearlike Gersons had resisted invasion all too well. Before the coming of the Ichtons, the Gerson planet had been blanketed by rich farmlands and lush forests almost primeval by most worlds' standards, its land masses girdled by wide seas teeming with life. Modest technological achievement had given the Gersons reasonable commerce with their nearest neighbors in the galactic core, but had also made their world ripe for exploitation by a race whose imperative was to expand, whatever the cost to other life-forms.

Now the Gerson world was a smoldering cinder. The Ichtons destroyed what would not submit. Impersonal and efficient, the Ichtons simply overwhelmed whatever stood in their path, no matter the level of indigenous civilization. This was not mere policy; it was a fact of existence. They had been hurt too much to sacrifice any warriors or ships to preserving resources while subduing a new planet. Any resistance by cities or military installations provoked immediate neutralization by antimatter and other bombing, followed by occupation of egg colony sites and the beginning of the stripping and exploitation of all the planet's resources.

The unvarying pattern of Ichton expansion then became a cold, methodical extermination of all higher life-forms. The dead were eaten, whatever their species; all plant life likewise became fodder for the expanding Ichton colonies. Like the legendary Terran locusts they somewhat resembled, the Ichtons left nothing living where their swarms had passed. Forbearance and compassion were not terms within the Ichton comprehension.

Shaking his head, Commander Anton Brand punched the Cancel button on the arm of his recliner and laid his head back, though he did not close his eyes. He had seen the recording too many times already, and the scenes he had cut short already haunted what little sleep he managed to steal between bouts of battle. The slagged

Gerson cities and barren, windswept plains were bad enough. But the worst was the final scene—an aerial glimpse of a cowering Gerson female trying desperately to shield her cub from the notice of half a dozen Ichton soldiers advancing through a burning village. The first time Brand had watched the Ichtons dismember the pair and begin devouring them alive, he had been all but physically ill.

The twittering sound of his intercom broke the intensity of unwanted memory and recalled him to the present, where the Ichtons were threatening to add another world to the string of stripped and lifeless husks already left in their wake. The little ready room adjacent to the command bridge was his personal hideaway for snatching a few minutes' respite from the tension of command, but it was also conveniently close enough that he could never really escape.

Thumbing the response plate, he said, "Brand here."

"Tashi here, Commander," said his second-in-command. "Ah—we have an incident developing down on Yellow Two, in one of the destroyer bays. It seems a couple of dozen Gersons, all armed, are asking for one of the destroyers. I've already got a security team on the scene, and so far it hasn't gotten ugly, yet. Now the Gersons are demanding to speak to you specifically. The leader's name is Hooth. He was the commander of that last ship that came in with the Gerson survivors. Shall I have security gas the lot and then clear the bay, or do you want to talk to them?"

"Let me talk to them," Brand said, sitting upright and swinging his feet to the floor. "The Gersons have been through enough, without their own allies turning on them. Who's the security officer in charge?"

"Tucker, sir. He's a level head, and he likes the Gersons, as you know, but it's getting really touchy."

"On my way," Brand said.

Shaking his head, he buckled on his side arm and headed out the door. This move by the Gersons did not really surprise him. He supposed it was only natural to want to strike back at least one small blow for Gerson pride. Out of a onetime population of close to three billion, something less than one hundred Gersons remained. The sheer scale of the genocide carried out by the Ichtons was simply beyond the comprehension of most sentient beings. The Gersons were a noble race, and had seemed to accept their situation with more stoic resignation than one might have expected, but Brand knew how easily anger and helplessness could shift into heroic but futile gesture.

The grav-lift doors were just closing as he approached, and he jogged a few steps to touch the call plate before the lift could leave. The doors immediately retracted to the turning form of a medical officer, who grinned and nodded as she saw him. Anton Brand was, had been, one of the Fleet's rising stars. Tall, and always thin, he had crossed into the painfully thin category months earlier. He had retained the sparkle in his bright blue eyes, but it was surrounded with the wrinkles and dark spots you can only gain from too much responsibility and too little sleep.

" 'Lo, Anton," she said. "That bad?"

"I hope not," he muttered as he ducked in beside her and added, in the direction of the lift's computer, "Deck Yellow Two, command override."

"Right," she said, she and Brand both steadying themselves on grab handles as the lift began to drop with stomach-wrenching speed. "Forget I asked."

Brand gave her a sidelong look and a mirthless smile. Before the war, Maggie Conroy had been a medical planning specialist—no minor function on a ship the size of the *Stephen Hawking*. Of late, however, emergency trauma management had become the specialty of no choice for nearly all Fleet medical personnel. She was wearing a tan lab coat over blue surgical scrubs, with a medical field kit slung over one shoulder.

"Sorry, Maggie. Busy in your section?"

"When is it anything else, these days?" she replied. "I've just been up to the command bridge to make certain everybody's still alert. How're you doing?"

"Ask me in about an hour," he said. "Sheer adrenaline cancels out a lot of ordinary fatigue."

She cocked her head at him. "Sounds serious. Can I help?"

"Depends on how much you know about Gersons. They're asking for a destroyer. What do you want to bet they're considering a suicide run?"

The lift came to a halt with another queasing of stomachs, and the doors sighed open on an impatient-looking security lieutenant and a sergeant at arms.

"Too late, Commander," the lieutenant said, gesturing down a right-angle corridor and already heading out. "Tucker just gave the order to flood the bay with knockout gas. They were trying to take the ship."

"Tell him to belay that order, *now!*" Brand retorted, breaking into a run.

He could hear the lieutenant relaying the message, was aware of the sergeant at arms and Maggie following close behind him as he ran. There were several more security officers in the little control module outside the series of airlocks that led into the docking bay in question, and Brand could hear the whine of large turbo fans starting up as he reached the module.

"Sorry, Commander, but everybody's down," one of the men said. "They started throwing riggers off the boarding ramp. They'd also captured a couple of access keys. If they'd gotten aboard, there wouldn't have been anything we could do to stop them taking the ship."

On one of the viewscreens of the bay's interior, Brand could see dozens of green clothed Gersons sprawled across the decks just outside the ship, security men in gas filter masks moving among them to remove weapons. The boarding ramp was choked with unconscious tech personnel, and security men were beginning to carry them off and lay them out in neat rows.

Brand took it all in and sighed. Sometimes, despite the best of intentions, things just didn't work out the way they should. The knockout gas would leave no permanent effects, but it was hardly conducive to leaving the Gersons in any positive frame of mind, when they came around.

"How much of a dose did they get?" Brand asked. "Has Med been called?"

"Yes to the last, sir, and I'd say everybody will be down for half an hour or so," the man said. "For the Gersons, it might be a little more or less. The gas is safe for a broad band of species, but I'm not sure exactly how the dosage works for them."

Brand glanced at Maggie. "What about it, Mags?"

She shook her head. "No problem. Larger body mass, smaller proportional dose. If anything, they'll recover more quickly than the humans, barring unusual reactions of individuals. Do you want me to start checking them, while we wait for the Meds?"

"Let's do that," he said. They headed for the set of airlocks that led into the docking bay in question. Because the bays were routinely opened to hard space, inside entrance and egress to them was protected by not one but two airlocks set in serial. As they entered the first lock and its safety doors sighed closed behind them, the doors ahead parted on a tall, sandy-haired security captain with a gas filter mask pushed up on top of his head.

"Tuck, I'm disappointed," Brand said, already moving forward. "Didn't they tell you I was on my way down?"

"Aye, sir, they did," Tucker replied, turning to accompany them back into the intermediate lock he had just left. "Unfortunately, the Gersons had already decided to take matters into their own hands by then. I stopped the gas as soon as I got your counter-order, but it was too late. Everybody should be up and about in a little while, though."

"Were they really trying to take the ship?" Maggie asked as they came through the last of the doors and into the bay, heading for the downed Gersons sprawled all around the ship.

"Sure looks that way," Tucker said. As Maggie knelt to check the nearest Gerson, he returned his attention to Brand. "Apparently they came in just as the tech crew had finished rearming it, and wanted to know how to rig the warp engines to overload."

Maggie glanced up sharply at that, but Brand only shook his head.

"Can't say I blame them," he said. "But I haven't got destroyers to spare. You think they were serious?"

"Sure sounds that way," Tucker replied. "They talked most with one of the tech crew, before we got called in. He's over there." He gestured toward the sprawled figure of a balding little man whose sleeve patches proclaimed him a Spec-5 armorer. "Name's Max Faber. His argument was actually making a lot of sense, before we had to gas everybody."

Brand cast his eyes over the clutter of sleeping humans and Gersons and shook his head.

"All right. I've got to get back up to the command bridge. Tuck, when they're awake again, I want to see the ringleaders in the ward room. Give me Hooth and a couple or three of his head honchos. Include Mr. Faber, too. I'd like to hear his arguments to justify a suicide run by the last of a race. And, Maggie, can you bird-dog this for me, make certain everybody's recovered before I start chewing ass?"

"I'll take care of everything," she said. "Give us a couple of hours, though. You've heard of people who wake up as grumpy as a bear that's been woken out of hibernation? Well, the Gersons bear more than a physical resemblance to their ursine forbears—if you'll pardon the multiple plays on words."

Brand grimaced and made a gesture of dismissal, then headed back out of the docking bay.

Captain Tashi did not glance back as Brand stepped out of the darkened passage that was the transition from the bright-lit outside corridor to the dim lighting of the command bridge, but Brand knew his arrival had been noted. Command staff wore personal coders that not only admitted them to the bridge but broadcast a short sequence of pips in the earphones of duty personnel, so that visual attention need not be diverted from what could be vital continuity in a battle situation.

It was always far quieter than Brand expected it to be, for the virtual nerve center of the *Hawking*. The bridge was mostly dark, lit primarily by the several dozen numbered status screens ranged to either side of the central command plinth and the enormous holotank set close to the far wall. Command staff manned five workstations in the pit between the tank and the command plinth. Two of them were battle tacticians when the *Hawking* was on alert, each provided with computer links to the ship's battle bridge and her gun decks; the other three were technicians who oversaw nondefense aspects of the ship's operation.

Alert status also meant that the command bridge duplicated many of the functions of fire control, over on the battle bridge, necessary for overall coordination when the *Hawking* was under periodic attack. Colored dots floated in the tank to mark the location of the ships engaged in the battle: white for Fleet ships, blue for allies, and red for the Ichton forces. The images in the tank kept changing as Tashi shifted first one screen and then another into the tank to get a fresh perspective, occasionally speaking softly into a tiny microphone attached to an earpiece in one ear.

Not speaking, Brand mounted the three steps of the command plinth and crouched beside the command chair, glancing at the information display screen embedded in the left chair arm and then letting his gaze range quickly over the large status screens and then on to the huge three-dimensional tank that showed the battle under active consideration. Near the center of the tank, not to scale, floated a small, semitransparent greenish sphere meant to represent the besieged Emry planet, closely surrounded by moving red dots, some of them far larger than others and pulsing. The latter were Ichton mother ships, most desirous of all targets because they carried the precious Ichton eggs, whose protection was the sole focus of the Ichton support fleet.

Once the mother ships landed on a planet and began setting up egg colonies, and especially once they became entrenched, they were much more difficult to destroy. Most desirable was to destroy such ships while still in space, since this also eliminated thousands of future Ichton soldiers. But even heavy damage to one would draw off Ichton escort vessels in an attempt to save the eggs—which lessened the number of ships available to resist Alliance forces as they swept in on desultory raids.

Such a raid was in progress now. From far on the right of the tank, a cluster of perhaps eight small blue dots was crawling toward one of the Ichton mother ships, small red dots beginning to swarm outward from it toward the blue ones.

"Emry?" Brand asked quietly.

"Yes," Tashi murmured, not taking his eyes from the tank. "They aren't going to make it, though." He hit a switch in his right armrest. "Abort. Break off."

At first nothing seemed to happen, but then the last four blue dots veered off in an oblique line, away from the advancing red dots. But the other four continued on.

"Call them off, damn it! They aren't going to get through," Tashi said into his mike.

But the blue dots kept going, now engaging with the Ichton ships. Where red and blue dots touched, a tiny flash always left only one dot lit. The blue dots lost three, but the red dots lost five. The remaining blue dot continued on, now heading directly toward the closest mother ship, its former escort blue dots now swarming in behind it to weave erratically among the defending red dots—and far more of the red dots went out than blue ones.

"God, they're brave little suckers, but it isn't going to work," Tashi whispered, now clenching his left fist to his mouth, trying to will the blue dots to hold on. The blue dot heading for the Ichton mother ship was still on course, two more red dots flicking out as Brand and Tashi watched. But when the blue dot finally touched the mother ship, it was the blue dot that disappeared.

"Damn!" Tashi whispered.

But even as he shook his head in denial, Brand was touching his sleeve and gesturing toward the tank, where one of the tacticians had changed the scene to a closer perspective of the Ichton mother ship. Actual visual contact was not possible at this distance, but from the movements of the many red dots now converging on the mother ship, it soon became clear that the last Emry ship had not been the only casualty of the ultimate engagement.

"I think they may just have holed her," Brand said, calling up a display on the chair-arm screen and scanning the readout. "By God, they did. And that's almost better than a kill, because they have to swarm in and try to save as many eggs as possible. Dirty fighting, but it may be all we've got."

They watched the display for another few seconds; then one of the tacticians had shifted to another perspective, another battle in progress, and Tashi regained his objectivity. After another little while, Brand took over, figuring he might as well give his second a break until it was time to go and deal with the Gersons.

He knew what the Gersons probably had in mind; just like what the Emry had just done, but on a larger scale. A destroyer rigged to overload its warp engines in the middle of an Ichton battle formation could wreak unbelievable havoc. The firepower of a destroyer, in and of itself, was formidable; but the energy contained in a destroyer's warp drive could be made to explode almost like a small star, if it was all released at once. It was not something that could be done by remote control; but it could be done by a willing crew, determined to settle at least a small part of the debt incurred by the enemy on a world many light-years away. But the Gersons were the last of their race. Not only that, destroyers were in short supply.

He ran battles for another three hours, by which time he was ready to let Tashi take over again. He was beginning to be concerned as to why he had not yet heard from Tucker about the Gersons. He hoped Maggie had not underestimated the effect of the knockout gas; the Gersons were aliens, after all. He had retreated to his ready room and was just preparing to call Security and get an update when the speaker twittered on his intercom. The sound startled him, for he had been just about to press his thumb to the button. He pushed the Receive button instead.

"Brand here."

"Anton, it's Maggie," said a familiar voice. "Would you like to come down to the ward room? I think we may have worked out a compromise solution to your problem."

"What compromise?" he replied. "What problem? They're the last of their race, Maggie. I can't let them go on a suicide mission, even if I could spare a ship."

"Just come to the ward room," she said. "They've gotten over their mad about the gas. But they've got some interesting arguments. Out."

He did up the collar of his tunic to reinforce an appearance of authority, told Tashi where he would be, and headed for the ward room. Two of Tucker's security men were standing guard outside, and came to attention as he approached.

"No one's armed except you, Commander," one of the men said, just before he activated the control that made the door retract.

They were standing around a small conference table over to one side of the room, Tucker and Maggie flanking the chair reserved for him. A slight, balding man in Fleet uniform sat to Tucker's left, his head resting on one hand, and four of the bear-like Gersons occupied the other end of the table, one of them a female. Gerson males towered over most humans by nearly a head, but the females were more delicately boned and rarely came past Brand's shoulder. Brand thought he recognized this particular one: Joli, Hooth's mate. It was certainly Hooth at the other end of the table: a glossy, black-furred Gerson obviously in his prime, proud and impressive.

All eyes turned in Brand's direction as he entered the room. Tucker looked very grim, Maggie more wistfully expectant. The human tech raised his head but did not stand, probably nursing the grandfather of all hangovers from the knockout gas, though all of the Gersons seemed fine. As Brand sat between Tucker and Maggie and everyone else also sat, he touched the Translator button on his collar to activate it.

"*Hoidah, Hooth, Gersonu,*" he said, which totally exhausted his command of the Gersons' language.

Hooth lifted his sleek muzzle in what might have been an expression of disbelief in a human. Brand suspected it had something to do with his accent, but the other Gersons' great bear-jaws parted in what he imagined were grins, or at least small smiles, pleased that he had made the effort. His translator's flat, uninflected voice whispered, *Greetings, Hooth, People of Gerson.* The Gersons were adjusting little speaker buttons in their rounded, furry ears, their black shoe-button eyes darting back and forth among themselves.

"Commander Brand," Hooth said. "I offer friendship." What he actually said sounded like a series of growls and whines, but the translator gave him an electronic basso voice with a trace of a Germanic accent.

"And I offer friendship to the Gersons," Brand acknowledged as he turned his attention to the human specialist. "And you are?"

"Spec-5 Max Faber, Commander," the little man said. "Ah—sorry about the little contretemps down on Green deck. The—ah—Gersons wanted me to turn over the *Prince Buthelezi* and destruct-rig it."

"So I understand." Brand turned his attention back to Hooth. "Would you mind telling me exactly what you proposed to do with a destruct-rigged destroyer, Hooth?"

"We want to take it into the center of the Ichton fleet," Hooth's translated voice said. "Since we would not be planning to come out again, we can divert all energy to the shields until we are very close to a mother ship, using the ship's missiles and lasers to keep the enemy at bay as we go. When we overload the warp engines, the explosion will destroy many Ichton ships."

Brand leaned back in his chair. "I can't let you do it, Hooth. Aside from the fact that I haven't got any extra destroyers to intentionally blow up, you're the last of your race. I won't be a party to genocide."

Hooth looked away for a moment, exchanging a poignant glance with his mate, then back at Brand.

"Commander, we Gersons have loved life as well as any other sentient creature. But the Ichtons have destroyed our world. They have destroyed our race. Now they will destroy the Emry and perhaps many other races, if they are not stopped. If we can prevent the destruction of even one other race, then perhaps our own obliteration will not have been for nothing."

Brand glanced at the other three Gersons, especially at the female, with one pawlike hand laid protectively over her stomach, then back at Hooth.

"Hooth, this is a noble thing you ask to do, but I can't allow it. If you go like this, you finish what the Ichtons started."

"If we stay, the same thing is accomplished," Hooth replied. "And yet—" He glanced at Maggie. "Commander, we are but eighty-four individuals remaining. Only twenty-six are females. Three of those are past breeding age. But—" He glanced uneasily at Maggie again. "I cannot explain, Doctor."

Maggie nodded, turning back to Brand. "Theoretically, we have the medical technology to possibly reestablish the Gerson race, Commander. With a pool of only twenty-three breeding females, it won't be easy or fast—but it won't happen at all, if we lose this war.

"So what I'm proposing is a way to give the Gerson race their best chance of survival, and still allow Hooth and some of his people to make a more direct contribution to the war effort. If we can preserve the full gene pool from all the remaining Gersons, a future in vitro fertilization program might be possible. To even have a chance of starting it, we'd need to collect and freeze sperm donations from all the males who elect to go on the mission Hooth is proposing. Needless to say, none of the females could go. Even then, there's no guarantee that we'll ever be given the opportunity to try the in vitro project. But at least it's a chance."

Brand was shaking his head by the time she finished. "Maggie, this is crazy," he said. "Oh, I know enough about in vitro fertilization to know that it should be theoretically possible to reestablish a race from such a small sample, but—" He shook his head again. "It still doesn't justify sending a shipload of Gerson males to their deaths. I've got enough to worry about without that on my conscience. I may have to commit the *Hawking* to battle—and that *still* might not be enough to win."

"Defeatist talk, Anton," Maggie said.

And Hooth said, "If the allies lost the Battle of Emry, and the Gersons had not given fully of their efforts, we would always hold ourselves partially responsible for the annihilation of another race besides our own. And if the Alliance does lose this battle, and eventually the war, it will not matter what any of us do today. You have seen the swath of destruction the Ichtons leave in their wake. If the Ichtons are not stopped, they will eventually reach the home worlds of the Alliance itself."

Brand sighed, knowing that in this last, at least, the Gerson was right; and knowing that he had no choice but to grant the request of these gallant beings who were willing to put everything on the line to stop an enemy that annihilated whole races. Even if he couldn't spare a destroyer. He glanced at Faber.

"What about it, Mr. Faber? If I did allow what the Gersons ask, could it really make that much difference?"

Faber nodded. "Oh, yes. Depending on how deeply they were able to penetrate the Ichton fleet, they could do an enormous amount of damage. They might take out two, maybe three mother ships, and who knows how many escorts and even light cruisers. Furthermore, they could open a breach in the Ichton line to give us the opportunity for follow through. It could be the best bet we've got to break the impasse."

"*Could*, Mr. Faber?" Brand asked. "Or *would*?"

Faber shrugged and shook his head. "It's just too close to call, Commander."

Brand pursed his lips and let out a low whistle, then glanced uncomfortably at the waiting Hooth.

"All right," he said quietly. "I can't say I'm happy about this. But if you're determined to do it, I can't deny the possible value to the Alliance. I shall miss your courage, Hooth—yours and all your people."

Hooth inclined his shaggy bear-head.

"It is easy enough to be brave going into battle, knowing you will die," he said, slowly reaching across to take his mate's hand. "I think perhaps it is harder to live, to stay behind and one day become the mother of the race."

"No!" Joli said fiercely. "I will not let you go without me. This right I claim, who have borne you eight healthy cubs but have not the will to live without you."

"Hush, we will speak of this later," Hooth said. "Commander Brand, I apologize for my mate's impetuous words. I ask that you make all necessary arrangements as soon as possible, for I know that this battle weighs heavily upon you, and wondering whether the *Hawking* itself must eventually be called into battle. Dr. Conroy, we will go to my people now, to explain what is required."

"She'll join you in a few minutes," Brand said, staying Maggie with a gesture as Hooth and his companions rose. "Mr. Tucker, why don't you show them where to go?"

"Med Blue, Tuck," Maggie said, sitting back down.

When they had gone, Brand glanced at Faber. "How long will it take to rig the ship?"

"Four to six hours. You really want me to do it?"

Brand nodded. "I have to let them try it. It really could make the difference in the war. Do we have a choice of destroyers?"

Faber shook his head. "The others are out on patrol. I'd have picked the *General Schwartzkopf*—she's already taken a lot of battle damage—but the *Prince Buthelezi* is what's available. A pity, because she's the best of the lot."

"Well, perhaps that's what they need, to give them the best chance to make their sacrifice count for something. Make sure they have a full complement of missiles, everything they can possibly throw at the Ichtons on their way in. Do the Gersons have the technical ability to operate the ship at full efficiency?"

"Well, it isn't what they're used to, but I can jury-rig something, simplify some of the controls. That's part of what will take a while. She's already armed, though. It's mainly a matter of disengaging the fail-safes and rigging so that the warp drive will blow when Hooth is ready, and not before. When it does blow, we'd better be farther out than we are now, and warn any other of our vessels likely to be in close."

"You'd better get on it, then."

When Faber had gone, Brand glanced at Maggie.

"I might have known you'd come up with something like this," he said. "Will it really work?"

She shrugged. "Given ideal conditions and some peace, it might," she said. "Meanwhile, if Hooth and his crew are determined to make this gesture—which could well make the major difference we've been praying for—they've also done everything they could to ensure the survival of their race. Their genetic heritage survives, even if the individuals don't—at least so long as the *Hawking* survives. And if they *are* to end here—well, I think it means a lot to them to be able to do *something*, as a final statement of their race. It isn't a terrible memorial, you know. *Here died the last of the Gerson race, who offered up their lives to buy the survival of the Emry and all other races who otherwise might have fallen to Ichton oppression.*"

"Yeah," Brand whispered. "'*Dulce er decorum est, pro patria mori.*'"

"No, 'Greater love hath no man than this: that he lay down his life for his friends,'" Maggie said. "That's a lot closer to the Gerson philosophy, regardless of the fact that they'd never heard of Christianity until the Ichtons had nearly wiped them out."

"What about Hooth's mate—Joli, is it?"

"What about her?"

"Will he let her go? I should think she's still of breeding age."

"Oh, she is. We've already taken specimens from her and from Hooth. We had to make certain that the in vitro procedure would work as well for Gersons as it does for humans."

"Does it?"

She grinned. "I'm happy to report that we have several dozen Hooth and Joli zygotes tucked away in our freezers, and we'll hit him up for another donation for the Gerson sperm bank after we've done everybody else who's going. We decided to go ahead and take all of Joli's eggs while we were at it, but she can still be a surrogate mother when the time comes."

"Not if she goes with Hooth."

"Oh, she isn't going."

"She thinks she is."

Maggie smiled. "Hooth says she isn't. I had to promise him that I'd make certain she didn't, or he wouldn't agree to any of the rest."

"God, what a tangled web, Maggie."

"Survival, Anton. It's the strongest instinct there is, no matter what the species." She patted his arm and rose. "But I'd better get back to the lab and supervise. I have to say that the thought of a room full of giant teddy bears— well, let's just say that it isn't exactly the kind of family practice I used to have. Still, it beats emergency trauma."

Brand managed to restrain a grin until she had left the room, but his mirth had totally died away by the time he called Tashi and two of the gunnery officers to the ward room to brief them on the plan that was taking shape in his mind.

"I'm trying to avoid committing the *Hawking*, as you know, but we may not have that option," he said when he had finished telling them what the Gersons wanted to do. "Sacrificing the *Buthelezi* may give us the edge we need. It isn't the sort of thing I could *ask* anyone to do, but since the Gersons have not only volunteered but practically insisted, it behooves us to make the most of what it will cost them."

The mood was sober in the little ward room, and one of the gunnery officers tapped a finger on the tabletop in agitation.

"It's a big gamble," she said. "If Hooth can get the *Buthelezi* in close enough to waste a mother ship or two, that's only to the good, but it's hard to predict how the Ichtons would react to destruction on that scale. Their usual pattern is to swarm to the rescue of wounded egg ships, and not pay much attention to anything else. I'm not sure they really understand the idea of vengeance. But if we wreak enough destruction among the mother ships—"

"Yeah," said the other gunnery officer. "They might just pull out, flatten what's left of the planet, and move out for their next destination—cut their losses. That gets them out of here, but bad luck for the Emry."

"How close could we get, if I wanted to piggyback the *Buthelezi* in, give it a head start?" Brand asked.

The two gunners exchanged dubious looks.

"Big risk, Commander," said the woman. "Emerging from warp in occupied space could be disaster for us and them. On the other hand, a mere close encounter could simply disrupt the drives of nearby smaller Ichton escorts. I presume you'd warp in and out as quickly as possible—unless you're thinking to do with the *Hawking* what the Gersons intend with the *Buthelezi*."

"I didn't have it in mind to take us on a suicide run," Brand said sourly. "But if the ship didn't have to carry anything but missiles and could overcharge all the turrets because they didn't need to conserve fuel, one ship might make a difference. How long would we have to be in close, to safely disgorge the *Buthelezi*, give it time to make distance, and get us out of there?"

The male gunner cocked his head. "Five minutes? Eight, at the outside. Our shields will hold for that long against anything short of a dreadnought, and surprise will be on our side. The last thing they'll be expecting is to have the *Hawking* suddenly pop into normal space right in the middle of their fleet. But even if our shields protect us from most of what they could throw at us, they could do a lot of damage. As we have already seen, they wouldn't hesitate to ram us. The cost could be high."

They continued discussing options for another quarter hour, after which Brand gave them his decision and then retired to get some sleep. The Gersons' farewell appearance was nothing he intended to entrust to anyone else aboard the *Hawking*. It was a privilege as well as a burden of command. He slept badly, and woke to the sight of Maggie perching on the foot of his recliner, inspecting him with a physician's eye.

"Howdy, Skipper," she said quietly. "The Gersons tell me it's a good day for a battle."

He let out a sigh and closed his eyes briefly, massaging the bridge of his nose to clear the cobwebs from his brain.

"Is it time?" he asked.

"Just about," she said. "The Meds have done their part. The ship is rigged, and the tech staff are briefing the Gerson crew." For just an instant her professional demeanor slipped. "Oh, Anton, they're so personable, so quick and eager to learn. I hate to see us lose them."

"Yeah," Brand said, "war's a bitch." He sat up, rubbing both hands across his face. "How are the remaining Gersons handling it?"

Maggie shrugged, back in control. "They're not happy, as you can imagine. I've had to sedate a few, including Joli. I took the liberty of commandeering one of the staff lounges and having a direct feed piped in from battle ops, so that at least they can watch the battle sequence. I wasn't going to do it, but one of the old-timers said she wanted to be able to tell cubs of later generations how their ancestors died for a good cause."

Brand buried his face momentarily in one hand. "Are there going to be later generations, Mags?" he asked.

"If we don't fight this battle and win it, there certainly won't be," she replied. "Are you okay?"

"Yeah," he said, getting to his feet. "Just not in a hurry to send that ship out. Is Tashi on the bridge?"

"He is." She set a hypospray against his wrist and triggered it before he could object. "That's just a bit of stimulant. You should feel it in a few seconds."

He could feel it already, a pleasant coolness spreading up his arm and through his body, clearing his brain like a wave of ice water. He drew a deep breath and let it out with a whoosh. His body was ready to cope, even if the task ahead was one of the most difficult he had ever had thrust his way.

"Okay," he said. "Let's go."

Up on the bridge, Tashi gave way immediately as Brand and Maggie came out of the transit passage, though he crouched down beside the command chair as Brand took his seat.

"Mind if I stay?" Tashi asked. "I've done the setup. I'd like to be here for the resolution."

For answer, Brand gestured for him to open one of the pull-out seats that allowed someone to sit on either side of the command chair. He opened the other one for Maggie. The tech support crew were glancing up from the command pit as Brand put on a headset and settled in, running his fingers over the control pad under his right hand and already calling up a readout under his left.

"All right, ladies and gentlemen, this is not a drill," Brand said, flashing through a sequence of battle perspectives in the tank ahead and then narrowing on a red-lit view of the command cabin of the *Buthelezi*. "Hooth, this is Brand. Is everything to your satisfaction?"

The Gerson leader swiveled in his command chair and looked directly into the camera pickup. The red lighting softened the ursine lines of his muzzle and rounded ears and made him look far less alien than he did in person.

"We are well pleased, Commander," Hooth's translated voice said. "We cannot thank you enough for this opportunity to save both our race and our pride. May Harsha of the Battles smile on all our endeavors today."

"A bit of Gerson theology," Maggie murmured, close by Brand's ear. "The first time it's come out. God, we had so much to learn from them. And now there's no time."

With a gesture to desist, Brand made the camera pan around the *Buthelezi*'s control room. The other Gersons in sight were all mature males as well, some of them almost white-muzzled. As the camera panned back to Hooth, Brand raised a hand open-palmed in the universal gesture of friendship and farewell.

"Hail and farewell, Hooth," he said, keeping his voice steady with an effort.

"There may not be time when we enter normal space and launch you. You're sure you want to go through with this?"

Hooth only nodded slowly, then touched a button that put the destroyer's ID number on the screen instead of the view of the control room. Respecting their wish for privacy, Brand shifted his perspective to a view outside the *Buthelezi*, from near the security lock.

"How many?" he asked Maggie as he memorized every line of the doomed destroyer.

"Thirty-one, down from the usual forty," she replied. "Faber was able to eliminate some of the normal crew positions. Other than Hooth, they're the older ones, as you saw."

"Does that leave you enough to work with?" he asked.

She shrugged. "It's what I've got. It will have to be enough. We have the crew's donations on ice, though. There isn't a whole lot more we can do, for now."

"Right." He slapped his controls and put up a view of a perspective from the *Hawking* toward the beleaguered Emry planet. Out beyond the white-glowing horizon that was the *Hawking*'s reference point, scores of white and blue dots were scattered like diamonds against a field of void. And far beyond, the faintly green-glowing pip that was the Emry planet, surrounded by a reddish glow.

"Helm, do we have that course plotted in?"

"Aye, sir," one of the stations replied as a new schematic came up in the holotank with a white-flashing light in the midst of red and blue ones. "Insertion at the point indicated should give us very close to three minutes to get the *Buthelezi* away and even launch some SBs that have just returned to rearm to provide a diversion, if everything goes according to plan."

"What is the chance we will drop back in an acceptable location?" the station's commander demanded of his chief navigation officer. If they dropped back too close, there was a chance of the *Hawking*'s warp drive interacting with one of the Ichton ships. The result would be a spectacular explosion and total disaster.

"There is no way to tell, sir," the Khalian replied honestly. "We've never done anything like this before. But my instincts say we will."

"What's the risk to the *Hawking*?" Brand then asked the gunnery chief.

"Less than losing Emry, sir," the tall Perdidan lieutenant answered with the typical bluntness of his culture. "We can pretarget the plasma cannons and missile tubes in a general way, and even let loose with the laser belts, once we're there. Give cover fire, until the *Buthelezi*'s far enough away for us to warp out again."

"Fleet standing by?"

"Aye, sir," came another voice. "We've got both battle plans ready to go, depending on your orders."

"Very well." Brand keyed a switch on his console. "All sections, rig for battle stations. Sound general quarters. This is not a drill. Emergency services, stand by. All sections, report."

His words produced action that set off alarm signals all over the ship. The winking lights on a tote board up on his left told of stations securing, section by section. The civilians aboard were not going to be happy, but it couldn't be helped.

"Stand by, Helm," he said as the last of the lights lit to green. "Prepare to go hyperspace on my mark—now!"

He felt the ship leap to his command, the jarring shudder of megatons of matter being wrenched into another dimension, the accompanying surge of vertigo that was the body's way of acknowledging that shift of existence. All the exterior screens had gone to white, for a ship in hyperspace jump was blind and deaf.

He found himself almost holding his breath as he counted out the mere seconds that the jump would last, for the battle zone he had selected was only light-seconds from where they had begun.

The ship wrenched again, and they were back in normal space. Instantly the screens lit back to life, reading out new data. Not more than a few hundred kilometers away, three of the oak leaf-shaped Ichton mother ships were hanging in formation amid a cloud of lesser escort ships, the disk of the Emry planet huge behind them. A tally to his right told of the destroyer bay already opening to let the *Buthelezi* into space.

The *Hawking* shuddered as the two massive plasma cannons at either pole began firing toward the Ichton ships, dozens of small, swift fighters now streaming out of the *Hawking*'s fighter bays to engage the enemy. As the missile tubes laid down covering fire, the belts of laser cannons also opened up, picking off Ichton escort vessels and splashing harmlessly off the strong shields of the three mother ships, now turning ponderously to head away from the growing battle.

Soon the *Buthelezi* was physically clear, though not yet clear of the *Hawking*'s mag fields if the latter attempted to warp out. Brand ceased fire in the *Buthelezi*'s direction as she moved out, already heading straight for the mother ships, picking up speed as she launched her own covering screen of missiles to clear a path before her. Other Ichton ships were being drawn to the mother ships' defense, several light cruisers and a dreadnought, which suddenly diverted when it noticed the *Hawking* and began closing fast.

"How long until we can warp?" Brand demanded, watching the dreadnought close. "Get that guy."

The *Hawking* adjusted attitude and the massive spinal-mounted plasma cannons spoke, sending bolt after bolt against the dreadnought's shields. Brand could see its shields starting to overload, but would it be in time? More Ichton ships were aware of the *Hawking*'s presence now, turning increasing firepower upon her.

Beyond, the *Buthelezi* was almost clear of the *Hawking*'s shields. Any second now—

"Helm, go hyperspace at will," he said. "Helm, you're cutting this awfully close—"

The wrench of the hyperdrive kicking in coincided almost exactly with the shield overload on the approaching dreadnought. As the ship steadied into hyperspace, Brand was sure they must have taken some damage. Alarm lights blinking on several of his tote boards confirmed it.

"Damage Control, give me status reports," he demanded. "Can you sustain return warp?"

Mercifully, the responses coming in confirmed that damage thus far was slight. But meanwhile, they were deaf and blind to the fate of the *Buthelezi*. He glanced again at the helmsman, aware that this was a slightly longer jump, calculated to bring them out almost directly opposite from where they had first departed. The ship wrenched again, and they were back in normal space.

Frantically he searched for the display that would show the *Buthelezi* going after the mother ships. An automatic touch of the correct button transferred it to the holotank.

Even as he watched, two red dots flared and disappeared. The screens on one of the mother ships were glowing brighter, edging into blue—

"Go, Hooth!" Brand found himself whispering, one clenched fist pounding gently on the display screen in his chair arm. "Get the bastards!"

As if in answer to his prayer, the screens flared into violet and then white incandescence. A cheer went up among the bridge staff as the screen cleared and the mother ship was gone. Already the *Buthelezi* was forging on toward the next mother ship—and hordes of smaller Ichton escorts were converging on the attacker.

"No," Brand whispered. "Let him get another one. Helm, stand by to reengage."

"Commander?"

"Pick me a spot nearby, and be ready to engage!" Brand snapped. "Prepare to redirect every ship we've got, to follow through. Hooth is opening us a window. Let's use the chance he's buying us at such a cost."

He could see the screens on the *Buthelezi* starting to overload now. The red dots were converging on the beleaguered Fleet destroyer. Soon it would be too late to turn it into a miniature sun. If Hooth waited too long—

Suddenly the entire screen lit up in a gigantic wash of brilliant white light. The tank sensors stopped down immediately to damp the glare, but for just a few seconds circuits overloaded and the entire tank went dark. As a murmur of consternation whispered among the bridge staff, emergency circuits kicked in and the tank relit. It took a second to reorient.

As the image steadied, one thing became immediately clear. The *Buthelezi* was gone, but so were both the remaining mother ships and nearly every Ichton escort that had been on the screen.

"Well done, Hooth!" Brand whispered, almost in awe of what the Gerson had accomplished. "All right, Helm. Let's make it count for something. Is the Fleet ready to shift?"

"Aye, sir."

"Then go FTL—now."

In the weeks and months to come, the battle for Emry would be cited as one of the greatest Fleet victories in the war against the Ichtons. Commander Anton Brand's bold move in taking the *Stephen Hawking* directly into battle was questioned in command circles, but no one could question the result. The *Hawking* sustained heavy damage, especially in the civilian sectors, but the back of the Ichton fleet was broken. Of the five remaining mother ships either on the surface or in orbit around the Emry planet, only one escaped, with a ragtag escort of less than a dozen small ships. Losses in the rest of the Alliance fleet were minimal: one destroyer and perhaps a score of fighters.

But that this had been made possible by the bravery and self-sacrifice of the Gerson crew of the *Buthelezi*, no one could deny. Later that evening, when the battle was over and the worst of the emergencies were under control, deep in space, where the *Hawking* had withdrawn to lick her wounds, Brand went down to the room where the rest of the Gersons were waiting. Maggie Conroy came with him, still blood-spattered from dealing with the injured.

Utter silence settled over the room as Brand came in. The last fifty-three Gersons in the universe slowly stood as Brand moved among them, the low mutters of their comments unintelligible by Brand's translator. They quieted as he turned to survey them, fifty-three pairs of black shoe-button eyes fixed on him in hope and fear.

"You—saw what happened today," Brand said quietly, gesturing toward the large viewscreen across one wall, now blank. "I'm not certain you understood what you saw, but the Emry planet has been saved. Not only that, but the Ichton fleet was routed and mostly destroyed. We know of only one mother ship that got away, along with a very small number of escorts."

He paused to glance at his feet and draw a fortifying breath.

"Unfortunately, a lot of other good people died in today's battle. But I can tell you that the bravest of them all were your Gerson loved ones who went out of here to avenge the death of your planet and put their lives on the line to save another race from a like fate. I stand in awe of what Hooth and the others did today. I want you to know that the Alliance appreciates the sacrifice they made. We will not forget."

He could not go on at that point, but one of the Gerson females came closer with a cub in tow, ducking her head in commiseration. Through the dull numbness of his grief, Brand realized that it was Joli, Hooth's mate.

"We will not forget either, Commander Brand," she said, the nasal growl of her actual voice coming through the translator as a pleasant alto. "And we will not forget what you and the Healer Maggie have made possible. We came to the Alliance convinced that our race was doomed to extinction, but you have given us hope that the Gerson might become a people once again."

Maggie pursed her lips. "It's a long shot, Joli. I told you that when we started."

Joli's bear-jaws trembled, the shoe-button eyes moist with tears.

"It was a 'long shot,' what Hooth and the others attempted to do," she said. "But they succeeded. And we shall succeed. We shall do it in their memory. You will see, when peace is restored."

She turned away at that, heavy shoulders shuddering in the ursine equivalent of weeping, and Brand had never felt so helpless. He was turning too when the Gerson cub came close enough to put its furry paw in his hand, turning liquid black eyes to his. It said nothing, but no words were needed. This was why the Alliance had fought today. Not for this particular Gerson cub, but for all the young of all the races under threat of annihilation by the Ichton. Brand supposed that the Ichtons might offer the same argument—that their expansion had to do with the young of their race. But the Ichtons must be taught moderation. There was room in the universe for all beings, if each race learned to respect the right of others to exist.

There would be more mere battles to see which side could kill the most of their opponents, but ultimately communication must be established to make the Ichtons understand. As Brand stroked a hand gently across the Gerson cub's head, he decided that perhaps all of today's sacrifices had been worthwhile, if that message eventually got through.

BEQUEST

The battle of Emry was a tactical success. The Ichton fleet was shattered and the Emry home world saved. On another level it had been a painfully Pyrrhic victory. The Fleet had suffered losses that more than balanced out all the reinforcements they had received so far. Further, many of the surviving warships were far from combat worthy. The *Hawking* itself had suffered major damage on virtually all levels. Over three hundred crewmen and civilians had died when a force of thirty Ichton fighters had made suicidal plunges at the battlestation. Six had broken through the defenses and smashed through the hull. Worse yet, one of the massive plasma cannon was disabled and couldn't be repaired without parts only available in the Alliance.

Two weeks later Commander Brand called a meeting of the Squam, Emry, and other allied commanders. Anton Brand had to admit that what remained of their combined forces could not win another such battle. He also presented new intelligence showing that the Ichtons were massing another fleet off the ruins of the Gerson home world. This new fleet was already half again larger than the one they had just defeated. Brand had requested more reinforcements, but there was a limit to what the Alliance, surrounded by potentially hostile neighbors, could spare. Nor was he sure the Senate would much longer support a losing cause.

Intelligence was still erratic. They had no idea how many worlds the Ichtons controlled. Nor if they were even facing the bulk of the invader's forces. The insectoids could well have a dozen more fleets farther up the spiral arm than these had disgorged from. Emry was now too devastated to supply any of the parts or metals needed for repairs. They would have to move the *Hawking* and her fleet close to another intact world and hope the Ichtons did not return to Emry before they had accumulated sufficient strength to meet them.

The *Hawking* had arrived three years earlier hoping to create a military solution to the threat. The idea had then been to make it too costly for the Ichtons to continue their rampage. They had since achieved, at best, mixed results. Of the three races the battlestation had come to assist, two had virtually ceased to exist and the home world of the third lay in ruins.

Although they had completely destroyed one Ichton armada at great cost, the only visible result was that another larger fleet was forming as they spoke. The conclusion was painfully obvious. Any purely military solution was impossible. They could hurt the Ichtons, but were losing a war of attrition. Another approach was needed.

The obvious solution was to convince the Ichtons it was to their advantage to cease pillaging the galaxy. Something no other race had demonstrably ever achieved. And something they certainly had just failed to do militarily. After more hours of debate the diplomats were called in. They too were forced to admit there seemed no way to get the Ichtons to talk, much less of moderating their instinct-driven behavior. All that could be suggested was a holding action. Holding until another way presented itself. If it ever did.

Fortunately the needed solution presented itself only a few months later.

FAILURE MODE
by David Drake

In the mirror-finished door to the admiral's office, Sergeant Dresser saw the expression on his own face: worn, angry, and—if you looked deep in the eyes—as dangerous as a grenade with the pin pulled.

"You may go in, sir," repeated Admiral Horwarth's human receptionist in a tart voice.

Dresser was angry.

Because he'd gone through normal mission debriefing and he should have been off duty. Instead he'd been summoned to meet the head of Bureau 8, Special Projects.

Because it had been a tough mission, and he'd failed.

And because he'd just watched a planet pay the price *all* life would pay for the mission's failure. Even the Ichtons would die, when they'd engulfed everything in the universe beyond themselves.

"The admiral is *waiting*, Sergeant," said the receptionist, a blond hunk who could have broken Dresser in half with his bare hands; but that wouldn't matter, because bare hands were for when you were out of ammo, your cutting bar had fried, and somebody'd nailed your boots to the ground . . .

Dresser tried to stiff-arm the feral gray face before him. The door panel slid open before he touched it. He strode into the office of Admiral Horwarth, a stocky, middle-aged woman facing him from behind a desk.

On the wall behind Horwarth was an Ichton.

If Dresser had had a weapon, he'd have shot the creature by reflex, even though his conscious mind knew he was seeing a holographic window into the Ichton's cell somewhere else on the *Stephen Hawking*. The prisoner must be fairly close by, because formic acid from its exoskeletal body tinged the air throughout Special Projects' discrete section of the vessel.

People like Dresser weren't allowed weapons aboard the *Hawking*. Especially not when they'd just returned from a mission and the Psych readout said they were ten-tenths stressed—besides having to be crazy to pilot a scout boat to begin with.

"Sit down, Sergeant," Admiral Horwarth said. She didn't sound concerned about what she must have seen on Dresser's face. "I'm sorry to delay your down-time like this, but—"

She smiled humorlessly.

"—this is important enough that I want to hear it directly from you."

Dresser grimaced as he took the offered chair. "Yeah, I understand," he said. "Sir."

And the hell of it was, he did. Even tired and angry—and as scared as he was—Dresser was too disciplined not to do his duty. Scouts without rigid self-discipline didn't last long enough for anybody else to notice their passing.

"I suppose it was a considerable strain," Horwarth prodded gently, "having to nursemaid two scientists and not having a normal crew who could stand watches?"

Dresser had been staring at the Ichton. He jerked his gaze downward at the sound of the admiral's voice. "Sorry, sir," he muttered. "No, that wasn't much of a problem. For me. The trip, that's the AI's job. There's nothing for human crews to do. I—"

Dresser looked at his hands. He waggled them close in front of his chest. He'd been told you could identify scouts because they almost never met the eyes of other human beings when talking to them. "Scouts, you know, anybody who's willing to do it more than once. Scouts keep to themselves. The boat isn't big enough to, to interact."

He raised his eyes to the Ichton again. It was walking slowly about its cell on its two lower pairs of limbs. The top pair and their gripping appendages were drawn in tight against the creature's gray carapace.

"The scientists," Dresser continued flatly, "Bailey and Kaehler . . . they weren't used to it. I think they were pretty glad when we got to the landing point, even though it didn't look like the right place . . ."

"You've done something wrong, Dresser!" snarled Captain Bailey as *Scout Boat 781*'s braking orbit brought the vessel closer to the surface of the ruined planet. "This place hasn't beaten off an Ichton attack. It's been stripped!"

"At this point, sir," Dresser said, "I haven't done anything at all except initiate landing sequence. The artificial intelligence took us through sponge space to the star that the—source—provided. There's only one life-capable planet circling that star, and we're landing on it."

He couldn't argue with Bailey's assessment, though. Mantra—properly, the name of the project file rather than the nameless planet itself—was utterly barren. Only the human-breathable atmosphere indicated that the planet's lifelessness resulted from an outside agency rather than incapacity to support life.

The agency had almost certainly been a swarm of Ichtons. The chitinous monsters had devoured the surface of the planet, to feed themselves and to build a fleet of colony ships with which to infect additional worlds. The Ichtons were a cancer attacking all life . . .

Mantra was gray rubble, waterless and sterile. Before they left, the invaders had reduced the planet to fist-sized pellets of slag, waste from their gigantic processing mills. The landscape over which the scout boat sizzled contained no hills, valleys, or hope.

"Chance wouldn't have brought us to a solar system, Captain," Kaehler said. She was small for a woman, even as Bailey was large for a man; and unlike her companion, she was a civilian without military rank. "It must be the correct location."

When Dresser thought about Kaehler, it appeared to him that she'd been stamped though a mold of a particular shape rather than grown to adulthood in the normal fashion. Events streamed through the slight woman without being colored by a personality.

Dresser thought about other people only when they impinged on his mission.

Dresser remembered that he wasn't dealing with scout crewmen. "Hang tight," he said. Even so, he spoke in a soft voice.

The AI pulsed red light across the cabin an instant after Dresser's warning. A heartbeat later, the landing motors fired with a harsh certainty that flung the three humans against their restraints.

Approach thresholds for scout boats were much higher than the norm for naval vessels, and enormously higher than those of commercial ships. The little boats might have to drop into a box canyon at a significant fraction of orbital velocity in order to survive. The hardware was stressed to take the punishment, and the crews got used to the experience—or transferred out of the service.

SB 781 crunched down at the point Dresser had chosen almost at random. They were in the mid-latitudes of Mantra's northern hemisphere. That was as good as any other place on the featureless globe.

"Well, sirs . . ." Dresser said. The restraints didn't release automatically. Scout boats were liable to come to rest at any angle, including inverted. The pilot touched the manual switch, freeing himself and the two scientists. "Welcome to Mantra."

"Was there a problem with the equipment?" Admiral Horwarth asked. "The Mantra Project was the first field trial, as I suppose you know."

She gave the scout a perfunctory smile. "I don't imagine that information stays compartmented within a three-man unit."

The Ichton turned to face the pickups. It seemed to be staring into the admiral's office, but that was an illusion. The link with the prisoner's cell was certainly not two-way; and in any case, the Ichton's multiple eyes provided a virtually spherical field of view, though at low definition by human standards.

"The equipment?" Dresser said. "No, there wasn't any difficulty with the equipment."

He laughed. He sounded on the verge of hysteria.

❖ ❖ ❖

"There," Kaehler called as the pole set a precise hundred meters from the imaging heads locked into focus on her display. "We have it."

"I'll decide that!" Captain Bailey replied from the support module twenty meters away. He shouted instead of using the hard-wired intercom linking the two units.

The breeze blew softly, tickling Dresser's nose with the smell of death more ancient than memory. He watched over Kaehler's shoulder as the image of the pole quivered and the operator's color-graduated console displays bounded up and down the spectrum—

Before settling again into the center of the green, where they had been before Bailey made his last set of adjustments.

"There!" Captain Bailey announced with satisfaction.

They'd placed the imaging module twenty meters from *SB 781*'s side hatch. The support module containing the fusion power supply and the recording equipment was a similar distance beyond. A red light on top of the fusion bottle warned that it was pressurized to operating levels.

Though there was a monitor in the support module, Bailey had decreed that in the present climate they needn't deploy the shelters that would have blocked his direct view of the imaging module's the meter display. If Kaehler had an opinion, the captain didn't bother to consult it.

Kaehler folded her hands neatly on her lap. "What has this proved?" Dresser asked, softly enough that he wouldn't intrude if the scientist was really concentrating instead of being at rest as she appeared to be.

Kaehler turned. "We've calibrated the equipment," she said. "We've achieved a lock on the target post, one second in the past. We'll be able to range as far back as we need to go when the artificial intelligence harmonizes the setting with the actual output of the power supply."

"That's what the captain's doing?" Dresser asked with a nod.

"The artificial intelligence is making the calculation," Kaehler said. "Captain Bailey is watching the AI while it works. I presume."

Dresser looked from Kaehler to the pole, then to the horizon beyond. "I don't see how it could work," he said to emptiness. "A second ago—the planet rotates on its axis, it circles the sun, the *sun* moves with its galaxy. Time is distance. Time isn't—"

He gestured toward the distant target.

"—the same place on a gravel plain."

Kaehler shrugged. "In this universe, perhaps not," she said. "We're accessing the past through the Dirac Sea. The normal universe is only a film on the—"

She shrugged again. It was the closest to a display of emotion Dresser had seen from her.

"—surface. Time isn't a dimension outside the normal universe."

"Kaehler!" Captain Bailey shouted. "Stop talking to that taxi driver and begin the search sequence. We've got a job to do, woman!"

The target pole hazed slightly in Dresser's vision, though the holographic image remained as sharp as the diamond-edged cutting bar on the scout's harness.

"I wanted to learn what it did," Dresser said in the direction of the image on the admiral's wall display. "I don't like to be around hardware and not know what it does. That's dangerous."

Admiral Horwarth glanced over her shoulder to see if anything in particular was holding the scout's attention. The Ichton rubbed its upper limbs across its wedge-shaped head as though cleaning its eyes. It raised one of its middle pair of legs and scrubbed with it also.

Horwarth looked around again. "Captain Bailey was able to find the correct time horizon, then?" she prompted.

"Not at first," Dresser said in his husky, emotionless voice. "You said five thousand years."

"The source believed the event occurred five thousand standard years ago," the admiral corrected. "But there were many variables."

"Kaehler went back more than ten thousand," Dresser said, "before she found anything but a gravel wasteland . . ."

"There," Kaehler said. Bailey, watching the monitor in the support module, bellowed, "Stop! I've got it!"

Dresser was watching the display when it happened. He might not have been. The search had gone on for three watches without a break, and Mantra's own long twilight was beginning to fall.

The pulsing, colored static of the huge hologram shrank suddenly into outlines as the equipment came into focus with another time. The score of previous attempts displayed a landscape that differed from that of the present only because the target pole was not yet a part of it. This time—this Time—the view was of smooth, synthetic walls in swirls of orange and yellow.

Kaehler rocked a vernier. The images blurred, then dollied back to provide a panorama instead of the initial extreme close-up. Slimly conical buildings stood kilometers high. They were decorated with all the hues of the rainbow as well as grays that might be shades beyond those of the human optical spectrum. Roadways linked the structures to one another and to the ground, like the rigging of sailing ships. Moving vehicles glinted in the sunlight.

"Not that!" Bailey shouted. "Bring it in close so that we can see what they look like."

Kaehler manipulated controls with either index finger simultaneously. She rolled them—balls inset into the surface of her console—off the tips and down the shafts of her fingers. The scale of the image shrank while the apparent point of view slid groundward again.

Dresser, proud of the way he could grease a scout boat in manually if he had to, marveled at the scientist's smooth skill.

"Get me a close-up, damn it!" Bailey ordered.

The huge image quivered under Kaehler's control before it resumed its slant downward. "We're calibrating the equipment," she said in little more than a whisper. "We're not in a race . . ."

Pedestrians walked in long lines on the ground among the buildings. Vehicles zipped around them like balls caroming from billiard cushions instead of curving as they would have done if guided by humans.

The locals, the Mantrans, were low-slung and exoskeletal. They had at least a dozen body segments with two pairs of legs on each. They carried the upper several segments off the ground. A battery of simple eyes was set directly into the chitin of the head.

Kaehler manually panned her point of view, then touched a switch so that the AI would continue following the Mantran she had chosen. The alien was about two meters long. Its chitinous body was gray, except for a segment striped with blue and green paint.

"They have hard shells, too," Kaehler commented. "You'd think the Ichtons might treat them better."

"The Ichtons don't spare anything," Dresser said softly. He had once landed on a planet while an Ichton attack was still going on. Then he added, "On our bad days, humans haven't been notably kind toward other mammaliforms."

"Kaehler, for God's sake, start bringing the image forward in time!" Captain Bailey shouted. "We aren't here as tourists. We won't see the locals' superweapon until after the Ichtons land. Get with the program, woman!"

Kaehler began resetting the controls on her console. Her face was expressionless, as usual.

"Humans," Dresser said, looking over the stark landscape, "haven't always done real well toward other humans."

Dresser glanced at Admiral Horwarth, then shifted his gaze to the captive again. He continued to watch the admiral out of the corners of his eyes.

"They had a high tech level, the Mantrans," Dresser said. "I made myself believe that they could have built something to defeat the Ichtons. But I knew they hadn't, because—"

Dresser swept both hands out in a fierce gesture, palms down.

"—I could *see* they hadn't," he snarled. "There was nothing. The Ichtons had processed the whole planet down to waste. There was nothing! Nothing for us to find, no reason for us to be there."

"Our source was very precise," Horwarth said gently. "The Ichtons have genetic memory, which our source is able to tap. Mantra was a disaster for them, which has remained imprinted for, you say *ten*, thousands of years."

The "source" was an Ichton clone, controlled by a human psyche. Dresser knew that, because the psyche was Dresser's own.

The scout began to shiver. He clasped his hands together to control them. With his eyes closed, he continued, "It took Kaehler an hour to get dialed in on the moment of the Ichton assault. Bailey badgered her the whole time . . ."

"I think—" Kaehler said.

A bead of blue fire appeared at the top of the image area. The terrain beneath was broken. The Ichton mother ship had appeared in the southern hemisphere. *SB 781*'s navigational computer told Dresser that the vector was probably chance. The Ichtons didn't appear to care where they made their approach.

The display turned white.

"Kaehler!" Bailey shouted. "You've lost the—"

"No!" Dresser said. "They follow an antimatter bomb in. That's how they clear their landing zones."

The white glare mottled into a firestorm, roaring to engulf a landscape pulverized by the initial shock wave. For an instant, rarefaction from an aftershock cleared the atmosphere enough to provide a glimpse of the crater, kilometers across and a mass of glowing rock at the bottom.

The Ichton mother ship continued to descend in stately majesty. A magnetic shield wrapped the enormous hull. Its Bux gradient was so sharp that it severed the bonds of air molecules and made the vessel gleam in the blue and ultraviolet range of the spectrum.

Kaehler's right hand moved to a set of controls discrete from those that determined the imaging viewpoint in the physical dimensions. As her finger touched a roller, Captain Bailey ordered, "Come on, come on, Kaehler. Advance it so that we can see the response! It's—"

The display began to blur forward, if Time had direction. Bailey continued to speak, though it must have been obvious that Kaehler had anticipated his command.

"—the response that's important, not some explosion."

The glowing mother ship remained steady. The Mantran reaction to being invaded was violent and sustained. War swirled around the huge vessel like sparks showering from a bonfire.

Kaehler advanced the temporal vernier at an increasing rate, letting the ball roll off her finger and onto the palm of her hand. She reached across her body with the other hand and switched a dial that increased the log of the rate.

A convoy of Ichton ground vehicles left the mother ship while the rock of the crater still shimmered from the antimatter explosion. The twenty vehicles had not escaped the frame of the display when the Mantrans engaged them from air and ground.

Ichton weapons fired flux generators like those that served the creatures as armor. The shearing effect of their magnetic gradients—particularly those of the heavy weapons mounted on the mother ship—wreaked havoc with the defenders, but the quickly mounted Mantran counterattack nonetheless overwhelmed the convoy vehicle by vehicle. The last to disintegrate in a fluorescent fireball was a gigantic cylinder carrying the eggs that were to be the basis of a new colony.

The Ichtons didn't send out further convoys. Instead, they ripped at the defenders with their flux generators. At intervals, the mother ship lofted missiles that exploded with the flash and actinics of antimatter when the Mantrans blew them up. Very rarely, a missile disappeared from Kaehler's display without being destroyed.

Mantran earthworks grew around the mother ship like mosaic virus expanding across a tobacco leaf. The defenders' weapons bombarded the vessel ceaselessly, but the Ichton armor absorbed even fusion bombs without damage.

"This isn't where they'll develop it," Bailey said abruptly. "We need to check their arsenals, their laboratories."

Kaehler didn't react. She continued to move the image in time without changing the spatial point of focus.

"This is where they'll deploy any weapon," Dresser snapped. "This is where we need to be for now."

Bailey was in command of the expedition and the scout's superior by six grades. Dresser didn't care. The command had been foolish. One of the reasons Dresser was a scout was his inability to suffer fools in silence, whatever the fools' rank.

On the display, seasons blurred between snow and baked, barren earth. All life but that armored within the mother ship and the defenders' lines was blasted away by the mutual hellfire. The sky above *SB 781* darkened, but the huge hologram lighted the boat and the watching humans.

"Stop playing with the scale, Kaehler," Captain Bailey ordered. "I'll tell you if I want a close-up."

Kaehler looked startled. Her hands were slowly working the temporal controls, but she hadn't touched the spatial unit since she initially focused on the mother ship.

"It's not the scale that's changing," Dresser said. "It's the ship. It's expanding the volume covered by its shields, despite anything the Mantrans can do."

The innermost ring of Mantran defenses crumbled as the blue glare swelled, meter by meter. Seasons washed across the landscape like a dirty river . . .

❖ ❖ ❖

Dresser unclenched his hands. He looked at Admiral Horwarth in embarrassment for being so close to the edge. "It was like gangrene, sir," he said. "Have you seen somebody with gangrene?"

She shook her head tautly. "No," she said. "I can imagine."

"You can't cure it," the scout said, speaking toward the Ichton again. The creature was huddled in a corner of its cell. "They just keep cutting pieces off and hope they got it all. Which they probably didn't."

"But the Mantrans *were* able to hold?" Horwarth prompted.

The scout shrugged. "For years," he said, "but it didn't matter. The fighting was poisoning the whole planet. The atmosphere, the seas . . . The land for hundreds of kilometers from the mother ship was as dead as the floor of Hell. The Ichtons didn't care. The whole Mantran infrastructure was beginning to break down."

Dresser laced his fingers again. "Then the Ichtons sent out another convoy . . ."

Dresser looked from Kaehler to Bailey. Both scientists were glassy-eyed with fatigue.

"Ah, Captain Bailey?" Dresser said.

Bailey didn't reply. He may not even have heard. The display was a fierce blue glare that sparkled but never significantly changed. It was like watching the play of light across the facets of a diamond, mesmerizing but empty.

"Cap—"

Thousand-meter fireballs rippled suddenly at the north side of the mother ship's shields. Through them, as inexorable as a spear cleaving a rib cage, rocked a column of Ichton vehicles.

The leading tank spewed a stream of flux projectiles that gnawed deep into the Mantran defenses until a white-hot concentration of power focused down on the vehicle. The tank ripped apart in an explosion greater than any of those that destroyed it, widening the gap in the Mantran defensive wall.

The convoy's second vehicle was also a tank. It continued the work of destruction as it shuddered onward. The defenders' fire quivered on the Ichton shield, but the Mantrans couldn't repeat the concentration that had overwhelmed the leader.

"They can't stop it," Dresser whispered. "It's over."

The image volume went red/orange/white. The dense jewel of the mother ship blazed through a fog that warped and almost hid its outlines. The blur of seasons was lost in the greater distortion.

"Kaehler, what have you done, you idiot?" Bailey shouted. He stepped out of his module; hands clenched, face distorted in the light of the hologram. Except for the blue core, the image could almost be that of the display's standby mode-points of light in a random pattern, visual white noise.

Except for the Ichton mother ship at the blue heart of it.

"It wasn't . . ." Kaehler said as her hands played across her controls with a brain surgeon's delicacy, freezing the image and then reversing it in minute increments.

" . . . me!" The last word was a shout, the first time Dresser had heard Kaehler raise her voice.

The image froze again in time. A disk of the planet's surface, hundreds of kilometers in diameter, slumped and went molten. Its center was the Ichton vessel. Vaporized rock, atmospheric gases fused into long chains, and plasma bursting upward from subterranean thermonuclear blasts turned the whole viewing area into a hellbroth in which the states of matter were inextricably blended.

The scout understood what had happened before either of the scientists did. "They blew it down to the mantle," Dresser said. "The Mantrans did. Their weapons couldn't destroy the Ichtons, so they used the planet to do it."

And failed, but he didn't say that aloud.

Kaehler let the image scroll forward again, though at a slower rate of advance than that at which she had proceeded before. The Ichton convoy vanished, sucked into liquescent rock surging from the planet's core. Plates of magma cooled, cracked, and up-ended to sink again into the bubbling inferno.

Sulfur compounds from the molten rock spewed into the stratosphere and formed a reflective haze. The sky darkened to night, not only at the target site but over the entire planet. Years and decades went by as the crater slowly cooled. Night continued to cloak the chaos.

"Bring it back to the point of the explosion, Kaehler," the captain said. Bailey spoke in what was a restrained tone, for him. For the first time during the operation he used the intercom instead of shouting his directions from the support module. "Freeze it at the instant the shock wave hit them. That must have been what destroyed the ship."

"It didn't destroy the ship," Kaehler said. Her voice had even less effect than usual. The image continued to advance.

The magnetic shields of the Ichton vessel provided the only light. The ship floated on a sea of magma, spherical and unchanged.

"They're dead inside it!" Bailey shouted. "Focus on the micro-second of the first shock wave!"

"You damned fool!" Kaehler shouted back. "I don't have that degree of control. We've got a hundred-millimeter aperture, or have you forgotten?"

Dresser watched Kaehler's profile as she spoke. She didn't look angry. Her face could have been a death mask.

The display continued to crawl forward. Lava crusted to stone. Cracks between solid blocks opened less frequently to cast their orange light across the wasteland. Century-long storms washed the atmosphere cleaner if not clean.

Bailey blinked and sat down in his module. Kaehler turned back to her controls. "Their own people," she said in a voice that might not have been intended even for Dresser. "There were thousands of them in the defenses. They all died."

There had been millions of Mantrans in the defense lines.

"They couldn't pull them out," the scout said softly. "The defenses had to hold until the last instant, so that the mantle rupture would get all the Ichtons."

"Did they know they were going to die?" Kaehler whispered.

"They knew they'd all die anyway," Dresser said.

Everything in the universe would die.

The mother ship released a sheaf of missiles, bright streaks across the roiling sky. Their antimatter warheads exploded in the far distance, flickers of false dawn.

Three convoys set out from the mother ship simultaneously. Mantran forces engaged one convoy while it was still within the display area, but the vain attempt lighted the hummocks of lava as briefly as a lightning flash . . .

"I knew it was over then," Dresser said to his hands in the admiral's office. "I'd *known* it before. They don't quit. The Ichtons don't quit."

He looked at the captive again. It now lay on its back. Its six limbs moved slowly, as though they were separate creatures drifting in the currents of the sea.

"It may have been the failure of conventional techniques that forced the Mantrans to develop their superweapon," Horwarth suggested. She wasn't so much arguing with the scout as soothing him.

Dresser shook his head. "There was never a superweapon on Mantra, Admiral," he said. "Just death."

"Move us forward faster, Kaehler," Captain Bailey ordered over the intercom. "And—change the spatial viewpoint, I think. Follow a moving column."

For once, Dresser thought the captain had a point. There was nothing useful to be seen in the neighborhood of the mother ship.

Three more convoys set out across the cooling lava. These met no resistance.

Kaehler remained fixed, as though she were a wax dummy at her console.

There was nothing useful to be seen anywhere on the planet.

"Kaehler?"

The female scientist began to change settings with the cool precision of a machine that had just been switched on again. She did not speak.

The images on the display flip-flopped through abrupt changes in time and place. An image of all Mantra hung above the console. Half the planet was in sunlight. Yellow-lit cities of the indigenes and the blue speckles of Ichton colonies studded the remaining hemisphere.

For the moment, the colonies were small and there were only a few of them visible. For the moment.

Kaehler's fingers searched discrete blocks of time and space like an expert shuffling cards, throwing up images for a second or less before shifting to the next:

A barren landscape with neither Ichtons nor Mantrans present.

A distant nighttime battle, plasma weapons slamming out bolts of sulfurous yellow that made Ichton shields pulse at the edge of the ultraviolet. Just as Kaehler switched away, an antimatter warhead obliterated the whole scene.

Ichton machinery with maws a kilometer wide, harvesting not only a field of broad-leafed vegetation but the soil a meter down. Enclosed conveyors snaked out of the image area, carrying the organic material toward an Ichton colony. The invaders' tanks oversaw the process, but their waiting guns found no targets.

A Mantran city looming on the horizon—

"There!" Bailey called. "There, hold on that one!"

Kaehler gave no sign that she heard her superior, but she locked the controls back to a slow crawl again. Perhaps she'd intended to do that in any case.

Mantran resistance had devolved to the local level. This city was ringed with fortifications similar to those that the planet as a whole had thrown up around the Ichton mother ship. Though the defenses were kilometers deep, they were only a shadow of those that the invaders had breached around their landing zone.

The Ichton force approaching the city was a dedicated combat unit, not a colonizing endeavor. Turreted tanks guarded the flanks and rear of the invaders' column, but the leading vehicles were featureless tubes several hundred meters long. They looked like battering rams, and their purpose was similar.

The city's defenders met the column with plasma bolts and volleys of missiles. A tank, caught by several bolts and a thermonuclear warhead simultaneously, exploded. The failure of its magnetic shields was cataclysmic, rocking nearby vehicles as the Mantran bombardment had not been able to do.

For the most part, Ichton counterfire detonated the missiles before they struck. Plasma bolts could at best stall an Ichton target for a few moments while the vehicle directed the whole output of its power supply to the protective shields.

The tubular Ichton vehicles were built around flux generators as large as those of the mother ship's main armament. Three of them fired together. A section of the Mantran defenses vanished in a sun-bright dazzle. It shimmered with all the hues of a fire opal.

The gun vehicles crawled closer to the city. The height of the flux gradient of their projectiles was proportional to the cube of the distance from the launcher's muzzle. Even at a range of several hundred meters, the weapons sheared the intra-atomic bonds of the collapsed metal armoring the defenses.

All the available Mantran weaponry concentrated on the gun vehicles. The ground before their treads bubbled and seethed, and the nearest of the indigenes' fortifications began to slump from the fury of the defensive fire.

The Ichtons fired again; shifted their concentrated aim and fired again; shifted and fired. The gap before them was wide enough to pass the attacking column abreast. Counterfire ceased, save for a vain handful of missiles from launchers that hadn't quite emptied their magazines.

The column advanced. An inner line of plasma weapons opened up—uselessly.

In the ruins of the outer defenses, a few Mantrans thrashed. Muscles, broiled within their shells by heat released when nearby matter ionized, made the Mantrans' segmented bodies coil and knot.

Sergeant Dresser turned his head. He was a scout. He was trained to observe and report information.

There was nothing new to observe here.

"Kaehler!" Captain Bailey shouted from the edge of Dresser's conscious awareness. "Bring us forward by longer steps, woman! This isn't any good to us."

When Dresser faced away from the holographic display, he could see stars in the sky of Mantra. He wondered if any of them had planets that had escaped being stripped by the Ichton ravagers . . .

"Bailey figured," Dresser said in a voice too flat to hold emotion, "that we'd be able to tell when the superweapon was developed by its effect on the Ichtons. When we saw signs of the Ichtons retreating, of their colonies vanishing, then we'd know something had happened and work back to learn what."

Admiral Horwarth nodded. "That sounds reasonable," she said.

"They should've taken a break, Bailey and Kaehler," the scout added in a non sequitur. His mind, trapped in the past, bounced from one regret to another. "Going straight on, I knew it was a mistake, but I wasn't in charge."

Horwarth looked over her shoulder at the captive Ichton. The movement was a way of gaining time for her to decide how to respond. The Ichton still lay full length on the floor of its cell. Its limbs wrapped its torso tightly.

Horwarth turned again. "Should we have sent more than one team?" she asked. "Was that the problem?"

"No," Dresser said sharply. The harshness of his own voice surprised him.

"No, sir," he said, meeting the admiral's eyes in apology. "I don't think so. Time wasn't that crucial. Bailey got focused on finding the superweapon. The more clear it was that no such weapon existed—"

Dresser's anger blazed out unexpectedly. "The planet was a wasteland!" he snarled. "We knew that from the prelanding survey!"

"The Mantrans could have developed their weapon when it was too late to save their planet, you know," Horwarth suggested mildly. "What we have is evidence that the Ichtons were traumatized by the contact—not that the Mantrans survived it."

Dresser sighed. "Yeah," he said to his hands, "I told myself that. But Bailey—and I think maybe Kaehler, too, though it didn't hit her in the same way. They weren't focused on the long-term result anymore."

He shook his head at the memory. "They were too tired, and it was getting toward dawn . . ."

Captain Bailey walked toward them from the support module. For a moment, Dresser saw his head silhouetted against the telltale on top of the fusion bottle. The red glow licked around the captain's features like hellfire.

Bailey didn't speak. Kaehler had ignored the last several of his commands anyway.

On the display, two Mantrans huddled together on a plateau as invaders approached from all sides. There were probably fewer than a thousand indigenes surviving at this time horizon.

Kaehler waited like a statue. Her fingers poised above the controls. The apparatus scrolled forward at one second/second.

"How long has it been since the Ichtons landed?" Dresser asked quietly. He wasn't sure she would answer him either.

"Six hundred standard years," Kaehler replied without moving more than her lips. "At the time we're observing, the Mantran year was at two-eighty-one standard. The Ichtons took so much mass with them that the planet shifted to an orbit longer by forty days."

The atmosphere on the holographic display was so foul that the sun shone wanly even at noon. Nevertheless the image area was lighted vividly by the six Ichton colonies visible from this point. Each colony had grown as large as the mother ship was when it landed.

When the time was right—when everything useful on Mantra had been processed into Ichton equipment or Ichton flesh—the myriad colonies would blast off from the stripped planet. Each would be the mother ship of a fresh brood, capable of destroying a further world in logarithmic progression.

"What sort of equipment do the defenders have?" Captain Bailey asked. He was looking at Kaehler.

"They don't have anything, sir," Dresser replied. He knew—all three of them knew—that Kaehler wasn't going to speak. "I thought they were dead, but a few minutes again, they moved a little."

Military operations on Mantra had ceased generations before. The Ichton columns grinding away the rock on which the pair of indigenes sheltered were miners, not troops.

"Pan back a little ways, Kaehler," Bailey said. "I want to get a view of the enemy."

Kaehler didn't respond.

The Mantrans were life-size images above the purring console. One of them coiled more tightly. Bright yellow blotches of fungus were the only color on either body. Illumination from the Ichton colonies turned the hue to sickly green.

Bailey cursed under his breath. He stamped back toward the support module.

When her superior was halfway to his proper position, Kaehler adjusted her controls. The apparent viewpoint lifted, giving Dresser a view of the approaching Ichtons.

The plateau on which the pair of Mantrans lay was artificial. Mining equipment ground away the rock from six directions, lowering the surface of the plain—of the planet—by twenty meters. A snake of tubing connected each of the grinding machines to one of the Ichton colonies that squatted on the horizon. There the material would be sorted, processed, and built into the mother ship growing at the heart of each colony.

The closed conveyors gleamed with magnetic shields. Such protection was now unnecessary. Not even rain fell. Separate conveyor lines carried tailings, the waste that not even Ichton efficiency could use, into the ocean basins already drained by the invaders' requirements.

Cutting heads snuffled up and down the face rock, then moved in a shallow arc to either side with the close of each stroke. An Ichton in shimmering body armor rode each machine, but there was no obvious need for such oversight. The cutters moved like hounds casting, missing nothing in a slow inexorability that was far more chilling than a cat's lithe pounce.

Bits of the upper edge of the plateau dribbled into the maw of a cutter rising to the top of its stroke. One of the Mantrans coiled because the ground was shifting beneath its segmented body. Dresser wasn't sure that the movement was conscious. Certainly the indigene made no concerted effort to escape.

Not that escape was possible.

Kaehler touched her controls, focusing down on the two Mantrans. The images swelled to larger than life size. Edges lost definition.

One of the creatures was chewing on a piece of cloth. Its chitinous jaws opened and closed with a sideways motion. The fabric, a tough synthetic, remained unaffected by the attempt to devour it.

"The left one has a weapon!" Captain Bailey suddenly cried. "Increase the resolution, Kaehler! This must be it!"

Dresser could see that the Mantran, writhing as the plateau disintegrated beneath it, didn't have a weapon. The yellow fungus had eaten away much of the creature's underside. Most of its walking legs were withered, and one had fallen off at the root. That, hard-shelled and kinked at an angle, was what Bailey's desperation had mistaken for a weapon,

Kaehler turned toward her superior. "I can't increase the resolution with a hundred-millimeter aperture," she said in a voice as empty as the breeze.

Bailey stood at the edge of his module. His head was silhouetted by the telltale behind him. "You could if you were any good at your job!" he shouted. "I'm tired of your excuses!"

The cutting head rose into sight on the display. The Ichton riding it pointed his weapon, a miniature version of the flux generators that had devoured armor denser than the heart of a star.

Kaehler stared at Bailey. Her left hand raised a panel on the front of her console. She didn't look down at it.

Dresser touched the woman's shoulder with his left hand. He was icy cold. "Ah, ma'am?" he said.

"All right, Captain," Kaehler said in a voice like hoarfost. "I'll enlarge—"

"Wait!" Bailey shouted.

Dresser didn't know what was about to happen, but he wouldn't have lived as long as he had without being willing to act decisively on insufficient data. He gripped Kaehler and tried to lift her out of her seat.

Kaehler's hand yanked at the control that had been caged within the console. Dresser saw Captain Bailey's face lighted brilliantly in the instant before another reality enveloped the imaging module and the two humans within it.

The Ichton fired, knocking the head off the nearer indigene with the easy nonchalance of a diner opening a soft-boiled egg. Rock beyond the Mantran disintegrated also, spraying grit into Dresser's face as his right hand snatched his cutting bar.

The air was foul with poisons not yet reabsorbed by ten thousand years of wind blowing through a filter of porous waste. The sky was black, and the horizon gleamed with Ichton colonies gravid with all-destroying life.

Kaehler had opened the viewing aperture to the point that it enveloped herself, her equipment—

And Sergeant Dresser, who hadn't carried a gun on a lifeless *desert*, for God's sake, only a cutting bar that wouldn't be enough to overload Ichton body armor. Dresser lunged for the monster anyway as it turned in surprise.

A stream of flux projectiles blew divots out of stone as the Ichton brought its weapon around. Kaehler didn't move.

Dresser's powered, diamond-toothed blade screamed and stalled in the magnetic shielding. He tried to grab the Ichton weapon but caught the limb holding it instead. The scout's fingers couldn't reach a material surface. Though he knew his arm was stronger than the exoskeletal monster's, his hand slipped as though he were trying to hold hot butter.

Dresser looked down the muzzle of the Ichton weapon.

He thought, when he hit the ground an instant later, that he was dead.

Instead, he was sprawled beside *SB 781*. Plasma spewing from the fusion bottle formed a plume that melted the upper surfaces of the support module. It was brighter than the rising sun . . .

Dresser met Admiral Horwarth's eyes. "He'd vented the containment vessel," the scout said. "Bailey had. He knew it'd kill him, but it was the only way to shut the apparatus off fast enough from where he was."

"I've recommended Captain Bailey for a Fleet Cross on the basis of your report, Sergeant," Horwarth said quietly. "The—cause of your transition through the aperture will be given as equipment failure, though."

Dresser shrugged. His eyes were wide and empty, with a thousand-meter stare that took in neither the admiral nor the image of the motionless Ichton on the wall behind her.

"It wasn't Kaehler's fault," the scout said. His voice sank to a hoarse whisper. "She cracked, people do that. It wasn't a fault."

He blinked and focused on Horwarth again. "Is she going to be all right?" he asked. "She wouldn't talk, wouldn't even move on the trip back."

"I'll have a report soon," Horwarth said, a bland placeholder instead of an answer.

Dresser wrapped his arms tightly around his torso. "Maybe it wasn't Bailey's fault either," he said. "I figure he cracked, too. Even me, I'm used to the Ichtons, but it bothered me a bit. He wasn't ready to see the things he saw on Mantra."

"A bit" was a lie obvious to anyone but the man who said it.

Dresser's smile was as slight and humorless as the point of a dagger. "I brought his feet back in cold storage. Everything above the ankles, that the plasma got when he dumped the bottle."

"There doesn't appear to have been any flaw in the equipment itself, though," Horwarth said. "Until the damage incurred in the final accident."

"I was the one who screwed up," Dresser said to his past. "I should've grabbed her quicker. *I* was supposed to be the scout, the professional."

"When the equipment can be rebuilt," Admiral Horwarth said, clamping the scout with the intensity of her gaze, "there'll have to be a follow-up mission to complete the reconnaissance."

"No," said Dresser.

Horwarth ignored the word. "I'd appreciate it if you would consent to pilot the mission, Sergeant," she said. "You know better than almost anyone else how impor—"

"No!" Dresser shouted as he lurched to his feet. "*No*, you don't need a follow-up mission! We'd completed the mission, and we'd *failed*. That's why it happened, don't you see?"

"What I see is that the incident aborted Captain Bailey's mission before it reached closure," the admiral said.

She rose also and leaned forward on her desk, resting on her knuckles. Her voice rose as either her facade cracked or she let some of her real anger and frustration out as a means of controlling the scout. "What I see is that we *have* to find the weapon the Ichtons fear, because you've proved that no conventional weapon can defeat them in the long term."

"Admiral," Dresser begged.

He turned to the closed door behind him, then turned again. He didn't realize that he was crying until a falling tear splashed the back of his hand. "Sir. The coordinates were wrong, something was wrong. The only thing left to learn on Mantra was whether the last of the indigenes died of disease or starvation before the Ichtons got them."

Horwarth softened. She'd skimmed the recordings the expedition brought back. She didn't need Psych's evaluation of the two survivors to understand how the images would affect those who'd actually gathered them.

"Sergeant," she said, "something happened to the Ichtons before they spread from Mantra. It made memory of the place a hell for them ten thousand years later. We have to learn what."

"Sir . . ." Dresser whispered. He rubbed his eyes angrily, but he was still blind with memory. "Sir, I'll go back, I'll do whatever you want. But we failed, sir, because there was nothing there to succeed with. And since I watched Mantra eaten, I know just how bad we failed."

"We've got to try, Ser—" Admiral Horwarth began.

The electronic chime of an alarm interrupted her. Horwarth reached for a control on her desk.

Dresser's gaze focused on the holographic scene behind the admiral. Three humans wearing protective garments had entered the Ichton's cell. They stumbled into one another in their haste.

"Duty officer!" Admiral Horwarth snarled into her intercom. "What the hell is going on?"

Two of the attendants managed to raise the Ichton from the floor of the cell. The creature was leaking fluid from every joint. It was obviously dead.

The chitinous exoskeleton of the Ichton's torso was blotched yellow by patches of the fungus whose spores had traveled with Sergeant Dresser from the surface of a dying planet.